FLIGHT
OF THE
FALCON

WILBUR SMITH

FAWCETT CREST • NEW YORK

Once again this book is for my wife
Danielle Antoinette

1860

Africa crouched low on the horizon, like a lion in ambush, tawny and gold in the early sunlight, seared by the cold of the Benguela Current.

Robyn Ballantyne stood by the ship's rail and stared toward it. She had been standing like that since an hour before dawn, long before the land could be seen. She had known it was there, sensed its vast enigmatic presence in the darkness, detected its breath, warm and spicy-dry, over the clammy cold exhalations of the current on which the great ship rode.

It was her cry, not that of the masthead, which brought Captain Mungo St. John charging up the companionway from his stern quarters, and the rest of the ship's company crowding to the ship's side to stare and jabber. For seconds only, Mungo St. John gripped the teak rail, staring at the land, before whirling to call his orders in the low but piercing tone which seemed to carry to every corner of the ship.

"Stand by to go about!"

Tippoo the mate scattered the crew to their duties with knotted rope end and clubbed fists. For two weeks, furious winds and low, sullen skies had denied them a glimpse of sun or moon, or of any other heavenly body on which to establish a position. On dead reckoning the tall clipper should have been one hundred nautical miles farther west, well clear of this treacherous coast with its uncharted hazards and wild deserted shores.

The captain was freshly awakened, the thick dark mane of his hair tangled, rippling now in the wind, his cheeks lightly flushed with sleep, and also with anger and alarm beneath the smooth darkly tanned skin. Yet his eyes were clear, the whites contrasting starkly against the golden-flecked yellow of the iris. Once again, even in this moment of distraction and confusion, Robyn wondered at the sheer physical presence of the man— a dangerous, disturbing quality that at the same time both repelled and attracted her intensely.

His white linen shirt had been stuffed hastily into his breeches, and the front was unfastened. The skin of his chest was dark and smooth also, as if it had been oiled, and the hair upon it was crisp and black, tight whorls of it that made her blush, reminding her too clearly of that morning early in the voyage— the first morning that they had run into the warm blue waters of the Atlantic Ocean below latitude 35° north, the morning which for her had been the subject of much torment and troubled prayer since.

That morning, she had heard the splash and drum of water on the deck above her, and the clank of the ship's pump. She had left the makeshift desk in her tiny cabin on which she was working at her journal, slipped a shawl over her shoulders and gone up on to the main deck, stepping unsuspectingly into the bright white sunlight and then stopping aghast.

There were two seamen working the pump lustily, and the clear seawater hissed from its throat in a solid jet. Naked, Mungo St. John stood beneath it, lifting his face and his arms toward it, the water sleeking his black hair down over his face and neck, flattening his body hair over his chest and the muscled plane of his belly. She had stood and stared, completely frozen, unable to tear her eyes away. The two seamen had turned their heads and grinned lewdly at her while they kept the handles pumping the hissing water.

Of course she had seen a man's naked body before, laid out on the dissection table, soft white flesh collapsing over bone, and with belly pouch slit open and the internal organs spilling out of it like butchers' offal, or between the grubby blankets of the fever hospital, sweating and stinking and racked with the convulsions of onrushing death—but never like this, not healthy and vital and overwhelming like this.

This was a marvelous symmetry and balance of trunk to

2

long powerful legs, of broad shoulders to narrow waist. There was a luster to the skin, even where the sun had not gilded it. This was not an untidy tangle of masculine organs, half hidden by a bush of coarse hair, shameful and vaguely revolting. This was vibrant manhood, and she had been struck with sudden insight as to the original sin of Eve, the serpent and the apples, here offered again, and she had gasped aloud. He had heard her and stepped from under the thundering jet of water, and flicked the hair from his eyes. He saw her standing near, unable to move or tear her eyes away, and he smiled that lazy, taunting smile, making no move to cover himself, the water still streaming down his body, and sparkling like diamond chips on his skin.

"Good morning, Dr. Ballantyne," he had murmured. "Perhaps I am to be the subject of one of your scientific studies?"

Only then had she been able to break the spell, to whirl and rush back to her smelly little cabin. She expected to be greatly disturbed, as she threw herself on the narrow planks of her bunk, waiting to be overwhelmed by a sense of sin and shame, but it did not come. Instead, she was confused by a contraction of her chest and lungs that left her breathless, and a remarkable warmth of her cheeks and the skin of her throat, a prickling of the fine dark hairs at the nape of her neck, and the same warmth of other parts of her body which had so alarmed her that she flung herself hurriedly off the bunk and onto her knees to plead for a proper sense of her own unworthiness and a true understanding of her essential baseness and irretrievable wickedness. It was an exercise she had undertaken a thousand times in her twenty-three years, but seldom with so little success.

For the thirty-eight days of the voyage since then, she had tried to avoid those flecked yellow eyes and that lazy taunting smile, and had taken to eating most of her meals in her cabin, even in the daunting heat of the equator, when the taint of the bucket behind the canvas screen in the corner of the cabin had done little to pique her appetite. Only when she knew that heavy weather would keep him on deck did she join her brother and the others in the ship's small saloon.

Watching him now as he conned his ship off the hostile coast, she felt that disturbing prickle once again, and she turned away quickly to the land that was now swinging across the bows. The tackle roared through the blocks and the yards creaked and crackled, the canvas flogged and then filled again with a crash like cannon.

3

At the sight of the land she almost overcame those earlier memories and was instead filled with such a sense of awe that she wondered if it were possible that the land of birth could call so clearly and so undeniably to the blood of its children.

It did not seem possible that nineteen years had passed since, as a four-year-old waif clinging to her mother's long skirts, she had last seen that great flat-topped mountain that guarded the southernmost tip of the continent sink slowly beneath the horizon. It was one of the only clear memories of this land that she retained. She could still almost feel the coarse cheap stuff that a missionary's wife must wear and hear the sobs that her mother tried to stifle and feel them shake her mother's legs beneath the skirts, as she clung closer. Vividly she recalled the fear and confusion of the little girl at her mother's distress, understanding with childlike intuition that their lives were in upheaval, but knowing only that the tall figure that had been up to that time the center of her small existence was now missing.

"Don't cry, baby," her mother had whispered. "We will see Papa again soon. Don't cry, my little one." But those words had made her doubt that she would ever see her father again, and she had pushed her face into the coarse skirt, too proud even at that age to let the others hear her wail.

As always it had been her brother Morris who had comforted her, three years her senior, a man of seven years, born like her in Africa, on the banks of a far wild river with a strange exotic name, Zouga, which had given him his middle name. Morris Zouga Ballantyne—she liked the Zouga best and always used it, it reminded her of Africa.

She turned her head back toward the quarterdeck, and there he was now, tall but not as tall as Mungo St. John, to whom he was speaking excitedly, pointing at the lion-colored land, his face animated. The features he had inherited from their father were heavy but strong, the nose bony and beaked and the line of the mouth determined, harsh perhaps.

He lifted the glass to his eye again and studied the low coastline, scanning it with the care that he took with any project from the smallest to the greatest, before lowering it and turning back to Mungo St. John. They spoke together quietly. An unlikely relationship had developed between the two men, a mutual though guarded respect each for the other's strengths and accomplishments. But if the truth be told, it was Zouga who pursued the relationship most assiduously. Always one to profit by any opportunity, he had milked Mungo St. John of

4

his knowledge and experience. He had done it with an exercise of charm, but since leaving Bristol Harbor he had drawn from the captain most of what he had learned in many years of trading and voyaging along the coasts of this vast savage continent, and Zouga had written all of it down in one of his calf-bound ledgers, storing knowledge against the day.

In addition to this, the captain had genially undertaken to instruct Zouga in the mystery and art of astronomical navigation. Each day local apparent noon would find the two of them huddled on the sunny side of the quarterdeck with brass sextants poised, waiting for a glimpse of the fiery orb through the layers of cloud, or, when the sky was clear, eagerly sighting it, swaying to the ship's motion, to hold the sun in the field of the lens as they brought it down to the horizon.

At other times they cut the monotony of a long tack with a contest of arms, taking turns at empty corked brandy bottles thrown over the stern by a crewman, using a magnificent pair of percussion dueling pistols that Mungo St. John brought up from his cabin still in their velvet-lined case, and loaded with care on the chart table.

They shouted with laughter, and congratulated each other as the bottles burst in midair in an explosion of shards bright as diamond chips in the sunlight.

At other times Zouga brought up the new Sharps breech-loading rifle, a gift from one of the sponsors of the expedition, "the Ballantyne Africa Expedition," as the *Standard*, that great daily newspaper, had named it.

The Sharps was a magnificent weapon, accurate up to the incredible range of eight hundred yards, with the power to knock down a bull bison at a thousand. The men who were wiping out the great herds of buffalo from the American prairie at this very time had earned the title "Sharpshooters" with this weapon.

Mungo St. John towed a barrel at the end of an eight-hundred-yard length of cable to act as a target, and they shot for a wager of a shilling a bout. Zouga was an accomplished marksman, the best in his regiment, but he had already lost over five guineas to Mungo St. John.

Not only were the Americans manufacturing the finest firearms in the world (already John Browning had patented a breech-loading repeating rifle that Winchester was evolving into the most formidable weapon known to man), but the Americans were also far and away the finest marksmen. This pointed up the difference between the tradition of the frontiersman with

5

his long rifle and that of massed British infantry firing smooth-bore muskets in strictly commanded volleys. Mungo St. John, an American, handled both the long-barreled dueling pistol and the Sharps rifle as though they were extensions of his own body.

Now Robyn turned away from the two men, looked back at the land and felt a small dismay to see it already sinking lower into the cold green sea.

She yearned toward it with a quiet desperation, as she had ever since that day of departure so long ago. Her whole life in the intervening years seemed to have been a long preparation for this moment, so many obstacles overcome, obstacles made mountainous by the fact that she was a woman; there had been so much struggle against temptation to give in to despair, a struggle that others had read as willfulness and vaunting pride, as stubbornness and immodesty.

Her education had been gleaned with such toil from the library of her Uncle William, despite his active discourage-ment. "Too much book learning will only plague you, my dear. It is not a woman's place to trouble herself with certain things. You would do better to assist your mother in the kitchen and learn to sew and knit."

"I can do both already, Uncle William."

Later, his reluctant and grumbling assistance changed only slowly into active support when he at last assessed the depth of her intelligence and determination.

Uncle William was her mother's eldest brother, and he had taken in the family when the three of them had returned almost destitute from that far savage land. They had only the father's stipend from the London Missionary Society, a mere fifty pounds per annum, and William Moffat was not a wealthy man, a physician at Kings Lynn with a small practice, hardly sufficient for the ready-made family with which he found himself saddled.

Of course, later—many years later—there had been money, a great deal of money, some said as much as three thousand pounds, the royalties from Robyn's father's books, but it had been Uncle William who had shielded and sustained them through the lean times.

William had somehow found the money to purchase Zouga's commission in his regiment, even selling his two prized hunters and making that humiliating journey to Cheapside and the moneylenders to do so.

With what William could raise, it was perforce not a fashion-able regiment, and not even the regular army, but the 13th

Regiment of Madras Native Infantry, a line regiment of the East India Company.

It was Uncle William who had instructed Robyn until she was as advanced in formal education as he was himself, and who had then aided and abetted her in the great deception of which she could never bring herself to be ashamed. In 1854 no hospital medical school in all of England would enroll a woman among their student body.

With her uncle's help and active connivance, she had enrolled, using his sponsorship and the assertion that she was his nephew, at St. Matthew's Hospital in the East End of London.

It helped that her name needed only changing from Robyn to Robin, that she was tall and small-breasted, that her voice had a depth and huskiness that she could exaggerate. She had kept her thick, dark hair cropped short, and learned to wear trousers with such panache that ever since the tangle of petticoats and crinolines around her legs had irritated her.

The hospital governors had only discovered the fact that she was a woman after she had obtained her medical qualification from the Royal College of Surgeons at the age of twenty-one. They had immediately petitioned the Royal College to withdraw the honor, and the ensuing scandal had swept the length and breadth of England, made more fascinating by the fact that she was the daughter of Dr. Fuller Ballantyne, the famous African explorer, traveler, medical missionary and author. In the end, the governors of St. Matthew's had been forced to retreat, for Robyn Ballantyne and her Uncle William had found a champion in the small, rotund person of Oliver Wicks, editor of the *Standard*.

With a true journalist's eye, Wicks had recognized good copy, and in a scathing editorial had called upon the British tradition of fair play, ridiculed the dark hints of sexual orgies in the operating rooms and pointed up the considerable achievement of this bright and sensitive young girl against almost insurmountable odds. Yet even when her qualification had been confirmed, it was for her only a short step along the road back to Africa, on which she had determined so long ago.

The venerable directors of the London Missionary Society had been considerably alarmed by the offer of the services of a woman. Missionary wives were one thing, were indeed highly desirable to shield the missionaries themselves against physical blandishments and temptations among the unclothed heathen, but a lady missionary was another thing entirely.

There was a further complication which weighed heavily

7

against Dr. Robyn Ballantyne's application. Her father was Fuller Ballantyne, who had resigned from the society six years previously before disappearing once again into the African hinterland; in their eyes he had completely discredited himself. It was clear to them that the father was more interested in exploration and personal aggrandizement than in leading the benighted heathen into the bosom of Jesus Christ. In fact, so far as they were aware, Fuller Ballantyne had made only one convert in all his thousands of miles of African travel, his personal gunbearer.

He seemed to have made himself a crusader against the African slave trade, rather than an emissary of Christ. He had swiftly changed his first missionary station in Africa into a sanctuary for runaway slaves. The station at Koloberg had been on the southern edge of the Kalahari Desert, a little oasis in the wilderness where a clear, strong spring of water gushed from the ground, and it had been founded with an enormous expenditure of the society's funds.

Once Fuller had made it a slave refuge, the inevitable had happened. The Trek Boers from the little independent republics which ringed the mission station to the south were the original owners of the slaves to whom Fuller Ballantyne gave sanctuary. They called "Commando," the medium through which the Trek Boers dispensed frontier justice. They came riding into Koloberg an hour before dawn, dark swift horsemen, a hundred of them, dressed in coarse homespun, bearded and burned by the sun to the color of Africa's dark earth. The bright flashes of their muzzle-loaders lit the dawn, and then the burning thatch of the buildings of Fuller Ballantyne's mission station made it bright day.

They roped the recaptured slaves together with the station servants and freedmen into long lines, and drove them away southward, leaving Fuller Ballantyne standing with his family huddled about him, a few pathetic possessions which they had managed to save from the flames scattered at their feet, and the smoke from the smoldering, roofless buildings drifting in eddies about them.

It had confirmed in Fuller Ballantyne his hatred of the institution of slavery, and it had given him the excuse for which he had unwittingly been searching, the excuse to rid himself of the encumbrances which had until then prevented him from answering the call of the vast, empty land to the north.

His wife and two small children were packed off back to England for their own good, and with them went a letter to the

8

directors of the London Missionary Society. God had made his will clear to Fuller Ballantyne. He was bidden to journey to the north, to carry God's word across Africa, a missionary at large, no longer tied to one small station, but with the whole of Africa as his parish.

The directors were greatly troubled by the loss of their station, but they were further dismayed by the prospect of having to mount what seemed to be a costly expedition of exploration into an area which all the world knew was merely a vast desert, unpeopled and unwatered except around the littoral, a burning sand desert which stretched to the Mediterranean Sea four thousand miles northward.

They wrote hurriedly to Fuller Ballantyne, uncertain where exactly the letter should be addressed, but feeling the need to deny all responsibility and to express their deep concern; they ended by stating strongly that no further funds other than his stipend of fifty pounds per annum could be voted for Fuller Ballantyne's highly irregular activities. They need not have expended their energy and emotions, for Fuller Ballantyne had departed. With a handful of porters, his Christian gunbearer, a Colt revolver, a percussion rifle, two boxes of medicines, his journals and navigational instruments, Fuller Ballantyne had disappeared.

He emerged eight years later, down the Zambezi River, appearing at the Portuguese settlement near the mouth of that river, to the chagrin of the settlers there who, after two hundred years of occupation, had pushed no farther than a hundred miles upstream.

Fuller Ballantyne returned to England and his book *A Missionary in Darkest Africa* created a tremendous sensation. Here was a man who had made the "Transversa," the overland passage of Africa from west to east coast, who had seen, where there should be desert, great rivers and lakes, cool pleasant grassy uplands, great herds of game and strange peoples—but most of all he had seen the terrible depredations of the slave raiders upon the continent, and his revelations rekindled the antislavery zeal of Wilberforce in the hearts of the British people.

The London Missionary Society was embarrassed by the instant fame of their prodigal, and they hurried to make amends. Fuller Ballantyne had chosen the sites for future missionary stations in the interior, and at the cost of many thousands of pounds they gathered together groups of devoted men and women and sent them out to the selected sites.

The British Government, prevailed upon by Fuller Ballantyne's description of the Zambezi River as a wide roadway to the rich interior of Africa, nominated Fuller Ballantyne Her Majesty's Consul, and financed an elaborate expedition to open this artery of trade and civilization to the interior.

Fuller had returned to England to write his book, but during this period of reunion with his family, they saw almost as little of the great man as when he was in the depths of Africa. When he was not locked in Uncle William's study writing the epic of his travels, he was in London hounding the Foreign Office or the directors of the L.M.S. And when he had gained from these sources all that he needed for his return to Africa, then he was traveling about England lecturing in Oxford or preaching the sermon from the pulpit of Canterbury Cathedral.

Then abruptly he was gone again, taking their mother with him. Robyn would always remember the feel of his spiky whiskers as she stooped to kiss his daughter farewell for the second time. In her mind her father and God were somehow the same person, all-powerful, all-righteous, and her duty to them was blind, accepting adoration.

Years later, when the missionary sites chosen by Fuller Ballantyne had proved to be deathtraps, when the surviving missionaries had stumbled back to civilization, their fellows and spouses dead of fever and famine, killed by wild animals and by the wilder men whom they had gone out to save, then Fuller Ballantyne's star had begun to fade.

The Foreign Office expedition to the Zambezi River, led by Ballantyne, had faltered and failed upon the terrible rapids and deep falls of the Kaborra-Bassa gorge through which the Zambezi crashed and roared, dropping a thousand feet in twenty miles. Men wondered how Ballantyne, who had claimed to have followed the Zambezi down from its source to the sea, could have not known of such a formidable obstacle to his dreams. They began to question his other claims, while the British Foreign Office, parsimonious as ever, was considerably miffed by the waste of funds on the abortive expedition and withdrew the title of consul.

The London Missionary Society wrote another of their lengthy letters to Fuller Ballantyne, requesting him in future to confine his activities to the conversion of the heathen and the propagation of God's word.

Fuller Ballantyne had replied by posting them his resignation, thereby saving the society fifty pounds per annum. At the same time he had penned a letter of encouragement to his two children urging them to show fortitude and faith, and sent the manuscript, in which he vindicated his conduct of the expedition, to his publisher. Then he had taken the few guineas that remained from the huge royalties that his other books had earned and had disappeared once more into the interior of Africa. That was eight years previously and no one had heard from him since.

Now here was this man's daughter, already nearly as notorious as the father, demanding admission to the society as a working missionary.

Once again, Uncle William had come to Robyn's aid, dear mild bumbling Uncle William with his thick pebble spectacles and wild gray bush of untamable hair. With her he had gone before the board of directors and reminded them that Robyn's grandfather, Robert Moffat, was one of the most successful of all African missionaries, with tens of thousands of conversions to his credit. Indeed the old man was still working at Kuruman and had only recently published his dictionary of the Sechuana language. Robyn herself was dedicated and devout, with medical training and a good knowledge of African languages taught her by her now deceased mother, daughter of the same Robert Moffat, and by virtue of the reverence with which the said Robert Moffat was regarded by even the most warlike African king, Mzilikazi of the Ndebele, or as some people called them, the Matabele, the granddaughter would find immediate acceptance among the tribes.

The directors had listened stonily.

Then Uncle William had gone on to suggest that Oliver Wicks, the editor of the *Standard* who had championed the girl against the attempt by the governors of St. Matthew's Hospital to deprive her of her medical qualification, would be interested in their reasons for refusing her application to the society.

The directors sat up and listened with attention, conferred quietly and accepted Robyn's application. They had then seconded her to another missionary movement who in turn sent her to the industrial slums of northern England.

It was her brother Zouga who had found the way back to Africa for both of them.

He had returned from India on leave, a man of considerable achievement, already a major in the Indian Army, promotion that he had won in the field, with the reputation of being a

11

soldier and military administrator of great promise for one so young.

Despite this, Zouga was every bit as dissatisfied with his lot as was Robyn. Like their father, they were both lone wolves, responding badly to authority and regimentation. In spite of the promising start to his military career, Zouga recognized the fact that he had already made powerful enemies in India, and he had begun to doubt that his future lay on that continent. Like Robyn, he was still a searcher, and they had greeted each other after the parting of years with a warmth that they had seldom displayed during their childhood.

Zouga took her to dinner at the Golden Boar. It was such a change from Robyn's daily surroundings that she accepted a second glass of claret and became gay and sparkling.

"By God, sissy, you really are a pretty thing, you know," he had told her at last. He had taken to swearing now, and though it had shocked her at first, she had grown accustomed to it quickly enough. She had heard a lot worse in the slums where she worked. "You are too good to spend your life amongst those ghastly crones."

It changed the mood between them instantly, and she was able to last to lean close to her brother and pour out all her frustrations. He listened sympathetically, reaching across the table to squeeze her hand so that she went on quietly but with utter determination.

"Zouga, I have to get back to Africa. I'll die if I don't. I just know it. I will shrivel up and die."

"Good Lord, sissy, why Africa?"

"Because I was born there, because my destiny is there— and because Papa is there, somewhere."

"I was born there also." Zouga smiled, and when he did so it softened the harsh line of his mouth. "But I don't know about my destiny. I wouldn't mind going back for the hunting, of course, but as for Father—don't you often think that Papa's main concern was always Fuller Ballantyne? I cannot imagine that you still harbor any great filial love for him."

"He is different from other men, Zouga, you cannot judge him by the usual yardstick."

"There are many who might agree with that," Zouga murmured dryly. "At the L.M.S. and at the Foreign Office—but as a father?"

"I love him!" she said defiantly. "After God, I love him best."

"He killed Mother, you know." Zouga's mouth hardened

into its usual grim line. "He took her out to the Zambezi in fever season and he killed her as certainly as if he'd put a pistol to her head."

Robyn conceded after a short, regretful silence, "He was never a father nor a husband—but as a visionary, a blazer of trails, as a torchbearer . . ."

Zouga laughed and squeezed her hand.

"Really, sissy!"

"I have read his books, all his letters, every one he ever wrote to Mother or to us, and I know that my place is there. In Africa, with Papa."

Zouga lifted his hand from hers and carefully stroked his thick side whiskers. "You always had a way of making me feel excited—" Then, seemingly going off at a tangent, "Did you hear that they have found diamonds on the Orange River?" He lifted his glass and examined the lees in the bottom of it attentively. "We are so very different, you and I, and yet in some ways so much alike." He poured fresh wine into his glass and went on casually. "I am in debt, sissy."

The word chilled her. Since her childhood she had been taught a dread of it.

"How much?" she asked at last quietly.

"Two hundred pounds." He shrugged.

"So much!" she breathed, and then, "You haven't been gambling, Zouga?"

That was one of the other dread words in Robyn's vocabulary.

"Not gambling?" she repeated.

"As a matter of fact, I have," Zouga laughed. "And thank God for that. Without it I would be a thousand guineas under."

"You mean you gamble—and actually win?" Her horror faded a little, became tinged with fascination.

"Not always, but most of the time."

She studied him carefully, perhaps for the first time. He was only twenty-six years old, but he had the presence and aplomb of a man ten years older. He was already a hard, professional soldier, tempered in the skirmishes on the border of Afghanistan where his regiment had spent four years. She knew there had been cruel encounters against fierce hill tribes, and that Zouga had distinguished himself. His rapid promotion was proof of that.

"Then how are you in debt, Zouga?" she asked.

"Most of my brother officers, even my juniors, have private

fortunes. I am a major now, I have to keep some style. We hunt, we shoot, mess bills, polo ponies—" He shrugged again.

"Will you ever be able to repay it?"

"I could marry a rich wife," he smiled, "or find diamonds."

Zouga sipped his wine, slumped down in his chair, not looking at her, and went on quietly.

"I was reading Cornwallis Harris's book the other day—do you remember the big game we saw when we lived at Koloberg?"

She shook her head.

"No, you were only a baby. But I do. I remember the herds of springbok and wildebeest on the trek down to the Cape. One night there was a lion, I saw it clearly in the light of the campfire. Harris's book described his hunting expeditions up as far as the Limpopo—nobody has been further than that, except Papa, of course. A damned sight better than potting pheasant or black buck. Did you know that Harris made nearly five thousand pounds from his book?"

Zouga pushed his glass away, straightened up in his seat and selected a cigar from his silver case. While he prepared and lit it, he was frowning thoughtfully.

"You want to go to Africa for spiritual reasons. I probably need to go to Africa, for much better reasons, for blood and for money. I make you a proposal. The Ballantyne Expedition!" He lifted his glass to her.

She laughed then, uncertainly, thinking he was joking, but lifted her own glass, which was still almost full, "My word on it. But how? Zouga, how do we get there?"

"What was the name of that newspaper fellow?" Zouga demanded.

"Wicks," she said, "Oliver Wicks. But why should he help us?"

"I'll find a good reason why he should." And Robyn remembered how, even as a child, he had been an eloquent and persuasive pleader of causes.

"You know I rather think you might."

They drank then, and when she lowered her glass, she was as happy as she could ever remember being in all her life.

It was another six weeks before she saw Zouga again, striding toward her through the bustle of London Bridge Station as she clambered down from the carriage. He stood tall above the crowd, with the high beaver top hat on his head and the three-quarter-length paletot cloak flaring from his shoulders.

"Sissy!" he called, laughing at her, as he lifted her from her feet. "We are going—we really are going."

He had a cab waiting for them, and the driver whipped up the horses the moment they were aboard.

"The London Missionary Society were no use at all," he told her, still with his arm around her shoulders as the cab clattered and lurched over the cobbles. "I had them down on my list for five hundred iron men, and they nearly had apoplexy. I had the feeling they would rather Papa stayed lost in darkest Africa, and they would pay five hundred to keep him there."

"You went to the directors?" she demanded.

"Played my losing tricks first," Zouga smiled. "The next was Whitehall—actually managed to see the First Secretary. He was damned civil, took me to lunch at the Travellers', and was truly very sorry that they were not able to give financial assistance. They remembered Papa's Zambezi fiasco too clearly, but he did give me letters. A dozen letters, to every conceivable person—to the governor at the Cape, to Kemp the admiral at Cape Town, and all the others."

"Letters won't get us far."

"Then I went to see your newspaper friend. Extraordinary little man. Smart as a whip. I told him we were going to Africa to find Papa—and he jumped up and clapped his hands like a child at a Punch and Judy show." Zouga hugged Robyn tighter. "To tell the truth, I used your name shamelessly—and it did the trick. He will have all the story rights to our diaries and journals, and the publishing rights to both books."

"Both books?" Robyn pulled away from him and looked into his face.

"Both." He grinned at her. "Yours and mine."

"I am to write a book?"

"You certainly are. A woman's account of the expedition. I have already signed the contract on your behalf."

She laughed then, but breathlessly. "You're going too far, much too fast."

"Little Wicks was in for five hundred, and the next on the list was the Society for the Extinction of the Slave Trade— they were easy. His Royal Highness is the society's patron, and he had read Papa's books. We are to report on the state of the trade in the interior of the continent north of the Tropic of Capricorn, and they came up with another five hundred guineas."

"Oh, Zouga, you are a magician."

15

"Then there was the Worshipful Company of London Merchants Trading into Africa. For the last hundred years they have based all their activities on the west coast, I convinced them that they needed a survey of the east coast. I have been appointed the Worshipful Company's Agent, with instructions to examine the market in palm oil, gum copal, copper and ivory—and they have come up with the third and last five hundred guineas—and a presentation Sharps rifle."

"One thousand five hundred guineas," Robyn breathed, and Zouga nodded.

"We are going back home in style."

"When?"

"I have booked passage on an American trading clipper. We sail from Bristol in six weeks, for Good Hope and Quelimane in Mozambique. I have written asking leave from my regiment for two years—you will have to do the same with the L.M.S."

It had all happened with dreamlike rapidity after that. The directors of the L.M.S., perhaps relieved that they were not to pay for her passage nor the expense of relocating Robyn in the African interior, in a flush of extravagance decided to continue her stipend during the period she was away, and made a guarded promise to review the position at the end of that time. If she proved herself capable, then there would be a permanent post in Africa thereafter. It was more than she had ever expected, and she had thrown herself wholeheartedly into assisting Zouga with the preparations for departure.

There was so much to do that six weeks was barely sufficient, and it seemed only days had passed before the mountain of the expedition's equipment was being swayed down into the holds of the big graceful Baltimore clipper.

The *Huron* proved as swift as she looked, another wise choice by Zouga Ballantyne, and under Mungo St. John's skillful navigation she made good her westings before attempting to cross the belt of the doldrums at their narrowest point. They were becalmed not a single day and sped across the line at 29° west and immediately Mungo St. John put her on the port tack to stand down across the southeast trades. *Huron* clawed her way southward with the flying fish sailing ahead of her, close on the wind until she broke from their grip at last with Ilha da Trinidade on the horizon. The northwester came howling at them and *Huron* fled before it, under low, sullen, scudding skies day after day that denied them sight of sun or moon or stars, until she almost hurled herself ashore two hundred miles up the west coast of Africa from her destination at the Cape of Good Hope.

"Mr. Mate!" Mungo St. John called in his clear, carrying voice as *Huron* settled down to reach across the wind, pulling swiftly away from the land.

"Captain!" Tippoo bellowed back from the foot of the mainmast, a great blurt of sound from the bull chest.

"Take the name of the masthead watch."

Tippoo ducked his cannonball head on its thick neck like a bare-knuckle fighter taking a punch, and looked up the mast, slitting his eyes in the heavy folds of flesh.

"Twenty minutes more and he would have had us on the beach." St. John's voice was cold, deadly. "I'll have him on the grating before this day is out, and we will get a peep of his backbone."

Tippoo licked his thick lips involuntarily, and Robyn, standing near him, felt her stomach heave. There had been three floggings already on this voyage and she knew what to expect. Tippoo was half Arab, half African, a honey-colored giant of a man with a shaven head that was covered with a mesh of tiny pale scars from a thousand violent encounters. He wore a loose embroidered highnecked tunic over his huge frame, but the forearms that protruded from the wide sleeves were thick as a woman's thighs.

Robyn turned quickly to Zouga as he came down the deck toward her.

"We had a good look at the land, sissy. Our first definite fix since Ilha da Trinidade. If this wind holds we will be in Table Bay in another five days."

"Zouga, can't you intercede with the captain?" she demanded, and Zouga looked startled.

"He is going to flog that poor devil."

"Damn right too," Zouga growled. "The man nearly had us on the rocks."

"Can't you stop him?"

"I wouldn't dream of interfering with his running of this ship—and nor will I allow you to."

"Do you have no humanity at all?" she demanded of her brother coldly, but there were bright hot spots of anger on her cheeks, and her eyes snapped clear angry green. "You call yourself a Christian."

"When I do, I speak softly though, my dear." Zouga made

17

the reply he knew would annoy her most. "And I don't flaunt it at every turn in the conversation."

Their arguments were always sudden as summer thunderstorms on the African veld, and as spectacular.

Mungo St. John sauntered forward to lean his elbow on the railing of his quarterdeck, a long Havana cheroot of coarse black tobacco held between white teeth. He mocked her silently with those flecked yellow eyes, infuriating her further, until she heard her own voice going shrill and she turned from Zouga, and rounded on him.

"The man you had flogged last week could be crippled for life," she shouted at him.

"Dr. Ballantyne—how would you like Tippoo to carry you down and lock you in your cabin?" Mungo St. John asked. "Until you regain your temper and your manners."

"You cannot do that," she flared at him.

"I can, I assure you—that and much more."

"He's right," Zouga assured her softly. "On this ship he can do virtually anything he wants." He laid his hand on her upper arm. "Steady now, sissy. The fellow will be lucky to get away with the loss of a little skin."

Robyn found she was panting with anger and a sense of helplessness.

"If you are squeamish, Doctor, I will excuse you from witnessing punishment," Mungo St. John mocked her still. "We must make allowance for the fact that you are a woman."

"I have never asked for consideration on that score, not once in all my life." She tried to get her anger back under control, and she shook off her brother's hand and turned away from them.

She walked with stiff back and squared shoulders up into the bows, trying to maintain an aloof dignity, but the ship's motion was awkward and her damned skirts fluttered around her legs. She realized she had thought the word, and she would ask forgiveness later—but not now, and suddenly she said it aloud.

"Damn you, Captain Mungo St. John, damn you to hell!"

She stood in the bows, and the wind pulled her hair out of the neat chignon at the nape of her neck and flicked it in her face. It was her mother's thick silken dark hair, shot with tones of russet and chestnut, and as a pale ray of greenish sunlight at last broke through the cloud cover, it turned to a glowing halo around her small neat head.

She stared ahead angrily, hardly noticing the hellish beauty of the scene about her. The cold, green waters, smoked with mist banks, opened and closed about the ship like pearly curtains. Wisps of mist trailed from the sails and yards as though she was on fire.

In patches, the surface of the sea simmered and darkened, for these waters were rich in microscopic sea life, which supported vast shoals of sardine that rose to the surface to feed, to be fed on in turn by flocks of shrieking seabirds that plunged upon them from high above, hitting the water in little cotton puffs of spray.

A thicker bank of mist took the tall ship in its damp cold grip so that when Robyn glanced back she could only just make out the ghostly figures of the captain and her brother on the quarterdeck.

Then just as suddenly they plunged out again into open sea, and sunny skies. The clouds which had covered them for all these weeks rolled away toward the south while the wind itself increased in strength and veered swiftly into the east, whipping the tops from the waves in graceful ostrich plumes of curling spray.

At the same moment Robyn saw the other ship. It was startlingly close, and she opened her mouth to shout—but a dozen other voices forestalled her.

"Sail oh!"

"Sail fine on the port quarter."

She was close enough to make out the thin, tall smokestack between the main and mizzenmasts. Her hull was painted black with a red line below her gunports; five guns each side.

The black hull had a sinister air to it, and the pile of her canvas was not shimmering white like that of *Huron,* but was sullied dirty gray by the belchings from her smokestack.

Mungo St. John played the field of his telescope swiftly over her. Her boilers were unlit, there was not even a tremble of heat from the mouth of her stack. She was under easy canvas only.

"Tippoo!" he called softly, and it seemed that the mate's bulk appeared beside him with the magical speed of a genie.

"Have you seen her before?"

Tippoo grunted and turned his head to spit over the lee rail.

"Lime juicer," he said. "I seen her last in Table Bay eight years back. She called *Black Joke.*"

"Cape Squadron?"

Tippoo grunted, and at that moment the gunboat bore up

sharply and at the same time her colors broke out at the mast-head. The crisp white and bright scarlet of her ensign shrieked a challenge, a challenge that all the world had learned to heed, and heed swiftly. Only the ships of one nation on earth need not heave to the instant that challenge was flown. The *Huron* was immune, she had only to hoist the Stars and Stripes, and even this importunate representative of the Royal Navy would be forced to respect it.

But Mungo St. John was thinking swiftly. Six days before he sailed from Baltimore Harbor, in May 1860, Abraham Lincoln had been nominated presidential candidate for the United States of America. If elected, as seemed highly likely, he would be invested early in the new year, and then one of his first actions would surely be to grant to Great Britain the privileges agreed by the Treaty of Brussels, including the right of search of American ships upon the high seas which previous American presidents had so steadfastly denied.

Soon, perhaps sooner than he expected, Mungo St. John might have to run his clipper in deadly earnest against one of these ships of the Cape Squadron. It was a heaven-sent opportunity to match his ship, and to observe the capabilities of the other.

He swept one last glance about him, that took in the sea, the wind-driven lines of foam upon it, the piled white pyramids of canvas above him and the evil black hull to leeward—and then his decision was made easier. On the wind came the thud of a gun, and a long feather of gunsmoke spurted from one of the gunboat's bow chasers, demanding instant obedience.

Mungo St. John smiled. "The insolent bastard!" To Tippoo he said, "We'll try him on a few points of sailing," to the helmsman beside him, softly, "Put the helm down." And as *Huron* paid off swiftly before the wind, beginning to point directly away from the threatening black ship, "Shake out all reefs, Mr. Mate. Set fore and maintop, hoist studding sails and skysails, crack on the main royal—yes, and flying jib too. By God, we'll show that grubby little coal-guzzling lime juicer how they build them down Baltimore way!"

Even in her anger, Robyn was thrilled by the manner in which the American worked his ship. With his crew swarming out across the yards to the reefing points, the mainsails swelled out to their full extent, dazzling white in the sunshine, and then high above, seemingly at the very base of the aching blue heaven itself, new unfamiliar-shaped sails popped open like overripe cotton pods and the long, graceful hull reacted instantly to the pressures thrust upon her.

"By God, she sails like a witch," Zouga shouted, laughing with excitement, as she knifed into the crests of the Atlantic rollers and he hustled his sister back from the bows before the first green sheets of water came aboard and swept *Huron*'s decks.

More and still more canvas burst open, and the thick trees of her masts began to arch like drawn longbows under the unbearable pressures of thousands of square feet of spread sails. Now *Huron* seemed to fly, taking off from the crest of each roller and smashing into the face of the next with a crash that shocked her timbers and jarred the teeth of her crew in their skulls.

"A cast of the log, Mr. Mate," Mungo St. John called, and when Tippoo bellowed back, "A touch better than sixteen knots, Cap'n!" the captain laughed aloud, and strode to the stern rail.

The gunboat was falling astern as though she was standing still, although every inch of her gray canvas was spread. Already she was at extreme cannon range.

Again powder smoke bloomed briefly on her black bows, and this time it seemed that it was more than merely a warning, for Mungo St. John saw the fall of shot. It struck the crest of a roller two cable lengths astern and skipped across the green torn waters, before plunging beneath the surface almost alongside *Huron*'s tall side.

"Captain, you are endangering the lives of your crew and passengers." The voice arrested him and St. John turned to the tall young woman who stood beside him, and he raised one thick black eyebrow in polite inquiry.

"That is a British man-of-war, sir, and we are acting like criminals. They are firing live shot now. You have only to heave to, or at the very least show your colors."

"I think my sister is right, Captain St. John." Zouga stood beside her. "I do not understand your behavior either."

Huron staggered violently to a larger crest, driven wild by the mountainous press of sail, Robyn lost her balance and fell against the captain's chest, but instantly pulled away, coloring fiercely at the contact.

"This is the coast of Africa, Major Ballantyne. Nothing is what it appears to be. Here only a fool would accept a strange armed vessel at its face value. Now if you and the good doctor will excuse me, I must attend to my duties."

He strode forward to gaze down at the main deck, judging

the mood of his crew and the wild abandon of his ship. He unhooked the key ring from his belt and tossed it to Tippoo. "The arms chest, Mr. Mate, a pair of pistols to you and the second mate. Shoot any hand who attempts to interfere with the setting of the sails." He had recognized the fear which gripped the crew. Most of them had never seen a ship driven like this, there might easily be an attempt to shorten sail rather than have her run herself under.

At that moment *Huron* put her shoulder into the Atlantic and took it aboard in a solid roaring green wall. One of the topmast men was not quick enough on to the rat lines. The water plucked him up and flung him down the length of the deck, until he crashed into the side, and lay huddled against the bulwark like a clump of uprooted kelp on a storm-driven beach.

Two of his fellows tried to reach him, but the next wave drove them back as it came pouring aboard waist deep and then cascading in a roaring white torrent over the side, and when it was gone the fallen topmast man was gone with it and the deck was empty.

"Mr. Tippoo, look you to those skysails, they are not drawing as they should."

Mungo St. John turned back to the stern rail, ignoring Robyn Ballantyne's horrified and accusing glare.

Already the British gunboat was hull down and her sails were barely discernible among the gray beards of the breaking Atlantic rollers, but suddenly Mungo St. John saw something change, and he reached quickly for the telescope in its slot under the chart table. There was a fine black line, as though drawn in Indian ink, extending from the tiny cone of the Englishman's sails for a short way across the bumpy horizon.

"Smoke! She has her boiler fired at last," he grunted, as Tippoo appeared at his shoulder, with the pistols thrust into his belt.

"One screw. She no catch us." Tippoo nodded his round shaven head.

"No, not downwind in a full gale," Mungo St. John agreed. "But I'd like to try her on the wind. We'll harden up now, Mr. Mate, on the port tack again. I want to see if I can run up to windward of her and pass her out of cannon shot."

The unexpected maneuver caught the gunboat commander completely off guard, and he was a few minutes slow in altering course to cut the shorter leg of the triangle and prevent the *Huron* from wresting the weather gage from him.

Huron went streaming past him at extreme cannon shot hard on the wind, her yards sheeted around as close hauled as she would sail. He tried a shot across her dipping, plunging bows with no visible fall of shot, and then he came around to follow her into the wind, and immediately the flaws in the design and construction of his ship were pointed up as clearly as they had been while both ships were running before the wind.

In order to accommodate the heavy boiler and machinery to drive the big bronze screw under her counter, serious compromise had been made with the design of her masts and the amount of canvas she could carry.

Within five miles it became clear that with all sail set and the boilers belching a solid greasy slug of coal smoke over the stern the *Black Joke* could not point as high into the wind as the beautiful tall ship ahead of her. She was drifting steadily away to leeward, and although the difference in their speeds was not as dramatic as when running before the wind, yet *Huron* was headreaching on her steadily.

The gunboat's commander pointed her higher and higher, trying desperately to hold the bigger ship directly over his bows, but all his sails were shaking and luffing before he could do so.

In a fury of frustration, he took in all his canvas, stripping his poles bare and relying only on the drive of his steam boiler pointed up directly into the very eye of the wind, much much higher than *Huron* could sail. But the gunboat's speed bled away when her screw received no help from her sails. Even though her mast and rigging were bare, the storm whistled and howled head on through them, acing as a great drogue that slowed her further and *Huron* forged ahead more swiftly.

"A bastard contraption." Mungo St. John watched her battle with all his attention, judging her performance at every point of the wind. "We are toying with her. As long as there is a breath of wind we'll romp away from her."

Astern, the gunboat's commander had abandoned his attempt to run the clipper down with steam power alone, and had come back onto a fine reach with all his canvas set, plugging along stubbornly in *Huron*'s streaming wake—until abruptly, with no warning at all, *Huron* sailed into a deep hole in the wind.

The line of the gale was drawn clearly across the surface of the sea. On one side, the water was darkened and furrowed

23

by the talons of the wind, on the other, the humped backs of the rollers in the calm had a polished velvety gloss to them.

As *Huron* crossed that line of demarcation, the clamor of the wind, which for week after week had battered their ears, fell to an eerie unnatural silence, and the ship's motion changed from the vital charge of a living, straining sea creature to the patternless rolling and wallowing of a dead log.

Overhead her canvas volleyed and flapped in the direction-less eddies created by her own rolling and pitching, and her tackle crashed and clattered so that it seemed that she might roll her masts clean out of her hull.

Far astern, the black-painted gunboat scrambled on eagerly, swiftly beginning to narrow the distance between them, the black column of coal smoke now rising straight up into the stillness of air, giving her a jubilant and menacing air.

Mungo St. John ran to the forward rail of the quarterdeck, and stared over his bows. He could see the wind two or three miles ahead clawing at the sea and ruffling it to a somber shade of indigo, but between them was the oily undulating surface of the calm.

He swung back and the gunboat was closer, sending her smoke spurting high against the bright windswept blue of the sky, so certain of herself now that her gunports were swinging open and the stubby barrels of her thirty-two-pounder cannon protruding from the black sides of her hull, the churning wash of her screw tumbling out from under her counter and sparkling whitely in the sunlight.

With no way upon *Huron*, the helmsman could not hold any course, and the clipper drifted around broadside to the onrushing man-of-war putting her bows directly into the rollers.

They could make out the individual figures of the three officers on the gunboat's bridge now. Again the bow chaser fired, and the shell lifted a tall column of water so high and close under the *Huron*'s bows that it collapsed upon the deck and streamed out through the scuppers.

Mungo St. John took one last despairing sweep of the ho-rizon, hoping even now for a resurgence of wind, and then he capitulated.

"Hoist the colors, Mr. Tippoo," he called, and as the gaudy scrap of cloth drooped from the mainyard in the windless air, he watched through the lens of his telescope the consternation it caused upon the gunboat's bridge. That was the last flag they had hoped to see.

They were now close enough to discern the individual
24

expressions of chagrin and alarm and indecision of the naval officers.

"There'll be no prize money for you—not this time around," Mungo St. John murmured with grim satisfaction, and snapped the telescope shut.

The gunboat came on and then rounded up to *Huron*, within easy hail, showing her full broadside, the long thirty-two-pounder cannon gaping menacingly.

The tallest officer on her bridge seemed also the oldest, for his hair was white in the sunlight. He came to the gunboat's near rail and lifted the voice trumpet to his mouth.

"What ship?"

"Huron, out of Baltimore and Bristol," Mungo St. John hailed back. "With a cargo of trade goods for Good Hope and Quelimane."

"Why did you not answer my challenge, sir?"

"Because, sir, I do not acknowledge your right to challenge ships of the United States of America on the high seas."

Both captains knew just what a thorny and controversial question that reply posed, but the Englishman hesitated only a second.

"Do you, sir, accede to my right to satisfy myself as to your nationality and your ship's port of registry?"

"As soon as you run in your guns you may come aboard for that purpose, Captain. But do not send one of your junior officers."

Mungo St. John was making a fine point of humiliating the commander of the *Black Joke*. But inwardly he was still seething at the fluke of wind and weather which had allowed the gunboat to come up with him.

The *Black Joke* launched a longboat on the heavy swell with an immaculate show of seamanship, and it pulled swiftly to *Huron*'s side. While the captain scrambled up the rope ladder, the boat's crew backed off and rested on their oars.

The naval officer came in through the entry port, so lithe and agile that Mungo St. John realized his error in thinking him an elderly man. It was the white-blond hair that had misled him; he was evidently less than thirty years of age. He did not wear a uniform coat, for his ship had been cleared for action, and he was dressed in a plain white linen shirt, breeches and soft boots. There was a pair of pistols in his belt and a naval cutlass in its scabbard on his hip.

"Captain Codrington of Her Majesty's auxiliary cruiser *Black Joke,"* he introduced himself stiffly. His hair was bleached in

25

silverwhite splashes from the salt and the sun, with darker streaks beneath, and it was tied with a leather thong in a short queue at the nape of his neck. His face was weathered to honey-golden brown by the same sun, so that the faded blue of his eyes was in pale contrast.

"Captain St. John, owner and master of this vessel."

Neither man made any move to shake hands, and they seemed to bristle like two dog wolves meeting for the first time.

"I hope you do not intend to detain me longer than is necessary. You can assure yourself that my government will be fully apprised of this incident."

"May I inspect your papers, Captain?" The young naval officer ignored the threat, and followed St. John on to the quarterdeck. There he hesitated for the first time when he caught sight of Robyn and her brother standing together at the far rail, but he recovered immediately, bowed slightly and then turned his full attention to the packet of documents that Mungo St. John had ready for his inspection on the chart table.

He stooped over the table, working swiftly through the pile until with a shock of discovery he straightened.

"Damn me—Mungo St. John—your reputation precedes you, sir." The Englishman's expression was strained with strong emotion. "And what a noble one it is, too." There was a bitter sting in his voice. "The first trader ever to carry more than three thousand souls across the middle passage in a single, twelve-month period; small wonder you can afford such a magnificent vessel."

"You are on dangerous ground, sir," Mungo St. John warned him with that lazy, taunting grin. "I am fully aware of the lengths to which the officers of your service will go for a few guineas of prize money."

"Where are you going to pick up your next cargo of human misery, Captain St. John?" the Englishman cut in brusquely. "On such a fine ship you should be able to pack in two thousand." He had gone pale with unfeigned anger, actually trembling slightly with the force of it.

"If you have finished your investigation—" St. John's smile did not slip, but the naval officer went on speaking.

"We have made the west coast a little too hot for you now, have we? Even when you hide behind that pretty piece of silk," the naval officer glanced up at the flag on the mainyard, "so you are going to work the east coast now, are you, sir? They tell me you can get a prime slave for two dollars—two for a ten-shilling musket."

"I must ask you to leave now," St. John took the document from his hand, and when their fingers touched, the Englishman wiped his hand on his own thigh as though to cleanse it of the contact.

"I'd give five years' pay to have the hatches off your holds," he said bitterly, leaning forward to stare at Mungo St. John with those pale fierce eyes.

"Captain Codrington!" Zouga Ballantyne stepped toward the group. "I am a British subject and an officer in Her Majesty's army. I can assure you that there are no slaves aboard this vessel." He spoke sharply.

"If you are an Englishman, then you should be ashamed to travel in such company," Codrington glanced beyond Zouga. "And that applies equally to you, madam!"

"You overreach yourself, sir," Zouga told him grimly. "I have already given you my assurance."

Codrington's gaze had flicked back to Robyn Ballantyne's face. Her distress was evident, unfeigned. The accusation had shattered her, that she, the daughter of Fuller Ballantyne, the great champion of freedom and sworn adversary of slavery— she, the accredited agent of the Society for the Extinction of the Slave Trade, should be traveling aboard a notorious slaver.

She was pale, the green eyes huge and liquid with the shock of it.

"Captain Codrington," her voice was husky and low, "my brother is right—I also assure you that there are no slaves aboard this ship."

The Englishman's expression softened, she was not a beautiful woman, but there was a freshness and wholesomeness about her which was difficult to resist.

"I will accept your word, madam." He inclined his head. "Indeed, only a madman would carry black ivory towards Africa, but"—and his voice hardened again—"if only I were able to enter her holds, I'd find enough down there to run her into Table Bay under a prize crew and have her condemned out of hand at the next session of the Court of Mixed Commission."

Codrington swung on his heel to face Mungo St. John again.

"Oh yes, I know that your slave decks will be struck to make way for your trade cargo, but the spare planks are aboard and it won't take you a day to set them up again," Codrington almost snarled, "and I'll wager there are open gratings under those hatch covers," he pointed down at the main deck, but without taking his eyes from Mungo St. John's face, "that there

27

are shackles in the lower decks to take the chains and leg irons—"

"Captain Codrington, I find your company wearying," Mungo St. John drawled softly. "You have sixty seconds to leave this ship, before I have my mate assist you over the side."

Tippoo stepped forward, hairless as an enormous toad, and stood a foot behind Codrington's left shoulder.

With a visible effort, the English captain retained his temper, as he inclined his head toward Mungo St. John.

"May God grant we meet again, sir." He turned back to Robyn and saluted her briefly.

"May I wish you a pleasant continuation of your voyage, madam."

"Captain Codrington, I think you are mistaken," she almost pleaded with him. He did not reply but stared at her for a moment longer, the pale eyes direct and disturbing—the eyes of a prophet or a fanatic—then he turned and went with a gangling boyish stride to *Huron*'s entry port.

Tippoo had stripped off the high-necked tunic and oiled his upper body so it gleamed in the sunlight with the metallic luster of the skin of some exotic reptile.

He stood stolidly on flat bare feet, balancing effortlessly to the *Huron*'s roll, his thick arms hanging at his side and the lash of the whip coiled on the deck at his feet.

There was a grating fixed at the ship's side and the sailor who had been at the masthead lookout when they had raised the African coast, was spreadeagled upon it like a stranded starfish on a rock exposed at low tide. He twisted his head awkwardly to look back over his shoulder at the mate, and his face was white with terror.

"You were excused witnessing punishment, Dr. Ballantyne," Mungo St. John told her quietly.

"I feel it my duty to suffer this barbaric—"

"As you wish," he cut her short with a nod, and turned away. "Twenty, Mr. Tippoo."

"Twenty it is, Cap'n."

With no expression at all Tippoo stepped up behind the man, hooked his finger into the back of his collar and ripped the shirt down to the belt. The man's back was pale as suet pudding, but studded with fat purple carbuncles, the sailor's affliction, caused by salty, wet clothing and the unhealthy diet.

Tippoo stepped back and flicked out the lash so that it extended to its full length along the seamed oak planking.

"Ship's company!" Mungo St. John called. "The charge is inattention to duty, and endangering the ship's safety." They shuffled their bare feet, but not one of them looked up at him. "The sentence is twenty lashes."

On the grating the man turned his face away and closed his eyes tightly, hunching his shoulders.

"Lay on, Mr. Tippoo," Mungo St. John said, and Tippoo squinted carefully at the bare, white skin, through which the knuckles of the spine showed clearly. He reared back, one thickly muscled arm thrown high above his head, and the lash snaked higher, hissing like an angry cobra, then he stepped forward into the stroke, pivoting the full weight and force of his shoulders into it.

The man on the grating shrieked, and his body convulsed in a spasm that smeared the skin from his wrists against the coarse hemp bonds.

The white skin opened in a thin bright scarlet line, from one side of his ribs to the other, and one of the angry purple carbuncles between his shoulder blades erupted in a spurt of yellow matter that ran down the pale skin and soaked into the waistband of his breeches.

"One," said Mungo St. John, and the man on the grating began to sob quietly.

Tippoo stepped back, shook out the lash carefully, squinted at the bloody line across the white shuddering flesh, reared back and grunted as he stepped forward into the next stroke.

"Two," said Mungo St. John. Robyn felt her gorge rise to choke her. She fought it down, and forced herself to watch. She could not allow him to see her weakness.

On the tenth stroke the body on the grating relaxed suddenly, the head lolled sideways and the fists unclenched slowly so that she could see the little bloody half-moon wounds where the nails had been driven into the palms. There was no further sign of life during the rest of the leisurely ritual of punishment.

At the twentieth stroke, she almost flung herself down the ladder to the main deck and was feeling for the pulse before they could cut the body down from the grating.

"Praise be to God," she whispered as she felt it fluttering under her fingers, and then to the seamen who were lifting the man down, "Gently now!" She saw that Mungo St. John had got his wish, for the white porcelain crests of the spinal column were jutting up through the sliced meat of the back muscles.

She had a cotton dressing ready and she placed it across the

29

ruined back as they laid him on to an oak plank and hustled him toward the forecastle.

In the narrow, crowded forecastle, thick with the fumes of cheap pipe tobacco and the almost solid reek of bilges and wet clothing, of unwashed men and moldering food, they laid the man on the mess table and she worked as best she could in the guttering light of the oil lamp in its gimbals overhead. She stitched back the flaps and ribbons of mushy, torn flesh with horsehair sutures and then bound up the whole in weak phenol solution, treatment which Joseph Lister had recently pioneered with much success against mortification.

The man was conscious again and whimpering with pain. She gave him five drops of laudanum, and promised to visit him the following day to change the bindings.

As she packed away her instruments and closed her black valise, one of the crew, a little pockmarked bosun named Nathaniel, picked it up and when she nodded her thanks, he muttered with embarrassment, "We are beholden, missus."

It had taken all of them time to accept her ministrations. First it had been only the lancing of carbuncles and sea boils, calomel for the flux and the grippe, but later, after a dozen successful treatments, which included a fractured humerus, an ulcerated and ruptured eardrum and the banishing of a venereal chancre with mercury, she had become a firm favorite among the crew, and her sick call a regular feature of shipboard life.

The bosun climbed the companionway behind her, carrying the valise, but before they reached the deck, an idea struck her and she stooped to him, placing a hand on his shoulder.

"Nathaniel," she asked urgently, but in a low voice, "is there a way of entering the ship's hold without lifting the main-deck hatches?"

The man looked startled, and she shook his shoulder roughly. "Is there?" she demanded.

"Aye, ma'am, there is."

"Where? How?"

"Through the lazaretto, below the officers' saloon—there is a hatchway through the forward bulkhead."

"Is it locked?"

"Aye, ma'am, it is—and Captain St. John keeps the keys on his belt."

"Tell nobody that I asked," she ordered him, and hastened up on the main deck.

At the foot of the mainmast, Tippoo was washing down the lash in a bucket of seawater that was already tinged pale pink;

he looked up at her, still stripping the water off the leather between thick hairless fingers—and he grinned at Robyn as she passed, squatting down on thick, brown haunches with his loincloth drawn up into his crotch, swinging his round bald head on its bull neck to follow her.

She found herself panting a little with fear and revulsion, and she swept her skirts aside as she passed him. At the door of her cabin she took the valise from Nathaniel with a word of thanks, and then slumped down upon her bunk.

Her thoughts and her emotions were in uproar, for she had still not recovered from the sudden avalanche of events that had interrupted the leisurely pattern of the voyage.

The boarding by Captain Codrington of the Royal Navy overshadowed even her anger at the flogging or her joy at her first view of Africa in nearly two decades—and now his accusations rankled and disturbed her.

After a few minutes' rest she lifted the lid of her traveling chest that filled most of the clear space in the tiny cabin, and had to unpack much of it before she found the pamphlets from the antislavery society with which she had been armed in London before departure.

She sat down to study them once again, a history of the struggle against the trade up to the present time. As she read, her anger and frustration reawakened at the tale of unenforceable international agreements, all with built-in escape clauses: laws that made it an act of piracy to indulge in the trade north of the equator, but allowed it to flourish unchecked in the southern hemisphere; treaties and agreements signed by all nations, except those most actively engaged in the trade, Portugal, Brazil, Spain. Other great nations—France—using the trade to goad their traditional enemy, Great Britain, shamelessly exploiting Britain's commitment to its extinction, trading political advantage for vague promises of support.

Then there was America, a signatory to the Treaty of Brussels which Britain had engineered, agreeing to the abolition of the trade, but not to the abolition of the institution of slavery itself. America agreed that the transport of human souls into captivity was tantamount to active piracy, and that vessels so engaged were liable to seizure under prize and condemnation by courts of Admiralty or Mixed Commission, agreed also to the equipment clause, that ships equipped for transport of slaves, although not actually with a cargo of slaves on board at the time of seizure, could be taken as prize.

There was America agreeing to all of this—and then denying to the warships of the Royal Navy the right of search. The most America would allow was that British officers could assure themselves of the legality of the claim to American ownership, and if that was proven, they could not search, not even though the stink of slaves rose from her holds to offend the very heavens, or the clank of chains and the half-human cries from her tween decks came near to deafening them—still they could not search.

Robyn dropped one pamphlet back into her chest, and selected another publication from the society.

ITEM, in the previous year, 1859, an estimated 169,000 slaves had been transported from the coasts of Africa to the mines of Brazil, and the plantations of Cuba, and to those of the Southern States of America.

ITEM, the trade in slaves by the Omani Arabs of Zanzibar could not be estimated except by observation of the numbers passing through the markets of that island. Despite the British treaty with the sultan as early as 1822, the British consul at Zanzibar had counted almost two hundred thousand slaves landed during the previous twelve-month period. The corpses were not landed, nor were the sick and dying, for the Zanzibar customs dues were payable to the sultan per capita, live or dead.

The dead and those so enfeebled or diseased as to have little hope of survival were thrown overboard, at the edge of the deep water beyond the coral reef. Here a permanent colony of huge man-eating sharks cruised the area by day and by night. Within minutes of the first body, dead or still living, striking the water, the surface around the dhow was torn into a seething white boil by the great fish. The British consul estimated a 40 percent mortality rate among slaves making the short passage from the mainland to the island.

Robyn dropped that pamphlet and before picking up the next, she reflected a moment on the sheer multitudes involved in the whole grisly business.

"Five million since the turn of the century," she whispered, "five million souls. No wonder that they call it the greatest crime against humanity in the history of the world."

She opened the next pamphlet and skimmed quickly over an examination of the profits that accrued to a successful trader.

In the interior of Africa, up near the lake country where few white men had ever reached, Fuller Ballantyne had discovered—her father's name in print gave her a prickle of pride and of melancholy—Fuller had discovered that a prime slave

32

changed hands for a cupful of porcelain beads, two slaves for an obsolete Tower musket that cost thirteen shillings in London, or a Brown Bess musket that cost two dollars in New York.

At the coast the same slave cost ten dollars, while on the slave market in Brazil he would sell for five hundred dollars. But once he was taken north of the equator, the risks to the trader increased and the price rose dramatically: a thousand dollars in Cuba, fifteen hundred in Louisiana.

Robyn lowered the text, and thought swiftly. The English captain had challenged that *Huron* could carry two thousand slaves at a time. Landed in America, they would be worth an unbelievable three million dollars, an amount which would buy fifteen ships like *Huron*. A single voyage would make a man rich beyond mundane dreams of greed; all risks were acceptable to the traders to win such vast wealth.

But had Captain Codrington been justified in his accusations? Robyn knew the counteraccusations that were made against the officers of the Royal Navy, that their zeal arose from the promise of prize money rather than a hatred of the trade and a love of humanity. That every sail they raised was considered a slaver, and that they were swift to apply the Equipment Clause in the widest possible interpretation.

Robyn was searching for the pamphlet that dealt in detail with this Equipment Clause and she found it next on the pile before her.

To enable a ship to be seized as a slaver under the clause, she need only satisfy one of the stipulated conditions. She could be taken if her hatches were equipped with open gratings to ventilate her holds; if there was dividing bulkheads in her holds to facilitate the installation of slave decks; if there were spare planks aboard for laying as slave decks; if she carried shackles and bolts, or leg irons and cuffs; if she carried too many water casks for the number of her crew and passengers; if she had disproportionally large numbers of mess tubs, or her rice boilers were too big, or if she carried unreasonable quantities of rice or farina.

Even if she carried native matting that might be used as bedding for slaves, she could be seized and run in under a prize crew. These were wide powers given to men who could profit financially by seizure.

Was Captain Codrington one of these, were those pale fanatical eyes merely a mask for avarice and a desire for personal gain?

Robyn found herself hoping they were, or at least that in

the case of *Huron* he had been mistaken. But then why had Captain St. John put down his helm, and run for it the moment he sighted the British cruiser?

Robyn was confused and miserable, haunted with guilt. She needed comfort and she slipped a lace Stuart cap over her head and shoulders before venturing out onto the deck again, for the wind had risen to an icy gale and *Huron* was always a tender ship; she heeled heavily as she beat southward, flinging spray high into the falling night.

Zouga was in his cabin, dressed in shirtsleeves and smoking a cigar as he worked over the lists of the expedition's equipment that would still have to be obtained once they reached Good Hope.

He called to her to enter when she knocked, and rose to greet her with a smile.

"Sissy, are you well? It was a most unpleasant business, even though unavoidable. I hope it has not unsettled you."

"The man will recover," she said, and Zouga changed the subject as he settled her on his bunk, the only other seating in the cabin.

"I sometimes think we would have been better off with less money to spend on this expedition. There is always such a temptation to accumulate too much equipment. Papa made the Transversa with only five porterloads, while we will need a hundred porters at the least, each carrying eighty pounds."

"Zouga, I must speak to you. This is the first opportunity I have had."

An expression of distaste flickered across the strong, harsh features as though he sensed what she was about to say. But before he could deny her she blurted out, "Is this ship a slaver, Zouga?"

Zouga removed the cigar from his mouth and inspected the tip minutely before he replied.

"Sissy, a slaver stinks so you can smell it for fifty leagues downwind, and even after the slaves are removed there is no amount of lye that will get rid of the smell. *Huron* does not have the stench of a slaver."

"This ship is on her first voyage under this ownership," Robyn reminded him quietly. "Codrington accused Captain St. John of using his profits from previous voyages to purchase her. She is still clean."

"Mungo St. John is a gentleman." Zouga's tone had an edge of impatience to it now. "I am convinced of that."

"The plantation owners of Cuba and Louisiana are amongst

the most elegant gentlemen that you could find outside the court of St. James's," she reminded him.

"I am prepared to accept his word as a gentleman," Zouga snapped.

"Are you not a little eager, Zouga?" she asked with a deceptive sweetness, but his tone had kindled sparks in her eyes like the green lights in an emerald. "Would it not seriously impede your plans to find ourselves shipped on board a slaver?"

"Damn me, woman, I have his word." Zouga was getting truly angry now. "St. John is engaged in legitimate trade. He hopes for a cargo of ivory and palm oil."

"Have you asked to inspect the ship's hold?"

"He has given his word."

"Will you ask him to open the holds?"

Zouga hesitated, his gaze wavered a moment, and then he made his decision.

"No, I will not," he said flatly. "That would be an insult to him and, quite rightly, he would resent it."

"And if we found what you are afraid to find, it would discredit the purpose of our expedition," she agreed.

"As the leader of this mission, I have made the decision—"

"Papa would never let anything stand in his way either, not even Mama or the family—"

"Sissy, if you still feel that way when we reach the Cape, I will arrange for passage on another vessel to Quelimane. Will that satisfy you?"

She did not reply but continued to stare at him with a flat accusing gaze.

"If we did find evidence," he waved his hands with agitation, "what could we do about it?"

"We could make a sworn deposition to the Admiralty at Cape Town."

"Sissy," he sighed wearily at her intransigence, "don't you understand? If I were to challenge St. John, we could gain nothing. If the accusation is unwarranted we would place ourselves in a damned awkward position, and if in the very unlikely event that this ship is equipped for the trade, we would then be in considerable danger. Do not underestimate that danger, Robyn. St. John is a determined man." He stopped and shook his head decisively, the fashionable curls dangling over his ears. "I am not going to endanger you, myself—or the whole expedition. That is my decision, and I will insist that you abide by it."

After a long pause, Robyn slowly dropped her gaze to her hands, and intermeshed her fingers.

"Very well, Zouga."

His relief was obvious. "I am grateful for your compliance, my dear." He stooped over her and kissed her forehead. "Let me escort you to dinner."

She was about to refuse, to tell him she was tired and that, once again, she would dine alone in her cabin, and then an idea struck her, and she nodded.

"Thank you, Zouga," she told him, and then looked up with one of those sudden smiles so brilliant, so warm and so rare as to disarm him completely. "I am fortunate to have such a handsome dinner companion."

She sat between Mungo St. John and her brother, and had her brother not known better, he might have suspected her of flirting outrageously with the captain. She was all smiles and sparkles, leaning forward attentively to listen whenever he spoke, recharging his glass whenever it was less than half filled with wine and laughing delightedly at his dry sallies.

Zouga was amazed and a little alarmed by the transformation, while St. John had never seen her like this. He had covered his original surprise with an amused half smile. However, in this mood Robyn Ballantyne was an attractive companion. Her stubborn, rather sharp face softened to the edge of prettiness, while her best features, her hair, her perfect skin, her eyes and fine white teeth, gleamed and flashed in the lamplight. Mungo St. John's own mood became expansive, he laughed more readily and his interest was clearly piqued. With Robyn plying his glass, he drank more than on any other night of the voyage, and when his steward served a good plum duff he called for a bottle of brandy to wash it down.

Zouga had also been infected by the strangely festive air of the dinner, and he protested as vigorously as St. John when suddenly Robyn declared herself to be exhausted and stood up from the board, but she was adamant.

In her cabin she could still hear the occasional shouts of laughter from the saloon, as she went quietly about her preparations. She slid the locking bar into place to assure her privacy. Then she knelt beside her chest and wormed her way down to the bottom layers, from which she retrieved a pair of man's moleskin breeches, a flannel shirt and cravat, with a high-buttoned monkey jacket to go over them, and well-worn half boots.

This had been her uniform and her disguise as a medical student at St. Matthew's Hospital. Now she stripped herself naked, and for a moment enjoyed the wicked freedom of the feeling, even indulging herself to the extend of gazing down at her nudity. She was not too certain if it was a sin to enjoy one's own body, but she suspected that it was. Nevertheless she persisted.

Her legs were straight and strong, her hips flared with a graceful curve and then narrowed abruptly into her waist, her belly was almost flat with just an interesting little bulge below the navel. Now here was definitely sinful ground; of this there was no doubt. But still she could not deny the temptation to let her gaze linger a moment. She understood fully the technical purpose and the physical workings of all her body's highly complicated machinery, both visible and concealed. It was only the feelings and emotions which sprang from this source which both confused and worried her, for they had taught her none of this at St. Matthew's. She passed on hurriedly to safer ground, lifting her arms to pile the tresses of her hair on to the top of her head and hold them in place with a soft cloth cap.

Her breasts were round and neat as ripening apples, so firm as hardly to change their shape as she moved her arms. Their resemblance to fruit pleased her and she spent a few moments longer than was necessary in adjusting the cloth cap upon her head looking down at them. But there was a limit to self-indulgence, and she swept the flannel shirt over her head, pulled the tails down around her waist, stepped into the breeches—how good they felt again after so long in those hobbling skirts—and then, sitting upon the bunk, she pulled on the half boots and buckled the ankle straps of the breeches under the arch of her foot, before standing to clinch the belt at her waist.

She opened her black valise, took out the roll of surgical instruments and selected one of the sturdier scalpels, folded out the blade and tested it with her thumb. It was stingingly sharp. She closed the blade and slipped it into her hip pocket. It was the only weapon available to her.

She was ready now, and she closed the shutter on the bull's-eye lantern, darkening the cabin completely before climbing, fully dressed, into her bunk, pulling the rough woollen blanket to her chin and settling down to wait. The laughter from the saloon became more abandoned, and she imagined that the brandy bottle was being cruelly punished by the men. A long while later she heard her brother's heavy, uneven footsteps on the companionway past her cabin and then there was only the creak and pop of the ship's timbers as she heeled to the wind, and far away the regular tapping of some loose piece of equipment.

She was so keyed, with both fear and anticipation, that there was never any danger of her falling asleep. However, the time passed with wearying slowness. Each time that she opened the shutter of the lantern to check her pocket watch, the hands seemed hardly to have moved. Then, somehow, it was two o'clock in the morning, the hour when the human body and spirit are at their lowest ebb.

She rose quietly from her bunk, picked up the darkened lantern and went to the door of her cabin. The locking bolt clattered like a volley of musketry, but then it was open and she slipped through.

In the saloon a single oil lamp still burned smokily, throwing agitated shadows against the wooden bulkheads, while the empty brandy bottle had fallen to the deck, and rolled back and forth with the ship's motion. Robyn squatted to pull off her boots and, leaving them at the entrance, she went forward on bare feet, crossed the saloon and stepped into the passageway that led to the stern quarters.

Her breath was short, as though she had run far, and she paused to lift the shutter of the bull's-eye lantern and flash a narrow beam of light into the darkness ahead. The door to Mungo St. John's cabin was closed.

She crept toward it, guiding herself with one hand on the bulkhead and at last her fingers closed over the brass door handle.

"Please God," she whispered, and achingly slowly twisted the handle. It turned easily, and then the door slid open an inch along its track, enough for her to peep through into the cabin beyond.

There was just light to see, for the deck above was pierced for a repeating compass so that even while in his bunk the master could at a glance tell his ship's heading. The compass was lit by the dull yellow glow of the helmsman's lantern and the reflection allowed Robyn to make out the cabin's central features.

The bunk was screened off by a dark curtain and the rest of the furnishings were simple. The locked doors of the arms chest to the left, with a row of hooks beyond from which hung a boat cloak and the clothing that St. John had been wearing at dinner. Facing the door was a solid teak desk with racks to hold the brass navigational instruments, sextant, straightedge, dividers, and on the bulkhead above it were affixed the barometer and the ship's chronometer.

The captain had evidently emptied his pockets onto the desk top before undressing. Scattered among the charts and ship's papers were a clasp knife, a silver cigar case, a tiny gold inlaid pocket pistol of the type favored by professional gamblers, a pair of chunky ivory dice—Zouga and St. John must have fallen to gaming again after she left them—and then, most important, what she had hoped to find, the bunch of ship's keys, that St. John usually wore on a chain from his belt, lay in the center of the desk.

An inch at a time Robyn slid the door farther open, watching the dark alcove to the right of the cabin. The curtain billowed slightly with each roll of the ship and she screwed her nerves tighter as she imagined the movement to be that of a man about to leap out at her.

When the door was open enough to allow her to pass through, it required a huge effort of will to take the first step.

Halfway across the cabin she froze; now she was only inches from the bunk. She peered into the narrow gap in the curtaining and saw the gleam of naked flesh, and heard the deep regular breathing of the sleeping man. It reassured her and she went on swiftly to the desk.

She had no way of learning which keys fitted the lazaretto and the hatch to the main hold. She had to take the whole heavy bunch, and realized that it would mean returning to the cabin later. She did not know if she would have the courage to do that, and as she lifted the bunch her hand shook so it jangled sharply. Startled, she clutched it to her bosom and stared fearfully at the alcove. There was no movement beyond the curtains, and she glided back toward the door on silent bare feet.

It was only when the door closed again that the curtains of the alcove were jerked open, and Mungo St. John lifted himself on one elbow. He paused only a moment and then swung his legs out of the bunk and stood up. He reached the desk in two quick strides and checked the top.

"The keys!" he hissed, and reached out for his breeches hanging on the rack beside him, pulling them on swiftly and then stooping to open one of the drawers in his desk.

He lifted the lid of the rosewood case and took out the pair of long-barreled dueling pistols, thrust them into his waistband and started for the door of the cabin.

* * *

Robyn found the correct key to the lazaretto on the third attempt and the door gave reluctantly, dragging on the hinge with a squeal that sounded to her like a bugle call commanding a charge of heavy cavalry.

She locked the door behind her again, feeling a rush of relief to know that nobody could follow her now, and she opened the shutter of the lantern and looked about her swiftly.

The lazaretto was no more than a large cupboard used as a pantry for the officers' personal stores. Sides of smoked ham and dried polonies hung from hooks in the deck above, there were fat rounds of cheese in the racks, boxes of tinned goods, racks of black bottles with waxed stoppers, bags of flour and rice, and, facing Robyn, another hatch with the locking bar chained in place by a padlock the size of her doubled fists.

The key, when she found it, was equally massive, as thick as her middle finger, and the hatch so heavy that it took all of her strength to drag it aside. Then she had to double over to get through the low opening.

Behind her, Mungo St. John heard the scrape of wood on wood and dropped silently down the steps to the door of the lazaretto. With a cocked pistol in one hand, he laid his ear to the oak planking to listen for a moment before trying the handle.

"God's breath!" he muttered angrily as he found it locked, and then turned away and raced on bare feet up the companionway to the cabin of his first mate.

At the first touch on his thickly muscled shoulder, Tippoo was fully awake, his eyes glistening in the gloom like those of a wild animal.

"Someone has broken into the hold," St. John hissed at him, and Tippoo reared up out of his bunk, a huge dark figure.

"We find him," he grunted, as he bound the loincloth around his waist. "Then we feed fish with him."

The main hold seemed vast as a cathedral. The beam of the lantern could not reach into its deepest recesses, and a great mass of cargo was piled high, in some places as high as the main deck fifteen feet above her.

She saw at once that the cargo had been loaded in such a way that it could be unloaded piecemeal, that any single item could be identified and swung up through the hatches without the necessity of unloading the whole. This, of course, must be essential in a ship trading from port to port. She saw also that the goods were carefully packaged and clearly labeled. Flashing the lantern around her she saw that the cases of equipment for

40

their own expedition were packed here, "Ballantyne Africa Expedition" stenciled in black on the raw, white wood.

She clambered up the rampart of cases and bales and balanced on the peak, turning the lantern upward toward the square opening of the hatch, trying to see if there was an open grating, and immediately she was frustrated for the white canvas cover had been stretched around the lower surface also. She stood at full stretch to try to touch the hatch, to feel for the shape of a grating under the canvas, but her fingertips were inches short of the hatch and a sudden wild plunge of the ship under her sent her flying backward into the deep aisle between the piles of cargo. She managed to keep her grip on the lantern, but hot oil from its reservoir splashed over her hand, threatening to blister the skin.

Once again she crawled up and over the mountains of cargo, searching for the evidence that she hoped not to find. There was no dividing bulkhead in the hold, but the mainmast pierced the deck above and came through the hold to rest its foot on the keel, and there were stepped wedges fixed to the thick column of Norwegian pine.

Perhaps they were there to hold the slave decks. Robyn knelt beside the mast and sighted across the hold to the outward curved side of the ship. In line with the wedges on the mast were heavy wooden ledges, like shallow shelves, and she thought that these might be supports for the outer edges of the slave decks. She guessed that they were between two and a half and three feet apart, which she had read was the average height of the between decks in a slaver.

She tried to imagine what this hold might look like with those decks in place, tiers of low galleries just high enough for a man to crawl into doubled over. She counted the shelves and there were five of them—five piles of decks, each with its layer of naked black humanity laid out sardine fashion, each one in physical contact with his neighbor on either side, lying there in his own filth and that of the slaves above him which leaked through the seams of the deck. She tried to imagine the heat of the middle passage when the ship lay becalmed in the baking doldrums, she tried to imagine two thousand of them vomiting and purging with seasickness as the ship reared and plunged in the wild seas where the Mozambique current scoured the Agulhas bank. She tried to imagine an epidemic of cholera or smallpox taking hold of that mass of misery, but her imagination could not rise to the task, and she pushed the hideous images aside and crawled on over the heaving cargo, flashing her lantern into each corner, searching for more solid evidence than the narrow ledges.

If there was planking on board it would be laid flat upon the deck, below this cargo, and there was no way in which Robyn could reach it.

Ahead of her she saw a dozen huge casks bolted to the forward bulkhead. They could be water barrels, or they could be filled with trade rum, or the rum could be replaced with water when the slaves were taken on board. There was no means of checking the contents, but she knocked on the oak with the hilt of her scalpel and the dull tone assured her that the casks contained something.

She squatted down on one of the bales and slit the stitching with the scalpel; thrusting her hand into the opening she grasped a handful and pulled it out to examine it in the lamplight.

Trade beads, ropes of them strung on cotton threads; a *bitil* of beads was as long as the interval between fingertip and wrist, four *bitil* made a *khete*. These beads were made of scarlet porcelain; they were the most valued variety called *sam-sam*. An African of the more primitive tribes would sell his sister for a *khete* of these, his brother for two *khete*.

Robyn crawled on, examining crates and bales—bolts of cotton cloth from the mills of Salem, called *merkani* in Africa, a corruption of the word "American" and the checkered cloth from Manchester known as *kaniki*. Then there were long wooden crates marked simply "Five Pieces," and she could guess that they contained muskets. However, firearms were common trade goods to the coast, and no proof of the intention to buy slaves; they could just as readily be used to purchase ivory or gum copal.

She was tired now with the effort of climbing and blundering around over the heaving slopes and peaks of cargo, and with the nervous tension of the search.

She paused to rest a moment, leaning back against one of the bales of *merkani* cloth, and as she did so something dug painfully into her back, forcing her to change her position. Then she realized that cloth should not have hard lumps in it. She shuffled around and once again slit the sacking cover of the bale.

Protruding from between the folded layers of cloth, there was something black and cold to the touch. She pulled it out and it was heavy iron, looped and linked, and she recognized it instantly. In Africa they were called "the bracelets of death." Here, at last, was proof, positive and irrefutable, for these steel slave cuffs with the light marching chains were the unmistakable stigmata of the trade.

Robyn tore the bale wider open; there were hundreds of the iron cuffs concealed between layers of cloth. Even if it had been possible, a perfunctory search by a naval boarding party was highly unlikely to have uncovered this sinister hoard.

She selected one set of cuffs with which to confront her brother and she started aft toward the lazaretto, filled suddenly with desire to be out of this dark cavern with its menacing shadows, and back once more in the safety of her own cabin.

She had almost reached the entrance to the lazaretto when suddenly there was a loud scraping sound from the deck above, and she froze with alarm. When the sound was repeated, she had enough of her wits still about her to douse the snuffer of her lantern, and then immediately regretted having done so for the darkness seemed to crush down upon her with a suffocating weight and she felt panic rising up to take possession of her.

With a crash like a cannon shot the main hatch flew open, and as she swung back toward it she saw the white pinpricks of the stars outlined by the square opening. Then a huge, dark shape dropped through, landing lightly on the piled bales beneath, and at almost the same instant the hatch thudded closed again, blotting out the starlight.

Now Robyn's terror came bubbling to the surface. There was somebody locked in the hold with her, and the knowledge held her riveted for long, precious seconds, before she plunged back toward the lazaretto hatch, suppressing the scream that choked up into her throat.

The shape she had glimpsed for a moment was unmistakable. She knew that it was Tippoo in the hold with her, and it spurred her terror. She could imagine the great hairless toadlike figure, moving toward her in the darkness, with repulsive reptilian swiftness, could almost see the pink tongue flickering out over thick cruel lips, and her haste became uncontrolled. She lost her footing in the darkness and fell heavily, tumbling backward into one of the deep gullies between banks of cargo, cracking the back of her skull on a wooden case, half stunning herself so that she lost her grip on the extinguished lantern and could not find it when she groped for it. When she scrambled to her knees again, she had lost all sense of direction in the total blackness of the hold.

She knew that her best defense was to remain still and silent until she could place the man who was hunting her, and she crouched down in a crack between two crates. Her pulse beat

43

in her ears like a drum, deafening her—and her heart seemed to have crammed up into her throat so that she must fight for each breath.

It took many minutes and all her determination to bring herself under control, to be able to think again.

She tried to decide in which direction lay the lazaretto hatch, her only means of escape, but she knew that the only way she would be able to find it would be to grope her way to the ship's wooden side and follow it around. The prospect of doing this, with that grotesque creature hunting her in the darkness, was appalling. She shrank down as far as she could into the narrow space and listened.

The hold was filled with small sounds that she had not noticed before, the heave and creak of the ship's timbers, the shifts of the cargo against its retaining ropes and netting—but then she heard the movement of a living thing close behind her and she caught the shriek of terror before it reached her lips, as she lifted her arm to protect her head. Frozen like that, she waited for a blow which never came.

Instead she heard another movement pass behind her turned shoulder, a whisper of sound, yet so chilling that she felt all power of movement drained from her legs. He was here, very close in the blackness, toying with her, cruel as a cat. He had smelled her out. With some sort of animal sense, Tippoo had found her unerringly in the darkness, and now he crouched over her ready to strike and she could only wait.

Something touched her shoulder, and before she could jerk away it swarmed up over her neck, brushed her face. She flung herself backward and screamed, striking out wildly with the steel chain and handcuffs which she still held in her right hand.

The thing was furry and quick, and it squealed sharply, like an angry piglet as she struck again and again. Then it was gone, and she heard the scamper of small feet across the rough wood of the crate and she realized that it had been one of the ship's rats, big as a tomcat.

Robyn shuddered, revolted, but with a lift of relief that was short-lived.

There was a flash of light, so unexpected that it almost blinded her, and a lantern beam was thrown in a single swift sweep about the hold, and then extinguished, so that the darkness seemed even more crushing than before.

The hunter had heard her scream, and had flashed his lantern in her direction, had probably seen her, for she had clambered out of her niche between the crates. Now at least she knew in

44

which direction to move: The brief flash of light had orientated her once again; she knew where to find the hatch.

She threw herself over a pile of soft bales, clawing herself toward the hatch, then checking her flight to think a moment. Tippoo must have known how she had entered the hold and would know that she would try to escape in the same direction. She must move with care, with stealth, ready for the moment when he flashed the lantern again, taking care not to rush headlong into the trap he was certainly setting for her.

She changed her grip on the iron chain, only then realizing its potential as a weapon, much more effective than the short-bladed scalpel in her pocket. A weapon! For the first time she was thinking of defending herself, not merely crouching like a chicken before the stoop of the hawk. "Robbie was always the plucky one." She could almost hear her mother's voice, troubled but touched with pride, when she had defended herself effectively against the village ruffians, or joined her brother on some of his more hair-raising escapades, and she realized she needed all of that pluck now.

With the chain gripped in her right hand, she started steathily back toward the hatch, crawling, slithering forward on her belly, pausing to listen every few seconds. It seemed like a complete round of eternity before her outreaching fingers touched the solid planking of the after bulkhead. She was within feet of the hatch now, and that was where he would be waiting for her.

She crouched down, with her back firmly against the planking, and waited for the flutter of her heart to abate enough to allow her to hear, but any noise her hunter made was covered by the creak and pop and groan of the working wooden hull, and the thud and hiss of the sea as *Huron* beat up hard to the wind.

Then she wrinkled her nose at a new smell that overlaid the pervading reek of the bilges. It was the hot oil smell of a shuttered lantern burning very close by, and now when she listened for it, she thought she could hear the pinkle and tick of the heated metal of the lantern. He must be close, very close, guarding the hatchway, ready to flash the lantern at the moment he could place her whereabouts accurately.

With the slowness of spreading oil she rose to face into the darkness where he was, she slipped the scalpel into the palm of her left hand, and she drew back her right arm with the chain and iron cuff dangling from her fist, ready to strike.

Then she pitched the scalpel with a short underhanded throw,

45

judging the distance to drop it close enough to force him to move again, but far enough to make him move away from her.

The tiny missile struck something soft, the sound muted, almost lost in other small sounds, but then it slithered softly along the deck, like a hesitant footfall and instantly light flooded the hold.

. Tippoo's monstrous shape sprang out of the darkness, huge, menacing, unbelievably close. He held the unhooded lantern high in his left hand, and the yellow light glistened on the bare round dome of his yellow skull, and on the broad plane of his back, the muscle rippling and tensing into valleys and ridges as he swung back the heavy club in his right hand, his head hunched down on the thick corded neck. He was facing away from her, but only for an instant. As he realized that there was nobody in front of him, he reacted with animal swiftness, ducking the great round head onto his chest, beginning to swing away.

She moved entirely by instinct. She swung the heavy iron manacle on the length of chain. It hummed in a glittering circle in the lamplight, and it caught Tippoo high on the temple with a crack like a branch breaking in a high wind, and the thin layer of yellow scalp opened like the mouth of a purse with a crimson velvet lining. Tippoo swayed drunkenly on straddled legs that started to buckle under him. She pulled back the chain and swung again with all the weight of her body and the strength of her fear behind the stroke. Again a deep red wound bloomed on the polished yellow dome of his skull and he went down slowly onto his knees, an attitude she had seen him adopt so often as he prayed on the quarterdeck, making the Moslem obeisance toward Mecca. Now again, his forehead touched the deck, but this time with his blood dribbling into a puddle under it.

The lantern clattered on to the deck, still burning, and in its light Tippoo rolled heavily on to his side with his breath snoring in his throat and his eyes rolled up into his head, glaring ghastly white and unseeing, his thick legs kicking out convulsively.

Robyn stared at the prostrate giant, aghast at the damage she had done, already feeling the need to administer to any hurt or crippled being; but it lasted for only seconds, as Tippoo's eyes rolled back into their deep sockets, and she saw the pupils beginning to focus. The yellow gleaming body heaved, the movement of limbs was no longer spasmodic but more

46

coordinated and determined, the head lifted, still lolling, but swinging questingly from side to side.

Unbelievably, the man was no longer crippled by those two cutting blows, had been stunned for seconds only, in seconds more he would be fully conscious and in his fury more dangerous than ever. With a sob Robyn flew at the open hatch of the lazaretto. As she passed him, cruel fingers hooked at her ankle, pulling her off balance so she almost fell before she could kick herself free and dive through the opening.

Tippoo was on hands and knees in the light of the fallen lantern, creeping toward her as she threw all her weight against the hatch. As it thudded into its jamb, she dropped the locking bar into its seating, and at that moment Tippoo's shoulder crashed into the far side of the hatch with a force that shook it in its frame.

Her frantic fingers were so clumsy that it took three attempts to secure the padlock and chain, and only then could she sink to the deck and sob away her fear until her relief came to buoy her up and give her renewed strength.

When she dragged herself to her feet, she was lightheaded, intoxicated with the strange fierce jubilation that she had never felt before. She knew it sprang from having fought herself out of danger, from the unfamiliar experience of inflicting punishment on a hated adversary—and she knew she would feel guilt for it later, but not now.

The keys were still in the door between the lazaretto and saloon where she had left them. She pushed the door open quickly and paused in the opening an instant, feeling the quick flare of alarm overtake her feeling of elation.

She had only an instant of time to realize that somebody had trimmed the saloon lamp, and then fingers seized her wrist from behind and swung her off balance, bearing her down heavily to the deck and holding her there with one arm twisted up between her shoulder blades.

"Keep still, damn you—or I'll twist your head off your shoulders." Mungo St. John's voice was low and fierce in her ear.

Her arm holding the chain was trapped under her, and now her captor shifted his weight over her, placing his knee in the small of her back and bearing down so painfully that she wanted to cry out with the agony that flared up her curved spine.

"Tippoo flushed you out quickly enough," St. John murmured with grim satisfaction. "Now let's have a look at you— before we stretch you out on the grating."

He reached forward and pulled off the cloth cap that covered her head, and she heard his little grunt of surprise as her hair tumbled loose in a slippery shining mass in the lamplight. His grasp slackened and the pressure of his knee into the base of her spine eased. Roughly he grasped her shoulder to turn her on to her back so he could see her face.

She rolled easily toward him and then as her trapped arm came free, she hurled the chain at his face. He threw up both hands to catch the blow. As slippery as an eel she wormed out from under him and flew at the door to the saloon.

He was quick, quicker than she was, and his fingers were steely; they caught in the thin worn flannel of her shirt and it ripped from collar to hem. She turned and lashed at him with the chain again, but now he was ready for her, and he caught her wrist, trapping it.

She kicked wildly at his shins, and succeeded in hooking an ankle behind his heel and they went down together in a tangle onto the wooden deck, and Robyn found herself carried along by a fierce uncaring madness. She was hissing and snarling like a cat as she raked at his eyes with her nails, raising a bloody line down his neck. The tatters of her shirt flapped around her waist and the coarse dark hair of his chest rasped against the tender points of her naked breasts so that dimly in her madness she realized that he wore only breeches, and the man smell of his body filled her nostrils as he tried to smother her wild struggles with his body.

She reached up toward him with her open mouth, trying to sink her teeth into that flushed handsome face, but he caught a handful of her hair at the back of her head and twisted it. The pain seemed to flow down through her body and explode at the base of her belly in a warm soft spasm that took her breath and crammed it down into her lungs.

He held her helpless and she felt the strength going out of her, to be replaced by spreading languor, and she stared up into his face with a kind of wonder as though she had never seen it before. She saw his teeth were very white, his lips drawn back into a rictus of emotion, and fierce yellow eyes unfocused and smoky with a kind of madness that matched her own.

She made one last feeble effort to repel him, driving her knee upward, aimed at the fork of his lower body, but he trapped it between his thighs and then holding her thus he reared up over her and looked down at her bared bosom.

"Sweet Mother of God!" he croaked, and she saw the cords

48

strain tight in his throat, saw the hot yellow fire in his eyes and she could not move, not even when he freed his hooked fingers from the twisted tresses of her hair and ran them slowly down her body, cupping first one tight small breast and then the other in the palm of his hand.

She felt his touch had gone, though the memory lingered on her skin like butterflies' wings. Then his fingers were back, tugging demandingly at the fastenings of her breeches. She closed her eyes and refused to let her mind consider what was about to happen. She knew that there was nothing she could do to escape, and cried out softly with the strange elation of the martyr.

But her cry seemed to touch something deep in him, the smoky yellow eyes focused for a moment, the predatory expression of the face became uncertain and then tinged with horror as he looked down at her spread white body. Swiftly he rolled away from her.

"Cover yourself!" he said harshly, and she was overwhelmed with a cold avalanche of loss, followed immediately by as great a rush of shame and of guilt.

She scrambled to her knees, clutching her clothing around her, suddenly shivering, but not with cold.

"You should not have struggled," he said and though he was obviously fighting to control it his voice shook as hers did.

"I hate you," she whispered foolishly, and then it became true. She hated him for what he had aroused in her, for the sickness and the guilt that followed it, and for the sense of loss and bereavement with which he had left her.

"I should kill you," he muttered, not looking at her. "I should have Tippoo do it."

She felt no fear at the threat. She had rearranged her clothing as best she could, but still she knelt opposite him.

"Go!" he almost shouted at her. "Get back to your cabin."

She rose slowly, hesitated a moment and then turned to the companionway.

"Dr. Ballantyne!" he stopped her, and she turned back. He had risen and now he stood beside the door to the lazaretto, the keys in his one hand, the slave cuff and chain in the other. "It would be best not to tell your brother of what you discovered tonight." His voice was controlled now, cold and low. "I would not have the same scruples with him. We will be at Cape Town in four days," he went on. "After that you may do as you will.

Until then you will not provoke me again. One chance is already too many."

She stared at him mutely, feeling small and helpless.

"Good night, Dr. Ballantyne."

She hardly had time to pack her breeches and torn shirt away in the bottom of her chest, inspect and rub a salve on her bruises, pull on her nightdress and climb into her narrow bunk before someone pounded on the cabin door.

"Who is it?" she called huskily and breathless, not yet fully recovered from the night's stresses.

"Sissy, it's me." Zouga's voice. "Someone has beaten Tippoo's skull in. He's bleeding all over the deck; can you come?"

Robyn glowed with a fierce spark of pagan glee, which she tried immediately to suppress with less than complete success.

"I'm coming."

There were three men in the saloon, Zouga, the second mate and Tippoo. Mungo St. John was not there. Tippoo sat stolidly on a stool under the oil lamp, naked except for his cotton loincloth, and his neck and shoulders ran with sheets of dark slick blood.

The second mate held a wad of grubby cotton to his skull and when Robyn lifted it away the wounds began spurting merrily.

"Brandy," she demanded, and rinsed her hands and her instruments in the spirit—she was an admirer and believer in the teachings of Jenner and Lister—before she probed the points of her forceps into the open wound. She gripped the vessels and twisted them closed. Tippoo made no move, his expression never changed—and she was still carried along on the pagan mood, in direct defiance to the oath of Hippocrates which she had sworn.

"I must clean the wounds," she told him, and quickly, before her conscience could prevent it, she tipped the raw brandy into the wounds and swabbed them out.

Tippoo sat still as a temple carving of a Hindu devil, making no acknowledgment of the harsh spirit burning open tissue.

Robyn tied off the vessels with silk thread, leaving an end hanging from the wounds, and then she sutured the lips closed, laying precise neat stitches and pulling them up tightly so that the smooth bald scalp came up in a sharp little peak of flesh with each tug.

"I will pull the thread when the vessels mortify," she told him. "The stitches will be ready to come out in a week." She would not deplete her stock of laudanum, she decided, the man obviously was impervious to pain, and she was still in the throes of un-Christian spite.

Tippoo lifted the round head. "You good doctor," he told her solemnly, and she learned then a lesson that would last her throughout her life: the stronger the purge, the more astringent or foul-tasting the medicine and the more radical the surgery, then the more impressed with the surgeon's skill was the African patient.

"Yes," Tippoo nodded gravely, "you one bloody fine doctor." And he opened one huge paw. In his palm lay the scalpel that Robyn had lost in *Huron*'s hold. Without expression he placed it in Robyn's own unresisting hand, and with that eerie swiftness was gone from the saloon, leaving her staring after him.

Huron flew southward, meeting the long South Atlantic rollers and spurning them carelessly, brushing them aside with her shoulder and letting them cream over her rail and then tumble away astern in a long smooth wake.

There were seabirds in company with them now, beautiful gannets with yellow throats and black diamonds painted around their eyes, coming in from the east and soaring above their wake, shrieking and diving for the galley scraps when they were thrown overboard. There were seals too, lifting their whiskered heads high above the surface to stare curiously after the towering clipper as she burst the sea open with her sharp bows in her flight into the south.

Smeared across the brilliant blue water were long serpentine trails of sea bamboo, torn from the rocky shoreline by the gales and storms of this uneasy and troubled sea.

All these were indications of the land which was always just below the eastern horizon, and Robyn spent many hours of each day alone at the port rail staring toward it, longing for another glimpse of it, smelling the dryness and the spiced aroma of its grass and herbs on the wind, seeing its blown dust in the marvelous reds and glowing gold of the sunsets, but denied sight of it by the offing that St. John was making before coming back onto the starboard tack for the final run into Table Bay.

However, as soon as Mungo St. John appeared on his quarterdeck Robyn would hurry below without another glance in his direction, and she locked herself in her cabin, brooding there alone so that even her brother sensed that something

51

troubled her. He tried a dozen times to draw her out. She sent him away each time, refusing to open the cabin to him.

"I'm all right, Zouga. I just want to be alone."

And when he tried to join her in her solitary vigils at the ship's rail, she was short and unbending, exasperating him so that he stamped away and let her be.

She was afraid to talk to him, afraid that she would blurt out her discovery of slaving equipment in *Huron*'s hold and put him in deadly danger. She knew her brother well enough not to trust his temper and not to doubt his courage. Neither did she doubt Mungo St. John's warning. He would kill Zouga to protect himself; he could do it himself, she had seen him handle a pistol, or he could send Tippoo to do the work in the night. She had to protect Zouga, until they reached Cape Town, or until she did what she had to do.

"Vengeance is mine, saith the Lord." She found the passage in her Bible and studied it carefully, and then she had prayed for guidance which had not been given—and she had ended more confused and troubled than she had begun.

She prayed again kneeling on the bare deck beside her bunk until her knees ached, and slowly her duty became clear to her.

Three thousand souls sold into slavery in a single year; that was what the Royal Navy captain had accused him of. How many thousands before that, how many thousands more in the years to come if *Huron* and her captain were allowed to continue their depredations, if nobody could prevent them from ravaging the east coast of Africa, her land, her people, those peoples whom she was sworn to protect and minister to and to lead into the fold of the Savior.

Her father, Fuller Ballantyne, was one of the great champions of freedom, the unrelenting adversary of this abominable trade. He had called it "the running sore on the conscience of the civilized world that must be rooted out with all the means at our disposal." She was her father's daughter, had made her oath in the sight of God.

This man, this monster, epitomized the sickening evil and monstrous cruelty of the whole filthy business.

"Please show me my duty, O Lord," she prayed, and always there was her own guilt and shame. Shame that his eyes had probed her half-naked body, that his hands had touched and fondled her, shame that he had debased her further, by stripping bare his own body. Hastily she thrust the image aside, it was too clear, too overpowering. "Help me to be strong," she prayed quickly.

There was shame and there was guilt, a terrible corrosive guilt in the fact that his gaze, his touch, his body, had not revolted and disgusted her, but had filled her instead with a sinful delight. He had tempted her to sin. For the first time in all her twenty-three years she had encountered real sin, and she had not been strong enough. She hated him for that.

"Show me my duty, O Lord," she prayed aloud and rose stiffly from her knees to sit on the edge of the bunk. She held her well-worn leather-bound Bible in her lap and whispered again.

"Please give unto your faithful servant guidance." And she let the book fall open, and with her eyes closed placed her forefinger on the text. When she opened her eyes again she gave a start of surprise: guidance obtained by this little ritual of hers was usually not so unequivocal, for she had chosen Numbers 35:19. "The revenger of blood himself shall slay the murderer: when he meeteth him, he shall slay him."

Robyn had no illusions as to the difficulty she would have in performing the heavy duty placed upon her by God's direct injunction, or how easily roles might be reversed and she become herself the victim rather than the avenger.

The man was as dangerous as he was wicked and time was against her. The accurate observation of the sun that Zouga had made at noon that day placed the ship within a hundred and fifty miles of Table Bay, and the wind stood fair and boisterous. Dawn the next day would reveal that great flat-topped mountain rising out of the sea. She had no time for elaborate planning. Whatever she did must be direct and swift.

There were half a dozen bottles in her medicine chest whose contents would serve—but no, poison was the most disgusting of deaths to inflict. She had seen a man die of strychnine poison when she was at St. Matthew's. She would never forget the arching spine as his back muscles convulsed until the man stood on the top of his head and on his heels like a drawn bow.

It must be some other means. There was the big naval Colt revolver which Zouga kept in his cabin—he had instructed her in its loading and discharge—or there was the Sharps rifle, but both of those belonged to her brother. She did not want to see him swinging from the gallows on the parade ground below the castle at Cape Town. The more uncomplicated and direct the plan, the greater was its chance of success, she realized, and at the thought she knew just how it must be done.

There was a polite knock on her cabin door, and she started.

"Who is it?"

"Jackson, Doctor." He was the captain's steward. "Dinner is served in the saloon."

She had not realized how late it had grown.

"I will not be dining tonight."

"You must keep your strength up, ma'am," Jackson entreated through the closed door.

"Are you the doctor, then?" she asked tartly, and he went shuffling off down the companionway.

She had not eaten since breakfast, but she was not hungry; her stomach muscles were rigid with tension. She lay awhile on her bunk, gathering her resolve, and then she stood up, selected one of her oldest dresses, in a dark heavy wool. It would be the least loss to her wardrobe, and the dark color would make it less conspicuous in the shadows.

She left her cabin and went quietly up to the main deck. There was no one but the helmsman on the quarterdeck, his weathered brown face lit faintly by the binnacle lamp.

She moved quietly across to the skylight of the saloon and looked down.

Mungo St. John sat at the head of the table, with a joint of steaming salt beef in front of him. He was carving thin slices of meat, laughing across the board at one of Zouga's sallies. One quick glance was enough. Unless there was a call from the lookout or a need to change sail, Mungo St. John would not move for another half hour at the least.

Robyn went back down the ladder, past her own cabin and down the companionway to the after quarters. She reached Mungo St. John's quarters and tried the door. Once again it slid open easily; she stepped through and closed it behind her again.

It took her only a few minutes to find the case of pistols in the drawer of the teak desk. She opened it on the desk top and took out one of the beautiful weapons. The mottled Damascus steel barrels were inlaid with bright gold, a hunting scene with horses and hounds and huntsmen.

Robyn sat down on the edge of the bunk, held the weapon muzzle up between her knees while she unscrewed the silver powder flask and measured the fine powder into the cup. It was a familiar chore, for Zouga had spent hours in her instruction. She rammed the charge down into the long, elegant barrel under the felt wad, and then selected a perfect sphere of lead from the ball compartment of the case, wrapped that in an oiled

54

patch of felt to give it a close fit in the rifled barrel and then rammed it down on top of the powder charge.

Then she reversed the pistol, pointing it down at the deck while she fitted one of the copper percussion caps over the nipple of the breech, drew back the hammer until it clicked at full cock, and laid it on the bunk beside her. She did the same with the other pistol, and when they were both loaded and cocked, she placed them on the edge of the desk, butts toward her, ready for immediate use.

Then she stood and, in the center of the cabin, lifted her skirts around her waist and loosened the drawstring of her drawers. She let them fall to the deck, and the air was cool on her naked buttocks so that she felt the little goose pimples rise on her skin. She dropped her skirts and picked up the cotton undergarment. Holding it across her chest she tore it half through and threw it across the cabin, then she took the fastenings of her bodice in both hands and ripped them down almost to her waist, the hooks and eyes hung on the torn threads of cotton.

She looked at herself in the polished metal mirror on the bulkhead beside the door. There was a luster in her green eyes and her cheeks were flushed.

For the first time in her life, she thought her image beautiful—not beautiful, she corrected herself, but proud and wild and strong as an avenger should be. She was glad he would see her like this before he died, and she lifted her hand and rearranged one of the thick tresses of hair that had broken free of its retaining ribbon.

She sat back on the bunk and picked up a loaded pistol in each hand; she aimed first the one and then the other at the brass handle of the door, and then laid them in her lap and settled down to wait.

She had left her watch in her own cabin so she could not tell how long she waited. The voices and laughter from the officers' saloon were completely muffled by the closed door, but every time a plank creaked or some part of the ship's gear clattered, her nerves sprang tight and she lifted the pistols to cover the doorway.

Then suddenly she heard his footsteps, there was no mistaking them for any other man aboard. They reminded her somehow of a caged leopard pacing its bars, quick, light and alert. He was on the deck above her, but the footsteps were so close that it seemed he was in the cabin with her. She looked up at the deck, swinging her head slightly to follow his turns from one side of the quarterdeck to the other.

She knew what he was doing, she had watched him on a dozen other nights. First he would talk quietly with the helmsman, checking the slate on which the ship's course was chalked before going back to inspect the log trailing astern. Then he would light one of his thin black Havana cigars and begin pacing the deck, with his hands clasped in the small of his back as he walked, darting quick glances up at the trim of his sails, studying the stars and the clouds for signs of change in the weather, pausing to feel the scend of the sea and the run of the ship under him before pacing on again.

Suddenly the footsteps stopped and Robyn froze; the moment had come. He had paused to flip the stub of his cigar over the rail and watch it fizzle into darkness as it hit the surface of the sea.

There was still time for her to escape, and she felt her resolve weaken. She half rose. She could still reach her own cabin if she moved now, but her legs would not carry her across the cabin. Then she heard his footsteps cross the deck above her with a different tread. He was coming down. It was too late.

Almost choking on her own breath, she sank back on to the bunk and lifted both pistols. They wavered uncertainly and she realized that her hands were shaking. With a tremendous effort she stilled them. The door slammed open and Mungo St. John stooped into the cabin, and then stopped as he saw the dark figure and the twin barrels that menaced him.

"They are loaded and cocked," she said huskily. "And I will not hesitate."

"I see." He straightened slowly, so the dark head just brushed the deck overhead.

"Close the door," she said, and he pushed it closed with his foot, his arms folded on his chest, and that mocking half smile on his lips. It made her forget her carefully rehearsed speech, and she stuttered slightly, and was immediately furious with herself.

"You are a slaver," she blurted, and he inclined his head, still smiling. "And I have to stop you."

"How do you propose doing that?" he asked with polite interest.

"I am going to kill you."

"That should do it," he admitted, and now he smiled, a flash of white teeth in the gloom. "Unfortunately they would probably hang you for it, if my crew didn't tear you to pieces before that."

"You assaulted me," she said. She glanced at her torn drawers lying near his feet and then with the butt of one pistol touched her torn bodice.

"A rape, by God!" Now he chuckled aloud, and she felt herself blushing vividly at the word.

"It's no laughing matter, Captain St. John. You have sold thousands of human souls into the most vile bondage."

He took one slow pace toward her and she half rose, panic in her voice.

"Don't move! I warn you."

He took another pace and she thrust both pistols toward him at the full stretch of her arms.

"I shall fire."

The smile never wavered on his lips and the yellow flecked eyes held hers steadily as he took another lazy pace closer.

"You have the most beautiful green eyes I have ever seen," he said, and the pistol shook in her hands.

"Here," he said gently. "Give them to me."

He took the two gold-worked barrels in one hand and turned their muzzles upward, pointing them at the deck above them. With the other hand he gently began to open her fingers, untangling them from trigger and butt.

"This is not why you came here," he said, and her fingers went slack. He took the pistols out of her hands and uncocked them before laying them back in their velvet-lined nests within the rosewood case.

His smile was no longer mocking, and his voice was soft, almost tender, as he lifted her to her feet.

"I am glad you came."

She tried to turn her face away, but he took her chin between his fingers and lifted it. As he brought his mouth down to hers, she saw his lips opening, and the warm wet touch was a physical shock.

His mouth tasted slightly salty, perfumed with cigar smoke. She tried to keep her lips closed, but the pressure of his own lips forced them gently open and then his tongue was invading her. His fingers were still on her face, stroking her cheek, smoothing her hair back from her temples, touching lightly her closed eyelids—and she lifted her face higher to his touch.

Even when he slowly unfastened the last hooks of her bodice and eased it down off her shoulders, her only response was to feel the strength go out of her thighs so she had to lean against his hard chest for support.

Then he lifted his mouth from hers, leaving it empty, cooling after the warmth, and she opened her eyes. With a sense of disbelief, she saw that his head was bowing to her breast, and she was looking down on the thick dark curls that covered the back of his neck. She knew it must stop now, before he did what she could hardly believe he was about to do.

When she tried to protest, it was only a whimper in her throat. When she tried to seize his head and thrust it away from her, her fingers merely curled into the springing crisp curls the way a cat claws a velvet cushion, and instead of thrusting him away, she drew his head down and arched her back slightly so that her breasts rose to meet him.

Yet she was unprepared for the feel of his mouth. It seemed as though he were about to suck her very soul out through the swollen, aching tips. It was too strong, she tried not to cry out, remembering that the last time she had done so, it had broken the spell—but it was too strong.

It was a sobbing choked-up little cry, and now her legs gave way under her. Still holding his head she sagged backward onto the low bunk, and he knelt beside the bunk without lifting his mouth from her body. She arched her back and raised her buttocks off the bunk at his touch and allowed him to draw out her billowing skirts from under her and drop them to the deck.

Suddenly, he pulled abruptly away and she almost screamed to him not to go away again—but he had crossed to the door and locked it. Then, as he came back to where she lay, his own clothing seemed to fall away from his body like morning mist from mountain peak, and she came up on one elbow to stare at him openly. She had never seen anything so beautiful, she thought.

"The devil is beautiful also." A tiny inner voice tried to warn her, but it was far away and so small that she could ignore it. Besides it was too late, far too late to listen to warnings now—for already he was coming over her.

She expected pain, but not the deep splitting incursion that racked her. Her head was flung back and her eyes flooded with the tears of it. Yet even in the stinging agony of it there was never a thought to reject this stretching, tearing invasion and she clung to him with both her arms about his neck. It seemed that he suffered with her, for except for that single swift deep stroke, he had not moved, trying to alleviate her agony by his utter stillness; his body was rigid as hers, she could feel the muscles taut to the point of tearing, and he cradled her in his arms.

Then suddenly she could breathe again, and she took in air

with a great rushing sob, and immediately the pain began to change its shape, becoming something she could not describe to herself. It started as a spark of heat, deep within her, and flared slowly so she was forced to meet it with a slow voluptuous movement of her hips. She seemed to break free of earth and rise up through flames, that flickered redly through her clenched eyelids. There was only one reality—and that was the hard body that rocked and plunged above her. The heat seemed to fill her until she could not bear it any longer. Then at the last moment when she thought she might die of it, it burst within her—and she felt herself falling, like a tumbling leaf, down, down, at last, to the hard narrow bunk in a half-dark cabin in a tall ship on a wind-driven sea.

When next she could open her eyes his face was very close to hers. He was staring at her with a thoughtful, solemn expression.

She tried to smile, it was a shaky unconvincing effort.

"Please don't look at me like that." Her voice was even deeper, more husky than it usually was.

"I don't think I ever saw you before," he whispered and traced the line of her lips with his fingertip. "You are so different."

"Different from what?"

"Different from other women." His reply gave her a pang.

He made the first movement of withdrawing from her, but she tightened her grip on him, panic-stricken at the thought of losing him yet.

"We will only have this one night," she told him, and he did not reply. He lifted one eyebrow, and waited for her to speak again.

"You don't dispute it," she challenged. There was that mocking little smile beginning to curl his lip again, and it annoyed her.

"No, I was wrong, you are like all other women," he smiled. "You have to talk, always you have to talk."

She let him go, as punishment for those words, but as he slithered free of her she felt a terrible emptiness and she regretted his going fiercely, beginning to hate him for it.

"You have no God," she accused him.

"Isn't it strange," he chided her gently, "that most of the worst crimes in history have been committed by men with God's name upon their lips."

The truth of it deflated her momentarily, and she struggled into a sitting position.

"You are a slaver."

"I don't really want to argue with you, you know." But she would not accept that.

"You buy and sell human beings."

"What are you trying to prove to me?" He chuckled now, further angering her.

"I'm telling you that there is a void between us that can never be bridged."

"We have just done so, convincingly," and she flushed bright scarlet down her neck on to her bosom.

"I have sworn to devote my life to destroy all you stand for," she said fiercely, pushing her face close to his.

"Woman, you talk too much," he told her lazily, and covered her mouth with his own, holding her like that while she struggled, gagging her with his lips so her protests were muffled and incomprehensible. Then when her struggles had subsided he pushed her easily backward onto the bunk and came over her again.

In the morning when she woke, he was gone, but the bolster beside her was indented by his head. She pressed her face into it and the smell of his hair and of his skin still lingered, though the heat of his blood had dissipated and the linen was cool against her cheeks.

The ship was in the grip of intense excitement. She could hear the voices from the deck above as she scurried down the empty passageway to her own cabin, dreading meeting a member of the crew, or more especially meeting her brother. What excuse could she have for being abroad in the dawn, with her cabin unslept in and her clothing torn and rumpled?

Her escape was a matter of seconds only, for as she locked and leaned thankfully against the door of her cabin, Zouga beat upon it with his first from the far side.

"Robyn, wake up! Get dressed. Land is in sight. Come and see!"

Swiftly she bathed her body with a square of flannel dipped into the enameled jug of cold seawater. She was tender, swollen and sensitive and there was a trace of blood on the cloth.

"The trace of shame," she told herself severely, but it was difficult to sustain the emotion. Instead she felt a soaring sense of physical well-being—and a hearty appetite for her breakfast.

Her step was light, almost skipping as she went up on to the main deck and the wind tugged playfully at her skirts.

Her first concern was for the man. He stood at the weather rail, in shirt sleeves only, and immediately a storm of conflicting feelings and thoughts assailed her, the chief of which was that he was so lean and dark and devil-may-care that he should be kept behind bars as a menace to all womankind.

Then he lowered the telescope, turned and saw her by the companionway and bowed slightly, and she inclined her head an inch in reply, very cool and very dignified. Then Zouga hurried to meet her, laughing and excited, and took her arm as he led her to the rail.

The mountain towered out of the steely green Atlantic, a great gray buttress of solid rock, riven and rent by deep ravines and gullies choked with dark-green growth. She had not remembered it so huge, seeming to fill the whole eastern horizon and reaching up into the heavens, for its summit was covered in a thick shimmering white mattress of cloud. The cloud rolled endlessly over the edge of the mountain like a froth of boiling milk pouring over the rim of the pot, but as it sank so it was sucked into nothingness, disappearing miraculously to leave the lower slopes of the mountain clear and close, each detail of the rock face finely etched and the tiny buildings at its foot as startling white as the wing feathers of the gulls that milled the air about the clipper.

"We'll dine tonight in Cape Town," Zouga shouted over the wind, and the thought of food flooded Robyn's mouth with saliva.

Jackson, the steward, had the hands spread a tarpaulin to break the wind and they breakfasted under its lee, in the sunshine. It was a festive meal, for Mungo St. John called for champagne and they toasted the successful voyage and the good landfall in the bubbling yellow wine.

Then Mungo St. John ended it. "The wind comes through there, funneled down that break in the mountain." He pointed ahead, and they saw the surface at the mouth of the bay seething with the rush of it. "Many a ship has been dismasted by that treacherous blast. We'll be shortening sail in a few minutes." And he signaled to Jackson to clear away the trestles that carried the remains of their breakfast, excused himself with a bow and went back to his quarterdeck.

Robyn watched him strip the canvas off the upper yards, taking in two reefs in the main and setting a storm jib so that *Huron* met the freak wind readily and ran in for Table Bay,

61

giving Robben Island a good berth to port. When the ship had settled onto its new heading, Robyn went up on to the quarterdeck.

"I must speak with you," she told him, and St. John cocked his eyebrow at her.

"You could not have chosen a better time—" and with the eloquent spread of his hands indicated wind and current and the dangerous shore close under their bows.

"This will be the last opportunity," she told him quickly. "My brother and I will be leaving this ship immediately you drop anchor in Table Bay."

The mocking grin slid slowly from his lips.

"If you are determined, then it seems that we have nothing more to say to each other."

"I want you to know why."

"I know why," he said, "but I doubt that you do."

She stared at him, but he turned away to call a change of heading to the helmsman and then to the figure at the foot of the mainmast.

"Mr. Tippoo, I'll have another reef on her, if you please."

He came back to her side, but not looking at her, his head tilted back to watch the miniature figures of his crew on the mainyards high above them.

"Have you ever seen sixteen thousand acres of cotton with the pods ready for plucking?" he asked quietly. "Have you ever seen the bales going downriver on the barges to the mills?"

She did not answer, and he went on without waiting. "I have seen both, Dr. Ballantyne, and no man dare tell me that the men who work my fields are treated like cattle."

"You are a cotton planter?"

"I am, and after this voyage I will have a sugar plantation on the island of Cuba—half my cargo to pay for the land and half of it to work the cane."

"You are worse than I thought," she whispered. "I thought you were merely one of the devil's minions. Now I know you are the devil himself."

"You are going into the interior." St. John looked down at her now. "When you get there, if you ever do, you will see true human misery. You will see cruelties that no American slaveowner would dream of. You will see the slaughter of human beings by war and disease and wild beast that will balk your belief in heaven. Beside this savagery, the barracoons and the slave quarters are an earthly paradise."

"Do you dare suggest that by catching and chaining these

62

poor creatures you do them favor?" Robyn demanded, aghast at his effrontery.

"Have you ever visited a Louisiana plantation, Doctor?" Then answering his own question, "No, of course, you have not. I invite you to do so. Come down to Bannerfield as my guest one day—and then compare the state of my slaves to the savage blacks you will see in Africa, or even to those damned souls that inhabit the slums and workhouses of your own lovely little green island."

She remembered those raddled and hopeless human creatures with whom she had worked in the mission hospital. She was speechless. Then suddenly his grin was wicked again. "Think of it only as forced enlightenment of the heathen. I lead them out of the darkness into the ways of God and civilization—just as you are determined to do—but my methods are more effective."

"You are incorrigible, sir."

"No, ma'am. I am a sea captain and a planter. I am also a trader in, and an owner of, slaves—and I will fight to the death to defend my right to be all of those things."

"What *right* is that you speak of?" she demanded.

"The right of the cat over the mouse, of the strong over the weak, Dr. Ballantyne. The natural law of existence."

"Then I can only repeat, Captain St. John, that I will leave this ship at the very first opportunity."

"I am sorry that is your decision." The hard fierce look in the yellow eyes softened a little. "I wish it were otherwise."

"I shall devote my life to fighting you and men like you."

"And what a waste that will be of a lovely woman." He shook his head regretfully. "But then your resolve may give us reason to meet again; I must hope that that is so."

"One final word Captain St. John: I shall never forgive last night."

"And I, Dr. Ballantyne, will never forget it."

Zouga Ballantyne checked his horse at the side of the road, just before it crossed the narrow neck between the crags of Table Mountain and Signal Hill, one of its satellite promontories.

He swung down out of the saddle to rest his mount, for it had been a hard pull up the steep slope from the town, and he tossed the reins to the Hottentot groom who accompanied him on the second horse. Zouga was sweating lightly and there was a residual pulse of dullness behind his eyes from the wine he

63

had drunk the night before, the magnificent rich sweet wine of Constantia, one of the most highly prized vintages in the world, but capable of delivering as thick a head as any of the cheap and common grogs they sold in the waterfront bars.

In the five days since they had disembarked, the friendliness of the Cape Colony citizens had almost overwhelmed them. They had slept only the first night at a public inn in Buitengracht Street, then Zouga had called upon one of the Cape Colony's more prominent merchants, a Mr. Cartwright. He had presented his letters of introduction from the directors of the Worshipful Company of London Merchants Trading into Africa, and Cartwright had immediately placed at their disposal the guest bungalow set in the gardens of his large and gracious home on the mountain slope above the old East India Company's gardens.

Every evening since then had been a gay whirl of dinners and dances. Had Robyn and Zouga not insisted otherwise, the days would have been filled with equivalent frivolity—picnics, sailing and fishing expeditions, riding in the forest, long leisurely lunches on the lawns under spreading oak trees that reminded him so vividly of England.

However, Zouga had avoided these diversions and had managed to accomplish much of the work of the expedition. Firstly there had been the supervising of the unloading of equipment from *Huron*—in itself a major undertaking as the crates had to be swayed up from the hold and lowered into lighters alongside before making the perilous return through the surf to land on the beach at Rogger Bay.

Then he had to arrange temporary warehousing for the cargo. Here again Mr. Cartwright had been of assitance. Still Zouga found himself fiercely resenting his sister's insistence that had made all this heavy work necessary.

"Damn me, sissy, even Papa used to travel in the company of Arab slave traders when he had to. If this fellow St. John *is* a trader, we would do well to learn all we can from him— his methods and sources of supply. No one could give us better information for our report to the society."

None of his arguments had prevailed, and only when Robyn had threatened to write home to the society's directors in London, and to follow that up with a frank talk to the editor to the *Cape Times*, had Zouga acceded, with the worst grace possible, to her demands.

Now he looked down longingly at *Huron*, lying well out from the beach, snubbing around on her anchor cable to point into the rumbustious southeasterly wind. Even under bare poles she seemed on the point of flight.

Zouga guessed that St. John would be sailing within days, leaving them to await the next ship that might be bound for the Arab and Portuguese coasts.

Zouga had already presented his letter of introduction from the foreign secretary to the admiral of the Cape Squadron of the Royal Navy, and been promised all consideration. Nevertheless, he spent many hours of each morning visiting the shipping agents and owners in the port in hope of an earlier passage.

"Damn the silly wench," he muttered aloud, thinking bitterly of his sister and her foibles. "She could cost us weeks, even months."

Time was, of course, of the very essence. They had to be clear of the fever-ridden coast before the monsoon struck and risk of malaria became suicidal.

At that moment there was the crack of cannon shot from the slopes of the hill above him, and as he glanced up he saw the feather of gunsmoke drifting away from the lookout station on Signal Hill.

The gunshot was to alert the townsfolk that a ship was entering Table Bay, and Zouga shaded his eyes with his cap as the vessel came into view beyond the point of land. He was not a seaman but he recognized instantly the ugly silhouette and single smokestack of the Royal Navy gunboat that had pursued *Huron* so doggedly. Was it really two weeks ago? he wondered; the days had passed so swiftly. *Black Joke*, the gunboat, had her boilers fired and a thin banner of dark smoke drifted away downwind as she rounded up into the bay, her yards training around as she pointed through the wind and she passed within half a mile of where *Huron* was already at anchor. The proximity of the two ships raised interesting possibilities of the feud between the two captains being revived, Zouga realized, but his immediate feeling was of intense disappointment. He had hoped that the vessel might have been a trader that could have offered the expedition further passage up the east coast—and he turned away abruptly, took the reins from the groom and swung up easily into the saddle.

"Which way?" he asked the servant, and the little yellow-skinned lad in Cartwright's plum-colored livery indicated the left branch of the road that forked over the neck and dropped down across the dragon's back of the Cape peninsula to the ocean shore on the far side.

65

It was another two hours' ride, the last twenty minutes along a rutted cart track, before they reached the sprawling thatched building hidden away in one of the ravines of the mountain slope behind a grove of milkwood trees. The slopes behind the building were thick with protea bushes in full flower and the long-tailed sugarbirds haggled noisily over the blazing blooms. To one side a waterfall smoked with spray as it fell from the sheer rock face and then formed a deep green pool on which a flotilla of ducks cruised.

The building had a dilapidated air to it, the walls needed white-washing and the thatch hung in untidy clumps from the eaves. Under the milkwood trees were scattered items of ancient equipment, a wagon with one wheel missing and the woodwork almost entirely eaten away by worms, a rusty hand forge in which a red hen was sitting upon a clutch of eggs, and moldering saddlery and ropes hung from the branches of the trees.

As Zouga swung down from the saddle, a pack of half a dozen dogs came storming out of the front porch, snarling and barking around Zouga's legs so that he lashed out at them with his riding whip and with his boots, changing the snarls to startled yelps and howls.

"Who the hell are you and what do you want?" A voice carried through the uproar, and Zouga took one more cut at a great shaggy Boerhound with a ridge of coarse hair fully erect between his shoulders, catching him fairly on the snout and forcing him to circle out of range, with fangs still bared and murderous growls rumbling up his throat.

Then he looked up at the man on the stoep of the building. He carried a double-barreled shotgun in the crook of his arm, and both hammers were at full cock. He was so tall that he had to stoop beneath the angle of the roof, but he was thin as a blue gum tree, as though the flesh and fat had been burned off his bones by ten thousand tropical suns.

"Do I have the honor of addressing Mr. Thomas Harkness?" Zouga called over the clamor of the dog pack.

"I ask the questions here," the lean giant bellowed back. His beard was as white as the thunderhead clouds of a summer's day on the highveld and it hung to his belt buckle. Hair of the same silver covered his head and flowed down to the collar of his leather jerkin.

His face and his arms were burned to the color of plug tobacco, and were speckled by the raised blemishes like little moles and freckles, where years of the fierce African sun had destroyed the upper layers of his skin. The pupils of his eyes

66

were black and bright as drops of fresh tar, but the whites were smoky yellow, the color of the malarial fevers and the pestilences of Africa.

"What is your name, boy?" His voice was strong and deep. Without the beard he might have been fifty years of age, but Zouga knew with certainty that he was seventy-three. He carried his one shoulder higher than the other and the arm on that side hung at an awkward angle to the joint. Zouga knew that a lion had chewed through the shoulder and through the bone of the upper arm before Harkness had been able to reach his hunting knife on his belt with the other hand and stab it between the forelegs, up into the heart. That had been forty years before and the injury had become the Harkness hallmark.

"Ballantyne, sir." Zouga shouted to make himself heard above the dogs. "Morris Zouga Ballantyne."

The old man whistled once, a fluting double note that stilled the dogs and brought them back around his legs. He had not lowered the shotgun and a frown puckered his sharp features.

"Fuller Ballantyne's pup, is it?"

"That's right, sir."

"By God, any son of Fuller Ballantyne's is good enough for a charge of my buckshot in the rump. Don't cock your butt when you get back on that horse, boy, for I'm a man who tempts very easily."

"I've ridden a long way to see you, Mr. Harkness." Zouga smiled that frank and winning smile of his, standing his ground. "I'm one of your greatest admirers. I've read everything that has ever been written about you and everything you have written yourself."

"I doubt that," Harkness growled, "they burned most of mine. Too strong for their lily livers." But the hostile glint in his eyes turned to a twinkle and he cocked his head as he studied the young man before him.

"I have no doubt that you're as ignorant and arrogant as your daddy, but you've got a fairer turn of speech." And he stared again at the toes of Zouga's boots, and let his gaze move up slowly.

"Priest," he asked, "like your daddy?"

"No, sir, soldier."

"Regiment?"

"Thirteenth Madras Foot."

"Rank?"

"Major."

Harkness's expression eased with each reply until his gaze once more locked with Zouga's.

"Teetotal? Like your daddy?"

"Perish the thought!" Zouga assured him vehemently and Harkness smiled for the first time as he let the muzzles of the shotgun droop until they pointed at the ground. He tugged at the long spikes of his beard for a moment, then reached a decision.

"Come." He jerked his head and led the way into the house. There was one huge central room, the high ceiling of dried reed stems kept it cool and the narrow windows kept it gloomy. The floor was of peach-pit shells set into a plaster of mud and cow dung and the walls were three feet thick.

Zouga paused in the threshold and blinked with surprise at the collection of strange articles that covered the walls, were piled on every table and chair and packed to the rafters in the dark corners.

There were books, thousands of books, cloth- and leather-bound books, pamphlets and journals, atlases and encyclopedias. There were weapons—assegai of Zulu, shield of Matabele, bow of Bushman with its quiver of poisoned arrows and, of course, guns—dozens of them in racks or merely propped against the walls. There were hunting trophies, the beautiful zig-zag-striped hide of zebra, the dark bush of the lion's mane, the elegant curved horn of Harris buck, teeth of hippopotamus and warthog, and then the long, yellow arcs of ivory thicker than a woman's thigh and taller than a man's head. There were rocks, piles of rocks that glittered and sparkled, crystal rocks of purple and green, metallic nodules, native copper redder than gold, hairy strands of raw asbestos—all of it covered with a fine layer of dust and piled untidily wherever it had fallen.

The room smelled of skins and dogs and damp, of stale brandy and fresh turpentine, and there were stacks of new canvases already stretched in their wooden frames, while other canvases stood on their easels with the subjects sketched in charcoal outline, or partly blocked in with bright oil paint. On the walls were hung some finished pictures.

Zouga crossed to examine one of them while the old man blew into a pair of glass tumblers and polished them on his shirttail.

"What do you think of my lions?" he asked, as Zouga studied a huge canvas entitled. "Lion Hunt on the Gariep River. Feb. 1846."

Zouga made an appreciative sound in the back of his throat.

68

Zouga was himself a dauber and scribbler, but he considered that the meticulous reproduction of the subject was the painter's duty, while these paintings had a guileless, almost childlike joy in every primitive line. The colors also were gay and made no pretense to imitate nature, while the perspectives were wildly improbable. The mounted figure with the flowing beard in the background dominated the pride of lions in the foreground. Yet Zouga knew that these strange creations had remarkable value. Cartwright had paid ten guineas for a fanciful landscape. Zouga could only believe it was a fad among the colony's fashionable set.

"They say my lions look like English sheepdogs." Harkness glowered at them. "What do you think, Ballantyne?"

"Perhaps," Zouga started, then saw the old man's expression change. "But tremendously ferocious sheepdogs!" he added swiftly, and Harkness laughed out loud for the first time.

"By God, you'll do!" He shook his head as he half filled the tumblers with the dark brown local brandy, the fearsome "Cape Smoke," and brought one glass to Zouga.

"I like a man who speaks his mind. Rot all hypocrites." He raised his own glass in a toast. "Especially hypocritical preachers who don't give a damn for God, for truth or for their fellow men."

Zouga fancied that he recognized the description, but raised his glass. "Rot them!" he agreed, and managed to suppress a gasp as the liquor exploded in his throat and sizzled behind his eyes.

"Good," he said hoarsely, and Harkness wiped his silver mustache, left and right, with his thumb before he demanded, "Why have you come?"

"I want to find my father, and I think you may be able to tell me where to search."

"Find him?" fulminated the old man. "We should all be extremely grateful he is lost, and pray each day that he remains that way."

"I understand how you feel, sir," Zouga nodded. "I read the book that was published after the Zambezi expedition."

Harkness had accompanied Fuller Ballantyne on that ill-fated venture, acting as second in command, expedition manager and recording artist. He had been caught up in the squabbling and blame-fixing that had marred the enterprise from the beginning. Fuller Ballantyne had dismissed him, accusing him of theft of the expedition stores, trading on his own account, artistic incompetence, neglecting his duties to hunt for ivory, and total ignorance of the countryside and its trails, of the tribes and their customs, and had included these accusations in his account of the expedition, implying that the blame for the expedition's failure could be laid on Thomas Harkness's uneven shoulders.

Now even mention of that book brought the color to the sunraddled face and made the white whiskers twitch.

"I crossed the Limpopo for the first time in the year that Fuller Ballantyne was born. I drew the map that he used to reach Lake Ngami." Harkness stopped and made a dismissive gesture. "I might as well try and reason with the baboons barking from the tops of the kopjes." Then he peered more closely at Zouga.

"What do you know about Fuller? Since he sent you home to the old country, how often have you seen him? How much time have you spent in his company?"

"He came home once."

"How much time did he spend with you and your mother?"

"Some months—but he was always in Uncle William's study writing, or he was up at London, Oxford or Birmingham to lecture."

"But you, nevertheless, conceived a burning filial love and duty for the sainted and celebrated father?"

Zouga shook his head. "I hated him," he said quietly. "I could hardly bear the days until he went away again."

Harkness tilted his head on one side, surprised, speechless for a moment, and Zouga drank the last few drops of liquor in the glass.

"I never told anybody that before." He seemed puzzled himself. "I hardly even admitted it to myself. I hated him for what he did to us, to me and my sister, but especially to my mother."

Harkness took the empty tumbler from his fingers, refilled it and handed it back. He spoke quietly.

"I also will tell you something that I have never told another man. I met your mother at Kuruman, my God, so long ago. She was sixteen or seventeen and I was nearly forty. She was so pretty, so shy and yet so filled with a special quality of joy. I asked her to marry me. The only woman I ever asked." Harkness stopped himself, turned away to his painting, and peered at it. "Damned sheepdogs!" he snapped, and then without turning back to face Zouga, "So why do you want to find your father? Why have you come out to Africa?"

70

"Two reasons," Zouga told him. "Both good. To make my own reputation and my own fortune."

Harkness swiveled to face him. "Damn me, but you can be direct." There was a tinge of respect in his expression now. "How do you plan to achieve those very desirable ends?"

Zouga explained swiftly: the newspaper sponsorship, that of the Society for the Extinction of the Slave Trade.

"You'll find much grist for your mill," Harkness interjected. "The coast is still rife with the trade, despite what you'll hear in London town."

"I am also an agent for the Worshipful Company of London Merchants Trading into Africa, but I have my own goods to trade, and five thousand cartridges for my Sharps rifle."

Harkness wandered across the dim room and stopped before one of the gigantic elephant tusks propped against the far wall. It was so old and heavy that there was very little taper from root to tip, the point worn blunt and rounded. One third of its length was smooth and a clear lovely butter-yellow color, where it had been buried in the jaw of the beast, the rest of it was stained dark with vegetable juices and scarred from the battles and foragings of sixty years.

"This one weighs one hundred and sixty pounds; its value in London is six shillings a pound." He slapped it with his open palm. "There are still bulls like that out there, thousands of them. But take a tip from an old dog: forget your fancy Sharps, and use one of the ten-bore elephant guns. They throw a ball that weighs a quarter of a pound, and though they kick like the devil himself, they drive better than any of these new-fangled rifles." There was a lightness in the worn old features, a sparkle in the dark eyes. "Another tip: get in close. Forty paces at the outside, and go for the heart. Forget what you'll hear about the brain shot, go for the heart—" He broke off suddenly and waggled his head, grinning ruefully. "By God, but it's enough to make a man want to be young again!"

He came back and studied Zouga directly, and a thought occurred to him with a suddenness that struck him like a physical blow, taking him so by surprise that he almost spoke it aloud.

"If Helen had given me a different answer, you could be my son." But he held back the words, and asked instead:

"How can I help you, then?"

"You can tell me where I can start to search for Fuller Ballantyne."

71

Harkness threw up his hands, palms uppermost. "It's a vast land—so big that you could travel across it for a lifetime."

"That's why I have come to you."

Harkness went to the long table of yellow Cape deal that ran nearly the full length of the room and with the twisted arm swept a clear space among the books and papers and paint pots.

"Bring a chair," he instructed, and when they sat facing each other across the cleared space, he recharged both their glasses and placed what remained in the bottle between them.

"Where did Fuller Ballantyne go?" Harkness asked, and took a silver tress from the thick beard and began to twist it around his forefinger. The finger was long and bony and covered with the thick ridges of ancient scar tissue where the recoil of overheated or overcharged firearms had driven the trigger guard to the bone.

"Where did Fuller Ballantyne go?" he repeated, but Zouga realized the question was rhetorical, and he said nothing.

"After the Zambezi expedition, his fortune was exhausted, his reputation all but destroyed—and to a man like Fuller Ballantyne that was unbearable. His entire life had been an endless hunt for glory. No risk, no sacrifice was too great, his own or others'. He would steal and lie—aye, even kill for it."

Zouga looked up sharply, challenging.

"Kill," Harkness nodded. "Anybody who stood in his way. I have seen him, but that is another tale. Now we want to know where he went."

Harkness stretched out and selected a roll of parchment from the cluttered tabletop, checked it quickly and grunted with approval as he spread it between them.

It was a map of Central Africa, east to west coast, south to the Limpopo, north to the lakes, drawn in India ink, and the borders were illuminated by Harkness's characteristic figures and animals.

Instantly Zouga coveted it with his very soul. All that Harkness had accused his father of he felt in his own heart. He had to have this, even if it was necessary to steal—or, by God, kill. He had to have it.

The map was huge—at least five feet square—hand-drawn on the finest-quality linen-backed paper. It was unique, the detail enormous; the notations were profuse but succinct, the observations firsthand, the details precise, written in a tiny elegant script that needed a reading glass to be deciphered with ease.

"Here heavy concentrations of elephant herds during June to September."

"Here I sampled gold reef in ancient workings at two ounces to the ton."

"Here rich copper is worked by Gutus people."

"Here slave convoys depart for the coast in June."

There were literally hundreds of these notations, each in a neatly numbered box, that corresponded to the exact location on the map.

Harkness watched Zouga's face, with a sly half-smile on his face, and then handed him a reading glass to continue his examination.

It took Zouga a few minutes to realize that the pink shaded areas indicated the "fly corridors" of the high African plateau. The safe areas through which domestic animals could be moved to avoid the tsetse-fly belts. The terrible Ngana disease which the fly carried could decimate the herds. Knowledge of these corridors had been gathered by the African tribes over hundreds of years, and here it was faithfully recorded by Thomas Harkness. The value of this knowledge was incalculable.

"Here Mzilikazi's border impis kill all travellers."

"Here there is no water between May and October."

"Here dangerous malarial vapours during October to December."

The areas of greatest hazard were signposted, while the known routes to the interior were clearly marked, though there were few enough of these.

The cities of the African kings were marked, as was the location of their military kraals, the areas of influence of each were defined and the names of the subservient chiefs noted.

"Here concession to hunt elephant must be obtained from Chief Mafa. He is treacherous."

Harkness watched the young man eagerly poring over the priceless document. His expression was almost fond, and he nodded his head once as a memory passed like a shadow behind his eyes. He spoke at last.

"Your father would be trying to restore his reputation at a single stroke," Harkness mused. "He would have to feed that monstrous ego. There are two areas that come immediately to mind. Here!"

He placed his open hand across an enormous area to the north and west of the defined shape of Lake Marawi. In this area the copious and authoritative notations were replaced by

73

meager, hesitant observations obtained from hearsay or native legend, and by speculation followed by a question mark.

"Sheikh Assab of the Omani Arabs reports River Lualaba runs north and west. Possible flow into Lake Tanganyika." The dotted outlines of rivers, instead of crisp detail. "Pemba, the chief of the Marakan, reports huge lake shaped like butterfly twenty-five days' march from Khoto Khota. Called Lomani. Possible source of Luapula and of Herodotus fountain." The lake was sketched in. "Question. Is Lake Tanganyika connected to Lake Albert? Question. Is Lake Tanganyika connected to Lake Lomani? If so, Lomani is ultimate source of Nile River?"

Harkness touched the two question marks with his gnarled and bony finger.

"Here," said Harkness. "The big question marks. The Nile River. That would attract Fuller. He spoke of it often." Harkness chuckled. "Always with the same introductory words: '*Of course, the fame matters not at all to me.*'" The old man shook his silver head. "It mattered not less than the air he breathed. Yes, the source of the Nile River and the fame that it would bring its discoverer—that would fascinate him."

Harkness stared for a long time at the empty spaces, dreaming perhaps, visions awakening behind the bright black eyes. He aroused himself at last, shaking his shaggy head as if to clear it.

"There would be only one other feat that would attract as much attention, would be greeted with as much acclaim." Harkness ran his spread hand southward down the parchment to cover another vast void in the web of mountains and rivers. "Here," he said softly. "The forbidden kingdom of the Monomatapas."

The name itself had an eerie quality. *Monomatapa*. The sound of it raised the fine hair on the back of Zouga's neck.

"You have heard of it?" Harkness asked.

"Yes," Zouga nodded. "They say it is the Ophir of the Bible, where Sheba mined her gold. Have you traveled there?"

Harkness shook his head. "Twice I started out," he shrugged. "No white man has traveled there. Even Mzilikazi's impis have not raided that far east. The Portuguese made one attempt to reach the Emperor Monomatapa. That was in fifteen sixty-nine. The party was wiped out, and there were no survivors." Harkness made a sound of disgust. "As you could expect of the Ports, they abandoned any further attempt to reach Monomatapa. For the two hundred years since then they have been content to sit in their seraglios at Tete and Quelimane, breeding

74

half-castes, and picking up the slaves and ivory that filter down out of the interior."

"But still there are the legends of the Monomatapa. I heard them from my father. Gold and great walled cities."

Harkness stood up from the table with the grace of a man half his age and crossed to an iron-bound chest against the wall behind his chair. The chest was not locked but the lid required both the old man's skinny arms to lift it.

He came back with a drawstring bag made of softly tanned leather. It was obviously weighty for he carried it in both hands. He pulled the mouth open, and upended the contents on to the linen map.

There was no mistaking the lovely yellow metal, it had the deep glowing luster which was bewitched mankind for thousands of years. Zouga could not resist the urge to reach out and touch it. It had a marvelous soapy feeling against his fingertips. The precious metal had been beaten into heavy round beads, each the size of the top joint of Zouga's little finger, and the beads had been strung onto animal sinew to form a necklace.

"Fifty-eight ounces," Harkness told him, "and the metal is of unusual purity, I have had it assayed."

The old man lifted the necklace over his own head and let it lie against the snowy fall of his beard. It was only then that Zouga realized that there was a pendant on the string of golden beads.

It was in the shape of a bird, a stylized falconlike shape with folded wings. It was seated upon a rounded plinth that was decorated with a triangular design, like a row of shark's teeth. The figure was the size of a man's thumb. The gold metal was polished by the touch of human skin over the ages so that some of the detail had been lost. The eyes of the bird were glassy green chips.

"It was a gift from Mzilikazi. He has no use for gold, nor for emeralds—yes, the stones are emeralds," Harkness nodded. "One of Mzilikazi's warriors killed an old woman in the Burnt Land. They found the leather pouch on her body."

"Where is the Burnt Land?" Zouga asked.

"I'm sorry." Harkness fiddled with the little golden bird. "I should have explained. King Mzilikazi's impis have laid waste to the land along his borders, in some places to a depth of a hundred miles and more. They have killed all who lived there and they maintain it as a buffer strip against any hostile force. The Boer commandos from the south particularly, but from any other hostile invader also. Mzilikazi calls it the Burnt Land, and it was here, to the east of his kingdom, that his border guards killed this solitary old woman. They described her as a very strange old woman, not of any known tribe, speaking a language they did not understand."

Harkness lifted the necklace from his neck and dropped it carelessly back into the bag, and Zouga felt bereft. He would have liked to feel the full weight and the texture of the metal in his hands for a little longer. Harkness went on quietly:

"Of course you have heard the talk of gold and walled cities, like everybody else. But that is the closest I have ever come to corroboration."

"Did my father know about the necklace?" Zouga asked, and Harkness nodded. "Fuller wanted to purchase it, he offered me almost twice its gold value."

They were both silent for a long while, each brooding on his own thoughts until Zouga stirred.

"How would a man like my father try to reach the Monomatapa?"

"Not from the south nor from the west. Mzilikazi, the Matabele king, will let no man pass through the Burnt Land. I feel that Mzilikazi has some deep superstition attached to the land beyond his eastern border. He does not venture there himself, nor does he allow others to do so." Harkness shook his head. "No, Fuller would have to try from the east, from the Portuguese coast, from one of their settlements." Harkness began to trace out the possible approach marches on the linen chart. "Here there are high mountains. I have seen them at a distance and they seemed a formidable barrier." Outside, night had already fallen, and Harkness interrupted himself to order Zouga, "Tell your groom to off-saddle the horses and take them to the stables. It is too late to return. You will have to stay overnight."

When Zouga returned a Malay servant had drawn the curtains, lit the lanterns and laid a meal of yellow rice and chicken cooked in a fiery curry—and Harkness had opened another bottle of the Cape brandy. He went on talking as though there had been no interruption. They ate the meal and pushed the enameled tin plates away to return to the map, and the hours passed unnoticed by either of them.

In the intimate lantern light, the sense of drama and excitement that gripped them both was heightened by the brandy they drank. Once in a while Harkness would rise to fetch some souvenir of his travels to reinforce a point, a sample of quartz

76

rock in which the seams of native gold were clearly visible in the lamplight.

"If there is visible gold, it's rich," Harkness told Zouga.

"Why did you never mine the reefs you found?"

"I could never stay long enough in one place," Harkness grinned ruefully. "There was always another river to cross, a range of mountains or a lake that I had to reach—or I was following a herd of elephant. There was never time to sink a shaft, or build a house, or raise a herd."

When the dawn was rising, peeping into the huge gloomy room around the curtains, Zouga exclaimed suddenly, "Come with me. Come with me to find Monomatapa!" And Harkness laughed.

"I thought it was your father you were intent on finding."

"You know better!" Zouga laughed with him. Somehow he felt at home with the old man, as if he had known him all his life. "But can you imagine my father's face when you come to rescue him?"

"It would be worth it," Harkness admitted, and then the laughter faded, and gave way to an expression of such deep regret, of such consuming sorrow that Zouga felt a compulsion to reach out across the table and touch the misshapen shoulder.

Harkness pulled away from his touch. He had lived alone too long. He would never again be able to take comfort from a fellow man.

"Come with me," Zouga repeated, letting his hand drop to the tabletop between them.

"I have made my last journey into the interior," Harkness said tonelessly. "Now all I have are my paint pots and my memories."

He lifted his eyes to the ranks of framed canvas with their brilliant joyous images.

"You are still strong, vital," Zouga insisted. "Your mind is so clear."

"Enough!" Harkness's voice was harsh, bitter. "I am tired now. You must go. Now, immediately."

Zouga felt his anger rise hotly to his cheeks at the abrupt rejection, this sudden change of mood, and he stood quickly. For a few seconds he stood looking down at the old man.

"Go!" said Harkness again.

Zouga nodded abruptly. "Very well." His eyes slid down to the map. He knew he must have it at any price, though he

77

sensed that there was no price that Harkness would accept. He must plan and scheme for it, but he would have it.

He turned and strode to the front door, and the dogs that had slept around their feet rose and followed him.

"Garniet!" Zouga shouted angrily. "Bring the horses." And he stood in the doorway rocking impatiently on his toes and heels, hands clasped behind his back, his shoulders stiff, not looking around at the thin stooped figure who still sat at the table in the lamplight.

The groom brought the horses at last, and still without turning Zouga called roughly, "Good day to you, Mr. Harkness."

The reply was in a frail old man's quaver that he hardly recognized.

"Come again. We have more to discuss. Come back—in two days."

The stiffness went out of Zouga's stance. He started to turn back, but the old man waved him away with a brusque gesture and Zouga stamped down the front steps, vaulted into the saddle and whipped his mount into a gallop along the narrow rutted track.

Harkness sat at the table until long after the hoofbeats had faded. Strange that the pain had receded to the very back of his consciousness during the hours that he had sat with the youngster. He had felt young and strong, as though he had suckled upon the vigor and the youth of the other.

Then it had come back with a savage rush at Zouga Ballantyne's invitation, almost as if to remind him that his life was no longer his, that it was already forfeit to the hyena that lived deep in his belly, each day growing stronger, bigger, as it fed upon his vitals. When he closed his eyes he could imagine it, the way that he had seen it so often in the light of a thousand campfires—up there in the wonderful land that he would never visit again. The thing within him had the same furtive slinking presence and he could taste the fetid breath of it in his throat. Now he gasped as the full strength of the pain returned, as the beast buried its fangs deeper into his gut.

He knocked over the chair in his haste to reach the precious bottle in the back of the cabinet and he gulped a mouthful of the clear pungent liquid without measuring it into the spoon. It was too much, he knew that, but each day he needed more to keep the hyena at bay, and each day the relief took longer to come.

He clung to the corner of the cabinet and waited for it. "Please," he whispered, "please let it end soon."

There were half a dozen messages and invitations awaiting Zouga on his return to the Cartwright estate that morning, but the one which gave him most excitement was on official Admiralty paper, a polite request to call upon the Honorable Ernest Kemp, Rear Admiral of the Blue, Officer Commanding the Cape Squadron.

Zouga shaved and changed his clothing, selecting his best jacket for the occasion although it was a long dusty ride to Admiralty House. Despite missing a night's sleep, he felt vital and alert.

The admiral's secretary kept him waiting only a few minutes before showing him through, and Admiral Kemp came around from behind his desk to greet Zouga amiably, for the young man came highly recommended and Fuller Ballantyne's name still commanded respect in Africa.

"I have some news which I hope will please you, Major Ballantyne. But first, a glass of Madeira?"

Zouga had to curb his impatience while the admiral poured the syrupy wine. The admiral's study was decorated richly, with velvet furnishings and a fashionable profusion of ornaments, small statues, bric-a-brac, stuffed birds in glass showcases, family portraits in ornate frames and pretty ceramics, potted plants and the kind of paintings which Zouga admired.

The admiral was tall but stooped, as though to accommodate his long frame to the limited headroom between the decks of one of Her Majesty's ships. He seemed old for the responsible appointment he held, guarding the Empire's lifeline to India and the East, but the aging may have been caused by ill health rather than years. There were dark-toned pouches of skin below his eyes and other marks of sickness carved around his mouth and evident in the distended blue veins on the back of his hands as he handed a glass of Madeira to Zouga.

"Your good health, Major Ballantyne." And then, after he had tasted his own wine, "I think I have a berth for you. A ship of my squadron anchored in Table Bay yesterday, and as soon as she has replenished her coal bunkers and revictualed I shall detach her for independent duty in the Mozambique channel."

Zouga knew from his meetings with the directors of the Society for the Extinction of the Slave Trade that one part of the admiral's standing orders read:

"You are requested and required to dispose the ships of your squadron in such manner as most expediently to prevent vessels of whatever Christian nation from engaging in the slave trade on the coast of the African continent south of the equator."

Clearly Kemp intended a sweep of the eastern seaboard with elements of his squadron, and Zouga felt awakening delight as the Admiral went on genially, "It will not need much of a diversion for my ship to call at Quelimane, and to land you and your party."

"I cannot thank you sufficiently, Admiral." His pleasure was transparent, and Admiral Kemp smiled in sympathy. He had put himself out more than his usual wont, for the youngster was attractive and likable, deserving of encouragement, but now there were other matters awaiting his attention and as he pulled out his gold hunter and consulted it pointedly he went on,

"You should be ready to sail in five days' time." He returned the watch to the fob of his uniform coat. "I hope we will see you on Friday? My secretary did send you an invitation, did he not? Your sister will be with you, I hope."

"Indeed, sir." Zouga stood in obedience to his dismissal. "And my sister and I are honored."

In fact Robyn had said, "I do not waste my evenings, Zouga, and I have no intention of enduring the company of a fleet of tipsy sailors nor of suffering the wagging tongues of their wives."

The Cape wives were agog with the presense in their midst of the notorious Robyn Ballantyne who had impersonated a man and invaded, successfully, an exclusively masculine preserve. Half of them were deliciously scandalized, and the rest were awed and admiring. However, Zouga was certain that she would pay this price for their passage to Quelimane.

"Very well then." Admiral Kemp nodded. "Thank you for calling on me." And then, as Zouga started for the door, "Oh, by the way, Ballantyne. The ship is the *Black Joke,* Captain Codrington commanding. My secretary will give you a letter for him, and I suggest you call upon him to introduce yourself and to learn the date of sailing."

The name came as a shock, and Zouga checked his stride as he thought quickly of the complication which the choice of ship might bring.

Zouga was sensitive to any threat to the expedition, and Codrington had struck him as being a hotheaded, almost fanatical character. He could not afford any slur to his leadership, and Codrington had seen him sailing in company with a suspected slaver. He could not be sure what Codrington would do.

It was a delicate decision: accept the berth and risk Codrington's denunciation, or refuse the offer of passage and perhaps wait for months in Cape Town before another vessel offered them another.

If they were delayed that long, it would mean missing the cooler and drier period between the monsoons, they would have to cross the pestilential and fever-ridden coastal lowlands in the most dangerous season.

Zouga made his decision. "Thank you, Admiral Kemp. I will call on Captain Codrington as soon as possible."

Thomas Harkness had asked Zouga to return on the second day, and the map was more important even than swift passage to Quelimane.

Zouga sent Garniet, the Cartwrights' groom, down to the beach with a sealed letter addressed to Captain Codrington and with instructions to take one of the water boats out to *Black Joke* and deliver it personally to Codrington. It was a warning, couched in the most polite terms, that Zouga and Robyn would call on the captain the following morning. Zouga had become aware that his sister had an effect on men quite out of proportion to her physical appearance—even Admiral Kemp had asked for her personally—and he had no compunction in using her to take the edge off Codrington's temper. He would have to warn her to exert her charm, but now there was more important business.

He had mounted on Cartwright's big bay gelding and ridden halfway down the graveled drive between the oaks, when a thought struck him and he swung the horse's head and cantered back to the guest bungalow again. The naval Colt revolver was on the top layer of his chest, already fully loaded and with caps on the nipples. He carried it under the tail of his coat while he went back out to the tethered gelding, and then slipped the revolver surreptitiously into the saddlebag as he swung up into the saddle.

He knew he had to have the Harkness map at any price, but he deliberately refused to think what that price might be.

He pushed his mount hard up the steep road to the neck between the peaks, and gave him only a few minutes to blow before starting down the far slope.

The air of dilapidation which hung over the thatched building in the milkwood grove seemed to have deepened. It seemed totally deserted, silent and desolate. He dismounted and threw his reins over a milkwood branch and stooped to ease the girth.

Then he quietly unfastened the buckle of the saddlebag and slipped the Colt into his waistband and pulled his coat over it.

As he started toward the stoep, the big ridge-backed Boerhound rose from where it had lain in the shadows and came to meet him. In contrast to its previous ferocity, the animal was subdued, its tail and ears drooping and it whined softly when it recognized Zouga.

He went up on to the stoep and hammered on the front door with his fist, and heard the blows reverberate through the room beyond. Beside him, the Boerhound cocked its head and watched him expectantly, but silence settled again over the old building.

Twice more Zouga beat upon the door, before he tried the handle. It was locked. He rattled the brass lock and put his shoulder to the door; but it was heavy teak in a solid frame. Zouga jumped down off the stoep and circled the house, squinting his eyes at the fierce reflected sunlight from the whitewashed walls. The windows were shuttered.

Beyond the farmyard stood the old slave quarters, now used by Harkness's servant, and Zouga called loudly for him, but his room was deserted and the ashes cold in the cooking place. Zouga went back to the main house and stood by the locked kitchen door.

He knew that he should go back to his horse and ride away, but he needed the map, even if just for long enough to make a copy. Harkness was not here, and in three days, perhaps less, he would be sailing out of Table Bay.

There was a pile of broken rusted garden tools in the corner of the stoep. Zouga selected a hand scythe, and carefully probed the metal point of the blade into the crack between jamb and door. The lock was old and worn, the tongue slipped back easily under the blade and he jerked the door open with his free hand.

It was still not too late. He paused in the doorway for many seconds, and then he took a deep breath and stepped quietly into the gloom of the interior.

There was a long passage leading past closed doors toward the front room. Zouga went down it, opening doors quietly as he passed. In one room was a huge four-poster bedstead with the curtains opened and the bedclothes in disorder.

Quickly Zouga passed on to the main room. It was in semidarkness and he stopped to let his eyes adjust, and immediately was aware of a low sound. The hive murmur of insects seemed to fill the high room. It was a disturbing, almost menacing sound, and Zouga felt the skin prickle on his forearms.

"Mr. Harkness!" he called hoarsely, and the hum rose to a loud buzzing. Something alighted on his cheek and crawled across his skin. He struck it away with a shudder of revulsion and stumbled across to the nearest window. His fingers were clumsy on the fastening of the shutters. A shaft of white sunlight burned into the room as the shutter swung open.

Thomas Harkness sat in one of the carved wingback chairs across the cluttered table, and stared at Zouga impassively.

The flies crawled over him, big metallic blue and green flies that glittered in the sunlight. They swarmed with evident glee upon the deep dark wound in the center of his chest. The snowy beard was black with clotted blood, and blood had formed a congealed pool beneath his chair.

Zouga was rooted by the shock for many seconds, and then reluctantly he took a step forward. The old man had propped one of his big-bored elephant guns against the table leg, reversing the weapon so the muzzle pressed into his own chest and his hands were still locked around the barrel.

"What did you do that for?" Zouga demanded stupidly, speaking aloud, and Harkness stared back at him.

Harkness had removed the boot from his right foot, and depressed the trigger with his bare toe. The massive impact of the heavy lead ball had driven the chair and the man in it back against the wall, but he had retained his death grip on the barrel.

"That was a stupid thing to do." Zouga took a cheroot from his case and lit it with a Swan Vesta. The smell of death was in the room, coating the back of his throat and the roof of his mouth. Zouga drew deeply on the tobacco smoke.

There was no reason at all to feel grief. He had known the old man for a single day and night. He had come here for one reason only: to get the map the best way he was able. It was ridiculous now to have the deep ache of sorrow turning his legs leaden and stinging the backs of his eyes. Was he mourning the passing of an era perhaps, rather than the man himself? Harkness and the legends of Africa were interwoven. The man had been history itself.

Slowly Zouga approached the figure in the chair, and then reaching out drew his palm slowly down over the old face, ruined by the elements and by pain, closing the lids down over the staring black eyes.

The old man looked more peaceful that way.

Zouga hooked one leg over the corner of the cluttered table, and smoked the cheroot slowly, in almost companionable silence with Thomas Harkness. Then he dropped the stub in the big copper spittoon beside the chair and went through to the bedroom.

He took one of the blankets off the bed and brought it back.

He brushed the flies away into an angry buzzing circle, and threw the blanket over the seated figure. As he drew it up over the head, he murmured softly, "Get it close, old man, and go for the heart," the advice that Harkness had given him as a farewell. Then he turned away briskly to the laden table, and began shuffling through the jumbled pieces of canvas and paper, and slowly his impatience turned to alarm—and then to panic as he hunted through pile after pile without finding the map.

He was panting when at last he straightened up and glared at the blanket-covered figure.

"You knew I was coming for it, didn't you!"

He left the table and went to the chest, lifted the lid against groaning hinges, and the leather bag with its golden contents was gone also. He ransacked the chest down to its floorboards, but it was not there. Then he started to search in earnest, going carefully through any possible hiding place in the crowded room. An hour later he went back and perched on the edge of the table once more.

"Damn you, for a cunning old bastard," he said quietly. He took one more slow look about the room, making certain that he overlooked nothing. The painting of the lion hunt was no longer on the easel, he noticed.

Suddenly the humor of the situation struck him, and his scowl lightened, he began to chuckle ruefully to himself.

"You had the last joke on the Ballantynes, didn't you? By God, but you always did things your way, Tom Harkness, I'll grant you that."

He stood up slowly, and placed his hand on the blanket-covered shoulder. "You win, old man. Take your secrets with you then." He could feel the twisted old bones through the cloth and he shook him gently and then he went out quickly to his horse for there was much to do. It took him the rest of the day to cross the neck again and reach the magistrate's court, then to get back with the coroner and his assistants.

They buried Thomas Harkness that evening, wrapped in the blanket, under the milkwood grove, for the heat was oppressive in the valley and they could not wait for a coffin to be carted out from the city.

Zouga left the coroner to take charge of the estate, to list the equipment and livestock in the yard and put his seals on the doors of the old house until the contents could be taken in.

Zouga rode home in the golden Cape dusk, his boots dusty and his shirt sticky with sweat. He was exhausted from the day's exertions, and low in spirits, still oppressed by grief for the old man and angry with him for the last trick he had played.

The groom took his horse in front of the bungalow.

"Did you deliver the letter to Captain Codrington?" Zouga demanded, and hardly waited for the reply as he went up into the house. He needed a drink now, and while he poured whiskey into a cut-crystal glass, his sister came into the room, and reached up casually to kiss his cheek, wrinkling her nose at the tickle of his whiskers and the smell of his sweat.

"You had best change. We are dining with the Cartwrights tonight," Robyn told him. "I could not avoid it." And then as an afterthought, "Oh, Zouga, a colored servant delivered something for you this morning, just after you had left. I had it put in the study."

"Who is it from?"

Robyn shrugged. "The servant spoke only kitchen Dutch and he seemed terrified. He fled before I could find someone to question him."

With the whiskey glass in his hand Zouga crossed to the door of the study, and stopped there abruptly. His expression changed, and he strode through the doorway.

Minutes later Robyn heard his shout of triumphant laughter, and curiously she crossed to the open door. Zouga stood beside the heavy carved stinkwood desk.

On the desk top lay a drawstring bag of tanned and stained leather from which spilled a heavy necklace of gleaming gold; beside the bag was spread a magnificently illustrated map on a backing of linen parchment, and Zouga stood with his back to her. He held at arm's length a flamboyant picture in oils in a large frame, a figure on horseback with a band of ferocious wild animals in the foreground, and as she watched, Zouga reversed the picture. There was a message freshly carved into the wood of the frame.

For Zouga Ballantyne. May you find the road to all your Monomatapas—would only that I could have gone with you.

Tom Harkness.

Zouga was laughing still, but there was a strange quality to the laughter and when he turned toward her she realized with a shock that her brother's eyes were bright with tears.

Zouga brushed the crumbs from his lips with the damask table napkin and chuckled as he picked up the sheet of newsprint and shook it open again at the second page.

"Damn me, sissy, I should have known better than to leave you alone." He read further and laughed outright. "Did you really say that to him? Did you really?"

"I cannot remember my exact words," Robyn told him primly. "You must remember it was in the heat of battle."

They sat on the terrace of the bungalow under the pergola of vines, through which the early sun flicked golden coins of light upon the breakfast table.

The previous day the editor of the *Cape Times*, with a speculator's eye to making a profit on Dr. Robyn Ballantyne's notoriety, had invited her on a tour of the military hospital at Observatory, and in innocence, Robyn had believed that the visit was at the invitation of the Colony's administration and she had welcomed the opportunity to widen her professional experience.

The visit had succeeded beyond the editor's most extravagent expectations, for the surgeon general of the Colony had scheduled a tour for the same day and he had walked into the hospital's main operating room, followed by his staff, at the moment that Robyn was expressing herself on the subject of sponges to the hospital matron.

The surgeon's sponges were kept in pails of water, clean water from the galvanized rainwater tanks at the rear of the building. The pails were under the operating table, where the surgeon could reach them readily, and after swabbing away blood and pus and other matter the sponge was dropped into a collection tray, later to be washed out and returned to the original pail of fresh water.

"I assure you, Doctor, that my nurses wash the swabs out most thoroughly." The matron was a formidable figure with the flattened features of a bulldog bitch and the same aggressive thrust to her jaw. She stooped, plunged her hand into the pail, and selected one of the sponges and proffered it to Robyn.

"You can see for yourself how soft and white they are."

"Just like the soft white germs that swarm in them." Robyn was angry, with red spots of color in her cheeks. "Have none of you here ever heard of Joseph Lister?"

The surgeon general answered her question from the doorway.

"The answer to that question, Dr. Ballantyne, is NO we have never heard of that person, whoever he may be. We do not have time to concern ourselves with the opinions of every crank or, for that matter, with male impersonators."

The surgeon general had a very good idea of the identity of the young woman before him. He had followed the gossip which was the Colony's main recreation, and he did not approve of Robyn.

On the other hand, Robyn had no idea as to the identity of the elderly gentleman with the bushy gray whiskers and beetling brows, though by the dried bloodstains on the front of his frock coat she guessed that he was a surgeon of the old school, one who operated in his street clothes and let the stains advertise his profession. Here was a much more worthy adversary than the hospital matron, and she rounded on him with the battle light bright in her eyes.

"Then, sir, I am amazed that you admit so readily your ignorance and your bigotry."

The surgeon general spluttered for breath and a ready answer.

"By God, madam, you do not truly expect me to look for dangerous poisons in each speck of dust, in each drop of water, on my own hands even." He held them up for her inspection, shaking them in Robyn's face. There were dark rinds of dried blood under the nails, for he had operated that morning. He pushed his face close to hers, and she drew back a little as his spittle flew angrily.

"Yes, sir," she told him loudly. "Look for them there, and on each breath you exhale, on those filthy clothes."

The editor scribbled delightedly in his shorthand notebook, as the exchanges became more violent, more loaded with personal insult. He had not bargained for anything so spectacular, but the climax came when Robyn had goaded her adversary until he used an oath as potent as his rage.

"Your choice of words is as foul as these lowly little white sponges of yours," she told him, and let him have the sponge full in the face, hurling it with all her strength so that water flew and dripped from his whiskers on to the front of his frock coat as Robyn marched from the operating room.

"You hit him?" Zouga lowered the newspaper, and stared across the table at his sister. "Really, sissy, sometimes you are no lady."

"True," Robyn agreed unrepentantly. "But that is not the first time you have made that observation. Besides, I had no idea that he was the surgeon general."

Zouga shook his head in mock disapproval and read to her. "His considered opinion of you, as expressed to the editor, is that you are a fledgling doctor of dubious qualification very recently obtained from an obscure school of medicine, by even more dubious means."

"Oh, rich!" Robyn clapped her hands. "He's a better orator than a surgeon."

"He goes on to say that he is considering going to law to obtain redress."

"For assault with a sponge." Robyn laughed lightly as she stood up from the breakfast table. "A fig for him, but we must hurry if we are to keep our appointment with Captain Codrington."

Her mood was still gay as she stood beside Zouga in the stern of the water lighter when they came alongside the steel side of the gunboat.

The southeast wind had raked the surface of Table Bay into a cottonfield of whitecaps, and had spread a thick white tablecloth of cloud upon the flat-topped mountain. The people of the Colony called this wind "the Cape Doctor," for without it the summers would have been oppressive and enervating. However, it provided a constant hazard to shipping and the bottom of the bay was littered with wrecks. *Black Joke* had two men on her anchor watch as she lunged and fretted against her cable.

As the lighter came alongside, the thick canvas hoses were passed down and a dozen men on the pumps began to transfer the cargo into the gunboat's boiler-room tanks, before any attempt was made to take visitors aboard.

As Robyn came up through the entry port to the main deck she looked immediately to the quarterdeck. Codrington was in shirtsleeves, he was a head taller than the group of warrant officers around him, and his sun-bleached blond hair shone in the sunlight like a beacon.

The group was giving its attention to the coal lighter which was secured against the port side of the ship.

"Have the hands secure a tarpaulin over the buckets," Codrington shouted down to his boatswain in the lighter, "else you'll have us looking like a party of chimneysweeps."

The deck was alive with the purposeful pandemonium of revictualing, bunkering and watering, and with Zouga beside her, Robyn picked her way through the litter. Codrington turned away from the rail and saw them.

He seemed younger than Robyn remembered, for his expression was relaxed and his manner easy. He had an almost boyish air when contrasted to the grizzled and weatherbeaten sailors about him, but the illusion was dispelled the moment he recognized his visitors. Suddenly his features were stern and the line of his mouth altered, the eyes chilled to the hardness of pale sapphires.

"Captain Codrington," Zouga greeted him with his most studied charm. "I am Major Ballantyne."

"We have met before, sir," Codrington acknowledged, making no effort to return the smile.

Zouga went on unruffled, "May I present my sister, Dr. Ballantyne?"

Codrington glanced back at Robyn. "Your servant, ma'am." It was more a nod than a bow. "I have read something of your further exploits since our last meeting in this morning's news sheet." For a moment the stern expression cracked, and there was a mischievous spark in the blue eyes. "You have strong views, ma'am, and an even stronger right hand."

Then he turned back to Zouga. "I have orders from Admiral Kemp to convey you and your party to Quelimane. No doubt you will find our company dull, after your previous traveling companions." Deliberately Codrington turned and looked across a half mile of wind-creamed green water to where *Huron* still lay at her anchor, and for the first time Zouga fidgeted uncomfortably as he followed the direction of the Captain's eyes. Codrington went on. "Be that as it may, I would be grateful if you could present yourselves aboard this ship before noon on the day after tomorrow, when I expect a fair tide to leave the bay. Now you must excuse me. I must attend to the management of my ship." With a nod, not offering to shake hands or make any other civility, Codrington turned away to his waiting warrant officers, and Zouga's charm deserted him. His face darkened and seemed to swell with anger at the abrupt dismissal.

"The fellow has a damnable cheek," he growled fiercely to Robyn. For a moment he hesitated and then with a curt, "Come, let us leave," he turned, crossed the deck, and clambered down into the water lighter, but Robyn made no move.

She waited quietly until Codrington had finished the discussion with his boatswain, and looked up again, feigning surprise to see her still there.

"Captain Codrington, we left *Huron* on my insistence. That is why we are now seeking other passage." She spoke in a low husky voice, but her manner was so intense that his expression wavered.

"You were correct. That ship is a slaver and St. John is a slavemaster. I proved it."

"How?" he demanded, his manner altering instantly.

"I cannot speak now. My brother—" She glanced back at the entry port, expecting her brother to reappear at any moment. He had given her strict instructions as to how he expected her to act toward Codrington.

"I will be at the landing place at Rogger Bay this afternoon," she went on quickly.

"What time?"

"Three o'clock," she said, and turned away, lifted her skirts above her ankles and hurried to the ships side.

Admiral Kemp sat impatiently in the immense carved abbot's chair which his junior officers referred to as the "throne." The size of it emphasized the thinness of the old man's body. It seemed his shoulders were too narrow to support the mass of gold lace which decorated his blue uniform. He clasped the arms of the chair to keep from fidgeting, for this young officer always made him uneasy.

Clinton Codrington leaned forward toward him and spoke quickly, persuasively, using the finely shaped hands to emphasize each point. The admiral found this much energy and enthusiasm wearying. He preferred men with less mercurial temperament, who could be relied on to carry out orders to the letter without introducing startling improvisations.

Officers with a reputation for brilliance he viewed with deep suspicion. He had never had that reputation as a young man; in fact his nickname had been "Slogger" Kemp, and he believed that the word brilliance was a pseudonym for instability.

The nature of duty on this station made it necessary for young men like Codrington to be detached for months at a time on independent service, instead of being kept with the battle fleet under the strict eye of a senior officer, ready with a signal of rebuke to check any hotheadedness.

Kemp had an uneasy conviction that he was going to be seriously embarrassed by this particular officer before his appointment of commander to the Cape Squadron terminated, and allowed him to collect his knighthood and retire to the peace and beloved seclusion of his Surrey home. That his future plans had not already been prejudiced by young Codrington was only a matter of the utmost good fortune, and Kemp had difficulty keeping his expression neutral when he remembered the Calabash affair.

Codrington had run down on the slave barracoons at Calabash on a clear June morning so that the five Argentinian slave ships had spotted his topsails while he was thirty miles out, and had immediately begun frantically relanding their cargoes of slaves on the beach.

By the time *Black Joke* reached them, the five captains were grinning smugly, their holds empty, and nearly two thousand miserable slaves in clear view squatting in long lines on the shore. To add to the slavers' complacency they were a good twenty nautical miles south of the equator, and therefore at that time beyond the jurisdiction of the Royal Navy. The barracoons had been sited at Calabash to take full advantage of this provision in the international agreements.

The slavers' complacency turned to indignation when the *Black Joke* ran out her guns, and under their menace sent boats with armed seamen on board them.

The Spanish masters, under their Argentinian flags of convenience, protested vigorously and volubly the presence of armed boarding parties.

"We are not a boarding party," Codrington explained reasonably to the senior captain. "We are armed advisers, and our advice is that you begin taking aboard your cargo again—and swiftly."

The Spaniard continued his protests until the crack of a gun from the *Black Joke* drew his attention to the five nooses already dangling from the gunboat's yardarm. The Spaniard was certain that the nooses could not be put to the use for which they were very obviously intended; then he looked once more into the chilled sapphire eyes of the very young silver-haired English officer and decided not to make any bets on it.

Once the slaves were reembarked the Englishman, their self-appointed armed adviser, gave them his next piece of unsolicited advice. That was that the slave fleet up-anchor and set a course which five hours later intercepted the equatorial line.

Here Captain Codrington made a very precise observation of the sun's altitude, consulted his almanac and invited the Spanish captain to check his workings and confirm his finding that they were now in 0°05′ north latitude. Then the Englishman immediately arrested him and seized the five vessels; the armed advisers changing their status, without visible pain or discomfort, to that of prize crews.

When Codrington sailed his five prizes into Table Bay, Admiral Kemp listened aghast to the Spaniard's account of his capture, and then immediately retired to his bed with bowel spasms and migraine headache. From his darkened bedroom he dictated first the order confining Codrington to his ship and the ship to its anchorage, and then his horrified report to the First Lord of the Admiralty.

The episode, which might so easily have ended with Codrington court-martialed and beached for life and with the abrupt termination of Admiral Kemp's dogged advance toward his knighthood and retirement, had in fact brought both men riches and advancement.

The sloop carrying Kemp's dispatch to the First Lord passed another southbound in midocean, which in its turn bore dispatches for the Admiral Commanding the Cape Squadron from not only the First Lord but the Foreign Secretary as well.

Kemp was requested and required in the future to apply the Equipment Clause to the ships of all Christian nations—with the glaring exception of the United States of America—in all latitudes, both north *and* south of the equatorial line.

The dispatches were dated four days previous to Codrington's raid upon the Calabash barracoons, making his actions not only legal but highly meritorious.

From the very brink of professional disaster, Admiral Kemp had been snatched back, with his knighthood assured and a large sum of prize money paid into his account at Messrs. Coutts of the Strand. The five Spaniards were condemned at the next session of the Court of Mixed Commission at Cape Town. Kemp's own share of the prize money had amounted to several thousand pounds, that of his junior captain to nearly twice that amount, and both officers had received personal letters of commendation from the First Lord.

None of this had done anything to increase Kemp's trust or liking for his junior, and now he listened with mounting horror to the suggestion that he sanction the boarding and search of the American trading clipper, which was at present enjoying the hospitality of the port.

For some sickening moments Kemp contemplated his place in history as the officer who had precipitated the second war with the former American colonies. There was nothing equivocal about the view of the American Government as to the sanctity of their shipping, and there were specific sections of Kemp's Admiralty orders covering the subject.

"Admiral Kemp," Codrington was clearly burning with enthusiasm for the enterprise, "it is absolutely beyond question that the *Huron* is a slaver, and is equipped for the trade in terms of the act. She is no longer upon the high seas, but lying at anchor within British territorial waters. I can be aboard her within two hours, with impartial witnesses, a Supreme Court judge even."

Kemp cleared his throat noisily. He had in fact tried to speak, but so appalled was he that the words had not reached his lips. Codrington seemed to take the sound as encouragement.

"This man, St. John, is one of the most infamous slavers of modern times. His name is a legend on the coast. They say he carried over three thousand slaves one year across the middle passage. It's a golden opportunity for us."

Kemp found his voice at last. "I dined at Government House on Wednesday. Mr. St. John was in the company as His Excellency's personal guest. I considered Mr. St. John to be a gentleman, and I know he is a man of considerable substance and influence in his own country," he said flatly, no trace of emotion in his voice. His self-control surprised even himself.

"He is a slaver." Robyn Ballantyne spoke for the first time since she had seated herself at the window of the admiral's study. The two men had forgotten her existence, but now they both turned to her.

"I have been inside the *Huron*'s main hold and she is fully equipped for the trade," she said, her voice low but clear, and Kemp felt a sour feeling rising within him. He wondered that he had thought this young woman enchanting at their first meeting. Kemp liked young females and he had personally instructed his secretary to send the invitations to the Ballantynes, brother and sister, but now he regretted it. He could see, of course, that what he had mistaken for spirit was in fact the mischievousness of the born troublemaker, and that far from being pretty she was in fact downright plain, with a large nose and heavy jaw. He had found her a refreshing change from the simpering and giggling young ladies of the Colony—and realized now that the preference had been unwise. He wondered if he could have his secretary withdraw the invitation.

"I would think, Admiral Kemp, that it was your duty to send a search party aboard the *Huron*," Robyn told him—and Kemp leaned back in the big chair and breathed heavily through his mouth. As an admiral of the blue it had been some years since anybody had dared point out his duty for him. His grip on his self-control slackened.

He stared at the young person. Did he detect a peculiar venom in her voice? He wondered. She had been a passenger on *Huron*. She had left the ship the instant it reached Table Bay. There was no doubt the woman was "fast" and that Captain St. John was a handsome man.

There was a fine story here, Kemp concluded, as he asked dryly, "Is it true, Miss Ballantyne, that you assaulted the surgeon general in a fit of ungovernable rage?"

Robyn gaped at him for a moment, the change of direction taking her completely off balance, and before she could reply he went on, "You are clearly a highly emotional young lady. I would have to consider very carefully committing a hostile act against an important citizen of a friendly nation on your unsupported testimony."

He pulled the gold watch from his fob pocket, and consulted it with his full attention.

"Thank you for calling on me, Miss Ballantyne." Once again he did not use her professional title. "We look forward to seeing you tomorrow evening. Perhaps you would allow me a private word with Captain Codrington."

Robyn felt her cheeks burning as she rose from the window seat.

"Thank you, Admiral, you have been very kind and patient," she said tightly, and swept from the room.

Kemp was not so mild with Codrington. While the young captain stood at attention before him, he leaned forward in the throne and the veins stood out like twisted blue ropes in the back of his hands as he gripped the arms of the chair.

"You were misguided in bringing that young person here to discuss Navy business," he snapped.

"Sir, I needed to convince you."

"That's enough, Codrington. I have heard all you have to say. Now you listen to me."

"Aye, aye, sir."

"You are naïve not to take into account the changed circumstances in the American administration. Are you not aware that Mr. Lincoln is likely to be elected to the presidency?"

"I am, sir."

"Then even you may be dimly aware that very delicate considerations are in the balance. The Foreign Office is confident that the new administration will have a markedly changed attitude to the trade."

"Sir!" Codrington agreed stiffly.

"Can you imagine what it will mean to us to have full right of search of American shipping on the high seas?"

"Sir."

"We will have that—once Mr. Lincoln takes the oath, and if no junior officers of this service take independent action to prejudice the attitude of the Americans."

"Sir." Codrington stood rigid, staring over the admiral's head at a painting of a lightly veiled Venus on the paneled wall behind him.

"Codrington"—Kemp spoke now with cold menace—"you have had one very close shave at Calabash. I swear to you, if you let your wild nature get the better of you once more, I will have you hounded from the service."

"Sir."

"You are now under the strictest injunction not to approach closer than a cable's length to the trade clipper *Huron*, and if you should encounter her again at sea, you will pay her passing honors and give her a wide berth. Do I make myself sufficiently clear?"

"Sir." Only Codrington's lips moved, and the admiral took two long controlled breaths before going on.

"When will you sail for the Mozambique channel?" he asked, his voice more reasonable.

"I have your orders to take the flood on Saturday, sir."

"Can you advance that sailing?"

"Yes, sir, but it would mean leaving without fully charged magazines; we expect the powder barge alongside at dawn on Saturday."

Kemp shook his head, and sighed. "I would feel better with you at sea," he muttered. "But very well then, I will look to see you flying the Blue Peter at first light on Saturday morning."

Robyn Ballantyne was waiting for him in the borrowed Cartwright carriage, under the portico of Admiralty House.

Codrington came down the steps, with his cocked hat under his arm, and climbed stiffly into the buttoned leather seat beside her. The Hottentot coachman flicked his whip at the shiny rumps, and they swayed in unison as the carriage jerked away down the treelined driveway. Neither of them spoke until they had left the Admiralty grounds, and were whirling down the hill toward the Liesbeeck bridge with the coachman holding them on a light brake.

"What do we do now?" Robyn asked.

"Nothing," said Clinton Codrington.

Twenty minutes later, as they came around the shoulder of the mountain and looked down at the bay where *Huron* rode at anchor, Robyn spoke again.

"Can't you think of anything to stop this monster?"

"Can you?" he asked sharply, and neither of them spoke again until they reached the landing place.

The fishing boats were in and beached already, their catch laid out on the sand, a glittering silver and ruby-red pile around which the housewives and their servants bartered and bargained with the brown bare-legged fishermen, while the fish horns blared to summon more customers down from the town. The two in the parked carriage watched the commotion with unnatural attention, avoiding each other's eyes.

"You will be at the Admiralty ball tomorrow night? I heard Slogger Kemp say so."

"No," Robyn shook her head fiercely. "I cannot abide the frivolous chatter and silly behavior of these occasions, and I particularly do not want to be again the guest of that man."

Codrington turned to her for the first time since they had reached the landing. She was a fine-looking woman, he thought, with that clear luster to her skin and the thoughtful dark-green eyes under their dark curved brows. He liked a tall strong woman, and he had learned enough of her spirit to accord her respect, a respect that could easily become fascination, he realized.

"Could I prevail upon you to change your mind?" he asked quietly, and she glanced at him, startled. "I would undertake to provide sober conversation and a dignified dancing partner."

"I do not dance, Captain."

"That is a great relief," he admitted. "For neither do I, when I have a choice." He smiled. She could not remember seeing him smile before. It changed him completely. The coldness went from the pale blue eyes and they darkened with merriment while two deep laughter lines formed at the corner of his mouth and arched up to touch the thin straight nose.

"Slogger Kemp keeps a wonderful chef." He was wheedling now. "Fine food and serious conversation."

His teeth were porcelain white and very regular against the deepwater tan. She felt the corners of her own mouth tugging upward, and he saw the change in her and pressed his advantage.

"I may have further news, some further plan for *Huron* to discuss with you."

"That makes it irresistible." She laughed outright at last, with surprisingly unforced gaiety that made some of the nearest bystanders glance around at her and smile in sympathy.

"I will call for you. Where? When?" He had not realized how attractive she truly was until she laughed.

"No." She laid her hand on his forearm. "My brother will accompany me, but if you are there I look forward to our momentous conversation." She felt the devil in her again, and squeezed his arm, finding pleasure in his immediate response, the way the muscles in his forearm corded under her fingertips.

"Wait," she told the coachman and watched the slim tall figure go down the beach to where *Black Joke*'s whaler waited for him.

He was wearing his dress uniform for the visit to his commanding admiral. The gold lace epaulettes emphasized the breadth of his shoulders and his sword belt nipped his waist. Abruptly, she wondered whether his body hair was as blond as the queue that was twisted up at the nape of his neck—and then instantly was shocked and agitated at herself. She would never have harbored a thought like that before. Before what? she asked herself, and the answer was clear: before that night on *Huron*. Mungo St. John had much to answer for. Comfortably placing blame where it belonged, she pulled her eyes away from the lithe figure to Clinton Codrington and leaned forward to tell the coachman, "Home, please."

She would not attend the admiral's ball, she decided, and then she began to recite silently to herself the Christian articles of faith.

However, Zouga prevailed over her good intentions. The two of them shared the open carriage with the eldest, unmarried Cartwright daughter, for it was one of the balmy nights of a Cape autumn.

Cartwright and his wife followed in the closed carriage, in serious discussion for the entire journey.

"I am sure he is quite taken with Aletta," Mrs. Cartwright had stated.

"My dear, the fellow has no fortune whatsoever."

"Expectations," Mrs. Cartwright told him benignly. "I understand he will make thousands from his expedition. He is one of those young men who will get on in life, I am certain of that."

97

"I prefer money in the bank, my dear."

"He has created quite a stir, I assure you—such a serious and sensible young man, and so very attractive. It would be quite a feather in Aletta's cap, and you could make a place for him in the firm."

Every lamp in Admiralty House was lit and a blaze of golden light welcomed the guests. There were colored lanterns hung in the trees to illuminate the garden.

The Marine band in scarlet and gold had converted the open gazebo into a bandstand, and already there were dancers on the open-air dance floor whirling furiously through the opening waltz, waving and calling greetings to the latecomers in the carriages as they trotted up the curved driveway and took their turn to alight under the portico of the main entrance.

Bewigged footmen in household uniform with silken hose and buckled shoes placed the steps and handed down the ladies onto the welcoming red carpet. At the head of the stairs the majordomo announced each group in a low throaty bellow.

"Major and Dr. Ballantyne. Miss Cartwright."

Robyn had not grown altogether accustomed to the scandalized ripple of feminine interest that followed her entrance to any public gathering here in the Colony. The quick exchange of glances, the nods and murmurs behind covering fans. It still left her with a heightened pulse and a feeling of bitter disdain for all of them.

"Did you bring your sponge, sissy? They expect you to hit somebody with it," Zouga murmured, and she shook his arm to silence him, but he went on: "or to drop your skirts and run up the staircase in your breeches."

"You are wicked." She felt the tension go out of her, and she smiled her thanks at him and they were into the throng of uniforms, gold lace on navy blue or dress scarlet, with, here and there, the dead black of evening dress relieved by the high stock and white-lace ruffles of silk shirts.

The women's skirts were taffeta and flounced silk over pyramids of petticoats. However, they were at least two years behind the London fashions, for only the most daring ladies had bared their shoulders and powdered them dead white.

Robyn's own dress made no concession to fashion, for it was years old, the only one that she possessed even vaguely suitable for the occasion. The cloth was wool, the skirt narrow, the bodice adorned with neither seed pearls nor sequins. There were neither ostrich feathers nor diamantines to sparkle in her

98

hair. She should have been dowdy, but instead she was strikingly different.

When she had told Codrington that she did not dance it was because she had never had the occasion, and she regretted it now as she watched Zouga lead Aletta Cartwright onto the floor and swirl away in the graceful dip and turn of the waltz.

She knew that nobody would invite her to dance, and that if they did she would be awkward and untutored. She turned away quickly, seeking a familiar or friendly face. She did not want to be left standing alone in the crowd. She began bitterly to regret that she had not stood by her resolution to stay away.

Her relief came with such a rush that she could have thrown her arms around his neck and embraced him. Instead she said evenly, "Ah, Captain Codrington. Good evening."

He really was one of the better-looking men in the room, she thought. She could sense the resentment of some of the younger women, so quite deliberately she took his arm as he offered it, but was surprised that he led her immediately through into the garden.

"He's here!" he said quietly, as soon as they were out of earshot of the others.

She did not have to ask who, and she felt the little jolt of shock that kept her silent for a moment.

"You've seen him?"

"He arrived five minutes before you did—in the governor's carriage."

"Where is he now?"

"He went into Slogger's study—with the governor." Clinton's face was set and hard. "The fellow flaunts himself."

A servant approached them with a silver tray of champagne flutes. Robyn shook her head distractedly but Clinton took a glass and drank it in two gulps.

"The devil of it is that nobody can touch him," he fumed.

When the evening turned chill, the Marine band moved on to the orchestral balcony above the ballroom floor and punched out the dance tunes with a bouncing martial air that set the dancers spinning and prancing.

One dancer stood out above the others, not merely because of his physical height. When the others hopped and strained with gasping breath and flushed faces, Mungo St. John seemed to turn and dip and glide with measured, unhurried grace although he completed a circuit of the ballroom floor more swiftly than any other dancer. Always there was one of the prettiest women in the room swinging in the circle of his arms, laughing

99

up at him, cheeks flushed with excitement, and a dozen others watching him with covert envy over the shoulders of their own partners.

Clinton and Robyn watched him also, from the raised and colonnaded balcony that surrounded the dance floor. They stood in a small circle of Clinton's brother officers and their ladies, making no serious effort to contribute to the light chatter around them.

Robyn found herself hoping that St. John would look up at her, would catch her eye so that she could flash her hatred at him; but he never glanced once in her direction.

She even thought of suggesting to Clinton Codrington that they should dance, despite her earlier protestations, but quickly decided against it. She knew that as a dancer, the naval captain would not be able to stand comparison with the elegant American.

When she went in to dinner on Clinton's arm, she saw St. John ahead of them. He had a blond woman on his arm, notoriously the Colony's prettiest, richest and most voracious widow. Her coiffure was an elaborate creation of diamanté and ostrich feathers, her shoulders were bared and she showed more of her bosom than she concealed beneath a brocaded bodice stiff with seed pearls.

Mungo St. John wore simple black-and-white evening dress with more panache than any of the most elaborate military uniforms around him.

Robyn watched the woman tap his shoulder with her fan to attract his attention and then reach up on tiptoe to whisper in his ear, while St. John stopped gravely to listen.

"The woman's a brazen whore," Robyn hissed, and beside her Clinton covered his shock at the word, and then nodded.

"And he's the very devil himself."

It was as though St. John heard them, for he glanced up and saw them watching him across the room. He bowed and smiled at Robyn.

It was such an intimate, completely knowing smile that she felt as though he had stripped her naked again, the way he had in the stern cabin of *Huron,* and immediately she felt the same feeling of helplessness overwhelm her.

With a huge effort she managed to turn away, but Clinton had been watching her. She could not meet his eyes, she felt he would be able to read it all if she did.

* * *

Two hours after midnight the Marine band was playing the less strenuous airs for the lovers and romantics who still circled the ballroom floor, but most of the company had gone to the cardrooms on the first floor, if not to play themselves, then to crowd around the tables and watch with hushed attention and the occasional bursts of applause at a particularly audacious or successful coup.

In the largest room the game was whist and the players were Slogger Kemp and the older guests. In the second room the younger set were at the lighthearted chemin-de-fer and Zouga smiled at Robyn as she passed. He and Aletta Cartwright were playing a single hand between them, and the girl squealed with glee as she won a handful of silver shillings.

Robyn and Clinton passed on into the third and smallest salon. Here it was the game that had once been popular only in America. Recently, however, it had come into sudden vogue at court when the Queen had found it fascinating, and in consequence it was all the rage around the Empire despite the odd name—poker.

In spite of Her Majesty's interest in it, it was still not considered a game for ladies to play in mixed company. Only men sat at the green baize, although the ladies fluttered around them like bright butterflies.

Mungo St. John sat facing the doorway so that Robyn saw him the instant she stepped into the room. He lazed in his chair, the waves of his dark hair unruffled and sleeked down as if carved from polished ebony, holding a tight fan of cards low against the snowy lace front of his shirt. There was a long black unlit cheroot between his teeth, and as Robyn watched the blond widow leaned across his shoulder displaying the creamy cleavage between her breasts and held a vesta to the cheroot.

St. John sucked flame into the tip of the cheroot, blew a long feather of blue smoke and thanked her with a slant of his eyes before he made his next bid.

He was an obvious winner, a careless pile of gold spilled across the table in front of him, each coin embossed with the Grecian-style head of Queen Victoria looking much younger than her forty-one years—and as they watched, he won again.

Excitement seemed to exude from the man like a tangible substance, infecting the women about the table so they exclaimed at every wager he made, and sighed with disappointment if he folded his cards and declined to play a hand. The same excitement spread to the five other men at the table. It was obvious in the glitter of the eyes, in the white knuckles of the fingers that held their cards, in the rash calls and the imprudent urge that made them remain in play long after chance and the odds were evidently against them. It was clear that all of them saw St. John as the main adversary, and the tension went out of each hand if he was not in play.

Robyn felt herself held by the same fascination, and unconsciously tightened her grip on Clinton's arm as the suspense mounted in each hand and the gold coins tinkled in the center of the table, and she heard herself gasp with chagrin or relief at the show of cards that ended each hand.

Unconsciously, she had moved closer to the table drawing Clinton with her, so that when one of the players exclaimed with disgust, "Fifty guineas is enough for one night. Will you excuse me, gentlemen?" gathered his few remaining coins from the table and pushed back his chair, they had to stand back to allow him to leave.

With surprise Robyn felt Clinton disengage her fingers from his arm, and then he slipped quietly into the vacant chair.

"May I join you, gentlemen?"

There were preoccupied grunts of acknowledgment but only St. John looked up and asked civilly,

"Are you aware of the stakes, Captain?"

Clinton did not reply but took a roll of five-pound notes from an inside pocket and placed them beside him. The amount surprised Robyn, it could not have been less than one hundred pounds. Then she remembered that Clinton Codrington had been for many years one of the most successful blockade commanders on the slave coasts. Her brother had repeated to her the rumor that during that period he had won prize money in excess of ten thousand pounds, yet somehow she had never thought of him as a rich man.

Then with sudden intuition Robyn realized that by that gesture Clinton had laid down a silent challenge, and with a little smile Mungo St. John had accepted it.

Robyn felt a flare of alarm. She was certain that Clinton Codrington had chosen an opponent too experienced and skilled. She remembered that Zouga, who relied on gambling to eke out his regimental pay, had been no match for the man, even with moderate stakes, and in his frustration Clinton had been drinking steadily during the evening. She was sure his judgment would be faulty even if he had any knowledge of the game.

Almost immediately St. John subtly altered the style of his play, doubling the stakes before the draw, crowding the game, dominating it, playing from the strength and confidence of his already considerable winnings, and Clinton seemed immediately uncertain of himself, hesitant in accepting the doubled stakes, discarding rather than going at risk for more than a few guineas, lacking the nerve to meet St. John head on.

Robyn moved slightly to a position from which she could watch both men. Clinton was pale under the deepwater tan, the rims of his nostrils bloodless and his lips compressed into a thin line, and she remembered that he had drunk a dozen glasses of champagne during the evening.

He was nervous, indecisive, every watcher could sense it, and their disappointment was evident. They had hoped for a dramatic confrontation when Clinton had made the flamboyant gesture of placing a hundred pounds on the table, but when the amount was slowly whittled away by unexciting overcautious play, their interest was transferred to a lively exchange between Mungo St. John and one of the Cloete sons, the family that owned half the Constantia Valley with its fabled vineyards.

They laughed at the light banter with which the two men made their bets, and admired the grace of the loser and the easy manner of the winner. The other players at the table were almost forgotten, picking up an uncontested ante or falling before the aggression of the leading pair.

Robyn could only pity Clinton, nervous and pale—when he fumbled his cards to expose prematurely one of his few winning hands and suffer the chuckles of the spectators as he picked up odd guineas instead of the fifty that might have been his if he had played it correctly.

Robyn tried to catch his eye, to make him leave before he was further humiliated, but Clinton played on doggedly, refusing to look up at her.

Cloete won a hand with four of a kind and as was his right called for a pot to celebrate his good fortune.

"Three of a kind to open the pot and guinea sweeteners," he announced and grinned across the table at St. John. "To your liking, sir?"

"Very much so," St. John smiled back, and the other players tried to cover their discomfiture. It was a dangerous game— requiring one of the players to be dealt an initial three of a kind to commence the game, but for every unsuccessful deal each player had to contribute a guinea to the pot, and when a lucky player achieved the minimum requirement, he could advance the stakes by as much again as was in the center of the table. It could amount swiftly to a huge sum, and there was no option of withdrawal—a very dangerous game.

Ten times the deal failed to produce an opening hand, and then with the pot at seventy guineas Mungo St. John announced quietly, "She is open, gentlemen, as wide open as my mother-in-law's mouth."

Play had stopped at the other tables in the room as St. John went on, "It will cost you another seventy iron men to stay in the game." He had doubled the pot, and the watchers applauded the bet and then looked eagerly to the other players.

"I am your man," said Cloete, but at last there was a breathlessness to his voice. He counted out the notes and gold coins and spilled them into the considerable pile in the center.

Three other players withdrew, dropping their cards with alacrity, clearly relieved to have gotten out of danger for a mere ten guineas, but Clinton Codrington hunched miserably over his cards and St. John had to prod him gently for his decision.

"Please don't hurry, Captain. We have all evening."

And Clinton looked up at him and nodded jerkily, not trusting his voice, then pushed a sheaf of notes into the center of the table.

"Three players," St. John said, and swiftly counted the money in the pot. "Two hundred and ten guineas!"

The next bid could double that amount, and the one after could redouble it. The room was silent now, the players at the other tables in the room had left their seats to watch as the dealer gave two cards to Mungo St. John to replace those he tossed into the center of the table. He was buying honestly, trying to add to the triplets with which he had opened the pot, neither faking a flush nor a full house. Cloete bought three cards, evidently looking for a third to a high pair—and then it was Clinton's turn to request cards.

"One," he mumbled, and held up a single finger. The finger quivered slightly. The dealer slid the card across to him and he covered it with his hand unable to bring himself to look at it yet. It was all too obvious that he was attempting to find the missing card to a flush or straight.

"The opener to bet," said the dealer. "Mr. St. John."

There was a pause as St. John fanned open his cards, and then he said evenly without a change of expression, "The bet is doubled."

"Four hundred and twenty guineas," said somebody loudly, and this time nobody applauded but every eye swiveled to Cloete as he consulted his cards. Then shook his head abruptly, and let them drop. He had not found another king to go with the original pair.

Now everybody looked to the remaining player. A transformation had come over Clinton Codrington, it was hard to define it exactly. There was just a touch of color under the tanned cheeks, his lips were slightly parted and for the first time he was looking directly at St. John—but somehow confidence and a barely suppressed eagerness shone from him. There was no mistaking it. The man positively glowed.

"Double again," he said. "Eight hundred and forty guineas." He could hardly contain himself, and every man in the room knew he had found the card he needed to transform his hand from worthlessness to a certain winner.

St. John did not have to deliberate more than a few seconds.

"Congratulations," he smiled. "You found what you were looking for, I must concede this one to you."

He dropped his cards and pushed them away from him.

"May we see the cards you required to open the pot?" Clinton asked diffidently.

"I beg your pardon." St. John's tone was lightly ironical, and he flipped his hand, face upward. There were three sevens and two odd cards.

"Thank you," said Clinton. His manner had changed again. The trembling eagerness, the nervous indecision, both had disappeared. He was calm, almost icy, as he began to gather in the piles of scattered gold and bank notes.

"What cards did he have?" demanded one of the women petulantly.

"He does not have to show them," her partner explained. "He beat the others out without a showdown."

"Oh, I'd die to see them," she squeaked.

Clinton paused in gathering his winnings and looked up at her.

"I beg of you, madam, not to do so," Clinton smiled. "I would not wish to have your life on my conscience."

He turned his cards face upward on the green baize, and it took the company many seconds to realize what they were looking at. There were cards of every suit, and not one of them matched another.

There were delighted exclamations, for the hand was utterly worthless. It could have been beaten by a single pair of sevens, to say nothing of the triple sevens which St. John had discarded.

With this valueless hand the young naval captain had beaten the American, outsmarting him for almost nine hundred gui-

neas. It was a spectacular coup. The company gradually realized how carefully it had been engineered, how Clinton had
lured his adversary, how he had made a pretense at fumbling
uncertainly until exactly the right moment, the moment when
he had struck boldly and decisively. They burst into sponta-
neous applause, the ladies oohing with admiration and the men
calling congratulation.

"Oh, jolly good play, sir!"

St. John held the smile, but his lips drew tighter with the
effort, and there was a savage glitter in his eyes as he stared
at the cards and realized how he had been duped.

The applause subsided, some of the spectators were beginning to turn away still discussing the hand, and St. John began
gathering the cards to shuffle when Clinton Codrington spoke.
His voice was low but clear, so that nobody about the tables
could miss a word of it.

"Even a blackbirder's luck can run out at last," he said. "I
must admit, I would rather have caught you at your dirty slaver's game than beaten you out of a few guineas tonight."

The company froze, gaping at Clinton with expressions of
horror and comical amazement. The silence in the room seemed
impenetrable, the only sound was the ripple and click of the
cards as Mungo St. John began to shuffle them, splitting the
pack with a click and then running them into each other his
thumbs in a blur of movement.

He did not look down at his hands as he rippled the cards.
He never removed his gaze from Clinton's face, and his smile
had still not slipped; only there was a flush of color under the
dark suntouched skin.

"You like to live dangerously?" St. John smiled the question.

"Oh, no." Clinton shook his head. "I am in no danger. In
my experience, slavers are all cowards."

Mungo St. John's smile disappeared, extinguished instantly,
and his expression was coldly murderous, but his fingers never
broke the rhythm of cut and ripple, and the cards flowed under
his fingers as Clinton went on evenly, "I was led to believe
that so-called Louisiana gentlemen had some exalted code of
honor," he shrugged. "I suggest, sir, that you are a living
contradiction of that notion."

Every listener was stunned. Not one of them could doubt
what they were hearing: the accusation of slave dealing. To an
Englishman, there could be no worse insult.

The last English duels had been fought in 1840 when Lord

Cardigan shot Captain Tuckett, and in 1843 when Munro shot his brother-in-law Colonel Fawcett. In consequence of these encounters, the Queen had made her desire for reform known, and the articles of war were amended in the following year, making dueling an offense. Of course, gentlemen still went abroad, mostly to France, to settle affairs of honor with pistol or sword. But this was Cape Colony, one of the jewels of the Empire, and the naval captain was one of Her Majesty's commissioned officers. The evening had proved diverting beyond any expectations, and now there was the promise of blood and violent death charging the gaming room.

"Gentlemen," an urgent persuasive voice interrupted them. The admiral's flag captain had come through from the whist room at the admiral's orders. "There has been some misunderstanding."

But neither of the two men as much as glanced in his direction.

"I don't think there has been any misunderstanding at all," Mungo St. John said coldly, his gaze still locked with Clinton's. "Captain Codrington's insults cannot possibly be misinterpreted."

"Mr. St. John, may I remind you that you are on British soil, subject to Her Majesty's laws." The flag captain was becoming desperate.

"Oh, Mr. St. John sets little store by laws. He sails his slave ship, fully equipped, into a British harbor." Clinton stared at the American with cold blue eyes. He would have gone on, but St. John interrupted him harshly, speaking to the flag captain but addressing the words to Clinton Codrington. "I would not dream of abusing Her Majesty's hospitality. In any event I will sail with the tide before noon this day, and in four days I shall be far beyond Her Majesty's territory, in latitude thirty-one degrees thirty-eight minutes south. There is a wide river mouth there, between tall bluffs of stone—a good landing and a wide beach. It is unmistakable." St. John stood up. He had recovered his urbane air, and now he adjusted the ruffles of his shirt front and gave the lovely widow his arm. He paused for a moment to look down at Clinton. "Who knows but that you and I may meet again, when we must certainly discuss the question of honor once more. Until then I give you good morrow, sir."

He turned away and the spectators fell back ahead of him and seemed to form a guard of honor as St. John and his lady sauntered casually from the room.

The flag captain flung one furious glare at Clinton.

"The admiral wishes to speak with you, sir," and then he hurried after the departing couple, followed them down the curve of the staircase and caught up with them at the double doors of carved teak.

"Mr. St. John, Admiral Kemp asked me to convey his compliments. He sets no store by the rash accusations of one of his junior captains. If he did, he would be obliged to send a party aboard your ship."

"None of us would like that," St. John nodded. "Nor the consequences."

"Indeed," the flag captain assured him. "Nevertheless the admiral feels that, in the circumstances, you should take advantage of the next fair wind and tide to proceed on your passage."

"Please return my compliments to the admiral—and convey my assurance that I will clear the bay before noon."

At that moment the widow's coach came up, and St. John nodded distantly to the flag captain and handed the lady up the steps.

From the deck of *Black Joke* they watched the clipper raise her anchor, her master skillfully backing and filling his topsails to run up on her cable, and break the anchor flukes out of the mud and sand of the bottom of the bay. As soon as it was free, he piled on his canvas, sail after sail ballooning in quick successive explosions of brilliant white, and *Huron* tore eagerly out of Table Bay on the southeast wind.

She would be out of sight beyond the lighthouse to Mouille Point for almost four hours before *Black Joke* was ready to follow her out of the bay. The Admiralty powder barge was alongside, and all the elaborate precautions for taking on explosives were in force. The red swallowtail warning flag at the masthead, the boiler fires in the engine room extinguished, the crew barefooted, the decks kept wet with a constant stream from the hoses to prevent a chance spark, and each powder barrel carefully inspected for leakage as it came aboard.

While the engineer refired his boilers the last members of the Ballantyne expedition came aboard. Once again, Zouga's letters of introduction had proved invaluable, and together with his persuasive manner had provided him with the most valuable addition so far to his expedition.

Old Tom Harkness had warned him during the long night discussion, "Don't try to cross the Chimanimani Mountains without a force of trained men. Beyond the narrow coastal belt there is only one law and it is promulgated from the muzzle of a gun."

On the strength of the letters, the commander of the Cape Town garrison had allowed Zouga to ask for volunteers from his regiment of Hottentot Infantry. "They are the only natives of Africa who understand the working of a firearm," Harkness had told him. "They are the devil with drink and women, but they can fight and march, and most of them are hardened to fever and famine. Pick them carefully and watch them every moment, night as well as day."

Zouga's request for volunteers had been most enthusiastically received. By reputation the Hottentots could scent plunder or a willing lady from fifty miles, and the pay and rations that Zouga offered were almost thrice that of the British army. They had volunteered to a man and Zouga's difficulty had been in selecting ten of them.

Zouga had taken an instant liking to these wiry little men, with their almost oriental features, slanted eyes and high cheek-bones. Despite appearances, they were more African than almost any other breed. They were the original inhabitants that the first navigators had found on the beach at Table Bay—and they had taken readily to the white man's ways, and more than readily to his vices.

Zouga had solved his problem by making one selection only. This was a man with an ageless face, it might have been forty years or eighty, for the skin was the color and texture of papyrus, each wrinkle seemed to have been eroded into it by wind and driven dust, but the little peppercorns of hair that covered his skull were untinged with silver.

"I taught Captain Harris to hunt elephant," he boasted.

"Where was that?" Zouga demanded, for Cornwallis Harris was one of the most famous of the old African hunters. His book *The Wild Sports of Africa* was the great classic of the African chase.

"I took him to the Cashan Mountains." Harris's expedition to the Cashan Mountains, which the Boers now called Magaliesberg, was in 1829, thirty-one years previously. That would make the little Hottentot somewhere between fifty and sixty years old, if he were telling the truth.

"Harris did not mention your name," he said. "I have read his account carefully."

"Jan Bloom—that was my name then." Zouga nodded. Bloom had been one of Harris's most intrepid hunter-retainers.

"Why is your name Jan Cheroot now?" Zouga asked and the dark eyes had twinkled with pixie merriment.

"Sometimes a man gets tired of a name, like he does of a woman, and for his health or his life he changes both."

The long military-issue Enfield rifle was as tall as Jan Cheroot, but it seemed part of his wizened little body.

"Pick nine other men. The best," Zouga told him, and Sergeant Cheroot brought them aboard while the gunboat was working up a head of steam in her boilers.

Each man carried his Enfield over his shoulder, his worldly possessions in the haversack on his back and fifty rounds in the pouches on his belt.

It needed only the "Rogue's March" to welcome them, Zouga thought wryly, as he watched them come in through the entry port, each one bestowing upon him a beatific grin and a salute so vigorous that it nearly swung the donor off his feet.

Sergeant Cheroot lined them up at the rail. Their original scarlet uniform jackets had suffered strange mutations to ten different shades, ranging from sun-faded pink to dusty puce, and each peppercorn head wore its brimless infantry cap cocked at a different angle from all the others. Thin shanks were bound up with grubby puttees, and brown bare feet slapped the oak planking of the deck in unison as Cheroot brought them to attention, Enfields at the slope and happy grins on each puckish face.

"Very well, Sergeant." Zouga acknowledged the salute. "Now let's have the packs open, and the bottles over the side."

The grins wilted, and they exchanged crestfallen glances; the major had looked so young and gullible.

"You hear the major, *julle klomp dom skaape.*" Gleefully Jan Cheroot likened them to "a herd of stupid sheep" in the kitchen Dutch of the Cape, and as he turned back to Zouga there was for the first time a gleam of respect in the black eyes.

There are two passages from which a ship may choose when sailing the southeastern coast of Africa. The master may stay outside the one-hundred-fathom line which marks the edge of the continental shelf, for here the opposing forces of the Mozambique current and the prevailing winds can generate a sea which seamen call with awe the "hundred-year wave," a wave over two hundred feet from crest to trough, which will overwhelm even the sturdiest vessel as though it were a drifting autumn leaf. The alternative and only slightly less hazardous passage lies close inshore, in the shallows where the rocky reefs await a careless navigator.

For the sake of speed Clinton Codrington chose the inshore passage, so that always the land was in sight as they bustled northward. Day after day the shimmering white beaches and dark rocky headlands unreeled ahead of *Black Joke*'s bows, sometimes almost lost in the smoky blue sea fret, and at other times brutally clear under the African sun.

Clinton kept steam in his boilers and the single bronze screw spinning under his counter with every sail set and trained around to glean the smallest puff of the wind, as he drove *Black Joke* on to the rendezvous that Mungo St. John had set. His haste was symptom of a compulsion that Robyn Ballantyne only began fully to understand during those days and nights that they drove east and north, for Clinton Codrington sought her company constantly and she spent many hours of each day with him, or all of it that could be spared from the management of the vessel—beginning with the assembly of the ship's company for morning prayers.

Most naval captains went through the motions of divine service once a week, but Captain Codrington held prayers every morning and it did not take Robyn long to realize that his faith and sense of Christian duty was, if anything, greater than her own. He did not seem to experience the terrible doubts and temptations to which she was always such a prey, and if it had not been un-Christian to do so she would have felt envy for his sense and secure faith.

"I wanted to go into the church, like my father and my elder brother, Ralph, before me," he told her.

"Why did you not?"

"The Almighty led me into the path He had chosen for me," Clinton said simply, and it did not seem pretentious when he said it. "I know now He meant me to be a shepherd for His flock, here in this land," and he pointed at the silver beaches and blue mountains. "I did not realize it at the time, but His ways are wonderful. This is the work He has chosen for me."

Suddenly she realized how deep was his commitment to the war he was waging against the trade, it was almost a personal crusade. His whole being directed at its destruction, for he truly believed that he was the instrument of God's will.

Yet, like many deeply religious men, he kept his belief closely guarded, never flaunting it in sanctimonious posturing or biblical quotation. The only time he spoke of his God was during the daily prayers and when he was alone with her on

111

his quarterdeck. Quite naturally, he assumed that her belief matched, if not outstripped, his own. She did nothing to disillusion him, for she enjoyed his patent admiration, his deference to the fact that she had been appointed as a missionary, and when she was truthful to herself, which was more and more often these days, she liked the way he looked, the sound of his voice, and even the smell of him. It was a man's smell, like tanned leather or the pelt of an otter she had once had as a pet at Kings Lynn.

He was good to be near, a man, as the pale missionary initiates and medical students she had known had not been men. He was the Christian warrior. She found a comfort in his presence, not like the wicked excitement of Mungo St. John, but something deeper and more satisfying. She looked upon him as her champion, as though the deadly assignation to which he was hurrying was on her behalf, to wipe out the knowledge of sin and to atone for her disgrace.

On the third day they passed the settlement on the shore of Algoa Bay, where the five thousand British settlers brought out by Governor Somerset forty years before in 1820 had landed and still eked a hard existence from the unforgiving African earth. The white flecks of painted walls looked pitifully insignificant in that wilderness of water and sky and land, and at last Robyn started to come to some small understanding of the vastness of this continent and how puny were the scratches that man had made upon it. For the first time she felt a small cold dread at her own temerity that had brought her so far, so young and so inexperienced, to venture she was not sure what. She hugged her shawl about her shoulders and shivered in the cutting wind that poured in off the green sea. The Africa she had dreamed of so often seemed harsh and unwelcoming now.

As *Black Joke* closed swiftly with the rendezvous that St. John had appointed, Clinton Codrington became quieter, and was more often alone in his cabin. He understood clearly the ordeal that faced him. Zouga Ballantyne had discussed it with him on almost every occasion that presented itself. Zouga was unwavering in his opposition to the meeting.

"You have chosen a formidable opponent, sir," he told Clinton bluntly. "And I mean no offense when I say I doubt you are a match for him with either pistol or sword—but he'll choose pistols, you can wager on that."

"He challenged," Clinton said quietly. "My weapon is the naval cutlass. We will fight with those."

"I cannot support you there." Zouga shook his head. "If

there was a challenge, and I could make a case against that—but if there was one, it came from you, sir. If you fight, it will be with pistols."

Day after day he tried to persuade Clinton to miss the rendezvous.

"Damn it, man. Nobody fights duels anymore, especially against a man who can split the cheroot in your mouth with either hand, at twenty paces." Or again, "There was no challenge, Captain Codrington, I was there, and I would stake my honor on it." At another time, "You will lose your commission, sir. You have Admiral Kemp's direct order to avoid the meeting, and it is obvious that Kemp is waiting for an opportunity to haul you before a court-martial." Then again, "By God, sir, you will serve no one—least of all yourself—by being shot to death on some deserted and godforsaken shore. If St. John is a slaver, then your chance to take him at more favorable odds will come later."

When Zouga's best arguments made no dent on Clinton's resolve Zouga went to Robyn in her cabin.

"You seem to have some influence on the fellow. Can you not persuade him, sissy?"

"Zouga, why are so determined to prevent Captain Codrington defending his honor?"

"He's a likable enough chap, and I do not wish to see him pipped."

"And if he were, you might find it difficult to reach Quelimane. Is that not so?" Robyn asked sweetly. "Your concern is most Christian."

"St. John can choose which of his eyes he will put a ball into. You have seen him shoot." Zouga ignored the accusation.

"I believe it is Captain Codrington's duty to destroy that monster. God protects the righteous."

"In my experience He protects only those who shoot fastest and straightest," Zouga growled with frustration.

"That is blasphemy," Robyn told him.

"You deserve to hear some real blasphemy for your stubbornness," Zouga told her curtly and strode out of the cabin. He had learned through long experience when he was wasting his time.

They passed the mouth of the Kei River—the frontier of British influence and beyond it was the wilderness, unclaimed and untamed, peopled by the tribes which had been driven back inexorably by the white advance, and by scattered bands of renegades and bastards, wandering hunters and hardy travelers and traders.

Even the trekking Boers had bypassed this land, going on into the interior, circling out beyond the mountain massif that divided the littoral from the highland plateau.

Far to the north they had turned back and crossed the mountains again and reached the coast, fighting and shattering the impis of the Zulu nation, beginning to settle the fertile coastal strip until the British ships had sailed into Port Natal, following them up from the Cape Colony, from whence they had trekked so long and so hard to avoid British rule. The Boers had loaded their wagons once more, and driving their herds before them, climbed back over the range that they called the Dragon mountains and abandoned the land they had wrested from the Zulu king Dingaan with the flame and smoke of their muskets.

However, this coast along which *Black Joke* now steamed lay between the English colonies of Cape and Natal, claimed by none, except the wild tribesmen who watched the black-hulled vessel pass almost within arrow shot.

Clinton Codrington had marked the point where latitude 31°38′ south intersected the coast, and the estuary was shown on the chart with the notation "St. John's River," named, probably, by one of the early Portuguese navigators, but it was ironic that it should bear the same name as the man they were hastening to meet. When *Black Joke* steamed around the last headland the description that St. John had given of his namesake was instantly recognizable.

Steep, heavily wooded hills rose almost sheer about a wide lagoon. The forest was very dense green, with tall galleries of trees, festooned with lianas. Through the telescope could be made out the troops of little gray vervet monkeys and the brilliant plumage of exotic birds that sported and fluttered through the top branches.

The river came down a deep rocky gorge torn through the barrier of hills, filling the reed-lined lagoon and then flowing out over the bar between the curved white pillows of a sandy beach.

To dispel any doubt that this was the rendezvous, *Huron* lay at anchor a cable's length beyond the first line of breakers, in the deep, where the shoal water turned from pale green to blue.

Clinton Codrington examined her carefully through his telescope, then without a word passed the instrument to Zouga.

114

While he in turn glassed the big clipper, Clinton asked softly, "Will you act for me?"

Zouga lowered the glass with surprise. "I expected one of your own officers."

"I could not ask them." Clinton shook his head. "Slogger Kemp would mark their service records if he ever heard of it."

"You do not have the same qualms about my career," Zouga pointed out.

"You are on extended absence from your regiment, and you have not been expressly ordered, as I and my officers have been."

Zouga thought quickly: dueling was not so seriously considered in the army as it was in the Royal Navy, in fact the Army manuals still contained no express prohibitions, and a chance to meet with St. John was also a last chance to avert this ridiculous affair that so seriously threatened the continuance of his expedition.

"I accept, then," Zouga said shortly.

"I am extremely grateful to you, sir," said Clinton as shortly.

"Let us hope you are as grateful after the business is over," Zouga told him dryly. "I had best go across to *Huron* right away. It will be dark in an hour."

Tippoo caught the line as it was thrown from the gunboat's whaler, and held it while Zouga gathered his cloak and jumped the gap of surging green water to the boarding ladder, clambering up before the next swell could soak his boots.

Mungo St. John waited for him at the foot of the mainmast. He held himself unsmiling and aloof, until Zouga hurried to him and offered his right hand, then he relaxed and returned the smile.

"Damn it, Mungo, cannot we make an end to this nonsense?"

"Certainly, Zouga," Mungo St. John agreed. "An apology from your man would settle it."

"The man is a fool," Zouga shook his head. "Why take the risk?"

"I don't consider there is any risk, but let me remind you he called me a coward."

"There is no chance then?" The two of them had become good friends during the weeks they had spent together and Zouga felt he could press further. "I admit the fellow is a prig, but if you kill him, you'll make it damned awkward for me, don't you know?"

Mungo St. John threw back his head and laughed delightedly. "You and I could work together, do you know that,

Zouga? You are a pragmatist, like I am. I make a prophecy: you'll go a long way in this world."

"Not very far, if you kill the man who is taking me."

And Mungo St. John chuckled again and clapped a friendly hand upon his shoulder. "I'm sorry, my friend. Not this time," and Zouga sighed with resignation.

"You have a choice of weapons."

"Pistols," said St. John.

"Of course," Zouga nodded. "Dawn tomorrow on the beach there." He pointed to the land with his chin. "Will that suit you?"

"Admirably. Tippoo here will act for me."

"Does he understand the conventions?" Zouga asked doubtfully, as he glanced at the half-naked figure that waited near at hand.

"He understands enough to blow Codrington's head off at the shoulders if he levels his pistol a moment before the signal." Mungo St. John flashed that cruel white smile. "And that's all he needs to know, as far as I am concerned."

Robyn Ballantyne slept not a minute during the night and it still lacked two hours of dawn when she bathed and dressed. On an impulse she chose her old moleskin breeches and man's woolen jacket. There would be the need to disembark through the surf from the ship's boat and skirts would hamper her, added to which the morning was damp and chill and her jacket was of good thick Scottish tweed.

She laid out her black leather bag and checked its contents, making certain she had everything she needed to cleanse and staunch a bullet wound, to bind up torn flesh or hold together shattered bone, and to reduce the agony of either man.

All of them had taken it without question that Robyn would be on the beach that morning. The gunboat did not rate a surgeon, and neither did *Huron*. She was ready with an hour to wait, and she opened her journal and began making the previous day's entry, when there was a light tap on her door.

When she opened it, Clinton Codrington stood in the opening, his face pale and strained in the smoky lamplight, and she knew intuitively that he had slept as little as she had. He recovered swiftly from the first shock of seeing her in breeches, dragging his eyes up to her face again.

"I hoped I might speak with you," he muttered shyly. "It will be the last opportunity before . . ."

She took his arm and drew him into the cabin. "You have not breakfasted?" she asked sternly.

"No, ma'am." He shook his head and his eyes dropped to her trousered legs, and then jerked up guiltily to her face again.

"The medicine worked?" she asked.

He nodded, too embarrassed to reply. She had administered a purge the evening before, for as a surgeon she could dread the effects of a pistol ball through a full bowel or through a belly loaded with breakfast.

She touched his forehead. "You are warm, you have not taken a chill?" She felt protective toward him, like a mother almost, for he seemed once again so young and untried.

"I wondered if we might pray together." His voice was so low that she barely caught the words, and she felt a warm, almost suffocating rush of affection for him.

"Come," she whispered, and she took his hand.

They knelt together on the bare deck of the tiny cabin, still holding hands, and she spoke for both of them, and he made the responses in a soft but firm voice.

When they rose stiffly at last, he kept her hand in his for a while longer.

"Miss Ballantyne—I mean, Dr. Ballantyne—I cannot tell you now what a profound effect meeting you has had on my life."

She felt herself blushing and tried feebly to disengage her hand, but he clung to it.

"I would like to have your permission to talk to you again in this vein after," he paused, "if this morning goes as we hope it will."

"Oh, it will," she said fiercely. "It will—I know it will." Hardly knowing what she was doing she pressed herself swiftly to him and reaching up kissed him full on the mouth. For a moment he froze, and then clumsily he crushed her to him so that the brass buttons of his coat dug into her bosom and his teeth crushed her lips until she felt them bruising.

"My darling," he whispered. "Oh, my darling."

The strength of his reaction startled her, but almost immediately she found she was enjoying the strength of his embrace, and she tried to free her arms to return it—but he misunderstood her movements and released her hurriedly.

"Forgive me," he blurted out. "I don't know what came over me."

Her disappointment was sharp enough to turn instantly to

117

annoyance at his timidity. Buttons and teeth notwithstanding, it had felt very pleasant indeed.

Both boats left the two ships at the same time, and they converged through the thin pearly morning mist as their crews pulled for the low lines of breaking surf and the pale outline of the beach in the dawn.

They landed within a hundred yards of each other, surfing in on the crest of the same low, green wave and the oarsmen leaped out waist-deep to run the boats high up the white sand.

Both parties moved separately over the crest of the sandbar and then down to the edge of the lagoon, screened from the boat crews by the intervening dunes and the stands of tall fluffy-headed reeds. There was a level area of firm damp sand at one edge of the reeds.

Mungo St. John and Tippoo halted at one end, and Mungo lit a cheroot and stood with both hands on his hips staring out at the crests of the hills, ignoring the activity about him. He was dressed in black tight-fitting breeches and a white silk shirt with full sleeves, open at the throat to reveal the dark curls of his body hair. The white shirt would give his opponent a fair aiming point: he was observing the conventions scrupulously.

Robyn watched him covertly as she stood beside Clinton Codrington at the further end of the clearing. She tried to capture the hatred she felt for St. John, to hold on to her outrage at the way he had abused her, but it was a difficult emotion to sustain. Rather, she was excited and with a strange sense of elation; the satanic presence of this man heightened the feeling. She caught herself staring openly and dragged her eyes off him.

Beside her Clinton stood very erect. He wore his blue uniform jacket with the gold lace of his rank gleaming even in the soft pink light of early dawn. He had scraped the sun-bleached hair back from his forehead and temples and bound it at the nape of his neck, leaving clean the purposeful line of his jaw.

Zouga went forward to meet Tippoo, who carried under his arm the rosewood case of pistols. When they met in the center of the level ground, he opened the case and proffered it, standing straddle-legged and attentive, while Zouga took each weapon from its velvet nest and loaded it with a carefully measured charge of black powder before ramming home the dark-blue leaden ball and setting the cap on the nipple.

The sight of the long-barreled weapons reminded Robyn

forcefully of that night aboard *Huron*, and she bit her lip and shifted uncomfortably.

"Do not fret yourself, Miss Ballantyne." Clinton mistook her emotion, and whispered soothingly to comfort her while he unbuttoned his jacket and shrugged out of it. Beneath it he also wore a plain white shirt to give St. John a fair aim. He handed her the jacket and would have spoken again but Zouga called.

"Will the principals come forward."

And Clinton gave her another tightly strained smile before he strode out, his heels leaving deep prints in the damp yellow sand.

He faced Mungo St. John, holding his gaze steadily, both of them completely expressionless.

"Gentlemen, I appeal to both of you to settle this affair without bloodshed." Zouga went through the ritual attempt as reconciliation. "Captain Codrington, as challenger, will you tender an apology?"

Clinton shook his head once, curtly.

"Mr. St. John, is there any other way in which we can avoid bloodshed?"

"I think not, sir," St. John drawled as he carefully tapped half an inch of gray ash from his cheroot.

"Very well," Zouga nodded and went on immediately to set the conditions of the meeting. "At the command 'Proceed' each of you gentlemen will take ten paces, which I will count aloud. Immediately after the count of ten I will give the command 'Fire' upon which you will be at liberty to turn and discharge your weapon."

Zouga paused and glanced at Tippoo: there was a long-barreled muzzle-loading pistol thrust into the waistband of his baggy breeches.

"Both seconds are armed." Zouga laid his right hand on the butt of the Colt pistol in his own belt. "If either principal attempts to fire before the command to do so, then he will immediately be shot down by the seconds."

He paused again looking from one to the other. "Is that clearly understood, gentlemen?" They both nodded. "Do either of you have a question?" Zouga waited in silence for a few seconds then went on. "Very well, we will proceed. Mr. St. John, you have first choice of weapon."

Mungo St. John dropped the cheroot and ground it into the sand with his heel, before stepping forward. Tippoo offered him the rosewood case and after a momentary hesitation St.

John lifted out one of the beautifully inlaid weapons. He pointed at the sky and cocked the hammer with a sweep of his free hand.

Clinton took the remaining pistol and weighed it experimentally in his hand, settling the butt deeply into the V formed by thumb and forefinger, turning half away and lifting the pistol at full stretch of his arm to aim it at one of the black and bright-yellow bishop birds that chattered in the reeds nearby.

With relief Robyn watched the familiar ease with which her champion handled the weapon, and she felt completely certain of the outcome now. Good must triumph, and she started to pray again, silently, only her lips moving as she recited the Twenty-third Psalm. "'Though I walk through the valley of the shadow of death.'"

"Take your positions, gentlemen." Zouga stepped back and gestured to Robyn. Still praying, she hurried to where Zouga stood, and fell in a few paces behind him, well out on the flank from the lines of fire of the two principals.

Beside Zouga, Tippoo drew the long, clumsy-looking pistol from the sash around his waist and cocked the big ornate hammer; the bore of the barrel gaped like a cannon as he lifted it into the present position. Zouga drew his own Colt revolver and stood quietly while the two principals walked the last few paces toward each other and then turned back to back.

Beyond them the early sun was gilding the hilltops with bright gold, but leaving the lagoon still in shadow so the still dark waters steamed with wisps of mist. In the silence a ghostly gray heron croaked hoarsely and then launched into flight from the edge of the reed bank with slow wingbeats, its neck drawn back into a snakelike S to balance the long beak.

"Proceed!" called Zouga, so loudly that Robyn started violently.

The two men stepped out, away from each other, with deliberate strides, heeling heavily in the yielding sand, pacing to the count that Zouga called.

"Five." Mungo St. John was smiling softly, as though at some secret joke, and his white silk sleeve fluttered like a moth's wing around the uplifted arm that held the slim steel-blue barrel pointed at the dawn sky.

"Six." Clinton leaned forward, stepping out with long legs clad in white uniform breeches. His face was set, pale as a mask, his lips drawn into a thin determined line.

"Seven." Robyn felt the beat of her heart crescendo, thumping painfully against the cage of her ribs so that she could not breathe.

"Eight." She noticed for the first time the patches of sweat that had soaked through the armpits of Clinton's white shirt, despite the chill of the dawn air.

"Nine." Suddenly she was deadly afraid for him, all her faith dissolved in a sudden premonition of disaster rushing down upon her.

"Ten!" She wanted to scream to them to stop. She wanted to rush forward and throw herself into the space between the two men. She didn't want them to die, either of them. She tried to fill her lungs but her throat was closed and dry, she tried to drive her legs forward but they were locked rigidly under her, beyond her control.

"Fire!" shouted Zouga, his voice cracking with the tension that gripped all the watchers, and out on the damp dark-yellow sand both men turned, like a pair of dancers in a meticulously rehearsed ballet of death.

Their right arms outflung toward each other in a gesture like that of parted lovers, the left hand on the hip to balance, the classic stance of the expert marksman.

Time seemed suspended, the movements of the two men graceful but measured, without the urgency of onrushing death.

The silence was complete, there was no wind to rustle the reeds, no bird nor animal called from the looming forest across the lagoon, the footfalls of the two men were deadened by the yielding sand; the world seemed to hold its breath.

And then the crash of pistol fire awoke the echoes and sent them bounding and booming across the gorge, leaping from cliff to cliff, startling the birds into raucous flight.

The two shots were within one hundredth of a second of each other, so that they blended into a single blurt of sound. From the leveling blue barrels the dead-white powder smoke spurted, and then the barrels were flung upward in unison with the shock of discharge.

Both men reeled backward, keeping their feet, but Robyn had seen the smoke fly from the muzzle of Mungo St. John's pistol a fraction of a second earlier, and then an instant later Mungo's big dark head flinched as though he had been struck with an open hand across the cheek.

After that one staggered pace backward, he steadied, drawing himself to his full height, the pistol still smoking in his raised hand, staring at his adversary, and Robyn felt a rush of relief. Mungo was unscathed. She wanted to run to him, and

121

then suddenly the joy withered, a dark red snake of blood slithered from the thick hair at his temple down the smoothly shaven olive skin of his cheek and dripped with slow sullen drops onto the white silk of his shirt.

She lifted her hand to her mouth to cover the cry that rose within her, and then her attention was distracted by another movement in the corner of her vision and she swung her head with a jerky movement toward Clinton Codrington.

He also had been standing erect, with almost military bearing, but now he began to bow slowly forward at the waist. The right hand holding the pistol hung at his side and now his fingers opened and the ornate weapon dropped into the sand at his feet.

He lifted the empty hand and placed it across his chest with fingers outspread in a gesture that seemed reverential and slowly his body bent forward and now his legs gave way under him and he dropped to his knees, as though in prayer. Kneeling, he lifted his hand away from his chest and examined with an expression of mild surprise the small smear of blood that coated his fingers and then he pitched forward face down on to the sand.

At last Robyn could move. She raced forward and dropped to her knees beside Clinton's fallen body, and with strength of panic rolled him onto his back. The front of the white linen shirt was damp with a little blood around the neat puncture in the cloth six inches to the left of the line of mother of pearl buttons.

He had been half turned to fire and the ball had taken him low and left, at the level of the lungs, she saw instantly. The lungs! She felt despair overwhelm her. It would mean death, no less certain because it was slow and agonizing. She would have to watch this man drown inexorably in his own blood.

Sand crunched beside her and she looked up.

Mungo St. John stood over her, his shirt a mess of wet blood. He was holding a silk kerchief to his temple to staunch the copious flow where the pistol ball had stripped a long ribbon of scalp off his skull above the ear.

His eyes were bleak, his expression forbidding and his voice cold and distant as he told her quietly.

"I trust you will be satisfied at last, madam." Then he turned abruptly up the white dune toward the beach. She wanted to run after him, to restrain him, to explain—to explain she knew not what, but her duty was here, with the man more gravely stricken. Her fingers shook as she unbuttoned the front of

Clinton's shirt and saw the dark-blue hole punched into the pale flesh from which a little thick slow blood oozed. So little blood at the mouth of the wound; it was the worst indication: the bleeding would be inside, deep inside the chest cavity.

"Zouga, my bag," she called sharply.

Zouga came to her, carrying the bag and went down on one knee beside her.

"I am but lightly struck," murmured Clinton. "I have no pain. Just a feeling of numbness here."

Zouga did not reply. He had seen a multitude of gunshot wounds in India; pain was no indication of the severity. A ball through the hand or foot was unbearable agony, another through both lungs was only mildly discomforting.

Only one thing puzzled him and that was why Mungo St. John's shot had been so wide. At twenty paces he would surely have taken the head shot, aiming between the eyes with an expectation of the ball deviating less than an inch from the point of aim, yet the shot had taken Clinton low in the chest.

While Robyn pressed a dressing over the wicked little blue mouth of the wound, Zouga picked the pistol out of the sand. The barrel was still warm and there was the peppery whiff of burned powder as he examined it and saw instantly why Mungo's shot had struck wide.

There was a bluish smear of bright new lead on the steel trigger guard.

Mungo St. John had indeed aimed at the head, but Clinton had lifted the pistol to his eye at the same instant directly in the line of sight. St. John's ball had struck the metal guard and been deflected downward.

That would account for the fact that Clinton's own ball had been high, for as a less expert marksman he would surely have aimed for St. John's chest. The strike of the ball had thrown his weapon upward at the moment of discharge.

Zouga looked up and handed the pistol to Tippoo, who waited impassively close at hand. Without a word, Tippoo took the weapon, turned away and followed his master over the dunes.

By the time four seamen from the gunboat could carry Clinton Codrington down the beach using his boat cloak as a hammock, St. John was climbing up from the *Huron*'s whaler on to his main deck, and before they could rig a block and tackle to lift the prostrate form of her captain into *Black Joke*, *Huron* had broken out her anchor and was spreading sail before the southwesterly breeze and bearing away with the sunrise transforming her into a vessel etched in golden fire.

For twenty-four hours Clinton Codrington surprised Robyn with the strength of his recovery. She looked to see blood on his lips, and she expected him to experience the agony of breathing as the damaged lung collapsed. Every few hours she listened with her sounding trumpet to his chest, stooping over the bunk in his cabin to catch the hiss and saw of his breathing, listening for the bubbling sound of blood, or for the dry rubbing of the lung against the rib cage, and was puzzled when none of these symptoms occurred.

Indeed Clinton was unaccountably resilient for a patient with ball through the chest cavity. He complained only of stiffness reaching up into his left armpit and semiparalysis of that arm—and he was vociferous in his advice to his surgeon.

"You will bleed me, of course?" he asked.

"I will not," Robyn told him shortly as she cleaned the area around the wound and then lifted him into a sitting position to bandage his chest.

"You should take at least a pint," Clinton insisted.

"Have you not bled enough?" Robyn asked witheringly, but he was undaunted.

"There is black rotten blood that must be taken off." Clinton indicated the massive bruise that was spreading around his chest like some dark parasitic plant around the smooth pale trunk.

"You must bleed me," Clinton insisted, for all his adult life he had been exposed to the ministrations of naval surgeons. "If you don't, fever is sure to follow."

He offered Robyn the inner curve of his elbow where the thin white scars over the blue blood vessels marked where he had been bled before.

"We no longer live in the dark ages," Robyn told him tartly. "This is eighteen-sixty," and she pushed him down on the bolster and covered him with a gray ship's blanket against the shivering and chilling nausea which she knew must soon accompany such a wound. It did not come, and for the next twenty hours he continued to manage the ship from his bunk, and he chafed at the restraint she placed on him. However, Robyn knew the pistol ball was still in there and that there must be drastic consequences. She wished that there was some technique that could enable a surgeon to locate the whereabouts of a foreign body accurately, and then allow him to enter the rib cage and remove it.

That evening she fell asleep in the rope chair beside his bunk, awakening once to hold the enamel cup of water to his lips when he complained of thirst and noting the dryness and heat of his skin, and in the morning all her fears were confirmed.

He was only semiconscious, and the pain was fierce. He moaned and cried out at the smallest movement. His eyes were sunken into plum-colored cavities, his tongue was thickly coated with white and his lips were dried and cracked. He pleaded for drink and his skin was hot, the heat increasing every hour until it seemed to be burning out the core of his being, and he was restless and flushed, tossing in the narrow bunk, fighting off the blankets with which she tried to keep him covered, and whimpering in his delirium at the agony of movement. His breath was sawing painfully in his swollen and bruised chest, his eyes were glittering bright, and when Robyn unwound the bandage to sponge his body with cool water there was only a little pale fluid staining the dressing, but her nostrils flared as she smelled it. It was so horribly familiar, she always thought of that stench as the fetid breath of death itself.

The wound had shrunk, but the crust that had formed over it was so thin that it cracked at one of Clinton's restless movements and through it rose a thick droplet of custard-colored matter. Immediately the smell was stronger. This was not the benign pus of healing, but the malignant pus that she so dreaded to see in a wound.

She swabbed it away carefully, and then with cold seawater sponged his chest and the hard hot swollen flesh below his armpit. The bruising was extensive and it had changed color, dark blue as storm clouds, tinged with the yellow of sulfur and the virulent rose of some flower from the gardens of hell itself.

There was one area just below the point of his shoulder blade that was particularly sensitive, for he screamed when she touched it, and a sparse prickle of sweat broke out across his forehead and among the find golden bristles of his unshaven cheeks.

She replaced the bandage with a fresh dressing and then forced between his dry lips four grams of laudanum mixed with a warm draft of calomel. She watched while he fell into a restless drug-induced sleep.

"Another twenty-four hours," she whispered aloud, watching him toss and mutter. She had seen it so often. Soon the pus would suffuse his whole body, building up steadily around the ball deep in his chest. She was helpless. No surgeon could enter the rib cage, it had never been done before.

She looked up as Zouga stooped into the cabin. He was grave and quiet, standing beside her chair for a moment and placing a hand on her shoulder comfortingly.

"He improves?" he asked softly.

She shook her head, and he nodded as though he had expected the answer.

"You must eat." He offered her the pannikin. "I brought you some pea soup. It has bacon in it, it's very good."

She had not realized how hungry she was and she ate gratefully, breaking the hard ship's bread into the broth, and Zouga went on quietly, "I loaded the pistols with less than a full charge, as little as I dared." He shook his head irritably. "Damned bad luck. After Mungo's ball hit the trigger guard, I'd not have expected it to have entered the chest; it must have lost most of its power."

She looked up quickly. "It struck the trigger guard—you did not tell me."

He shrugged. "It's not important now. But the ball was deflected."

She sat very still in her chair for ten minutes after he was gone, and then purposefully she stood over the bunk and stripped back the blanket, unwound the bandage and examined the wound again.

Very carefully she began to sound the ribs beneath it, pressing in with thumb gently to feel for the give of shattered bone. The ribs were all firm, yet there was no proof that the ball had not driven between two of them.

She pressed her thumb into the swelling toward the outside of his chest, and although he thrashed around weakly, she thought she felt the rasp of bone against bone—as though the rib had been chipped or even as if a long splinter had been cracked off it.

She felt a little flutter of excitement, and extended her examination gradually backward, guided by his delirious cries of pain, until once again she reached the lower point of his shoulder and he came upright in the bunk with another wild yell of agony, breaking out once more into the burning sweat of high fever. But with the tip of her finger she thought she had felt something, something that was neither bone nor knotted muscle.

The excitement quickened her breathing. From the angle at which Clinton had stood, half turned away from Mungo St.

John, she now believed that it was possible that the ball had followed a different path from that which she had assumed.

If the pistol had been undercharged with powder, and if the ball had struck the trigger guard, it was just possible that it had not had the velocity to penetrate the rib cage, it had been turned by the bone and plowed along under the skin, skidding along the groove between two ribs following the track that she had just probed, and lodging at last in the thick bed of the *latissimus dorsi* and *tenes major* muscle.

She stood back from the bunk. She could be very wrong, she realized, but if she was he would die anyway, and that very soon.

"I will cut for it," she decided, the decision direct and swift. She glanced up at the skylight in the roof of the cabin. There was only an hour or two of good daylight left.

"Zouga!" she called as she raced from the cabin. "Zouga! Come quickly!"

Robyn administered another five grams of laudanum before they moved Clinton. It was as large a dose as she dared, for he had taken nearly fifteen grams in the preceding thirty-six hours. She waited as long as she could in the failing light for the drug to begin taking effect. Then she passed the word to Lieutenant Denham to shorten sail, reduce engine revolutions and make the ship's motion as easy as possible.

Zouga had chosen two seamen to assist them. One was the boatswain, a burly and graying sailor, the other was the officer's steward who had impressed Robyn with his quiet, controlled manner.

Now as the three of them half lifted Clinton and rolled him on to his side, the steward spread a sheet of fresh white canvas on the bunk under him to receive the spilled blood, then Zouga swiftly knotted the lengths of soft cotton rope around Clinton's wrists and ankles. He had chosen cotton in preference to the coarse hemp which would tear the skin, and he made the bowline knots that would not slip under pressure.

The boatswain helped him to tie down the ends at the head and foot of the bunk, stretching out the almost naked white body so that for an instant it reminded Robyn of the painting of the crucifixion that stood in Uncle William's study at Kings Lynn—the Roman legionaries spreadeagling Christ upon the cross before driving home the nails. She shook her head irritably, driving the memory from her mind, concentrating all her attention on the task ahead.

127

"Wash your hands!" she ordered Zouga, indicating the bucket of almost boiling water and yellow lye soap the steward had provided.

"Why?"

"Do it," she snapped, in no mood to aruge. Her own hands were pink with the heat of the water and tingled with the harsh soap, as she wiped her instruments with the cloth dipped in a mug of pungent ship's rum, laying them out on the shelf above the bunk, and then the same cloth swabbed the hot discolored flesh at the base of Clinton's shoulder blade. He jerked against his bonds and muttered an incoherent protest, but she ignored it and nodded to the boatswain.

He seized Clinton's head, drawing it back slightly, and thrust a thick pad of felt, a piece of wadding for the main-deck cannon, between his teeth, holding it in place.

"Zouga!"

He took Clinton's shoulders and locked them in his powerful fingers, preventing Clinton from rolling onto his belly.

"Good."

Robyn took one of the razor-sharp scalpels from the shelf, and then with the forefinger of her other hand probed brutally down to where she had felt that hard foreign body.

Clinton's back arched and he let out a shattering cry that was muffled by the wadding, but Robyn felt it clearly this time, hard and unyielding in the swollen flesh.

She cut swiftly, without hesitation, opening the skin cleanly, following the direction of the muscle fiber beneath, dissecting down through layer after layer of muscle, separating the bluish membrane capsules that covered each of the muscles with the hilt of the scalpel, probing deeper and deeper with her fingers toward that elusive lump in the flesh.

Clinton writhed and heaved at his bonds, his breathing rasping in the back of his throat, his teeth locked into the felt wadding in a fierce rictus so that cords of muscle stood out along his jawline and white spittle frothed upon his lips.

His wild lunges made her task that much more difficult, and her fingers were slippery with blood in his hot flesh, but she found the rubbery pulsing snake of the lateral thoracic artery and worked past it gently, pinching off the smaller spurting blood vessels with the forceps, and tying them with a loop of catgut, torn between the need for speed and the danger of doing greater damage.

Finally she had to use the blade again, and she reversed the

128

scalpel and paused a moment to locate the lump with the tip of her forefinger.

She could feel the sweat sliding down her cheek, and she was aware of the strained tense faces of the men who held Clinton as they watched her work.

She guided the scalpel down into the open wound, and then cut down firmly and a sudden bright yellow fountain spouted up through her fingers, and the cloying stomach-twisting stench of corruption that filled the hot little cabin made her gasp.

That sharp rush of pus lasted only a second, and then there was something black and sodden blocking the wound. She picked it out with the forceps, releasing another, lesser welling up of the thick custardy matter.

"The wad," Zouga grunted with the effort of holding down the struggling naked body. They all stared at the soft rotten object in the teeth of her forceps.

The patch of cloth had been carried deeply into the flesh by the passage of the ball, and Robyn felt a surging lift of relief: she had been right.

Quickly she went back to work, running her finger into the tunnel cut by the ball until she felt it with her fingertip.

"There it is!" She spoke for the first time since she had cut, but the metal pellet was slippery and heavy, she could not prise it loose and she had to cut again and then lock the teeth of the pair of bone forceps over it. It came out with reluctant suck of clinging tissue, and she dropped it impatiently on the shelf. It made a heavy clunk against the wood. There was a temptation to come out immediately, to sew up and bind up—but she resisted and took an extra ten seconds to probe the wound thoroughly. She was almost immediately justified, there was another rotting and stinking tatter of cloth in the wound track.

"A piece of the shirt." She identified the white shreds, and Zouga's face mirrored his disgust. "Now we can come out," Robyn went on complacently.

She left a bristle in the wound to allow the remaining pus to drain off. It stuck out stiffly between the stitches with which she closed up.

When she stood back at last she was smugly satisfied with her work. There had been nobody at St. Matthew's who could lay down stitches so neatly and regularly; not even the senior surgeons could match her.

Clinton had collapsed with the shock of deep surgery. His body was wet and slick with his sweat, and the skin at his wrists and ankles had been smeared away where he had fought against his bonds.

"Let him loose," she said softly. She felt a vast pride, almost of ownership, in him now, as though he were her special creation, for she believed that she had dragged him back almost bodily from the abyss. Pride was sin, she knew, but it did not make the sensation any the less agreeable, and in the circumstances, she decided, she had earned the pleasure of a little sin—if he recovered.

Clinton's recovery was almost miraculous. By the next morning he was fully conscious, and the fever had abated to leave him white and shaky, with just enough strength to argue bitterly when she had him carried up into the sunshine and laid behind the canvas wind shelter that the carpenter had rigged under the poop.

"Cold air is bad for gunshot wounds, everybody knows that."

"And I suppose I should bleed you before closing you up in that hot little hellhole you call a cabin," Robyn asked tartly.

"A Navy surgeon would do so," he muttered.

"Then thank your Maker that I am not one."

On the second day he was sitting up unaided and eating voraciously, by the third he was managing the ship from his litter, and on the fourth day he was on his quarterdeck once more, although his arm was in a sling and he was still gaunt where the fever had wasted away the flesh from his face, but strong enough to keep on his feet for an hour at a time before resorting to the rope chair the carpenter had rigged at the rail. That day Robyn withdrew the bristle from the wound and was relieved at the tiny quantity of benign pus that followed it out. They watched the little town of Port Natal come up ahead of them, the primitive buildings huddled under the whale-backed mountain they called the Bluff like chickens under the wing of the hen. *Black Joke* did not call, even though this was the furthest outpost of the British Empire on this coast, but steamed on briskly into the north, each day becoming perceptibly warmer with the sun standing higher at noon and the sea changing to the darker azure of the tropics beneath *Black Joke*'s bows, and once again the flying fish sported ahead of them on filmy silver wings.

The evening before they reached the Portuguese settlement of Lourenço Marques on the deep bight of Delagoa Bay, Robyn dressed the stitches in Clinton's side, making small cooing and

130

clucking sounds of satisfaction and approval as she saw how cleanly they were healing.

When she helped him into his shirt and then buttoned it for him, like a mother dressing her child, he told her gravely, "I am aware you have saved my life."

"Even though you do not approve of my methods?" she asked with a smile.

"I ask your forgiveness for my impertinence." He dropped his eyes. "You have proved yourself to be a brilliant physician."

She made a modest murmur of denial, but when he insisted, "No, I truly mean that. I think you are gifted," Robyn protested no further, but moved slightly to make it easier for him to reach her with his good arm, but his declaration of faith in her skills seemed to have exhausted his courage for the moment.

That evening she vented some of her frustration by confiding to her journal, "Captain Codrington is clearly a man that can be trusted by a woman, in any circumstances—though a bit more boldness would make him a great deal more attractive."

She was about to close the journal and lock it away in her chest, when another thought occurred to her. She thumbed back through the preceding pages each crammed with her small neat script, until she reached the single sheet that had become a milestone in her life. The entry for the day before *Huron* reached Cape Town she had left blank. What words were there to describe it? Each moment of it would be engraved forever on her memory. She stared for many minutes at the empty sheet, and then she made a silent calculation, subtracting one date from another. When she had the answer she felt a chill of foreboding, and went over the calculation again, reaching the same answer.

She closed the journal slowly and stared at the lantern flame.

She had missed her lunar courses by almost a week, and with a prickle of dread lifting the fine hair at the nape of her neck she laid her hand upon her own belly as if there was something to feel there—like the pistol ball in Clinton's flesh.

Black Joke called at Lourenço Marques for coal bunkers, despite the town's notoriety as a fever port. The swamps and mangroves that half circled the town to the southward spread miasmic airs across the port.

Although Robyn had only very limited firsthand experience of the peculiar fevers of Africa, she had made a close study of all the writings on the subject—the most notable of these being probably those of her own father. Fuller Ballantyne had written a long paper for the British Medical Association, in which he recognized four distinct types of African fever—the recurrent fevers with a definite cycle he divided into three categories—quotidian, tertian and quartan—by the length of the cycle. These he called the malarial fevers. The fourth type was the black vomit, or the yellow jack.

In his own unmistakable style, Fuller Ballantyne had shown that these diseases were neither contagious nor infectious. He had done so by a horrifying but courageous demonstration to a group of skeptical brother physicians at the military hospital at Algoa Bay.

While the other physicians watched, he had collected a wineglass of fresh vomit from a victim of the yellow jack. Fuller had toasted them with the awful draft and then drunk it down at a single swallow. His colleagues had waited with a certain keen anticipation for his demise and had some difficulty in hiding their disappointment when he showed no ill effects and set off a week later to walk across Africa. Fuller Ballantyne was a man easier to admire than to like. The episode had become part of the legend that surrounded him.

In his writings her father insisted that the disease could only be contracted by breathing the night air of tropical areas, particularly those airs released by swamps or other large bodies of stagnant water. However, some individuals most certainly had a natural resistance to the disease, and this resistance was probably hereditary. He cited the African tribes who lived in known malarial areas, and his own family and that of his wife who had lived and worked in Africa for sixty years with only mild afflictions.

Fuller wrote of the "seasoning fever"—the first dose of which either killed or gave partial immunity to the subject. He used the example of the high mortality rate among newly arrived Europeans in Africa. He quoted the case of Nathaniel Isaacs, who in 1832 left Port Natal in a party with twenty-one newly arrived white men to hunt hippopotamus in the estuary and swamps of St. Lucia River. Within four weeks nineteen had perished—while Isaacs and the other survivor were so wracked with the disease that they were invalids for almost a year thereafter.

These losses were unnecessary, Fuller Ballantyne pointed out. There was a preventative and a cure that had been known for hundreds of years though under various names, Peruvian bark, or chinchona bark, more recently called essence of quinine when manufactured in powder form by the Quaker brothers

Luke and John Howard. Taken at the dosage of five grains daily it was a highly effective preventative, for even if the disease was subsequently contracted, it was in such mild form as to be no more dangerous than a common cold and responded immediately to a more massive dose of twenty-five grains of quinine.

Of course, Robyn had heard the accusation that her father played down the dangers of the disease to further his grand design. Fuller Ballantyne had a vision of Africa settled by colonists of British stock, bringing to the savage continent the true God, and all the benefits of British justice and ingenuity. His catastrophic expedition to the Zambezi had been in pursuit of this vision, for the great river was to have been his highway to the high and healthy plateau of the interior where his Englishmen would settle, driving out the slavers, bringing the warring and godless tribes to order, and taming and cultivating the savage earth.

Part of his vision had died upon the terrible torrents and rapids of the Kaborra-Bassa gorge.

With a sneaking sensation of disloyalty Robyn admitted to herself that there was probably some shred of justification in the accusation, for she had as a child seen her father in the grip of a malarial fever brought out by the cold of an English winter. It had not seemed as mild as a common cold then. Despite this, there was no one in the medical profession who doubted that Fuller Ballantyne was probably one of the world's leading authorities on the disease and that he had a real talent in diagnosing and treating it. So she followed his dictates faithfully, administering the daily five grains of quinine to herself, to Zouga and under protest to Captain Codrington. She had no success with Zouga's Hottentot musketeers, however. At the first dose Jan Cheroot had begun staggering in circles, clutching his throat and rolling his eyes horribly, crying to all his Hottentot gods that he had been poisoned. Only a tot of ship's rum saved him, but none of the other Hottentots would touch the white powder after that. Not even the thought of a tot of rum would tempt them, which was a measure of their opposition to the cure. Robyn could only hope that they possessed the resistance to the fever that her father spoke of.

Her store of quinine was meant to last for the duration of the expedition, possibly as long as two years, so she had reluctantly to refrain from pressing any of it on *Black Joke*'s seamen. She stilled her conscience with the fact that none of them would be spending a night ashore, therefore they would not be exposed to the dangerous airs. She prevailed upon Clinton Codrington to anchor in the outer roads where the onshore breeze kept the air sweet and, as an added attraction, the distance offshore prevented the swarms of mosquitoes and other flying insects from coming on board during the night.

The first night at anchor, the sound of music, of drunken laughter and the shrill cries of women at play and at work carried across the still waters to the nine Hottentot musketeers in their corner of the forecastle, and the lights of the brothels and bars along the waterfront were as irresistible to the nine as a candle to a hawkmoth. Temptation was made unbearable by the weight and heat of the golden sovereign that each of them carried in some secret place upon his person, the princely advance that Major Ballantyne had made against their salaries.

Sergeant Cheroot woke Zouga a little before midnight, his features a mask of outrage.

"They are gone." He was shaking with anger.

"Where?" Zouga was still more asleep than awake.

"They swim like rats," stormed Cheroot. "They all go drinking and awhoring." The thought of it was unsupportable. "We must catch them. They will burn their brains out on smoke and pox themselves—" His rage was mixed with an equal portion of raw envy, and once they were ashore his enthusiasm for the chase was almost a frenzy. Cheroot had an unerring instinct that led him directly to the lowest dives on the waterfront.

"You go in, Master," he told Zouga. "I'll wait around the back," and he twitched the short oaken club in his hand with gleeful anticipation.

The tobacco smoke and the fumes of cheap rum and gin were like a solid wall, but the musketeers saw Zouga the moment he stooped through the doorway into the yellow lantern light. There were four of them. They overturned two tables and smashed a dozen bottles in their eagerness to depart, jamming in a solid knot in the doorway to the rear alley before bursting out into the night beyond.

It took Zouga half a minute to push and wrestle his way through the crowd. The women of a dozen rich shades between gold and ebony reached out to pluck shamelessly at the more private areas of his anatomy as he passed, forcing him to defend himself, and the men deliberately blocked his path until he drew the Colt revolver from under his coattails; only then they sullenly opened a way for him to pass. When he reached the back door Sergeant Cheroot had the four Hottentots laid out in a row in the filth and dust of the alley.

"You haven't killed them?" Zouga asked anxiously.

"*Nee wat!* They got heads of solid bone." Cheroot tucked the club back in his belt, and stooped to pick up one of the bodies. The strength of his wiry little body was out of all proportion to its size. He carried them down to the beach one at a time as though they were bags of straw, and dumped them headfirst into the waiting whaler.

"Now we find the others."

They ferreted them out, singly and in pairs, from the fan-tan parlors and the gin hells, tracking down the ninth and last to the embrace of an enormous naked Somali lady in one of the shacks of mud walls and corrugated iron roofs behind the waterfront.

It was almost dawn when Zouga climbed wearily out of the whaler on to *Black Joke*'s deck and booted the ninth Hottentot down the forecastle ladder. He started for his own cabin, red-eyed and irritable, aching with fatigue, when it occurred to him that he had not noticed Sergeant Cheroot among the dark figures in the whaler, and his penetrating voice and biting sarcasm had been silent on the return from the beach.

Zouga's mood was murderous as he landed once again, and picked his way through the narrow filth-choked alleys to the mud and iron shack. The woman made up four of Jan Cheroot. She was a mountain of polished dark flesh, gleaming with oil, each of her widespread thighs thicker than his waist, her great mammaries each as large as his head, and Jan Cheroot's head was buried between them as though he was drowning himself in exotic and abundant flesh so that his ecstatic cries were almost smothered.

The woman looked down at him fondly, chuckling to herself as she watched Sergeant Cheroot's upended buttocks. They were skinny and a delicate shade of buttercup yellow, but they seemed to blur with the speed of movement, and the shock waves they created were transferred into the mountain of flesh beneath him, creating ripples and waves that undulated through the woman's belly and elephantine haunches, traveling up to agitate the pendulous folds that hung from her upper arms, and at last breaking in a wobbling heaving surf of gleaming black flesh around Sergeant Cheroot's head.

On the final return to the gunboat, Sergeant Cheroot sat, a small dejected figure, in the bows of the whaler, his postcoital tristesse considerably enhanced by the buzzing in his ears and the ache in his head. Only Englishmen had the alarming habit of bunching up a hand suddenly, and then hitting with more effect than a man wielding a club or hurling a brick. Sergeant Cheroot found his respect for his new master increasing daily.

"You should be an example to the men," Zouga growled at him as he hoisted him up the ladder by the collar of his uniform jacket.

"I know that, Master," Cheroot agreed miserably. "But I was in love."

"Are you still in love?" Zouga said harshly.

"No, Master, with me love don't last too long."

"I am a modestly wealthy man," Clinton Codrington told Robyn seriously. "Since my days as a midshipman I have saved as much of my pay as I did not need to live by, and of recent years I have been fortunate in the matter of prize money. This, together with the legacy of my mother, would enable me to care very comfortably for a wife."

They had lunched with the Portuguese governor at his invitation and the *vinho verde* that had accompanied the meal of succulent seafood and tasteless stringy beef had given Clinton a flush of courage.

Rather than returning immediately to the ship after the meal, he had suggested a tour of the principal city of the Portuguese possessions on the east coast of the African continent.

The governor's dilapidated carriage rumbled over the rutted roads and splashed through the puddles formed by the overflow from the open sewers. A raucous flock of ragged child beggars followed them, dancing in their dirty rags to keep pace with the bony, swaybacked mule that drew the carriage, and holding up their tiny pink-palmed hands for alms. The sun was fierce but not as fierce as the smells.

It was not the appropriate setting for what Clinton Codrington had in mind, and with relief he handed Robyn down from the carriage, scattered the beggars by hurling a handful of copper coins down the dusty street and hurried her into the cool gloom of the Roman Catholic cathedral. The cathedral was the most magnificent building in the city, its towers and spires rising high above the hovels and shacks that surrounded it.

However, Robyn had difficulty in concentrating on Clinton's declaration in these popish surroundings, among the gaudy idols, saints and virgins in scarlet and gold leaf. The reek of incense and the flickering of the massed banks of candles distracted her; even though what he was saying was what she

136

wanted to hear, she wished he had chosen some other place to say it.

That very morning she had been taken by a sudden spell of vomiting, and a mild nausea persisted even now. As a physician she knew exactly what that heralded.

Before the courtesy visit to the Portuguese governor's moldering palace, she had tentatively decided that she would have to take the initiative. That attack of vapors had convinced her of the urgency of the situation, and she had pondered how she could induce Clinton Codrington to stake some sort of claim to the burden she was convinced she was carrying.

When Zouga had still lived at Kings Lynn with Uncle William, she had discovered a cheaply printed novel of a most disreputable type concealed among the military texts on Zouga's desk. From a furtive study of this publication she had learned that it was possible for a woman to seduce a man, as well as the other way around. Unfortunately, the author had not provided a detailed description of the procedures. She had not even been certain if it were possible in a carriage, or whether anything should be said during the process, but now Clinton was obviating the necessity for experiment by a straightforward declaration. Her relief was tinged with shades of disappointment: after having been forced into the decision to carry out his seduction, she had found herself looking forward to the experience.

Now, however, she forced herself to assume an attentive expression and, when he hesitated, to encourage him with a nod or a gesture.

"Even though I am without powerful friends in the service, yet my record is such that I would never expect half-pay appointment, and although it might sound immodest I would confidently look forward to hoisting my own broad pennant before I am fifty years of age."

It was typical of him that he was already thinking twenty-five years ahead. It required an effort to prevent her irritation from showing, for Robyn preferred to live in the present, or at least the immediately foreseeable future.

"I should point out that an admiral's wife enjoys a great deal of social prestige," he went on comfortably, and her irritation flared higher. Prestige was something she had always intended to win at first hand—crusader against the slave trade, celebrated pioneer in tropical medicine, writer of admired books on African travel.

She could not contain it longer, but her voice was demure. "A woman can have a career as well as being a wife."

Clinton drew himself up stiffly. "A wife's place is in the home," he intoned, and she opened her mouth, then slowly closed it again. She knew she was bargaining from weakness, and when she was silent Clinton was encouraged. "To begin with a comfortable little house, near the harbor in Portsmouth. Of course, once there are children one would have to seek larger premises—"

"You would want many children?" she asked still sweetly, but with color mounting in her cheeks.

"Oh yes, indeed. One a year," and Robyn recalled those drabs with whom she had worked, women with brats hanging from both breasts and every limb, with another one always in the belly. She shuddered, and he was immediately concerned.

"Are you cold?"

"No. No, please go on." She felt trapped, and not for the first time resented the role that her sex had forced upon her.

"Miss Ballantyne—Dr. Ballantyne—what I have been trying to say to you—is that I would be greatly honored if you could find it in yourself to consent to become my wife."

Now when it came she was not really ready for it, and her confusion was genuine.

"Captain Codrington, this comes as such a surprise—"

"I do not see why. My admiration for you must be apparent, and the other day you led me to believe—" He hesitated, and then with a rush, "You even allowed me to embrace you."

Suddenly she was overcome with the urge to burst out laughing, if only he had known her further intentions toward him— but she skittered away from the subject, her expression as solemn as his.

"When would we be able to marry?" she asked instead.

"Well, on my return to—"

"There is a British consul at Zanzibar, and you are bound there, are you not?" she interrupted quickly. "He could perform the ceremony."

Clinton's face lit with slow, deep joy. "Oh, Miss Ballantyne, does this mean—can I take it that—" He took a pace toward her, and she had a vivid image of the tiny house in Portsmouth bursting at the seams with little blond replicas of himself, and she took a quick pace backward and went on hurriedly.

"I need time to think."

He stopped, joy faded and he said heavily, "Of course."

"It means such a change in my life, I would have to abandon all my plans. The expedition—it's such a big decision."

"I could wait—a year, longer if necessary. Until after the expedition, as long as you wished," he told her earnestly, and she felt a flutter of panic deep in her belly.

"No, I mean I need a few days, that is all," and she laid her hand on his forearm. "I will give you an answer before we reach Quelimane. I promise you that."

Sheikh Yussuf was a worried man. For eight days the big dhow-rigged vessel had lain within sight of land, the single huge lateen sail drooped from the long yard, the sea about her was velvet-smooth during the day and afire with phosphorus during the long moonless, windless nights.

So deep and utter was the calm that not the slightest swell moved the surface. The dhow lay so still that she might have been hard aground.

The Sheikh was a master mariner who owned a fleet of trading vessels and who for forty years had threaded the sea-ways of the Indian Ocean. He knew intimately each island, each headland and the tricks of the tides that swirled around them. He knew the roads that the currents cut across the waters the way a post coachman knows each turn and dip of the road between his stages, and he could run them without compass or sextant, steering only by the heavenly bodies a thousand miles and more across open water, making his unerring landfalls on the Horn of Africa, on the coast of India and back again on the island of Zanzibar.

In forty years he had never known the monsoon wind to fail for eight successive days at this season of the year. All his calculations had been based on the wind standing steady out of the southeast, day and night, hour after hour, day after day.

He had taken on his cargo with that expectation, calculating that he could discharge again on Zanzibar Island within six days of loading. Naturally, a man expected losses, they were an integral part of his calculations. Ten percent losses was the very least, twenty was more likely, thirty was acceptable, forty was always possible and even losses of fifty percent would still leave the voyage in profit.

But not this. He looked up at the stubby foremast from which drooped the fifteen-foot-long scarlet banner of the Sultan of Zanzibar, beloved of Allah, ruler of all the Omani Arabs and overlord of vast tracts of eastern Africa. The banner was faded and soiled as the lateen sail, both of them veterans of fifty such voyages, of calms and hurricanes, of baking sun and the driving torrential rains of the high monsoon. The golden Arabic script that covered the banner was barely legible now, and he had lost count of the number of times it had been taken down from the masthead and carried at the head of his column of armed men deep into the interior of that brooding land on the horizon.

How many times had that banner wafted out proudly, long and sinuous as a serpent on the breeze, as he brought his vessel up under the fort at Zanzibar Island. Sheikh Yussuf caught himself dreaming again. It was an old man's failing. He straightened up on the pile of cushions and precious rugs of silk and gold thread, and looked down from his command position on the poop deck. His crew lay like dead men in the shade of the sail, their grubby robes folded up over their heads against the heat. Let them lie, he decided, there was nothing mortal man could do now, except wait. It was in the hands of Allah now. "There is one God," he murmured. "And Mohammed is his prophet." It did not occur to him to question his fate, to rail or pray against it. It was God's will, and God is great.

Yet he could not help feeling regret. It was thirty years since he had taken such a fine cargo as this, and at prices that compared with those of thirty years before.

Three hundred and thirty black pearls, each one perfectly formed, young, by Allah, not one of them over sixteen years of age. They were of a people he had never encountered before, for he had never before traded so far south. It was only in this last season that he had heard of the new source of black pearl from beyond the Djinn Mountains, that forbidden land from which no man returned.

A new people, well favored and beautifully formed, strong and tall, sturdy limbs, not those sticklike legs of the people from beyond the lakes; these had full-moon faces and good strong white teeth. Sheikh Yussuf nodded over his pipe, the water bubbled softly in the bowl of the hookah at each inhalation and he let the smoke trickle out softly between his lips. It had stained his white beard yellow at the corners of his mouth, and at each lungful he felt the delightful lethargy steal through his old veins and take the edge off the cold frosts of age which seemed always now to chill his blood.

There was suddenly a higher-pitched shriek that rose above the low hubbub which enveloped the dhow. The sound was part of the ship, day and night it came up from the slave hold below the dhow's main deck.

Sheikh Yussuf removed the mouthpiece from his lips and cocked his head to listen, combing his fingers through his scraggling white beard—but the shriek was not repeated. It was perhaps the final cry from one of his fine black pearls.

Sheikh Yussuf sighed, the din from belowdecks had slowly decreased in volume while the dhow lay becalmed, and he was able to judge accurately how high his losses were by that volume. He knew he had already lost half of them. Another quarter at the very least would perish before he could reach Zanzibar, many more would go even after they were landed; only the very hardiest would be fit for the market, and then only after careful convalescence.

Another indication of his losses, though not as accurate, was the smell. Some of them must have gone on the very first day of the calm and without the wind the heat had been blinding. It would be even worse in the holds, the corpses would be swollen to twice life size. The smell was bad, he could not recall a worse stench in all his forty years. It was a pity that there was no way in which to remove the bodies, but this could only be done in port.

Sheikh Yussuf dealt only in young females. They were smaller and much hardier than males of the same age, and could be loaded more densely. He had been able to reduce the clearance between each deck by six inches, which meant an entire extra deck could be built into the hold.

Females had a remarkable ability to go without water for longer periods than the males, like the camel of the desert they seemed able to exist on the accumulated fat in their thighs, buttocks and bosoms, and to make the Mozambique passage even in the fairest conditions of wind and tide required five days without water.

Another consideration was the loss of males destined for China and the Far East by the necessary surgery. The Chinese buyers insisted that all male slaves be castrated before they would purchase. It was a logical precaution to prevent breeding with local populations, but one that entailed additional losses to the trader who must perform the operation.

The final reason that Sheikh Yussuf dealt only in comely young females was that they commanded a price almost twice that of a young male slave in the Zanzibar market.

Before Sheikh Yussuf loaded his wares, he allowed them to fatten for at least a week in his barracoons, with as much

141

to eat and drink as they could force down their throats. Then they were stripped naked, except for light chains, and at low tide taken out to the dhow where it lay high and dry on the shoaling beach.

The first girls aboard were made to lie on the bare boards of the hull in the bottom of the hold, each on her left side with her knees raised slightly so that the knees of the girl behind her could fit against the back of her legs, the front of her pelvis against buttocks, belly against back, like a row of spoons in a rack.

At intervals the chains were snapped into the ring bolts already set into the deck. This was not only for security but also to prevent the layer of human bodies sliding about in rough weather, piling up in heaps and crushing those beneath.

Once the bottom of the hold was covered with a layer of humanity, the next deck was placed in position over them, so close that they could not attempt to sit upright nor roll over. The next layer of girls was laid over them, and the next deck over them again.

To reach the lower decks meant laboriously unchaining and unloading each layer of humanity, and lifting the intervening decks. It could not even be attempted at sea. However, with the trade wind standing fair, it was a straight run down the channel and the wind blowing in through the canvas scoops and ports kept the air belowdecks breathable, and the heat bearable.

Sheikh Yussuf sighed again and lifted his rheumy eyes to the unbroken blue line of the eastern horizon.

"This will be my last voyage," he decided, whispering aloud in the way of old men. "Allah has been good and I am a rich man with many strong sons. Perhaps this is his sign to me. This will indeed be my last voyage."

It was almost as though he had been overheard, for the scarlet banner moved lazily, like an adder emerging from long hibernation, then slowly reared its head, and Sheikh Yussuf felt the wind on his seared and wrinkled cheek.

He stood up suddenly, quick and supple as a man half his age, and stamped his bare foot on the deck.

"Up," he cried. "Up, my children. Here is the wind at last." And while his crew scrambled to their feet, he took the long tiller under his arm and threw back his head to watch the sail bulge outward, and the thick clumsy pole of the mainmast heel slowly across a horizon suddenly dark with the scurry of the trade wind.

Clinton Codrington caught the first whiff of it during the night. It woke him from a nightmare that he had lived through on many other nights, but when he lay sweating in his narrow wooden bunk the smell persisted and he threw a boat cloak over his bare shoulders and hurried up on deck.

It came in gusts out of the darkness, for minutes at a time the warm sweet rush of the trade wind brought only the iodine and salt smell of the sea, then suddenly there was another curdled whiff of it. It was a smell that Clinton would never forget, like the smell of a cage full of carnivorous beasts that had never been cleaned, the stench of excrement and rotten flesh, and his nightmare came rushing back upon him in full strength.

Ten years before, when Clinton had been a very junior midshipman aboard the old *Widgeon*, one of the very first gunboats of the antislavery squadron, they had taken a slaver in northern latitudes. She was a schooner of three hundred tons' burden, out of Lisbon, but flying a Brazilian flag of convenience, with the unlikely name of *Hirondelle Blanche*, the *White Swallow*. Clinton had been ordered into her as prize master with orders to run her into the nearest Portuguese port and deliver her to the Courts of Mixed Commission to be condemned as a prize.

They had made the capture a hundred nautical miles off the Brazilian coast, after the *Hirondelle Blanche* and her five hundred black slaves had almost completed the dreaded middle passage. Under orders, Clinton had turned the schooner and sailed her back to the Cape Verde Islands, crossing the equator to do so and lying three days becalmed in the doldrums before breaking from their suffocating grip.

In the harbor of Praia, on the principal island of São Tiago, Clinton had been refused permission to land any of his slaves, and they had lain sixteen days waiting for the Portuguese president of the Court of Mixed Commission to reach a decision. Finally, the president had decided, after strenuous representation by the owners of the *Hirondelle Blanche* that he had no jurisdiction in the case, and ordered Clinton to sail her back to Brazil and submit the vessel to the Brazilian courts.

However, Clinton knew very well what a Brazilian court would decide, and instead set a course for the British naval station on St. Helena Island, once more crossing the equator with his burden of human misery.

By the time he dropped anchor in Jamestown roads, the

surviving slaves aboard had made three consecutive crossings of the terrible middle passage. There were only twenty-six of them still alive, and the smell of a slaver had become part of the nightmares which still plagued Clinton ten years later.

Now he stood on the darkened deck and flared his nostrils, the same smell coming to him out of the tropical night, horrible and unmistakable. He had to drag himself away with a physical effort to give the orders to fire *Black Joke*'s furnace and work up a head of steam in her boilers, ready for the dawn.

Sheikh Yussuf recognized the dark shape with a sense of utter disbelief, and the dismay of one finally deserted by Allah.

She was still five miles distant, indistinct in the dusty pink light of the dawn, but coming up swiftly, a thick column of black smoke smearing away on her beam, carried low over the green waters of the inshore channel by the boisterous trade wind. The same wind spread out her ensign to full view from the poop of the dhow, and in the field of Sheikh Yussuf's ancient brass and leather-bound telescope it snapped and flickered, the snowy white field crossed by bold bright scarlet.

How he hated that flag, the symbol of an arrogant, bullying people, tyrants of the oceans, captors of continents. He had seen gunboats like this one in Aden and Calcutta, he had seen that same flag flying in every far corner of every sea he had ever sailed. Very clearly he knew what it all meant.

He put up the helm, in that gesture acknowledging the final end to a disastrous voyage, the dhow came around reluctantly, creaking in every timber, the sail flogging before it could be trimmed to take the wind over the stern.

There had seemed to be so little risk, he thought with weary resignation. Of course, the treaty that the Sultan had made with the Zanzibar consul of these dangerous infidels allowed his subjects to trade in the black pearls, between any of the Sultan's possessions, with the proviso that only Omani Arabs loyal to the Sultan could indulge in the lucrative traffic. No person of Christian European extraction, not even a converted Moslem, could sail under the Sultan's flag, and not even an Omani Arab might trade beyond the borders of the Sultan's possessions.

The Sultan's African possessions had been very carefully defined in the treaty, and here was he, Sheikh Yussuf, with a cargo of three hundred and thirty living, dying and dead slaves at least one hundred and fifty miles south of the furthest of the Sultan's borders, with a British gunboat bearing down upon him. Truly the ways of Allah were wonderful, passing the comprehension of man, Sheikh Yussuf thought with only the slightest taste of bitterness in his throat, as he hung grimly onto the tiller and made his run for the land.

A gun thumped from the gunboat's bows, powder smoke flew bright as a seabird's wing in the first rays of the low sun, and Sheikh Yussuf spat passionately over the lee bulwark and said aloud, "El Sheetan, the Devil," using for the first time the name with which, in time, Captain Clinton Codrington would be known through the length of the Mozambique channel, and as far north as the great Horn of Africa.

The bronze screw under *Black Joke*'s counter thrashed out a long wide wake behind her. She still had main and jib set, but Codrington would shorten to "fighting sail" just as soon as he had made the adjustment to counter the dhow's turn away toward the land.

Zouga and Robyn were on the quarterdeck to watch the chase, infected by the restrained businesslike excitement which gripped the vessel so that Zouga laughed aloud and called, "Gone away! Tallyho!" as the dhow turned, and Clinton glanced at him with a conspiratory grin.

"She's a slaver. Apart from the stink, that turnaway proves it beyond doubt."

Robyn strained forward to watch the filthy little vessel, with its discolored and patched sail, the unpainted timbers of the hull marked with zebra stripes of human excrement and other wastes. It was her first view of a slaver actually carrying on its grisly trade, and she felt herself filled with a new purpose; she had come so far for this moment, and she tried to capture every detail of it all for her journal.

"Mr. Denham, give him a gun, if you please," ordered Clinton.

The bow chaser thudded, but the dhow held to her new course.

"Be ready to round up and send the boat away on the instant." Clinton's excitement had given way to obvious anxiety. He turned to look across at his boarding party. They had been issued with cutlass and pistol, and waited now in the waist under the command of a young ensign.

Clinton would dearly have liked to command the boarding party himself, but his arm was still in its sling and the stitches still in the wound. To go aboard a dhow in a rough sea and fight its crew required both hands and the agility which his

145

wound denied him. Reluctantly he had put Ferris in charge of the boarders.

Now he looked back at the dhow, and his expression was grim.

"He is going to beach."

They were all silent now, staring ahead, watching the slaver run in toward the land.

"But there is a coral reef." Robyn spoke for them all, pointing to the black ridges that broke the surface a quarter of a mile short of the land itself, they looked like a necklace of shark's teeth, and the surf broke and swirled about them as it was driven in upon the trade wind.

"Yes," Clinton agreed. "They will run it up on the coral and escape across the lagoon."

"But what about the slaves?" Robyn asked, horrified, and nobody answered her.

Black Joke rushed on purposefully, but with the wind almost dead astern the dhow trained her long boom around to go on to her best point of sailing. The boom was longer than the hull itself, and the huge triangular mainsail bulged far out, almost touching the surface of the water as she hurled down upon the reef.

"We may just cut her off," Zouga said loudly, but he did not have the seaman's eye for bearing and speed, and Clinton Codrington shook his head angrily.

"Not this time."

But it was very finely run. Clinton held his course up until the very last moment, and the dhow passed a mere two hundred yards ahead of his bows. So close that they could clearly make out the features of the helmsman on the vessel's poop deck, a skinny old Arab in long, flowing robe and with the tasseled fez on his head that declared that he had made the pilgrimage to Mecca. On his belt glittered the gold filigree hilt of the short curved dagger of a sheikh, and his long scraggling white beard fluttered in the wind as he leaned on the tiller and turned his head to watch the high black hull bearing down on him.

"I could put a bullet through the bastard," Zouga growled.

"It's too late for that," Clinton told him, for the dhow had passed beneath their bows and the gunboat was as close to the menacing fangs of coral as she dared go. Clinton called to his quartermaster at the gunboat's wheel, "Heave to! And bring her head to wind." Then, spinning on his heel, "Away, the boarding party!"

There was a squeal of davits as the crowded whaler dropped

out of sight toward the choppy green sea alongside, but already the dhow was pitching wildly in the lines of seething white surf that guarded the reef.

It was two days since that dead flat calm had broken, and since then the trades had worked up a goodly swell. It came sweeping in across the inshore channel, in low green humps with dark wind-scarred backs, but as soon as they felt the tilt of the land, they peaked up eagerly, the crests turning opaque as green jelly, shivering and wobbling, and then collapsing on themselves and surging in tumultuous white water up onto the black fangs of the reef.

The dhow caught one of the taller swells, threw up her stern and went racing down upon it like a surf boat, with the skinny old Arab at the tiller prancing like a trained monkey on the stick of the tiller to hold her in the wave, but the dhow was not built for this work, and she dug her shoulder rebelliously into the sliding, roaring chute of water, breaching so fiercely to the wave that the water poured aboard her in a green wall and she wallowed broadside, half swamped before she took the reef with a force that snapped off her single mast at deck level and sent yard and sail and rigging crashing over the side.

In an instant she was transformed into a broken hulk, and clearly the watchers on *Black Joke*'s deck could hear the crackle and rending of her bottom timbers.

"There they go!" Clinton muttered angrily, as the dhow's crew began to abandon her, leaping over the side and using the swells to carry them over the reef into the quieter waters of the lagoon, thrashing and kicking until the beach shelved up beneath them.

They saw the old Arab steersman among the survivors. He waded ashore, beard and robe plastered against his body with seawater, and then lifted his robes to his waist, exposing skinny legs and shrunken buttocks as he scampered up the white beach with the agility of a goat and disappeared among the palm groves.

Black Joke's whaler pulled swiftly into the first line of breakers, the ensign in the stern peering over his shoulder to judge the surf, and then catching his wave taking her in with a rush, swinging sharply into the lee of the dhow's stranded hull where there was calmer water.

They watched the ensign and four of his men go up over the side, pistols and cutlasses drawn, but by this time the last of the Arab crew were staggering up the beach and into the sanctuary of the palm grove a quarter of a mile away across the lagoon.

The ensign led his men belowdecks, and they waited on *Black Joke*'s quarterdeck, watching the abandoned dhow through the telescope. A minute passed before the ensign appeared on deck again. He crossed quickly to the dhow's rail and leaned against it to vomit over the side, then straightened up and wiped his mouth on the back of his sleeve, before shouting an order down to the oarsmen in the whaler.

Immediately the whaler shot out from the lee of the hull, and pulled lustily back through the surf toward *Black Joke*.

The boatswain came in through the entry port, and knuckled his forehead to his captain.

"Mr. Ferris's compliments, sir, and he needs a carpenter to get the slave decks open, and two good men with bolt cutters for the chains." He had gabbled this out on a single breath, and he paused to refill his lungs. "Mr. Ferris says as how it's fierce bad belowdecks, and some of them is trapped—and he needs the doctor—"

"I'm ready to go," Robyn cut in.

"Wait," Clinton snapped, but Robyn had gathered her skirts and run.

"If my sister goes, I'm going too."

"Very well, then, Ballantyne, I'm obliged for your assistance," Clinton nodded. "Tell Ferris we have an incoming tide, full moon tonight, so it will make springs. There is a twenty-two-foot tidal fall on this coast. He will have less than an hour in which to work."

Robyn appeared on deck again, lugging her black leather valise, and she exchanged skirts for breeches once more. The seamen on deck gawked at her legs curiously, but she ignored them and hurried to the ship's side. The boatswain gave her a hand and she scrambled down into the whaler with Zouga carrying her valise behind her.

The ride in through the surf was terrifying and exhilarating at the same time; the whaler tilted forward at an alarming angle, the water hissing and creaming alongside, with a belly-swooping rush that ended alongside the dhow's heavily canted side.

The deck was running with water and listed so steeply that Robyn had to crawl up it on her hands and knees, and each time a wave struck the hull, it quivered and shook and more water came streaming down over the deck.

The ensign and his boarding party had ripped the hatches off the main hold, and as she reached them, Robyn gagged

148

and choked with the solid stench that came out of that square opening. She had believed herself hardened to the smell of death and corruption, but never had she experienced anything like this.

"Did you bring the bolt cutters?" the ensign demanded, whitefaced with nausea and horror.

The bolt cutters were heavy-duty shears, used for cutting the shrouds and halyards from a dismasted vessel. Two men wielded them now, as they lifted a bunch of small black bodies through the hatch, all of them fastened together at wrist and ankle by the clanking black steel links. It reminded Robyn of the cut-out paper dolls she had amused herself with as a child, fashioning with scissors a single figure from the folded sheet, and then pulling out a chain of identical dolls. The cutters crunched through the light chain and the limp little bodies fell apart.

"They are children," she cried out aloud, and the men around her worked in grim silence, dragging them out of the hatch, cutting them free and dropping them onto the tilted wet deck.

Robyn seized the first of them, a skeletal stick figure, crusted and streaked with dried filth, vomit, feces, head lolling as she lifted it into her lap.

"No." There was no life. The eyeballs had dried already. She let the head drop and a seaman dragged it away.

"No," and "No," and "No again." Some of them were already in an advanced state of putrification; at a word from the ensign, the seamen began dropping the wasted corpses over the side, to make room for those still coming up from below.

Robyn found her first live one, there was feeble pulse and fluttering breath, but it did not need a physician's instinct to tell that the hold on life was tenuous. She worked swiftly, apportioning her time to where the chance of life seemed greater.

Another taller wave struck the dhow, and it tilted sharply, the timbers crackled and snapped deep inside her.

"Tides flooding. Work faster," shouted the ensign. They were into the hull now. Robyn could hear the thud of sledge-hammers and the rip of irons as they began to tear the slave decks out of her.

Zouga was in there, stripped to the waist, leading the attack on the wooden barricades. He was an officer, with the easy way of command, and his natural leadership was swiftly acknowledged by the seamen around him.

The hubbub reminded Robyn of a rookery at sundown, the shrieks of the returning birds and the answering cries from the

149

chicks in the nests. The mass of black girls were aroused from
the lethargy of approaching death by the dhow's wild antics,
the crash of breaking timbers and the flood of cold salt water
into the hold.

Some of those lying in the bilges were already drowning as
the hold flooded, and some of them had realized that there was
a rescue team aboard, and cried aloud with the last strength of
waning hope.

Alongside the slaver, the whaler was moored, and she was
almost filled with the wasted bodies in which some life still
burned, while on the surface of the lagoon bobbed a hundred
or more corpses with gas-swollen bellies like the corks on a
fishing-net.

"Take them to the ship," the ensign shouted down to his
oarsmen in the whaler, "and come back for more." As he spoke,
another white-crested wave struck the dhow solidly and she
heeled, but she was pinned down by the spikes of coral driven
through her bottom timbers, otherwise she would have turned
turtle.

"Robyn!" Zouga shouted at her from the hatch. "We need
you!"

For a moment she did not even glance at him, but shook
her head at the sailor beside her.

"No, she's gone." Expressionlessly the sailor picked up the
frail body and dumped it over the side.

Then Robyn scrambled up to the hatch and dropped through
it.

It was a descent into the pit, dark after the brilliant noontide,
so that she paused for a moment to let her vision adjust.

The tilting deck beneath her feet was slippery with human
waste, so that she had to cling for a handhold.

The air was so thick that for a minute she nearly panicked,
as though she were being smothered by a stinking damp pillow.
She almost fought her way back into the sweet sunlight, but
then she forced herself to take a gulp of it, and though her guts
heaved and she tasted the bitter flooding into the back of her
throat, she kept it down.

Then her own discomfort was forgotten as she made out the
chaos about her.

"That last wave," Zouga grunted as he steadied her with an
arm about her shoulder, "the decks have collapsed."

Like a house of cards they had folded in upon each other,
raw splinters of timber thrusting up out of the gloom, balks
crossed like the blades of a scissors, with small bodies trapped

in the jaws, others crushed by the fallen beams, squashed so that they were no longer recognizable as human, others dangling head down on their ankle-chains, suspended in space, writhing weakly as crippled insects, or hanging quietly, swinging to the dhow's movements.

"Oh, sweet Mother of God, where to begin?" Robyn whispered. She let go her handhold, starting forward, and her feet shot out from under her on the slick-coated deck, and she went plunging down into the hold.

She struck heavily and pain flared in her back and lower body, but she dragged herself onto her knees. Her own pain seemed insignificant in this terrible prison.

"Are you all right?" Zouga asked anxiously, but she shrugged his hands away.

There was one girl screaming, Robyn crawled to her. Her legs were crushed below the knees, trapped under a balk of hand-hewn timber.

"Can you move that?" she asked Zouga.

"No, she's done for. Come, there are others—"

"No." Robyn crawled back to where her bag had fallen. The pain was bad, but she forced it below the surface of her consciousness.

She had only seen a leg amputation performed once before. When she started the girl threw off the seamen who held her and attacked Robyn like a tortured wildcat. Her nails raked skin from Robyn's cheek, but by the time Robyn had freed the first leg below the knee, the child was silent and limp. She died before Robyn had reached the bone of the second leg, and Robyn was weeping chokingly to herself as she left the body still hanging in the grip of the timber balk.

She scrubbed her hands together, they were bloodied to the elbows, her palms sticky against each other. She felt consumed by guilt at her failure, without the strength to move. Dully, she stared about her now.

The hold was more than half flooded, the tide pounded remorselessly at the ship's hull.

"We have to get out," Zouga called to her urgently, and when she did not turn her head, he seized her shoulder and shook her roughly. "There's nothing more we can do. It will capsize at any moment."

Robyn was staring down into the stinking black waters which sloshed from one end of the hold to the other, a single hand broke through the surface directly below her, a child's hand with soft pink palm and pretty tapered fingers spread in a gesture of appeal. The iron cuff seemed too large for the narrow wrist, and weighted it down so the hand sank gently, disappearing from her sight. She stared after it with infinite regret, then Zouga hauled her roughly to her feet.

"Come on, damn it!" His face was savage, haunted with the horrors he had experienced in this fetid, half-flooded hull.

The next wave hit the swamped hull, and this time it broke the grip of the coral. Timber squealed as it twisted and tore, and the dhow began to roll, the filthy waters rose up into a steep wave and burst about them, shoulder-deep.

The damaged slave decks broke free, sliding down over each other, tumultuous and lethal, releasing a fresh layer of tightly packed bodies to tumble loosely into the flooded depths.

"Robyn! We'll be trapped." He dragged her up toward the square of brilliant sunlight, clambering over timbers and bodies.

"We can't leave them," Robyn resisted.

"They're finished, damn it. The whole thing is going. We have to get out."

She pulled her arm free, stumbled, collapsed backward, hit something so that pain flared through her lower body again and she cried out with the strength of it. She was lying on her side, couched on a pile of linked bodies, and there was a face a foot from hers. It was alive, she had never seen such eyes, cat fierce, falcon bright, the color of boiling honey.

"This one is strong enough!" Robyn thought, and then she shouted. "Help me, Zouga."

"For God's sake, Robyn."

She crawled forward and reached the child, and the deck tilted viciously under her, fresh cold water bursting into the hull.

"Leave her," shouted Zouga.

The fresh flood swirled up around Robyn's head, and the chained girl disappeared below it.

Robyn lunged for her, groping blindly below the surface, feeling panic rise in her when she could not find the child.

Ducking her head under, choking as the pain in her belly made her gasp and she swallowed water, she at last got a grip on the girl's shoulder, feeling her struggling as desperately as she.

Together they came out above the surface, coughing and gasping weakly, Robyn holding the girl's mouth just clear of the surface, but when she tried to lift her further the chain anchored them both and she screamed.

152

"Zouga, help me!"

Another surge of water, smelling like raw sewage, filled her mouth and both of them went under once more.

She thought she would never come up again, but stubbornly she held on, sliding one arm under the girl's armpit, and with the other hand gripping her chin, forcing it up so that when they broke out again the girl's face was lifted to take another precious breath of the awful air, and Zouga was with them.

He took a double turn of the chain around his wrists and threw all his weight onto it. In the gloom of the hull he towered over them, the light from the hatch highlighting the bulging wet muscles in his arms and shoulders as he strained at the chain, his mouth opened in a silent scream of effort, sinewy cords standing out of his throat.

Another wave hissed over them, and this time Robyn was not ready for it, she felt the burn of it in her lungs and knew she was drowning. She need only release her hold on the girl's head and shoulders and she would be free to breathe, but she held on stubbornly, determined suddenly that she would never let this little soul go. She had seen it in the girl's eyes, the fierce will to live. This one she could save, this one out of three hundred or more was the only one she could be certain of saving. She had to have her.

The wave receded and Zouga was still there, his hair streaming with water, slicked down over his face and into his eyes, and now he shifted slightly, jamming his legs against one of the heavy timbers, and he reared back once more against the chain, and a low bellow broke from his throat in the agony of effort.

The ring bolt that held the loop of chain to the deck ripped out cleanly, and Zouga dragged both women clear of the water, the chain slithering after them for ten feet or more before coming up hard against the next ring bolt.

Robyn had never suspected Zouga capable of such strength; she had never seen his naked upper body—not since he was a child—had not realized that he had the lean hard muscle of a prizefighter. But even so, he could not repeat the effort, and the girl was still chained. They had won only a temporary respite. Zouga was bellowing now, and the young naval ensign scrambled down through the open hatch. To reenter the doomed hull was an act of courage in itself, Robyn realized, as she saw that the ensign carried the cutting shears, lugging the heavy tool with him as he floundered toward the struggling group in the bottom of the hold.

The hull rolled through another five degrees, the water swirling higher toward them hungrily, it sucked at their at their bodies. Had not Zouga given them the extra few feet of chain they would be far below the surface now.

Zouga stooped over her and helped her hold the girl's head above the water, while the ensign groped for the chain links and fed them into the jaws of the shears. But the blades had been blunted and chipped by the heavy work they had already done, and the ensign was still only a lad. Zouga pushed him aside.

Again muscle bunched in his shoulders and upper arms and the chain parted with a metallic clunk. Zouga cut twice at ankle and at wrist, then he dropped the shears, picked the frail naked body up against his chest and climbed frantically up toward the hatch.

Robyn tried to follow him, but something tore deep in her belly, she felt it go, tearing like brittle parchment, and the pain was a lance that transfixed her. She doubled over it, clutching herself, unable to move, and the wave hit her, knocking her down, swirling her over the broken timbers into the water, and the void began to fill her head. There was temptation to let go now, to let the water and darkness take her, it would be so easy, but she gathered her anger and her obstinacy to her and went on fighting. She was still fighting when Zouga reached her, and dragged her up toward the light.

As they crawled out through the hatch into the sunlight, so the dhow rolled all the way, flinging them as though from a catapult over the side into the shocking cold of the green waters.

When the dhow capsized the last faint cries from within her were extinguished, and the hull began to break up under the remorseless hammer of the sea. When Robyn and Zouga surfaced, still clinging together, the whaler was hovering over them, the ensign risking all to come in over the reef for the pickup.

Strong hands reached down, and the overladen boat heeled dangerously as they were pulled aboard. Then the ensign swung the bows to meet the next boiling line of surf and they climbed its steep side and crashed over the top, the seamen pulling frantically to hold her bows on.

Robyn crawled to where the girl lay on a heap of other bodies in the bottom of the boat, her relief at finding her aboard and still alive outweighing the pain of her sodden lungs and the deep ache in her belly.

Robyn rolled the girl on to her back, and lifted her lolling head to cushion it from the pounding of the whaler's hull over the steep swells that threatened to crack her skull against the floorboards.

She saw immediately that the girl was older than she had imagined, although the body was desiccated and wasted. Yet her pelvis had the breadth of maturity, She would be sixteen years old at least, Robyn thought, and pulled a corner of the tarpaulin over her body to screen her from the men's gaze.

The girl opened her eyes again, and stared at Robyn solemnly. Those eyes were still the color of dark honey, but the ferocity had dimmed to some other emotion as she looked up into Robyn's face.

"Ngi ya bonga," the girl whispered, and with a shock Robyn realized that she understood the words. She was transported in an instant to another land and another woman, her mother, Helen Ballantyne, teaching her those same words, repeating them to her until Robyn had them perfected

"Ngi ya bonga, I praise you!"

Robyn tried to find a reply, but her mind was as battered as her body, and it had been so long ago that she had learned the language, the circumstances so different that the worlds came only haltingly.

"Velapi wena, who are you and from where do you come?"

The girl's eyes flew wide with shock.

"You!" she whispered. "You speak the language of the people."

They had taken on board twenty-eight living black girls. By the time *Black Joke* got under way again and turned from the land, toward the open sea, the dhow's hull had burst open and the planking and timbers swung and pitched end over end as they sawed across the exposed reef.

A squawking raucous flock of seabirds squabbled over the reef, hovering above the gruesome remnants that were mixed in the floating debris of the wreck, dropping to seize a tidbit and rise again on delicate fans of pearly wings.

In the deeper water along the seaward side of the reef, the shark packs were gathering, lashing themselves into a frenzy, the stubby rounded triangles of their dorsal fins crisscrossing the sweep of the current, while every few seconds a long torpedo-shaped body would break clear of the surface in an ecstasy of greed, falling back heavily with a boom like distant cannon as it struck the surface.

Twenty-eight from three hundred and more was no great

haul, Robyn thought, as she hobbled along the line of barely living bodies, her own bruised limbs protesting every step, and her despair deepened as she realized how far gone they were. It was easy to see which of them had already lost the will to resist. She had read her father's treatise on the sick African, and she knew how important was the will to resist. A perfectly healthy man could will himself to die, and once he did so there was nothing that could save him.

That night, despite Robyn's constant attention, twenty-two of the girls died and were carried aft to be dropped over *Black Joke*'s stern. By morning, all the others were sinking into the coma and fever of renal failure, their kidneys, shriveled and atrophied by lack of fluid, were no longer filtering the urinal wastes from the bodies' systems. There was only one treatment and that was to force the patient to drink.

The little Nguni girl resisted strongly. Robyn knew that she belonged to the Nguni group of peoples, although she was uncertain of which tribe, for many of them spoke variations of the original Zulu, and the girl's accent and pronunciation had been strange to Robyn's ear.

Robyn had tried to keep her talking, keep her conscious and keep the will to resist burning in her. She had conceived an almost maternal possessiveness for the child, and though she tried to spread her attention fairly among the other survivors, she always returned to where the girl lay under a strip of tarpaulin and held the pannikin of weak sugar solution to her lips.

They shared only a few hundred words in which to converse, as the girl rested between each painful sip of fluid.

"I am called Juba," the child whispered, in answer to Robyn's question. Even the sound of it brought back to Robyn the memory of the cooing of the plump blue-gray ring-necked doves in the wild fig trees that grew above the mission cottage in which she had been born.

"Little Dove. It is a pretty name." And the girl smiled shyly, and went on in that dry tortured whisper. Much of it Robyn could not follow, but she listened and nodded, realizing with a pang that the sense of it was going, Juba was sinking into delirium, that she was talking to phantoms from her past. Now she tried to resist when Robyn forced her to drink, muttering and crying out in fear or anger, gagging on the tiny mouthfuls of liquid.

"You must rest yourself," Zouga told Robyn brusquely.

"You have been with her for almost two days without sleeping. You're killing yourself."

"I am quite well, thank you," Robyn told him, but her face was gray with fatigue and pain.

"At least let me take you down to your cabin."

By this time Juba was the only girl still alive, all the others had gone over the stern to feed the following shark pack.

"Very well," Robyn agreed, and Zouga carried the child down from the makeshift shelter on the aft deck which Robyn had used as a surgery.

The steward brought a canvas pallet filled with straw and laid it on the deck of Robyn's tiny cabin. There was only just room for it, and Zouga laid the naked body upon it.

Robyn was tempted to stretch out on her own narrow bunk to rest for a while, but she knew that if she let go now, even for a moment, she would fall into a deathlike sleep, and her patient would die of such neglect.

Alone in the cabin, she sat cross-legged on the straw pallet, wedged her back against the sea chest, and lifted Juba into her lap. Doggedly she went on with the task of forcing liquid between the girl's lips, drop by drop, hour after hour.

Through the single port, the light turned to a ruby glow at the short tropical sunset and then it swiftly faded. It was almost completely dark in the cabin when suddenly Robyn felt a copious warm flood soak through her skirts into her lap, and she smelled the strong ammoniacal taint of the girl's urine.

"Thank you, God," she whispered. "Oh, thank you, God!" The girl's kidneys were functioning again, she was safe. Robyn rocked the girl in her lap, feeling no revulsion from her soaked skirts, welcoming them as the promise of life.

"You did it," she whispered. "You did, with sheer pluck, my little dove."

She had just enough strength left herself to wipe down the child's body with a cloth soaked in seawater, then she stepped out of her soiled dress and collapsed facedown on her hard narrow bunk.

Robyn slept for ten hours, until the cramps woke her groaning. Her knees were drawn up against her chest by the severity of the pain, and her belly muscles were as hard as stone and it felt as though she had been clubbed across the back, a deep bruised sensation that alarmed her seriously.

For many minutes after waking she believed herself seriously stricken, and then with a rush of relief and joy that was far stronger than the pain she realized what was happening to her. She dragged herself across the cabin, doubled over with the pain, and bathed in the bucket of cold seawater. Then she knelt beside Juba on the pallet.

The girl's fever had abated. The skin felt cooler to the touch. Her continued recovery added to Robyn's sense of relief. Now she would have to find the right moment to tell Clinton Codrington that she would not marry him, and the vision of the little house above the Portsmouth harbor receded. Despite the pain, she felt free, light of body, like a bird poised on the point of flight.

She filled the pannikin with water and lifted Juba's head.

"We will be all right now," she told the girl, and Juba opened her eyes.

"We'll both be all right now," she repeated, watching the girl drink thirstily, smiling happily to herself.

Juba's recovery was swift. Soon she ate with a robust appetite. Her body filled almost before Robyn's eyes, her skin took on the luster of health and youth again, her eyes regained the sparkle of high spirits—and Robyn realized with proprietorial approval that she was a pretty girl, no more than that, she had natural grace and poise, the voluptuous curve of bosom and buttock which ladies of high fashion tried to achieve with bustle and padded bodice. She possessed also a sweet moon face, the big wide-set eyes and full sculptured lips that were exotic and strangely beautiful.

Juba could not understand Robyn's concern with having her cover her breasts and legs, but Robyn had seen the seamen's eyes when the girl followed her up onto the deck with only a scrap of canvas covering the most vital point of her anatomy and showing no concern at all when the wind lifted the canvas and fluttered it like a beckoning flag. Robyn commandeered one of Zouga's oldest shirts. It hung to Juba's knees and she belted it at the waist with a bright ribbon that had the child cooing with the eternal feminine delight in pretty things.

She followed Robyn about like a puppy, and Robyn's ear tuned to the Nguni language. Her vocabulary expanded swiftly, and the two of them chatted late every night, sitting side by side on the straw pallet.

Clinton Codrington began showing acute signs of jealousy. He had become used to having more of her company, and Robyn was using the girl as an excuse to taper off their relationship, preparing him for the news that she must deliver before they reached Quelimane.

Zouga also disapproved of her growing intimacy with the girl.

"Sissy, you must remember that she is a native. It never pays to let them get too familiar," Zouga told her gravely. "I've seen that happen too often in India. One has to keep one's reserve. After all, you are an Englishwoman."

"And she is a Matabele of Zanzi blood, which makes her an aristocrat, for her family came up with Mzilikazi from the south. Her father was a famous general and she can trace her bloodline back to Senzangakhona, the King of the Zulu, and the father of Chaka himself. We, on the other hand, can trace our family as far as great-grandfather, who was a cattleherd."

Zouga's expression stiffened. He did not enjoy discussing the family origins.

"We are English. The greatest and most civilized people in the world's history."

"Grandfather Moffat knows Mzilikazi," Robyn pointed out, "and thinks him a great gentleman."

"You are being foolish," Zouga snapped. "How can you compare the English race to these bloodthirsty savages?" But he stooped out of the cabin for he did not wish to continue the discussion. As usual, Robyn had her facts correct and her logic was infuriating.

His own grandfather, Robert Moffat, had first met Mzilikazi back in '29 and over the years the two men had become firm and trusted friends. The King relied on Moffat, whom he called Tshedi, for counsel in his dealings with the world beyond his borders and for medical treatment for the gout which plagued him as he grew older.

The route northward to the land of the Matabele always passed through Robert Moffat's mission station at Kuruman. A prudent traveler would ask for a safe conduct from the old missionary, and the Matabele impis guarding the Burnt Land along the border would honor that safe conduct.

Indeed, the ease with which Fuller Ballantyne had moved through the wild, untamed tribes along the Zambezi River as far west as Lake Ngami, unmolested and unharmed, was in great part due to his relationship with Robert "Tshedi" Moffat. The mantle of protection which the Matabele King spread over his old friend extended to his immediate family, and was recognized by all the tribes within range of the Matabele long arm, an arm that wielded the assegai, the terrible stabbing spear which King Chaka of the Zulu had first conceived, and with which he had conquered his known world.

In his pique at Robyn's comparison of the ancestry of his family and that of the pretty half-naked black girl, Zouga at first missed the significance of what she had told him. When it struck him, he hurried back to Robyn's cabin.

"Sissy," he burst out excitedly. "If she comes from Mzilikazi country—why! that's almost a thousand miles due west of Quelimane. She must have passed through the land of Monomatapa to reach this coast. Get her to tell about it."

He regretted his childhood inattention to the language when his mother had taught them. He concentrated savagely now as the two girls chatted animatedly, and began recognizing some of the words, but it needed Robyn to translate the full sense for him.

Juba's father was a famous induna, a warrior who had fought the Boers at Mosega, and a hundred other battles since then; his shield had been thick with the tassels of cow tails, black and white, each of which signified a heroic deed.

He had been granted the headring of the induna when he was still a young man of less than thirty summers, and had become one of the highest elders in the council of the nation. He had fifty wives, many of them of pure Zanzi blood like his own, a hundred and twelve sons and uncounted daughters. Although all the cattle of the nation belonged to the King, yet over five thousand were put in charge of Juba's father, a mark of the King's high favor.

He was a great man—perhaps too great for his own safety. Somebody whispered the word "treason" in the King's ear, and the King's executioners had surrounded the kraal in the dawn, and called out Juba's father.

He had stooped out through the low entrance of his thatched beehive hut, naked from the embrace of his favorite wife.

"Who calls?" he cried into the dawn, and then he saw the ring of black figures, tall in their feather headdresses, but standing motionless, silent and menacing.

"In the King's name," a voice answered him, and out of the ranks stepped a figure he recognized immediately. It was one of the King's indunas also, a man named Bopa, a short powerful man with a deep-muscled bare chest and a head so heavy that the broad features seemed to have been carved out of a chunk of granite from the kopjes across the Nyati River.

There was no appeal, no escape, not that either consideration even passed briefly through the old induna's mind.

"In the King's name." That was sufficient. Slowly he drew himself to his full height. Despite the gray cap of his hair, he was still a finely built warrior with broad rangy shoulders and the ridged battle scars crawled across his chest and flanks like live serpents.

"The Black Elephant," he began to recite the praise names of his King. "Bayete! The Thunder of the Heavens. The Shaker of the Earth. Bayete!"

Still calling the King's names he went down on one knee, and the King's executioner stepped up behind him.

The wives and elder children had crawled from their huts now, and huddled together in dread, watching from the shadows, their voices blending in a single cry of horror and sorrow as the executioner drove his short thick-bladed assegai between the induna's shoulder blades, and two hands' breadth out of his chest. As he withdrew the blade, there was the crude sucking sound of steel leaving flesh and the old induna's life blood spurted head-high as he fell forward onto his face.

With his smeared red blade the King's executioner commanded his warriors forward, for the sentence of death included the old man's wives, every one of their sons and daughters, the household slaves, and their children, every inhabitant of the large village, three hundred or more souls.

The executioners worked swiftly, but there was a change in the ancient ritual of death. The old women, the gray-headed slaves, died swiftly, not honored with the blade but clubbed to death with the heavy knobkerries that each warrior carried. The infants, and unweaned toddlers were snatched up by the ankles, and their brains were dashed from their skulls against the trunk of a tree, against the heavy poles of the cattle enclosure or against a convenient rock. It was very swift, for the warriors were highly trained and disciplined troops and this was something they had done many times before.

Yet this time there was a difference: the younger women, the adolescent children, even those on the verge of puberty, were hustled forward and the King's executioner glanced at them appraisingly, and with a gesture of the bloody spear sent them left or right.

On the left hand was swift death, while those who were sent right were forced into a trot and led away toward the east, toward the sunrise as the girl Juba explained it to Robyn.

"Many days we traveled," her voice sinking, the horror of it still in the brown eyes. "I do not know how long it was. Those who fell were left where they lay, and we went on."

"Ask her what she remembers of the country," Zouga demanded.

"There were rivers," the girl replied. "Many rivers and great mountains." Her memories were confused, she could make no estimates of distance, they had encountered no other people, no villages nor towns, they had seen no cattle nor standing crops. Juba shook her head to each of Zouga's questions, and when he showed her the Harkness map in a forlorn hope that she might be able to point out features upon it, the child giggled in confusion. Drawn symbols on parchment were beyond her comprehension, she could not begin to relate them to features of landscape.

"Tell her to go on," he ordered Robyn impatiently .

"At the end we passed through deep gorges in high mountains where the slopes were covered with tall trees, and the rivers fell with white spray, until at last we came to where the *bunu*—the white men—waited."

"The white men?" Robyn demanded.

"Men of your people," the girl nodded. "With no color skin and eyes. There were many men, some white and others brown or black men, but dressed as the white men were dressed, and armed with the *isibamu,* with guns." The Matabele people knew well the power and effect of firearms, they had encountered enemies armed with them at least thirty years before. Even some of the Matabele indunas carried muskets, although they always handed these to a servant to carry when there was serious fighting in the offing.

"These people had built kraals, such as we build for our cattle, but these were filled with people, a multitude of people, and with them we were bound with the *insimbi,* the links of iron." She rubbed her wrists instinctively at the memory, and the callouses raised by the slave cuffs still blemished the skin of her forearms.

"Each day that we stayed at this place in the mountains, more people came. Sometimes only as many as the fingers on both your hands, on other days there were so many we could hear their lamentations at a distance. And always there were warriors guarding them.

"Then before the sun one morning, at the time of the horns—" Robyn recalled the expression for the time of dawning when the horns of the cattle first show against the morning sky—"they led us from the kraals, wearing the *insimbi,* and we formed a snake of people so long that the head was out of sight ahead of me in the forest while the tail was still up in the clouds of the mountains when we came down the Hyena Road."

"The Hyena Road, *Ndlele unfisi.*" It was the first time that

Robyn had heard the name spoken. It conjured up an image of a shadowed trail through the forests, beaten by tens of thousands of bare feet, with the loathsome eaters of dead flesh slinking along beside it, chuckling and shrieking their inane chorus.

"Those that died, and those that fell and could not rise again were released from their chains and dragged to one side. The *fisi* have grown so bold along the road that they rushed out of the bushes and devoured the bodies while we passed in full sight. It was worst when the body still lived."

Juba broke off and stared unseeingly at the bulkhead across the cabin. Slowly her eyes filled with tears, and Robyn took her hand and held it in her lap.

"I know not how long we followed the Hyena Road," Juba went on, "for each day became as the one before it, and as the one that followed it, until at last we came to the sea."

Afterward Zouga and Robyn discussed the girl's story.

"She must have gone through the kingdom of Monomatapa, and yet she says there were no towns nor signs of occupation."

"The slavers might have avoided contact with Monomatapa's people."

"I wish she had seen and remembered more."

"She was in a slave caravan," Robyn pointed out. "Survival was her only concern."

"If only these damned people could even read a map."

"It's a different culture, Zouga," and he saw the flash in her eye, and sensed the drift of the conversation and turned it aside swiftly.

"Perhaps the legend of Monomatapa is only a myth, perhaps there are no gold mines."

"The important thing about Juba's story is that the Matabele are dealing in slaves; they have never done so before."

"Nonsense!" grunted Zouga. "They are the biggest predators since Genghis Khan! They and all the Zulu splinter tribes— the Shángaan, the Angoni and the Matabele. War is their way of life, and plunder is their main crop. Their whole nation was built on a system of slave-taking."

"But they have never sold them before," said Robyn mildly. "At least as far as we know from all that grandfather and Harris and the others have written."

"The Matabele never found a market before," Zouga replied reasonably. "Now they have at last made contact with the slavemasters, and found an opening to the coast. That was all it lacked before."

"We must witness this, Zouga," Robyn spoke with quiet determination. "We have to bear witness to this terrible crime against humanity and carry word back to London."

"If only the child had seen evidence of the Monomatapa, or the gold mines," muttered Zouga. "You must ask her if there were elephant." He pored over the Harkness map, lamenting the blank spaces. "I cannot believe that it does not exist. There is too much evidence." Zouga looked up at his sister. "One other thing: I seem to have forgotten almost every word of the language that mother taught us, except some of the nursery rhymes and lullabies.

" '*Munya, mabili zinthatu, Yolala umdade-wethu,*' 'One, two, three, Go to sleep, my little sister,'" he recited, and then chuckled and shook his head. "I shall have to study it again; you and Juba will have to help me."

The Zambezi comes to the sea through a delta of vast swampland, and a hundred confused shallow channels spread out for thirty miles down the low featureless coastline.

Floating islands of papyrus grass break free from the main pastures which blanket the waters of the delta and are carried out to sea on the dirty brown water. Some of these islands are many acres in extent and the roots of the plants so entangled that they can support the weight of a heavy animal. On occasions small herds of buffalo are trapped and carried twenty miles out to sea before the action of the waves smashes up the islands and plunges the great bovine animals into the water, prey for the big sharks which cruise the tainted estuary waters for just such a prize.

The muddy smell of the swamps carries far from the land when the wind is right, and the same wind carries strange insects with it. There is a tiny spider no bigger than the head of a wax vesta which lives in the papyrus banks of the delta. It spins a gossamer web on which it launches itself into the breeze in such numbers that gossamer fills the sky in clouds, like the smoke from a raging bush fire, rising many hundreds of feet and eddying and swirling in misty columns that are touched by the sunset into lovely shades of pink and mauve.

Where the river pours a muddy brown effluent into the sea, silt enriched with the bodies of drowned animals and birds, the huge Zambezi crocodiles join the shark packs at the feast.

Black Joke found the first of these hideous creatures ten miles from land, wallowing in the low swells like a log, the rough scales glittering wetly in the sunlight until the gunboat

164

approached too closely and the reptile dived with a lash and swirl of its powerful ridged tail.

Black Joke steamed obliquely across the multiple mouths of the river, none of which offered passage for a vessel of her size. She was headed further north for the Congone channel which was the only passage upriver to the town of Quelimane.

Clinton Codrington planned to enter it the following morning, after having lain hove to during the night off the mouth. Robyn knew that she must remove the stitches from the wound under his armpit, though she would have liked to leave them a few days longer. They must come out before she left the gunboat at Quelimane.

She decided to use the same opportunity to give him the answer for which he had waited so patiently. It was going to be painful for him to hear that she would not marry him, and she felt guilty that she had so encouraged him. It was alien to her nature to inflict suffering on another, and she would try to tell him as gently as possible.

She ordered him to her cabin for the removal of the horsehair stitches, seating him on the narrow bunk naked to the waist, with his arm raised. She was delighted with the way the wound had healed, and proud of the neatness of her work. She cooed over each knot as she snipped it with the pointed scissors, then seized it with the forceps and gently tugged and worried it free of his flesh. The stitches left twin punctures, one on each side of the raised purple welt of the scar, and they were clean and dry. Only one of them leaked a single drop of blood which she swabbed away gently.

Robyn was training Juba as her assistant, teaching her to hold the tray of instruments, and receive the discarded and soiled dressing or instruments. Now she stood back and appraised the healed wound, without looking at Juba.

"You may go now," she said quietly. "I will call you when I need you."

Juba smiled like a conspirator, and murmured in the language they shared, "He is truly beautiful, so white and smooth," and Robyn blushed pinkly, for that was exactly what she had been thinking. Clinton's body, unlike that of Mungo St. John, was hairless as a girl's but finely muscled, and the skin had an almost marble sheen to it.

"His eyes are like two moons when he looks at you, Nomusa," Juba went on with relish, and Robyn tried to frown at her but her lips kept puckering into a smile.

"Go swiftly," she snapped, and Juba giggled.

"There is a time to be alone," and she rolled her eyes lewdly. "I shall guard the door, and hardly listen at all, Nomusa." Robyn found it impossible to be angry when the child used that name, for it meant "daughter of mercy," and Robyn found it highly acceptable. She would have had difficulty picking a better name for herself, and she was smiling as she hurried Juba from the cabin with a gentle slap and a push.

Clinton must have had some idea of the exchange, for he was buttoning his shirt as she turned back to him, and looking embarrassed.

She drew a deep breath, folded her arms and began.

"Captain Codrington, I have thought unceasingly of the great honor you have done me by inviting me to be your wife."

"However," Clinton forestalled her, and she faltered, the prepared speech forgotten, for her next word would indeed have been "However."

"Miss Ballantyne, I mean Dr. Ballantyne, I would rather you did not say the rest of it." His face, intense, was beautiful now, she thought, with a pang. "That way I can still cherish hope."

She shook her head vehemently, but he lifted a hand.

"I have come to realize that you have a duty, to your father and the poor unhappy people of this land. I understand and deeply admire that."

Robyn felt her heart go out to him, he was so good and so perceptive to have understood that much about her.

"However, I feel sure that one day, you and I shall..."

She wanted to spare him pain.

"Captain," she began, shaking her head again.

"No," he said. "Nothing you say will ever make me abandon hope. I am a very patient man, and I realize that now is not the time. But I know in the depths of my soul that our destiny binds us together, even if I must wait ten or fifty years."

A time span of that magnitude no longer frightened Robyn. She relaxed visibly.

"I love you, my dear Dr. Ballantyne, nothing will ever alter that, and in the meantime I ask only your good opinion, and friendship."

"You have both," she said, with truth and relief. It had been easier than she had expected, yet strange that a shadow of regret lingered.

There was no further opportunity to speak privately, for Clinton was fully occupied with bringing *Black Joke* into the

166

treacherous channel, with its shifting banks and uncharted shoals guarding the mouth. The channel meandered twenty miles through the mangrove forests to the port of Quelimane on the northern bank.

The heat in the delta was rendered scarcely bearable by the humid effluxion of mud and rotting vegetation that rose from the mangrove forests. The weird shapes of the mangroves fascinated Robyn, and she stood by the rail and watched them slide past. Each tree stood clear of the slick chocolate-colored mud on its pyramid of roots, like the multiple legs of a grotesque insect reaching up to join the thick pulpy stem which in turn extended upward to the roof of poisonous green foliage. Among the roots skittered the purple and yellow fiddler crabs, each of them holding aloft a single disproportionally huge claw, and waving it in menace or ponderous greeting at the passing vessel.

Black Joke's wake spread across the channel, flopping wavelets on the mud banks and startling the small green-and-purple night herons into laborious flight.

Around a bend in the channel the decaying buildings of Quelimane came into view, dominated by the square towers of the stucco church. The plaster was falling away in unsightly chunks and the whitewash was streaked and splotched with gray and green mold, like a ripening cheese.

This port had once been one of the most busy slave ports on the entire African Coast. The Zambezi River had acted as a highway to the interior for the slavemasters, and the Shire River, its major tributary, led directly to Lake Marawi and the highlands which had been the mother lode from which hundreds and thousands of black slaves had poured.

When the Portuguese, under British pressure, had signed the Brussels Agreement, the barracoons at Quelimane and Lourenço Marques and Mozambique Island had been closed down. However, the slaving dhow that *Black Joke* had intercepted proved that the abominable trade still flourished covertly along the Portuguese coast. That was typical of these people, Clinton Codrington thought.

Clinton curled his lip with distaste. In 'the many hundreds of years since their great navigators had opened up this coast, the Portuguese had clung to the narrow unhealthy strip of the littoral, making only one halfhearted effort to penetrate the interior and since then, lying here like their disintegrating buildings and crumbling empire, content with the bribes and extortions of petty officialdom and their seraglios of women, tolerant of any crimes or evil as long as there was a little dash or profit in it.

As he worked *Black Joke* in toward the quay, he could see them gathering already, gaudy vultures, in their fool's motley of uniform, tarnished gold braid and ornate swords sported by even the lowliest customs officer.

There would be endless forms and declarations, unless he was firm, and always the open palm and the leering wink. Well, this time there would be none of that. This was a ship of the Queen's Navy.

"Mr. Denham," Clinton called sharply, "issue pistols and cutlasses to the anchor watch, and nobody comes aboard without the express permission of the officer of the watch."

He turned away to shake hands briefly with Zouga; they had found little in common during the voyage and the parting was cool.

"Never thank you enough, sir," said Zouga briskly.

"Only my duty, Major." But already Zouga's eyes were following Sergeant Cheroot as he assembled his men on the foredeck. They were in full marching order, eager to be ashore after the tedious voyage.

"I must see to my men, Captain," Zouga excused himself and hurried forward.

Clinton turned to Robyn and looked steadily into her green eyes.

"I beg a small token of remembrance," he said quietly.

In response to his request she reached up and took one of the cheap paste earrings from her lobe. As they shook hands, she slipped the little ornament into his palm, and he touched it briefly to his lips before slipping it into his pocket.

"I will wait," he repeated, "ten or even fifty years."

Black Joke had come upchannel on the flood, unloaded the mountainous stores of the Ballantyne Africa Expedition onto the stone quay during slack water, and two hours later thrown off her mooring ropes and swung sharply across the ebb, pointing her high bows down the channel.

From his position on the quarterdeck, Clinton Codrington stared across the widening gap at the slim, tall figure in long skirts standing on the very edge of the quay. Beyond her, her brother did not look up from his lists as he checked the stores and equipment. Sergeant Cheroot stood armed guard with his little pug-featured Hottentots, and the idlers and watchers kept well clear.

The Portuguese officials had treated the red-wax seals and ribbons which decorated Zouga's letters of authority from the Portuguese ambassador in London with respect. Even more important was the fact that Zouga was an officer of Queen Victoria's army, that he had arrived in a Royal Navy gunboat, and lastly that there was every reason to believe that the same gunboat would remain in the area for the foreseeable future.

The governor of Portuguese East Africa himself would not have commanded more respect. Already minor officials were scampering about the squalid little town arranging the best accommodation, securing warehousing for the stores, commandeering river transport for the next leg of the journey upriver to Tete, the last outpost of Portuguese empire on the Zambezi, drafting orders to have bearers and guides meet the expedition at Tete, and doing everything else that the young British officer casually demanded as though it were his God-given right.

In this termoil of activity Robyn Ballantyne stood alone, staring after the blue-clad figure on *Black Joke*'s quarterdeck. How tall he was, and his hair caught the sunlight in a flash of white gold as he lifted his hand in farewell. She waved until *Black Joke* disappeared behind a palisade of trees, though her masts and fuming smokestack stayed in view for a long time after. She watched until they, too, dwindled to nothingness, and only the smear of smoke lay low over the tops of the green mangrove.

Clinton Codrington stood on his deck, hands clasped loosely at the small of his back, with an expression of near-rapture. In this temper the knight-errant of old must have ridden out at chance, Clinton thought.

He did not find the notion at all melodramatic. He felt truly ennobled by his love, sensing somehow that he must earn something so precious, and that the opportunity to do so lay ahead of him. The earring that Robyn had given him was suspended by a thread around his neck, lying under his shirt against his skin. He touched it now, peering impatiently ahead down the channel. It seemed to him that for the first time he had a steady direction in his life, constant as the polestar to the navigator.

This gallant mood was still strong five days later when *Black Joke* rounded the headland of Ras Elat and steamed into the anchorage. There were eight large dhows keeled over on the exposed sanbar at low tide. The tidal fall on this coast at full springs was twenty-two feet. These craft were designed to take the ground readily, and it facilitated loading. The long ranks of chained slaves were being goaded out to the stranded vessels, slipping and splashing through the shallow tidal pools, to await patiently their turn to climb the ladder up the side of the dhow.

Black Joke's unannounced arrival caused pandemonium, and the beach was alive with running, stumbling figures, the screams and shrieks of the slaves, the pop of the kurbash whips, and the frantic cries of the slavemasters carried clearly to *Black Joke*'s deck as she dropped her anchor just beyond the reef and rounded up to the wind.

Clinton Codrington stared longingly at the heeled vessels and the concourse of panicky humanity, the way a slum child stares at the display in the window of a food shop.

His orders were clear, had been spelled out by Admiral Kemp with painful attention to detail. The admiral remembered with lingering horror his young captain's capture of the slaving fleet at Calabash after forcing the masters to load the cargoes and sail north of the equator. He wanted no repetition of this type of risky action on this patrol.

Black Joke's commander was strictly adjured to respect the territorial integrity of the Sultan of the Omani Arabs, and the exact letter of the treaty that the British consul had negotiated at Zanzibar.

Clinton Codrington was strictly forbidden to interfere with any subject of the Sultan who was engaged in trade between any of the Sultan's dominions. He was denied even the right of search of any vessel flying the red-and-gold flag of Omani on any of the Sultan's recognized trade routes, and these were carefully defined for Captain Codrington's benefit.

He was to confine his patrol to intercepting only vessels that did not belong to the Sultan, particularly vessels of the European powers. Naturally no American vessel might be searched on the high seas. Within these limits, Captain Codrington had powers of independent action.

Far from being allowed to seize or search the Sultan's vessels, Clinton was ordered to use the first opportunity to make a courtesy call on the port of Zanzibar. There he would take counsel from the British consul as how best to use his influence to reinforce the existing treaties, and especially to remind the sultan of his own obligations under those treaties.

So now Clinton paced his deck like a caged lion at feeding time and glowered helplessly, through the pass in the coral reef, at the slaving fleet of Omani engaged in legitimate trade, for the Gulf of Elat was very much part of the Sultan's possessions, and had so been recognized by Her Majesty's Government.

After the first wild panic ashore, the beach and dhows were now deserted, but Clinton was aware of the thousands of watchful eyes upon him from the mud-walled town and the shadows of the coconut groves.

The thought of hauling his anchor and sailing away filled him with bitter chagrin, and he stood bareheaded and stared with cold hungry blue eyes at the prize spread before him.

The palace of the Sheikh of Elat, Mohamed Bin Salim, was an unpainted mud-walled building in the center of the town. The only opening in the parapeted wall was the gate, closed by thick, brass-studded double doors in carved teak, which led through to the dusty central courtyard.

In this courtyard, under the spreading branches of an ancient takamaka tree the Sheikh was in earnest conclave with his senior advisers and the emissaries of his supreme sovereign—the Sultan of Zanzibar. They were discussing the matter, literally, of life or death.

Sheikh Mohamed Bin Salim had the plump smooth body of the *bon vivant*, the bright-red lips of the sensualist, and the hooded eyes of a falcon.

He was a very worried man, for his ambition had led him into dire danger. His ambition had been quite simply to accumulate the sum of one million gold rupees in his treasury, and he had very nearly satisfied that reasonable goal when his overlord, the omnipotent Sultan of Zanzibar, had sent his emissaries to call the Sheikh to account.

Sheikh Mohamed had begun to satisfy his ambition ten years previously by very gently mulching the Sultan's tithe, and each year since then he had increased his depredations. Like all greedy men, one successful coup was the signal for the next. The Sultan had known this, for though he was old, he was also exceedingly cunning. He knew that the missing tithes were safely stored for him in the Sheikh's treasure-house, to be collected whenever he felt inclined. He need only benignly feign ignorance of the Sheikh's manipulations until he was so deeply in the trap that no squirming or squealing would get him out again. After ten years that moment had arrived. The Sultan would collect not only his due but the Sheikh's own accumulations.

Further retribution would be a lengthy business. It would begin with a beating on the soles of the Sheikh's bare feet, until all those delicate little bones were cracked or fractured, making it extremely painful for the Sheikh to be marched into the Sultan's presence. There, the final judgment would be read, and it would end with the knotted strip of buffalo hide wound up tighter and tighter around the forehead, until first the Sheikh's falcon eyes popped from their sockets and then his skull collapsed like a bursting melon. The Sultan truly enjoyed these spectacles, and had been looking forward to this particular one for ten years.

Both men knew the ritual, and it had begun with the polite visit of the Sultan's emissaries who even now were sitting opposite the Sheikh under the takamaka, sipping thick black coffee from the brass thimbles, munching the coconut sweetmeats, and smiling at the Sheikh with cold passionless eyes.

It was into this chilling atmosphere that the messengers from the harbor came running to fling themselves prostrate and gabble out the news of the British warship, whose guns threatened the harbor and the town.

The Sheikh listened quietly and then dismissed the messengers, before turning back to his distinguished guests.

"This is a serious business," he began, relieved to be able to change the subject under discussion. "It would be wise to view this strange vessel."

"The Ferengi have a treaty with our master," pronounced one graybeard, "and they set great store by these pieces of paper."

They all nodded, none of them showing the agitation which filled all of their breasts. Although this coast had received only passing attention from these brash northern people, still it had been enough to engender fear and apprehension.

The Sheikh deliberated for a few minutes, stroking his thick curly beard, hooding his eyes as the ideas began to flow. His mind had been almost paralyzed with the extent of the disaster which had overtaken him, but now it began to work again.

"I must go out to this warship," he announced. There was an immediate hubbub of protest, but he held up his hand to silence them. He was still the Sheikh of Elat, and they had, perforce, to hear him out.

"It is my duty to ascertain the intentions of the commander and to send word immediately to our master."

Clinton Codrington had almost resigned himself to give the order to weigh anchor. There had been no sign of life on the beach for many hours, and there was nothing he could accomplish here. His hope that he might catch a European slaver, actually taking on slaves in the anchorage, had proved forlorn. He should have sailed hours ago, the sun was halfway down the sky already and he did not want to run the dangers of the inshore channel in darkness, but some instinct had kept him here.

He kept returning to the starboard rail, and glassing the flat-roofed mud buildings that just showed among the palm trees. Each time his junior officers stiffened expectantly, then relaxed as he turned away without a word or change of expression.

This time Clinton saw movement, the flash of white robes in the deserted, single street of the town, as he watched through the telescope he felt a prickle of excitement and a lift of self-congratulation. A small deputation was emerging from the grove and coming down the beach.

"Pass the word to my steward to lay out my number ones and sword," he ordered without lowering his glass. The party on the beach was led by a portly figure in blindingly white robes and a full headdress that gleamed with gold. Behind him a bearer carried the long floating banner, scarlet and gold, of the Sultan.

"We'll treat him as a governor," Clinton decided. "And give him four guns." With that he turned on his heel and went to his cabin to change his uniform.

The Arab climbed out of the little felucca and came in through the entry port puffing for breath, assisted by two house slaves. As his foot touched the deck, the first gun of the salute crashed out unexpectedly, and the Sheikh let out a whinny like a wild stallion and leaped two feet straight up in the air, the high color flying from his cheeks leaving them ashen and trembling.

Clinton stepped forward, resplendent in cocked hat, blue-and-gold jacket, white breeches and sword, and took the Sheikh's arm to steady him through the rest of the salute, and to prevent him from stampeding back into the crazily rocking felucca where the oarsmen were in equal terror.

"Will you step this way, Your Excellency," Clinton murmured and without releasing his iron grip on the Sheikh's pudgy arm marched him briskly down to his cabin.

Translation was a problem, but one of the Sheikh's entourage had a smattering of French and some English. It was almost night before Clinton was able to see through the flowery verbiage and the atrocious rendering of his mother tongue. When it came it was like a light filling the cabin, and Clinton found himself buoyed up with a savage, warlike glee.

The fat Sheikh, governor of Elat, with his soft, red lips, was asking for the protection of her Britannic Majesty against the injustices and tyrannies of the Sultan of Zanzibar.

"Dites-lui je ne peux pas—oh, damn it, tell him I can only protect him if he declares Elat free of the Sultan's dominions, *comprenez-vous?"*

"Je m'excuse, je ne comprends pas."

It was tedious, especially in view of Clinton's eagerness to remove the province of Elat from under the sway of Zanzibar.

The Foreign Office had provided all commanders of the Atlantic antislavery squadrons with blank treaty forms, drawn up with deference to protocol and in correct legal terminology. These were for signature of any indigenous chiefs, warlords, petty princes and native kings who could be induced to place their mark upon them.

These documents started with a declaration of mutual recognition between Her Majesty's Government and the signatory, went on in vague terms to promise protection and free trade and ended in very specific terms with a round condemnation of the slave trade and the granting of rights to Her Majesty's Government to search, seize and destroy all ships engaged in such trade within the signatory's territorial waters. Further it granted rights to Her Majesty's Navy to land troops, destroy barracoons, free slaves, arrest slavemasters and do any such other act as should be deemed necessary to the extinction of the trade in all the signatory's lands and possessions.

Admiral Kemp in Cape Town had overlooked the fact that Captain Codrington had a good supply of these documents in his possession. They had been intended for use entirely on the West African coast north of the equator. The good admiral would have been a very worried man indeed if he had realized that he had detached his most brilliant but mercurial junior on independent patrol armed with anything so explosive.

"He must sign here," Clinton explained briskly, "and I will give him an order on the British treasury for a hundred guineas." The treaty made provision for annual tribute to be paid to the signatory. Clinton considered a hundred guineas sufficient. He was not sure of what authority he had to write treasury orders, but Sheikh Mohamed was delighted. He had negotiated for life alone, and received not only the protection of this fine warship but the promise of good gold as well. He was smiling happily, pursing his red lips as he signed his long signature under his

new title "Prince and Supreme Ruler of the sovereign possessions of Elat and Ras Telfa."

"Good," said Clinton briskly, rolling his copy of the treaty
and slipping the retaining ribbon over it as he hurried to the
door of his cabin.

"Mr. Denham," he bellowed up the companionway, "I want
a landing party, muskets, pistols, cutlasses and carrying com-
bustibles, forty men ready to go ashore at first light tomorrow!"
He was grinning as he turned back and told the Sheikh's translator, "It would be best if His Excellency remained on board
tonight. We will see him safely installed at noon tomorrow."
And for the first time the Sheikh felt a thrill of apprehension.
This Ferengi had the cold blue merciless eyes of a devil. "El
Sheetan," he thought, "the very devil." And made the sign
against the evil eye.

"Sir, may I speak?" Mr. Denham, *Black Joke*'s first lieutenant, looked puzzled in the light of the binnacle. It was an
hour short of sunrise and he glanced down at the ranks of armed
seamen squatting on the foredeck.

"Speak your heart," Clinton invited him magnamimously.
Lieutenant Denham was not accustomed to this jovial mood
from his captain, and he expressed himself cautiously. In essence Lieutenant Denham's views came very close to those of
the admiral in Cape Town.

"If you would like to make a protest against my orders,
Lieutenant," Clinton interrupted him cheerfully, "I will be
pleased to enter it in the ship's log."

Thus absolved of responsibility for having been party to an
act of war on the territory of a foreign ruler, Lieutenant Denham
was so relieved that when Clinton told him, "I am taking command of the landing party. You will command the ship in my
absence," he shook Clinton's hand impulsively.

"Good luck, sir," he blurted.

They went ashore in two boats, the whaler leading through
the pass in the reef and the gig following two lengths astern.
The moment the keel touched, Clinton sprang knee-deep into
the bloodwarm water and the rush of armed men followed him
ashore. He drew his cutlass and his shoes squelched as he led
his team of five men to the nearest dhow at a dead run.

As he jumped down from the ladder onto the dhow's heavily
canted deck, an Arab watchman ducked out of the stern cabin
and aimed a long jezail at Clinton's head. The range was point
blank and Clinton struck out instinctively in an underhand parry,

just as the gun's lock clicked and smoke and spark shot from the pan under the steel and flint.

His blade clashed against the steel barrel, deflecting it upward as the jezail roared an instant after the snap of the lock, and a blinding billow of smoke and burning powder struck his face and singed his eyebrows, but the chunk of beaten potleg howled inches over his head. When his vision cleared the watchman had thrown his empty weapon aside, leaped over the side of the dhow and was hopping and hobbling across the sand toward the grove of palms.

"Search her, and then put fire into her," Clinton ordered brusquely.

It was the first chance he had had to look across at the other dhows of the fleet. One of them was already on fire, the flames bright in the early light, rising straight up with little smoke. The furled mainsail was blackening like a dried leaf, and he could hear the crackle of the tinder-dry timbers of the hull and stern cabin. His seamen were spilling out of her and straggling across to the next vessel.

"She's aflame, sir," his boatswain panted, and a hot gust of air struck Clinton's cheek at that moment and a quiver of heat hung over the main hatch.

"We'd best be getting on," he said mildly, and scrambled down the ladder on to the packed damp sand. Behind him the flames roared like a cageful of wild animals.

The biggest dhow, a two-hundred-tonner, lay ahead of them and Clinton reached it fifty paces ahead of his men.

"Make sure there is nobody below," he ordered, and one of the seamen came back on deck carrying a rolled silk prayer rug under his arm.

"Belay that!" snapped Clinton. "There'll be no looting."

Reluctantly the seaman dropped the precious burden back into the hatchway, and the flames sucked up in a hot breath to accept it as though it were an offering to Baal.

By the time they reached the tree line, all eight of the stranded vessels were burning fiercely, the stubby masts collapsing as they burned through at the base, the furled sails disappearing in bright explosions of flame. In one of the burning hulls a keg of powder went up with a thunderous crash of sound, and a tall column of smoke hovered over the beach for a few seconds, shaped like a gigantic gray octopus before it drifted slowly out across the reef, leaving the dhow shattered, its timbers scattered across the sand, the flames extinguished by the shock wave of the explosion.

"Was there anybody aboard her?" Clinton demanded quietly.

"No, sir." His boatswain was panting beside him, red-faced with excitement, and with a bared cutlass in his hand. "All accounted for."

Clinton hid his relief behind a cool nod, and spent a few precious minutes drawing his men into an orderly formation, giving them time to regain their breath, and getting them well in hand again.

"Check your muskets," he ordered, and there was the click of the locks. "Fix bayonets." Metal rattled on metal as the long blades were fitted to the barrels of the Enfield rifles. "If there is resistance we'll find it in the town, I fancy," and he ran an eye down the uneven ranks. They were neither marines nor lobsterbacks, he thought with quick affection. They might not be perfect in drill, but they were men with spirit and initiative, not parade-ground automatons.

"Come along then." He waved them forward into the dusty street between the mud-brown flat-roofed buildings. The town smelled of wood smoke and raw sewage, of rice cooked with saffron and of ghee, clarified butter.

"Shall we burn 'em?" His boatswain jerked a thumb at the buildings that flanked the deserted street.

"No, we are here to protect them," Clinton told him stiffly. "They belong to our new ally, the Sheikh."

"I see, sir," the boatswain grunted, looking mildly perplexed, and Clinton took pity on him.

"We are after the barracoons," he explained, as they trotted up the street in compact formation. They halted where the road branched left and right.

The heat was oppressive and the silence menacing. There was no wind and the coconut groves had stilled the eternal clatter of their fronds. From the beach far behind them came the faint popping of burning timbers, and overhead the ubiquitous pied crows of Africa circled and cawed raucously, but the buildings and dense coconut groves were deserted.

"I don't like this," one of the men croaked behind Clinton. He could understand the man's point of view. A seaman always felt awkward when parted from his ship, and there were a mere forty of them, out of sight of the beach and surrounded by thousands of unseen but none the less savage warriors. Clinton knew he must keep the momentum of surprise rolling through the town, yet he hesitated a moment longer until he realized that the amorphous sacklike shape lying on the edge of the right hand street was a human body, naked and black and very dead. One of the slaves trampled in the previous day's panic and left where he had fallen.

That way must lie the barracoons, he decided. "Quiet!" he cautioned his men, and cocking his head, listened with all his attention to the faint susurration on the still air. It might have been the wind except there was no wind, or the flames, except that the flames were behind them. It was the distant sound of human voices, he decided, many voices, thousands of voices.

"This way. Follow me." They went forward at a full run, taking the right fork and running immediately into the ambush which had been so carefully prepared for them.

The volley of musket fire crashed out from both sides of the narrowing track, and powder smoke rolled out toward them and hung like a thick, pearly curtain among the palm boles and the cashew nut trees.

Through the smoke danced the ethereal robed figures of the attackers, brandishing the long-barreled jezails or swinging the half-moon-bladed scimitars, with wild shrieks of *"Allah Akbar, Allah is great!"*

They rushed down on the little band of seamen, caught in enfilade on the narrow track. There were at least a hundred of them, Clinton judged instantly, and they were pressing in determinedly. Those scimitars were glittering bright; bare steel has a particularly chilling effect.

"Close up," Clinton shouted. "We'll give them a volley, then take the bayonet to them, through the smoke."

The first rank of racing Arabs were almost on top of the leveled Enfields. Incongruously, Clinton noticed that many of them had tucked up the skirts of their robes, leaving the legs bared to the thighs. Their skins varied from the color of ivory to that of tobacco, and there were wrinkled graybeards in the front rank, screaming and howling with rage and battle lust. They had just seen their livelihood burned to heaps of ash upon the beach. All that remained to them of their wealth was the contents of the barracoons set back among the groves of cashew nut and coconut trees.

"Fire!" roared Clinton, and the solid blast of sound deafened him for a moment. The gunsmoke wiped out all vision ahead of him and then hung on the windless morning in an impenetrable fog bank.

"Forward!" howled Clinton and led the charge into the smoke. He stumbled over the body of an Arab. The man's turban had unwound and come down over his eyes, soaked with blood like the Sultan's scarlet banner which Clinton could see waving ahead of him above the smoke.

A figure loomed ahead of him, and he heard the fluting whistle of a scimitar blade, like wild goose wings overhead. He ducked. The sharp breeze puffed a loose strand of hair into his eyes, as the blade passed an inch from his forehead, and Clinton straightened from the knees and put his whole body into the counterlunge.

The point of his blade went in with a dead, soggy feel, sliding grudgingly through flesh until the point grated on bone. The Arab dropped his scimitar and clutched the cutlass blade with bare hands. Clinton leaned back and jerked the cutlass free of flesh. As the blade slid through the Arab's nerveless fingers the tendons parted with a faint popping sound, and the man went down on his knees, holding his mutilated hands up in front of his eyes with a look of amazement on his face.

Clinton ran on to catch up with his seamen, and found them scattered in little groups among the grove, laughing and shouting with excitement.

"They've run like steeplechasers, sir," the boatswain called. "Grand National, ten to one the field!" He snatched up the fallen banner of the Sultan and waved it furiously over his head, completely overtaken by excitement.

"Did we lose anybody?" Clinton demanded. He also felt the dizzy euphoria of battle. The killing of the Arab, far from sickening him, had elated him. In that moment he was quite capable of turning back and taking the man's scalp. However, the question sobered them.

"Jedrow caught one in the belly, but he can walk. Wilson got a sword cut in the arm."

"Send them back to the beach. They can escort each other. The rest of you, come on!"

They found the barracoons a quarter of a mile further on. The guards had fled.

The slave pens stretched out for a half mile along both banks of a small stream that provided both drinking water and sewage disposal for the inmates.

They were unlike the barracoons that Clinton had captured and sacked on the west coast, for those had been built by European traders with an orderly eye. There was no resemblance in these sprawling compounds built of rough, unbarked forest poles, bound together with rope made from plaited palm fronds. Behind the outer barricades were open godowns with thatched roofs in which the chained slaves could find some shelter from sun and rain. The only thing the same was the smell. An epidemic of tropical dysentery had swept through the barracoons and most of the sheds contained the decomposing bodies of the victims. The crows and buzzards and vultures were waiting patiently in the palms and cashew trees, misshapen silhouettes against the hard bright blue of the morning sky.

Clinton met the new ruler of the state of Elat, Sheikh Mohamed, at the water's edge and escorted him up the beach. The incoming tide was dousing the piles of smoldering ash that marked the last resting places of eight fine dhows, and the Sheikh tottered uncertainly, like a man in deep shock, relying for support on the sturdy shoulder of one of his house slaves, looking about him with lugubrious disbelief at the carnage that had overtaken him. The Sheikh owned a one-third share in every one of those smoking piles of ash.

He had to rest when they reached the tree line above the beach. A slave placed a carved wooden stool in the shade, and another waved a fan of plaited palm fronds over his head to keep off the flies and to cool his heated brow that was dewed with the heavy sweat of despair.

His misery was completed by the lecture in broken French and pidgin English which "El Sheetan," the mad British sea captain was relaying to him through the shocked and incredulous interpreter. Such things could only be repeated in a hoarse whisper, and the Sheikh greeted each new revelation with a soft cry of "Waai!" and the upturning of his eyes to heaven.

He learned that the village blacksmiths had been dragged out of the bushes and were already knocking the fetters off long rows of perplexed slaves.

"Waai!" wailed the Sheikh. "Does the devil not realize that those slaves have already been purchased and that the tax has been collected?"

Comfortably Clinton explained that once the slaves were freed, they would be marched back into the interior, and the Sheikh would send guards with them to see them safely home, and to warn any slave caravans that they encountered on the down route that all the ports of Elat were now closed to the trade.

"Waai!" This time the Sheikh's eyes brimmed with tears. "He will beggar me. My wives and children will starve."

"El Sheetan counsels you to enlarge the trade in gum copal

180

and copra," explained the interpreter in a sepulchral voice. "And as your closest ally, he promises to call upon you regularly with his great ship of many guns, to make certain that you heed this advice."

"Waai!" The Sheikh plucked at his beard, so that long curly hairs came out between his fingers. "This ally makes one long for ordinary enemies."

Twenty-four hours later *Black Joke* sailed into Telfa Bay, forty miles further up the coast. Nobody had thought to warn the slaving fleet that was anchored there of the new policies of the state of Elat to which the territory now belonged.

The five dhows in the outer anchorage managed to cut their anchor cables and slip away into the maze of shallow coral channels and shoals to the north of the bay, where *Black Joke* could not follow.

However, there were another six smaller vessels on the beach and four magnificent double-decked oceangoing dhows lying in the inner anchorage. Clinton Codrington burned two of them and seized the four newest and biggest vessels, put prize crews into them and sent them south to the nearest British base at Port Natal.

Two days later, off the beach at Kilwa, Clinton Codrington exercised his ship at gunnery practice, running out his thirty-two-pounders and firing them in broadsides which set the surface of the lagoon seething and dancing with foam and white fountains of spray. The thunder of gunfire burst against the far hills and rumbled back across the sky like cannonballs rolled across a wooden deck.

The Sultan's local governor was reduced to a quivering jelly of terror by this display of might, and had to be carried bodily into *Black Joke*'s whaler to be rowed out to a conclave with the gunboat's captain. Clinton had the treaty forms already filled out and ready for signature when they carried the governor aboard to learn that he was heir to a kingdom to which he had never aspired, and a title which he knew was too grandiose not to bring with it certain retribution from somebody whose name he did not dare to breathe aloud.

Admiral Kemp, sitting in his study in the magnificent mansion of Admiralty House, overlooking the wide smoky-blue haze of the Cape flats to the far mountains of the Hottentots Holland, hopefully dismissed the first reports as the wild imaginings of some crazed subordinate who had served too long in the godforsaken outpost of Port Natal, and who was suffering from the bush madness of "El Cafard" that sometimes affects a person so isolated.

Then the details began to arrive with every dispatch from the north, and they were too graphic to be lightly dismissed. An armada of captured prizes was arriving in the bay of Port Natal, twenty-six sizable dhows to date, some of them loaded with slaves.

The lieutenant governor of Port Natal was desperate for the admiral's advice as to what should be done with the dhows. The slaves had been taken ashore, released and immediately been contracted as indentured laborers to the hardy and hopeful gentlemen who were attempting to raise cotton and sugarcane in the wilderness of the Umgeni Valley. The shortage of labor was critical, the local Zulu tribesmen much preferred cattle raiding and beer drinking to agricultural labor, so the governor would be delighted to receive as many freed slaves as the Royal Navy wished to send him. (The admiral was not entirely certain of the difference between indentured laborers and slaves.) However, what was the lieutenant governor to do with twenty-six— no, the latest figure was thirty-two—captured dhows? A further flotilla of six vessels had arrived as the governor was dictating his report.

Two weeks later, one of the captured dhows, which had been purchased into the Colonial Service by the lieutenant governor, arrived in Table Bay bearing a further batch of dispatches.

One of these was from Sir John Bannerman, H.M. Consul on the island of Zanzibar. Another was from the Sultan of Omani in person, with copies to the foreign secretary in London and, quite remarkably, to the governor general in Calcutta. The Sultan evidently believed that as the representative of the Queen of England the governor general would have some jurisdiction in the Indian Ocean, which was virtually his front garden.

Admiral Kemp split the seals on both packets with a queasy feeling of impending doom.

"Good God!" he groaned, as he began reading, and then, "Oh sweet merciful Jesus, no!" And later, "It's too much, it's like some sort of nightmare!"

Codrington, one of the most junior post captains on the Admiralty list, seemed to have taken powers unto himself which would have made a Wellington or a Bonaparte pause.

He had annexed to the British Crown vast African territories, which hitherto had formed part of the Sultan's dominions. With a high hand he had negotiated with various local chiefs and

182

dignitaries of dubious title and authority, pledging recognition and good British gold. "Good God!" the admiral cried again in real anguish, "What will that blighter Palmerston have to say?" As a staunch Tory, Kemp had no great opinion of the new Whig Prime Minister.

Since the troubles in India, the sepoy risings of a few years previously, the British Government was very wary of accepting further responsibility for overseas territory and backward peoples. Their orders were specific, and Codrington's recent activity went far from the essence of those orders.

The scramble for Africa was still in the future, and the spirit of the Little Englanders motivated British foreign policy; of this Admiral Kemp was very painfully aware. Daunting as this was, yet it was far from the entire story, Kemp realized, as he read on into the consul's dispatch, his breath rasping hoarsely, his color rising steadily, and his eyes behind the gold wire-framed reading glasses swimming with tears of rage and frustration.

"When I get my hands on that puppy—" he promised himself.

Codrington seemed to have declared singlehanded war upon the Sultan. Yet even in his outrage the admiral felt a prickle of professional appreciation for the scope of his subordinate's operations.

There was a formidable list of over thirty separate incidents recited by H.M. consul. The puppy had stormed fortified castles, raided ashore to burn and destroy barracoons, released tens of thousands of slaves, seized slaving vessels on the high seas, burned others at their moorings and wreaked the kind of chaos worthy of a marauding Nelson himself.

The admiral's reluctant admiration for Codrington's technical conduct of the campaign in no way lessened his determination to exact vengeance for the disruption of his life and career that those actions presaged.

"Nothing can save him this time. Nothing!" the admiral rumbled, as he turned to study the Sultan's protest. This was obviously the work of a professional letter writer, and every paragraph began and ended with incongruous and flowery inquiries after Kemp's health, between which were sandwiched cries of anguish, screams of outrage, and protest against the broken promises and treaties of Her Majesty's Government.

At the very end the letter writer had not been able to resist adding a prayer for the admiral and the Queen's prosperity and health in this life, and happiness in the one to follow. This detracted a little from the tone of injury in which the protests and demands had been couched.

The Sultan assessed his losses at over fourteen lakhs of rupees, almost a million of sterling, in plundered shipping and released slaves, and that did not take into account the irreplaceable damage to his prestige, nor the breakdown of the entire trade along the coast. The confusion was such that some ports might never again be opened to the trade. The system of gathering slaves in the interior of the continent and the network of routes to the coastal ports had been so sadly disrupted that they might take years to reopen, to say nothing of the gross shortage of shipping resulting from the depredations of "El Sheetan." Those ports still open to the trade were swamped with patient slaves, waiting for the dhows which were already scattered wrecks upon the reefs and beaches of the Mozambique channel, or sailing southward under prize crews.

"Nothing can save him," repeated Admiral Kemp, and then paused. His own career was finished also. He realized that, and he felt the deep injustice of it. For forty years he had not put a single foot wrong, and his retirement was so close, so very close. He shook off the lethargy of despair, and began to draft his orders.

The first was to all ships of his squadron, to detach immediately and to steam in search of *Black Joke*. In despair he realized that it might take as much as six weeks for his orders to reach his commanders, for they were scattered across two oceans. It might also take as long again for them to search out the errant gunboat in the maze of islands and bays along the Mozambique channel.

However, when they did so, Captain Codrington was to be relieved of his command with immediate effect. Lieutenant Denham was to take over as temporary commander, with orders to bring *Black Joke* into Table Bay as soon as possible.

Admiral Kemp was confident that he could assemble sufficient senior officers on the Cape Station to convene an immediate courtmartial. It might help his own position a little if he could report to the First Lord that a savage sentence had already been handed down to Codrington.

Then there was a dispatch to H.M. consul in Zanzibar, suggesting he keep the sultan reassured and quiescent until the situation could once more be brought under control—and until instructions could be forwarded from the Foreign Office in London regarding possible redress and compensation, although naturally at this stage, no promises or commitments were to

184

be given the Sultan, beyond expressions of good faith and commiseration.

Then there was the onerous task of making his report to the Admiralty. There were no words to soften the actions of his subordinate, and his own responsibility. Besides, he had been a serving officer too long to make any such attempt. Yet when the bare facts were stated, even in the beloved unemotional jargon of the Navy, they seemed so magnified that Admiral Kemp was himself utterly appalled, all over again. The packet boat was delayed five hours while the admiral completed, sealed and addressed this missive. It would be in London in less than a month.

His last dispatch was addressed to the officer commanding Her Majesty's ship *Black Joke* in person. And in it Admiral Kemp allowed himself a sour sadistic pleasure in weighing the relative effectiveness of such words as "corsair" and "pirate"— or "malicious" and "irresponsible." He had his little master-piece of venom written out in five copies to be disseminated in every direction and by every available means that might most speedily bring the puppy to heel. Yet when they were sent, all he could do was wait—and that was the worst part of the affair. Uncertainty and inaction seemed to corrode his very soul.

He dreaded each new arrival in Table Bay, and whenever the signal gun on the hill above the town boomed its brief feather of gunsmoke, his spirit quailed and that sour ache of dread stabbed him in his guts.

Each new dispatch lengthened the toll of destruction and depredation, until at last there was a report from the culprit himself, sewn up in a package of canvas and addressed to Admiral Kemp, delivered by the prize crew of a particularly valuable dhow over eighty feet long and of a hundred-ton burden.

The tone in which Codrington listed his achievements in-furiated the admiral as much as the deeds themselves. In an almost casual opening paragraph, Captain Codrington recorded the addition of some million square miles of Africa to the Empire.

He had the grace to admit that his action may have exceeded his orders, and he explained away the discrepancy winningly. "It had been my firm intention to avoid scrupulously, whilst on this service, every act of a political nature. However, I was forced to accept the cession of the kingdoms of Elat and Telfa by the entreaties of the Sheikh and the Iman—together with that of their people, who seek refuge from the inimical and savage acts of the Sultan of Zanzibar."

This was hard fare to serve Their Lordships, especially the First Lord, Lord Somerset, who had always grudged the use of his men and ships to fight against slavery. However, much worse was to follow. Captain Codrington went on to lecture the admiral and to deliver a few homilies for Their Lordship's instruction.

"By God's providence, an Englishman with no other force than the character of his noble nation has brought to these poor people salvation. Their Lordships must pardon me for using an unfashionable argument"—a sneer at the Little Englanders—"however, it is as clear to me as the African sun that God has prepared this continent for the only nation on earth that has the public virtue sufficient to govern it for its own benefit, and for the only people who take the revealed word for their moral law."

Admiral Kemp gulped as he read it, swallowed the wrong way, and was prostrated with a coughing fit from which he recovered some minutes later to read on.

"In all the foregoing I have been influenced by no personal motive or interest, by no desire of vainglory, but my endeavours have solely been to use the powers granted me to the honour of my God, my Queen and to the benefit of my country and all mankind."

The admiral removed his reading glasses and stared at the glass case of stuffed songbirds on the wall opposite him.

"To write that, he is either the world's greatest fool—or a brave man or both," he decided at last.

Admiral Kemp was wrong in his estimate. In fact, Clinton Codrington was having an attack of cockiness and self-importance occasioned by the sense of limitless power which this command had given him. He had been wielding this power for many months, and his judgment and good sense had warped. Yet he still truly believed that he was fulfilling, in this order, the will of God, his patriotic duty and the spirit of his orders from the Lords of the Admiralty.

He was also fully aware that he had demonstrated superior professional ability in carrying out a series of land and sea actions, nearly always against superior numbers, without a single reverse and with the loss of only three men killed in action and fewer than a dozen wounded. There was only one area in which Clinton had any reservations regarding the success of the patrol up to this time.

Huron was still on the coast, he had intelligence of her from a dozen sources. Mungo St. John was trading, paying top prices for only the best merchandise, handpicked by either himself or his mate, the bald yellow giant, Tippoo. They were taking only healthy, mature men and women fit to withstand the long voyage back around Good Hope and across the middle passage, and there was a shortage of this type of merchandise.

For Clinton every dawn brought the hope that *Black Joke* would once again raise that towering pyramid of beautiful white sails, but each day the hope faded slowly with the passage of the fierce tropical sun across the heavens, to be extinguished each night as the huge red orb plunged into the sea, and to be resurrected again with the next dawn.

Once they missed the big American clipper by a single day. She had slipped out of the bay at Lindi twenty-four hours before *Black Joke*'s arrival, after taking on fifty prime slaves. The watchers from the beach said that they could not be certain if she had turned north or south, for she had made her offing below the horizon, and had been lost to sight from the shore before coming around onto her intended course.

Clinton guessed *Huron* would go south, and had steamed in pursuit for three days, over an empty sea, down a seemingly deserted coast with barren anchorages before admitting that St. John had sailed away from him again, and he was forced to abandon the hunt.

At the very least he knew that if *Huron* had turned north, St. John was still trading, and there was always a chance of another encounter. He prayed for it every evening. It was all that he needed to make this patrol a clean sweep, so that he could fly a broom from his masthead when he sailed into Table Bay again.

This time he had sworn and witnessed depositions of the men who had sold St. John his slaves as proof positive that *Huron* was trading. He did not have to rely on the Equipment Clause, or the dubious rights of search. He had his proof and somehow he knew his chance would come.

The tide was running at full flow for Clinton. He was imbued with a new sense of worthiness, a new, ironclad confidence in himself and his own good fortune. He carried himself differently, chin higher, shoulders squarer, and if his gait was not yet a swagger, it was at least an assured stride. He smiled more often and when he did there was a wicked curl to his upper lip. He had even grown a full mustache, golden and curling, that gave him a piratical air, and his crew, who had always respected his cold precise management of the ship, but felt little affection for him, now cheered him when he came back on board from one of his forays ashore.

"Good old Tongs!" It was his new nickname from "Hammer and Tongs." They had never had a pet name for him before, but now they were a proud ship, proud of themselves, and proud of their twenty-seven-year-old "old man."

"Give 'em hell, Tongs!" they cheered behind him, as he led them, naked cutlass in hand, over the outer stockade of a barracoon with musket smoke swirling around his lanky figure.

"At 'em, the Jokers!" they cheered themselves, as they leaped the gap between *Black Joke*'s rail and the deck of a slaving dhow, swinging their cutlasses, pistols popping as they drove the slavers down into their own holds and battened the hatches down on them, or chased them over the side where the sharks were cruising.

They knew they were creating a legend. Tongs and his Jokers sweeping the slavers from the Mozambique channel, a hell of a story to tell the nippers back home, and a good slice of prize money to prove the tale.

It was in this mood that *Black Joke* sailed into Zanzibar Harbor, the stronghold of the Omani Sultan, little Daniel into the lion's den. The gunners on the parapets of the fort, though they stood with the slow matches burning in their hands, could not bring themselves to touch them to the huge bronze cannon as the ugly little gunboat came fussing up the Zanzibar roads.

Black Joke had her yards manned with neatly uniformed seamen. A spectacular display, geometrical white ranks of men against the backdrop of tropical anvil-headed thunderclouds.

Her officers were in cocked hats and full ceremonial dress, uniform, swords, white gloves and white breeches, and as she made her turn into the inner harbor, *Black Joke* began firing her courtesy salute—which was a signal for most of the population to head for the hills, jamming the narrow alleyways of the old city with a lamenting torrent of refugees.

The Sultan himself fled his palace, and with most of his court took refuge in the British consulate, overlooking the harbor.

"I am not a coward," the Sultan complained to Sir. John Bannerman, "but the captain of that ship is a madman. Allah himself does not know what he will do next."

Sir John was a large man, of large appetite. He possessed

a noble belly like the glacis of a medieval castle and full mutton-chop whiskers around a florid face, but the clear intelligent eyes, and the wide friendly mouth of a man of humanity and humor. He was a noted oriental scholar, and had written books of travel and of religious and political appraisal of the East, as well as a dozen translations of minor Arabic poets.

He was also a confirmed opponent of the slave trade, for the Zanzibar markets were held in the square below the windows of his residence and from his bedroom terrace he could watch on any morning the slaving dhows unloading their pitiful cargoes on the stone wharf they called, with cruel humor, the "Pearl Gate."

For seven years he had patiently negotiated a series of treaties with the Sultan, each one nipping a few more twigs off the flourishing growth which he detested, but found almost impossible to prune effectively, let alone root out entirely.

In all the Sultan's territories Sir John had absolute jurisdiction only over the community of Hindu traders on the island, for they were British subjects, and Sir John published a bulletin requiring them to free all their slaves forthwith, against a penalty of one hundred pounds for noncompliance.

His bulletin made no mention of compensation, so the most influential of the merchants sent Sir John a defiance which was the Pashto equivalent of "The hell with you and your bulletins."

Sir John, with his one good foot, personally kicked in the merchant's door, dragged him out from under his charpoy bed, dropped him to his knees and with a full-blooded roundhouse punch, chained him around the neck and marched him through the city streets to the consulate and locked him in the wine cellar until the fine was paid and the slaves' manumission papers signed. There had been no further defiance and no takers for the Hindu merchant's subsequent, privately circulated offer to pay another hundred pounds to anybody who would stick a knife between Sir John's ribs during one of his evening promenades through the old city. Thus it was that Sir John was still bluff and hale as he stood on his terrace puffing a cigar; his only indisposition was the gouty foot thrust into a carpet slipper. He watched the little black-hulled gunboat coming up the channel.

"She behaves like a flagship," he smiled indulgently, and beside him, Said the Sultan of Zanzibar, hissed like a faulty steam valve.

"El Sheetan!" His wrinkled turkey neck turned bright red with impotent anger, his bony nose beaked like that of an unhappy parrot. "He sails here, into my harbor, and my gunners stand by their cannons like dead men. He who has beggared me, who has plunged my empire into ruins—what does he dare here?"

The answer that Tongs Codrington would have given him was quite simple. He was carrying out to the letter the orders given him in Cape Town many months previously by Admiral Kemp, the commander of the South Atlantic and Indian Ocean Squadron.

"You are further requested and required to take advantage of the first opportunity to call into the harbour of Zanzibar, where you will accord to His Royal Highness the Sultan of Omani full honours, while taking the advice of Her Majesty's Consul, Sir John Bannerman, as to reinforcing existing treaties between His Royal Highness and Her Britannic Majesty's Government."

Which, being translated, was an instruction to show the Union Jack against a background of thirty-two-pounder cannons, and by doing so remind the Sultan of his commitments under the various treaties.

"To teach the naughty old beggar to mind his P's and Q's," as Clinton explained cheerfully to Lieutenant Denham with a twirl of his new golden mustache.

"I would have thought, sir, that the lesson had already been given," Denham answered darkly.

"Not at all," Clinton demurred. "The treaties with the new sultans on the mainland no longer affect the Zanzibar fellow. We still have to ginger this old boy up a little."

Sir John Bannerman limped up onto *Black Joke*'s deck, favoring his gouty foot and cocked a lively eye at the young naval officer who stepped forward to greet him.

"Well, sir, you have been busy indeed," he murmured. My God, the fellow was little more than a boy, a fresh-faced youngster, despite the cocked hat and mustache. It was difficult to believe that he had created such havoc with this tiny ship.

They shook hands, and Bannerman found himself liking the boy, despite the turmoil that he brought into the consul's normally tranquil existence.

"A glass of Madeira, sir?" Clinton suggested.

"Damned decent of you, I must say."

In the small cabin, Bannerman mopped his streaming face and came directly to business.

"By God, you've put the cat amongst the pigeons." He wagged his big head.

190

"I don't see——"

"Now, listen to me," Bannerman snapped, "and I'll explain to you the facts of life as they apply to eastern Africa in general, and Zanzibar in particular."

Half an hour later, Clinton had lost much of his newfound bumptiousness.

"What should we do?" he asked.

"Do?" Bannerman asked. "What we do is take full advantage of the situation which you have precipitated, before these idiots in Whitehall come stumbling in. Thanks to you the Sultan is at last in a mood to sign the treaty I have been after for five years. I'll trade a handful of these utterly illegal, untenable treaties that you have made with nonexistent states and mythical princes for one that will truss the old goat up the way I've wanted him for years."

"Excuse me, Sir John"—Clinton looked slightly perplexed—"from what you said earlier, I understood that you heartily disapproved of my recent actions."

"On the contrary," Sir John grinned at him expansively, "you have stirred my blood, and made me proud to be an Englishman again. I say, do you have a little more of the Madeira?"

He raised the glass to Clinton. "My hearty congratulations, Captain Codrington. I only wish that I could do something to save you from the fate that so certainly awaits you, once the Admiralty and Lord Palmerston catch up with you." Sir John drank half the glass, smacked his lips. "Jolly good stuff," he nodded, set the glass aside and went on briskly, "Now, we have to work fast and get the Sultan to sign an ironclad treaty— before Whitehall rushes in with apologies and protestations of good faith which will put to naught all the fine work you have done to date. Something tells me that won't be very long," he added lugubriously, and then more brightly, "You could have your ship's guns run out whilst we are ashore. Do wear your sword. Oh, and one other thing, don't take your eyes off the old goat while I do the talking. There is already talk about your eyes—that extraordinary color of blue, don't you know—and the Sultan has heard about them already. As you probably know, they now call you 'El Sheetan' on this coast, and the Sultan is a man who sets great store by djinns and the occult."

Sir John's predictions as to the imminent arrival of tidings from higher sources was almost clairvoyant, for as he spoke H.M. sloop *Penguin,* with urgent dispatches on board for Sir John Bannerman, for the Sultan, and for Captain Codrington, was on a fair wind, which, if it held, would bring her into Zanzibar Harbor within the next two days. Time was shorter than even Sir John believed.

With some trepidation, the Sultan had moved back into his palace. He had only half believed Sir John's assurances, but, on the other hand, the palace was half a mile from the harbor where that evil black ship was displaying its formidable broadside of carronades, while the consulate was on the harbor front— or the front line of fire, depending on how one looked at it.

On Sir John's advice Clinton had come ashore with a bodyguard of a dozen picked seamen, who could be trusted to resist the temptations of the old city's red-light area, the grog and the women that seamen dream of. It was dusk when the party plunged into the labyrinth of narrow alleys, where the balconies almost met overhead, led by Sir John who despite his game leg set a good pace, picking his way around heaps of noisome garbage and avoiding the puddles in the uneven paving that looked like a cold minestrone soup and smelled a great deal higher.

He chatted affably with Clinton, pointing out the various sites and buildings of interest, relating the island's history and giving a quick perceptive character sketch of the Sultan and the more important men in his empire, including those unfortunate new princes who had signed Clinton's blank treaty forms.

"That's one thing, Sir John. I wouldn't want anything to happen to them," Clinton cut in for the first time. "I hope they won't be victimized for having, well, how can one say, for having seceded from the Sultan's empire—"

"Forlorn hope." Sir John waggled his head. "Not one of them will be alive by Ramadan. The old goat has a nasty streak."

"Couldn't we put a clause in the new treaty to protect them?"

"We could, but it would be a waste of paper and ink." Sir John clapped his shoulder. "Your concern is misplaced. The finest collection of ruffians, rogues and assassins south of the equator, or north of it, for that matter. One of the side benefits of the whole business, getting rid of that lot. Old goat will have a lovely time, compensate him for the loss of face when he straps their heads or hands them the cup of datura tea. Ghastly death, datura poisoning. Oh, by the way, you must look at these gates." They had reached the front of the palace. "One of the most magnificent examples of craftsmanship on the island."

The massive teak doors were fifteen feet high, intricately carved, but in accordance with Moslem law the carvings depicted neither human nor animal figures. They were the only impressive feature of the drab square building with its blank walls relieved by the wooden balconies high above street level, shuttered against the night air and the gaze of the curious.

The gates swung open at their approach, and the palace guards armed with ancient jezails were the first living beings they had seen since leaving the harbor. The city was still deserted, and cowering under the menace of *Black Joke*'s guns.

Clinton noticed, since Sir John had mentioned it, that the guards averted their gaze as he passed, one of them actually covering his face with the loose tail of his turban. So the business of the eyes was true. He was not sure whether to feel insulted or amused.

"You must see these." Sir John stopped him in the cavernous antechamber with guttering oil lamps suspended in heavy brass chandeliers from a ceiling lost in the gloom. "The heaviest recorded specimens in the world, one of them over three-hundred-pounds' weight."

They were a pair of African elephant tusks, suspended on the stone wall with retaining bands of copper, two incredible curves of ancient ivory, as thick as a girl's waist, taller than a man could reach, with hardly any taper from hilt to blunt tip, gleaming with the luster of precious porcelain.

"You have not hunted these beasts?"

Clinton shook his head, he had never even seen one of them, but the huge teeth impressed him none the less.

"Before my foot, I shot them in India and in Africa. No other sport to beat that, incredible animals." He patted one of the tusks. "The Sultan killed this one when he was a young man, with a jezail! But there aren't any monsters like that around anymore, more's the pity. Come along, mustn't keep the old goat waiting."

They went on through half a dozen chambers, each of them Aladdin's caves of rare treasures, carved jade, beautifully worked ivory carvings, a palm tree and suspended moon, the symbol of Mohammed, in solid gold, carpets of silk and thread of gold and silver, a collection of fifty priceless Korans in silver and golden containers set with precious and semiprecious stones.

"Look at that shiner." Sir John stopped again, and pointed out a native cut diamond in the hilt of an Arabian scimitar. The diamond was cushion-shaped and a little out of true, but burning with a weird blue and icy fire even in the semi-dark. "Legend says the sword was Saladin's; I doubt it, but the stone is one hundred and fifty-five carats. I weighed it myself." And then as he took Clinton's arm and stumped off again, "Old goat is rich as Croesus. He has been milking rupees out of the mainland for forty years, and his father for fifty years before that. Ten rupees for every slave, ten for every kilo of ivory, God knows how much for copra and gum-copal concessions."

Clinton saw instantly why Sir John called him the old goat. The resemblance was startling, from the white, pointed beard and square yellow teeth to the mournful Roman nose and elongated ears.

He took one look at Clinton, catching his eye for a split part of a second, before he looked away hurriedly, blanching visibly, as he waved his two visitors to the piles of velvet and silk cushions.

"Keep the old beady eye on him," Sir John counseled aside, "and don't eat anything." He indicated the display of sweetmeats and sugared cakes on the bronze trays. "If they aren't poisoned, they'll probably turn your stomach anyway. It's going to be a long night."

The prediction was accurate, the talk went on hour after tedious hour, in flowing Arabic hyperbole and flowery diplomacy, that concealed the hard bargaining. Clinton understood not a word. He forced himself not to fidget, though his bottom and legs soon lost all feeling from the unusual position on the cushions, yet he maintained a stern expression and kept his gaze fixed on the Sultan's wrinkled and whiskered visage. Sir John assured him later that it had helped greatly to shorten the negotiations, yet it seemed a full round of eternity before Sir John and the Sultan were exchanging polite fixed smiles and deep bows of agreement.

There was a triumphant gleam in Sir John's eye as he strode out of the palace. He took Clinton's arm affectionately.

"Whatever happens to you, my dear fellow, generations unborn will have reason to bless your name. We have done it, you and I. The old goat has agreed. The trade will wither and die out within the next few years now."

On the walk back through the narrow streets, Sir John was as lively and cheerful as a man returning from a convivial party rather than the bargaining table. His servants were still waiting his coming, and all the lamps in the consulate were burning.

Clinton would have liked immediately to go back aboard his ship, but Sir John restrained him with an arm about his shoulder, as he called for his Hindu butler to bring champagne.

On the silver tray with the green bottle and crystal glasses was a small package in stitched and sealed canvas. While the uniformed butler poured the champagne, Sir John handed Clinton the package.

"This came in earlier on a trading dhow. I did not have the opportunity to deliver it to you before we left for the palace."

Clinton accepted it warily, and read the address: "Captain Clinton Codrington, Officer Commanding Her Majesty's Ship *Black Joke*. Please forward to H.M. Consul at Zanzibar to await collection."

The address was repeated in French, and Clinton felt a quick thrill kindle his blood as he recognized the bold round script in which the package was addressed. It took an effort to restrain himself from ripping the package open immediately.

However, Sir John was handing him a glass of wine, and Clinton suffered through the toasts, the loyal toast to the Queen, and that ironical one to the Sultan and the new treaty, before he blurted out, "Excuse me, Sir John, I believe this is to be a communication of importance," and the consul waved him into his study and closed the door after him to give Clinton privacy.

On the leather top of the marquetry desk, Clinton slit the seals and stitching of the package with a silver knife from the consul's desk set. From it fell a thick sheaf of closely written notepaper, and a woman's earring of paste and silver, the twin to the one that Clinton wore under his shirt against his chest.

Black Joke groped her way out through the dark, unbuoyed channel an hour before the first flush of dawn in the eastern sky. Turning southward she set all canvas and worked up swiftly to her best speed.

She was making eleven knots when she passed the sloop *Penguin* a little before midnight the following night. *Penguin*, bearing her urgent dispatches, was hull down on the eastern horizon and her running lights were obscured by a heavy tropical deluge, the first fanfare of the coming monsoon that passed between the two vessels hiding them from each other's look-outs.

By dawn the two ships were fifty nautical miles apart, and rapidly widening the gap, while Clinton Codrington paced his quarterdeck impatiently, stopping at every turn to peer impatiently into the south.

He was hurrying to answer the most poignant appeal, the most pressing duty of a dutiful man, the call for succor from the woman he loved, a woman in terrible and pressing jeopardy.

The flow of the Zambezi had a majesty that Zouga Ballantyne had seen on no other great river, neither the Thames, nor the Rhine, nor the Ganges.

The water was the almost iridescent green of molten slag pouring down the side of a steel-yard dump, and it formed powerful, slowly turning vortices in the angles of the broad bends, while in the shallows it seemed to roil upon itself as though the leviathan of all the world sported below its mysterious surface. Here the main channel was more than a mile across, though there were other lesser channels, and other narrower mouths beyond the waving banks of papyrus and cotton-headed reeds.

The small flotilla of boats hardly seemed to move against the current. In the lead was the steam launch *Helen*, named after Zouga's mother.

Fuller Ballantyne had designed the vessel and had it manufactured in Scotland for the disastrous Zambezi expedition which had penetrated only as far as the Kaborra-Bassa gorge. The launch was almost ten years old now, and for most of that time had been the victim of the engineering prowess of the Portuguese trader who had purchased her from Fuller Ballantyne when the expedition was abandoned.

The launch's steam engine creaked and thudded, leaked steam from every pipe and joint, and sprayed sparks and thick black smoke from her wood-burning furnace, exerting herself far beyond the dictates of her age and maker's specifications as she towed the three deeply laden barges against the flow of the mighty river. They were making good a mere fifteen miles a day, and it was more than two hundred upriver from Quelimane to Tete.

Zouga had chartered the launch and her barges to carry the expedition upstream to the jump-off point at Tete. He and Robyn rode in the first barge, together with the most valuable and delicate equipment: the medical stores, the navigational equipment, sextants, barometers and chronometers, the ammunition and firearms, and the personal camping gear.

In the third and last barge, under the bright and restless eye of Sergeant Cheroot, were the few porters who had been recruited at Quelimane. Zouga was assured that the additional hundred porters that he needed could be procured at Tete, but it had seemed prudent to sign on these healthy and vigorous men as they became available. So far there had been no desertions, which was something unusual for the beginning of a long safari, when the proximity of home and hearth could be expected to exert sudden irresistible attractions on the weaker souls.

In the middle barge, on the towline directly behind Zouga, were the bulkier stores. In the main these were trade goods, cloth and beads, knives and axes, some cheap muskets and lead bars for ball, bags of black powder and flints. These were essential commodities with which to buy fresh provisions, to bribe local headmen for right to passage, to purchase concessions to hunt and prospect, and generally to sustain the expedition's objects.

In charge of this middle barge was Zouga's newest and most dubious acquisition, who had been hired as a guide, translator and camp manager. His slight admixture of blood showed in his skin, a smooth olive, and his hair, thick and lustrous as a woman's. His teeth were very white and he flashed them in a perpetually ready smile. Yet, even when he smiled, his eyes were as black as those of an angry mamba.

The governor in Quelimane had assured Zouga that this man was the most famous elephant hunter and traveler in all the Portuguese territories. He had ventured further into the interior than any other living Portuguese, and he spoke a dozen of the local dialects and understood the customs of the local tribes.

"You cannot travel without him," the governor assured Zouga. "It would be madness to do so. Even your own father, the famous Dr. Fuller Ballantyne, made use of his services. It was he who showed your sainted father the way to reach Lake Marawi."

Zouga had raised an eyebrow. "My father was the first man to reach Lake Marawi."

"The first *white* man," the governor corrected him delicately, and Zouga smiled as he realized that it was one of the subtle distinctions which Fuller Ballantyne used to protect the value of his discoveries and explorations. Of course, there had been men living on the shores of the lake for at least two thousand years, and the Arabs and mulattoes had traded there for two hundred years, but they were not *white* men. That made an enormous difference.

Zouga had at last acceded to the governor's suggestions when he had realized that this paragon was also the governor's nephew, and that the further course of the expedition would be much smoothed by employing somebody so well connected.

He had reason to reconsider this opinion within the first few days. The man was a braggart and a bore. He had an endless fund of tales, of which he was always the hero, and the evident disregard for the truth that these demonstrated made all his facts and information suspect.

Zouga was uncertain just how well the man spoke the tribal dialects. He seemed to prefer to communicate with the toe of his boot or the *sjambok* of cured hippopotamus hide which he always carried. As for his hunting prowess, he certainly expended a great deal of powder and shot.

Zouga was sprawled on the barge's afterdeck, in the shade of the canvas awning, and he was sketching on the board he held on his knees. It was a pastime he had taken up in India, and though he knew that he had no special talent, yet it filled the idle hours of camp life and served as a useful record of places and persons, of events and animals. Zouga intended to incorporate some of the sketches and watercolors in the book describing the expedition. The book which would make his fortune and reputation.

He was trying to capture on paper the river's immensity, and the tallness of that aching blue sky set with the afternoon's building thunderheads, when there was the sharp crack of a rifle shot, and he looked up frowning with annoyance.

"He is at it again." Robyn dropped her book into her lap and glanced back at the second barge.

Camacho Nuño Alvares Pereira sat high on the barge's cargo, reloading the rifle, ramrodding the charge down the long barrel. The high beaver hat sat on his head like a chimneystack and the bunch of white ostrich feathers plumed out above the crown like smoke from the furnace. Zouga could not see what he had fired at, but he guessed what would be his next target, for the steamer was being pushed out by the current to the outside of a broad bend in the river, and it was forced to steer between two low sandbanks.

The sand shone in the sunlight with the peculiar brilliance of an alpine snowfield, contrasting with the shapes upon it that looked like rounded granite boulders.

As the steamer slowly closed the gap, the shapes resolved into a troop of sprawling somnolent hippopotami. There were a dozen of them, one a huge scarred bull, lying on his side and exposing the expanse of his belly.

Zouga glanced back from the huge sleeping animals to the figure of Camacho Pereira on the second barge. Camacho lifted the plumed beaver and waved it in jovial salute, his teeth flashing like a semaphore even at that distance.

"You chose him," said Robyn sweetly, following the direction of his gaze.

"That's a comfort." Zouga glanced at his sister. "They told me he was the best sportsman and guide on the east coast."

They both watched Camacho finish loading the rifle and setting the cap on its nipple.

The sleeping hippopotami suddenly became aware of the approaching vessels. They scrambled upright with amazing alacrity for such clumsy-looking animals, and galloped over the white sand, scattering clouds of it under their huge feet and then entered the water in a high crashing cascade of thrown spray, disappearing swiftly, and leaving the water churned and flecked with foam. Standing in the bows of the first barge, Zouga could clearly see the shapes below the surface of the water, galloping in comical slow motion, their movements inhibited by the water. They were silhouetted against the lighter-colored sandbanks, and as he watched them, the ungainly creatures evoked his sympathy and amusement. He remembered a nursery rhyme that his Uncle William had recited to him as a child that began: "A hippo—what—amus?"

Zouga was still smiling as the bull hippo surfaced fifty paces from the barge's side. The bulky gray head broke clear, the flaps of flesh that sealed the nostrils flared open as he breathed and the small round ears fluttered like the wings of a bird as he cleared them of water.

For a moment he stared at the strange vessels through pinkly inflamed, piggy blue eyes. Then he opened the full gape of his jaws, a cavern the color and the texture of a rose. The tusks were yellow and curved to murderous cutting edges, quite capable of biting a bullock cleanly in half, and he no longer seemed fat and comical. Instead he looked exactly what he was, the most dangerous of all African big game.

Zouga knew that the hippopotamus had killed more human beings than all the elephant and lion and buffalo together. With ease they could crunch in the fragile hull of a dugout canoe, the ubiquitous *makoro* of Africa, and then cut in half the terrified swimmers. They would readily leave the water to chase and kill any human who they believed threatened a calf, and in areas where they had been hunted they would attack without any other provocation. However, the steel hulls of the barges were invulnerable even to the jaws and tusks of the massive creature, and Zouga could afford to watch with complete objectivity.

From the bull's gaping jaws came a challenging series of

bellows, each mounting in volume and menace as he moved closer to drive off the intruders who threatened his females and their young. Camacho put his hand up behind his head, and tilted the beaver hat at a jaunty angle over one eye. As always, he was smiling as he swung up the rifle and fired.

Zouga saw the strike of the bullet deep in the animal's throat, it severed an artery and instantly bright crimson blood gushed against the roof of the open mouth, discoloring the gleaming tusks, and pouring in a quick flood over the rubbery, bewhiskered lips. The bull's bellow rose into a piercing scream of agony, and he lunged half clear of the surface in a burst of white water.

"I keel heem!" roared Camacho, and his shout of laughter filled the sudden void of silence as the bull dived below the surface, leaving his blood to swirl away down the current.

Robyn had jumped up and was clinging to the barge's rail, a flush overlaying her sun-bronzed cheeks and throat.

"That was callous butchery," she said quietly.

"No point in it," Zouga agreed. "The animal will die below the surface and be washed out to sea."

But he was wrong, for the bull surfaced again, closer to the barge. His jaws still gaping and streaming gouts of blood, he thrashed and lunged in maddened circles, his bellows distorted by blood and water, as his death frenzy rose to a crescendo. Perhaps the bullet had damaged his brain, making it impossible for him to close his jaws or to control his limbs.

"I keel heem!" roared Camacho, dancing with excitement on the foredeck of the second barge, pouring shot after shot into the immense gray body, grabbing a rifle from his gunbearer or from his second loader as soon as it was primed.

His two black servants worked with the expertise of long practice, so it seemed that Camacho always had a loaded rifle ready to snatch and waiting hands ready to take the smoking weapon from him the moment he had fired.

Slowly the string of barges drew away upstream, leaving the stricken animal wallowing with increasing feebleness in its own expanding circle of blood-tinged waters, until at last it rolled belly upward, all four stubby legs sticking up toward the sky for a moment before it sank at last and the blood was diluted and swept away downstream.

"That was sickening," whispered Robyn.

"Yes, but he has trained those gunbearers of his damned well," said Zouga thoughtfully. "If one is going to hunt elephant, that is the way to do it."

Two hours before sunset the *Helen* edged in toward the south bank. For the first time since leaving Quelimane there was some feature on the shore, beyond the endless reed swamps and sandbanks.

The bank was steeper here, rising ten feet above the river, and game paths had been cut into the earth by thousands of sharp hooves, and polished to shiny clay by the sliding wet bellies of the long lizardlike shapes of the big crocodiles that came tobogganing down the almost vertical slope when they were disturbed by *Helen*'s churning propeller. The heavily armored reptiles with the staring yellow eyes set on a hard horny scale atop the long saurian head repulsed Robyn, the first African animal to do so.

There were trees on the bank now, not just waving stands of papyrus. Chief of these were the graceful palms with stems sculptured like a claret bottle.

"Ivory palms," Zouga told her. "The fruit has a kernel like a ball of ivory."

Then far beyond the palms, low against the ruddy evening sky, they could make out the first silhouette of hills and kopjes. They were leaving the delta at last, and that night the company would camp on firm ground, instead of soft white sand, and burn heavy logs on the campfires rather than the pulpy papyrus stems.

Zouga checked the sentries that Sergeant Cheroot had placed over the irreplaceable cargoes in the barges on which the whole expedition depended, then he supervised the siting of the tents before taking the Sharps rifle and starting out into the open forest and grassland beyond the campsite.

"I come weeth you," offered Camacho. "We keel something."

"Your job is to make camp," Zouga told him coolly, and the Portuguese flashed his smile and shrugged.

"I make one damn fine camp—you see."

But as Zouga disappeared among the trees, the smile slid off Camacho's face, and he hawked in his throat and spat in the dust. Then he turned back into the turmoil of men raising canvas on poles, or dragging in branches of freshly cut thorns to build the scherm against marauding lions or scavenging hyena.

Camacho lashed out at a bare black back. "Hurry, you one mother, twenty-seven fathers." The man cried out at the pain of the cured hippo-hide whip, redoubling his efforts as a purple welt, thick as a man's little finger, rose across his sweat-oiled muscles.

Camacho strode on toward the small grove of trees which Zouga had picked as the site for the tents of his sister and himself, and he saw that the tents had already been erected and that the woman was busy with the evening muster when she treated the ailments of the camp.

She had been seated at the collapsible camp table, but as Camacho approached, she rose and stooped to examine the foot of one of the bearers whose ax had slipped and almost severed a toe.

The Portuguese stopped abruptly, and his throat dried out as he watched her. As soon as they had left Quelimane, the woman had taken to wearing men's breeches. Camacho found them more provocative than naked flesh itself. It was the first time he had ever seen a white woman dressed like this, and he found it hard to take his eyes off her. Whenever she was in sight, he would watch her surreptitiously, waiting hungrily for the moment when she stooped or leaned forward and the moleskin stretched over her buttocks, as it was now. It lasted too short a time, for the woman straightened up and began speaking to the little black girl who seemed more of a companion to her than a servant.

Still Camacho leaned against the bole of one of the tall umsivu trees and watched her with those black eyes gone velvet and swimming with desire. He was carefully weighing the consequences of what he had dreamed about every night since they had left Quelimane. He had imagined every detail, every expression, every word, each movement and each sigh or cry.

It was not as improbable as it seemed at first. She was an Englishwoman, of course, daughter of a famous man of God; both facts should have been prohibitive to his intentions. However, Camacho had a canny instinct when it came to women, there was a sensuality about her eye and in the full soft lips, and she moved with animal awareness of her body. Camacho stirred restlessly and thrust his hands into his pockets, kneading and tugging gently at himself.

He was fully aware that he was a magnificent specimen of masculinity—those thick tresses of black hair, the gypsy feyness of eyes, the blazing smile, and powerful and well-proportioned body. He was attractive, perhaps irresistibly so, for more than once he had intercepted a quizzical appraising look from the woman. Often the admixture of his blood was attractive to white women, it was an exoticism, the attraction of the forbidden and dangerous, and he sensed in this woman a rebellious disregard for the rules of society. It was possible, no more than possible, Camacho decided, and there was unlikely to be a better opportunity than now. The cold stiff English brother was out of camp, would be so for another hour or more, and the woman had finished attending the little group of sick bearers. A servant had brought a kettle of boiling water to her tent, and she was closing the fly.

Camacho had watched this little ritual every evening. Once the oil lamp had cast her shadow upon the canvas, and he had watched her silhouette lowering those tantalizing breeches, and then using the sponge to— He shuddered deliciously at the memory, and pushed himself away from the tree trunk.

Robyn mixed the hot water from the kettle into the enamel basin. It was still scalding hot, but she liked it so that it reddened the skin and left her feeling glowing with cleanliness. She began to unbutton the flannel shirt, sighing with pleasant weariness, when something scratched on the fly of the tent.

"Who is it?" she called sharply, and felt a faint stir of alarm as she recognized the low voice. "What do you want?"

"I want talk you, missus." Camacho's tone was conspiratorial.

"Not now, I am busy." The man repelled her, and yet in a contrary manner fascinated her as well. She had found herself staring at him more than once—as she would at a beautiful but poisonous insect. She was annoyed that he had noticed and was vaguely aware that it was unwise to show even the vaguest interest in a man like that.

"Come back tomorrow." It suddenly occurred to her that Zouga was not in the camp, and she had sent little Juba on an errand.

"I cannot wait. I am sick."

That was one appeal she could not deny.

"Oh, very well. Wait," she called, and buttoned her shirt, and then as an excuse perhaps to delay the moment turned her attention to her instruments still spread on the table that had been carried into the tent. It reassured her to touch them, and rearrange the bottles and pots of medicines.

"Enter," she called at last, and faced the entrance of the tent.

Camacho stooped through the entrance, and for the first time she realized how tall he was. His presence in the small tent was almost overpowering, and his smile seemed to light up the interior. His teeth were startlingly white and perfect;

she found herself staring again, like a chicken at the dancing cobra perhaps. He was beautiful in a decadent, overblown way, he was bareheaded, all dark dancing hair and scalding eyes.

"What is the trouble?" she asked, trying to sound brisk and businesslike.

"I show you."

"Very well," she nodded, and he unbuttoned his shirt. His skin had the sheen of wet marble, but was deep olive in color, and his body hair grew in crisply springing whorls. His belly was molded like that of a greyhound and his waist narrow as a girl's. She ran her eyes down his body, quite certain that her gaze was level and professional, but there was no denying the fact that he was an extraordinary animal.

"Where is it?" she asked, and with a single movement he had unclinched and lowered the light duck trousers that were all he wore on his lower body.

"Where?" she asked, and realized that her voice croaked, and she could not go on with the question, for suddenly it dawned upon her that she had been the victim of a carefully planned ruse, and she was in a potentially dangerous position.

"Is that where it hurts?" she found her voice was still a husky whisper.

"Yes," his voice was a whisper also, and he made a slow stroking movement. "You can fix, maybe." He took a step toward her.

"I can fix, certainly," she said softly, and her hand dropped onto the array of surgical instruments. She actually experienced a twinge of real regret, for it was a superior example of nature's art, and afterward she was relieved that she had selected a needle probe—and not one of the razorlike scalpels that she had reached for.

The instant before she stabbed, he realized what was about to happen and an expression of utter terror blanched his swarthy, handsome face. He tried frantically to return it to whence it had come, but fear had slowed his hand.

He screamed like a teenage girl as the probe plunged into him, and kept on screaming as he spun around on the same spot as though one foot had been nailed to the ground. Now he was using both hands to hold himself, and once again, with cool professional interest, Robyn noticed the quite miraculous change that had taken place.

She advanced the probe once more into the ready position, and Camacho could no longer stand his ground. He snatched up his trousers, and with a last terrified howl, launched himself headfirst into the tent pole. The collision checked him only a moment, and then he was gone, and Robyn found herself trembling violently and yet she was strangely elated. It had been an unusual and instructive experience. However, she would have to use her own personal code when describing it in her journal.

From that evening onward the Portuguese kept well away from Robyn, and she was relieved not to have those hot eyes caressing her wherever she turned. She thought of telling Zouga of the incident, but decided that the embarrassment to both of them and the difficulty of finding the correct words was not worth it. Then there would be the extreme reaction which Zouga would almost certainly have, or that she expected he would have. She had learned never to expect the obvious reaction from her brother; behind the cool and reserved exterior she suspected there existed mysterious passions and turbulent emotions. After all, they were full-blooded brother and sister, and if she was so afflicted, why should he not be also?

On the other hand, she suspected that, like a cornered wild animal, the Portuguese could be a grave danger even to an experienced soldier and man of action like Zouga. She had a horror of forcing her brother into a position which might lead, if not to his death, then at least to serious injury. Besides which, she had effectively taken care of the man herself. He would be no further trouble, she decided comfortably, and she dismissed Camacho from her mind, and concentrated instead on the pleasure of the last few leisurely days of the voyage upstream.

The river had narrowed, and the flow was swifter, so that the rate of the convoy's advance slowed even further. The banks provided an ever-changing panorama. Sitting under the awning, with Zouga sketching or writing beside her, she was able to call his attention to the new birds and trees and animals and to have the benefit of his knowledge, gathered to be sure mostly from books, but still wide-reaching and interesting.

The hills of the escarpment rose in a series of cockscombs, so two-dimensional that they seemed to be cut out from thin sheets of some opaque material that allowed the colors of the sunrise to glow through with a weird luminosity. As the sun rose higher, the colors washed out to ethereal eggshell blues, and finally faded altogether in the heat haze of midday, to reappear in the late afternoon in a new suit of totally different colors—pale pinks and ash of roses, ripe plum and delicate apricot.

The hills formed a backdrop to the forests that now ran in a narrow belt along the riverbanks: tall galleries of trees, with spreading upper branches in which the troops of vervet monkeys frolicked. The trunks of these trees were daubed with multicolored lichens, sulfurous yellows, burnt oranges and the blues and greens of a summer sea. The tangled ropes of lianas, which as a child Robyn had called "monkey ropes," dangled down from the upper branches to touch the surface of the river or cascade into the dense greens of the undergrowth.

Beyond this narrow strip of vegetation, there were occasional glimpses of a different forest on the higher, drier ground, and Robyn saw again with a sharp nostalgic pang the ugly and bloated baobab tree with its scrubby bare little branches topping the huge swollen stem. The African legends that her mother had repeated to her so often explained how the Nkulu-kulu, the great great one, had planted the baobab upside down, with its roots in the air.

Nearly every baobab had a nest of one of the big birds of prey in its bare branches, each a shaggy mass of dried twigs and small branches looking like a small, airborne haystack. Often the birds were at the nest site, sitting on a lookout branch, with that typical raptorial stillness, or soaring above in wide circles, with only an occasional lazy flap of the spread wings, and the stiff tip feathers feeling the air currents like the fingers of a concert pianist upon the keys.

There was very little game along this part of the river, and the rare antelope rushed back into cover at the first distant approach—a pale blur of movement, with a mere fleeting glimpse of the tall corkscrew horns of a greater kudu, or the flirt of the white, powder-puff underside of a reedbuck's tail.

The game close to the river had been heavily hunted, if not by the Portuguese themselves then by their armed servants, for nearly two hundred years.

When Zouga asked Camacho, "Do you ever find elephant on this part of the river?" the Portuguese had flashed his smile and declared, "If I find heem, I keel heem."

A sentiment that was probably shared by nearly every traveler along this busy waterway, and which accounted for the timidity and scarcity of game in the area.

Camacho was reduced to firing at the roosting fish eagles on their fishing perches overhanging the water. These handsome birds had the same snowy white head, breast and shoulders of the famous American bald eagle, and a body of lovely russet and glistening black. When a shout of Camacho's laughter signaled a hit, a bird would tumble untidily over its disproportionately large wings as it fell into the water, reduced from imperial dignity to awkward and ungainly death by the strike of the lead bullet.

Within a few days Camacho had recovered from the peculiar bowlegged and deliberate gait with which he favored the injury that Robyn had inflicted on him, and his laughter regained its ringing timbre. But there were other injuries that did not heal so readily, those to his pride and his masculinity. His lust had been changed on the instant to burning hatred, and the more he brooded upon it the more corrosive it became and the deeper his craving for vengeance.

However, his personal considerations would have to wait. There was still much important work for him to do. His uncle, the governor of Quelimane, had placed much trust in him by assigning him to this task—and his uncle would be unforgiving of any failure. The family fortune was involved, and to a lesser extent the family honor, although this last was a commodity that through constant attrition had lost much of its luster. However, the family fortunes had suffered considerably since Portugal had been forced to heed the Brussels Treaty. What was left to the family had to be protected. Gold before honor, and honor only when it does not affect the profits—this might have been the family motto.

His uncle had been perceptive, as always, in recognizing in this English expedition a further threat to their interests. It was, after all, headed by the son of a notorious troublemaker who could be expected to aggravate the enormous damage done by the father. Furthermore, nobody could be sure of the real objects of the expedition.

Major Ballantyne's assertion that it was an expedition to find his missing father was, of course, utterly absurd. That explanation was much too simple and direct, and the English were never simple or direct. This elaborate expedition must have cost many thousands of English pounds, a huge sum of money, far beyond the means of a junior army officer, or the family of a missionary whose futile effort to navigate the Zambezi had ended in disgrace and ridicule, a sick old man who must have perished years ago in the uncharted wilderness.

No, there was another motive for all this activity—and the governor wanted to know what it was.

It was, of course, possible that this was a clandestine reconaissance by an officer of the British Army ordered by his overbearing government. Who knew what outrageous designs they had upon the sovereign territory of the glorious Portuguese empire? The avarice of this impudent race of shopkeepers and tradesmen was scarcely to be believed. The governor did not trust them, despite their traditional alliance with Portugal.

On the other hand, it might indeed be a private expedition, but the governor never lost sight of the fact that it was led by the son of that notorious old busybody who had possessed the scavenging eye of a vulture. Who knew what the old devil had stumbled upon out there in the unknown land, a mountain of gold or silver, the fabled lost city of Monomatapa with all its treasures intact: anything was possible. Of course, the old missionary would have sent news of the discovery to his own son. If there was a mountain of gold out there, then the governor would be very pleased to know about it.

Even if there were no new treasures to discover, there were certainly old ones to protect. It would be Camacho Pereira's duty to steer the expedition away from certain areas, to prevent it from stumbling on secrets known not even to the governor's masters in Lisbon.

Camacho's orders were clear: distract the Englishman by accounts of the insurmountable difficulty of travel in certain directions, the swamps, the mountain ranges, the disease, the savage animals and even more savage men, and contrast that with the friendly people in pleasant lands, rich with ivory, that lay in other directions.

If this was unsuccessful—and Major Ballantyne had all the earmarks of arrogance and intractibility peculiar to his nation— then Camacho was to use what other means of persuasion came to hand. This was a euphemism perfectly understood by both the governor and his nephew.

Camacho had almost convinced himself that this was really the only sensible course of action. Beyond Tete there was no law except that of the knife, and Camacho had always lived by that law. Now he savored the thought. He had found the Englishman's unconcealed contempt as galling as the woman's rejection had been painful.

He had convinced himself that the reason for the attitude toward him of both brother and sister was his mulatto blood. This was a sensitive area of Camacho's self-esteem, for even in Portuguese territories where miscegenation was almost universal practice, mixed blood still carried a stigma. He would enjoy the work ahead, for not only would it wipe out the insults he had suffered, but it would bring rich pickings, and even after they had been shared out with his uncle and others, there would still be much profit in it for himself.

The equipment that the expedition carried represented, in Camacho's view, a vast fortune. There were bargeloads of excellent trade goods. Camacho had taken the first opportunity to check secretly the contents of the packs. There were firearms, and valuable instruments, chronometers and sextants, and there was a forged-steel field safe that the Englishman kept locked and guarded. The merciful God alone knew how many golden English sovereigns it contained, and if He did not know, then his good uncle the governor knew less. It would make the division of spoils more in Camacho's favor. The more he brooded upon it, the more he looked forward to the arrival at Tete, and the jump-off into the unexplored territory beyond.

To Robyn the tiny town of Tete marked her real arrival in Africa, and her return to the world for which she had trained so assiduously and yearned so deeply.

She was secretly glad that Zouga had used the unloading of the barges as an excuse not to accompany her.

"You find the place, sissy, and we'll go there together to-morrow."

She had changed back into skirts, for small and isolated as it was, Tete was still a backwater of civilized behavior and there was no point in giving offense to the local inhabitants. Though she found the heavy folds about her legs annoying, she soon forgot them as she walked the single, dusty street of the village where her father and mother must have walked together for the last time, and peered at the mud-walled trading stores built haphazardly along a rough line with the bank of the river.

She stopped at one of these little *dukas* and found that the storekeeper could understand a mixture of her basic Swahili, English and Nguni language, enough anyway to direct her on to where the village street petered out in a mere footpath that meandered off into the acacia forest.

The forest was hushed in the heat of the noon, even the birds were silent and the mood weighed on Robyn, depressing her and awakening the memories of long-ago mourning.

She saw a flash of white among the trees ahead, and stopped, reluctant to go on to what she knew she would find. For a moment she was transported to girlhood again, to a gray November day standing beside her Uncle William waving upward at the passenger decks of the departing ship, her eyes so dimmed with tears that she could not make out at the crowded rail the beloved face for which she searched, while the distance between ship and quay opened like the gulf between life and death.

Robyn shook the memory away and went on. There were six graves among the trees, she had not expected that, but then she recalled that there had been heavy mortality among the members of her father's Kaborra-Bassa expedition, four of disease, one drowned and a suicide.

The grave for which she searched stood a little apart from the others. It was demarcated by a square of whitewashed river stones and at the head was a cross built of mortar. It also had been whitewashed. Unlike the other graves, it had been kept cleaned of grass and weed, and the cross and stones freshly painted. There was even a small bunch of wilted wild flowers standing in a cheap blue china vase. They were not more than a few days old. That surprised Robyn.

Standing at the foot of the grave she read the still fully legible lettering on the plaster cross:

In loving memory of
Helen
beloved wife of Fuller Morris Ballantyne.
Born August 4th 1814. Died of fever December 16th 1852.
God's will be done.

Robyn closed her eyes and waited for the tears to come up from deep inside, but there were no tears, they had been shed long ago. Instead there were only the memories.

Little fragments of memory played over and over in her mind—the smell of strawberries as they gathered them together in Uncle William's garden, standing on tiptoe to place one of the lush red fruits between her mother's white teeth and then eating the half that was left especially for her; lying cuddled under her bedclothes as she listened drowsily to her mother's voice reading aloud to her in the candlelight; the lessons at the kitchen table in winter, under the elm trees in summer, and her own eagerness to learn and to please; her first pony ride, her mother's hands holding her in the saddle, her legs too short for the stirrups; the feel of the soapy sponge down her back as her mother stooped over the iron hip bath; the sound of her mother's laughter, and then at night the sound of her weeping beyond the thin partition beside her cot; then the final memory of the smell of violets and lavender as she pressed her face to her mother's bodice.

"Why must you go, Mama?"

"Because your father needs me. Because your father has sent for me, at last."

And Robyn's own terrible consuming jealousy at the words, mingled with the sense of impending loss.

Robyn knelt in the soft cushion of dust beside the grave, and began to pray, and as she whispered, the memories came crowding back, happy ones and sad ones together, and she had not felt so close to her mother in all the intervening years.

She did not know how long she had knelt there, it seemed an eternity, when a shadow fell across the earth in front of her and she looked up, jerked back to the present with a little gasp of surprise and alarm.

A woman and child stood near her, a black woman, with a pleasant, even pretty face. Not young, in her middle thirties possibly, though it was always difficult to guess an African's age. She wore European-style clothing, castoffs probably, for they were so faded that the original pattern was hardly visible, but starched and fastidiously clean. Robyn sensed that they had been donned for the occasion.

Although the child wore the brief leather kilt of the local Shangaan tribe, he was clearly not a full-blooded African. He could not have been more than seven or eight years of age, a sturdy boy, with a head of dusty-colored curls and oddly pale-colored eyes. There was something vaguely familiar about him that made Robyn stare.

He carried a small bunch of the yellow acacia flowers in his hands, and smiled shyly at Robyn before hanging his head and shuffling his feet in the dust. The woman said something to him and tugged at his hand, and he came hesitantly to Robyn and handed her the flowers.

"Thank you," she said automatically, and raised the bouquet to her nose. They were faintly but sweetly perfumed.

The woman hiked her skirts and squatted beside the grave, removed the wilted flowers and then handed the little blue china vase to the boy. He scampered away toward the riverbank.

While he was gone the woman plucked out the first green sprouts of weeds from the mound of the grave and then rearranged the whitewashed stones carefully. The familiar manner in which she performed the chore left no doubt in Robyn's mind that she was responsible for the upkeep of her mother's grave.

Both women maintained a friendly, comfortable silence, but when their eyes met they smiled and Robyn nodded her thanks. The child came trotting back, muddy to the knees and slopping water from the vase, but puffed up with self-importance. He had clearly performed this task before.

The woman took the vase from him and set it carefully on the grave, then both of them looked expectantly toward Robyn and watched her while she arranged the acacia flowers in the vase.

"Your mother?" said the woman softly, and Robyn was startled to hear her speak English.

"Yes." She tried to hide her surprise. "My mother."

"Good lady."

"You knew her?"

"Please?"

After the valiant opening, the woman had very little English, and their communication was halting, until Robyn, out of the habit of talking to little Juba, said something in Matabele. The woman's face lit with pleasure and she answered swiftly in a language which was obviously one of the Nguni group, and whose inflection and vocabulary differed very little from that to which Robyn was accustomed.

"You are Matabele?" Robyn demanded.

"I am Angoni," the woman put in hastily, for there was rivalry and hostility between even the closely related tribes of the Nguni.

Her tribe, the Angoni, had swept northward from their origins in the grassy hills of Zululand, and crossed the Zambezi River thirty years before, she explained in her lilting musical dialect. They had conquered the land along the northern shores of Lake Marawi. It was from there that the woman had been sold to one of the Omani slavemasters, and had come down the Shire River in chains.

Unable to keep up with the slave caravan, reduced by starvation and the fevers and hardships of the long journey, she had been freed of her chains and left for the hyenas beside the slave road. It was there that Fuller Ballantyne had found her and taken her into his own small camp.

She had responded to his rough nursing and when she was recovered, Fuller had baptized her with the Christian name of Sarah.

"So my father's detractors are mistaken," Robyn laughed, and spoke in English. "He made more than one convert."

Sarah did not understand but laughed in sympathy. By now

it was almost dusk and the two women, followed by the half-naked child, left the little cemetery and started back along the footpath, with Sarah still telling how when Robyn's mother, summoned at last by Fuller Ballantyne, arrived in Tete with other members of the Kaborra-Bassa expedition, Sarah had been presented to her by Fuller as a personal servant.

By now they had stopped at a fork in the path, and after a moment of hesitation Sarah invited Robyn to her village, which was only a short way off the path. Robyn glanced up at the sun and shook her head: it would be dark in an hour and Zouga would be certain to turn out the camp to search for her if she had not returned by then.

She had enjoyed the hours spent with the young woman and the bright sweet child, and when she saw Sarah's obvious disappointment, she said quickly, "Although I must go, I will return tomorrow at the same time. I wish to hear all you can tell me of my mother and father."

Sarah sent the little boy with her as far as the buildings of the village, and after the first few yards Robyn quite naturally took the boy's hand, and he skipped along beside her, chattering gay childish nonsense, which helped to lift her somber mood until Robyn laughed and chattered with him.

Before they reached the outskirts of Tete, Robyn's fears were confirmed. They met Zouga and Sergeant Cheroot. Zouga was armed with the Sharps rifle and angry with relief the moment he saw her.

"Damn me, sissy, but you have had us all beside ourselves. You've been missing for five hours."

The child stared at Zouga with wide eyes. He had never seen anything like this tall lordly man with the imperious manner and sharp commanding voice. He must be a great chief, and he slipped his hand out of Robyn's, retreated two paces, then turned and darted away like a sparrow from the circling hawk.

Some of Zouga's anger left him as he watched the child go, and a small smile touched his lips.

"For a moment I thought you'd picked up another stray."

"Zouga, I found Mama's grave." Robyn hurried to him and took his arm. "It's only a mile or so."

Zouga's expression changed again and he glanced up at the sun that was already on the tops of the acacia trees and turning deep smoldering red.

"We'll come back tomorrow," he said. "I don't like to leave the camp after dusk, there are too many jackals lurking about—

two-legged jackals." Firmly, he led her back toward the village, continuing his explanation as they walked.

"We are still having a great deal of difficulty obtaining porters, despite the fact that the governor of Quelimane assured me they would be readily available, and the good Lord knows there are àny amount of able-bodied men hereabouts. Yet that strutting poppinjay Pereira finds obstacles at every turn." The frown made him look much older than his years as did the full beard which he had allowed to grow since disembarking from *Black Joke*. "He says that the porters refuse to contract until they know the direction and duration of the safari."

"That seems logical," Robyn agreed. "I know I wouldn't carry one of those huge packs, unless I knew where I was going."

"I don't think at all that it's the porters; there is no reason why the destination should worry them. I am offering top wages, and not a single man has come forward."

"What is it, then?"

"Pereira has been trying to wheedle our intentions out of me ever since we left the coast. I think this is a form of blackmail: no porters until I tell him."

"Then why don't you tell him?" Robyn asked, and Zouga shrugged.

"Because he is too damned insistent. It's not a casual interest, and instinct warns me not to trust him with any information which it is not essential for him to know."

They walked on in silence until they reached the perimeter of the camp. Zouga had laid it out on the lines of a military base, with an outer stockade of acacia thorn branches, a Hottentot guard at the gate and the *boma* for the porters separated from the stored depot by the tent lines.

"It looks like home already," Robyn congratulated him, and would have left him for her own tent when Camacho Pereira hurried forward.

"Ah! Major, I wait for you with good news."

"That's a pleasant change," Zouga murmured dryly.

"I find man who has seen your father, not eight months ago."

Robyn turned back instantly, her excitement matching that of the flamboyant Portuguese, and she spoke directly to him for the first time since the incident in her tent.

"Where is he? Oh, this is wonderful news."

"If it's true," qualified Zouga, with considerably less enthusiasm.

214

"I bring the man, damned quick—you see!" Camacho promised, and hurried away toward the porters' *boma*, shouting as he went.

Within ten minutes he returned dragging with him a skinny old man dressed in greasy tatters of animal skins, and with his eyes rolling up into his head with terror.

As soon as Camacho released him, the old man prostrated himself before Zouga, who sat in one of the canvas camp chairs under the awning of the dining tent, and gabbled replies to the queries that Camacho shouted at him in hectoring tones.

"What dialect is that he speaks?" Zouga interrupted within the first few seconds.

"Chichewa," Camacho replied. "He no speak other."

Zouga glanced at Robyn, but she shook her head. They had to rely entirely on Camacho's rendition of the old man's replies.

It seemed that the old man had seen "Manali," the man with the red shirt, at Zimi on the Lualaba River. Manali had been camped there with a dozen porters, and the old man had seen him with his own eyes.

"How does he know it was my father?" Zouga asked.

Everybody knew Manali, the old man explained, he was a living legend from the coast to "Chona langa," the land where the sun sets.

"When did he see Manali?"

One moon before the coming of the last rains, which made it in October of the previous year, as Camacho had said, about eight months previously.

Zouga sat lost in thought, but his gaze fixed with such ferocity on the unfortunate who groveled before him that the old man suddenly burst out on a plaintive note that made Camacho's handsome face flush with anger and he touched the skeletal ribs with the toe of his boot, a threatening gesture that quieted the old man instantly.

"What did he say?" Robyn demanded.

"He swears he speak the truth only," Camacho assured her, resurrecting his smile with an effort.

"What else does he know of Manali?" Zouga asked.

"He speak with the porters of Manali, they say they go follow the Lualaba River."

It made some sense, Zouga thought. If Fuller Ballantyne was indeed seeking the source of the Nile River to recover his lost reputation, then that is where he would have gone. The Lualaba, which was reputed to run directly northward, was one of obvious choices for the source river.

215

Camacho questioned the old man for another ten minutes, and would have taken the hippo-hide to jog his memory, but Zouga stopped him with a gesture of annoyance. It was obvious that there was nothing further to learn from him.

"Give him a bolt of *merkani* cloth and a *khete* of beads—and let him go," Zouga ordered, and the old man's gratitude was pathetic to watch.

Zouga and Robyn sat later than usual beside the campfire, while it collapsed slowly upon itself in spasmodic torrents of rising sparks and the murmur of sleepy voices from the porters' *boma* died into silence.

"If we go north," Robyn mused, watching her brother's face, "we will be going into the stronghold of the slave trade, from Lake Marawi northward. From that area, into which no white man, not even Pater, has ever ventured, must come all the slaves for the markets of Zanzibar and the Omani Arabs—"

"What about the evidence of the trade to the south?" Zouga glanced across the clearing at the silent figure of Juba, waiting patiently by the entrance to Robyn's tent. "That girl is the living proof that a new trade is flourishing south of the Zambezi."

"Yes, but it seems to be nothing compared to the activity north of here."

"The northern trade has been fully documented. Father reached Marawi and followed the slave caravans down to the coast fifteen years ago, and Bannerman at Zanzibar has written a dozen reports on the Zanzibar market," Zouga pointed out, nursing a precious tumbler of his fast-dwindling supply of whiskey and staring into the ashes of the fire. "Whereas nobody knows anything about the trade with the Monomatapa and the Matabele south of here."

"Yes, I acknowledge that," Robyn admitted reluctantly. "However, in his *Missionary Travels* father wrote that the Lualaba was the source of the Nile and he would one day prove it by following it from its headwaters. Besides which, he has been seen in the north."

"Has he, though?" Zouga asked mildly.

"That old man—"

"—Was lying. Somebody put him up to it, and I don't need more than one guess," Zouga finished.

"How do you know he was lying?" Robyn demanded.

"If you live long enough in India you develop an instinct for the lie," Zouga smiled at her. "Besides, why would Father
216

wait eight years *after* he disappeared to explore the Lualaba River? He would have gone there directly—if he had gone north."

"My dear brother," Robyn's voice was stinging, "it would not be the legend of Monomatapa that makes you so stubbornly determined to go south of the river, would it? Is that gleam in your eye the gleam of gold?"

"That is a mean thought." Zouga smiled again. "But what does intrigue me is the determination of that great guide and explorer, Camacho Pereira, to discourage any journey to the south, and instead to lead us northwards."

Long after Robyn had disappeared into her tent and the lantern within was extinguished Zouga sat on beside the fire, nursing the whiskey in the tumbler and staring into the fading coals. When he reached his decision he drained the last drop of precious golden brown spirit in the glass and stood up abruptly. He strode down the lines to where Camacho Pereira's tent stood at the furthest end of the camp.

There was a lantern burning within even at this late hour, and when Zouga called out, a squeak of alarm in feminine tones was quickly hushed with a man's low growl and a few minutes later Camacho Pereira pulled the fly aside and peered out at Zouga warily.

He had thrown a blanket over his shoulders to cover his nudity, but in one hand he carried a pistol and relaxed only slightly as he recognized Zouga.

"I have decided," Zouga told him brusquely, "that we'll go north, up the Shire River to Lake Marawi—and then on to the Lualaba River."

Camacho's face shone like the full moon as he smiled.

"That is very good. Very good—much ivory, we find your father—you see, we find him damn soon."

Before noon the following day Camacho, with a great deal of shouting and swishing of the kurbash, marched a hundred strong healthy men into the camp. "I find you porters," he announced. "Plenty porters—damn good, hey?"

The Christian girl Sarah was waiting beside the grave again when Robyn came down through the acacia forest the following afternoon.

The child saw her first and ran to greet her. He was laughing with pleasure and Robyn was struck once again by the familiarity of his face. It was something about his mouth and his eyes. The resemblance to somebody she had known was so

217

forcible that she stopped dead and stared at him, but could not recapture the memory before the boy took her hand and led her to where his mother waited.

They went through the little ritual of changing the flowers on the grave and then settled side by side on a fallen acacia branch. It was cooler in the shade and in the branches above their heads a pair of shrikes hunted little green caterpillars. The birds were black and white across the back and wings, their breasts a striking shade of crimson that glowed like the blood of a dying gladiator, and Robyn watched them with rare pleasure while she and Sarah talked quietly.

Sarah was telling her about her mother, how brave and uncomplaining she had been in the terrible heat of the Kaborra-Bassa where the black ironstone cliffs turned the gorge into a furnace.

"It was the bad season," Sarah explained. "The hot season before the rains break." Robyn recalled her father's written account of the expedition in which he had laid the blame for the delays upon his subordinates, old Harkness and Commander Stone, so that they had missed the cool season, and entered the gorge in the suicide month of November.

"Then when the rains came, the fever came with it," Sarah went on. "It was very bad. The white men and your mother became sick very quickly." Perhaps her mother had lost much of her immunity to malaria during the years in England while she waited for her husband's summons. "Even Manali himself became sick. It was the first time I had seen him sick of the fever. He was filled with the devils for many days." The expression described vividly the delirium of malarial fever, Robyn thought. "So he did not know when your mother died."

They were silent again. The child, bored by the interminable talk of the two women, threw a stone at the birds in the acacia branches above their heads, and with a flash of their marvelous crimson breasts the two shrikes winged away toward the river, and again the child engaged Robyn's attention. It was as if she had known that face all her life.

"My mother?" Robyn asked, still watching the child.

"Her water turned black," said Sarah simply. Blackwater fever; Robyn felt her skin prickle. When malaria changed its course, attacking the kidneys and transforming them into thin-walled sacs of clotted black blood, that could rupture at the patient's smallest movement. The blackwater fever, when the urine changed to mulberry-colored blood, and few, very few, victims ever recovered.

218

"She was strong," Sarah went on quietly. "She was the last of them to go." She turned her head toward the other neglected graves. The curly pods of the acacia were scattered thickly over the unadorned mounds. "We buried her here, while Manali was still with his devils. But later, when he could walk, he came with the book and said the words for her. He built the cross with his own hands."

"Then he went away again?" Robyn asked.

"No, he was very sick, and new devils came to him. He wept for your mother." The thought of her father weeping was something so completely alien that Robyn could not imagine it. "He spoke often of the river that had destroyed him."

Through the acacia trees there were glimpses of the wide green river, and both their heads turned toward it naturally.

"He came to hate that river as though it was a living enemy that had denied him a road to his dreams. He was like a man demented, for the fever came and went. At times he would battle with his devils, shouting his defiance the way a warrior *giyas* at the enemy host." The *giya* was a challenge dance with which the Nguni warrior baits his adversary. "At other times he would speak wildly of machines that would tame his enemy, of walls that he would build across the waters to carry men and ships up above the gorge." Sarah broke off, her lovely moon face stricken with the memory, and the child sensed her distress and came to her, kneeling on the earth and laying his dusty little head in her lap. She stroked the tight cap of curls with an absentminded caress.

With a sudden little chill of shock Robyn recognized the child. Her expression changed so drastically that Sarah followed the direction of her gaze, looking down with all her attention at the head in her lap, then up again to meet Robyn's eyes. It did not really need words to pass, the question was posed and answered with silent exchange of feminine understanding, and Sarah drew the child toward her with a protective gesture.

"It was only after your mother . . ." Sarah began to explain and then fell silent, and Robyn went on staring at the little boy. It was Zouga at the same age, a dusky miniature Zouga. It was only the color of his skin which had prevented her from seeing it immediately.

Robyn felt as though the earth had lurched beneath her feet, then it steadied again and she felt a strange sense of release. Fuller Ballantyne was no longer the godlike figure hewn from

219

unforgiving, unbending granite that had overshadowed her entire life.

She held out both her hands to the child and he went to her unhesitatingly, trustingly. Robyn embraced him, and his skin was smooth and warm as she kissed him. He wriggled against her like a puppy, and she felt a deep glow of affection and gratitude to the child.

"He was very sick," said Sarah softly, "and alone. They had all gone or died, and he was sad, so that I feared for his life."

Robyn nodded understanding. "And you loved him?"

"There was no sin in it, for he was a god," said Sarah simply.

"No," thought Robyn with intense relief. "He was a man, and I, his daughter, am a woman."

In that moment she knew that she never need again feel shame and guilt for her body and the demands and desires which sprang from it. She hugged the child who was proof of her father's humanity, and Sarah smiled with relief.

For the first time in her life Robyn was able to face the fact that she loved her father, and she understood part of the compulsion that over the years had grown stronger rather than dwindling.

The longing she had felt for the father had been submerged completely by the awe and majesty of the legend. Now she knew why she was here, on the banks of this majestic river, on the very frontier of the known world. She had come not to find Fuller Ballantyne, but to discover rather the father and the self that she had never known before.

"Where is he, Sarah, where is my father? Which way did he go?" she demanded eagerly, but the woman dropped her eyes.

"I do not know," she whispered. "I woke one morning and he was gone. I do not know where he is, but I will wait for him, until he returns to me and his son." She looked up quickly. "He will come back?" she asked pathetically. "If not to me then for the child?"

"Yes," Robyn answered with certainty that she did not feel. "Of course he will come back."

The selection of porters was a lengthy business, and after Zouga had signaled his choice with a slap on the shoulder, the men were sent to Robyn's tent to be examined for signs of

220

disease or infirmity that might prevent them from performing their duties.

Then came the allocation of packs.

Although Zouga had already made up and weighed each pack, making sure that not one of them exceeded the stipulated eighty pounds weight, the newly engaged porters had to watch the loads reweighed publicly, and then there was interminable haggling over the size and balance of the burden that each of them would carry for months, perhaps even years ahead.

Although Zouga brusquely forbade Pereira to hasten the selection process with his kurbash, and entered good-naturedly into the spirit of banter and bargain, he was, in fact, using the occasion to assess the spirit of his men, to pick out the malcontents who would sour that spirit in the hardships ahead, and also to select the natural leaders to whom the others turned instinctively for decision.

The following day when planning the order of march, Zouga used the knowledge he had gained in this way. To begin with, seven of the more obvious troublemakers were given a *khete* of beads each and ordered out of the camp without explanation or apology. Then Zouga called out four of the brightest and best and made them captains of divisions of twenty porters each.

They would be responsible for maintaining the pace of the march, for preventing pilfering of the loads, making and breaking camp, distributing rations, and acting as the spokesmen of each division, presenting complaints to and transmitting orders from Zouga.

When the roll was complete there were one hundred and twenty-six names upon it, including Sergeant Cheroot's Hottentots, the porters who had come up from Quelimane, Camacho Pereira and the two principals—Robyn and Zouga himself.

It would be a slow and unwieldy caravan unless properly organized, that was bad enough—but on the march it would also be very vulnerable. Zouga gave much thought to defense of the column, and he and Sergeant Cheroot shared the last quarter bottle of whiskey as they pooled their experience and planned the order of march.

Zouga, with a small party of local guides and personal bearers, planned to travel independently of the main caravan, reconnoitering the terrain ahead and making himself free to prospect and hunt as the opportunity arose. He would return most nights to rejoin the march, but would be equipped to spend many days out of contact.

Camacho Pereira with five of the Hottentot musketeers would lead the van of the main column, and even when Robyn chaffed him lightly, Zouga saw nothing ludicrous in Camacho marching under the Union Jack.

"It's an English expedition, and we will carry the flag," Zouga replied stiffly.

"Rule, Britannia," Robyn laughed irreverently, and Zouga ignored her and went on describing the order of march.

The divisions of porters would remain separate but closed up, and Sergeant Cheroot with the remainder of his musketeers would form the rear guard of the column.

There was a simple system of signals to control the movements of the column, a prearranged series of blasts on the kudu-horn trumpets would sound the "march" or "halt," the "close up" or "form square."

For four days Zouga exercised the column in these evolutions and though proficiency would only come much later, at last he felt that they were ready to make a start, and he told Robyn so.

"But how are we to cross the river?" she asked looking across at the north bank.

The river was half a mile wide, and the heavy rainfalls over millions of square miles had drained into it. The flow was swift and powerful. If they were going northward to the Shire River and Lake Marawi they would need a flotilla of dugout canoes and many days to make the crossing to the north bank.

The steam launch *Helen* had long ago departed on the flood of the river, making good at least twenty knots with the current pushing her, so she would already be back to Quelimane.

"All the arrangements have been made," Zouga told her, and she had to be satisfied with that.

On the last day Robyn allowed Juba to accompany her to the cemetery for the first time, and both of them were laden with gifts: bolts of trade cloth and a thirty-five-pound bag of ceramic beads, the most sought-after scarlet *sam-sam* variety.

It was as much as she dared ask for from the expedition's stores without arousing Zouga's ire and interest.

She had thought of telling Zouga of Sarah and the child, but had wisely decided against it.

Zouga's reaction to finding a half-brother of mixed blood was terrible to contemplate. Zouga had acquired his opinions

222

on caste and color in the hard school of the Indian army, and to find that his own father had trespassed against these iron rules would be too much of a shock. Instead, Robyn had mentioned that she had met one of her father's former servants, who tended their mother's grave over the years. The gift would have to be in proportion to these services.

Sarah and her child were waiting by the grave, and she accepted the gifts with a gracious little curtsy and her palms held together at the level of her eyes.

"We leave tomorrow," Robyn explained, and saw the immediate regret in Sarah's eyes, followed by acceptance.

"It is God's will," and Robyn could almost hear her father saying it.

Juba and the child soon became involved in collecting the pods from a Kaffir boom tree nearby and stringing together the pretty scarlet lucky beans, each with its little black eye at the end, to make necklaces and bracelets. The two of them, girl and boy, made a delightfully uninhibited pair, their laughter and shrill happy voices a pleasant background to the talk under the acacia tree.

Robyn and Sarah had become friends in the short time they had known each other. Her father had written in his *Missionary Travels* that he preferred the company of black people to white, and certainly all the evidence seemed to point that way. It seemed that Fuller Ballantyne had done nothing but squabble with his own kind. Contact with other white men seemed to bring out in him all the pettiness, suspicion and jealousy of his complex nature; while he had spent the greater part of his life with black men, and received from them trust and honor and lasting friendships. His relationship with Sarah was only a natural extension of those feelings, Robyn realized. She contrasted these feelings with those of her brother, and knew that he could never cross the dividing line. A black man could possibly earn Zouga's liking and even his respect, but the gulf was too wide. For Zouga they would always be "those people," and she guessed that he could never change. If he lived on in Africa for another fifty years, he would never learn to understand them, while she, within weeks, had made real friendships. She wondered if, like her father, she would come one day to prefer them to her own kind. It didn't seem possible now, but she recognized in herself the capacity for adjustment.

Beside her, Sarah was speaking, so softly, so shyly that Robyn had to make an effort to tear herself away from her own thoughts and ask:

"What was that you said?"

"Your father, Manali, will you tell him about the boy when you find him?"

"He did not know?" Robyn was stunned, and Sarah shook her head.

"Why did you not go with him then?" Robyn demanded.

"He did not wish it. He said the journey would be too hard, but in reality, he is like an old bull elephant who does not like to stay too long with his cows but always must follow the wind."

Camacho Pereira towered above the wiry little tribesmen, checking off their names against the camp register. This evening he wore a jerkin of kudu skin that was decorated with fancy stitching and trade beads, and unfastened down the front to expose bulging hairy chest and the flat belly with its ridged muscles like the patterns in the sand of a windswept beach.

"We feed them too much," he told Zouga. "Fat nigger is lazy nigger." He chuckled when he saw Zouga's expression, for that word had already been the cause of dissension. Zouga had forbidden him to use it, particularly in front of the expedition's black servants; for some of them it was the only word of English they understood. "Feed small, kick heavy and they work hard," Camacho went on with relish.

Zouga ignored these gems of philosophy. He had heard them before, many times. Instead he turned to the captains of divisions, and watched them finish the rationing.

Two of them, their arms floury to the elbows, dipped into the bags of meal and doled it out to the shrinking line of porters. Each man had his calabash or chipped enamel basin to receive the scoop of stone-ground red-brown grain. Then one of the other captains slapped a split and smoked river fish on top of the pile. The fish looked like Scotch kippers, but their odor punched like a prizefighter. Weevils, maggots and all, they were a delicacy that the porters would miss once they left the river.

Pereira suddenly hauled a man out of the line and hit him a lusty clout across the back of the head with the stock of his kurbash.

"He come twice, try for double," he explained cheerfully, and took a playful kick at the man as he ran. If it had landed it would have knocked him off his feet, but all the porters had come to anticipate Camacho's flying boots.

Zouga waited until the last porter had been rationed, then he called to the captains.

"*Indaba!* Tell the men, *indaba.*"

It was the call to council, to discuss affairs of consequence, and the whole camp left the cooking fires and came hurrying, agog with excitement.

Zouga paced up and down before the ranks of intent squatting men, drawing out the moment, for he had come quickly to realize the African love of the theatrical. Most of them could understand the basic Nguni which Zouga now spoke with some fluency, for many of them were Shangaans or Angoni.

Now he spread his arms to his audience, paused for a second and then announced portentously,

"*Kusasa isufari,* tomorrow the march begins!"

There was a hive murmur of comment and excitement, and then one of the captains rose from the front rank.

"*Phi? Phi?* Where? Which way?"

Zouga lowered his arms, and let the suspense build up for a few moments, and then he stabbed out toward the far blue southern hills with a bunched fist.

"*Laphaya!* That way!"

They roared with approval, just as they would have done if Zouga had pointed north or west for that matter. They were ready to go now. The direction was not important. The captains of divisions, the indunas, were shouting out the translation to those who had not understood and the first roar of the crowd settled to a boisterous rumble of comment and speculation, but it died away suddenly, and Zouga turned.

Camacho Pereira had stepped beside Zouga, his face was swollen and dark with rage. This was the first time he had heard Zouga's intention to go southward. When he started to speak, it was so forcefully that droplets of spittle flew from his lips. He was using one of the local dialects, and speaking so swiftly that Zouga understood only a word here and there. The sense was unmistakable, however, and he saw the shock on the faces of the men who squatted before them.

Camacho was warning them of the dangers beyond the southern hills. Zouga heard the word "Monomatapa" and knew that he was speaking of the terrible armies of the legendary empire, merciless legions whose favorite sport was to cut off a man's genitals and force him to eat them himself. The shock of the listening black faces was changing swiftly to terror. Camacho had been speaking for only a few seconds; a minute more and nothing would induce the caravan to march, two minutes more and most of his porters would have deserted by morning.

There was nothing to be gained by arguing with the Portuguese except an unseemly shouting match, which would be watched with interest by the entire assembled camp. One thing that Zouga had learned was that the Africans, like the Asians he had come to know well in India, were immensely respectful of a victor and impressed by success. He could demonstrate neither quality by becoming embroiled in an undignified wrangle in a language that none of the spectators could understand.

"Pereira!" he snapped, in a tone that cut through the Portuguese's torrent of words, and for an instant stilled them. Zouga had the Englishman's peculiar sense of fair play which made him warn an enemy before an attack. As the Portuguese turned to face him, Zouga swung in toward him with two light steps and he flicked his left hand at Camacho's eyes, forcing him to throw up both hands to protect his face. As he did so, Zouga slammed his fist into his belly, just under the ribs, with a force that doubled him in the middle, his breath whooshing out of his gaping mouth in an agonized explosion of sound and his hand dropping to cover his injured belly, leaving his face open for the next blow.

It was a short chopping left-handed shot that took Camacho cleanly under the right ear, on the hinge of the jaw. The plumed beaver hat spun off his head. His eyes rolled up into his skull, leaving the whites glaring madly, and Camacho's knees gave way under him. He pitched forward, making no effort to cushion his fall and dropped face down on to the gray sandy soil.

The silence lasted only a second, and then a shout went up from the watchers. Most of them had felt Camacho's boots or his kurbash, and they hugged one another happily. The trepidation that Camacho's little speech had raised was completely lost in wonder at the swiftness and the effect of those two blows. Most of them had never seen a man strike with a bunched hand, and the novelty of this form of combat impressed and delighted them.

Casually, Zouga turned his back on the prone figure. Not a trace of anger showed on his face, in fact he was smiling slightly as he strolled down the front rank of men and lifted one hand to quieten them.

"There are soldiers who travel with us," he told them, in a low voice that yet reached clearly to every one of them, "and you have seen them shoot." He had made sure they had, and that news of the prowess in weapons of Sergeant Cheroot's men would travel ahead of them.

"You see that flag?" He flung one hand dramatically at the red-and-white-and-blue jack floating above the main tent on its improvised flag pole. "No man, no chief nor warrior dare—"

"Zouga!" shrieked Robyn. To the terrible urgency of her tone Zouga reacted instantly, spinning aside with two dancing paces, and the crowd exploded with a single word, a deep drawn-out "Jee!"

It is a blood-chilling sound, for it is the cry with which an African warrior encourages himself or another in the fatal moments of a battle to the death.

Camacho's stroke had been aimed at the small of Zouga's back. He was a man who had fought with the knife many times before, and he had not taken the more tempting target between the shoulder blades, where the point could turn against the ribs. He had gone for the soft area above the kidneys, and even with Robyn's warning, Zouga was not quite quick enough. The point raked his hip, slitting the cloth of his breeches in a six-inch rent, beneath which skin and flesh opened cleanly and the bright blood spread swiftly to the knee.

"Jee!" The deep sonorous chant of the watchers as Camacho reversed the stroke of his extended right hand, cutting sideways at Zouga's belly. The blade twinkled and hissed like an angry cobra, ten inches of tempered steel, and Zouga threw up his hands and sucked in his belly muscles as he jumped back. There was a sharp tug as the point caught in his shirt, but it did not touch the skin.

"Jee!" again as Camacho lunged. His face was bloated and mottled with purple and white, the eyes squinting with rage and the aftereffects of the blow to his jaw. Zouga felt the sting of the wound on his hip pulling open as he swayed back out of the path of the blade, and the stronger flood of warm blood down his leg.

He paused out of range of the knife for Zouga had heard the snap of a weapon being cocked and from the corner of his eye he saw Sergeant Cheroot leveling the Enfield, waiting for a clear shot at the Portuguese.

"No! Don't shoot!" Zouga called urgently. He did not relish a bullet in his own belly, for he and Camacho were dancing close together, with the weaving point of the knife seeming to bind them to each other.

"Don't shoot, Sergeant!" There was another reason why he could afford no interference. There were a hundred men judging

227

him now, men with whom he would march and work in the months and years ahead. He needed their respect.

"Jee!" sang the watchers, and Camacho was panting with rage. Again the blade in his right hand whispered like the wing of a swallow in flight, and this time Zouga overreacted, blundering back half a dozen paces, and then losing his balance for a moment he dropped on one knee and put a hand to the ground to steady himself. But as Camacho charged again, he rebounded to his feet and arched his hips aside, the way a matador swings out of the line of the bull's run. In the hand that had touched the ground, Zouga held a handful of the coarse gray sand.

His eyes were locked to those of the Portuguese, it was the eyes not the knife hand that would signal Camacho's intentions. They flickered left, while the hand feigned the other way, and Zouga moved in past the blade, and was ready again when Camacho rounded.

They faced each other, shuffling in a slow circle that stirred wisps of dust around their feet. Camacho kept the knife low, and stirred it gently as though he were conducting a slow passage of music, but Zouga studying his eyes saw the first small nervous flickers of uncertainty.

He jumped in, launching himself off the right foot.

"Jee!" roared the watchers, and for the first time Camacho broke ground, falling back and then turning hurriedly as Zouga checked and feinted to his open side.

Twice more Zouga drove him back with threats, until it needed only a feint with his upper body to make Camacho scramble away. The watchers were laughing now, mocking shouts of glee every time he gave ground, and the rage that had flushed Camacho's face had given way to fear, the angry purple mottling had chilled to white. Zouga was still watching his eyes, as they darted from side to side seeking an escape— but the knife kept weaving between them, bright and razor-sharp, broad as three fingers and grooved along its length to break the suction of clinging wet flesh once it was buried.

Camacho's eyes flickered away once more and Zouga moved, pulling the knife hand around as he crossed the man's front, holding out his empty hand for the eyes to follow, keeping the other low and moving in as close to the knife as he dared, then at the moment that Camacho lunged, using the momentum of his avoiding turn, he hurled the handful of coarse sand into Camacho's eyes, blinding him, and still in the same movement reversing his direction, and going straight in on the knife,

228

chancing it all on locking the wrist before the man could see again.

"Jee!" the crowd roared as Camacho's wrist slapped into Zouga's palm, and he locked it down with all his strength.

Tears were already streaming from Camacho's eyes, and his lids fluttered, grinding the sharp grains across the unseeing eyeballs. He could not judge nor meet Zouga's weight as, still locked grimly to the wrist, he threw him off balance. As Camacho went over, Zouga reared back, resisting with all his strength, holding the knife arm against the fall. Something went with a loud rubbery popping sound in Camacho's shoulder and he screamed, as he sprawled again, facedown, with the arm twisted up behind him.

Once again Zouga jerked viciously, and this time Camacho screeched like a girl and the knife dropped from his fingers. He made a feeble effort to snatch it with the other hand, but Zouga trod down on the blade with a booted foot, then scooped it up, released the damaged arm and stepped back holding the heavy weapon in his right hand.

"Bulala!" chanted the watchers. "Bulala! Kill him! Kill him!" They wanted to see the blood, for that was the fitting end and they hungered for it.

Zouga stabbed the blade deeply into the trunk of the acacia tree and then wrenched against the steel. It snapped at the hilt with a crack like a pistol shot, and he dropped the hilt contemptuously.

"Sergeant Cheroot," he said, "get him out of this camp."

"I should shoot him," the little Hottentot told him as he came up, and thrust the muzzle of the Enfield rifle into the fallen man's belly.

"If he tries to enter the camp again, you can shoot him. But now just get him out."

"Big mistake." Sergeant Cheroot's pug face took on a theatrically mournful expression. "Always stamp on the scorpion—before he stings."

"You are hurt." Robyn was running toward him.

"It's a scratch." Zouga unwound the bandanna from around his throat and pressed it to the wound in his hip as he strode away toward his tent, forcing himself not to favor it with a limp. He had to get away quickly for the reaction was on him, he felt dizzy and nauseated, the wound stung abominably and he did not want anybody to see that his hands were trembling.

* * *

229

"I reset the shoulder," Robyn told Zouga as she bound up his hip wound. "I don't think there is anything broken, and it went in again very neatly—but you," she shook her head, "you won't be able to march with that. Every step will pull against the stitches."

She was right, it was four days before the march could begin.

Camacho Pereira put that time to good use. He had left an hour after Robyn reset his dislocated shoulder, four paddlers taking a dugout canoe down the Zambezi with the current. When they would have pulled into the bank to make camp, Camacho snarled at them from the bow where he crouched, hugging the injured arm, that even after being set and strapped into a sling, still ached so fiercely that it lit little white sparks of agony behind his closed eyelids every time he tried to doze.

He also would have liked to rest, but his hatred drove him onward, and the dugout canoe arrowed downcurrent under a fat yellow moon that paled slowly at the coming of the new day.

Camacho went ashore on the south bank of the Zambezi at noon at the small native village of Chamba, a hundred miles below Tete. He paid off the crew of the dugout and hired two bearers to carry his rifle and blanket roll. Then he set off again immediately along the network of narrow footpaths that criss-cross the entire African continent like the blood vessels of a living body, laid down by wandering men and migrating animals over the centuries.

Two days later he reached the Road that runs from the Mountains of Dismay, Inyangaza, to the sea. The Hyena Road was a secret track. Although it paralleled the old road from the coast to Vila de Manica, it kept forty miles north of it, following the course of the Pungwe River so that there would be water for the multitudes who unwillingly used the road on their long, last journey from their homeland to other lands, other continents.

Vila de Manica was the last outpost of the Portuguese administration in East Africa. A decree by the governor in council forbade any man, black or white, Portuguese or foreigner, to journey beyond that clay-walled fort toward the haunting range of mountains with the chilling name. It was for this reason that the Hyena Road had been secretly opened by enterprising men, and pushed up through the dense forests of the lower slopes to the bleak and open grasslands atop the mountains.

The march from Chamba to the Pungwe River was a hundred and fifty miles. To make it in three days with the agony of a

230

healing shoulder was good going, and once they reached it, the temptation to rest was almost irresistible. But Camacho kicked his two bearers to their feet and drove them with stinging words and lash along the deserted road toward the mountains.

The road was twice as wide as any of the other footpaths they had followed to reach it, wide enough for a double column rather than the Indian file that was the usual order of African travel. Although the surface had been beaten hard by the passage of thousands of bare feet, it was a source of satisfaction to Camacho that the road had clearly not been used for many months, except by the occasional herd of antelope, and once, perhaps a week before, by an old bull elephant, whose huge piles of dung had long dried out.

"The caravan has not passed yet," Camacho muttered as he scanned the trees ahead for the shapes of the vultures and searched without success for the sly skulking shapes of hyena in the undergrowth beside the road.

True there were human bones scattered along the route, here and there the thick knuckle of the thigh bone that had defied even the iron jaws of the scavengers, or other splintered fragments that they had overlooked, but even these were dried out and bleached white. They were the debris of the previous caravan that had passed this way three months before.

He had reached the road in time, and now he hurried along it, pausing now and then to listen or to send one of the bearers up a tree to search ahead.

However, it was two days later that they heard the first faint sound of many voices, and this time Camacho himself climbed to the highest fork of one of the umsisa trees beside the track, and peering ahead he saw the vultures circling, a wide slow wheel of tiny black specks turning against the silver and blue ranges of cloud, as though caught in a hidden vortex of the high heavens.

He sat in the fork thirty feet above the ground, while the sound of voices grew stronger, became the sound of singing. This was no sound of joy, but a terrible mourning dirge, slow and heartbreaking, rising and fading as flukes of the breeze and folds of the ground blanketed the sound, but each time it came back a little stronger, until Camacho could make out far away the head of the column, like the head of a maimed serpent writhing out of the forest into an open glade a mile ahead.

He slid down the trunk of the umsisa and hurried forward. There was an armed party ahead of the main column, five blacks dressed in the tatters of cast-off European-style clothing

231

and carrying muskets, but at their head was a white man, a little man with a face like that of a vicious gnome, wrinkled and burned darkly by the sun. The thick drooping black mustache was laced with gray, but he stepped out with a bouncing elastic stride and he recognized Camacho from two hundred paces and snatched his hat off his head and waved it.

He shouted "Camacho!" and the two men ran to embrace, and then hold each other at arm's length, laughing with pleasure. It was Camacho who sobered first, the laughter changing to a scowl as he said, "Alphonse, my beloved brother, I have bad tidings—the worst possible."

"The Englishman?" Alphonse was still smiling, he had a tooth missing from the front of his upper jaw, which made the cold humorless smile seem less dangerous than it really was.

"Yes, the Englishman," Camacho nodded. "You know of him?"

"My father sent a message. I know." Alphonse was the governor of Quelimane's eldest surviving son, full-blooded Portuguese by the lawfully wedded bride who had come out forty years previously from Lisbon, a sickly mail-order bride, who had borne three sons in swift succession, the first two of which had succumbed to malaria and infantile dysentery even before the appearance of the little wizened yellowed mite whom they had named Alphonse José Vila y Pereira, and expected to bury with his brothers before the end of the rains. However, it was the mother they had buried in the end, and the child had flourished at the breast of a black wet nurse.

"He did not go north, then?" Alphonse demanded, and Camacho dropped his eyes guiltily, for he was speaking to the eldest, full-blooded and legitimate son.

Camacho himself was a bastard and a half-breed, son of one of the governor's once beautiful mulatto concubines, now fat and faded and forgotten in one of the back rooms of the seraglio. He was not even recognized as a son, but had to bear the ignominious title of nephew. This in itself was enough for him to show respect for the other, but added to this Alphonse was as determined as their father had been at the same age, though even crueler and harder. Camacho had seen him sing a plaintive fado as he flogged a man to death, accompanying the traditional love song with the flute and percussion of the lash.

"He did not go north," Camacho agreed uneasily.

"You were told to see that he did."

"I could not stop him. He is English"—Camacho's voice croaked a little—"he is stubborn."

232

"We will speak again of that," Alphonse promised coldly. "Now, swiftly tell me where he is and what he plans to do."

Camacho recited the explanation he had prepared, skirting delicately around the most offensive parts of the story, and dwelling on subjects such as the wealth that the Ballantyne Expedition carried with it rather than his own brutal beating at the Englishman's hands.

Alphonse had thrown himself down in the shade of a tree beside the track and listened broodingly, chewing at the straggling ends of his mustache, filling in for himself the conspicuous gaps in his half-brother's recital, and speaking again only at the end.

"When will he leave the valley of the Zambezi?"

"Soon," Camacho hedged, for the unpredictable Englishman might already be halfway to the escarpment. "Although I cut him deeply, it may be he has had himself carried in a *mushila* [litter]."

"He must not be allowed to enter the Monomatapa," Alphonse said flatly, and came to his feet with a single lithe movement. "The best place to do the business would be in the bad ground below the rim of the valley."

He glanced back along the winding road. The head of the column was a mile away still, across a glade of open golden grass. The shuffling double rank of bowed creatures, yoked at the neck, did not seem human, though the singing was sad and beautiful.

"I can spare fifteen men."

"It will not be enough," Camacho cut in swiftly.

"It will be," said his brother coldly, "if you do the business in the night."

"Twenty men," Camacho pleaded. "He has soldiers with him, trained soldiers, and he is a soldier himself."

Alphonse was silent, weighing risk and advantage—but the worst part of the Hyena Road already lay behind the column, and each mile nearer the coast, the land was tamer, the risk diminished and the need for guards less pressing.

"Twenty!" he agreed abruptly, and turned to Camacho. "But not one of the foreigners must escape." Looking into his brother's cold black eyes, Camacho felt his skin crawl. "Leave no sign, bury them deep, so the jackal and hyena do not dig them out. Use the porters to carry the expedition's equipment to the place in the hills, and when they have done so, kill them also. We will bring it down with the next caravan to the coast."

"*Sí. Sí.* I understand."

233

"Do not fail us again, my beloved cousin-brother." Alphonse made the endearment a threat, and Camacho swallowed with a nervous little gulp.

"I will leave as soon as I have rested."

"No," Alphonse shook his head. "You will leave immediately. Once that Englishman enters the land beyond the mountains, there will soon be no more slaves. It is bad enough that there has been no gold for twenty years and more, but if the river of slaves were to dry up, both my father and I would be displeased—very displeased."

At Zouga's order the long mournful blast of the kudu-horn trumpet shattered the silence of the utterly dark hour before the dawn.

The indunas took up the cry "Safari! We march!" and they prodded the sleeping porters off their reed sleeping mats. The campfires had burned down to dim red mounds of coals smothered in the soft gray powder of their own ash. As fresh logs were thrown upon them they flared up in a false dawn that lit the underside of the umbrella-shaped acacia trees with wavering yellow light.

The smell of roasting *ropoko* cakes rose on tendrils of smoke straight into the windless dark sky. The muted voices became louder, more cheerful, while the flames drove away the chills and the nightmares.

"Safari!" The cry was taken up, and the divisions assembled, ghostly figures in the gloom, emerging more clearly as the growing dawn light snuffed out the stars.

"Safari!" And the mass of men and equipment resolved itself and order grew out of chaos.

Like those long columns of big shiny black serowe ants that endlessly cross and recross the African earth, the stream of porters moved steadily away into the still gloomy forest.

As each of them passed Zouga and Robyn standing together at the gate of the thorn scherm, they shouted a greeting and executed a few prancing steps to demonstrate their loyalty and enthusiasm—while Robyn laughed with them and Zouga called encouragement.

"We no longer have a guide, and we don't know where we are going." She took Zouga's arm. "What is to become of us?"

"If we knew, it would take all the fun out of it."

"At least a guide."

"While you thought I was hunting I went out as far as the escarpment which is further than that swattering Portuguese

234

ever went, further than any white man, except of course Pater, has ever been. Follow me, sissy, I am your guide."

She looked up at him now in the strengthening light of coming dawn.

"I knew you were not hunting," she told him.

"The escarpment is rugged and very broken, but I have examined two passes through the telescope that I think will go—"

"And beyond that?"

He laughed. "We will find out." Then he squeezed her around the waist. "That is the whole fun of the thing."

She studied his face with full attention for a few moments. The new full beard emphasized the strong, almost stubborn, lines of his jaw. There was a piratical devil-may-care lift to the corner of his lips, and Robyn realized that no man of conventional mind would have proposed and engineered this expedition. She knew he possessed courage, his exploits in India had proved that beyond doubt, and yet when she looked at his sketches and watercolors and read the rough notes he was making for the book, she discovered a sensitivity and an imagination she had never before suspected. He was a difficult person to know and understand.

Perhaps she could have told him about Sarah and the child or even about Mungo St. John, and that night in the main cabin of *Huron*, for when he laughed like this, the stern features softened with humor and humanity, and green lights showed in his eyes.

"That's what we are here for, sissy, the fun of it all."

"And the gold," she teased, "and the ivory."

"Yes, by God, the gold and ivory as well. Come on, sissy, this is where it truly begins," and he limped after the column as its tail disappeared into the acacia forest, favoring his injured leg and using a freshly cut staff to move across the sandy earth. For a moment Robyn hesitated and then she shrugged aside her doubts and ran to catch up with her brother.

That first day the porters were rested and eager, the valley floor flat and the going easy, so Zouga ordered *tirikeza*, the double march, so that even at their slow pace the column left many miles of dusty earth behind them that day.

They marched until the heat came up in the middle of the morning and the merciless sun dried the sweat the moment it burst through their pores and left tiny salt crystals on the skin, like diamond chips. Then they found shade and lay like dead men through the heat of noon, stirring again only when the lowering sun gave the illusion of cooling the air and the blast of the kudu-horn trumpet forced them to their feet again.

The second stage of the *tirikeza* lasted until sunset when it became too difficult to see the ground under their feet.

The fires were dying and the voices of the porters in their thornbush scherms had slowly descended through the occasional mutter and soft murmur to ultimate silence before Zouga left his tent and limped silently as a night creature out of the camp.

He carried the Sharps rifle slung over his shoulder, the staff in one hand and a bull's-eye lantern in the other, while the Colt revolver hung in its holster upon his belt. Once clear of the camp, he stepped out as briskly as his leg would allow two miles along the freshly beaten footpath that the column had made that afternoon until he reached the fallen tree trunk that was the agreed rendezvous.

He stopped and whistled softly, and a smaller figure stepped out from the undergrowth into the moonlight, carrying a rifle at high port. The jaunty step and alert set of head on narrow shoulders was unmistakable.

"All is well, Sergeant."

"We are ready, Major."

Zouga inspected the ambush positions that Sergeant Cheroot had chosen for his men astride the path. The little Hottentot had a good eye for ground and Zouga found his trust and liking for him increasing with every such display of competence.

"A puff?" Jan Cheroot asked now, with the clay pipe already in his mouth.

"No smoking," Zouga shook his head. "They will smell it." And Jan Cheroot reluctantly buttoned the pipe into his hip pocket.

Zouga had chosen a position in the center of the line, where he could make himself comfortable against the trunk of the fallen tree. He settled down with a sigh, his leg thrust out stiffly ahead of him: after the *tirikeza* it was going to be a long wearying night.

The moon was a few days short of full, and it was almost light enough to read the headlines of a newspaper. The bush was alive with the scurry and rustle of small animals, and it kept their nerves tightened and their ears strained to catch the other sounds for which they waited.

Zouga was the first to hear the click of a pebble striking against another. He whistled softly and Jan Cheroot snapped his fingers, imitating the sound of a black scarab beetle to show that he was alert. The moon had dropped low upon the hills, and its light through the forest trees laid silver-and-black tiger stripes upon the earth and played tricks with the eye.

Something moved in the forest, and then was gone, but Zouga picked up the whisper of bare feet scuffling the sandy disturbed earth of the path, and then suddenly they were there, and very close, man shapes in file, hurrying, silent, furtive. Zouga counted them, eight—no, nine. Each of them straight-backed under the bulky burden he carried balanced upon his head. Zouga's anger simmered to the surface and yet at the same time he felt a grim sense of satisfaction that he had not wasted the night.

As the leading figure in the file came level with the fallen tree trunk, Zouga pointed the muzzle of the Sharps rifle straight into the air and pressed the trigger. The crash of the shot broke the night into a hundred echoes that bounced and rebounded through the forest, and the silence magnified it until it seemed like the thunder of all the heaven.

The echoes had not dispersed, and the nine figures were still frozen with shock when Jan Cheroot's Hottentots fell upon them from every direction in a shrieking pack.

The sound of their cries was so shrill, so inhuman, that it even startled Zouga, while the effect on the victims was miraculous. They let fall the burdens they carried and dropped to earth in a paralysis of superstitious awe, adding their wails and screams to the pandemonium. Then the thud and clatter of cudgels against skull and cringing flesh mingled with it all, and the screams and howls rose to a new pitch.

Jan Cheroot's men had spent much time and care on selecting and cutting their clubs and now they wielded them with a lusty glee, making up for a night of discomfort and boredom. Sergeant Cheroot himself was in the thick of it, and in his excitement he had almost lost his voice. He was yipping squeakily like a demented fox terrier with a cat up a tree.

Zouga knew he would have to stop it soon, before they killed or seriously maimed somebody, but the punishment was richly earned, and he gave it a minute more. He even joined in himself when one of the prostrate figures scrambled to its feet and tried to dart away into the undergrowth. Zouga swung his staff and brought him down again with a blow to the back of his knees, and when he sprang up again as though he were on springs, Zouga dropped him in the dust with a short right-handed punch to the side of the head.

Then, stepping back out of the fray, Zouga took one of his few remaining cheroots from his top pocket, and lit it from the chimney of the lantern, inhaling with deep satisfaction, while around him the enthusiasm of his Hottentots flagged a little as they tired and Jan Cheroot regained his voice and became coherent for the first time.

"*Slat hulle, kerels!* Hit them, boys!"

It was time to stop it, Zouga decided and opened the shutter of the lantern.

"That's enough, Sergeant," he ordered, and the thuds of blows became intermittent and then ceased while the Hottentots rested on the cudgels, panting and streaming with the honest sweat of their exertions.

The deserting porters lay moaning and whimpering in pitiful heaps, with their loot scattered about them. Some of the packs had burst open, and trade cloth and beads, flasks of gunpowder, knives, mirrors and glass jewelry were strewn about and trodden into the dirt. Zouga's fury returned at full strength when he recognized the tin box which contained his dress uniform and hat. He delivered a last kick at the nearest figure and then growled at Sergeant Cheroot, "Get them on their feet and clean it up."

The nine deserters were marched into camp, roped together and bearing not only the heavy burdens which they had stolen but also an impressive set of contusions, cuts and bruises. Lips were swollen and split, some teeth were missing, a good many eyes were puffed closed and most of their heads were as lumpy as newly picked Jerusalem artichokes.

More painful than their injuries, however, was the ridicule of the entire camp, which turned out to a man to jeer and mock them with laughter.

Zouga lined up the captives, with their booty piled in front of them, and in the presence of their peers made a speech in limping but expressive Swahili in which he likened them to sneaking jackals and lurking hyena and fined them each a month's wages.

The audience was delighted with the show, and hooted at every insult while the culprits tried physically to shrink themselves into insignificance. There was not one of the watching porters who would not have done the same thing. In fact, had the escape succeeded, most of them would have followed the next night, but now that it had been foiled, they could enjoy the vicarious pleasure of having escaped punishment, and the discomfort of their companions who had committed the sin of being caught.

During the noon rest that divided the two stages of the next day's *tirikeza*, the clusters of porters chatting in the shade of the mopani groves agreed that they had found a strong master to follow, one whom it would not be easy to cheat, and it gave them all confidence for the future of the safari. Coming directly after his defeat of the Portuguese, the recapture of the deserting porters added immeasurably to Zouga's standing.

The four indunas of the divisions agreed that it was fitting that such a man have a praise name. They conferred at length, and after considering many suggestions, finally decided on "Bakela."

"Bakela" means "the one-who-strikes-with-the-fist," for this was still the one of Zouga's many accomplishments which impressed them most.

Where Bakela led, they were now prepared to follow, and though Zouga spread a dragnet of his faithful Hottentots behind the column each of the following nights, no more fish swam into it.

"How many?" Zouga whispered, and Jan Cheroot rocked on his heels, sucking softly on the empty clay pipe and squinting his oriental eyes thoughtfully, before he shrugged, "Too many to count. Two hundred, three hundred, perhaps even four."

The ground had been plowed up into soft fluffy dust by the multitude of huge cloven hooves, and the pats of dung were round and shaped in little concentric circles, completely indistinguishable from those of domestic cattle, and the rank smell of cattle was heavy on the heated air of the Zambezi Valley.

For an hour they had followed a small herd through the open mopani forest, stooping under the low branches with the thick shiny double leaves, each of them shaped like the cloven spoor that they followed, and now where the spoor emerged from the forest it had been joined by another much larger herd.

"How close?" Zouga asked again, and Jan Cheroot slapped his own neck where one of the buffalo flies had settled. It was the size of a honeybee, but dull black and the long needle of its proboscis stung as though it was white-hot.

"We are so close that the flies that follow the herd still linger," and he pushed his forefinger into the nearest pat of wet dung, "and the body heat is still in the dung, but," Jan Cheroot went on as he wiped his finger on a handful of dry grass, "they have gone into bad ground—" and he pointed ahead with his chin.

A week before they had reached the escarpment of the valley, but each of the possible passes that Zouga had examined through the telescope had proved on closer inspection to be a dead end, the gorges pinching out into abrupt rock faces, or falling off into some terrifying abyss.

They had turned westward, following the edge of the escarpment, Zouga ranging ahead with his small scouting party. Yet day after day those impassable heights loomed at their left hand, rising sheer into the unknown. Even below the main escarpment, the ground was tortured and riven by deep gorges and ravines, by cliffs of dark rock and hills of enormous tumbled boulders. The ravines were choked with the drab gray stands of thorn, so densely interwoven that a man would have to crawl in on hands and knees, and his vision would be limited to a few feet ahead, yet the herd of many hundreds of buffalo that they were following had disappeared into one of these narrow gorges, their thick hides impervious to the cruel red-tipped thorn.

Zouga took the telescope from his haversack carried by his bearer, and carefully scanned the ground ahead. It had a wild and menacing beauty and for the hundredth time in the last few days he wondered if there was a way through this maze to the empire of Monomatapa.

"Did you hear that?" Zouga demanded, lowering the glass suddenly. It had sounded like the distant lowing of the milk herd as it returned to the farmyard.

"Ja!" Sergeant Cheroot nodded, as again the mournful sound echoed against the black ironstone cliffs, and was answered by the bleat of a calf. "They are lying up in the jessie bush. They won't move again until sunset."

Zouga glanced up at the sun. It was four hours or so from its zenith. He had over a hundred mouths to feed, and they had rationed out the last of the dried fish two days before.

"We will have to go in after them," he said, and Jan Cheroot removed the stem of the pipe from between yellow teeth and spat reflectively in the dust.

"I am a very happy man," he said. "Why would I want to die now?"

Zouga lifted the glass again, and while he scanned the ridges of higher ground about the choked valley, he imagined what it would be like in there. When the first shot was fired, the jessie bush would be filled with huge, furiously charging black animals.

The fluky breeze coming down the steep narrow valley brought with it another powerful whiff of the herd smell before it faded.

"The wind is down the valley," he said.

"They have not smelled us," Cheroot agreed, but that was not what Zouga had meant. Again he examined the nearest ridge of high ground. A man could work his way along the edge of it, up toward the head of the narrow valley.

"Sergeant, we are going to flush them out," he smiled, "like spring pheasant."

Zouga had found the native names of his personal bearers hard to pronounce and tiresome to remember. There were four of them, he had selected them with care, rejecting half a dozen others in the process, and he had rechristened them Matthew, Mark, Luke and John. They had earned enormous prestige by being so honored, and had proved keen and willing to learn their duties. In a few days they were already proficient at reloading, though not yet of the same standard as Camacho Pereira's gunbearers—but that would come.

Zouga carried the Sharps rifle, but each of the four bearers had one of the heavy four-to-the-pound elephant guns that Harkness had recommended to Zouga. At any time he had only to reach back over his shoulder and a loaded and primed weapon would be thrust into his hand.

Apart from the elephant guns, his bearers carried his blanket roll, water bottle, canvas food bag, spare ball and powder and the little clay firepot from which a smoldering ball of moss and wood pulp could be blown into flame in a few seconds. It was wise to conserve the amenities of civilization, such as Swan vestas, for the months and years ahead.

Zouga relieved Luke, the quickest and most wiry of the four, of all his equipment except the firepot, pointed out the path along the cliff and explained carefully to him what he was to do.

All of them listened with approval, even Sergeant Cheroot nodded sagely at the end. "My old mother tells me, before she throws me out, 'Jan,' she says, 'remember it's brains what counts.'"

In the mouth of the valley, where it debouched out into the mopani forest, was a low outcrop of rock, the ironstone boulders had been split into strange shapes by sun and erosion, and they formed a natural redoubt, with chest-high walls behind which a man could crouch. A hundred paces directly ahead, the dense palisade of iron-gray thorn blocked the valley, but the ground between was fairly open, with a few stunted second-growth mopani bushes and clumps of coarse dried razor grass as high as a man's shoulder.

Zouga moved his party into the lee of the rocks, and himself scrambled onto the highest point to follow through his glass the progress of the almost naked bearer as he picked his way cautiously along the rim of the cliff. Within half an hour he had worked so far up the escarpment that he had disappeared from Zouga's view.

It was another hour before, from the head of the valley, a thin tendril of pure white smoke rose gently into the heated air, and then bent into the elegant shape of an ostrich plume before the gentle breath of the breeze.

With miraculous suddenness the rising column of white smoke was surrounded by another living cloud, hundreds of tiny black specks that weaved and darted about and around it. The faint but excited bird cries carried down to where Zouga waited, and through the glass he could make out the rainbow, turquoise and sapphire plumage of the blue jay as they rolled and dived for the insects put to flight by the flames. Competing with them for the feast were the iridescent black drongos with their long forked tails catching the sunlight with metallic glitter as they swirled above the spreading smoke clouds.

Luke was doing his job well. Zouga grunted with satisfaction as new columns of smoke rose at intervals, sealing off the valley from side to side as they spread to meet each other. Now there was a solid wall of smoke from one cliff to the other, and as the smoke turned dirty black, billowing upward, spinning upon itself, carrying flaming fragments of leaves and twigs within it, it began to roll ponderously down the valley.

It reminded Zouga of a snow avalanche he had watched in the high Himalayas, the slow majestic progress gathering weight and momentum, building up its own windstorm as it sucked the valley of air.

He could see the tops of the flames now, leaping above the thorn, and hear the sound of them, like the whispering waters of a distant river. The alarm bellow of a bull buffalo rang like the blast of a war trumpet from the ironstone cliffs, and the whisper of flames rose swiftly to a dull crackling roar.

The smoke clouds rose across the sun, plunging them into an unnatural gloom, and Zouga felt a sharp drop in his spirits

242

at the extinction of the bright morning sun; that infernal swirling pall of dun smoke seemed to hold a world of menace.

From the edge of the jessie bush broke a herd of kudu, led by a magnificent bull with his corkscrew horns laid flat along his back. He saw Zouga standing on the pinnacle of rock and snorted with alarm, swinging away out of easy shot with his cows flying big-eared and scary behind him, their fluffy white tails flickered away among the mopani groves.

Zouga scrambled down from his too obvious position, and propped himself comfortably against the rock, checked the nipple on the cap of the Sharps and then cocked the big hammer.

Ahead of the flames a white dust cloud was rising over the tops of the jessie bush, and another sound was added to the roar of flames. It was a low thunder that made the earth tremble under their feet.

"They are coming," Jan Cheroot muttered to himself, and his little eyes sparkled.

A single buffalo burst from the palisade of thorn. He was an old bull, almost bald across the shoulders and rump, the dusty gray skin crisscrossed by a thousand ancient scars and scabby with the bites of bush ticks. The big bell-shaped ears were torn and tattered, and one thickly curved horn was broken off at the tip. He came out at a crabbing gallop, dust exploding at each hoof beat like miniature mortar bursts.

He was on a line to pass the rocky redoubt at twenty paces, and Zouga let him come on to twice that distance before he threw up the Sharps rifle.

He aimed for the fold of thick skin under the throat that marked the frontal aiming point for the heart and its complex of arteries and blood vessels. He hardly noticed the recoil nor the blurt of the shot as he watched for the strike of the lead bullet. There was a little spurt of dust off the gray hide precisely on his aiming point, and the sound of the hit was exactly like his headmaster swinging the Malacca cane against his school-boy backside, sharp and meaty.

The bull took the bullet without a stumble or lurch, instead it swung toward them, and seemed immediately to double in size as it lifted its nose into the high attitude of the charge.

Zouga reached for his second gun, but he groped in vain. Mark, his number two, showed the whites of his eyes in a flash of terror, let out a squawk, hurled the elephant gun aside, and went bounding away toward the mopani grove.

The bull saw him and swerved again, thundering ten feet past Zouga as it went after the fleeing bearer. Waving the empty

Sharps, Zouga shouted desperately for another rifle, but the bull was past him in a blur and it caught Mark as he reached the tree line.

The great bossed head dropped until the snout almost touched the earth, and then flew up again in a powerful tossing motion that bunched the muscle in the thick black neck. Mark was looking back over his shoulder, his eyes wide and glaring white in his face, rivulets of sweat pouring down his naked back, his mouth a pink gape as he screamed.

Then he was in the air. Legs and arms tumbling wildly, he went up like a rag doll thrown by a petulant child and disappeared into the thick green canopy of mopani foliage overhead. Without missing a stride, the bull drove on into the forest, but that was all that Zouga saw, for a cry from Sergeant Cheroot made him turn again.

"Hier kom hulle! Here they come!"

Across their whole front, the earth seemed to move, as though racked by the convulsions of an earthquake. Shoulder to shoulder, nose to rump, the main herd broke from cover, flattening the thorn bush under the wave of bodies, filling the valley from side to side.

They lifted behind them a dense curtain of dust, from which the front ranks seemed endlessly to emerge, their heads nodding in unison as they pounded on, long silver strings of saliva dangling from open jaws as they bellowed in alarm and anger, and the roar of their hooves drowned the sound of the flames.

Matthew and John, Zouga's two remaining bearers, had stood their ground, and one of them snatched away the empty Sharps and thrust the thick stock of an elephant gun into Zouga's hand.

The weapon seemed heavy and unbalanced after the Sharps, and the sights were crudely fashioned, a blunt cone for the foresight, and a deep V for the backsight.

The solid wall of bodies was bearing down upon them with frightening speed. The cows were chocolate color, and their horns were more delicately curved. The calves that raced at their flanks were sleek russet with crowns of reddish curls between the rudimentary little horn spikes. The herd was so tightly packed that it seemed impossible that they could split open to pass the rock. There was a tall rangy cow in the leading rank, coming straight on to Zouga.

He held half a bead aiming into the center of her chest, and squeezed off the shot. The firing cap popped with a tiny puff of smoke, and a heartbeat later the elephant gun vomited a deafening gust of powder and bright flame, the burning patches went spinning away over the heads of the charging buffalo and Zouga felt as though one of them had kicked in his shoulder. He staggered backward, the barrel thrown high by the recoil, but the big red cow seemed to run into an invisible barrier. A quarter of a pound of mercury-hardened lead drove into her chest, and brought her down in a rolling sliding tangle of hooves and horns.

"Tom Harkness! That one was yours!" Zouga shouted, offering the kill to the memory of the old white bearded hunter, and he grabbed the next loaded rifle.

There was a prime bull, big and black, a ton of enraged bovine flesh. It had seen Zouga, and was coming in over the rocks in a long scrambling leap—hunting him out, so close that Zouga seemed to touch it with the gaping muzzle of the four-to-the-pound. Again the clanging burst of sound and flame and smoke, and half the bull's head flew away in a gust of bone chips and bloody fragments. It reared up on its hind legs, striking out with forehooves, and then crashed over in a cloud of dust.

Impossibly, the herd split, galloping down each side of their rocky hide, a heaving, grunting, forked river of striving muscle and bone. Jan Cheroot was yipping shrilly with the fever of the chase, ducking down behind the rock to reload, biting open the paper cartridge with powder dribbling down his chin, spitting the ball into the muzzle and then plying the ramrod in a frenzy, before bobbing up again to fire into the solid heaving press of gigantic bodies.

It lasted for two minutes, which seemed to take a round of eternity, and then they were left choking and gasping in the swirling clouds of dust, surrounded by half a dozen huge carcasses, with the drumbeats of the herd fading away into the mopani forest, and a louder, more urgent din roaring down on them from in front.

The first tongue of heat licked across them, and Zouga heard the lock of sun-bleached hair that hung on his forehead frizzle sharply and smelled the stink of it. At the same instant, the dust cloud fell abruptly aside, and for seconds they stared at a spectacle which deprived them of power of movement.

The jessie bush was not burning, it was exploding into sheets of flame.

"Run!" shouted Zouga. "Get out of here!"

The sleeve of his shirt charred, and the air he breathed scorched his lungs painfully. As they reached the edge of the mopani forest, the shiny leaves about their heads shriveled and yellowed, curling their edges in the heat, and Zouga felt his eyeballs drying out as the clouds rolled over them. He knew that they were experiencing only the heat and smoke carried on the wind, but if the flames were able to jump the gap, then they were all doomed. Ahead of him, the Hottentots and the other bearers were shadowy wraiths, staggering forward but weakening and losing direction.

Then, as suddenly as they had been engulfed by them, the billowing smoke clouds lifted. The flames had not been able to jump the open ground, and the heat came only in gusts. A ray of sunshine pierced the thick gloom overhead, and a puff of sweet fresh air came through. They sucked at it gratefully, and huddled in awed silence, beating at their clothing, which still smoldered in patches. Zouga's face was blackened and blistered, and his lungs still convulsed in spasms of coughing. As he caught his breath, he grunted hoarsely,

"Well, the meat is cooked already," and he pointed back at the buffalo carcasses.

At that moment something fell limply out of the dense top branches of a mopani tree, and then picked itself up and limped painfully toward them. Zouga let out a husky growl of laughter.

"O thou swift of foot," he greeted Mark, the bearer, and the others took up the mockery.

"When you fly, the eagles are put to shame," Jan Cheroot hooted.

"Your true home is in the treetops," Matthew added with relish, "with your hairy brethren."

By evening they had hacked the buffalo carcasses into wet red chunks, and spread these on the smoking racks. The racks were waist-high, cross poles set in forked branches, with a slow smoking fire of wet mopani wood smoldering under it.

Here was meat for the caravan that would last them many weeks.

Camacho Pereira had no doubts that by simply following the line of the escarpment, keeping just below the bad broken ground, he must at last cut the spoor of the caravan. A hundred men, in column, would blaze a track that even a blind man would trip over.

His certainty dwindled with each day's march through the quivering, breathless heat that seemed to rebound from black kopjes and the ironstone cliffs which glittered in the aching sunlight like the scales of some monstrous reptile.

246

Of the men that his half-brother, Alphonse, had given him, he had already lost two. One had stepped on something that looked like a pile of dried leaves, but which had transformed itself instantly into six feet of infuriated Gaboon adder, thick as a man's calf, with a repulsively beautiful diamond-patterned back and a head the size of a man's fist. The gaping mouth was salmon pink, and the curved fangs three inches long. It had plunged them into the man's thigh and squirted half a cupful of the most toxic venom in Africa into his bloodstream.

After blowing the serpent to shreds with volleys of rifle fire, Camacho and his companions had wagered all their expectations of loot on exactly how long it would take the victim to die. Camacho, the only one who owned a watch, was elected timekeeper, and they gathered around where the dying man lay, either urging him to give up the useless struggle or pleading with him raucously to hang on a little longer.

When he went into back-arching convulsions, with his eyes rolled up into his skull, his jaws locked and he lost control of his sphincter muscle, Camacho knelt beside him, holding a bunch of smoldering tambouti leaves under his nostrils to shock him out of it, and crooning, "Ten minutes more—hang on for just ten minutes more for your old friend Machito!"

The last convulsion ended with a dreadful gangling expulsion of breath, and after the heart beat faded completely, Camacho stood and kicked the corpse with disgust.

"He always was a dung-eating jackal."

When they began to strip the corpse of all items of any possible value, five coins, heavy golden mohurs of the East India Company, fell out of the folds of his turban.

There was not one man in all that company who would not have willingly sold his mother into slavery for a single gold mohur, let alone five.

At the first gleam of gold, all their knives came out with a sardonic metallic snickering, and the first man to snatch for the treasure reeled away, trying to push his intestines back into the long clean slice through his stomach wall.

"Leave them lie," Camacho shouted. "Don't touch them until the lots are drawn!"

Not one of them trusted another, and the knives stayed out while the lots were cast, and grudgingly the winners were allowed one at a time to claim their prize.

The man with the belly wound could not march without his stomach falling out, and because he could not march, he was as good as dead. The dead, as everybody knows, have no need

247

of personal possessions. The logic was apparent to all. They left him his shirt and breeches, both torn and badly stained anyway, but stripped him of all else as they had stripped the first corpse. Then, with a few ribald pleasantries, they propped him against the base of a marula tree, with the naked corpse of the snakebite victim beside him for company, and they marched away along the line of the escarpment.

They had gone a hundred yards when Camacho was overcome by a rush of compassion. He and the dying man had fought and marched and whored together for many years. He turned back.

The man gave him a haggard grin, his dry crusted lips cracking with the effort. Camacho answered him with that marvelous flashing smile as he dropped the man's loaded pistol in his lap.

"It would be better to use it *before* the hyena find you tonight," he told him.

"The thirst is terrible," the man croaked, a tiny bead of blood appeared on his deeply cracked lower lip, bright as an emperor's ruby in the sunlight. He eyed the two-gallon water bottle on Camacho's hip.

Camacho resettled the water bottle on its strap so it was out of sight behind his back. The contents sloshed seductively.

"Try not to think about it," he counseled.

There was a point where compassion ended and stupidity began. Who knew where and when they would find the next water? In this God-blasted desolation, water was an item not to be wasted on a man who was already as good as dead.

He patted the man's shoulder comfortingly, gave him a last smile and then swaggered away among the gray iron-thorn scrub, whistling softly under his breath with the plumed beaver cocked over one eye.

"Camachito went back to make sure we had forgotten nothing," the one-eyed Abyssinian greeted him as he caught up with the column, and they shouted with laughter. Their spirits were still high, the water bottles more than half filled and the prospects of immense loot danced like a will-o'-the-wisp down the valley ahead of them.

That had been ten days ago, the last three of which without water, for you could not count the cupful of mud and elephant piss they had from the last puddled waterhold. Apart from the lack of water, the going had become appalling. Camacho had never marched through such broken and harsh terrain, toiling up one rocky slope and then battling down through tearing thorn to the next dry river course, and then up again.

Also, it now seemed highly probable that either the Englishman had changed his mind and gone north of the Zambezi River after all, in which case they had lost him, or else—and Camacho's skin crawled at the thought—or else they had crossed the spoor of the caravan in the early dawn or late evening when the light was too bad to make it out clearly. It was an easy mistake to make, they had crossed hundreds of game tracks each day, and the spoor could have been wiped by a herd of game, or one of the fierce short-lived little whirlwinds, the dust devils which ravaged the valley at this season of the year.

To cap all Camacho's tribulations, his band of noble warriors was on the point of mutiny. They were talking quite openly about turning back. There never had been an Englishman and a caravan of riches; even if there had, he was now far from here and getting further every day. They were exhausted by these switchback ridges and valleys and the water bottles were nearly all of them dry, which made it hard to maintain enthusiasm for the venture. The ringleaders were reminding the others that in their absence, their share of the profits of the slave caravan were blowing in the wind. Fifty slaves, for certain, were worth a hundred mythical Englishmen. They had many excellent reasons for turning back.

Camacho, on the other hand, had nothing to return for, apart from his half-brother's ire. He also had a score to settle, two scores. He still hoped that they might manage to take the Englishman and his sister alive, especially the woman. Even in the thirst and the heat, his groin swelled at the memory of her in men's breeches. He jerked himself back to reality, and he glanced over his shoulder at the straggling line of ruffians who followed him.

Soon it would be necessary to kill one of his men, he had decided hours ago. Dung eaters all of them—it was the only language they truly understood. He must make an example to stiffen their backbones, and keep them slogging onward.

He had already decided which one it would be. The one-eyed Abyssinian was the biggest talker, the most eloquent apostle of the return to the coast, and what made his choice even more attractive was that his left side was blind. The problem was that the job must be done properly. The others would be impressed by the knife but not the gun. However, the Abyssinian allowed no man into that blind spot. Without making it too obvious, Camacho had twice sidled up on his left, but each time the Abyssinian had swung his head with its frizzed-up halo of dense curly hair toward him, and given him a grin with a slow trickle of a tear running down his cheek from that obscenely empty eye socket.

However, Camacho was a persistent man, and an inventive one, for he noticed that whenever he moved out of the Abyssinian's blind spot the man relaxed, and immediately became more verbose and arrogant. Twice more Camacho tried an approach from the left, and twice more was met with a single cold beady stare. He was establishing a pattern, teaching the victim that threat came only from the left, and when they halted in the middle of the morning, he ostentatiously squatted on the right. The Abyssinian grinned at him as he wiped the spout of his almost empty water bottle on his sleeve.

"This is the place. I go no further." The one-eyed man announced in fluent Portuguese. "I make the oath on Christ's sacred wounds." And he touched the Coptic gold cross that hung around his neck. "Not another step forward. I am going back."

Fanning himself with the beaver hat, Camacho shrugged, and answered the cold grin with his own sunny smile. "Let's drink to your going then." With his free hand, he lifted his own water bottle, and shook it slightly. There was a cupful, no more. All their eyes went instinctively to the bottle. Here water was life, even the Abyssinian's single eye fastened on it.

Then Camacho let it slip from his fingers. It looked like an accident, the bottle rolled to the Abyssinian's feet with clear water glugging out onto the baked earth, and, with an exclamation, the man stooped for it with his right hand, his knife hand.

Nobody really saw Camacho move. He had been holding the knife in the lining of the beaver hat. Suddenly it seemed to reappear behind the Abyssinian's right ear, just the carved bone handle protruding, the blade completely buried. The Abyssinian lifted his hand with a mystified expression and touched the hilt of the knife, blinked his single eye rapidly, opened his mouth and then closed it firmly and fell forward on top of the water bottle.

Camacho was standing over them, a cocked pistol in each hand.

"Who else wishes to make an oath on Christ's sacred wounds?" he smiled at them, his teeth very big and white and square. "Nobody? Very well then, I will make an oath. I make it on the long-lost maidenheads of your sisters which they sold a hundred times for an escudo the bunch."

Even they were shocked by such blasphemy.

"I make it on your flaccid and puny manhoods which it will be my great pleasure to shoot off," he was interrupted, and broke off in midsentence.

There was a faint popping sound on the hushed heated morning, so distant, so indistinct, that for a moment none of them recognized it as the sound of gunfire. Camacho recovered first, he thrust the pistols into his waistband. They were no longer needed—and he ran to the crest of the rocky kopje on which they sat.

There was a column of dun-colored smoke rising into the washed-out blue sky far ahead. In this terrain, it lay a day's march away against the steep and fearsome edge of the escarpment.

Around him his men, once again loyal and filled with fire, were laughing and hugging each other with delight. It was a pity about the Abyssinian, Camacho conceded, like all his people he had been a good fighter, and now they had found the Englishman, he would be missed.

Camacho cupped the cheroot in both hands and inhaled deeply. Holding the smoke in his lungs, he squinted his eyes against the flat glare of rising noon. The sun had bleached all color from the landscape, only the shadows were cut clearly, very sharp edged and black below each tree and rock.

Across the narrow valley the long column of men he was watching moved at the pace of the slowest. Camacho doubted if they were making a single mile in an hour.

He removed the beaver hat from his head and blew the smoke into it gently, so that it dispersed into nothingness instead of standing in the still air to draw the eye of a watcher.

Camacho saw nothing odd in that the leading Hottentot musketeer in the column carried an English flag. Even in this barren, forsaken corner of the earth, although its gaudy folds were already dulled with dust and the ends shredded by grasping thorn, it was the promise of protection, a warning to those who might check their passage. All caravans in Africa went under a banner.

Camacho dragged on the black cheroot and considered once again how infallible was the advice of his brother Alphonse. The night was the only time to do the business. Here the column was spread out for more than a mile, there were wide gaps between each of the four divisions—and with himself he had eighteen men left. If he attacked in daylight, he would be forced to concentrate them on the detachments of Hottentot musketeers at the head and tail of the caravan. He imagined vividly what might happen at the first shot. One hundred porters would drop their packs and scatter away into the bush, and when the fighting was over he would have nobody to carry the loot.

It was necessary, furthermore, for him to wait until the Englishman rejoined the caravan. He guessed that Zouga Ballantyne was scouting or hunting, but that he would rejoin the column before nightfall.

The woman was there. He had another glimpse of her at that moment as she stepped up on to a log that lay across the path; for a moment she balanced there, long-legged, in those maddening breeches, and then jumped down off the log. Camacho passed a pleasant few minutes in erotic imaginings. He had been twenty days without a woman and it had put a razor edge to his appetite which even the hot hard trek had not dulled.

He sighed happily, and then squinted his eyes again as he concentrated on the immediate problems. Alphonse was right, they would have to wait until night. And tonight would be a good night for it, three days after the full moon, and yet the moon would rise very late, an hour or so after midnight.

He would let the Englishman come in, let the camp settle down, let the fires die, and let the Hottentot sentries drowse off. Then when the moon rose and the vitality of the camp was at its lowest ebb, he and his men would go in.

Every one of his men was good with the knife, the fact that they had lived so long showed that—Camacho smiled to himself—and they would have an opportunity to prove it again tonight. He personally would mark the position of the sentries while it was still light. They would start with them, Camacho did not expect more than three or four. After the sentries, then the Hottentot musketeers that were sleeping. They were the most dangerous, and after them there would be time for indulgence.

He would go to the woman's tent himself, he squirmed slightly at the thought and adjusted his dressing. It was just a terrible pity that he could not take care of the Englishman as well. He would send two of his best men to do that work. He had dreamed of driving a long wooden spike up between the Englishman's buttocks, and then taking wagers on how long he would take to die, amusing himself and the company while regaining some of his previous losses at the same time.

252

Then reluctantly, and prudently, he had decided not to chance such pleasures, not with a man like that. Best to cut his throat while he still slept. They could have their fun with the woman instead, Camacho decided firmly.

His single regret was that he would have only a short time with her before the others demanded their turns, though a few minutes would probably be enough for him. Strange how months of craving could be satiated so swiftly, and after that brief outpouring become indifference and even distaste. That was a very philosophical thought, Camacho realized. Once again he had astonished himself with his own wisdom and sensitivity to things of the mind. He had often thought that if he had ever learned to read and write he could have been a great man, like his father the governor. After all, the blood in his veins was that of aristocrats and dons, only slightly diluted.

He sighed, yes, five minutes would suffice and then the others could have her, and when they also had finished they could play the betting game with the long wooden stake—and, of course, there was a more amusing place to put it. He chuckled aloud at the thought and took a last draw on the cheroot, and the stub was so short that the ember scorched his fingers. He dropped it and crushed it under his heel. He moved like a panther, slipping quietly over the skyline and circling out stealthily to get ahead of the creeping caravan.

Zouga had left his bearers tending the smoking racks, feeding the fire with chips of wet wood, and turning the hunks of red meat so they cured evenly. It was wearisome work, for the racks had to be guarded at all times from the hyena and jackals, the crows and kites which hung about the camp, while there was always wood to cut and the baskets of mopani bark to weave in which the smoked meat would be carried.

Jan Cheroot was happy to escape with Zouga as he marched back to find the main caravan and guide it to the buffalo camp. Even the tsetse fly could not repress his high spirits. They had been in fly country for a week or more now. Tom Harkness had called these importunate little insects "the guardians of Africa," and certainly they made it impossible for man to move his domestic animals through vast tracks of country.

Here they were one of the many reasons why the Portuguese colonization had been confined to the low coastal littoral. Their cavalry had never been able to penetrate this deadly screen, nor had their draft animals been able to drag their war trains up from the coast.

They were the reason, also, why Zouga had not attempted to use wagons or beasts of burden to carry his stores. There was not even a dog with the caravan, for only man and wild game were immune to the dreadful consequences of the bite.

In some areas of the fly belt there were so few of the insects as to cause little annoyance, but in others they swarmed like hiving bees, plaguing and persecuting even during the moonlight periods of the night.

That day on the march back to rejoin the column, Zouga and Jan Cheroot suffered the worst infestation of fly they had yet met within the valley of the Zambezi. They rose from the ground to sit thickly upon their legs, and clustered on the backs of their necks and between their shoulder blades, so that he and Jan Cheroot took turns to walk behind each other and brush them off with a freshly cut buffalo tail.

As suddenly as they had entered it, they found themselves out of the fly belt and with blessed relief from the torment they settled down to rest in the shade. Within half an hour they heard distant singing, and as they waited for the caravan to come up, they smoked and chatted in the desultory fashion of the good companions they had become.

During one of the long pauses in their talk Zouga thought he saw vague movement on the far side of the shallow valley in front of them. Probably a herd of kudu or a troop of baboon, both of which were plentiful in the valley, but apart from the buffalo herd the only game they had encountered since leaving Tete.

The approaching caravan would have alarmed whatever it was, Zouga thought, removing his cap and using it to drive away the persistent cloud of tiny black mopani bees which hovered around his head, attracted by the moisture of his eyes and lips and nostrils. The movement in the forest opposite was not repeated. Whatever it was had probably crossed the ridge. Zouga turned back to listen to Jan Cheroot.

"The rains only stopped six weeks ago," Jan Cheroot was musing aloud. "The waterholes and rivers up on the high ground will still be full—not here, of course; this ground drains too steeply." He indicated the dry and rocky water course below them. "So the herds spread out, and follow their old roads." He was explaining the complete lack of elephant, or even recent evidence of elephant herds in the valley, and Zouga listened with attention, for here was an expert speaking. "The old elephant roads, they used to run from the flat mountain of Good Hope to the swamps of the far Sud," he pointed north. "But

254

each year they shrink as we, the *jagters* [hunters], and men like us, follow the herds and drive them deeper and deeper into the interior."

Jan Cheroot was silent again, and his pipe gurgled noisily as he sucked on it.

"My father told me that he killed the last elephants south of the Olifants River—the river of elephants—when he was still a young man. He boasted that he killed twelve elephants that day, he alone with his old *roer* [muzzle-loader] that was too heavy to hold to the shoulder. He had to rest it on the crutch of a forked stick he carried for it. Twelve elephants in one day—by one man. That is a feat." He gurgled his pipe again, and then spat a little yellow tobacco juice. "But then my father was even more famous as a liar than he was as a hunter," Jan Cheroot chuckled and shook his head fondly.

Zouga smiled, and then the smile vanished and his head jerked up. He narrowed his eyes, for a tiny dart of reflected sunlight had struck his eye coming from the same place across the valley. Whatever he had seen was still there, and it was neither kudu nor baboon. It had to be a man, for only metal or glass could have shot that reflection. Jan Cheroot had noticed nothing and he was musing on.

"When I rode with Cornwallis Harris, we found the first elephant on the Cashan Mountains, that's a thousand miles further north of where my father killed his herd. There was nothing in between; it had all been hunted bare. Now there are no elephant in the Cashan Mountains. My brother Stephan was there two years ago. He tells me that there are no elephant south of the Limpopo River. The Boers graze their herds where we hunted ivory; perhaps we will find no elephant even up there on the high ground, perhaps there are no elephant left in all the world."

Zouga was not really listening anymore. He was thinking about the man on the opposite side of the valley. It was probably somebody from the caravan, a party sent ahead to cut firewood for the night's bivouac, yet it was still early to think of making camp.

The singing of the bearers was louder now. There was a single voice carrying the marching song. Zouga recognized it. The man was a tall Angoni, with a fine tenor voice, and a poet who improvised his own verses, adding to them and altering them on the march. Zouga, cocking his head, could make out the words.

255

"Have you heard the fish eagle cry above Mar-
    awi?
  Have you seen the setting sun turn the snows of
    Kilimanjaro to blood?"

And then the chorus coming in after him, those haunting
African voices, so beautiful, so moving,

  "Who will lead us to these wonders, my brother?
  We will leave the women to weep,
  We will let their sleeping mats grow cold,
  If a strong man leads, we will follow him, my brother."

Zouga smiled at the next verse, as he recognized his name.

  "Bakela will lead us like a father leads his children,
  Bakela will give you a *khete* of *sam-sam* beads—
  Bakela will feed you upon the fat of the hippopotamus and
    meat of the buffalo—"

Zouga closed his mind against the distraction, concentrating
on the man across the valley. Here, a hundred miles from the
nearest habitations of men, it must have been somebody from
the caravan—woodcutter, honey hunter, deserter, who knew?
  Zouga stood up and stretched, and Jan Cheroot knocked out
his pipe and stood with him. The head of the column appeared
among the trees lower down the slope, the red, white and blue
banner flapped lazily open and then drooped again dejectedly.
  Zouga glanced once more at the opposite slope, it seemed
deserted again. He was tired, the soles of his feet felt as though
he had marched across burning embers, for they had been going
hard since dawn, and the barely healed knife wound in his hip
ached dully.
  He should really go up that slope to check what he had
seen, but it was steep and rocky. It would take another half an
hour of scrambling to reach the crest and return. They went
down to meet the caravan, and when Zouga saw Robyn striding
along with that easy coltish grace of hers behind the standard
bearer, he lifted his cap and waved it above his head.
  She ran to meet him, laughing like a child with delight. He
had been gone three days.
  Below a polished face of smooth black rock, that when the
river was in spate would be a roaring cascade, there was a bend
in the dry water bed filled with pure white sand.
  On the banks above it the wild mahogany stood tall and

vigorous, its roots in water, and the baboon had been scratching in the sand below the bank.

Robyn and Zouga sat together on the edge of the dry waterfall, watching the men that Zouga had set to digging for water.

"I pray there will be enough." Robyn watched them with interest. "I have not used my bath since we left Tete." Her enameled hip bath was the expedition's single bulkiest item of equipment.

"I'll be satisfied with enough for a pot of tea," Zouga replied vaguely, but he was clearly distracted.

"Something is worrying you?" she asked.

"I was thinking of a valley in Kashmir.".

"Was it like this?"

"Not really—it is just that . . ." he shrugged. In that faraway valley, when he had been a young ensign leading a patrol ahead of the battalion, he had seen something as he had today. Something of no account, a stray movement, a glint of light that might have been off a gun barrel or the horn of a wild goat. Then, as now, it had been too much trouble to check it. That night he had lost three men, killed while they fought their way out of the valley. The fight had earned praise from his colonel, but the men remained dead.

He glanced up at the slanting sun: there was an hour of light left. He knew he should have climbed that slope. While Robyn watched him with a puzzled expression, he wavered a few seconds longer and then with an exclamation of exasperation stood up wearily. His feet still ached abominably and he rubbed his hip where the knife-wound throbbed. It was going to be a long walk back down the valley.

Zouga used a deep and narrow ravine to get out of the camp unobtrusively, and once clear he scrambled out and kept to the thicker bush just above the riverbed until he reached a tangled barrier of driftwood carried down during the recent rains which blocked the dry water course from bank to bank.

He used this to cover his crossing, and started up the far slope. He went very carefully, dodging from one tree to another and watching and listening before each move.

On the crest there was a faint movement of cooler air, the evening breeze coming down the escarpment that cooled the sweat on his neck and almost made the hard climb worthwhile. It seemed that was all the reward he would get. The stony ground was too hard to carry sign, and it was deserted of life, animal or human. However, Zouga was determined to make up for his previous sloth. He stayed too long. It would be night before he reached camp again, moonrise was late, and he risked a broken leg moving over this sort of terrain in the pitch dark.

He turned to go back, and he smelled it before he saw it, and the hair prickled along his forearms and he felt his belly muscles contract, yet it was such a commonplace smell. He stooped and picked up the small squashed brown object. He had smoked the last of his own cheroots two days before, perhaps that was why his nose was so sensitive to the smell of tobacco.

The cigar had been smoked down to a thin rind, and crushed out so it resembled a scrap of dried bark. Without the smell to guide him, he would never have found it. Zouga shredded it between his fingers. There was still a little residual dampness of saliva in the chewed end. He lifted his fingers and sniffed them. He knew where he had smelled that particular scented type of Portuguese tobacco before.

Camacho left fifteen of his men well back off the crest, in a tumble of rock that looked like a ruined castle, and whose caves and overhangs gave shade and concealment. They would sleep, he knew, and he begrudged them the time. His own eyelids were drooping as he lay belly down in cover, on the other side of the ridge watching the caravan making camp.

He had only two of his men with him to help him mark the sentries and scherms, the watch fires and the tent sites. They would be able to lead the others in, even in the complete blackout before the moon, if that should become necessary. Camacho hoped not. In the dark mistakes could be made, and it needed only a shot or a single shout. No, they would wait for the moon, he decided.

The Englishman had come into camp earlier, just before the caravan halted. He had the Hottentot with him, and they both hobbled stiffly like men who had made long, hard marches. Good, he would sleep soundly, was probably doing so already, for Camacho had not seen him in the last hour. He must be in the tent beside the woman's. He had seen a servant carrying a steaming bucket of water to her.

They had watched the Hottentot sergeant only set two sentries. The Englishman must be feeling very secure, two sentries merely to watch against lions. They would probably both be fast asleep by midnight. They would never wake again. He, personally, would cut one of them, and he would send a good knife to cut the other. He smiled in anticipation.

The remaining Hottentots had built their usual lean-to shelter and thatched it in a rudimentary fashion. There was no chance of rain, not at this season and not with that unblemished egg-shell-blue sky. It was almost two hundred paces from the tents, a groan or a whimper would not carry that far. Good, Camacho nodded again. It was working out better than he had hoped.

As always, the two tents were set close together, almost touching. The gallant Englishman guarding the woman; Camacho smiled again, and felt his drowsiness lifting miraculously as his groin charged once more. He wished the night away, for he had already waited so long.

Night came with the dramatic suddenness of Africa, within minutes the valley was filled with shadows, the sunset made its last theatrical flare of apricot and old gold light and then it was dark.

For an hour more Camacho could see the occasional figure silhouetted by the flames of the campfires. Once the sound of singing carried softly and sweetly to the ridge, and the other camp sounds, the clank of a bucket, the thud of a log thrown on the fire, the drowsy murmur of voices, showed that the routine was unaltered, and the camp completely unaware.

The noises faded and the fires died. The silence was disturbed only by the piping lament of a jackal across the valley.

The star patterns turned slowly across the sky marking the passage of the hours, and then gradually faded before the greater brilliance of the rising moon.

"Fetch the others," Camacho told the man nearest him. He rose stiffly to his feet, stretching like a cat to relieve numbed muscles. They came silently and gathered close about Camacho to listen to his final whispered instructions.

When he finished, he looked from one to the other in turn. Their faces in the bright moonlight had the greenish hues of freshly exhumed corpses, but they nodded their agreement to his words, and then followed him down the slope, silent shapes like a troop of wolves; they reached the dry water course in the gut of the valley, and split into their prearranged groups.

Camacho moved up the newly beaten path toward the camp. He carried his knife in his right hand and his musket in the other, and his feet made a barely audible brushing sound through the short dry grass. Ahead of him, beneath the outspread branches of a makusi tree, he could make out the shape of the sentry, where he had been placed six hours before. The man was asleep, curled like a dog on the hard earth. Camacho nodded with satisfaction and crept closer. He saw the man had pulled a blanket over his head. The mosquitoes had bothered him. Camacho grinned and knelt beside him.

With his free hand he felt softly for the man's head through the blanket, then the hand stilled. He gave a little grunt of surprise, and jerked the blanket aside. It had been arranged over the exposed roots of the makusi tree to look like the shape of a sleeping man, and Camacho swore quietly but with great vehemence.

The sentry had chosen the wrong time to sneak away from his post. He was probably back in the lean-to shelter snoring happily on a mattress of dry grass. They would get him with the others, when they cleaned out the shelter. Camacho went on up the slope into the camp. In the moonlight the canvas of the tents shone ghostly silver, a beacon on which his lust could concentrate. Camacho slipped the sling of the musket over his shoulder as he hurried forward, toward the left-hand tent, and then checked as another figure emerged from the shadows, the knife in his right hand instinctively came up and then he recognized his own man, one of those whom he had sent to cut the Englishman's throat.

The man nodded jerkily, all was well so far, and they went forward together, separating only as they approached the two tents. Camacho would not use the fly opening of the woman's tent—for he knew it would be laced closed, and if there were any surprises they would be at the entrance. He slipped around the side of the tent, and stooped to one of the hooded ventilator openings. He ran the point of the blade into it and then drew it upward in a single stroke. Although it was heavy canvas, the blade had been whetted expertly, and the side wall split with only a whisper of sound.

Camacho stepped through the opening, and while he waited for his eyesight to adjust to the deeper darkness of the interior, he fumbled with the fastening of his breeches, grinning happily to himself as he made out the narrow collapsible cot and the little white tent of the muslin mosquito net. He shuffled toward it slowly, careful not to trip over the cases of medical stores that were piled between him and the cot.

Standing over the cot, he ripped the muslin netting aside violently, and lunged full length onto the cot, groping for the woman's head to smother her cries, the loose ends of his belt flapping at his waist, and his breeches sagging around his hips.

For a moment he was paralyzed with shock at the fact that the cot was empty. Then he groped frantically over every inch of it, before coming to his feet again and hoisting his breeches with his free hand. He was confused, disconnected, and wild ideas flashed through his mind. Perhaps the woman had left the cot to answer a call of nature, but then why was the fly carefully laced closed? She had heard him and was hiding behind the cases, armed with a scapel, and he swung round panicking to lash out with the knife, but the tent was empty.

Then the coincidence of the missing sentry and the empty cot struck him with force. Something was happening that he did not understand. He charged for the rent in the canvas, tripped and sprawled over one of the cases and rolled on to his feet again, nimble as a cat. He ran out, clinching his belt and looking about him wildly, unslinging his musket and only just preventing himself from calling aloud to his men.

He ran to the Englishman's tent, just as his man came running out of the long tear in the canvas side, brandishing his knife, his face fearful in the moonlight. He saw Camacho, screamed and struck out at him wildly with the long silver blade.

"Silence, you fool," Camacho snarled at him.

"He's gone," the man panted, craning to stare about into the deep shadows that the moon cast under the trees. "They've gone. They've all gone."

"Come!" snapped Camacho, and led him at a run down toward the lean-to that the Hottentot musketeers had built.

Before they reached it they met their companions running toward them in a disorderly bunch.

"Machito?" somebody called nervously.

"Shut your mouth," Camacho growled at them, but the man blurted on.

"The scherm is empty, they have gone."

"The Devil has taken them."

"There is nobody."

There was an almost superstitious frenzy of awe on them all, the silent empty camp turned them all into cowards. Camacho found himself, for once, without an order to give, uncertain of what to do. His men crowded around him helplessly, seeming to take comfort from each other's physical presence, cocking and fiddling with their muskets and peering nervously into the shadows.

"What do we do now?" A voice asked the question that Camacho had feared, and somebody else threw a log from the pile onto the smoldering watch fire in the center of the camp.

"Don't do that," Camacho ordered uncertainly, but instinctively they were all drawn to the warmth and comfort of the

261

orange tongue of flame that soared up brightly, blowing like a dragon's breath.

They turned their backs toward it, forming a half circle, and faced outward, looking into a wall which in contrast to the flames was suddenly impenetrably black.

It was out of this darkness that it came. There was no warning, just the sudden thunderous burst of sound and flame, the long line of spurting muzzle flashes, blooming briefly and murderously, and then the sound of the striking balls in their midst, like a handful of children's marbles hurled into a mud puddle, as the musket balls slogged into human flesh.

Immediately men were hurled lightly about by the heavy lead slugs, and the little band about the watch fire was thrown into struggling, shouting confusion.

One of them flew backward, at a run, doubled in the middle where a ball had taken him low in the belly. He tripped over the burning log and fell full length into the blazing watch fire. His hair and beard flared like a torch of pine needles and his scream rang wildly through the treetops.

Camacho threw up his musket, aiming blindly into the night from whence the Englishman's voice was chanting the ritual infantry orders for mass volley fire.

"Section one. Reload. Section two. Three paces forward. One round volley fire."

Camacho realized that the devastating blast of close range musketry that had just swept them would be repeated within seconds. With mild derision Camacho had watched on many a hot afternoon as the Englishman drilled his double line of red-jacketed puppets, the front rank leveling and firing on command, then the second rank taking three paces forward in unison, stepping through the gaps in the first rank and in their turn leveling and firing. The same evolutions which, when magnified ten thousand times, had broken the charge of French cavalry up the slope at Quatre Bras, now filled Camacho with unutterable terror, and he fired unsighted, in the direction of the cool, precise English voice. He fired at the same instant as one of his own men who had been knocked down by the first volley scrambled to his feet only lightly wounded, directly in front of Camacho's musket muzzle. Camacho shot him cleanly between the shoulder blades at a range of two feet, so close that the powder burn scorched the man's shirt. It smoldered in little red sparks as he sprawled at full length on his face once more, until the glowing sparks were quenched by the quick flow of the man's heart blood.

"Fool!" Camacho howled at the corpse, and turned to run.

Behind him the English voice called, "Fire!"

Camacho threw himself down on to hard earth, howling again as his hands and knees sank into the hot ash of the watch fire and he felt his breeches char and his skin blister.

The second volley swept over his head, and around him more men were falling and screaming, and Camacho rebounded to his feet at a dead run. He had lost both his knife and his musket.

"Section one, three paces forward, one round volley fire."

The night was suddenly filled with running, shouting figures, as the porters burst out of their encampment. There was no direction or purpose in their flight. They ran like Camacho, driven by gunfire and their own terrible panic, scattering away into the surrounding bush, singly and in small groups.

Before the command ordering the next volley of musket fire, Camacho ducked behind the hillock of porters' packs, which had been piled close to the Englishman's tent and covered with waterproof tarpaulin.

Camacho was sobbing with the agony of his scorched hands and knees, and with the humiliation of having walked so guilelessly into the Englishman's trap.

He found his terror giving way to bitter, spiteful hatred. As groups of terrified porters stumbled toward him he drew one of the pistols from his belt and shot the leader in the head and then leaped up howling like a demented ghost; they ran and he knew they would not stop until, miles away in the trackless wilderness, they dropped with exhaustion, easy prey for lion or hyena. It gave him a moment's sour satisfaction, and he looked around for some other damage he could wreak.

The pile of stores behind which he crouched and the dying fire in front of the Englishman's deserted tent caught his attention. He snatched a brand from the fire, blew it into flame and tossed it flaring brightly on to the high canvas-covered pile of stores and equipment, then flinched as another volley crashed out of the darkness, and he heard the Englishman's voice.

"As a line of skirmishers, take the bayonet to them now, men."

Camacho jumped down into the dry riverbed, and blundered through the crunching sugary sand to the far bank, where he scrambled thankfully into the dense riverine bush.

At the reassembly point on the ridge three of his men were waiting. Two of them had lost their muskets and all three were as shaken and sweaty and breathless as Camacho himself.

Two more came in while they regained their breath and power of speech. One was badly hit, his shoulder shattered by a musket ball.

"There won't be any others," he gasped, "those little yellow bastards caught them with bayonets as they were crossing the river."

"They'll be here any minute." Camacho dragged himself to his feet again, looking back down into the valley. He saw with grim satisfaction that the pile of stores was blazing brightly, despite the efforts of half a dozen tiny figures to beat out the flames. He had only moments to enjoy the spectacle, for lower down the slope came the thin but warlike cries of the Hottentot musketeers and the thud and flash of their musket fire.

"Help me," cried the man with the shattered shoulder. "Don't leave me here, my friends, my comrades, give me an arm," he pleaded, trying to struggle back on to his feet, but he was speaking to the empty night. As the rush of footsteps down the far slope of the hill dwindled, his knees buckled under him and he sank back onto the rock earth sweating with pain and the terror which lasted only until one of the Hottentots drove the point of a bayonet into his chest and out between his shoulder blades.

Zouga strode angrily through the camp in the rising heat and bright sunlight of morning. His face and arms were blackened with soot, his eyes still red and smarting from the smoke of the fires, his beard was scorched and his eyelashes burned half away from fighting the flames. They had lost most of their stores and equipment, for the fire had run away through the tents and thatched shelters. Zouga paused to glance at the charred and trodden scraps of canvas that were all that was left of the tents; they would miss them when the rains broke, but that was the very least of their losses.

He tried to make a mental list of the most grievous damage they had suffered. There were firstly only forty-six porters left out of more than one hundred. Of course, he could expect Jan Cheroot and his Hottentots to bring in a few more. They were at this moment scouring the valleys and hills around the camp for scattered survivors. He could still hear the kudu-horn trumpets calling in the stragglers. However, many would have risked the long and dangerous journey back to Tete rather than a recurrence of the night's attack, and they would have seized the opportunity to desert. Others would be lost after their midnight flight and panic. They would fall prey to wild animals

264

or succumb to thirst. Half a dozen had been killed by random musketry fire and by the retreating brigands who had deliberately fired into the masses of unarmed porters. Four others were so badly wounded that they would die before nightfall.

That was the most serious loss, for without porters they were helpless. Without porters to carry them, what remained of the carefully selected equipment and trade goods were as useless to them as if they had left them in London or dumped them overboard from *Huron*'s deck.

Of the equipment itself, it would take them hours to count their losses, to find what had burned and what they could salvage from the stinking, smoldering mass of cloth and canvas, what they could pick out of the trodden and dusty mess scattered down the rock hillside. The scene reminded Zouga forcefully of so many other battlefields, the terrible destruction and waste affronted him, as it had done before.

The few remaining porters were already at work, picking over the field like a line of harvesters, retrieving anything of value from the ash and the dust. Little Juba was with them, concentrating on the search for Robyn's medical stores, and books and instruments.

Robyn herself had set up an emergency clinic under the wide green branches of the makusi tree in the center of the camp, and when Zouga paused to look at the wounded men who still awaited her attention, and at the dead bodies laid out in a neat row and covered with a blanket or a scrap of charred and dirty canvas, he was angry with himself all over again.

Though what alternative had there been for him? he wondered.

If he had turned the camp into an armed fortress, it would have meant enduring a long drawn-out siege with Camacho's wolves skulking around the perimeter, sniping and harrying them until their opportunity came.

No, he had been right to set the trap and end it at a single stroke. At least now he could be certain that the Portuguese were still in full flight for the coast. But the price had been too high, and Zouga was still angry.

The expedition, so well conceived and lavishly equipped, had ended in disaster before it had achieved a single one of its objectives. The loss of equipment and life had been heavy, but that was not what burned so acidly in Zouga's stomach as he paused at the perimeter of the devastated camp and lifted his eyes longingly toward the high broken ground of the southern escarpment. It was the idea of having to give up, before he had begun, and when he was so close, so very close. Twenty, fifty, not more than a hundred miles ahead of him lay the frontier of the empire of Monomatapa. Behind him, one hundred miles to the north, was the dirty little village of Tete, and the wide river which was the beginning of the long ignoble road back to England, back to obscurity, back to a commission in a third-rate regiment, back to conformity and the wearying discipline of the cantonments of the Indian army. Only now that he was doomed to return to that life did he realize how deeply he had hated and resented it, just how much the desire to escape it had brought him here to this wild untouched land. Like a long-term prisoner who has tasted one day of sweet freedom, so the prospect of return to his cage was that much more painful now. The pain of it cramped his chest, and he had to breathe deeply to control it.

He turned away from the southern vista of ragged peaks and savage black rock cliffs, and he walked slowly to where his sister worked quietly in the shade of the makusi. Smudges of fatigue and strain showed under her green eyes. Her blouse was speckled with spots of her patients' blood, and her forehead appeared blistered with tiny beads of perspiration.

She had started work in the darkness, by the light of a bull's-eye lantern, and now it was midmorning.

She looked up wearily as Zouga stood over her.

"We won't be able to go on," he said quietly. She stared at him a moment without change of expression, then dropped her eyes and went on smearing salve on the badly burned leg of one of the porters. She had treated the worst cases first, and now was finishing with the burns and abrasions.

"We've lost too much vital equipment," Zouga explained. "Stores that we need to survive." Robyn did not look up this time. "And we've not enough porters to carry what is left."

Robyn began bandaging the leg with her full attention.

"Papa made the Transversa with four porters," she observed mildly.

"Papa was a man," Zouga pointed out reasonably, and Robyn's hands stilled ominously and her eyes narrowed, but Zouga had not noticed. "A woman cannot travel or survive without the necessities of civilization," he went on seriously. "That is why I am sending you back to Tete. I'm sending Sergeant Cheroot and five of his Hottentots to escort you. You'll have no difficulty, once you reach Tete. I will send with you what remains in cash, a hundred pounds for the launch downriver to Quelimane and a passage to Cape Town on a trader. There you can draw on the money I deposited in Cape Town to pay for a passage on the mail ship.."

She looked up at him. "And you?" she asked.

Until then he had not made the decision. "The important thing is what happens to you," he told her gravely, and then he knew what he was going to do. "You will have to go back and I am going on alone."

"It'll take more than Jan Cheroot and five of his damned Hottentots to carry me," she told him, and the oath was a measure of her determination.

"Be reasonable, sissy."

"Why should I start now?" she asked sweetly.

Zouga opened his mouth to reply angrily, then closed it slowly and stared at her. There was a hard uncompromising line to her lips, and the prominent, almost masculine, jaw was clenched stubbornly.

"I don't want to argue," he said.

"Good," she nodded. "That way you won't waste any more of your precious time."

"Do you know what you are letting yourself in for?" he asked quietly.

"As well as you do," she replied.

"We won't have trade goods to buy our way through the tribes."

She nodded. "That means we'll have to fight our way through if anyone tries to stop us."

He saw the shadow in her eyes at that, but there was no wavering of her determination.

"No tents for shelter, no canned food, no sugar or tea." He knew what that meant to her. "We will live straight off the land, and what we can't scavenge or kill or carry, we go without. We'll have nothing but powder and shot."

"You'd be a fool to leave the quinine," she told him quietly, and he hesitated.

"The bare minimum of medicines," he agreed, "and remember, it won't be for just a week or a month."

"We'll probably go a great deal faster than we have so far," she answered quietly, as she stood up and brushed off the seat of her breeches.

The choice of what to take and what to leave had been nicely balanced, Zouga thought, as he listed and weighed the new loads.

He had chosen paper and writing equipment in place of

267

sugar and most of the tea. His navigational instruments in place of spare boots, for the boots they wore could be resoled with raw buffalo hide. Quinine and other medicines together with Robyn's instruments in place of the extra clothing and blankets. Powder and shot in place of trade beads and cloth.

The pile of abandoned equipment grew steadily, cases of potted jams, bags of sugar, canned foods, insect nets, folding camp chairs and cots, cooking pots, Robyn's enamel hip bath and her flowered chamber pot, trade goods, *merkani* cloth and beads, hand mirrors and cheap knives. When the pile was complete, Zouga put fire into it, a token of finality and of determination. Yet they watched it burn with trepidation.

There were two small concessions Zouga had made: a single case of Ceylon tea for, as Robyn pointed out, no Englishman could be expected to explore undiscovered territories without that sovereign brew, and the sealed tin which contained Zouga's dress uniform, for their very lives might depend on impressing a savage African potentate. Otherwise they had divested themselves of all but the very essentials.

Chief of these essentials was the ammunition, the sacks of first-grade Curtis and May black powder and the ingots of soft lead, the bullet molds, the flask of quicksilver to harden the balls and the boxes of copper caps. Out of the remaining forty-six porters, thirty of them carried this powder and shot.

Jan Cheroot's musketeers were horrified when they were informed that their field packs would in future hold two hundred and not fifty, rounds of Enfield ammunition.

"We are warriors, not porters," his corporal told him loftily. Jan Cheroot used the metal scabbard of his long bayonet to reason with him, and Robyn dressed the superficial wounds in the corporal's scalp.

"They now understand the need for carrying extra ammunition, Major," Jan Cheroot reported to Zouga cheerfully.

It truly was interesting to realize how much fat they could shed, Zouga mused, as he watched the shorter, more manageable column start out. It was less than a hundred and fifty yards from head to tail, and the pace of its march was almost doubled. The main body nearly matched the speed of Zouga's advance party—falling only a mile or so behind during the first day's march.

That first day they reached the scene of the buffalo hunt before noon, and found more than bark baskets of cured black buffalo meat awaiting there. Zouga's head gunbearer, Matthew, came running to meet him through the forest and he was so excited as to be almost incoherent.

"The father of all elephant," he gibbered, shaking like a man in fever, "the grandfather of the father of all elephants!"

Jan Cheroot squatted beside the spoor and grinned like a gnome in a successful piece of sorcery, his slant eyes almost disappearing in the web of wrinkles and folds of yellow skin.

"Our luck has come at last," he exulted. "This is indeed an elephant to sing about."

He took a roll of twine out of the bulging pocket of his tunic and used it to measure the circumference of one of the huge pad marks. It was well over five feet, close to six feet around.

"Double that is how high he stands at the shoulder," Jan Cheroot explained. "What an elephant!"

Matthew had at last controlled his excitement enough to explain how he had awaked that dawn, when the light was gray and uncertain, and seen the herd passing close to the camp in deathly silence, three great gray ghostly shapes, moving out of the forest and entering the blackened and barren valley through which the fire had swept. They were gone so swiftly that it had seemed that they had never existed, but their spoor was impressed so clearly into the soft layer of fire ash that every irregularity in the immense footprints, the whorls and wavy creases of the horny pads, was clearly visible.

"There was one of them, bigger and taller than the others, his teeth were long as a throwing spear and so heavy that he held his head low and moved like an old man, a very old man."

Now Zouga also shivered with excitement, even in the stultifying heat of the burned-out valley, where it seemed the blackened earth had retained the heat of the flames. Jan Cheroot, mistaking the small movement, grinned wickedly around the stem of his clay pipe.

"My old father used to say that even a brave man is frightened three times when he hunts the elephant: once when he sees its spoor, twice when he hears its voice and the third time when he sees the beast—big and black as an ironstone kopje."

Zouga did not trouble to deny the accusation; he was following the run of the spoor with his eyes. The three huge animals had moved up the center of the valley, heading directly into the bad ground of the escarpment rim.

"We will follow them," he said quietly.

"Of course," Jan Cheroot nodded, "that is what we came for."

269

The spoor led them over the cold gray ash, among the blackened and bared branches of the burned-out jessie bush and up the rising funnel of the narrow valley.

Jan Cheroot led. He had discarded his faded tunic for a sleeveless leather jerkin with loops for the Enfield cartridges across the chest. Zouga followed him closely, carrying the Sharps and fifty extra rounds, together with his two-gallon water bottle. His gunbearers, in strict order of seniority, backed him, each with his burden of blankets and water bottles, food bag, powder flask and ball pouch, and of course the big smooth-bored elephant guns.

Zouga was anxious to see Jan Cheroot work. The man talked a very good elephant hunt, but Zouga wanted to know if he was as good on the spoor as he was at telling about it around the campfire. The first test came swiftly when the valley pinched out against another low cliff of impassable rock, and it seemed as though the beasts they followed had taken wing and soared away above the earth.

"Wait," said Jan Cheroot and cast swiftly along the base of the cliff. A minute later he whistled softly and Zouga went forward.

There was a smudge of ash on a block of ironstone, and another above it, seeming to lead directly into sheer rock face.

Jan Cheroot scrambled up over the loose scree at the foot of the cliff and disappeared abruptly. Zouga slung his rifle and followed him. The blocks of ironstone had fractured in the shape of a giant's staircase—each step as high as his waist so that he had to use a hand to climb.

Even the elephants would have extended themselves to make each step, rising on their back legs as he had seen them do at the circus, for an elephant is incapable of jumping. They must keep two feet on the earth before they can heave their ungainly bulks upward.

Zouga reached the spot where Jan Cheroot had disappeared and stopped short in amazement at the threshold of the stone portals, invisible from below, which marked the beginning of the ancient elephant road.

The portals were symmetrically formed in fractured rock, and had eroded through the softer layers, leaving straight joints so they seemed to have been worked by a mason. The opening was so narrow that it seemed impossible that such a large animal could pass through, and looking above the level of his own head, Zouga saw how over the centuries their rough skin had worn the stone smooth as thousands upon thousands of elephant had squeezed through the gap. He reached up and plucked a course black bristle, almost as thick as a Swan vesta, from a crack in the face. Beyond the natural gateway, the gap in the cliffs widened and rose at a more gentle pitch. Already Jan Cheroot was four hundred yards up the pathway.

"Come!" he called, and they followed him up.

The elephant road might have been surveyed and constructed by the corps of engineers, for never was the gradient steeper than thirty degrees and when there were natural steps they were never higher than a man—or an elephant could comfortably negotiate, although it seemed there were always accidents, for within a quarter of a mile they found where one of the big animals had missed his footing and struck the tip of one tusk against the ironstone edge.

The tusk had snapped above the point, and twenty pounds of ivory lay in the path. The fragment was worn and stained, so thick around that Zouga could not span it with both hands, but where it had sheared the fresh ivory was a lovely finely grained porcelain white.

Jan Cheroot whistled again when he saw the girth of the fragment of tusk. "I have never seen an elephant so big," he whispered, and instinctively checked the priming of his musket.

They followed the road out of the rocky pass on to forested slopes, where the trees were different, more widely spaced, and here the three old bulls had paused to strip off long slabs of bark from the msasa trunks before moving on. A mile further along the road, they found the chewed balls of bark still wet and smelling of elephant saliva, a rank gamy smell. Zouga held one of the big stringy balls to his nostrils and inhaled the elephant smell. It was the most exciting odor he had ever known.

When they rounded a shoulder of the mountain, there was a terrifying drop of open blue space before them in which the tiny shapes of vultures soared. Zouga was sure that it was the end of the road.

"Come!" Jan Cheroot whistled and they stepped out on to the narrow secret ledge, with the deep drop close at hand, and followed the road that had been smoothed for them by tens of thousands of roughly padded feet over the centuries.

Zouga at last was allowing himself to hope, for the road climbed always, and there seemed to be a definite purpose and direction to it—unlike the meandering game trails of the valley.

271

This road was going somewhere, climbing and bearing determinedly southward.

Zouga paused a moment and looked back. Far behind and below the sunken plain of the Zambezi shimmered in the blue and smoky haze of heat. The gigantic baobab trees seemed like children's miniatures, the terrible ground over which they had labored for weeks seemed smooth and inviting, and far away just visible through the haze the serpentine belt of denser vegetation marked the course of the great wide river itself.

Zouga turned his back upon it and followed Jan Cheroot up around the shoulder of the mountain, and a new and majestic vista opened around him as dramatically as though a theater curtain had been drawn aside.

Another steep slope stretched away above the cliffs, and there were luxuriant forests of marvelously shaped trees; the colors of their foliage was pink and flaming scarlet and iridescent green. These lovely forests reached up to a rampart of rocky peaks that Zouga was certain must mark the highest point of the escarpment.

There was something different with this new scene, and it took Zouga some moments to realize what it was. Then suddenly he drew a deep breath of pleasure. The air fanning down from the crest was sweet and cool as that on a summer's evening on the South Downs, but carrying with it the scent of strange shrubs and flowers and the soft exotic perfume of that beautiful pink-and-red forest of msasa trees.

That was not all, Zouga realized suddenly. There was something more important still. They had left the tsetse-fly belt behind them. It was many hours and a thousand feet of climbing since he had noticed the last of the deadly little insects. The land ahead of them now was clean, they were entering a land where man could live and rear his animals. They were leaving the killing heat of that harsh and forbidding valley for something softer and cleaner, something good, Zouga was certain of it, at last.

He stared about him with delight and wonder. Below him in the void a pair of vultures came planing in on wide-stretched pinions, so close that he could see every individual feather in their wingtips, and above the shaggy mound of their nest that clung precariously to a fissure in the sheer rock cliff they beat at the air, hovering, before settling upon the nest site. Clearly Zouga heard the impatient cries of the hungry nestlings.

On the rock shelf high above his head a family of hyrax, the plump rabbitlike rock dassie, sat in a row and stared down at him with patent astonishment, fluffy as children's toys, until at last they took fright and disappeared into their rocky warrens with the speed of a conjurer's illusion.

The sun, sinking through the last quadrant of its course, lit it all with richer and mellower light, and turned the cloud ranges to splendor, tall mushroom-shaped thunderheads of silver and brightest gold, touched with fleshy pink tongues and the tinge of wild roses.

Now at last Zouga could not doubt where the elephant road was leading him and he felt his spirits soaring; his body wearied from the climb was suddenly recharged with vigor, with vaulting expectations. For he knew that those rugged peaks above him were the threshold, the very frontiers, of the fabled kingdom of Monomatapa.

He wanted to push past Jan Cheroot on the narrow track, and run ahead up the broad beautiful forested slope that led to the crest, but the little yellow Hottentot stopped him with a hand upon his shoulder.

"Look!" he hissed softly. "There they are!"

Zouga followed his outflung arm and saw instantly. Far ahead among those magical red-and-pink groves something moved, vast and gray and slow, ethereal and insubstantial as a shadow. He stared at it, feeling his heartbeat quicken at this, his first glimpse of an African elephant in its savage habitat, but the slow gray movement was immediately screened by the dense foliage.

"My telescope." He snapped his fingers urgently behind his back, never taking his eyes from the spot where the beast had disappeared, and Matthew thrust the thick cylinder of cool brass into his hand.

With fingers that shook slightly he pulled out the sections of the spyglass, but before he could lift it to his eye the tree that had screened the elephant's body began to tremble and shake as though it had been struck by a whirlwind, and faintly they heard the rending crackle of tearing timber, the squealing protest of living wood, and slowly the tall tree leaned outward and then toppled with a crack that echoed off the cliffs like a cannon shot.

Zouga lifted the telescope and rested it on Matthew's patient shoulder. He focused the eyepiece. Abruptly, in the rounded field of the glass, the elephant was very close. His head was framed by the foliage of the tree he had uprooted. The ears seemed wide as a clipper's mainsail as they flapped lazily and

273

he could see the puffs of dust that their breeze raised from the massive gray withers.

Clearly he could see the wet tear path from the little eye down the sered and wrinkled cheek, and when the animal raised its head, Zouga drew breath sharply at the unbelievable size of the double arches of stained yellow ivories. One tip was foreshortened, broken off cleanly, and the ivory was brilliant snowy white in the fresh break.

As Zouga watched, the bull used his trunk, with its rubbery fingers of flesh at the tip, to pluck a handful of the delicate new leaves from the fallen tree. He used his trunk with the finesse of an expert surgeon, and then drooped open his triangular lower lip and thrust the leaves far down his own throat, and his rheumy old eyes wept with slow contentment.

An urgent tap on his shoulder disturbed Zouga and irritably he lifted his eye from the telescope. Jan Cheroot was pointing further up the slope.

Two other elephants had drifted into view from out of the forest. Zouga refocused upon them and then gasped. He had thought the first elephant massive. Here was another bull just as big; yet it was the third elephant which daunted his belief.

Beside him Jan Cheroot was whispering with suppressed tension making his voice hoarse and his slanted black eyes shine.

"The younger bulls are his two askaris, his indunas. They are his ears and his eyes. For in his great age he is probably almost deaf and more than half blind, but look at him. Is he not still a king?"

The oldest bull was tall and gaunt, taller by almost a head than his protégés, but the flesh seemed to have wasted off the ancient frame. His skin hung in baggy folds and creases from the massive framework of bones. He was thin in the way that some old men are thin; time had eroded him, seeming to leave only skin and stringy sinew and brittle bone. Matthew had been right in his description, the bull moved the way an old man moves, as though each joint protested with rheumatic pangs, and the weight of ivory he had carried for a hundred years was at last too much for him.

The ivory had once been the symbol of his majesty, and it was still perfect, flaring out from the lip and then turning in again so the points almost met. The gracious curves seemed perfectly matched, and the ivory was a lovely butter yellow, unblemished despite the dominance battles he had fought with them, despite the forest trees that the bull had toppled with them and stripped of their bark or the desert roots he had dug from stony soil with them.

But now, at last, these tusks were a burden to him, they wearied him and he carried his head low as they ached in his old jaws. It had been many years now since he had used them as fearsome weapons to keep control of the breeding herds. It had been as many years since he had sought the company of the young cows and their noisy squealing calves.

Now the long yellow ivories were a mortal danger to him, as well as a source of discomfort and pain. They made him attractive to man, his only enemy in nature. Always it seemed that the hunters were camped upon his spoor, and the man smell was associated with the flash and thudding discharge of muzzle-loading firearms, or the rude stinging intrusion of sharpened steel into his tired old flesh.

There were pieces of beaten iron pot leg and of round hardened lead ball deep in his body, the shot lying against the bone castle of his skull had become encysted with gristle and formed lumps as big as ripe apples beneath the skin, while the scars from arrows and stabbing spears, from the fire-hardened wood spikes of the dead-fall trap had thickened into shiny scars and become part of the rough, folded and creased mantle of his bald gray hide.

Without his two askaris he would long ago have fallen to the hunters. It was a strangely intimate relationship that knit the little herd of old bulls, and it had lasted for twenty years or more. Together they had trekked tens of thousands of miles, from the Cashan Mountains in the far south, across the burning, waterless wastes of the Kalahari Desert, along the dry riverbeds where they had knelt and with their tusks dug for water in the sand. They had wallowed together in the shallow lake of Ngami while the wings of the waterfowl darkened the sky above them, and they had stripped the bark from the forests along Linyati and Chobe, and crossed those wide rivers, walking on the bottom with just the tips of their trunks raised above the surface to give them breath.

Over the seasons they had swung in a circle through the wild land that lay north of the Zambezi, feasting on the fruits of different forests scattered over a thousand miles, timing their arrival as each crop of berries came into full ripening.

They had crossed lakes and rivers, had stayed long in the hot swamps of the Sud where the midday heat, reaching 120°, soothed the aches in the old bull's bones. But then the wanderlust had driven them on to complete the circle of their migration, south again over mountain ranges and across the low alluvial plains of the rivers, following secret trails and ancient passes that their ancestors had forged and which they had first trodden as calves at their mother's flank.

In these last dozen seasons, however, there were men where there had never been men before. There were white-robed Arabs in the north around the lakes, with their long-barreled jezails. There were big bearded men in the north, dressed in rough homespun and hunting from tough shaggy little ponies, while everywhere they met the tiny little Bushmen with their wicked poisoned arrows, or the Nguni regiments hunting a thousand strong, driving the game into set positions where the plumed spearmen waited.

With each round of the seasons, the elephant ranges were shrinking, new terrors and new dangers waited in the ancient ancestral feeding grounds, and the old bull was tired and his bones ached and the ivory in his jaws weighed him down. Still he moved on up the slope to the head of the pass with slow determination and dignity, driven on by his instincts, by the need for space about him, by the memory of the taste of the fruits he knew were already ripening in a distant forest on the shores of a faraway lake.

"We must hurry." Jan Cheroot's voice roused Zouga, for he had been mesmerized by the sight of the regal old animal, filled with a strange feeling of *déjà-vu*, as though he had lived this moment before, as though this meeting were part of his destiny. The old bull filled him with awe, with a sense of timelessness and grandeur, so he was reluctant to return to the reality of the moment.

"The day dies fast," Jan Cheroot insisted, and Zouga glanced over his shoulder to where the sun was setting like a mortally wounded warrior bleeding upon the clouds.

"Yes," he acknowledged, and then frowned as he realized that Jan Cheroot was stripping off his puttees and breeches, folding them and stuffing them together with his blanket and food bag into a crevice in the rock face beside him.

He answered Zouga's silent inquiry with a twinkling grin. "I run faster like this."

Zouga followed his example, leaving his own pack and pulling off the webbing belt from which hung knife and compass, stripping down to good running order, but he stopped short of removing his breeches. Jan Cheroot's skinny naked yellow buttocks were totally devoid of dignity and his dangling penis played hide-and-seek from under his shirttails. There

276

were some conventions that an officer of the Queen must observe, Zouga decided firmly, and one was to keep his breeches on in public. He followed Jan Cheroot along the narrow ledge, until they stepped off it onto the forested slope and immediately their forward vision was limited to a dozen yards by the lichen-covered tree trunks. From higher up the slope, however, they could hear the crackle and the ripping sound as the bull with the broken tusk fed on the uprooted tree.

Jan Cheroot worked out swiftly across the slope to avoid the askaris, to circle around him and come at the lead bull. Twice he paused to check the wind. It held steadily down the slope into their faces and the colorful leaves above their heads quivered and sighed at its passing.

They had gone a hundred yards when the sounds of the feeding bull ceased abruptly; again Jan Cheroot paused and the little group of hunters froze with him, every man instinctively holding his breath as they listened, but there was only the sound of the wind and the singing whine of a cicada in the branches above.

"He has moved on to join the others," Jan Cheroot whispered at last. Zouga was also certain that the bull could not yet have suspected their presence. The wind was steady, he could not have scented them. Zouga knew that the eyesight of the elephant was as weak as his hearing and sense of smell were acute, but they had made no sound.

Yet this was a clear demonstration of the benefits that the three old bulls derived from their association. It was always difficult for the hunter to place each of them accurately, especially in thick forest such as this, and the two askaris seemed always to take station on the lead bull to cover and protect him. To come at him, the hunter must penetrate the screen they threw around him.

Standing now, listening and waiting, Zouga wondered if a genuine affection existed between the three animals, whether they derived the pleasure of companionship from each other, and whether the askaris would mourn or pine when the old bull fell at last with the musket ball in his brain or his heart.

"Come!" Silently Jan Cheroot made the open-handed signal to advance and they went on up the slope, stooping under the low trailing branches, Zouga keeping four paces out on the Hottentot's flank to open his field of vision and fire, concentrating his whole being in his eyes and his ears. Far up the slope there was the snap of a breaking twig and it stopped them dead once more, breathing shallowly with the tension, but the sound fastened all their attention ahead so none of them saw the askari.

The elephant waited with the stillness of granite, his sered hide gray and rough as the lichen-covered tree trunks, the shadows thrown by the low sun barred him and broke up the shape of his great body so he blended into the forest, gray and unearthly as mist, and they tiptoed past him at twenty paces without seeing him.

He let the hunters pass and get up above the wind and when the acrid stench of carnivorous man was borne thickly down to him through the forest, he took it in his trunk and lifted it to his mouth and sprayed the tainted air over the little olfactory organs under his upper lip, and his smell buds flared open like soft wet pink rosebuds and the askari bull squealed.

It was a sound that seemed to bounce against the sky, and ring from the peaks above them, it was an expression of all the hatred and pain, the terrible memories of that acrid man smell from a hundred other encounters, and the askari bull squealed again and launched his huge body up the slope to destroy the source of that evil odor.

Zouga spun to the piercing din, his shocked eardrums still buzzing with the sound, and the forest shook with the bull's charge. The dense shiny vegetation burst open, like a storm surf running on to rock, and the bull came through.

Zouga was not conscious of his own movements, he was aware only that he was looking at the bull over the open sights of the Sharps rifle, and the blast of shot seemed muted and far off after the ringing squeal that initiated the charge. He saw dust fly from the bull's forehead in a brief little puff, saw the skin ripple like that of a stallion stung by a bee, and he reached back and found the stubby wooden stock of one of the big elephant guns in his hand. Again, there was no awareness of conscious movement, but over the crude V of the sight the elephant appeared much closer. Zouga seemed to be leaning back to look up at the gigantic head and the long shafts of yellow ivory reached out over him, blotting out the sky. Clearly he could see the bright white porcelain break in one point of the left-hand tusk.

He heard Jan Cheroot beside him, and heard his excited shrieks.

"Skiet hom! Shoot him!"

Then the heavy weapon leaped against his own shoulder, driving him back a pace, and he saw the tiny fountain of bright blood squirting out of the elephant's throat like a lovely scarlet flamingo feather. He reached back for the next loaded gun, although he knew there would be no time to fire again.

He was surprised that he felt no fear, although he knew he was a dead man. The elephant was on him, his life was forfeit, there could be no question, yet he went on with the motions of living, hefting the new gun, thumbing back the clumsy hammer as he swung the barrel up.

The shape of the huge animal above him had altered, it was no longer so close, and he realized with a thrill that the bull was turning, it had been unable to endure the fearful punishment of the heavy-bored guns.

He was turning, passing by them with blood streaming down his head and chest. As he passed, he exposed his neck and flank, and Zouga shot him a hand's span behind the joint of his shoulder on the line of the lungs and the ball slogged into his rib cage.

The bull was going, crashing away up the slope, and with the fourth gun Zouga hit him high in the back, aiming for the bony knuckles of the spine where they showed through the scabby hide of the sloping back and the bull whipped his thick tufted tail at the agony of the strike and disappeared into the forest, gone like a wraith in the failing light of the sunset.

Zouga and Jan Cheroot stared at each other speechlessly, each of them holding a smoking weapon at high port across his chest, and they listened to the run of the bull up the slope ahead of them.

Zouga found his voice first, he turned to his gunbearers.

"Load!" he hissed at them, for they also were paralyzed by the close passage of violent, thundering death, but his command liberated them and they each snatched a handful of black powder from the bag slung at their sides and poured it into the still-hot muzzles of the guns.

"The lead bull and the other askari will run," lamented Jan Cheroot, himself frantically busy with the ramrod of his Enfield.

"We can still catch them before the summit," Zouga told him, grabbing the first loaded gun. An elephant goes on a steep uphill at a very measured pace that a good runner can gain upon, but downhill he goes like a runaway locomotive; nothing can catch him, not even a good horse.

"We must catch them before the crest," Zouga repeated, and launched himself toward the incline. Weeks of hard going over bad terrain had toughened him, and the driving lust of the hunter was the spur. He flew at the slope.

Awareness of his own lack of experience that had resulted in such poor shooting made Zouga more fiercely determined to close with the lead bull and vindicate himself. He guessed that as a complete novice he had failed to find the vitals with any of the balls he had fired, he had missed brain and heart and lungs by inches, inflicting pain and mutilation, instead of the quick kill for which the true huntsman strives. He wanted desperately to have another chance to end it cleanly, and he pelted up the slope.

Before he had gone two hundred yards, he had evidence that his shooting had not been as wide as he had at first believed. He checked at a spot where it looked as though someone had thrown a bucket of blood across the stony earth. The blood was a peculiarly bright scarlet, and it frothed with tiny bubbles, lung blood. There was no question, that last ball fired into the bull's back as he went away up the slope must have raked the lungs. It was a killing shot, but a slow killer. The old bull was drowning in his own bright arterial blood, desperately trying to rid himself of it by squirting it through his trunk as it bubbled up into his throat.

He was dying, but it would take time still, and Zouga raced on after him.

He had not expected the bull to stand again. He expected him to run until he dropped, or until the hunters caught up with him. Zouga knew the folly of attributing human motives and loyalties to wild animals; even so it seemed that the stricken bull had determined to sacrifice himself in order to allow the lead bull and the second askari to escape across the pass at the crest of the mountains. Up the slope, he was waiting for Zouga, listening for him with those vast ears spread wide, his chest with the girth of a Cognac cask of Limousine oak racking and straining to force air into his torn lung.

He charged as soon as he heard the man, his huge ears cocked back and rolled at the tips, trunk curled at his chest, shrilling and squealing, blowing a fine red mist of blood from his trunk, pounding through the forest so the earth trembled with each massive footfall and the branches crackled and broke like a discharge of musketry.

Panting, Zouga stood to meet the charge, ducking his head and weaving for a clean shot through the thick forest. At the last moment the bull broke off the charge, and swerved up the slope again. Each time the hunters began to move forward, he launched another thunderous mock attack, forcing them to stand to meet him, and then breaking off again.

Minutes passed between each charge, and the hunters were pinned down, fretting with the knowledge that already the lead bull and his surviving protégé must have reached the crest and gone away in a rush like an avalanche down the far side.

Zouga was learning two hard lessons: the first, as old Tom Harkness had tried to teach him, was that only a novice or a fool underguns an elephant. The light ball of the Sharps might be highly effective on American bison, but the African elephant has ten times the body weight and resistance. Standing in the msasa forests, listening to the squealing and crashing of the wounded monster, Zouga determined never again to use the light American rifle on heavy game.

The second lesson he was learning was that if the first ball does not kill, then it seems to numb and anesthetize heavy game to further punishment. Kill cleanly, or the subsequent shots into heart and lungs seem to be without effect. It was not only anger and provocation which made a wounded animal so dangerous, it was also this shock-induced immortality.

After standing down half a dozen mock charges, Zouga abandoned caution and patience, and he ran forward shouting to meet the next charge.

"Whoa there!" he called. "Come on then, old fellow!"

This time he got in close, and crashed another ball through the bull's rib cage as he turned away. He had controlled his first wild excitement, and the ball struck precisely at the point of aim. He knew it was a heart shot, but the bull came again squealing, and Zouga fired a last time before the angry trumpeting and shrilling turned to a long sad bellow that echoed off the peaks and rang out into the blue void of sky beyond the cliffs.

They heard him go down, the impact of the heavy body against the earth made it shiver under their feet. Cautiously, the little group of hunters went forward through the forest and they found him kneeling, his forelegs folded neatly under his chest, his long, yellow ivories propping up the dusty wrinkled old head, still facing down the slope as though defiant even in death.

"Leave him," shouted Jan Cheroot. "Follow the others." And they ran on past him.

Night caught them before they reached the crest of the slope, the sudden impenetrably black night of central Africa, so they lost the spoor and missed the pass.

"We will have to let them go," Jan Cheroot lamented, his yellow face a blob at Zouga's shoulder.

"Yes," Zouga agreed. "This time we must let them go." But somehow he knew there would be another time. The feeling that the old bull was part of his destiny was still strongly with Zouga. Yes, there would be another time, of that he was certain.

That night for the first time Zouga ate the hunter's greatest delicacy: slices of elephant heart threaded onto a green stick with cubes of white fat cut out from the chest cavity, salted and peppered, and roasted over the slow coals of the campfire, eaten with cold cakes of stone-ground corn and washed down with a mug of tea, steaming hot, bitter, strong and unsweetened. He could not remember a finer meal, and afterward Zouga lay down on the hard earth, covered by a single blanket and protected from the chill of the wind by the huge carcass of the old bull, and slept as though he also had been struck down, without dreams, without rolling over even once in his sleep.

In the morning, by the time they had chopped out one of the tusks and laid it under the msasa trees, they could already hear the singing of the porters as the main body of the caravan filed along the narrow ledge, rounding the shoulder of the mountain and then came up onto the slope.

Robyn was a hundred paces ahead of the standard bearer, and when she reached the carcass of the bull she stopped.

"We heard the gunfire last evening," she said.

"He's a fine old bull," Zouga told her, indicating the freshly chopped tusk. It was the unbroken right-hand ivory, taller than Zouga, but a third of its length had been buried in the skull. This portion was smooth, unblemished white, whereas the rest of it was stained by vegetable juices.

"It will weigh almost a hundred pounds," he went on, touching the tusks with the toe of his boot. "Yes, he's a fine old bull."

"Not anymore he isn't," Robyn told him quietly, watching Jan Cheroot and the gunbearers hacking away at the enormous mutilated head. Little chips of white bone flew in the early sunlight, as they whittled away the heavy skull to free the second tusk. Robyn watched the butchery for a few seconds only before going on up the slope toward the crest.

Zouga was irritated and angry with her, for she had detracted from his own vaulting pleasure in his first elephant hunt. So, an hour later when he heard Robyn calling to him from higher up the slope, he ignored her cries. However, she was persistent, as always, and at last with an exclamation of exasperation, he followed her up through the forest. She came running down to meet him, with the unrestrained infectious joy of a child shining on her face.

"Oh, Zouga." She seized his hand, and began to drag him impetuously up the slope. "Come and see, you must come and see."

The old elephant road crossed the saddle, through a deep pass, guarded on each hand by buttresses of rough gray rock and as they took the last few paces over the highest point a new and beautiful world opened below and ahead of them. Zouga gasped involuntarily, for he had not anticipated anything like this.

Low foothills fell away from beneath their feet, regular as the swells of the ocean, covered with stately trees whose trunks were tall as the oaks of Windsor Park, and then beyond the hills the undulating lightly forested grasslands, golden as fields of ripe wheat, spread to a tall blue horizon. There were streams of clear water meandering through the glades of light colored grass, where herds of wild game drank or lazed upon the banks.

There were buffalo everywhere Zouga looked, black bovine shapes, standing shoulder to shoulder in masses under the umbrella branches of the acacia trees. Closer at hand a troop of sable antelope, that loveliest of all antelope, jet-black above but with snowy bellies, their long symmetrical curve of horn extended backward almost to touch the haunches, followed the herd bull in long file to the water, pausing unafraid to stare curiously at the interlopers, forming a frieze of stately, almost Grecian, design.

The endless stretch of land was dotted with hills like ruined natural castles of stone, seeming to have been built in past eons by giants and ogres from mammoth blocks of stone, and tumbled now in fantastic shapes, some with fairy turrets and spires, others again flat-topped, geometrically laid out as though by a meticulous architect with plumb line and theodolite.

This scene was lit by a peculiar pearly luminosity of the morning light, so that even the furthest hills, probably more than a hundred miles distant, were sharply silhouetted through the clean air.

"It's beautiful," Robyn murmured, still holding Zouga's hand.

"The kingdom of Monomatapa," Zouga answered her, his own voice husky with emotion.

"No," Robyn answered softly. "There is no sign of man here, this is the new Eden."

Zouga was silent, letting his eyes rove across the scene,

283

searching for, but not finding, any evidence of man. It was a land untouched, unspoiled.

"A new land, there for the taking!" he said, still holding Robyn's hand. They were as close, in that moment, as they had ever been or would ever be again, and the land awaited them, wide, limitless, empty and beautiful.

At last, reluctantly, he left Robyn at the head of the pass and went back through the rock portals to bring on the caravan. He found the second tusk removed, and both of them bound up with bark rope onto the carrying poles of newly cut msasa wood, but the porters had laid aside their packs and were indulging in an orgy of fresh meat, and that most sought after of African spoils, thick white globs of elephant fat.

They had cut a trapdoor into the belly of the elephant carcass, and pulled out the entrails, and these glistened in the early sunlight, huge rubbery tubes of purple and yellow guts, already swelling and ballooning with the trapped gases they contained.

Half a dozen porters, stripped mother-naked, had crawled into the interior of the elephant's carcass, disappearing completely from view and wading almost waist-deep in the clotting, congealing bath of trapped blood. They crawled out, painted with it from head to foot, eyes and grinning teeth startlingly white in the grisly shining wet red visages, their arms filled with tidbits of liver and fat and spleen.

These delicacies were hacked into pieces with the blade of an assegai and thrown on the glowing coals of one of half a dozen fires, then snatched up again, black on the outside and more than half raw within to be wolfed down with every appearance of ecstatic pleasure.

There would be no moving them until they were satiated, Zouga realized. So he left instructions to Jan Cheroot, himself already pot-bellied with the meat he had gorged, to follow as soon as the carcass had been either eaten or packed up for carrying, and taking the Sharps rifle returned back up the slope to where he had left Robyn.

He called for her, fruitlessly, for almost half an hour, and was really becoming concerned for her safety when her reply echoed off the cliffs, and looking upward he saw her standing on a ledge a hundred feet above him, waving him to come up.

Zouga climbed up swiftly to where she stood on the ledge, and checked the rebuke that he had ready for her when he saw her expression. She was a sickly grayish color, under the gilding of the sun, and her eyes were reddened and still swimming with tears.

"What is it, sissy?" he asked with quick concern, but she seemed unable to reply, the words choking in her throat so she had to swallow thickly and motion him to follow her.

The ledge on which they stood was narrow, but level—and was cut back under the cliff, forming a low long cavern. The cavern had been used before by other men, for the rocky roof was blackened with the sooty smoke of countless cooking fires, and the back wall was decorated with the lyrically childlike paintings of the little yellow Bushmen who over the centuries must have used this as a regular camp during their endless wanderings.

The paintings lacked both perspective and accurate form, but they captured the essential nature of all they recorded, from the graceful sweep of the giraffe's neck to the bulky shoulders of the Cape buffalo with the mournful drooping horns framing the lifted nose.

The Bushman artist saw himself and his tribe as frail, stick-like figures, with drawn bows, dancing and prancing about the quarry, and again, out of all proportion to the rest of the painting, each little man sported a massively erect penis. Even in the heat of the chase, such was the universal conceit of all male kind, Zouga thought.

Zouga was enchanted by the frozen cavalcade of man and beast which covered the walls of the cave, and he had already determined to camp here so that he could have more time to study and record this treasure-house of primitive art, when Robyn called him again.

He followed her along the ledge until they reached the point where it ended abruptly, forming a balcony over the dreaming land ahead of them. Zouga's attention was torn between this fresh vista of forest and glade and the cave art at his shoulder, but Robyn summoned him again impatiently.

There were strata of multicolored rock running horizontally through the rock face of the cliff. The different layers of rock varied in hardness, and the erosion of a softer layer had formed the long low cavern beyond the ledge.

This layer of rock was a soapy green color, where it had not been painted over by the Bushmen artists or discolored with the smoke of their fires, and here at the point overlooking the empire of Monomatapa someone had used a metal tool to scrape a smooth square plaque into the green soapstone. The freshly cut surface stood out rawly as though it had been done that very day, but the words gave the lie to that impression.

There was a simple Christian cross chiseled deeply into the stone, and below it the name and the date, the lettering very carefully cut and designed by an expert penman.

FULLER MORRIS BALLANTYNE

Zouga exclaimed aloud at seeing his father's name, so clearly rendered by his father's own hand.

Despite the apparent freshness of the cut, the date was seven years old—July 20, 1853. After that single exclamation they were both speechless, staring at the inscription, each of them gripped by differing emotion—Robyn by a resurgence of filial love and duty, by a crushing desire to be with her father again after so many years, the vast empty place in her life aching more excruciatingly at the prospect of being soon filled. Her eyes refilled with tears, and they broke from her eyelids and ran down her cheeks.

"Please, God," she prayed silently, "lead me to my father. Dear God, grant me that I am not too late."

Zouga's emotions were as strong, but different. He felt a corroding resentment that any other man, father or not, should have preceded him through these rocky gates into the kingdom of Monomatapa. This was his land, and he did not want to share it with another. Especially, he did not want to share it with that monster of cruelty and conceit that was his father.

He stared coldly at the inscription that followed the name and date, but inwardly he seethed with anger and resentment.

"In God's Holy name." The words were carved below his father's name.

It was typical of Fuller Ballantyne that he should carve his own name here with cross and credentials as the Lord's ambassador, as he had on trees and rocks at a hundred other places across the continent which he regarded as a personal gift from his God.

"You were right, Zouga dear. You are leading us to him, as you promised. I should never have doubted you."

If he had been alone Zouga realized that he might have defaced that inscription, scraped the rock bare with his hunting knife, but as he had the thought, he realized how futile it would be, for such an action would not wipe out the ghostly presence of the man himself.

Zouga turned away from the rock wall and its taunting

plaque. He stared out over the new land—but somehow his heady pleasure in it had been dimmed by the knowledge that another man had passed this way ahead of him. He sat down with his feet dangling over the sheer drop to wait for Robyn to tire of staring at her father's name.

However, the caravan of porters came before she did that. Zouga heard the singing from the forested slope behind the pass long before the head of the line crossed the saddle. The porters had voluntarily doubled their own loads, and they struggled up the slope under the enormous weight of elephant meat and fat and marrow bones, bound up in baskets of green msasa leaves and bark rope.

If Zouga had asked them to carry that weight of trade cloth or beads, or even gunpowder, he would have had an immediate mutiny to deal with, he thought grimly, but at least they were carrying the tusks. He could see them near the head of the line, each tusk slung on a long pole, a man at either end, but even here they had hung extra baskets of meat on the same pole as the tusk. The total weight must have been well over three hundred pounds, and they struggled up the slope uncomplainingly, even cheerfully.

Slowly, the caravan wound out of the forest and entered the gut of the pass, beginning to move directly under where Zouga sat, the figures of the porters and of Jan Cheroot's Hottentot musketeers foreshortened by the angle. Zouga rose to his feet; he wanted to order Jan Cheroot to camp just beyond the point where the pass debouched on to the foothills. From where Zouga stood, he could see a patch of green grass against the foot of the cliffs far below him, and a pair of pale-gray herons hunting frogs in this verdant marshy area. There was certainly a spring, and with the meat upon which they had gorged, his servants would be burning with thirst by nightfall.

The spring would be a good place to camp, and it would allow him the following morning to copy and record the Bushman paintings in the cavern. He cupped his hands to his mouth to hail Jan Cheroot—when a crash like the broadside from a ship of the line filled the pass with thunder that echoed and bounced back and forth between the cliffs.

For many seconds Zouga could not understand what was happening—for the thunderous bursts of sound were repeated, almost drowning the thin screams of his porters. They were throwing down their burdens and scattering like a flight of doves under the stoop of the falcon.

Then another movement caught his attention, a large round
287

shape went bounding down the scree slope below the cliffs, charging straight at his panic-stricken caravan. For a moment Zouga believed it was some sort of living predator that was attacking his servants, and, running along the lip of the ledge, he unslung the Sharps rifle, ready to fire down into the pass as soon as he could get a sight on one of the bounding shapes.

Then he realized that at each leap the thing struck sparks and fine gray smoke from the scree slope, and he could smell the faint smell, like burned saltpeter that the sparks left in the air. He realized abruptly that they were giant rounded boulders rolling down upon his caravan, not one but a dozen or more, each weighing many tons, an onslaught which seemed to spring from the very air itself, and he looked wildly about for its source, goaded by the screams of his men and the sight of the rolling boulders smashing open packs of his precious irreplaceable provisions and scattering them across the rocky ground of the saddle.

Far below him, he heard the thudding report of an Enfield rifle, and glancing back he saw the tiny figure of Jan Cheroot aiming almost directly upward at the sky, and following the direction of his rifle Zouga saw movement, just a flicker of movement on the edge of the cliff, outlined against the blue soaring vault of the heavens.

The deluge of huge boulders was coming from the very top of the cliff, and as Zouga stared, another and then another came raining down into the pass. Zouga squinted his eyes, head thrown back, as he studied the cliff rim. There was some animal up there. Zouga did not at first think of man, for he had already convinced himself that this new land was devoid of human presence.

He felt an almost superstitious chill of horror that some pack of giant apes was on top of the cliff, bombarding his men with huge rocks, then he shook himself free of the feeling, and looked quickly for some way to get higher up his side of the pass, to reach a position from where he could fire across the rocky gateway at the attackers on the opposite cliff and give some protection to his servants.

Almost immediately he discovered another ledge rising at a steep angle from the one on which he stood. Only a soldier's eye would have picked it out. The tiny feet of the little rock hyrax that used it had put a light sheen on the rock and it was this that had drawn Zouga's attention to the narrow pathway.

"Stay here!" he shouted at Robyn, but she stepped in front of him.

"Zouga, what are you going to do?" she demanded, and then before he could answer. "Those are men up there! You cannot fire upon them!" Her cheeks were still smeared with tears, but her pale face was set and determined.

"Get out of the way," he snapped at her.

"Zouga, it will be murder."

"That's what they are trying to do to my men."

"We must bargain with them." Robyn caught at his arm as he pushed past her, but he shook her off and ran to the higher ledge.

"It will be murder!" Robyn's cry followed him, and as he climbed, Zouga was reminded of the words of old Tom Harkness. The accusation that his father would not stop at killing anybody who stood in his way. This was what he had meant, Zouga was suddenly sure of it. He wondered if his father had fought his way through this pass, just as Zouga himself was about to do.

"If the champion of the Almighty can do it, then what a fine example to follow," he muttered to himself as he went up the steep ledge.

Below him the Enfield rifle thudded again, the sound muted by distance, almost lost in the roar of a new avalanche of murderous rock. Jan Cheroot could only hope to discourage his attackers with rifle fire from that angle; only if one of them actually leaned far out over the edge of the cliff would he be vulnerable to fire from the gut of the pass.

Zouga climbed in cold anger, stepping unhesitatingly over dangerous spots in the narrow ledge where small pieces of rock crumbled under his boots and went rattling down into the pass hundreds of feet below.

Abruptly he came out on to a broader ledge, formed by the strata of rock, which rose at a gentler pitch so that now Zouga could run along it without fear of losing his footing. He climbed swiftly, it was less than ten minutes since that first boulder had come crashing down into the pass; the attackers were continuing the bombardment, the hills reverberated with the crash and rumble of flying boulders.

Ahead of Zouga on the ledge, a pair of tiny klipspringer went bouncing up over broken rock, seeming to flit on the tips of their elongated hooves, terrified by the men and the rumble of falling rock. They reached the corner of the ledge and one after another they made what seemed suicidal leaps out into space, phenomenal leaps that carried them forty feet to the next sheer wall of rock, rock which seemed devoid of foothold, but

289

they clung to it like flies and scrambled swiftly up out of sight over the top of the cliff.

Zouga envied them that birdlike agility as he toiled up the steep incline, sweat soaking his shirt and streaming stingingly into his eyes. He could not stop to rest, for far below him a thin wailing scream of agony told him that at least one of the flying boulders had struck down a porter.

He turned another steep corner in the goat track, scrambled over the rim, and was suddenly out upon the flat tablelike summit, dotted with little clumps of broom bush and sparse stiff yellow grass like hedgehog quills.

Zouga threw himself down on the edge of the plateau, heaving and straining for breath, and he struck the sweat from his eyes, peering across the deep void of the pass at the cliffs on the opposite side. He found himself on a level with the heights opposite. It was three or four hundred yards across, easy range for the Sharps—though one of the smooth-bore four-to-the-pounds would have been hopelessly inaccurate at that distance.

While he primed the rifle, he studied the ground opposite him and saw almost immediately why the attackers had chosen that side of the pass in preference to the one on which Zouga lay.

They were on a flat-topped pinnacle of sheer rock, with no visible access to it from any direction; what path there was would be secret and highly defensible. The attackers had an inexhaustible supply of missiles for the rounded boulders were scattered everywhere upon the heights, varying in size from that of a man's head to that of an elephant carcass, and as Zouga watched them they were using heavy raw timber balks to lever one of these over the edge of the cliff.

Zouga's hands were shaking and he fought to bring them under control, but the Sharps rifle wavered as he tried to take a sight on the little group of men across the open void of space. There were not more than two dozen of them, all of them naked except for a brief kilt of leather, their skins polished with a sheen of sweat in the sunlight.

He was regaining his breath swiftly, and now he wriggled forward on his belly and propped the stock of the Sharps rifle on a rock in front of him. It was a dead rest, and as he leveled his gaze over the open sights the group of men succeeded in working the huge boulder over the edge of the cliff.

It went with a brief grating that carried clearly to Zouga, and then it fell with the soft rushing of eagle's wings until it struck again in the pass two hundred feet below—and once again the hills rang and rumbled to the force and weight of it.

The little group of black men had drawn back from the edge of the cliff, resting a moment before they selected another missile. Only one of them wore a headdress. It looked like a cap made from the mane of a male lion, long tawny hair tipped with black. It made the man taller than his companions, and he seemed to be giving orders to them, gesticulating and pushing those nearest to him.

"You'll do, my beauty!" Zouga whispered. He had regained his breath now, and the sweat was cooling his back and his neck. He pushed up the leaf of his backsight to its three-hundred-yard adjustment and then settled down on his elbows to peer over it. The rifle was rock-steady on its rest, while he took a fine bead on the man with the lion headdress.

He touched off the shot, and while the crack of it still stung his eardrums he saw a tiny chip of rock fly from the lip of the cliff across the valley. "Low, but very nicely on line," he told himself, opened the breech of the Sharps and forced the paper cartridge into it.

The shot had startled the little group of men. They peered about them, mystified, not certain of what it was or from where it had come. The tall figure in the headdress moved cautiously forward to the edge of the cliff and stooped to examine the fresh chip on the ironstone rim, touching it with one finger.

Zouga set the cap, and thumbed back the hammer. He gave it a full bead, and aimed at the waving yellow headdress, set the hair trigger and then with a lover's touch stroked the curved trigger.

The bullet told loudly, a meaty slap like a housewife beating a carpet, and the man in the lion headdress spun around sharply, his arms jerking out wide, his legs shuffling in a grotesque little dance; they collapsed under him and he flopped on the very edge of the cliff like a harpooned catfish.

His companions stood frozen, making no effort to help him as he slid toward the edge of the cliff, and a final spasmodic jerk of his legs tumbled him into the void. He fell for a long time, his outspread limbs spinning like the spokes of a wagon wheel, and there was another meaty thump as he landed at last on the broken scree slope far below.

Zouga fired again, into the tight knot of men, not attempting to single out one of them, and he hit two of them with a single bullet, for even at that range the Sharps could drive the hardened lead ball through a man's body with hardly any loss of velocity, and the group was bunched up.

As the ball whacked into them, they split into separate racing figures, their yells of fright carrying clearly to where Zouga lay, and before he could fire again, they had disappeared into a narrow rocky gulley with the miraculous speed of a troop of little furry hyrax.

The silence was sudden and startling after the uproar of falling boulders and heavy gunfire and it lasted for many minutes, broken at last by the shrill voice of Jan Cheroot calling up from the deep gut of the pass. Zouga stood up, and hanging on to the branch of a monkey orange tree, leaned out over the edge of the cliff.

"Take the caravan through, Sergeant." He pitched his voice to carry, and the echoes mocked him with his own words. "Sergeant—Sergeant—Sergeant—"

"I will cover you—cover you—cover you," taunted the echoes.

Zouga called the little Matabele maiden from the fireside where she knelt beside Robyn, helping her treat one of the porters who had been struck by a flying splinter of rock during the attack, and whose shoulder had been laid open to the bone.

"Juba," he told her, "I want you to come with me." And the girl glanced back at Robyn, hesitating to obey him. Zouga's irritation flared again. He and Robyn had not spoken again since Zouga had broken up the attack with rifle fire, and Jan Cheroot had reassembled the caravan and led it out of the deadly trap of the gorge to where it was camped now in the foothills beyond the pass.

"Come," Zouga repeated, and the child dropped her eyes at his tone and followed him submissively as he started back toward the pass.

Zouga moved back cautiously, pausing every fifty paces or so to survey the clifftops suspiciously, although he was fairly certain that there would be no renewal of the boulder rolling. However, he kept in close under the sheer rock face so that any boulder would fall beyond them.

The going was difficult over the loose scree, and through the thick scrub that covered it. It took them nearly an hour to get back to the spot where Zouga had marked the fall of the body of the warrior in the lion headdress, and then they had to search for nearly as long again before they found the corpse.

He had fallen into a deep crevice between two rocks, and

he lay at the bottom of it on his back. The body appeared unmarked except for the small black bullet hole low on the left side of his naked chest.

The eyes were still wide open, but he had lost his headdress.

After a moment Zouga turned to Juba inquiringly. "Who is he? Of what tribe is he?" he asked, and the child showed no concern at the presence of violent death. She had seen very much worse in her short life.

"Mashona!" she told Zouga scornfully. Juba was Matabele of Zanzi blood, and there was no more noble breeding outside the kraal of King Mzilikazi himself. She felt nothing but contempt for all the other tribes of Africa, especially for these people.

"Mashona!" she repeated. "Eaters of dirt."

It was the ultimate term of denigration that the Matabele applied to all the tribes that they had taken into slavery or driven to the very point of extinction.

"It is always the way these baboons fight." She indicated the dead man with a toss of her pretty head. "They stand on the hilltops and throw down stones."

Her eyes sparkled. "It becomes more difficult each year for our young men to blood their spears, and until they do so the King will not give them leave to marry." She broke off, and Zouga smiled ironically. The child's resentment was clearly not so much at the Mashona's alleged lack of sportsmanship, but at the havoc that this wrought on the Matabele marriage markets.

Zouga scrambled down into the rocky crevice and stooped over the dead warrior. Despite Juba's contempt, the man was well formed, with straight strong limbs, and handsome intelligent features. For the first time Zouga felt a twinge of regret at having fired the ball which had caused that innocuous-looking little wound. It was a good thing that the warrior lay upon his back for the exit would have been ghastly. A soldier should never examine the bodies of the men he kills in the heat of battle. Zouga had made that discovery long ago in India, for afterward there was always this moment of guilt and remorse. He shrugged it away, for he had not come either to gloat over the kill or to torture himself with it, but to merely identify his enemy.

Why had these warriors attacked the caravan without warning? he wondered. Were they the border guards of the fabled Monomatapa? It seemed the most likely explanation, though, of course, they could be ordinary bandits, like the dacoits of India with whom he had made bitter acquaintance.

Zouga stared moodily down at the corpse. Who had he been? And how much danger did his tribe still present to Zouga's caravan? But there was nothing more to learn and Zouga began to straighten up again when he noticed the necklace around the corpse's throat. He knelt again to examine it.

It was made of cheap trade beads on a thong of gut, a gaudy little trifle except for the pendant that had hung onto his chest but had slipped back under the armpit, half concealed so that Zouga noticed it now for the first time.

He pulled it free, examined it a moment and then slipped the entire necklace off over the man's head. When he put his hand around the back of the dead man's head to lift it he felt the pieces of skull grate together deep in his head like shards of broken pottery under his fingers. He lowered the shattered head and stood up with the necklace twined about his fingers, examining the pendant.

It had been carved from ivory that had yellowed with age, and tiny black cracks formed a fine web across its polished surfaces. Zouga held it to catch the sunlight, and turned it between his fingers to study it from every angle.

He had seen another figurine that was almost a twin to this one, a golden figurine that was now in a bank vault in Cape Town where he had deposited it before they had sailed on board the gunboat *Black Joke*.

This was the same stylized birdlike shape, perched on a round plinth. The plinth was decorated with the same triangular shark's-teeth pattern, and the bird had the same swelling chest and short, sharply pointed wings folded across its back. It could have been a pigeon or a dove, except for one detail. The beak was the curved and hooked weapon of a raptor.

It was a falcon, he knew it beyond any doubt, and it was certain that the heraldic bird had some deep significance. The golden necklace that Tom Harkness had left him must have belonged to a king or a queen or a high priest. The choice of material, gold, was an indication of that. Now here was the same shape, worn by a man who seemed to be a chieftain, and once again the shape was faithfully copied in a precious material, ivory.

The falcon of Monomatapa, Zouga wondered, studying the ancient pendant, ancient it must be, for the ivory had acquired a deep patina and luster.

Zouga looked up at the little Matabele girl standing almost naked above him and watching him with interest.

"Do you see this?" he asked.

"It is a bird."

"Have you seen it before?"

Juba shook her head, and her fat little breasts joggled at the movement.

"It is a Mashona thing," and she shrugged. What would a daughter of the sons of Senzangakhona and Chaka want with such a nonsense?

On an impulse, Zouga lifted the necklace and dropped it over his own head, letting the ivory falcon fall inside the V of his flannel shirt.

"Come!" he told Juba. "There is nothing more for us here," and he led the way back toward the camp beyond the pass.

The land into which the old bull had led them by the secret road through the pass was an elephant kingdom. Perhaps the pressure of the hunters moving up from the far southern tip of the continent had driven them into this unpeopled world. The herds were everywhere. Each day Zouga and Jan Cheroot hunting far ahead of the main caravan came up with the huge gray pachyderms, and they shot them down.

They shot and killed forty-eight elephant the first month and almost sixty the second, and Zouga meticulously recorded each kill in his journal, the circumstances of the hunt, the weight of each tusk, and the exact location of the cache in which they buried them.

His small band of porters could not carry even a small part of such a mass of ivory, and the distance and direction which they must still travel was uncertain. Zouga buried his treasure, always near a readily recognizable landmark, a distinctive tree, or an unusual rock, a hilltop or a confluence of rivers, to enable him to find it again.

He would return one day for it, and when he did, it would have dried off its excess moisture and be easier for the porters to carry.

In the meantime, he spent all his daylight hours in pursuit of the quarry, walking and running long distances until his body was hard and fit as that of a highly trained athlete, and his arms and face a deep mahogany brown, even his full beard and mustache gilded to shades of gold by the sun.

Every day he learned from Jan Cheroot the tricks of bush lore, until he could run a difficult spoor over rocky ground without a check. He learned to anticipate the turns and the twists that the driven herds made to get below the wind and take his scent. He learned to anticipate the pattern of their movements so that by cutting across the circuitous spoor he could save many hours of dogged pursuit. He learned to judge the sex and size and age and ivory of a beast by the mark of its rounded pads in the earth.

He found that if the herd was allowed to settle into that swinging gait between a trot and a canter, then they could keep it up for a day and a night without pause—whereas if they were taken in the full heat of noon, he could run them hard for the first five miles, winding them, bringing the tiny calves to a standstill so the cows stopped with them—flapping their huge ears to fan themselves, thrusting their trunk down their own throat to suck the water out of their belly and spray it over their head and neck.

He learned to find the heart and the brain, the lungs and the spine hidden in that amorphous mountain of gray hide and flesh. He learned to break the shoulder when the beast stood broadside, dropping him as though he had been struck by lightning, or to take the hip shot as he ran choking in the dust cloud behind the herd, shattering the hip joint and pinning the beast for an unhurried coup de grâce.

He hunted the herds on the hilltops where they had climbed to catch the soothing evening breeze. At dawn he hunted in the thick forests and the open glades, and at noon he hunted them in the old overgrown gardens of a vanished people. For the land that he had first believed devoid of human presence was not, and had never been so for unnumbered thousands of years.

Beyond the abandoned gardens where once man had planted his crops, but where now the elephant herds had returned to reclaim their heritage, Zouga found the remains of huge native cities, the long deserted keystones of a once-flourishing civilization, though all that remained were the circular outlines of the thatch-and-daub huts on the bare earth, the blackened hearthstones, and the charred fence poles of the cattle enclosures which must once have penned great herds. Judging by the height of the secondary growth in the ancient gardens, no man had farmed here for many decades.

It seemed strange to find these great gray herds of elephant ranging slowly through the ruined towns and fields. Zouga was reminded of a line from that strange exotic poetry that had been published in London the previous year, and which he had read just before sailing.

> They say the Lion and the Lizard keep
> The Courts where Jamshyd gloried and drank deep:
> And Bahram, that great Hunter—the Wild Ass
> Stamps o'er his Head, and he lies fast asleep.

Zouga scratched among foundations of the huts and found the deep ash which must once have been the wooden walls and thatched roofs. In one ancient village Zouga counted a thousand such dwellings before giving up the count. A numerous people, but where had they gone?

He found a partial answer in an ancient battlefield on the open ground beyond the thousand huts. The bones were white as daisies in the sunlight, bleached and dried out, most of them half buried in the rich red soil or covered by the dense fields of waving fluffy-topped grass.

The human remains covered an area of many acres and they lay in clumps and chains like newly cut wheat awaiting the reapers. Nearly every one of the skulls had been crushed in as if by a fierce blow with a club or mace.

Zouga realized that it was not so much a battlefield as a killing ground, for such slaughter could not be called warfare. If this toll had been repeated at each of the ruined towns he had stumbled upon, then the final total of the dead must have been in the tens or even hundreds of thousands. It was small wonder that what human presence remained was in tiny scattered groups, like the handful of warriors that had tried to prevent them crossing the pass of the elephant road. There were others. Occasionally, Zouga spied the smoke from a cooking fire rising from the highest point of one of the strangely shaped rock hillocks that dotted the land in all directions. If these were the survivors of the vanished civilization, then they still lived in terror of the fate that had overtaken their forebears.

When Zouga and his hunting party approached any of these tiny elevated settlements, they found the crests were fortified with built-up walls of rock, and they were greeted wth a hail of boulders rolled down the slope upon them, that forced them to retreat hurriedly. Often there were small cultivated gardens on the level ground below the fortified hilltops.

In the gardens grew millet, *ropoko* and big sweet yams, but, most important for Zouga, dark-green native tobacco. The soil was rich, the *ropoko* grew twice the height of a man and the corn sprays were loaded with red grain.

The tobacco leaves were thick-stemmed, the size of an elephant's ear. Zouga rolled the tip leaves into powerful cigars that had a rich distinction of taste and as he smoked them he pondered how the plant had reached this distant land from its far origins. There must once have been an avenue of trade between these people and the coast. The trade beads on the necklace he had taken from the body at the pass, and now these exotic plants, proved that, as did the tamarind trees, native of India, which grew among the ruins of the ancient villages.

Zouga wondered what a colony of British settlers with their industry and sophisticated agricultural technique, plow and crop rotation, seed selection and fertilization, might make of this lush rich soil, as he moved on slowly through the sparsely populated, well-timbered land that abounded with game and game birds, and was fed by strong clear streams of water.

Whenever he returned to the main body of the caravan, he made his meticulous observations of the sun and worked with chronometer and almanac to compute his exact positions, to add them, and his own succinct descriptions, to the map that old Tom Harkness had bequeathed him. The map increased in value, as new rivers were marked in, new boundaries set to the fly belts and the "fly corridors" extended, as Zouga's observations of the terrain, of soil and vegetation types began to cover the blank portions of the old parchment.

If he was not immersed in his map, then he worked as long as the light was good enough on his journal and the manuscript which was an adjunct to it—and while he did so, Jan Cheroot and the porters brought in the latest harvest of ivory, only just beginning to stink, and buried it.

Totaling the harvest from the lists in his journal, Zouga found that he had over twelve thousand pounds of tusks cached along his route. They were worth six shillings a pound in London, nearly four thousand pounds sterling. The trick was to get it to London. Zouga grinned to himself as he completed the calculation: a dozen wagons, or five hundred porters, and two thousand miles to carry it; that was all it required.

At each river crossing Zouga took the flat black iron pan, which doubled as laundry tub and cooking pot, and for miles in each direction along the riverbed he worked the gravel. He would fill the pan from a likely spot under the bank in the bend of the river, and then set the contents swirling awash, dipping and turning the pan, spilling a little of the lighter gravel at each turn, refilling with water and spinning it again until at last he was left with a smear of the finest and heaviest material lying around the bottom of the pan in a "tail." Always the tail was uninteresting, without the golden sparkle for which he longed so ardently.

When he detailed all these activities in his journal, only one thing gave Zouga a pause—and that was what to call this new and beautiful land. So far there was no evidence at all that it was the empire of Monomatapa, or even that Monomatapa existed. The timid, scattered and demoralized people he had so far encountered were certainly not the warriors of a powerful emperor. One other consideration decided him not to use that name. If he did so, it was tacit acknowledgment that the land had already been claimed, and each day that he traveled through the empty wilderness the dreams of himself claiming it for a queen and a nation seemed less far-fetched. Zouga began to use the name "Zambezia"—the land below the Zambezi River— and that was how he wrote it in his journal and in the thick bundle of pages of his manuscript.

With all this work to impede progress, the pace of the caravan was leisurely, or, as Robyn told Zouga furiously, "You would make a snail look like a Derby winner." For although Zouga might cover two hundred miles in the sweeping patterns of the hunt, the caravan camped and waited for his return, and then waited another four or five days as Jan Cheroot and the porters ferried in the loads of wet ivory.

"For all you know, Morris Zouga, your own father might be dying out there somewhere for want of a handful of medicine, while you—"

"If he has survived eight years already, the old devil is unlikely to turn up his toes for another few days." Zouga's light tone covered the irritation he felt. Since he had killed the Mashona at the pass on the elephant road, the feeling between brother and sister had been strained to the point where each of them found it difficult to maintain a civil tone of voice on the few occasions when they spoke together.

Zouga's long and frequent absences from the main body were not entirely on account of his dedication to the chase and exploration of the surrounding countryside. He found it less wearying on the nerves to be away from his sister. That ecstatic mood when they had stood like two children on Christmas morning, hand in hand, upon the heights of the escarpment, was months in the past.

Brooding beside his solitary campfire, with the hyena giggling and shrieking over the freshly killed elephant carcasses in the nearby forest, Zouga thought how it was really a miracle that two such definite personalities as his and Robyn's, whose objects were so widely divergent, should have come this far without serious disagreement. It had been too good to last indefinitely, and now he wondered how it might end. He should have followed his instincts and sent Robyn back to Tete and Cape Town when he had the excuse to do so, for the collision course on which they were so clearly set could only end in disaster for the entire expedition.

When he rejoined the main body the following day he would have it out with her, one way or the other. She would have at last to accept that he was the leader of the expedition and that as such his decisions were final. If she did so, then he could make some concession to her wishes, though the hunt for Fuller Ballantyne was very low on Zouga's list of priorities. It would probably be best for all of them, Fuller Ballantyne not excluded, if he had long ago been laid by his faithful bearers in a hero's grave.

The thought gave Zouga a prick of guilt, and he knew he would never write it, not even in the most private pages of his journal, nor would he voice it to his sister. But the idea persisted, even while he rolled into his blanket, with a small fire at his feet and another at his head to break the thick crunching white frost which would cover the earth and grass at dawn, serenaded by Jan Cheroot's snores which took the basso profundo to the soprano of the hyena packs. Zouga fell asleep at last.

Having made the decision to assert his authority, Zouga rolled out of his blanket in the frosty dawn determined on a forced march that would take them back to where he had left Robyn and the caravan twelve days previously. He reckoned it was forty miles, perhaps a little less, to the main campsite and he set a cruel pace, not even taking the usual noon break, but pushing on remorselessly.

Zouga had deliberately left the main body encamped below a distinctively shaped kopje, whose rocky spires could be clearly seen from many miles around and which Zouga had named Mount Hampden in memory of a childhood visit to that castle.

They were still far out when Zouga had his first misgivings. There was no smoke rising from the base of the hills, and there should have been. He had left almost a ton of elephant meat curing on the smoking racks, and on the outward march he had been able to look back and see the rising column of smoke long after the crests of the hills had disappeared below the tops of the forest trees.

"There is no smoke!" he told Jan Cheroot, and the little Hottentot nodded.

"I did not want to be the first to say that."

"Can Camacho have followed us this far?"

"There are other man-eating animals out here beside the Portuguese," Jan Cheroot said, and cocked his head at an inquisitive birdlike angle as Zouga began swiftly to strip down to light running order. Then, still without another word, Jan Cheroot followed his example, and handed his breeches and other traps to the bearers.

"Follow as fast as you can!" Zouga told them, snatching a spare powder bag from Matthew and turning away and breaking into a run.

Jan Cheroot fell in at his shoulder and they ran as they had run so often before, at the driving pace which could bring a breeding herd of elephant to a winded standstill within a few miles. All Zouga's feelings of antagonism toward his sister were swept away in the rush of deep concern for her safety. A series of horrific images flashed through his mind, of a sacked campsite, of mutilated bodies lying in the bloody trampled grass, shattered by the balls of the Portuguese muskets, or stabbed to death by the broad-bladed assegais of plumed and kilted warriors.

He found himself praying for her safety, repeating the formulas of his childhood which he had used so seldom since then, and unconsciously he increased the pace, until Jan Cheroot grunted a protest at his shoulder, and then slowly fell back, as Zouga forged powerfully ahead.

He reached the foot of the hill a mile ahead of Jan Cheroot, and turned to face the lowering red orb of the sun as he skirted the rocky base, crested a low rise and stopped there, hunting for breath, his chest swelling and subsiding and the sweat running down into his beard.

He stared down at the shaded dell, under the tall makusi trees where he had left the caravan and his heart plunged. He felt physically nauseated with horror. The campsite was deserted, the fires were cold black ash and the thatched lean-to shelters had already acquired that dejected air of all deserted habitation. Still fighting for breath, Zouga plunged down the gentle slope into the abandoned camp, and looked about him wildly for the bodies. There were none, and his first thought was of slavers. They would have taken them all, and he shuddered with horror at the thought of what Robyn must have suffered.

Zouga ran to her hut first. It was totally devoid of any trace of her. He ran to the next hut and the next—all of them were empty, but in the last hut he found a single body. It was curled on the sandy floor of the primitive shelter, and wrapped in a blanket. The blanket was drawn up over the head and wound tightly around the trunk.

Reluctant to discover his sister's horribly mutilated corpse, Zouga knelt beside it. Sweat half blinded him as he reached out a hand that trembled with dread and exhaustion and gently drew back the fold of a gray blanket that covered the still head.

The corpse came to life with a howl of fright and leaped two feet into the air, gibbering wildly, trying to throw off the blanket and lashing out with feet and fists to defend itself.

"Hellhound!" Zouga had so christened the laziest of his porters, a skinny fellow with a vast appetite for meat and less enthusiasm for anything that involved physical exertion. "What has happened? Where is Nomusa?"

Hellhound, once he had been quieted and had sufficiently recovered from shock, had a brief note to answer his questions. The single scrap of paper torn from Robyn's journal was double-folded and sealed with a splash of red wax; it read:

Dear Zouga,
I am of the opinion that further delay will seriously prejudice the interests of the sponsors of this expedition.
Accordingly, I have decided to move on at a speed better suited to achieving our objects before the onset of the rainy season.
I leave Hellhound to await your eventual return. Do follow at your own speed.

Your affectionate sister,
Robyn.

The note was dated ten days previously, and it was all she had left him. There was not even a pouch of salt or a bag of tea leaves, both of which commodities Zouga had been without for days.

Zouga's numbing shock lasted until Jan Cheroot reached the deserted camp, but by the time his exhausted bearers came, black rage had begun to replace all other emotion. He would have made a night march of it in pursuit of the caravan, but though he kicked their ribs as they lay and cursed them coldly, his bearers were so exhausted that they could not rise from where they had thrown themselves down.

Robyn had difficulty getting the bearers to break camp and take up their packs. Her first efforts to do so were greeted with amusement and light laughter, for none of them believed she was serious. Even Juba could not understand that Nomusa, a woman, was taking command of the caravan.

When all argument failed, Robyn took the hippo-hide kur-bash whip to the little yellow Hottentot corporal whom Jan Cheroot had left in command of his musketeers. The corporal shouted frantic orders to his men from the upper branches of the makusi where Robyn had him treed.

They were on the march within the hour, but the light laughter had given way to scowls and sulks. They were all convinced that the safari was now doomed, for who had ever heard of a woman, a young woman—worst of all, a young white woman—leading into the unknown? Within half a mile most of the porters were complaining of thorns in the feet or bad blood behind the eyes, afflictions common only to porters reluctant to advance.

Robyn got them to their feet again by firing a shot from the big naval Colt revolver over their heads; it almost sprained her wrist, but proved an amazingly effective cure for both feet and eyes, and finally they made a fair day's march of it, south and west, ten miles, as Robyn reckoned it as she marked her journal that night.

Despite the brave countenance she put on before the porters and musketeers, Robyn had her own doubts. She had watched closely as Zouga plotted a course with the prismatic compass, and she had mastered the technique of sighting a distant hill or other feature and marching upon it, before again sighting ahead on another feature. It was the only way to maintain a direct line of march in this rolling forested country.

She had studied, whenever she had the opportunity, the Harkness map, and had seen the wisdom of Zouga's choice of direction. He was aiming to traverse this wide unexplored land he had called Zambezia, and eventually to hit the road that their grandfather, Robert Moffat, had pioneered from his mission station at Kuruman to the town of the Matabele King, Mzilikazi, at Thabas Indunas.

However, Zouga's intention had been to cut south of the frontiers of the Matabele kingdom, avoiding the Burnt Land

303

where, according to Tom Harkness, the rapacious border impis of Mzilikazi killed all travelers. Neither she nor Zouga could trust to their relationship to Moffat to protect them.

Once they gained the wagon road to Kuruman, they would be back in the known world, and the road would lead them to the series of waterholes that Grandfather Moffat had marked. At Kuruman, after the family reunion, the road to Cape Town was long and wearying, but well traveled and in less than a year they could be back in London. The delicate part was to grope the way south of Matabele land, through the untold hazards still ahead, and to reach the road.

Robyn did not truly anticipate that she would be called upon to perform this feat of navigation entirely on her own. It could only be a matter of days before Zouga reached Mount Hampden camp and then hurried to catch up with the main body. There would be an interesting clash of wills then. However, at the end of it, she was certain that Zouga would be convinced that their father's whereabouts and safety were more important than the slaughter of animals, whose teeth could probably never be retrieved from their burial mounds.

This was a gesture of defiance only; soon Zouga would be with her once more. In the meantime, however, she had an unpleasantly hollow and lonely sensation beneath her ribs as she strode along in her tight-fitting breeches, the Hottentot standard bearer carrying the grubbied and tattered Union Jack a few paces behind her, and a sullen line of porters straggling along behind that again.

They camped the second night on the edge of a river that had been reduced to a string of still green pools in the sugary white sand of the riverbed. On the steep bank stood a small grove of strangler figs; the smooth pale trunk and branches had crept up like thick and sinuous pythons to smother the host trees. The parasites were now taller and more robust than the rotting remains that supported them had ever been, and the clusters of ripening figs covered their branches. Fat green pigeons came to feed on the fruits, flicked their wings and whistled their shrill cry, unlike that of any other pigeon, that to Robyn sounded like "Oh well, oh very well!" and they cocked their heads to peer down through the green leaves at the men camped below.

The porters had cut the scherms of thorn branches and lit the cooking fires when they all heard the lion roar. The sound checked the murmur of voices for only a few seconds, for it was very faint and distant, seeming to come from miles downstream, and it was a sound to which they had all long grown accustomed.

There had hardly been a night since they had crossed the pass on the elephant road that they had not heard the lions, and in the morning found the pugmarks, sometimes almost the size of a soup plate, in the soft earth around the camp where the big inquisitive cats had circled them during the night.

However, Robyn had never seen one of them for they are almost entirely nocturnal, and her first tremors of trepidation had long turned to indifference. She felt quite secure behind the scherm of thornbush, and now at the distant muttering rumble she hardly bothered to look up from her journal in which she was exaggerating only slightly the competent manner in which she had directed the day's march.

"We are making as good a time as we ever did when Z was leading," she wrote smugly, but did not go on to mention the mood of the porters.

The lion roared only once, and when it was not repeated, the sullen talk around the cooking fires was resumed and Robyn bowed her head once more over her journal.

A few hours after the setting of the sun the camp settled for the night, and lying under her hastily thatched shelter with Juba curled on the mattress of freshly cut grass beside her, Robyn listened to the melodious African voices of her porters fade gradually into silence. She sighed once, deeply, and fell instantly asleep—to wake with a confusion of sound and movement all around her.

She knew that it was late by the frostiness of the air, and her own sleep-drugged stupor. The night rang with the terrified shouts of men and the rush of their feet. Then there was the thudding report of a musket, the crash of heavy logs being thrown on the watch fires and then, heart-stoppingly, the screams of Juba close to her head.

"Nomusa! Nomusa!"

Still groggy with sleep, Robyn struggled up. She was not certain what she was dreaming and what was reality.

"What is it?"

"A devil!" shrieked Juba. "Devils have come to kill us all."

Robyn flung off her blanket, and ran out of the shelter barefoot, dressed only in her flannel nightgown with ribbons in her hair.

At that moment the new logs blazed up on the watch fire, and she saw naked yellow and black bodies, and terrified faces, whites of rolling eyes and open shouting mouths.

305

The little Hottentot corporal, stark naked, pranced beyond the fire, brandishing his musket, and as Robyn ran toward him he fired it blindly into the darkness.

Robyn caught his arm as he began to reload.

"What is it?" she shouted into his ear.

"*Leeuw!* Lion!" His eyes were glittering with fright and bubbles of spittle ran from the corners of his mouth.

"Where is it?"

"It has taken Sakkie! It pulled him out of his blankets."

"Quiet!" Robyn shouted. "Keep quiet, all of you!"

Now, at last, they all turned instinctively to her for leadership.

"Quiet!" she repeated, and the gabble of fright and uncertainty died swiftly.

"Sakkie!" she called in the silence, and the missing Hottentot's voice answered her faintly from below the steep bank of the riverbed.

"*Die leeuw het my!* The lion has me! *Die duiwel gaan my dood maak,* the devil is going to kill me," and he broke off with a shriek of agony.

Above the high-pitched shriek they all clearly heard the crunch of bone, and the muffled growl like that of a dog with food in its jaws. With a rush of horror that raised goose pimples along her arms, Robyn realized that she was listening to the sounds of a man being eaten alive not fifty yards from where she stood.

"*Hy vreet my bene,*" the voice out of the darkness rang with unbearable agony. "He is eating my legs," and the gruesome cracking, tearing sounds made Robyn's gorge rise to choke her. Without thinking, she snatched a burning brand from the fire and holding it aloft shouted at the Hottentot corporal. "Come on! We must save him!"

She ran forward to the lip of the bank before she realized she was alone and unarmed.

She looked back. Not one of the men around the fire had followed her. They stood in a tight group, shoulder to shoulder, clutching muskets or axes or assegais, but rooted where they stood.

"He is finished." The corporal's voice shook with fright. "Leave him. It's too late. Leave him."

Robyn hurled the burning brand she held down into the riverbed below her feet, and before its flames faded and pinched out she thought she saw something big and dark and terrifying on the edge of the shadows.

Robyn ran back to the group and snatched a musket from one of the Hottentots. Thumbing back the hammer, she ran once more to the riverbank and peered down into the dry bed. It was utterly black, until suddenly there was somebody at her shoulder, holding high a burning branch from the fire.

"Juba! Go back!" Robyn snapped at the child. Juba was naked except for a single string of beads about her hips, and the firelight glinted on her sleek body.

She could not answer Robyn, for tears were rolling down her plump cheeks and her throat was closed with terror, but she shook her head fiercely at the order to retreat.

Below them, outlined against the white sand of the dry river, was that grotesque shape, and the screams of the dying man blended with the grisly wet growls of the animal.

Robyn lifted the musket, but hesitated for fear of hitting the Hottentot. Disturbed by the light, the lion rose, becoming huge and black; swiftly it dragged the weakly wriggling body, dangling between his forelegs back into the darkness beyond the feeble circle of light from the flames.

Robyn drew a deep breath and the heavy musket shook in her hands, but she lifted her chin in a gesture of decision and, holding up the skirts of her long nightdress in one hand, went down the path into the riverbed. Juba followed her like a faithful puppy, pressing so hard against her that they nearly lost their balance, but she kept the burning brand on high, though it shook, and the flames wavered smokily.

"Brave girl!" Robyn encouraged her. "Good brave girl!"

They stumbled through the loose white sand that covered the ankles of their bare feet at each pace.

Ahead of them, at the extreme limit of their vision, moved the menacing black shadow, and the deep muttering growls seemed to fill the night around them.

"Leave it!" Robyn shouted, her voice quavering and breaking. "Drop it—this instant!"

Unconsciously she was using the same commands as she had given her terrier as a child when it refused to deliver the rubber ball.

Ahead of her Sakkie heard her, and bleated feebly. "Help me—for God's love, help me." But the lion pulled him away, leaving a long wet drag mark through the sand.

Robyn was tiring rapidly, her arms ached from the weight of the heavy weapon, each breath burned her throat as she panted, but she could not seem to get enough air, for an iron band of fear cramped her chest. She sensed that the lion would only retreat a certain distance before it lost patience with the shouting and harassment, and her instinct was right.

Suddenly she made out the full shape of the lion ahead of them. It had dropped the maimed body and stood over it now like a tomcat with its mouse, but it was as big as a Shetland pony, with the ruff of its mane fully erect, seeming to double its size.

In the light of the flames, its eyes glowed a bright ferocious gold, and it opened its jaws and roared. The very air dinned upon Robyn's eardrums, causing her actual physical pain as that gust of sound struck her. It rose to an unbearable pitch, so that involuntarily she reeled backward with Juba clinging to her. The child wailed with despair, losing control of her body and in the light of the flames her urine shot in sharp little spurts down her legs, and as the lion launched into its charge she dropped the torch into the sand.

Robyn lifted the musket in front of her, as a defensive reflex rather than a planned act of aggression, and when the barrel was at waist-level she pulled the trigger with all her strength. The cap flashed, flaring brightly in the blackness, and for an instant she saw the lion. It was so close that the long barrel of the musket seemed to touch its huge shaggy head. The mouth was wide open, still emitting those shattering gusts of sound, and the fangs that lined the deep, meat-red gape of jaws were long and white and cruel. The eyes burned yellow as living flames, and Robyn found that she was screaming, but the sound was lost completely in the roaring of the enraged animal.

Then an instant after the flash of the cap the musket fired, bucking so savagely in her hands that it almost tore itself from her grip, and the butt, not anchored against her shoulder, was driven back into her stomach with a force that expelled the air from her lungs and sent her reeling in the loose white sand. Juba, clinging to her legs and wailing with despair, tripped her and she went over backward, sprawling full length at the same moment that the full weight of the lion lunged into her.

If Robyn had not fallen, the charge would have stove in her ribs and snapped her neck, for the lion was over four hundred pounds' weight of driving bone and muscle. As it was, it knocked her out of her senses for she never knew how long, but she became conscious again, with the strong cat reek of the lion in her nostrils, and an immense weight crushing her into the sand. She wriggled weakly, but the weight was suffocating her, and gouts of hot blood, so hot it seemed to scald her, were spurting over her head and neck.

"Nomusa!" Juba's voice, high with anguish and very close, but those shattering roars were silent. There was just the unbearable weight and the rank smell of lion.

Robyn's strength came back to her with a rush, and she struggled and kicked, and the weight above her rolled loosely aside. slithering off her, and she dragged herself free of it. Immediately Juba clung to her again, throwing her arms about Robyn's neck.

Robyn comforted her as though she was an infant, patting her and kissing her cheek that was wet and hot with tears.

"It's over! There, now. It's all over," she mumbled, aware that her hair was sodden with the lion's blood, and that a dozen men, led cautiously by the Hottentot corporal, had lined the high riverbank, each of them holding aloft a torch of burning grass.

In the dim yellow light the lion lay stretched out beside Robyn in the sand. The ball from the musket had struck him full in the nose, passed cleanly through the brain and lodged in the base of his neck, killing the cat in midair, so the lifeless body had pinned Robyn to the sand.

"The lion is dead!" Robyn quavered as she called to the men, and they came down in a close bunch, timidly at first and then boldly when they saw the huge yellow carcass.

"It was the shot of a true huntress," announced the corporal grandly. "An inch high and the ball would have bounced off the skull, an inch lower and it would have missed the brain."

"Sakkie," Robyn's voice still shook, "where is Sakkie?"

He was still alive, and they carried him in his blanket up into the camp. His wounds were fearsome, and Robyn knew there was not the smallest chance of saving him. One arm from wrist to elbow had been chewed so that not a piece of bone bigger than the top joint of her finger remained. One foot was gone just above the ankle, bitten clean off and swallowed in one piece. He had been bitten through pelvis and spine, while through a tear in his diaphragm below the ribs the mottled pink of his lungs swelled out with each breath.

Robyn knew that to attempt to cut and sew that dreadfully torn flesh or to saw the splintered bone stumps would be inflicting futile agony on the little yellow man. She had him laid close to the fire, she plugged the worst holes gently, and then covered him with blankets and fur karosses. She administered a dose of laudanum so powerful as to be almost lethal in itself. Then she sat next to Sakkie and held his hand.

"A doctor must know when to let a man die with dignity,"

her professor at St. Matthew's had once told her. And a little before dawn Sakkie opened his eyes, the pupils dilated widely by the massive dose of the drug, and smiled at her just once before he died.

His brother Hottentots buried him in a small cave in one of the granite kopjes and they blocked the opening with boulders that the hyena could not roll aside.

When the corporal and his Hottentots came down from the hill, they indulged in a brief ritual of mourning which consisted mainly of emitting loud theatrical cries of anguish and firing their muskets in the air to speed Sakkie's soul on its journey, after which they ate a hearty breakfast of smoked elephant meat, and the corporal came to Robyn, dry-eyed and grinning broadly.

"We are now ready to march, Nomusa!" he told her, and with a stamp of his right foot, which began with the knee lifted under his chin, he gave her one of those widely extravagant salutes, a mark of deep respect that up to that date had been reserved exclusively for Major Zouga Ballantyne.

During that day's march, the porters sang again for the first time since leaving Zouga's camp at Mount Hampden.

> "She is your mother and your father too,
> She will dress your wounds
> She will stand over you while you sleep
> We, your children, greet you, Nomusa,
> The girl child of mercy."

It was not only the caravan's rate of advance under Zouga that had irritated and annoyed Robyn. It was also their complete failure to make contact with any of the indigenous tribes, with any of the inhabitants of the scattered and fortified villages.

To her it seemed completely logical that the only way that they would be able to trace Fuller Ballantyne through this wilderness was by asking questions of those who must have seen him pass, and almost certainly had spoken and traded with him.

Robyn could not believe that her father would have adopted the same high-handed actions to force a passage past anybody or anything that stood in the way of the caravan as Zouga had done.

When she closed her eyes she could still see clearly in her mind's eye the tiny falling body of the black man in the tall headdress, shot down ruthlessly by her brother. She had rehearsed in her mind how she or her father would have passed through the elephant road without gunfire and slaughter. The tactful withdrawal, the offering of small gifts, the cautious parley and eventual agreement.

"It was plain bloody murder!" she repeated to herself for the hundredth time. "And what we have done since then has been blatant robbery."

Zouga had helped himself to the standing crops of the villages they had passed, to tobacco, millet and yams, not even bothering to leave a handful of salt or a few sticks of dried elephant meat as token payment.

"We should try to communicate with these people, Zouga," she had remonstrated.

"They are a sullen and dangerous people."

"Because they expect you to rob and murder them—and, as God is my witness, you have not disappointed them, have you?"

The same argument had run its well-worn course many times, neither of them relenting, each holding stubbornly to their own view. Now at least she was free to attempt to establish contact with these people, Mashona, as Juba called them disparagingly, without her brother's impatience and arrogance to distract her and alarm the timid black people.

On the fourth day after leaving Zouga's camp, they came in sight of an extraordinary geological formation. It was as though a high dam wall had been constructed across the horizon, an enormous dyke of rock running almost exactly north and south to every limit of the eye.

Almost directly in their line of march was the only breach in this rampart, and from the altered vegetation, the denser growth and deeper green, it was clear that a river flowed through the gap. Robyn ordered a small adjustment in their line of march and headed for the pass.

When they were still some miles distant Robyn was delighted to make out the first signs of human habitation that they had come across since leaving Mount Hampden.

There were fortified walls on the cliffs above the breach in the long low hill, high above the riverbed, and as they drew closer, Robyn could see the gardens on the banks of the river, defended by high brush and thorn barriers with little thatched lookout huts standing high on stilts in the center of the lucious green stands of young millet.

"We will fill our bellies tonight," the Hottentot corporal gloated. "That corn is ripe enough to eat."

"We will camp here, Corporal," Robyn told him firmly.

"But we are still a mile—"

"Here!" Robyn repeated.

They were all puzzled and resentful when Robyn forbade entry to the tempting gardens, and confined them all to the perimeter of the camp, except for the water and wood parties. But resentment turned to genuine alarm when Robyn left the camp herself, accompanied only by Juba, and as far as they could see completely unarmed.

"These people are savages," the corporal tried to intercept her. "They will kill you, and then Major Zouga will kill me."

The two women entered the nearest garden, and carefully approached the lookout hut. On the earth below the rickety ladder that rose to the elevated platform a fire had burned down to ash, but flared again when Robyn knelt and fanned it. Robyn threw a few dry branches upon it and then sent Juba for an armful of green leaves. The column of smoke drew the attention of the watchers on the cliff above the gorge.

Robyn could see their distant figures on the skyline, standing very still and intent. It was an eerie feeling to know that so many eyes were upon them, but Robyn was not relying entirely on the fact that they were women, nor was she relying on their patently peaceful intentions, nor even upon the prayers which she had offered up so diligently to protect them. On the principle that the Almighty helps those who show willing, she had Zouga's big Colt pistol stuffed into the waistband of her breeches and covered by the tail of her flannel shirt.

Next to the smoking beacon fire, Robyn left a half pound of salt in a small calabash gourd, and a bundle of sticks of black smoked elephant meat which was the last of her stock.

Early the next morning Robyn and Juba again visited the garden and found the meat and salt had been taken, and that there were the fresh footprints of bare feet overlaying their own in the dust.

"Corporal," Robyn told the Hottentot with a confidence she did not feel, "we are going out to shoot meat."

The corporal grinned beatifically. They had eaten the last of the smoked meat, weevils and all, the previous eveing, and he flung her one of his more flamboyant salutes, his right arm quivering at the peak of his cap, his fingers spread stiffly, the stamp of his right foot raising dust, before he hurried away shouting orders to his men to prepare for the hunt.

Zouga had long ago declared the Sharps rifle to be too light for elephant, and left it in camp, favoring the big four-to-the-

312

pound smooth bores to the more expensive breech-loading rifle. Robyn took it now and inspected it with trepidation. Previously she had only fired it at a target, and now in the privacy of her grass hut she rehearsed loading and cocking the weapon. She was not sure that she would be capable of cold-bloodedly aiming it at a living animal, and had to reassure herself of the absolute necessity of procuring food for the many mouths and stomachs that now depended upon her. The corporal did not share her doubts, he had seen her shoot a charging lion between the eyes, and trusted her now implicitly. Within an hour's walk they found a herd of buffalo in the thick reed beds along the river. Robyn had listened to Zouga talking of the hunt with enough attention to know the necessity of keeping below the wind—and in the reeds with visibility down to a few feet and with the commotion created by two hundred cows and bleating calves they crept up to a range at which nobody could miss.

Her Hottentots blazed away with their muskets, while Robyn herself fired grimly into the galloping bellowing bodies that charged wildly past her after the first shot had startled them.

After the dust had settled and the thick bank of powder smoke had drifted away on the faint breeze, they found six of the big black animals lying dead in the reedbeds. Her entourage was delighted, hacking the bodies into manageable chunks which they slung on long poles and carried singing up to the camp. Their delight turned to amazement when Robyn ordered that an entire haunch of fresh buffalo be taken out and left next to the hut in the millet garden.

"These people are eaters of roots and dirt," Juba explained patiently. "Meat is too good for them."

"To kill this meat we have risked our lives," the corporal began his protest, then caught the look in Robyn's eye, broke off and coughed and shuffled his feet. "Nomusa, could we not give them a little less than a haunch? The hooves make a good stew, and these people are savages, they will eat anything," he pleaded. "A whole haunch . . ."

She sent him away muttering and shaking his head sorrowfully.

During the night, Juba woke her, and the two of them sat and listened to the faint throb of drums and the singing that carried down from the hilltop village, clearly the sounds of feasting and jubilation.

"They have probably not seen so much meat at one time in all their lives," Juba murmured sulkily.

In the morning Robyn found, in place of the buffalo meat,

a bark basket, conttaiing fifteen hen's eggs the size of pigeon's eggs, and two large earthen pots of millet beer. The look of the bubbling thin gray gruel almost turned Robyn's stomach. She gave the beer to the corporal to distribute, and her followers drank it with such obvious relish, smacking their lips and nodding over it like connoisseurs over an ancient bottle of claret, that Robyn controlled her heaving stomach and tasted some; it was tart and refreshing and strong enough to set the Hottentots chattering and laughing raucously.

With Juba following her, each of them carrying a bundle of half-dried buffalo meat, Robyn returned to the gardens, certain that the exchange of gifts had proved it possible to establish friendly contact. They sat under the shelter and waited. The hours passed without a sign of the Mashona appearing. The hushed heat of noon gave way to long, cool shadows of evening—and then, for the first time, Robyn noticed a gentle stir among the millet plants that was neither wind nor bird.

"Do not move," she cautioned Juba.

Slowly a human shape showed itself, a frail bent figure dressed in tatters of a skin kilt. Robyn could not tell whether it was man or woman, and she didn't dare stare openly for fear of frightening it away.

The figure emerged from the stand of millet, crouched down on its haunches, and it hopped hesitantly toward them, with long pauses between each tentative hop. It was so thin and wrinkled and dried out that it looked like one of the unbandaged mummies that Robyn had seen in the Egyptian section of the British Museum.

It was definitely a man, she realized at last, sneaking a glance in his direction, for with each hop his shriveled and stringy genitals flapped out from under the short kilt.

Closer still, Robyn saw that his cap of woolly hair was pure white with age, and in the seamed and pouched sockets his eyes wept slow tears of fright, as though these were the last drops of liquid that his desiccated old body contained.

Neither Juba nor Robyn moved or looked directly at him until he squatted a dozen paces from them, then slowly Robyn turned her head toward him. The old man whimpered with fear.

It was clear to Robyn that he had been selected as an emissary because he was the least valuable member of the tribe, and Robyn wondered what threats had been made to force him to come down from the hilltop.

Moving very slowly and calmly, as though she were dealing with a timid wild creature, Robyn held out a stick of half-cured buffalo meat. The old man stared at it, fascinated. As Juba had told her, these people probably existed almost entirely on their meager crops and such roots and wild fruit as they could glean in the forest. Meat was a rare treat, and such an unproductive member of the tribe would be given only a very little of what there was.

The way he stared at the piece in Robyn's hand made her believe that the old man had not had so much as a taste of the buffalo haunch. He was more than half starved. He rolled his tongue loosely around in his toothless mouth, gathering his courage, and then shuffled close enough to hold out the claws of his bony fingers, palms cupped upward in the polite gesture of acceptance.

"There you are, dearie." Robyn placed the stick in his hands and the man snatched it to his mouth, sucking noisily upon it, worrying it with his smooth gums, drooling silver strings of saliva as his mouth flooded, his eyes streaming again, this time with pleasure rather than fear.

Robyn laughed with delight, and the old man rapidly blinked his eyes and then cackled around the stick of meat, the sound so comical that Juba laughed also, the laughter of the two younger women rippling and tinkling without restraint. Almost immediately, the dense leaves of the millet garden stirred and rustled, as other half-naked figures came slowly forward, their anxiety relieved by the sound of laughing women.

The hilltop settlement consisted of not more than a hundred individuals, men, women and children, and every one of them came out to stare and laugh and clap as Robyn and Juba climbed the steep twisting path. The old silver-headed man, almost unbearably proud of his achievement, led Robyn by the hand possessively, screeching out explanations to those around, pausing every now and then to perform a little shuffling dance of triumph.

Mothers held up their infants to look at this marvelous being, and the children ran forward to touch Robyn's legs and then squeal with their own courage, skipping away ahead of her up the path.

The pathway followed the contours of the hillside, and it passed between defensive gateways and under terraced walls. Above the path at every steep place were piled boulders, ready to be hurled down upon an enemy, but now Robyn's ascent was a triumphant progess, and she came out into the village surrounded by a welcoming throng of singing, dancing women.

The village was laid out in a circular pattern of thatched

and windowless huts. The walls were of plastered clay with low doorways and beside each hut was a granary of the same materials but raised on poles to protect it from vermin. Apart from a few diminutive chickens, there were no domestic animals.

The space between the huts and the central courtyard was swept, and the whole village had an air of order and cleanliness. The people themselves were handsome, though none of them carried any excess flesh or fat. Robyn was reminded by their slim, lithe bodies that they were almost exclusively vegetarian.

They had alert and intelligent faces, and the laughter and singing with which they welcomed her was easy and unaffected.

"There are the people whom Zouga shot down like animals," she thought, looking around her with pleasure.

They had set a low carved stool in the shade for her and Juba squatted beside her. As soon as Robyn was seated, the old man squealed importantly and a giggling young girl brought her a pot of the millet beer. Only when she had drunk a mouthful of the beer did the crowd fall silent and draw aside to let a commanding figure come through.

On his head was a tall headdress of animal fur, similar to the one worn by the chieftain on the elephant road pass. He wore a cloak of leopard skin over his shoulders, the skins so worn that they must have been very old, probably the heredity symbol of his chieftainship. He sat down on another stool facing Robyn. He was a man of middle age, with a pleasant humorous face and a lively imagination—for he followed Robyn's sign language with attention, and then acted out his own replies with facial expressions and gestures that Robyn understood readily.

This way he asked her from where she came and she showed him the north and made a circle of her hands toward the sun for each day's travel. He wanted to know who was her husband and how many children she had. That she was both unmarried and childless was a source of amazement to the whole village.

More beer was brought out in the clay pots and Robyn felt slightly light-headed, and her cheeks turned pink and her eyes shone. Juba was contemptuous of their hosts.

"They do not have even a goat!" she pointed out scornfully.

"Perhaps your brave young men have stolen them all," Robyn answered tartly, and raised her beer pot in salute to the chief.

The chief clapped his hands, signaling his drummers to stoop to their instruments. The drums were hollowed tree trunks, beaten with a pair of short wooden clubs to a frantic rhythm

316

that soon had the drummers running with rivulets of sweat and glassy-eyed with the mesmeric effects of the beat. The chieftain threw off his leopard-skin cloak and launched himself into the dance, swirling and leaping until his necklaces and bracelets jangled and rattled.

On his chest he wore a pendant of ivory, snowy-white polished ivory, and it caught the firelight, for by now the sun was long set. Robyn had not noticed the ornament before for it had been covered by the cloak, but now she felt her eye drawn repeatedly to the bouncing white disc.

The disc seemed too perfectly shaped, and as the chief came bounding up to her stool to perform a solo pass before her Robyn saw that it was decorated with a regular pattern around its border. The next moment her heart raced with excitement for the decoration was writing, she was not sure in what language, but it was Latin script, that was certain. Then the chief had gone, leaping away to prance in front of his drummers, exhorting them to greater efforts.

Robyn had to wait until the chief exhausted himself, and staggered panting back to his stool to quaff a pot of the thick gray beer, before she could lean forward and get her first close look at the ornament.

She had been mistaken. It was not ivory but porcelain, and its perfect shape and whiteness was immediately accounted for. It was an item of European manufacture, the lid of a small pot, the type in which tooth powder or potted meats are sold. The writing was English; printed in neat capitals were the words:

PATUM PEPERIUM —THE GENTLEMAN'S RELISH.

She felt her skin go clammy with excitement. Clearly she remembered her father's rage when the pantry at Kings Lynn had been bare of this delicacy. She remembered as a small girl running down the village street in the rain to the grocer to buy another pot.

"It is my one weakness, my only weakness"—she remembered her father's exact words while he spread the savory paste on his toast, his anger mollified so that he came near to making a joke of it. "Without my Gentleman's Relish, I doubt I would have had strength for the Transversa."

When Robyn's mother left for Africa on that last ill-fated voyage, there had been a dozen cases of the relish in her luggage. There was only one possible way that the porcelain lid could have reached here.

317

Robyn stretched out a hand and touched it, but the chief's expression changed instantly and he jumped back, out of reach. The singing and drumming came to an abrupt halt, and the consternation of the entire village made Robyn realize that the porcelain lid was a charm of great personal magic, and that it was a disaster that another hand had touched it.

She made an attempt to mollify the chief, but swiftly he covered himself with his leopard cloak and stalked away to his hut at the end of the village. The festivities were clearly ended. The rest of the villagers were subdued and crept away after the chief, leaving only the silver-haired toothless ancient, possessive as ever, to lead Robyn to the hut which had earlier been set aside for her.

She lay awake most of the night on the plaited reed sleeping mat, excited at the evidence that her father had passed this way, and worried that she had ruined her relationship with the Mashona chief and would learn no more of the ornament and, through it, of her father.

She did not have an early opportunity to meet the chief again and make amends for her breach of manners. The villagers kept away from her, obviously hoping she would go, but she stayed on stubbornly in the hilltop village, attended only by the faithful old man. For Robyn was the most important thing that had ever happened in his long life, and he was not going to relinquish her for the chief or for anybody else.

In the end, there was nothing for it but to send the chief an extravagant gift. She used the last *khete* of *sam-sam* beads and one of the double-bladed axes.

The chief could not resist such princely bribes, and though his attitude was cooler and more reserved than at first, he listened attentively while Robyn asked her questions, acting out little charades, which the chief discussed seriously with his elders, before giving his answers.

The answer was southward again, south for five circles of the sun, and the chief would send somebody to guide Robyn. He was obviously pleased to be rid of her at last, for, though her gifts were welcome, the chief was still deeply troubled by the ill fortune that her sacrilegious action must bring upon the tribe.

For a guide the chief chose the silver-headed old man, ridding himself of a useless mouth and an unwelcome visitor at one stroke.

* * *

Robyn had doubted that her guide's thin legs could carry him either very fast or very far. However, the old man surprised her. He armed himself with a long throwing spear which looked as old and frail as he did himself and on his head he balanced a rolled sleeping mat and a clay cooking pot—these his total worldly possessions. He girded up his tattered kilts and set off southwards at a pace that had Robyn's porters grumbling again. Robyn had to restrain him.

It took a little time to get the old man to understand that he was now her language tutor. As they marched she pointed at herself, and everything around them, naming them clearly in English, and then looking at him inquiringly. He returned the look with equal inquiry in his rheumy old eyes. However, she persevered, repeating her own name "Nomusa" as she touched her chest, and suddenly he understood.

He slapped his own chest. "Karanga," he squeaked. "Karanga!" Once again his enthusiasm for this new activity was such that she had to restrain him. Within a few days Robyn had dozens of verbs and hundreds of nouns which she could begin stringing together, much to old Karanga's delight.

However, it was four days before Robyn realized that there had been an initial misunderstanding. Karanga was not the old man's name, but the name of his tribe. It was too late to rectify, because by that time everybody in the caravan was calling him "Karanga," and the old man answered to it readily. It was difficult to get him to leave Robyn's side. He followed her wherever she went, much to Juba's disgust and undisguised jealousy.

"He smells," she told Robyn virtuously. "He smells very bad." Which was true, Robyn had to admit.

"But after a while you do not notice it so much." There was one thing, however, which could not be so readily overlooked: it appeared from under the old man's kilts whenever he squatted, which he did whenever at rest. Robyn solved this by giving old Karanga a pair of Zouga's woolen underwear and taking her chances with her brother's wrath later. The underwear filled old Karanga with almost unbearable pride. He preened and strutted like a peacock, as they flapped around his long thin legs.

Old Karanga led them cautiously wide of every occupied village along their route, although he assured Robyn they were also of the same tribe. There seemed to be no trade nor commerce between these settlements, each perched on its fortified hilltop in suspicious and hostile isolation.

By this time, Robyn could speak enough of the language to find out from Karanga more about the great wizard from whom the chief had received the magical porcelain talisman, and the story filled her with excitement and anticipation.

Many rainy seasons ago, old Karanga was not sure how many, at his age every season blurred into the one before or the one after, anyway, at some not too far distant date an extraordinary man had come out of the forest, even as she had come, and like her he had been fair-skinned. However, his hair and beard were the color of flames (he showed her the campfire), and he was without doubt a magician and prophet and rain-maker, for the day he arrived the long drought had broken with thunderous storms that filled the rivers for the first time in many years.

This pale wizard had performed other rare and wonderful feats, transforming himself first into a lion and then into an eagle, raising the dead from the grave, and directing the lightning with a wave of his hand. The tale had lost nothing in the retelling, Robyn noted wryly.

"Did anybody speak to him?" Robyn asked.

"We were all too afraid," Karanga admitted, shaking the-atrically with terror, "but I myself saw the wizard as an eagle fly over village and drop the talisman from the sky." He flapped his skinny old arms in pantomime.

The strong anchovy smell would have attracted the bird to the discarded pot, Robyn reflected, but when it proved inedible the bird would have dropped it, by chance over Karanga's village.

"The wizard stayed a short time near our village and then went away to the south. We have heard that he traveled swiftly, obviously in his guise as a lion.

"We heard of his miracles, the word shouted from hilltop to hilltop or tapped out by the drums. How he cured others sick to death, how he challenged spirits of the Karanga in their most sacred places, shouting abuse at them so all who heard him trembled.

"We heard also how he slew the high priestess of the dead, an Umlimo of vast power in her own stronghold. This pale magician slew her and destroyed her sacred relics."

In fact he had raged through the land like a man-eating lion, which of course he was, until finally he came to rest upon a dark hilltop far to the south, the Mountain of Iron, Thaba Simbi, where he stayed to perform diverse curses and miracles so that the people came to him from far and wide to buy his services with corn and other offerings.

"Is he still there?" Robyn demanded.

Old Karanga rolled his watery eyes and shrugged. "It is always difficult and dangerous to predict the comings and goings of wizards and magicians," that eloquent gesture seemed to say.

The journey was not so straightforward as Robyn had hoped, for the further he went from his own village the less certain old Karanga became of his direction, or of the exact location of the Iron Mountain which he had told her of.

At the beginning of each day's march, he informed Robyn confidently that they would reach their destination that day, and as they went into camp each evening he told her apologetically that it would be the next day for certain.

Twice he pointed out rocky kopjes, "That is indeed the Iron Mountain," but each time they were driven off with a hail of boulders and throwing spears from the heights.

"I was mistaken," Karanga mumbled, "there is a darkness in my eyes sometimes, even under the noonday sun."

"Have you verily and truly seen this mountain?" Robyn demanded sternly, almost at the end of her patience, and Karanga hung his silver-wrinkled head and busily picked at his nostrils with a bony finger to hide his discomfiture.

"It is true that I have not personally seen this place, not with my own eyes, but I have been told by one who spoke with a man who himself—" he admitted, and Robyn was so angry that she shouted at him in English.

"You naughty old devil, why did you not say so before!"

Old Karanga understood the tone, if not the words, and his misery was so apparent that she could not sustain her anger for more than an hour; his gratitude when she once more allowed him to carry her water bottle and food bag was pathetic to see.

Robyn was now consumed with impatience. She had no way of knowing how far behind her was Zouga and his hunting party. He might have returned to the camp at Mount Hampden and found her note the very day after her departure, or he might still be killing elephant a hundred miles away, completely unaware that she had marched without him.

Her disapproval of her brother, and her anger at his recent actions, had gradually evoked a sense of competition in her. She had come so far and accomplished so much on her own—from the contact with the Karanga village to following the traces of her father so far and so doggedly—that she fiercely resented the idea of his arrival when she was at the very point of making the prayed-for and long-delayed reunion with Fuller Ballantyne. She guessed how the tale would be told in Zouga's journal, and in the book that would follow it. She knew who would get all the credit for the arduous search and its brilliantly successful conclusion.

Once she had thought that fame and praise meant little to her; she believed she would be content to leave that to her brother. She had believed that her own reward would be her father's embrace, and the deep personal knowledge that she had brought some comfort or some surcease to the suffering black peoples of Africa.

"I still do not know myself all that well," she admitted, as she called the third successive *tirikeza*, double-marching her porters relentlessly to keep ahead of Zouga, wherever he might be.

"I want to find Pater, I want to find him alone, and I want the world to know I found him."

"Pride is sinful, but then I have always been a sinner. Forgive me, sweet Jesus, I will make it up in a thousand other ways. Only forgive this one small unimportant sin," she prayed in her rude grass shelter, and as she did so she listened with one ear for the shouts of Zouga's bearers coming into camp, and her heart tripped at each sudden noise. She was tempted to break camp and call a night march toward the next distant hill they had seen on the horizon at sunset and which old Karanga had once again confidently declared to be the Iron Mountain. The moon was full and would rise in an hour; that one march might be all that was necessary to keep ahead of her brother.

However, her porters were exhausted, even Juba was complaining of thorns in her feet. It seemed that only she and old Karanga were able to maintain this pace for day after day. She must let them rest.

The next morning, she had them away when the grass was still bent under the weight of dewdrops, and before she had gone a mile her breeches were soaked to the thighs. During the last few days' march the character of the land had altered. The elevated plateau of rolling grasslands and open forest across which they had marched so long now seemed to be dipping southward, and the single peak which she had seen the night before slowly evolved into a whole series of hills stretching across her horizon from west to east, and she felt her spirits sag.

What chance would she ever have of finding one man's camp, one single hilltop, among so many? But she slogged on doggedly, and she and Karanga reached the first foothills before noon well ahead of the column. She checked Zouga's barometer nestling in its velvet-lined wooden case, and found that the altitude was still well over twelve hundred feet, though they had dropped two hundred feet in the last two days' march.

Then, followed closely by Karanga, and at a little distance by Juba, she climbed the rocky shoulder of one of the foothills and from its height had a clearer view ahead over the confused and broken ground. She could see that the hills descended sharply into the south. Perhaps they had crossed the highlands and before them lay the descent to one of the known rivers that Tom Harkness had marked upon his map. She tried to remember the names, Shashi and Tati and Macloutsi.

Suddenly she was starting to feel very lonely and uncertain again. The land was so vast she felt like a tiny insect pinned to an endless plain beneath the high pitiless blue sky. She turned and looked back into the north, using the long, brass-bound telescope to search for any signs of Zouga's party. She was not certain if she was relieved or disappointed to find none.

"Karanga!" she called, and he scrambled to his feet readily and looked up at her on the pinnacle of rock on which she stood. His expression was trusting as that of a pet dog.

"Which way now?" she demanded, and he dropped his eyes and stood on one bird-thin leg, scratching his calf with the other foot as he pondered the question. Then with an apologetic gesture he indicated the nearest half dozen promontories along the skyline ahead with a hesitant all-embracing gesture, and Robyn felt her heart sink further. She had to admit at last that she was lost.

She knew then that she would have to do one of two things: either camp where she was until Zouga came up, or turn back along her own spoor until she met him. Neither alternative was attractive, and she put off the decision until the morrow.

There was water in the riverbed below her, the usual shallow warm green pools, foul with bird and animal droppings.

Suddenly she felt very tired. While the expectations of success had buoyed her up she had not noticed it, but now she felt deflated and the marrow of her bones ached with weariness.

"We will camp here," she told the corporal. "Take two men and find meat."

They had marched so hard and long since leaving Karanga's village that there had been no time to hunt. By this time the

323

last of the dried buffalo meat smelled like badly cured hides and was full of bacon beetles. She could only eat it in a strong curry and the curry powder was almost finished. They needed fresh meat desperately, but she was too dispirited to lead the hunting party.

The porters had not finished thatching the low lean-to roof that would be her home for the night when she heard a fusillade of musket fire close by in the forest, and an hour later the corporal came into camp. They had found a large herd of the lovely sable antelope, Harris buck, as Zouga insisted on calling them, and had succeeded in bringing down five fat chocolate-colored cows. The porters, chattering happily, left en masse to help bring in the meat, and Robyn wandered listlessly down the riverbed, accompanied only by Juba, until she found a secluded pool.

"I must smell as good as old Karanga," she thought, scrubbing herself with handfuls of white sand, for she had weeks previously used the last of her soap. She washed out her clothing and spread it to dry on the smooth, water-worn rocks around the pool. Then, still naked, she sat in the sunlight and Juba knelt behind her and combed out her hair so that it could dry.

Juba was obviously pleased to have Robyn to herself again, without old Karanga hovering nearby, even though Robyn was silent and dejected. Juba loved to play with her hair and delighted in the reddish lights that flared in the sunlight as the comb stroked through it.

She chattered merrily as she worked and gurgled with laughter at her own sallies, so that neither of them heard the footsteps in the sand, and it was only when the shadow fell at Robyn's feet that she realized that they were not alone. With a cry of alarm she rose, snatching up her still wet breeches and holding them to her breast to cover her nudity.

The woman who stood before her was unarmed, nervous as she was and shy. Not a young woman, though her skin was smooth and unlined and she had all her teeth still. She was almost certainly Mashona with the finer, more Egyptian features than the Nguni, and she wore the short kilt that left her upper body bare. Her naked breasts were large, out of proportion to the slim upright body; the nipples were raised and drawn out as though she had recently been nursing an infant.

"I heard the guns," she whispered shyly, and Robyn felt a lift of relief when she understood the language. It was Karanga. "I came when I heard the guns. I came to lead you to Manali."

324

Robyn felt the quick rush of tears scald her eyes at the name, and the leap of her heart made her gasp aloud.

Manali, the man who wears a red shirt; her father had always stoutly maintained that the color red discouraged tsetse fly and other stinging insects, and that good thick flannel staved off the ague of fever.

Robyn jumped to her feet, completely oblivious now of her nudity, and rushed to the woman, seizing her arm and shaking it.

"Manali!" she cried, and then in English, "Where is he? Oh, take me to him this instant."

It was more than mere chance, and old Karanga's faltering guidance, that had led her, Robyn decided exultantly as she followed her new guide along one of the narrow winding game paths. It was blood calling to blood. Instinctively, like a migrating swallow, she had flown straight to her father.

She felt like shouting aloud, singing her joy to the forest while the woman went swiftly ahead of Robyn; her narrow, smoothly muscled back and shoulders hardly moved above the gliding roll of her hips, that graceful walk of the African woman trained from childhood to carry a burden upon her head so smoothly that not a drop spills from a brimming pot.

She did not move swiftly enough for Robyn's expectations. Already Robyn could imagine the powerful figure of her father striding toward her, the flaming bush of his beard, the deep compelling voice as he called her name and swung her high as he had when she was a child, then the crushing embrace of his arms.

She imagined his joy matching hers, and after the first heady moments of reunion, then the serious hours of discussion, the recital of the long years between, the growing trust and intimacy between them that they had lacked before, so that finally they could march together to a common goal. In the long years ahead, he could hand the torch to her, confident that his faith and work would go forward in loving and loyal hands.

What would be his first words when he saw and recognized her? How immense his surprise? She laughed aloud breathlessly; of course, he would be deeply touched and grateful that she had come so far, so determinedly to be with him, and she, Robyn, knew that she would not be able to hold back her own tears of joy; she could imagine her father tenderly wiping them away. The tone of his voice would betray the pent-up love of all the intervening years that had parted them, and which would be so sweet that she could hardly bear it.

Ahead of her, in the fading light of a dying day, the Mashona woman led them on to a steep pathway, climbing at a traverse across the western slope of the highest hill. Robyn laughed again when she realized that it was the same hill that old Karanga had pointed out from twenty miles away. He had been right in the end, she must praise him lavishly for that. In her own happiness she wanted to give joy to all the world.

The path came out on a level shelf just below the crest, with a shallow cliff at the back of it and the slope of the hill falling away steeply toward the sunset, and a breathtaking view across the forest and savannah. The entire land turned pink and gold in the low sun and the stupendous flat-topped thunderheads of cloud rose along the dark-blue horizon. The setting was right for this magical moment, but Robyn glanced at it only once and then her full attention fastened on what lay ahead of her.

In the face of the cliff was the mouth of a low cave; the slanting rays of the sun struck fully into it, showing that it was not very deep but had been occupied for a long time. The roof and walls were blackened with the soot of the cooking fire, the floor had been swept bare except for the fire at the entrance, with its circle of blackened hearthstones and a small clay pot standing upon them.

The clearing in front of the cave was bare also, trodden by feet over many years, and there was the offal of human occupation scattered about it, the bare bones of small animals, scraps of fur, chips of wood and shards of broken pottery. There was the odor of rotting food fragments, unwashed leather garments, woodsmoke and human excrement that confirmed the other evidence that men had lived here for a long time.

There was a single human figure crouched over the smoky little fire, an old crone, bowed by age, a mere bundle of filthy fur blankets, motheaten and ragged, looking more like an ancient ape than a human being. It did not stir, and Robyn barely glanced at it, for something else held her attention.

In the back of the cave, lit by the last fleeting sunlight, stood a bed. It was made of rudely cut poles, and tied together with bark rope, yet it stood on four legs in European style, not the African sleeping mat, and it was piled with a stained fur kaross that might have contained a human shape.

On a ledge directly above the bed stood a brass telescope, a teak box similar to the one that held Zouga's sextant and chronometer, but scarred and battered with age, and a small cheap tin chest. The chest was much battered also, most of the original paint chipped away so the bare metal showed.

Robyn remembered that box so vividly, open in Uncle William's study at Kings Lynn, the papers from it overflowing onto the desk top and her father bowed over them, steel-rimmed spectacles on the end of his beaked nose, tugging at his thick red beard as he worked.

Robyn gave a little choking cry, and ran forward passing the old crone sitting at the fire, crossing the cave, and flinging herself on her knees beside the crude bedstead.

"Pater!" Her voice husked over with emotion rasped her own throat. "Pater! It's me—Robyn."

There was no movement beneath the fur blanket and she put out a hand, then stopped before it touched.

"He is dead," she thought miserably. "I am too late!"

She forced her hand to move again, and touched the malodorous pile of old furs. They collapsed under her touch, and it took her seconds to realize that she had been mistaken. The bed was empty, the discarded blanket had fallen in the shape of a man, but the bed was empty.

Bewildered, Robyn rose to her feet and turned back toward the entrance of the cave. The Karanga woman stood by the fire, watching her expressionlessly, while little Juba hung back fearfully at the far side of the clearing.

"Where is he?" Robyn spread her hands to emphasize the question. "Where is Manali?"

The Karanga woman dropped her eyes. For a moment Robyn did not understand, and then she too looked down at the grotesque figure that crouched by the fire at her feet.

She felt a cold steel band lock about her chest and squeeze her heart so that it took an effort of will to force her feet to move back across the swept floor of the cave.

The Mashona woman was watching Robyn expressionlessly. She had clearly not understood the English question, but she waited with the endless patience of Africa. Robyn was about to appeal to her again when the skeletal figure across the smoky little fire started to rock from side to side agitatedly, and a querulous slurred old man's voice began to chant some strange litany, like a magical incantation.

It took Robyn some moments to realize that the accents were faintly Scots and the words, though blurred and jumbled, were a parody of the Twenty-third Psalm.

"Yea! Though I walk through the valley of the shadow of death, I shall fear no evil."

As suddenly as it had begun the chanting broke off, and the rocking ceased. The frail figure froze into stillness and silence again. Across the fire, the Mashona woman stooped and, gently as a mother with a child, she drew back the kaross from the head and shoulder of the figure at her feet.

Fuller Ballantyne had shriveled, his face lined and roughened like the bark of an old oak. It seemed as though the smoke of the fire had etched his skin, collecting in the creases, crusting it with soot.

His hair and beard had fallen out in clumps, as though from some disgusting disease, and what was left of it was pure white but stringed and darkened with dirt to a tobacco yellow at the corners of the mouth and at the nostrils.

Only his eyes still seemed to live, they rolled in their sockets, and it needed only one look at them for Robyn to realize that her father was mad.

This was not Fuller Ballantyne, this was not the great explorer, the powerful evangelist and enemy of slavery. He had gone long ago, leaving a filthy shriveled lunatic in his place.

"Pater," she stared at him in disbelief, feeling the world spin and lurch beneath her. "Pater," she repeated, and across the fire the crouched figure gibbered with abrupt falsetto girlish laughter, and then began to rave incoherently, snatches of English giving way to a half-dozen dialects of Africa, the cries becoming more agitated, his thin pale arms thrown wildly in the air.

"I have sinned against thee, my God," he screamed and clawed at his own beard, a tuft of the thin pale hair coming away in the hooked fingers. "I am not worthy to be thy servant." He tore at himself again, this time leaving a thin livid scratch down the pouched and wrinkled cheek, though it seemed that the wasted body had no blood left to shed.

The Mashona woman leaned over him and caught the bony wrist, restraining him. The action was so familiar that she must have performed it often. Then gently she stooped and lifted him. The body seemed to weigh no more than that of a child for she carried him without visible effort to the crude pole bed. One of his legs was bound up in a rudimentary splint and stuck straight out ahead of him.

Robyn stayed on beside the fire, hanging her head. She found that she was still shivering, until the woman came back to her, touching her arm.

"He is very sick."

Only then could Robyn force back her revulsion and her
328

horror. She stood, hesitated only a moment longer, and then went to her father. With Juba and the Mashona woman helping her, she began her examination, taking refuge behind her professional rituals and procedures while she regained control of her emotions. He was thinner than she had ever seen a living human body, thinner than the starved brats of gin-soaked slum sluts.

"There has been little food," said the woman, "and what there is, he will not eat. I have had to feed him like a small baby." Robyn did not then understand what she meant, but she went on grimly with her examination.

The starved body was verminous, the bunches of little white nits hanging like grapes in the thin white pubic hair, and his whole body was crusted with filth and traces of his own incontinence.

Feeling under the staring rib cage her fingertips encountered the hard distended shape of liver and spleen, and Fuller Ballantyne screamed when she did so. The swelling and extreme tenderness were certain indications of massive malarial infection of long duration, and evidence of terrible neglect.

"Where is the medicine, the *umuthi*, of Manali?"

"It was long ago finished, together with the powder and shot for the gun. Everything was finished long ago"—the woman shook her head—"long, long ago, and when it was finished, the people no longer came with gifts to feed us." It was suicidal to remain in a malarial area without supplies of quinine. Fuller Ballantyne of all people knew that. The acknowledged world expert on malarial fever and its treatment—how could he have neglected his own often-repeated advice? She found the reasons almost immediately, as she opened his mouth, forcing open his lower jaw despite his feeble protests.

Most of his teeth had been rotted out by the disease, and his throat and palate were covered by the characteristic lesions. She released his jaw, allowing him to close the ruined mouth, and gently she touched the bridge of his nose, feeling the soggy collapsing bone and gristle. There could be no doubt at all, the disease was far advanced, had long ago begun its final assault upon the once magnificent brain. It was syphilis, in the terminal stages, the general paralysis of the insane. The disease of the lonely man that led inevitably to the lonely madman's death.

As Robyn worked, so her horror and revulsion gave way swiftly to the compassion of the healer, to the sympathy of one who had lived with human weakness and folly and had come far along the road of understanding. She knew now why her

329

father had not turned back when his supplies of vital medicines ran perilously low: the half-destroyed brain had not recognized the dangers which he had previously described so clearly.

She found herself praying for him as she worked, praying silently but with the words coming more readily than they usually did.

"Judge him as he was, O Lord, judge him by his service in your name—not by his small sins, but by his great achievements. Look not upon this ruined pathetic thing, but on the strong and vital man who carried your work forward without flinching."

As she prayed, she lifted the heavy kaross off his legs, and the smell of corruption made her blink and the frail figure began immediately to struggle with renewed strength that needed both Juba and the Mashona woman to control.

Robyn stared at the legs, and realized the other reason why her father had never left this land. He had been physically unable to do so. The splints that held the leg had been whittled out of native timber. The leg had been fractured, probably at more than one place below the hip. Perhaps the hip joint itself had gone, that vulnerable neck of the femur. But what was certain was that the breaks had not mended cleanly. Perhaps the bindings of the splints had been too tight, for the deep suppurating ulcerations went down to the very bone, and the smell was a solid jarring thing.

Quickly she covered his lower body; there was nothing she could do until she had her medical chest and instruments, and now she was merely inflicting unnecessary pain and humiliation. Her father was still struggling and bleating like a petulant child, rolling his head from side to side, the toothless mouth agape.

The Mashona woman leaned over him, and took one of her own dark tight breasts in her hand, squeezing out the nipple between her fingers, and then she paused and looked up shyly, imploringly, at Robyn.

Only then did Robyn understand, and respecting the privacy of the woman and the poor maimed thing that had been her father, she dropped her eyes and turned away toward the entrance of the cave.

"I must fetch my *umuthi*. I will return here later tonight."

Behind her, the childlike bleats gave way abruptly to small snuffling sounds of comfort.

Robyn felt no shock or outrage as she went down the steep pathway in the moonlight. Instead she felt immense pity for

Fuller Ballantyne who had made the full circle back to infancy. She felt also a deep gratitude to the woman, and a sense of wonder at her loyalty and dedication. How long had she stayed on with Fuller Ballantyne after all reason for staying was gone?

She remembered her own mother, and her devotion to the same man, she remembered Sarah and her child still waiting patiently beside a far-off river. And then there was Robyn herself, come so far and so determinedly. Fuller Ballantyne always had the power to attract as powerfully as he could repel.

Holding Juba's hand for her own comfort as well as that of the child, Robyn hurried along the moonlit path on the bank of the river, and with relief saw the glow of the campfires in the forest ahead of her. On the return journey she would have bearers to carry her medical chest, and armed Hottentot musketeers as escort.

Her relief was short-lived, for as she answered the challenge of the Hottentot sentry and entered the circle of firelight, a familiar figure rose from beside the campfire and came striding to meet her, tall and powerful, golden-bearded and handsome as a god from Greek mythology, and every bit as wrathful.

"Zouga!" she gasped. "I didn't expect you."

"No," he agreed icily. "I'm sure that you did not."

"Why?" she thought desperately. "Why must he come now? Why not a day later, when I have had time to clean and treat my father? Oh God, why now? Zouga will never understand—never! Never! Never!"

Robyn and her escort could not hope to keep pace with Zouga. They fell swiftly behind him as he climbed the pathway in the night, months of hard hunting had toned him to the peak of physical condition and he ran at the hill.

She had not been able to warn him. What words were there to describe the creature in the cave on the hilltop? She had told him simply, "I have found Pater."

It had deflected his anger instantly. The bitter accusations shriveled on his tongue, and the realization dawned in his eyes.

They had found Fuller Ballantyne. They had accomplished one of the three major objectives of the expedition. She knew that Zouga was already seeing it in print, almost composing the paragraph that would describe the moment, imagining the newspaper urchins shouting the headlines in the streets of London.

331

For the first time in her life she came close to hating her brother, and her voice was crisp as hoarfrost as she told him, "And don't you forget it was me. I was the one who made the march and broke trail, and I was the one who found him."

She saw the shift in his green eyes in the firelight.

"Of course, sissy." He smiled at her thinly, an obvious effort. "Who could ever forget that? Where is he?"

"First I must assemble what I need."

He had stayed with her until they reached the foot of the hill, and then had been unable to restrain himself. He had gone at the slope at a pace that none of them had been able to equal. Robyn came out in the little clearing in front of the cave. Her heart was racing and her breathing ragged from the climb so that she had to pause and fight for breath, holding one hand to her breast.

The fire in front of the cave had been built up to a fair blaze, but it left the depths of the cave in discreet shadow. Zouga stood in front of the fire. His back to the cave.

As Robyn regained her breath, she went forward. She saw that Zouga's face was deathly pale, in the firelight his sunbronzing had faded to a muddy tone. He stood erect, as though on the parade ground, and he stared directly ahead of him.

"Have you seen Pater?" Robyn asked. His distress and utter confusion gave her a sneaking and spiteful pleasure.

"There is a native woman with him," Zouga whispered, "in his bed."

"Yes," Robyn nodded. "He is very sick. She is caring for him."

"Why did you not warn me?"

"That he is sick?" she asked.

"That he had gone native."

"He's dying, Zouga."

"What are we going to tell the world?"

"The truth," she suggested quietly. "That he is sick and dying."

"You must never mention the woman." Zouga's voice, for the first time that she could remember, was uncertain, he seemed to be groping for words. "We must protect the family."

"Then what must we tell about his disease, the disease that is killing him?"

Zouga's eyes flickered to her face. "Malaria?"

"The pox, Zouga. The French sickness, the Italian plague— or, if you prefer it, syphilis, Zouga. He is dying of syphilis."

Zouga flinched, and then he whispered, "It's not possible."

332

"Why not, Zouga?" she asked. "He was a man—a great man, but a man nevertheless."

She stepped past him. "And now I have work to do."

An hour later when she looked for him again, Zouga had gone back down the hill to the camp beside the river pools. She remained to work over her father for the rest of that night and most of the following day.

By the time she had bathed and cleaned him, shaved off the infested body hair and trimmed the stringy beard and locks of yellowed hair, treated the ulcerations of his leg, she was exhausted both physically and emotionally. She had seen approaching death too many times not to recognize it now. She knew that all she could hope for was to give comfort and to smooth the lonely road that her father must travel.

When she had done all that was possible, she covered him with a clean blanket and then tenderly caressed the short soft hair which she had so lovingly trimmed. Fuller opened his eyes. They were an empty shade of blue, like an African summer sky. The last sunlight of the day was washing the cave, and as Robyn leaned over him, it sparkled in her hair in chips of ruby light.

She saw something move in the empty eyes, a shadow of the man who had once been there, and Fuller's lips parted. Twice he tried to speak and then he said one word, so husky and light that she missed it. Robyn leaned closer to him.

"What is it?" she asked.

"Helen!" This time clearer.

Robyn felt the tears choke up her throat at the sound of her mother's name.

"Helen." Fuller said it for the last time, and then the flicker of comprehension in his eyes was gone.

She stayed on beside him, but there was nothing more. That name had been the last link with reality and now the link was broken.

As the last light of the day faded, Robyn lifted her eyes from her father's face and for the first time realized that the tin chest was missing from the ledge at the back of the cave.

Using the lid of his own writing case as a desk, screened from the camp by the thin wall of thatch, Zouga worked swiftly through the contents of the chest.

His horror at the discovery of his father had long ago been submerged by the fascination of the treasures which the chest contained. The disgust, the shame, would return again when

333

he had time to think about it, he knew that. He knew also that there would be hard decisions to make then, and that he would have to use all his force of personality and of brotherly superiority to control Robyn, and make her agree to a common version of the discovery of Fuller Ballantyne and a tactful description of the circumstances to which he had been reduced.

The tin chest contained four leather-and-canvas-bound journals, each of five hundred pages, and the pages were covered on both sides either with writing or with hand-drawn maps. There was also a bundle of loose sheets, two or three hundred of them tied together with plaited bark string, and a cheap wooden pen case with a partition for spare nibs, and cutouts for two ink bottles. One bottle was dry, and the pen nibs had obviously been sharpened many times, for they were almost worn away. Zouga sniffed the ink in the remaining bottle. It seemed to be an evil-smelling mixture of fat and soot and vegetable dyes that Fuller had concocted when his supplies of the manufactured item were exhausted.

The last journal and most of the loose pages were written with this mixture, and they had faded and smeared, making the handwriting that much more difficult to decipher, for by this stage Fuller Ballantyne's hand had deteriorated almost as much as his mind. Whereas the first two journals were written in the small, precise and familiar script, this slowly turned into a loose sloping scrawl as uncontrolled as some of the ideas expressed by it. The history of his father's madness was plotted therein with sickening fascination.

The pages of the leather-bound journals were not numbered, and there were many gaps between the dates of one entry and the next, which made Zouga's work easier. He read swiftly, an art he had developed when acting as regimental intelligence officer with huge amounts of reading-reports, orders and departmental manuals—to get through each day.

The first books of writing were ground that had been traveled before, meticulous observations of celestial position, of climate and altitude, backed up by shrewdly observed descriptions of terrain and population. Sandwiched between these were accusations and complaints about authority, whether it were the directors of the London Missionary Society, or "The Imperial Factor," as Fuller Ballantyne referred to the foreign secretary and his department in Whitehall.

There were detailed explanations of his reasons for leaving Tete and traveling south with a minimally equipped expedition, and then, quite suddenly, two pages devoted to an account of a sexual liaison with an ex-slave girl, an Angoni girl whom Fuller had christened Sarah and who he suspected was about to bear his child. His reasons for abandoning her at Tete were direct and without pretence. "I know that a woman, even a hardy native, carrying a child would delay me. As I am on God's work, I can brook no such check."

Although what Zouga had seen on the hilltop should have conditioned him for this sort of revelation, still he could not bring himself to terms with it. Using his hunting knife, whetted to a razor edge, he slit the offending pages from the journal, and as he crumpled them and threw them in the campfire he muttered, "The old devil had no right to write this filth."

Twice more he found sexual references which he removed from the journal, and by then the handwriting was showing the first deterioration, and passages of great lucidity were followed by wild ravings and the dreams and imaginings of a diseased mind.

More often Fuller referred to himself as the instrument of God's wrath, his blazing sword against the heathen and the ungodly. The weirdest and patently lunatic passages Zouga cut from the journal and burned. He knew he must work swiftly, before Robyn came down from the hilltop. He knew that what he was doing was right, for his father's memory and place in posterity and also for those who would have to live on after him, Robyn and Zouga himself, and their children and children's children.

It was a chilling experience to see his father's great love and compassion for the African people, and the very land itself, changing and becoming a bitter unreasoning hatred. Against the Matabele people, who he referred to as the Ndebele—or the Amandebele—he railed: "These leonine peoples who acknowledge no God at all, whose diet consists of the devil's brew and half-cooked meat, both in vast quantities, and whose greatest delight is spearing to death defenceless women and children, are ruled over by the most merciless despot since Caligula, the most grossly blood-besotted monster since Attila himself."

Of the other tribes he was at least as scornful. "The Rozwis are a sly and secret people, the timid and treacherous descendants of the slave-trading and gold-mad kings they called the Mambos. Their dynasties destroyed by the marauding Ndebele and their monstrous Nguni brothers the Shangaans of Gungundha and the blood-smattered Angoni."

The Karangas were "cowards and devil-worshipers, lurking

in their caves and hilltop fortresses, committing unspeakable sacrilege and offending in the face of the Almighty by their blasphemous ceremonies in the ruined cities where once their Monomatapa held sway."

The reference to Monomatapa and ruined cities checked Zouga's eyes in the middle of the page. Then he read on eagerly, hoping for elaboration of the mention of ruined cities, but Fuller's mind had flown on to other ideas, the theme of suffering and sacrifice which has always been the spine of Christian belief.

"I thank God, my Almighty Father, that he has chosen me as his sword, and that as the mark of his love and condescension he has made his mark upon me. This dawn when I awoke there were the stigmata in my feet and hands, the wound in my side, and the bleeding scratches from the crown of thorns upon my forehead. I have felt the same sweet pain as Christ himself."

The disease had reached that part of his brain that affected his eyes, and sense of feeling. His faith had become religious mania. Zouga cut out this and the following pages and consigned them to the flames of the campfire.

Ranting madness was followed by cool sanity, as though the disease had tides which ebbed and flowed within his brain. The next entry in the journal was dated five days after that claiming the stigmata. It began with a celestial observation that placed him not far from where Zouga sat reading the words, always making allowances for the inaccuracy of a chronometer that had not been checked for almost two years. There was no further reference to the stigmata. They had healed as miraculously as they had bloomed. Instead there was a brisk and businesslike entry in the old neat script.

"The Karanga people practice a form of ancestor worship, which calls for sacrifice. It is extremely difficult to make any one of them discuss either this ceremony or even the basic precepts of this abominable religion. However, my command of the Karanga language is now sufficient to have earned the respect and trust of those members of the tribe with whom I have succeeded in making contact. The spiritual center of their religion is in a place which they refer to as 'the burial place of the kings,' or in their language 'Zimbabwe' or 'Simbabwee' where the idols which represent their ancestors stand.

"It would seem that this place is situated to the south and east of my present position.

"The head of this foul belief is a priestess, referred to as the 'Umlimo' who once dwelt in the 'burial place of the kings' but fled from there at the coming of the Angoni marauders. She lives in another sacred place, and commands such sway that even the godless Ndebele, that sanguine tyrant Mzilikazi, send gifts for her oracle.

"So deeply ingrained is the power of this evil belief into the minds of all these people, that they are strongly resistant to the word of Christ which I bear.

"It has come to me in a revelation which can only be the voice of God Almighty himself that he has chosen me to march upon this citadel of evil, this 'Simbabwee,' and to throw down the images of the ungodly—even as Moses threw down and destroyed the golden calf on his descent from the mountain.

"God Almighty has further revealed to me that I have been chosen to seek out the High Priestess of evil in her secret place and to destroy her, and by so doing break the hold that she has over the minds of these people, that they might become receptive to the Holy Word of Christ which I bring them."

Zouga raced on through the pages; it seemed as though they were being written by two different men, the rational being with the neat script and the raving religious maniac with the wild looping hand. In some passages the change came from one line to the next, in others the one character was maintained for page after page. Zouga could not afford to miss a word of it.

It was well after noon, and his eyes felt grainy and tender from continually scanning the cramped sheets, blurred and faded from the improvised ink which Fuller was now using.

"November 3rd. Position 20° 05 S. 30° 50 E. Temperature 103° in the shade. Heat unbearable. Rain threatens each day and never comes. Have reached the lair of the Umlimo."

The single laconic entry electrified Zouga. He almost missed it, for it was squeezed into the bottom of a page. He turned that page and on the next the madman had taken over again, writing in vaunting hyperbole and thunderous religious ecstasy.

"I praise God, my Maker. The one true and Almighty Saviour for whom all things are possible. Thy will be done!

"The Umlimo knew me as the instrument of God's wrath when I confronted her in that reeking charnel house, for she spoke in the voices of Belial and Beelzebub, the hideous voices of Azazel and Beliar, all Satan's myriad alter egos.

"But I stood before her strong and proud in God's word, and when she saw she could not move me, she fell silent.

"So I slew her, and cut off her head and carried it out into the light. And God spoke to me in the night and said in his

337

small still voice 'Go on, my faithful and well-beloved servant. You cannot rest until the graven images of the godless are cast down.'

"So I rose, and God's hand held me up and carried me onwards."

How much of this was fact, and how much was the ranting of madness, fantasy of a diseased brain, Zouga could not know, but he read on furiously.

"And the Almighty guided me until I came at last alone to the foul city where the devil-worshipers commit their sacrilege. My bearers would not follow me, terrified of the devils. Even old Joseph who was always at my side could not force his legs to carry him through the gateway in the high stone wall. I left him cringing in the forest, and went in alone to walk between the high towers of stone.

"As God had revealed to me, I found the graven images of the heathen all decked with flowers and gold, the blood of the sacrifice not yet dried, and I broke them and cast them down and no man could oppose me for I was the sword of Zion, the finger of God's own hand."

The entry broke off abruptly, as though the writer had been overwhelmed by the strength of his own religious fervor, and Zouga flipped through the next one hundred pages of the journal searching for further reference to the city and its gold-decked images, but there was none.

Like the miraculous blooming of the stigmata upon Fuller's hands and feet and body and brow, perhaps this was also the imaginings of a lunatic.

Zouga returned to the original entry, describing Fuller's meeting with the Umlimo, the sorceress whom he had slain. He wrote the latitude and longitude into his own journal, copied the rough sketch map and made cryptic notes of the text, pondering it for clues that might lead or guide him. Then, quite deliberately, he cut out the pages from Fuller's own journal and held them one at a time over the fire, letting them crinkle and brown, then catch and flare before he dropped them and watched them curl and blacken. He stirred the ashes to dust with a stick before he was satisfied.

The last of the four journals was only partially filled, and contained a detailed description of a caravan route running from "the blood-soaked lands where Mzilikazi's evil impis hold sway" eastward five hundred miles or more "to where the reeking ships of the traders surely wait to welcome the poor souls who survive the hazards of this infamous road."

"I have followed the road as far as the eastern rampart of mountains, and always the evidence of the passing of the caravans is there for all the world to see. That grisly evidence which I have come to know so well, the bleaching bones and the circling vultures. Is there not a corner of this savage continent which is free from the ravages of the traders?"

These revelations would interest Robyn more than they did him. Zouga glanced through them swiftly and then marked them for her attention. There was a great deal on slavery and the traders, a hundred pages or more — and then the penultimate entry.

"We have today come up with a caravan of slaves, winding through the hilly country towards the east. I have counted the miserable victims from afar, using the telescope, and there are almost a hundred of them, mostly half-grown children and young women. They are yoked together in pairs with forked tree trunks about their necks in the usual manner.

"The slavemasters are black men, I have been unable to descry either Arabs or men of European extraction amongst them. Although they wear no tribal insignia, no plumes nor regalia, I have no doubt they are Amandebele, for their physique is distinctive, and they come from the direction of that tyrant Mzilikazi's kingdom. They are furthermore armed with the broad-bladed stabbing spears and long oxhide shields of that people, while two or three of them carry trade muskets.

"At this moment they are encamped not more than a league from where I lie, and in the dawn they will continue their fateful journey towards the east where the Arab and Portuguese slavemasters no doubt wait to purchase the miserable human cattle and load them like cargo for the cruel voyage half across the world.

"God has spoken to me, clearly I have heard his voice as he enjoined me to go down, and, like his sword, cut down the ungodly, free the slaves and minister to the meek and the innocent.

"Joseph is with me, that true and trusted companion of the years, and he will be well able to serve my second gun. His marksmanship is not of the best, but he has courage and God will be with us."

The next entry was the last. Zouga had come to the end of the four journals.

"God's ways are wonderful and mysterious, passing all understanding. He lifteth up and he casteth down. With Joseph beside me I went down, as God had commanded, to the camp of the slavemasters. We fell upon them, even as the Israelites fell upon the Philistines. At first it seemed that we must prevail for the ungodly fled before us. Then God in all his knowing wisdom deserted us. One of the ungodly leapt upon Joseph while he was reloading, and though I put a ball through his chest he impaled poor Joseph from breast bone to spine with that terrible spear, before himself falling dead.

"Alone I carried on the fight. God's fight, and the slavemasters scattered into the forest before my wrath. Then one of them turned and at extreme range fired his musket in my direction. The ball struck me in the hip.

"I managed, I do not know how, to drag myself away before the slavemasters returned to slay me. They did not attempt to follow me, and I have regained the shelter which I left to make the attempt. However, I am sorely smitten and reduced to dire straits. I have managed to remove the musket ball from my own hip, but I fear the bone is cracked through and I am crippled.

"In addition I have lost both my firearms, Joseph's musket lies with him where he fell, and I was so badly hurt as to be unable to carry my weapon off the field. I sent the woman back to find them, but they have been carried away by the slave-traders.

"My remaining porters, seeing the state to which I have been reduced and knowing that I could not prevent it, have all deserted, but not before they had looted the camp and carried away almost everything of value, not excluding my medicine chest. Only the woman remains. I was angry at first when she attached herself to my party, but now I see God's hand in this—for although she is a heathen, yet she is loyal and true beyond all others, now that Joseph is dead.

"What is a man in this cruel land without a musket or quinine? Is there a lesson in this for me and posterity, a lesson that God has chosen me to teach? Can a white man live here? Will he not always be the alien, and will Africa tolerate him once he has lost his weapons and expended his medicines?"

Then a single poignant cry of agony.

"Oh God, has this all been in vain? I came to bring your Word and nobody has listened to my voice. I came to change the ways of the wicked and nothing is changed. I came to open a way for Christianity, and no Christian has followed me. Please, my God, give me a sign that I have not followed the wrong road to a false destination."

Zouga leaned back and rubbed his eyes with the heels of

both hands. He found himself deeply moved, his eyes stinging not only from fatigue.

Fuller Ballantyne was an easy man to hate, but a hard man to despise.

Robyn chose the place with care. The secluded pools on the river, away from the main camp, where nobody would overlook or overhear them. She chose the time, in the heat of midday—when most of the Hottentots and all the porters would be asleep in the shade. She had given Fuller five drops of precious laudanum to quiet him, and left him with the Mashona girl and Juba to care for him while she went down the hill to Zouga.

They had barely exchanged a dozen words during the ten days since he had caught up with her. In all that time he had not returned to the cave on the hilltop, and she had seen him only once when she had gone down to the river camp for supplies.

When she had sent Juba down with a tersely worded note, demanding the return of Fuller's tin chest of papers, he had sent a porter with it immediately. In fact, with such alacrity that Robyn was immediately suspicious.

This distrust was a symptom of their rapidly deteriorating relationship. She knew that she and Zouga must talk, must discuss the future, before the opportunity to talk was past.

He was waiting for her beside the green river pools, as she had asked him to be, sitting in the mottled shade beneath a wild fig tree, quietly smoking a hand-rolled cheroot of native tobacco. He stood up courteously as soon as he saw her, but his expression was reserved and his eyes guarded.

"I do not have much time, Zouga dear." Robyn tried to lessen the tension between them by using the small endearment, and Zouga nodded gravely. "I must get back to Pater." She hesitated. "I did not want to ask you to come up the hill since you find it distasteful." She saw the green sparks in his eyes kindle immediately, and went on quickly. "We must decide what we should do now. Obviously we cannot stay on here indefinitely."

"What do you suggest?"

"Pater is much stronger. I have subdued the malaria with quinine and the other disease"—she worded it tactfully—"has responded to the mercury. It is only the leg that truly worries me now."

"You told me he was dying," Zouga reminded her levelly,

and she could not help herself: despite her good intentions she flared at him.

"Well, I am sorry to disappoint you, then."

Zouga's face stiffened into a handsome, bronzed mask. She could see the effort it took him to control his own temper, and his voice was thick with it as he answered.

"That's not worthy of you."

"I'm sorry," she agreed, and drew a deep breath. "Zouga, he has rallied strongly. Food and medicine, care and his own natural strength have made an immense difference. I am even convinced that if we could get him to civilization to a skilled surgeon, we could cure the ulceration of his leg, and possibly even induce the bone to mend."

Zouga was silent for a long time, and though his face was expressionless, she could see the play of emotion in his eyes.

He spoke at last. "Father is mad." She did not answer. "Can you cure his mind?"

"No." She shook her head. "That will get worse, but with care and skilled attention in a good hospital, we can improve his body and he could live for many years still."

"To what purpose?" Zouga insisted.

"He would be comfortable and perhaps happy."

"And all the world would know that he was a syphilitic madman," Zouga went on quietly for her. "Would it not be kinder to let the legend stand untarnished? No, more than that, to add to it by our own account, rather than drag back this poor diseased and demented thing for all his enemies, his numerous enemies, to mock?"

"Is that why you tampered with his journals?" Robyn's voice was shrill, even in her own ears.

"That's a dangerous accusation." He was losing his control also. "Can you prove it?"

"I don't have to prove it; we both know it's so."

"You cannot move him." Zouga changed direction. "He is crippled."

"He could be carried on a litter. We have more than enough porters."

"Which way would you take him?" Zouga demanded. "He would never survive the route over which we have traveled— and the route southwards is uncharted."

"Pater himself has charted the slave road in his journal. We will follow that. It will lead us directly to the coast."

"With the major objectives of the expedition unfulfilled?" Zouga asked quickly.

342

"The major objectives were to find Fuller Ballantyne, and report on the slave trade, both of which we can accomplish if we march down the slave road to the sea." Robyn broke off, and then made a show of dawning comprehension. "Oh, dear, how silly of me, you mean the gold and the ivory. Those were the major objectives all along, were they not, my dear brother?"

"We have a duty to our sponsors."

"And none to that poor sick man up there?" Robyn flung out one hand dramatically, and then spoiled the effect by stamping her foot. Angry with herself as well as with him, she yelled at him. "I am taking Pater down to the coast, and quickly as I can."

"I say you are not."

"And I say the hell with you, Morris Zouga Ballantyne!" The oath gave her a grim pleasure, and she turned and strode away from him, long-legged in her tight-fitting breeches.

Two days later Robyn was ready to march. All exchanges between Zouga and herself since their final meeting at the river had been in the form of written notes, and Robyn realized that her brother would be keeping copies of all his correspondence to justify his actions later.

She had briefly repudiated his written command not to attempt to march with the sick man. Zouga had listed half a dozen reasons, each neatly enumerated, why she should remain. Once he had her written defiance, his next note sent up the hill in Juba's sweating little hand was magnanimous, written for future readers other than herself, Robyn decided sourly.

"If you insist on this folly," he began, and he went on to offer her the protection of the entire force of Hottentot musketeers—with the exception of Sergeant Cheroot, who had expressed a desire to remain with Zouga. Under the corporal they would form an escort capable, as Zouga worded it, "of bringing you and your charge safely to the coast, and protecting you from any hazards upon the way."

He insisted that she take most of the remaining porters. He would keep five porters to carry his essential stores, together with his four gunbearers, Matthew, Mark, Luke and John.

He also ordered her to take the Sharps rifle and all the remaining stores, "leaving me only sufficient powder and shot, and the bare minimum of medicines to enable me to complete the further objectives of this expedition which I deem to be of prime importance."

His final note reiterated all his reasons for keeping Fuller

Ballantyne on the hilltop, and asked her once more to reconsider her decision. Robyn saved him the trouble of making fair copies by simply turning over the note and scribbling on it. "My mind is made up. I will march at first light tomorrow for the coast." Then she dated and signed it.

The next morning, before sunup, Zouga sent a team of porters up the hill, carrying a litter of mopani poles. The poles had been peeled of their rough bark and bound together with rawhide strips from the hide of a freshly killed roan antelope, and the body of the litter was made from the same interwoven hide strips. Fuller Ballantyne had to be strapped into the litter to prevent him from throwing himself out of it.

When Robyn brought them down again, walking beside the litter to try to calm the crazy old man on it, the Hottentot escort and the porters were ready to join her on the march. Zouga was waiting also, standing a little aside as though he had already dissociated himself, but Robyn went to him directly.

"At least we know each other now," she said huskily. "We may not be able to rub along together, Zouga. I doubt we ever could have, or ever will be able to, but that does not mean I do not respect you, and love you even more than I respect you."

Zouga flushed and looked away. As she should have known, such a declaration could only embarrass him.

"I have made sure that you have a hundred pounds of gunpowder, that is more than you could ever need," he said.

"Do you wish to say farewell to Pater?"

Zouga nodded stiffly, and followed her to the litter, avoiding looking at the Mashona woman who stood beside it, and spoke formally to Fuller Ballantyne.

"Good-bye, sir. I wish you a swift safe journey and a speedy return to good health."

The wizened toothless face, revolved toward him upon its scrawny neck. The shaven head had a porcelain gloss in the gray dawn light, and the eyes were bird-bright, glittering with madness.

"God is my shepherd, I shall fear no evil," Fuller cawed, mouthing the words so they were barely understandable.

"Quite right, sir," Zouga nodded seriously. "No doubt at all about that." He touched his cap in a military salute and stepped back. He nodded to the porters and they lifted the litter and moved away toward the orange and yellow sunrise.

Brother and sister stood side by side for the last time watching the column of escort and porters file past, and when the final one had gone and only little Juba remained beside her, Robyn reached up impulsively and threw her arms around Zouga's neck, embraced him almost fiercely.

"I try to understand you, won't you do the same for me?"

For a moment she thought he might unbend, she felt the hard erect body sway and soften, and then Zouga straightened again.

"This is not good-bye," he said. "Once I have done what is necessary, I shall follow you. We'll meet again."

Robyn dropped her arms to her sides, and stood back.

"Until then," she agreed wistfully, sad that he had not been able to make even a show of affection.

"Until then," she repeated, and turned away. Juba followed her away into the forest, after the departing column.

Zouga waited until the singing of the porters dwindled, and the only sound was the sweet wild bird chorus that greets each dawn in Africa, and the distant melancholy whooping of a hyena slinking away to its earth.

There were many emotions warring in him. Guilt that he had let a woman, however well supported, attempt the journey to the coast; worry that once she reached it, her accounts would be the first to reach London; doubt as to the authenticity of the clues which Fuller Ballantyne had left for him to follow, but overlying it all a sense of relief and excitement that he was at last answerable only to himself, free to range as fast and far as hard legs and harder determination would take him.

He shook himself, a physical purging of guilt and doubt, leaving only the excitement and soaring sense of anticipation, and he turned to where Sergeant Cheroot waited at the perimeter of the forlorn and deserted camp.

"When you smile, your face makes the children cry," Zouga told him, "but when you frown . . . What troubles you now. O mighty hunter of elephants?"

The little Hottentot lugubriously indicated the bulky tin box that contained Zouga's dress uniform and hat.

"Say not another word, Sergeant," Zouga warned him.

"But the porters complain, they have carried it so far."

"And they will carry it to the gates of hell itself, if I say so. Safari!" Zouga raised his voice, elated with the sense of excitement still strongly upon him. "We march!"

Zouga was prepared for wide discrepancies in the positions that his father had fixed by celestial observation, and his own.

A few seconds of error in the chronometers would put them many miles out.

So he treated with suspicion the terrain features which he saw ahead and which seemed to match with uncanny accurancy the sketch maps he had copied from Fuller's journals.

Yet as each day's march that he made opened up country that fitted his father's descriptions, he became more confident, more certain that the Umlimo and the ruined city were real and that they lay not many days' march ahead.

It was beautiful country they passed through, though the air was more sultry as they descended the sloping plateau toward the south and west. The long dry season, now drawing to its close, had seared the grasslands to the color of fields of ripening wheat, and turned the foliage of the forests to a hundred shades of plum reds and soft apricots. Many of the trees were bare of all leaves, lifting arthritically contorted limbs to the sky as if beseeching it for the relief of rain.

Each day the thunderheads built up, tall silver ranges of cloud turning purple and sullen leaden blue, threatening rain but never making good that threat, though the thunder muttered, and in the evenings the lightning flickered low on the horizon as though armies were locked in battle far to the east.

The big game was concentrated on the remaining water, the deeper river pools and the strongest waterholes, so that each day's march was through a wonderland of wild animals.

In one herd Zouga counted thirty-two giraffe, from the old stinkbull almost black with age, his long neck taller than the trees on which he fed, to the beige-splotched calves on their disproportionately long legs, galloping away in that slow rocking gait with their long tufted tails twisted up over their backs.

Every clearing had its family of rhinoceros, the cows with the distinctively long slender nose horn running their calves ahead of them, guiding them with a touch of the horn on the flank. There were herds of Cape buffalo, a thousand strong, flowing in a black dense mass across the open glades, steaming with dust like the lava from an active volcano.

Then there were elephant. There was not one day they did not cut fresh spoor, veritable roads through the forest, tall trees pushed down or still standing but stripped of their bark so the trunks were naked and weeping with fresh sap, the earth beneath them strewn with chewed twigs and bunches of picked leaves only just beginning to wither, the huge piles of fibrous dung standing like monuments to the passing of the beasts, and the baboon and the plump brown pheasant scratching and

346

foraging enthusiastically in them for the half-digested wild nuts and other tidbits.

Zouga could seldom resist him when Jan Cheroot looked up from his examination of the pad marks and said, "A big bull, this one, walking heavy in the front quarters. Good teeth, I'd stake my sister's virtue on it."

"A commodity which was staked and lost many years ago," Zouga observed dryly. "But we will follow, none the less."

Most evenings they could cut teeth and, having buried them, carry the bleeding heart to where they had left the porters, two men to carry the forty-pound hunk of raw flesh slung on a pole between them, a feast for the whole party. Because of the hunt, progress was slow and not always direct, but steadily Zouga identified and passed the landmarks that his father had described.

Then at last, knowing he was close, Zouga withstood the temptation to hunt, for the first time refusing to follow the fresh spoor of three fine bulls, and disappointing Jan Cheroot most grievously by doing so.

"You should never leave a good elephant or a warm and willing lady," he advised dolefully, "because you never know where or when you are going to meet the next one."

Jan Cheroot did not yet know the new object of their quest and Zouga's behavior puzzled him. Zouga often caught him watching him with a quizzical sparkle in his bright little slitty eyes, but he avoided the direct question diplomatically and accepted Zouga's orders to abandon the spoor with only a little further grumbling, and they went on.

It was the porters who first balked. Zouga never knew how they guessed, perhaps old Karanga had spoken of the Umlimo around the campfire, or perhaps it was part of their tribal lore, although the gunbearers and most of the porters were from the Zambezi many hundreds of miles to the north. Yet Zouga had learned enough of Africa by now to recognize the strange, almost telepathic knowledge of far events and places. Whatever it was, and however they had acquired forewarning, there were thorns in the porters' feet for the first time in months.

At first Zouga was angry, and would have lived up to his nickname of Bakela, the Fist, but then he realized that their reluctance to continue toward the range of bald hills that showed above the horizon was confirmation that he was on a hot scent and close to his goal.

In camp that night, he drew Jan Cheroot aside and, speaking in English, explained what he was seeking and where. He was unprepared for the sickly expression that slowly spread over Jan Cheroot's wizened yellow features.

"Nie wat! Ik lol nie met daai goed nie!" The little Hottentot was driven in his superstitious terror to fall back on the bastard Cape Dutch. "No what! I don't mess around with that sort of thing," he repeated in English, and Zouga smiled tauntingly across the campfire at him.

"Sergeant Cheroot, I have seen you run, with a bare backside, right up to a wounded bull elephant, and wave your hat to turn him when he charged."

"Elephants," said Jan Cheroot without returning the smile, "is one thing. Witches is another thing." Then he perked up and twinkled like a mischievous gnome.

"Somebody must stay with the porters or they'll steal our traps and run for home."

Zouga left them camped near a muddy little waterhole, within an hour's march of the northernmost granite kopje. At the waterhole he filled the big enameled water bottle and wet its thick covering of felt to keep the contents cool, slung a freshly charged powder sack on one hip and a food bag on the other, and, with the heavy smooth-bore elephant gun over his shoulder, set out alone while the shadows were still long on the earth, and the grass wet with the dew.

The hills ahead of him were rounded domes of gray granite, smooth as a bald man's pate and completely free of vegetation. As he trudged toward them across the lightly forested plain, his spirit quailed at the task ahead of him.

With each step the hills seemed to rise higher and steeper, the valleys between them deeper and more sheer, the thorny bush that choked the gorges and ravines more dense. It could take months to search all of this broken wilderness, and he did not have a guide as his father had had. Yet, in the end, it was so easy that he was irritated with his own lack of foresight.

His father had written in the journals, "Even that sanguine tyrant Mzilikazi sends gifts for her oracle."

He struck the well-defined road, leading out of the west, broad enough for two men to walk along it, and aimed directly into the maze of smooth, granite hills. It could only be the road used by the emissaries of the Matabele King.

It led Zouga up the first gentle slope of ground, and then turned abruptly into one of the gorges between peaks. The path narrowed, and jinked between huge round granite boulders, the bush so thick on each side that he had to duck below the thorny branches that interlinked to form a gloomy tunnel over-head.

The valley was so deep that the sunlight did not penetrate to the floor, but the heat was thrown out by the granite as though it had been baked in an open fire, and the sweat soaked Zouga's shirt and slid in cool, tickling drops down his flanks. The bush thinned and the valley narrowed, and then pinched out into a narrow neck between the converging rock walls. It was a natural gateway where a few good spearsmen could have held a regiment. On a ledge high above was a small thatched watch hut, and beside it an idle blue tendril of smoke rising from a watch fire into the still hot air. But if there had been a guard he had deserted his post at Zouga's approach.

Zouga grounded the butt of his elephant gun, and leaned upon it to rest from the climb and at the same time surreptitiously to search the cliffs above him for a hidden enemy, or for the spot from which one could send the familiar boulders bounding and clanging down upon him.'

The gorge was silent, hot and deserted. There was not even the chittering of birds or the murmur of insects in the undergrowth. The silence was more oppressive than the heat and Zouga threw back his head and hallooed up at the deserted watch hut.

The echoes boomed grotesquely back and forth across the gorge, and then descended through confused whispers to the same foreboding silence. The last white man to pass this way was the Sword of God, in person, intent on decapitating the oracle, Zouga thought bitterly. He could not expect a hero's welcome.

He shouldered the gun again and went into the natural granite gateway, his instinct telling him that the bold approach was the only one open to him. The narrow passageway was floored with crunching gray sand, full of mica chips that sparkled like diamonds even in the subdued light. The passage curved gently until he could see neither the entrance behind him nor the end of it. He wanted to hurry, for this was like a cage, or a trap, but he controlled his feet and showed neither fear nor indecision in his tread.

Around the curve the passageway fanned open, and from one wall a small freshet rippled down the granite cliff, spilled with a tiny liquid gurgle into a natural basin of rock and then overflowed to run down into the hidden valley beyond. Zouga came out of the natural gateway and paused again to stare about

349

him. It was a pleasant valley, probably a mile long and half as wide. The rivulet watered it, and the grass was cool green.

In the center of the valley was a huddle of neatly thatched huts, around which scratched a few scrawny fowls. He went down to them. The huts were all deserted, although there was everywhere evidence of very recent occupation; even the porridge in the cooking pot was still hot.

Three of the largest huts were crammed with treasures— leather bags of salt, tools and weapons of iron, ingots of smelted red copper, a pile of small ivory tusks—and Zouga guessed that these were the tributes and gifts sent by petitioners and supplicants to the oracle. Payments made for her intercession with the rain gods, fees for a spell cast upon an enemy, or to soften a coquette's heart.

The fact that these treasures were left unguarded was proof of the Umlimo's power, and her own belief in that power. However, if Fuller Ballantyne's journal was the truth "the foul and midnight hag" as he referred to her was long ago dead, and her severed skull crunched by the hyenas or bleaching somewhere in the hot African sun.

Zouga stooped out through the low entrance of the last hut, into the sunlight once more. He called again, but again there was no answer. There were people here, many of them, but to make contact with them, and then to learn from them the location of the "burial place of the kings" was going to be more difficult than he expected.

Leaning on the long gun he turned his attention to the steep side of the valley, and again it was the pathway that caught his eye and led it to the entrance of the cave. For the path continued beyond the village, running down the center of the valley, and climbed the far slope of the valley, then came to an abrupt end against the granite cliff. The mouth of the cave was low and wide, a narrow horizontal gash in the base of the cliff like a toad's mouth, and the path led directly into it.

Zouga climbed the gentle slope to the cave entrance. He had left his food bag and water bottle at the village, and, lightly burdened, he strode upward, tall and lithe, his beard like gold thread in the sunlight, so that any hidden watcher could not have doubted that this was a chieftain and warrior to treat with respect.

He reached the cave entrance and checked, not from fatigue, for the climb had not taxed him, but merely to take his bearings. The cave entrance was a hundred paces or so wide, and the roof so low that he could reach up and touch the rough rock.

There was a guard wall built to close off the opening, a wall of dressed granite blocks, fitted so closely that it would have been impossible to drive a knife blade between the joints, clearly the work of skilled masons, but done long ago for in places the wall had tumbled, the blocks piled upon each other in disarray.

The path led into one of these gaps, and disappeared into the gloom beyond. It was a most unwelcoming entrance. Going in he would have the light at his back, and his eyes would be unaccustomed to the poor light, there would be many places where a man could wait with spear or ax. Zouga felt his first ardor cooling as he peered into that forbidding opening, and he called again in the Matabele language.

"I come in peace!"

He was answered almost immediately, in a childish piping voice speaking the same language, close behind his shoulder, so close that his heart tripped, and he whirled.

"White is the color of mourning and death," piped the voice, and Zouga looked about him in confusion. There was no child, no human, no animal even, the valley behind him was deserted, silent. The voice had emanated from the very air.

Zouga felt his mouth drying, and the skin on his forearms and at the base of his skull crawled with the loathsome little insects of fear, and while he stared another voice screeched from the cliff above him.

"White is the color of war."

It was the voice of an old woman, a very old woman, quavering and shrill. Zouga's heart jumped again, and then raced as he looked up. The cliff face was bare and smooth. His heart was fluttering against his ribs like a trapped bird, and his breath rasped and sawed in his throat.

"White is the color of slavery," sang a young girl's voice, filling the air about his head, having no direction and no substance, sweet and liquid as the burble of running water.

"She spoke in the voices of Belial and Beelzebub, the hideous voices of Azazel and Beliar, all Satan's myriad alter egos," his father had written, and Zouga felt the slow leaden spread of superstitious terror weighing down his legs.

Another voice, roaring like a bull, boomed from the mouth of the cave. "The white eagle has cast down the stone falcons."

He took a long slow breath, to bring his mutinous body under control, and he cast his mind back deliberately to a childhood memory. Brighton pier on August bank holiday, the small boy clutching his Uncle William's hand and staring up

351

in wonder at the magician on the stage who made a doll come to life and speak in a quaint piping voice, answering the voice from the box too small to contain even a rabbit. The memory steadied him, and he laughed. It was a clear firm laugh, surprising himself even.

"Keep your tricks for the children, Umlimo. I come in peace to speak with you as a man."

There was no reply, though he thought he caught the silken whisper of bare feet on stone, coming from beyond the ruined stone wall.

"See me, Umlimo! I lay aside my weapons."

He unslung the powder bag and dropped it at his feet, and then he laid the elephant gun across it and holding his empty hands before him advanced slowly into the cave.

As he reached the step in the wall, there was the crackling spitting snarl of an angry leopard from the shadows just ahead of him. It was a terrible sound, fierce and real, but Zouga had himself in hand now. He did not miss a pace but stooped under the sill through the gap, and straightened on the far side.

He waited for a minute while his eyes adjusted, and he could make out shapes and planes in the gloom. There were no other voices or animal sounds. A faint source of light showed somewhere ahead of him in the depths of the cave, and he could now make out a way among the scree and fallen rock that choked the cave, in some places as high as the low roof.

Zouga began to pick his way carefully forward. The light grew stronger, and Zouga realized that it was a single beam of sunlight, shining through a narrow crack in the roof.

Looking up, he stumbled and put out a hand to save himself. It was not rock that he touched but something sticklike that moved beneath his touch. There was a rattle, and a loose dry rush of debris. Zouga caught his balance and glanced down. A disembodied human skull gaped up at him from empty eye sockets, the cheekbones still covered with a parchment of dried skin.

In shock Zouga realized that what he had taken for loose scree and rock was instead piles of human remains, dried and desiccated corpses, lying in mounds and heaps, choking the passages and deepest recesses of the cave, here and there a single body, crouched or sprawled alone, bone shining dully from gaps in its covering of dark dried skin or through the rotting leather garments.

"That reeking charnel house," Fuller Ballantyne had called it.

Instinctively Zouga wiped the hand that had touched the long-dead skeleton, and then went on toward the light. There was the smell of smoke now, and of human presence, and another sweet mousy odor that was hauntingly familiar but which Zouga could not place at that moment. The floor of the cave sloped downward under his feet, and he turned a rocky shoulder and looked down into a small natural amphitheater, with a floor of smooth granite.

In the center of the floor burned a low fire of some aromatic wood, the smoke spiced the air and rose in a slow spiral toward the crack in the rocky roof, clouding the beam of sunlight with milky blue. There seemed to be other fingers of the cave leading further into the hillside, like the adits of a mine shaft, but Zouga's attention was focused on the figure that sat across the fire from him.

Zouga went slowly down onto the floor of the stone amphitheater without taking his eyes from the figure.

"That foul and midnight hag," his father had called the Umlimo. This was no hag. She was young, in full physical prime, and as she knelt facing him Zouga realized that he had seldom seen such a fine-looking woman, certainly not in India or Africa, and very seldom, if ever, in the northern lands.

She had a long regal neck on which her head balanced like a black lily on its stem. Her features were Egyptian, with a straight fine nose and huge dark eyes above high molded cheekbones. Her teeth were small and perfect, her lips chiseled like the flutes of a pink seashell.

She was naked, her body slim, her limbs long and fine, her hands and feet narrow and delicately shaped with tapered fingers and pale pink palms. Her small breasts rode high and were perfectly round, her waist narrow but flaring into hips like the curve of a Venetian vase. Her sex was a wide triangle, deeply cleft, the inner lips bursting out unashamedly, the wings of an exotic butterfly emerging from its woolly chrysalis.

She was watching him with those huge dark eyes, and when he stopped across the fire from her, she made a slow gracious gesture with the delicate fingers. Obediently Zouga squatted down opposite her and waited.

The woman took up one of the calabash gourds from the array beside her, holding it between the palms of her hands and poured from it into a shallow earthen bowl. It was milk. She set the calabash aside, and Zouga expected her to offer him the bowl, but she did not. She continued to watch him inscrutably.

353

"I come from the north," Zouga said at last. "Men call me Bakela."

"Your sire slew the one before me," said the woman. Her voice was compelling, for although the fluted lips barely moved, it was thrown with the power and timbre of the skilled ventril oquist. The sound of it seemed to quiver in the air long after she finished speaking and he knew now with certainty who had spoken in the voice of child and maid, of warrior and wild animal.

"He was a sick man," Zouga replied, not questioning the source of her knowledge. Not querying how she had known that he was the son of the father.

Her words explained much to Zouga, and it was logical that the Umlimo was a hereditary duty, the office of high priestess being passed on down the years. This magnificent woman was the latest bearer of the title.

"My father was driven mad by the sickness in his blood. He did not know what he did," Zouga explained.

"It was part of the prophecy." The Umlimo's statement shimmered against the cave walls, but she did not stir while the silence spun out over many minutes.

"These," Zouga spoke at last, indicating the dusty, crumbling piles of dead, "who were they, and how did they die?"

"They are the people of the Rozwi," said the woman, "and they died by fire and smoke."

"Who laid the fire?" Zouga persisted.

"The black bull from the south. The Angoni."

Zouga was silent again imagining the tribe fleeing here, to their holy place, their refuge, the women carrying the children, running like driven game ahead of the beaters, looking back over their shoulders for a glimpse of the waving tufts on the crowns of the war shields and the plumed headdresses of the Angoni *amadoda*.

He imagined them lying here in the dark listening to the ring of axes and shouts of the besieging warriors as they cut the timber and piled it in the mouth of the cave, and then the crackle of the flames as they put fire to it and the first choking acrid clouds of smoke boiled into the cave.

He could hear again in his imagination the screams and cries of the choking, dying victims, and the shouts and the laughter of the men beyond the flaming, smoking barricade of timber.

"That too was part of the prophecy," said the Umlimo and was silent. In the silence there was a soft rustling sound like a leaf blown by the breeze across the tiles at midnight, and Zouga's eyes turned toward the sound.

A dark thing flowed out of the shadows at the back of the cave, like a trickle of spilled blood, black in the gloom but catching the firelight in pinpricks of reflected light. It rustled softly across the stone floor, and Zouga felt his skin crawl and his nostrils flare at the sweetish mousy odor which he had noticed before, but which he recognized now.

It was the smell of snake.

Zouga stared at it, frozen with fascinated horror, for the reptile was as thick as his wrist and the full length of it was lost in the recesses of the cave. The head slid into the circle of orange firelight. The scales glittered with a marble luster, the lidless eyes fixed Zouga with an unblinking stare and from the slyly grinning lipless mouth the silken black tongue vibrated as it tasted his scent upon the air.

"Sweet Christ!" Zouga whispered hoarsely and dropped his hand to the hilt of his hunting knife on his belt, but the Umlimo did not move.

The snake lifted its head from the stone and dipped it over the bowl of milk. It began to drink.

It was a mamba, a black mamba, the most venomous of all the reptiles. The death it could inflict was swift but agonizing beyond all nightmares of pain. Zouga had not believed that a mamba could grow to such dimensions, for as he watched it drink half its length was still lost in the shadows.

After a minute the monstrous reptile lifted its head from the bowl and turned toward the Umlimo; it began to slide forward, the muscles under the glittering scales convulsing in little waves that came running down its length toward the broad spatulate head.

It touched the woman's bare knee with the flickering black tongue, seeming to use the tongue as a blind man uses his cane to grope its way along her thigh, licking briefly at the tips of her bulging sex, and then lifting itself up over her belly, over her breasts, still licking at her smoothly oiled skin, it rose up around her neck and then slid down over the other shoulder until it came to rest at last suspended around her neck, the head reaching out the length of a man's arm ahead of her at the level of her breasts; swaying slightly, it fixed Zouga once more with that cold ophidian stare.

Zouga licked his lips, and relaxed his grip on the hilt of the knife.

"I have come to seek wisdom," he said hoarsely.

"I know what you seek," replied the Umlimo. "But you will find more than you seek."

"Who will lead me?"

"Follow the little seeker of sweetness in the treetops."

"I do not understand." Zouga frowned, still watching the huge snake, and the Umlimo did not reply. Her silence was clearly an invitation to ponder the reply, and Zouga did so in silence, but found no explanation. He memorized the words, and would have asked another question but there was a silken rush out of the darkness near him, and he started half to his feet as a second snake slid swiftly past him.

It was another mamba, but a smaller snake, not much thicker than his thumb, and as long as twice the stretch of his arms. Half its length was raised arrow-straight in the air, and it sailed on its tail up to the kneeling woman with her grotesque living necklace.

The woman did not move, and the smaller snake stood before her, swaying gently from side to side, lowering itself gradually until it touched tongue to darting black tongue with the thick reptile around her neck.

Then it slid forward and began to roll itself around the body of the other snake, throwing turn after turn like a sailor lashing a sheet about a mast, and each time it rolled, it showed its soft white pulsating underbelly with the narrow scales reaching from flank to flank.

Neither the woman nor the bigger snake moved, nor removed their steadfast gaze from Zouga's fascinated pale face. The thinner, lighter-colored body of the second snake began a slow rhythmical and sensual movement, expanding and contracting about the thicker and darker body of the other, and Zouga realized that they were a mating pair.

Two thirds of the way down the underbelly of the male were the elongated scales that guarded the genital sac. As the male's excitement mounted, the scales gaped apart and the penis began to extrude. It was the color and shape of the bloom of a night-flowering cactus, a pale-lilac bellied flower that gleamed like wet satin.

Insistently the male caressed the thick, dark body, and gradually his ardor was rewarded. The female rolled a portion of her own length, the white belly throbbing softly in acquiescence, exposing the scaled genital purse.

With a long shuddering movement the male slid his length down hers, white belly pressed to belly, and the swollen lilac flower prised open the female sexual purse, distorting the lips.

356

The female mamba opened her mouth wide, and her throat was a lovely buttercup yellow. In her top jaw the small bony needles of her fangs were erect, each tipped with a pearly drop of venom, and she emitted a low sibilant hiss of ecstasy or pain as the male locked his penis deeply into her.

Zouga found he was sweating. A droplet slid down from his temple into his beard. The bizarre courtship and copulation had taken only minutes during which neither he nor the Umlimo had moved, but now she spoke.

"The white eagle has stooped on the stone falcons, and cast them to earth." She paused. "Now the eagle shall lift them up again and they will fly afar."

Zouga leaned forward, listening intently.

"There shall be no peace in the kingdoms of the Mambos or the Monomatapas until they return. For the white eagle will war with the black bull until the stone falcons return to roost."

While she spoke, the slow convulsing copulation of those interlocked bodies continued, giving her words an obscene and evil weight.

"Generation will war with generation, the eaglet will strive against the bull calf—white against black, and black against black, until the falcons return. Until the falcons return."

The Umlimo raised her narrow pink-palmed hands, and lifted the garland of intertwined serpents from off her own neck. She laid them gently on the stone floor of the cave and with a single flowing movement she stood erect, and the firelight glinted upon her oiled satin body.

"When the falcons return"—she spread her arms, and the round breasts changed shape at the movement—"when the falcons return, then once again the Mambos of Rozwi and the Monomatapa of Karanga will hold sway in the land." She lowered her arms and her breasts sagged weightily. "That is the prophecy. That is the whole prophecy," she said, and turned away from the fire and, with a gliding walk, moved across the irregular stone floor, her back straight and her naked buttocks swaying in stately rhythm.

She disappeared into the shadows that shrouded one of the fingers of the cave beyond the amphitheater.

"Wait!" Zouga called after her, scrambling to his feet and starting after her.

The huge female mamba hissed sharply, like the steam of a boiling kettle, and rose up as high as Zouga's head. The butter-yellow mouth gaped again, and a crest of glittering scales came angrily erect down the length of her neck.

357

Zouga froze, and the snake hissed again and flared a little higher, the raised body arching gently into a taut S shape. Zouga backed off, one pace and then another. The crest of scales subsided a little. He took another step backward and the tense bow of the serpentine body relaxed, the head lowered a few inches. He moved steadily backward toward the entrance of the cave, and before the amphitheater was obscured by the shoulder of rock he saw the huge snake coiled in a knee-high pile of glinting scales still locked in sexual congress with her deadly consort.

The prophecy of the Umlimo, cryptic and unrevealed, stayed with Zouga during the long march back to where Jan Cheroot waited with his porters.

That night, by the firelight, Zouga copied it word for word into his journal, and afterward the sweet smell of snakes haunted his nightmares—and lingered in his nostrils for long days after.

Now the wind turned fickle, sometimes completely still in the enervating hush and heat of noon, at other times dancing in the tall swaying vortex of the "dust devils" across the plains, lifting leaves and dried blades of grass hundreds of feet in the yellow columns of dust, then again it gushed in turn from every point of the compass, one minute firm out of the north and the next as firmly from out of the south.

It was impossible to come up with elephant while the wind played so loosely. Often when the spoor was hot and true, and they had already laid aside their heavy traps and stripped down to light running order, Zouga would feel the cool touch of the breeze upon the back of his sweating neck and almost immediately afterward hear the alarm squeal of an elephant ahead of them in the forest, and after that first alert, it was impossible to close with the herd, for they went into that long sloping gait that they could keep up for mile upon mile, hour upon hour, day upon night, that would kill a man who tried to match it for more than a few miles.

Thus they killed no elephant in the days following Zouga's meeting with the Umlimo, and once, when they had a good spoor which would have led them back into the north, away from the direction in which Zouga was convinced lay his quest, it was Zouga himself who called off the hunt. Jan Cheroot muttered for the rest of that day and the next while they made those seemingly aimless casts, eastward and then westward again, through the unmarked and uncharted wilderness.

Each day now the heat became fiercer, for the suicide month

358

that ushers in the rains was upon them. Not even Zouga could march during the hours before and after noon. They would find the best shade and throw themselves down under it, sweating out the worst of the heat, trying to sleep when the buffalo flies would let them, but it was an effort to speak, an effort to wipe away the sweat that welled up on their bodies and dried in white crystals on their skin and clothing. The salt rotted the fabric of Zouga's shirt and breeches so they tore like paper at the first touch of thorn or rock, and Zouga was gradually reduced to a beggar's rags, patched and stitched until little of the original material remained.

His boots had been resoled more than once with the rawhide peeled from the inner surface of an elephant's ear, and his belt and webbing, the sling of his elephant gun, renewed with uncured buffalo hide.

He made a strange gaunt figure, for hard hunting had burned all the fat and loose flesh from his body and limbs. His height was enhanced by his leanness and the breadth of his bony shoulders tapering sharply to his waist. The sun had burned his skin to leather, yet bleached his hair and beard to white gold. His hair hung to his shoulders, and he tied it at the back of his neck with a leather thong. He kept his beard and whiskers trimmed neatly, using scissors to cut and the heated blade of his hunting knife to singe them.

The sense of well-being from his superb physical condition, together with the vaunting anticipation of a successful outcome to his search, drove him onward so that the days seemed too short for him and yet when the night fell he lay down on the hard earth and slept, except for the occasional nightmare, the deep dreamless refreshing sleep of a child, to awake again long before the dawn's first glimmering, impatient for what the new day would bring forth.

However, the time was passing. After each hunt, the powder bags were lighter, and though he dug the spent musket balls from the carcasses of his victims and recast them, there was always wastage.

The precious little store of quinine dwindled as swiftly, and the rains were coming. No white man could survive the rains without ammunition and quinine. Soon he would have to abandon the search for the ruined city with its idols decked in gold. He would have to march to beat the rains, south and west, five hundred miles or more, if his observations were still accurate, to cut his grandfather's road and follow it down to the mission

359

station at Kuruman, which was the nearest outpost of European civilization.

The later he left it, the harder would be the march when he made it. Hard and fast, stopping for nothing, neither elephant nor gold, until he was out into the drier, safer land to the south.

The thought of leaving depressed him, for he knew with a certain deep gut feeling that there was something here, very close to where he now lay, and it irked him terribly that the oncoming rains would frustrate his search. But then he consoled himself that there would be another season, and he knew with the same deep gut certainty that he would return. There was something about this land— An insistent, irritating sound interrupted his thoughts. He pushed the cap up from his eyes and looked into the dense branches of the marula tree under which he lay. The harsh cries were repeated, and the drab little bird that uttered them hopped agitatedly from branch to branch, flirting its wings and tail with a sharp whirring. The bird was the size of a starling, its back dull brown and its chest and belly a muddy yellow.

Zouga rolled his head and saw that Jan Cheroot was awake also.

"Well?" he asked.

"I haven't tasted honey since we left Mount Hampden," Jan Cheroot answered. "But it's hot, and perhaps the bird is a liar, perhaps he will lead us to a snake or a lion."

"He only leads you to a snake if you cheat him of his share of the comb," Zouga told him.

"So they say," Jan Cheroot nodded and then they were silent, considering the effort involved in following the honey guide, and weighing it against the possible rewards. The bird will very often lead a badger or a human being to a wild hive, and wait for its share of the wax and honey and bee grubs. The legend is that if his payment is not made, then next time he will lead the man who cheated him to a venomous snake or a man-eating lion.

Jan Cheroot's sweet tooth got the better of him. He sat up and the bird's cries were immediately shriller and more excited. It flashed away across the clearing to the next tree, flitting wings and tail noisily, calling them impatiently, and when they did not follow it darted back to the branches above them and continued its display.

"All right then, old fellow," Zouga agreed resignedly, and stood up. Jan Cheroot took an ax from Matthew and the clay fire pot in its plaited-bark carrying net.

"Make camp here," Jan Cheroot told the bearers. "We will bring you honey to eat tonight."

Salt and honey and meat, the three greatest delicacies of the African bush. Zouga felt a twinge of guilt at wasting so much of the time that remained to him on this frivolous side journey, but his men had worked hard and traveled fast and honey would revive their flagging spirits.

The little brown and yellow bird danced ahead of them, burring and rattling, darting from tree to bush, turning as soon as it settled to make sure they were following.

For almost an hour it led them along a dry river course, and then it turned and crossed a rocky ridge of ground. At the saddle, they looked down into a heavily wooded valley bounded by the familiar rocky kopjes and hillocks.

"The bird is teasing us," Jan Cheroot grumbled. "How much further will it make us dance?"

Zouga shifted his elephant gun to the other shoulder. "I think you are right," he agreed, the valley ahead of him was forbidding, the floor choked with tall stands of the razor-edged elephant grass, higher than a man's head. It would be even hotter down there, and the dried seeds of the grass had arrowheads to them that could work themselves into the skin and cause festering little wounds.

"It comes to me that I am not so fond of honey as I thought I was," Jan Cheroot cocked his head at Zouga.

"We will turn back," he agreed. "Let the bird find another dupe. We will look for a fat kudu cow on the way back, meat instead of honey."

They started back down the ridge and instantly the bird flashed back, and renewed its entreaties above their heads.

"Go and find your friend the *ratel*, [the honey badger]!" Jan Cheroot shouted at it, and the bird's contortions became frantic. It dropped lower and lower, until it was in the branches barely an arm's length above their heads, and its cries were irritating, and distracting.

"*Voetsak!*" Jan Cheroot yelled at it. The bird's cries would alert all wild game for miles about to the presence of man, and thwart any chance of killing an animal for the night's meal. "*Voetsak!*" He stooped and picked up a stone to shy at the bird. "Go away and leave us, little sugar mouth."

The name stopped Zouga in his tracks. Jan Cheroot had used the bastard Dutch, *"klein Suiker bekkie,"* and now he drew back his right arm to hurl the stone.

Zouga caught his wrist. "Little sugar mouth," he repeated,

and the Umlimo's voice rang in his ears, that strange shimmering tone that he had memorized, "the little seeker of sweetness in the treetops."

"Wait," he told Jan Cheroot. "Do not throw."

It was ridiculous, of course it was. He would not make himself ludicrous by repeating the Umlimo's words to Jan Cheroot. He hesitated a moment. "We have come so far already," he told the Hottentot reasonably, "and the bird is so excited that the hive cannot be far."

"It could be another two hours," Jan Cheroot growled, but lowered his throwing arm. "That makes six hours back to camp."

"You don't want to grow fat and idle," Zouga said. Jan Cheroot was lean as a whippet that had been coursing rabbit all season, and he had walked and run a hundred miles in the last two days. He looked pained at the accusation, but Zouga went on remorselessly, shaking his head in mock sympathy. "But when a man grows older, he cannot march as far or as fast, and he is slower with the women too."

Jan Cheroot dropped the stone, and went back up the ridge at a furious pace with the bird flitting and screeching ecstatically ahead of him.

Zouga followed him, smiling at the little man and at his own folly in placing any store on the words of that naked witch. Still the honey would be welcome, he consoled himself.

An hour later, Zouga was convinced that Jan Cheroot had been correct. The bird was a liar, and they were wasting what remained of the day, but there would be no turning Jan Cheroot now, he had been deeply insulted by Zouga's gibes.

They had crossed the valley, blundering through the stands of elephant grass, for the bird did not pick one of the game trails to follow. It moved on a direct line, and as they followed, the grass seeds showered upon them, working their way down the back of their shirts, and the sweat of their bodies activated them, as the first rains should have done, so that they began to worm like living things, trying to pierce the skin.

The view ahead was cut off by the tall grass, and they reached the far side of the valley with little prior warning. Suddenly there was a smooth rock cliff looming over them, almost obscured by the tall leafy trees of the forest, and by its own covering of lianas and dense climbing plants. It was not a very high prominence, perhaps forty feet, but it was sheer. They stopped below it and peered upward.

The wild beehive was almost at the top of the cliff. The

honey guide fluttered triumphantly above it, twisting its head to look down at them with a single bright beadlike eye.

The rock below the opening to the hive was stained with a dark dribble of old melted wax and the detritus of the hive, but it was almost entirely masked by a lovely creeping plant. The stem of the plant climbed the cliff, branching and twisting and doubling on itself, its leaves a cool green, but its blossoms a lovely shade of cornflower blue.

The bees leaving and returning to the hive caught the sunlight like golden dust motes, except their trajectory was swift and straight through the hot still air.

"Well, Sergeant, there is your hive," Zouga said. "The bird did not lie." He felt a deep sense of disappointment. Although he had told himself to place no store on the Umlimo's words, yet there had been a sneaking anticipation, the forlorn hope persisting against common sense, and now that sense had prevailed, there was this regret.

Zouga leaned his gun against the bole of a tree, shed his traps, and threw himself down to rest and watch Jan Cheroot making his preparation to rob the hive. Jan Cheroot cut a square of bark from a makusi tree, and rolled it into a smoking tube. He filled it with wood pulp scraped from a dead tree trunk.

Then he swung the clay fire pot on its carrying sling of bark rope, fanning it until the smoldering moss and wood chips that it contained burst into flame. He transferred fire to the smoking tube, and when it had fairly taken he hooked his ax over one shoulder and began climbing the interwoven branches of the flowering creeper up the sheer cliff.

The first of the defender bees buzzed fiercely about his head when he was a few feet from the opening to the hive, and pausing, Jan Cheroot lifted the bark tube to his mouth and blew a gentle stream of blue smoke toward his attacker. The smoke drove the insect away, and he resumed the climb.

Lying under the makusi tree, idly swatting at the buffalo flies, picking at the grass under his shirt, and harboring his disappointment, Zouga watched the Hottentot work.

Jan Cheroot reached the hive, and blew another stream of smoke over the hole in the cliff, stupefying the bees, which had now formed a swirling defensive cloud about him. One of them darted in, despite the smoke, and stung him in the soft of the neck. Jan Cheroot swore bitterly, but he did not make the mistake of slapping at the attacker, or of trying to scratch away the barbed sting lodged in his flesh. He worked on calmly, unhurriedly, with the smoke tube.

Minutes later, the hive was sufficiently smoke-drugged to allow him to begin cutting away the screen of flowering branches that hid the entrance, and he balanced on a fork of the creeper, using both hands to swing the ax, perched like a little yellow monkey forty feet above where Zouga lay.

"What the thunder . . ." He stopped after a dozen ax blows, and stared at the cliff face that he had exposed. "Master, there is devil's work here."

The tone of his voice alerted Zouga, and he scrambled to his feet.

"What is it?"

Jan Cheroot's body obscured the object of his amazement, and impatiently Zouga crossed to the foot of the cliff and climbed hand over hand up the serpentine stem of the creeper.

He reached Jan Cheroot's side and clung to a handhold.

"Look!" Jan Cheroot exhorted him. "Look at that!" He pointed at the stone face that he had exposed with the ax.

It took Zouga a few seconds to realize that the entrance to the hive was through a geometrically perfect, sculptured aperture, one of a series which pierced the cliff face in a broad horizontal band, that seemed to extend unbroken in both directions along the cliff face. The decorated band was in chiseled stone blocks, arranged in a chevron pattern, a latticework that was without question the work of a skilled stonemason.

The realization jolted Zouga so that he almost missed his handhold, and immediately afterward he saw something else that up to that moment had been hidden by the dense covering of climbing plants and the thick coating of old outpouring wax from the beehive.

The entire cliff face was formed of perfect blocks of dressed stone, small blocks, so neatly fitted that they had appeared on casual inspection to be a solid sheet of rock. Zouga and Jan Cheroot were suspended near the top of the massive stone wall, forty feet high, so thick and long that it had seemed to be a granite hillock.

It was a monumental work of stonemasonry, to compare with the outer wall of Solomon's Temple, a vast fortification which could only be the periphery of a city, a city forgotten and overgrown with trees and creepers, undisturbed over the ages.

"Nie wat!" whispered Jan Cheroot. "This is a devil's place— this is the place of Satan himself. Let us go, master," he pleaded. "Let us go far away, and very fast."

* * *

The circuit of the walls took Zouga almost an hour, for the growth was thicker along the northern curve of the stone rampart. The wall seemed to be laid out in an almost perfect circle, and without openings. At two or three likely points, Zouga hacked away the growth and searched the foot of the wall, looking for a postern or a gateway. He found none.

The decorative chevron pattern did not seem to extend around the entire circumference, but covered the eastern quadrant. Zouga wondered at the significance of that. The immediate explanation seemed to be that the decoration would face the rising sun. It seemed likely that the peoples who had built this massive edifice had been sun worshipers.

Jan Cheroot trailed him reluctantly, prophesying the wrath of the devils and hobgoblins who guarded this evil place, while Zouga hacked and chopped his way around the walls, completely oblivious to his advice.

"There must be a gateway," he grumbled. "How did they get in and out?"

"Devils got wings," Jan Cheroot pointed out broodingly. "They fly. Me, I wish I had wings also, to fly the hell away from here."

They came again to the point in the wall where they had discovered the beehive, and by then it was dusk, the sun had disappeared below the treetops.

"We'll search for the gate in the morning," Zouga decided.

"We are not going to sleep here?" Jan Cheroot demanded, horrified.

Zouga ignored the protest. "Honey for supper," he suggested mildly, and for once he did not sleep that deep hunter's sleep, but lay under his single blanket, his imagination filled with golden idols and treasure-houses built out of massive worked stone blocks.

Zouga resumed the search again when it was light enough to see the top of the wall silhouetted against the misty sky of dawn. The previous day he had been blinded by his own eagerness and careless in his haste. He had missed the area, only a few yards from where they were camped, where the creepers covering the wall had once been hacked away and then had regrown, even more thickly than before. Now, however, a lopped branch beckoned him like a finger, the clean cut unmistakably made by an ax.

"Jan Cheroot," Zouga called him from the cooking fire. "Clean out this rubbish." Zouga showed him the dense secondary growth, and Jan Cheroot sauntered away to fetch his ax.

While he waited for him to return, Zouga decided that only one person could possibly be responsible for these old overgrown and healed cut marks on the stems of the vine. Once again Fuller Ballantyne had been his guide, yet this time he did not resent it so fiercely; the experience of treading squarely in his father's footsteps was no longer new, and he had his excitement and anticipation to lessen the sting of it.

"Hurry," he called to Jan Cheroot.

"It's been here a thousand years. It's not going to fall down now," Jan Cheroot answered saucily, and spat on his palms before hefting the ax.

The little Hottentot was a great deal happier this morning. He had survived a night under the wall, without being assailed by even a single hobgoblin, and Zouga had passed the unsleeping hours in describing to him the treasures that might lie beyond that wall. Jan Cheroot's temporarily paralyzed avarice had revived sufficiently to imagine himself with his pants filled with gold coin seated in his favorite tavern on the Cape Town dockside with a dozen butter-yellow Hottentot beauties crowding close to him to hear the story, while the bartender prised the wax seal off another bottle of Cape Smoke. Now his enthusiasm almost matched that of Zouga himself.

He worked swiftly and when Zouga stooped and peered into the passage that he had cut through the dense secondary growth that had sprung up behind Fuller Ballantyne's ax, he saw the outline of the curved portals of the gateway, and the chiseled granite steps that led up to the narrow opening.

The steps had been worn into a smooth dish shape by the passage of thousands of feet over the centuries, but the gateway had been deliberately blocked with stone and rubble, not the neat stonework of the main wall, but a careless and hurried attempt to seal the entrance, probably in the face of an advancing enemy, Zouga thought.

Somebody, probably Fuller Ballantyne, had pulled down this barrier sufficiently to enter. Zouga followed his tracks, the loose stone rolling underfoot; he squeezed his way through the gateway, and found that it turned abruptly to the left, into a narrow vegetation-choked passage, between high walls open to the sky.

His disappointment was intense. He had hoped that once he forced the gateway, all the city and its wonders and treasures would lie before him. Instead there were many hours

366

of hard sweating labor facing him. It had been years, four years at least, since Fuller Ballantyne had entered through this gate and passageway, and it was as though he had never been.

Where the stonework had collapsed, Zouga clambered over it gingerly, the thought and dread of snakes was very much with him since the cave of the Umlimo. The long narrow passage, obviously constructed as a defensive measure against intruders, followed the curve of the main wall until abruptly it opened into a clear space, again choked with dense green thorny growth, and dominated by a tall cylindrical tower of lichen-covered granite blocks. The tower was immense, seeming in Zouga's excitement to reach to the very clouds.

Zouga started across the intervening courtyard, hacking impatiently at the bush and creepers, and halfway across he saw that there was a second tower, an identical twin to the first that had until that moment obscured it. Now his heart was pounding fiercely against his ribs, not from the exertion of swinging the ax—but with an intuitive belief that the towers were the center of this strange ancient city, and that they held the key to the mystery.

He stumbled in his haste, and went down on his knees, tearing another long rent in his breeches and abrading a strip of skin from his shin, so he swore in his impatience and his pain. He had lost the ax but when he groped for it in the tangled roots and interwoven branches, he found it almost immediately, and at the same time uncovered the stone that had tripped him.

It was not the granite of which the walls and tower had been constructed. That fact caught his attention, and still on his knees he used the ax to clear the bush around the stone. He felt his nerves thrill as he realized that it was a work of sculpture.

Jan Cheroot had come up behind him, and now he knelt also and tore at the plants with his bare hands; then the two of them rocked back on their heels, and still squatting examined the statue that they had uncovered. It was not large, probably weighed less than a hundredweight. It was carved in satiny, greenish soapstone, sitting on that familiar ornamental plinth, the simple pattern of triangles, like a row of shark's teeth.

The head was smashed off the statue, seemingly by a blow from a sledgehammer, but more likely from a rock used as a hammer. The body of the statue was still intact, the body of the raptor, with the folded pointed wings of a bird of prey, crouching on the point of flight.

367

Zouga slipped his hand into the opening of his shirt and drew out the little ivory charm on its leather thong that he had taken from the body of the Mashona chieftain he had killed at the pass of the elephant road.

He let it nestle in the palm of his hand, comparing it with the statue. Beside him Jan Cheroot murmured, "It is the same bird!"

"Yes," Zouga agreed softly. "But what does it mean?" He dropped the ivory charm back inside his shirt.

"It is from long ago," Jan Cheroot shrugged. "We will never know." And dismissing it thus, he would have risen to his feet again, but something else caught his beady bright eye and he darted forward, his hand pecking at the loose earth beside the statue like a greedy hen, and held it up between thumb and forefinger to catch the slanted morning light.

It was a perfectly round bead of metal, pierced for the string of a necklace, a tiny bead only slightly bigger than the head of a wax vesta, and it was irregular in shape, as though beaten out under the hammer of a primitive smithy, but the color was red-yellow, and its surface was undulled by either tarnish or corrosion; there is only one metal that has that peculiar luster and sheen.

Zouga held out his hand for it almost reverently, and it had the weight and the warmth of a living thing.

"Gold!" said Zouga, and beside him Jan Cheroot giggled ecstatically, like a young bride at her first kiss.

"Gold," he agreed. "Good yellow gold."

Zouga was always aware of the very limited time left to him, and every hour or so as they worked he would lift his head to the sky with the sweat streaming down his face and neck, and greasing the flat hard muscles of his naked upper body, and always the clouds were taller and blacker, the heat more punishing, and the wind sullen as a captive tribe on the point of rebellion.

In the night he would start awake, breaking up through the drugged surface of exhausted sleep, to lie and listen to the thunder growling below the horizon like a man-killing monster.

Each dawn he shook his men from their blankets and drove them in a suppressed frenzy of impatience to their labor, and when Matthew, the gunbearer, refused to rise again after the short rest which Zouga allowed them in the hottest hour of the day, Zouga dragged him to his feet and hit him once, a short, perfectly timed chopping blow that sent him spinning backward full length into his own excavation. Matthew crawled out again with blood dribbling from his chin, and picked up the crude sieve of plaited split bamboos with which he was sifting the earth from the digging, and began again working over the piles of loose earth and rubble.

Zouga drove himself harder than he drove his small band of temple plunderers. He worked shoulder to shoulder with them as they cut out all the undergrowth from the courtyard below the twin stone towers, exposing the broken cobbles and piles of loose rubble among which lay the fallen statues.

He found six more of the bird carvings virtually undamaged, except for minor chips and the attrition of the ages, but there were the fragments of others that had been broken with a savagery which could only have been deliberate, so that he was uncertain of the original number of statues. Zouga spent little time puzzling over them. The loose earth and rubble on which they lay was rich ground for his band to pick over, though they were handicapped by the lack of tools. Zouga would have paid a hundred guineas for a set of good picks and spades and buckets. However, they had to make do with sharpened wooden stakes, the tips hardened in the fire, to dig out the loose stuff, and Jan Cheroot wove baskets of split bamboo, like the flat baskets used by the African women to winnow the stamped cornmeal, and with these they sieved the fine earth after picking over it by hand.

It was tedious, backbreaking work, and the heat was murderous, but the harvest was rich. The gold was in small pieces, mostly in the pierced round beads, from which the string had long ago rotted away, but there were flakes and flecks of thinly beaten foil, which might once have been used to decorate a votive wooden carving, there were coils of fine gold wire, and more rarely small ingots of the metal the size and thickness of a child's finger.

Once the green stone birds must have stood in a circle, facing inward like the granite columns of Stonehenge, and the gold had probably formed some part of the offerings and sacrifices made to them. Whoever had thrown down the statues had scattered and trampled the sacrifice, and time had corroded all except that lovely yellow incorruptible metal.

Within ten days of first hacking away the undergrowth that choked the inner courtyard, the temple yard, as Zouga called it, they had gleaned over fifty pounds' weight of native gold, and the interior of the stone courtyard had been gutted, the earth rutted and harrowed as though a troop of wild bush pig had rooted it out.

Then Zouga turned his full attention to the twin towers. He measured them around the base, over a hundred paces, and inspected each joint in the masonry for a secret opening. There was none, so he built a rickety ladder of raw timber and bark rope and risking neck and limb reached the top of the tallest tower. From this vantage point he could look down into the roofless passageways and courtyards of the city. It was a maze, all of it choked with growth—but there was no other part as promising as the temple courtyard of the bird statues.

He turned his attention back to the tower on which he stood. There was again no sign of a secret opening, although he searched diligently for one. It puzzled him that the ancient architect would have built such a solid structure with no apparent use or motive, and the possibility occurred to him that it might be a sealed treasure-house, built around an inner chamber.

The work of trying to penetrate the massive stonework daunted even Zouga, and Jan Cheroot declared the attempt to be madness. But Zouga had exhausted the digging below the tower, and this seemed to be the only fruitful area left to him.

Complaining, a small team led by Matthew climbed the rickety ladder, and under Zouga's supervision began loosening small blocks from the summit of the tower. However, such was the skill and dedication of the original masons that progress in the demolition was painfully slow, and there was a long pause between each crash of one loose block into the courtyard below and the next. It needed three days' unremitting toil to break a jagged aperture through the first layer of dressed blocks and to discover that the interior of the tower consisted merely of a fill of the same gray granite.

Standing beside him on the summit of the tower, Jan Cheroot voiced Zouga's own disappointment.

"We are wasting our time. It's stone and more stone." He spat over the side of the tower and watched the speck of phlegm float down into the ransacked courtyard. "What we should look for is the place the gold came from."

Zouga had been so obsessed by his search and plunder of the ruined and deserted city that he had paid no thought to the mines which must lie somewhere beyond the walls. Now he nodded his head thoughtfully.

"No wonder your mother loved you," he said. "Not only are you beautiful, but you are clever too."

"Ja," Jan Cheroot nodded smugly. "Everybody tells me that."

At that moment a fat weighty drop of rain struck Zouga's forehead, and ran down into his left eyeball so that his vision blurred. The drop was warm as blood, warm as the blood of a man racked by malarial fever.

Beyond the high walls there were other ruins, none of such proportions or importance as the inner city, however, and all of them so scattered, so overgrown and thrown down as to make detailed exploration of them out of the question in the time still available to Zouga.

The kopjes around the city had been fortified, but were deserted, the caves empty as the eye sockets of a long-dead skull, smelling of the leopards and rock rabbits who were the latest tenants, but Zouga concentrated his search on the ancient mine workings which he had convinced himself had formed the backbone of this vanished civilization. He imagined deep shafts driven into a hillside, and dumps of loose rock like the ancient Cornish tin mines, and he scoured the densely wooded country for miles in each direction, eagerly checking each irregularity of ground, each eminence that could possibly be an abandoned mine dump.

He left Jan Cheroot to oversee the scratching and sweeping up of the last tiny scraps of gold in the temple yard, and all the men profited by the new relaxed supervision. They shared views with Jan Cheroot on the role of menial work in the life of a warrior and hunter.

The first spattering of rain had been only a warning of the fury to come, and it had barely wet Zouga's shirt through to the skin before passing, but it was a warning that Zouga realized he was ignoring at his own peril. Yet still the hope of the ancient mine workings with their fat golden seams of the precious metal tantalized him, and he spun out the days until even Jan Cheroot began to worry.

"If the rivers spate, we will be trapped here," he brooded beside the campfire. "Besides, we have taken all the gold. Let us now live to spend it."

"One more day," Zouga promised him as he settled into his single blanket, and composed himself to sleep. "There is a valley just beyond the southern ridge, it will take me only another day to search it—the day after tomorrow—" he promised sleepily.

* * *

Zouga smelled the snake first, the sweet sickening stench of it filled his nostrils, so he drew each breath with difficulty, yet trying not to gasp or choke lest he call the snake's attention. He could not move, he was pinned under an immense weight which threatened to crush his ribs and the smell of snake suffocated him.

He could barely turn his head toward the place from which he knew the snake would come, and it came flowing sinuously, coil upon thick undulating coil. Its head was lifted, its eyes were unblinking and glassily fixed in the cold and deadly reptilian stare, the ribbon of its tongue flickered in a soft black blur through the icy smile of its thin curved lips. Its scales scratched softly across the earth, and they glittered with a soft metallic sheen, the color of the polished gold foil that Zouga had gleaned from the temple courtyard.

Zouga could not move nor cry out, his tongue had swollen with terror to fill his mouth and choke him, but the snake slid past him, close enough to touch if he had had command of his arms to reach out. It slid on into the circle of soft wavering light, and the shadows drew back so the birds emerged from the darkness, each on its elevated perch.

Their eyes were golden and fierce, the cruel yellow curve of their beaks echoed by the proud pout of their russet-flecked breasts and the long pinions folded across their backs like crossed blades.

Though Zouga knew they were hunting falcons with belled tresses on their legs, yet they were the size of golden eagles. They were decked with garlands of flowers, crimson blossoms of King Chaka fire, and the snowy virginal white of arum lilies. They wore necklaces and chains of gold about their arrogant necks, and as the serpent slid into the midst of the circle they stirred upon their perches.

Then as the serpent raised its glittering head with the crest of scales erect upon the back of its neck, the falcons burst into thunderous flight and the blackness was filled with the roar of their wings and the plaintive lament of their wild hunting cries.

Zouga lifted his hands to shield his face, and wings beat all about him, as the flock of falcons took flight and the presence of the snake was no longer of significance; what was important was the departure of the birds. Zouga felt a tremendous sense of doom, of personal loss, and he opened his mouth, able to utter again. He shouted at the birds to call them back to roost.

He shouted, after the soaring, buffeting thunder of the birds' wings and his own shouts and the cries of his servants woke him from the coils of the nightmare.

He woke to find the night was thunderous with the wind of the storm that swept down upon the camp. The trees tossed and thrashed their branches overhead, showering them with leaves and small twigs, and the rush of air was glacially cold. It stripped the thatch from their crudely built huts and it scattered ash and live coals from the fire. The coals, fanned into new life, were the only source of light, for overhead, the stars were obscured by the thick rolling banks of cloud that pressed close upon the earth.

Shouting to each other above the wind, they scrambled to collect their scattered equipment.

"Make sure the powder bags are kept dry," Zouga bellowed, naked except for his tattered breeches, and groping for his boots. "Sergeant Cheroot, where are you?"

The Hottentot's reply was lost in the cannon's roar of thunder that drove in their eardrums, and the flash of lightning that followed immediately seared their eyeballs, and imprinted on Zouga's vision the unforgettable picture of Jan Cheroot dancing stark naked on one foot, a red hot coal from the scattered fire stuck to the sole of the other, his wild curses lost in the drawn-out roll of the thunder and his face contorted like that of a gargoyle on the parapet of Notre Dame cathedral. Then the darkness fell on them again, like an avalanche, and out of it came the rain.

It came in cutting horizontal sheets like the blade of a harvester's scythe, so thick that it filled the air with water and they coughed and gasped like drowning men. It came with such hissing force that it stung their naked skins as though coarse salt had been fired at them from a shotgun barrel, and the cold chilled them to the bone, so that they crawled into a forlorn huddle, crowding together for comfort and warmth with the sodden fur blankets pulled over their heads, and stinking like a pack of wet dogs.

The cold gloomy dawn found them still huddled from the silver streams of falling rain, under the swollen bruised sky that pressed down upon them like the belly of a pregnant sow. Scattered and sodden equipment floated or was submerged in the ankle-deep flood of water that poured through the wind-shattered camp. The lean-to shelters had been wrecked, the campfire was a muddy black puddle of ash, there was no prospect of rebuilding it, and with that went any chance of hot food or comfort for their stiff cold bodies.

Zouga had wrapped the powder bags in strips of oilskin, and he and Jan Cheroot had held them in their laps, like ailing infants, during the night. However, it was impossible to open the bags and check the contents for damp, for the rain still teemed down out of the low gray sky in long thin silver lances.

Slipping and sloshing in the muddy footing, Zouga drove his men to make up their loads for the outward march, while he made his own final preparations. In the middle of the morning they ate a miserable and hasty meal of cold millet cakes and the last scraps of smoked buffalo meat. Then Zouga stood, with a cloak of half-cured kudu skin draped over his head and shoulders, the rain dripping from his beard and plastering his patched clothing to his body.

"Safari!" he shouted.

"And not too damned soon either," muttered Jan Cheroot, reversing his musket on its sling so the barrel pointed at the ground and the rain could not run into the muzzle.

It was then that the porters discovered the extra burden that Zouga had for them. It was lashed to carrying poles of mopani wood with bark rope, and protected by a plaited covering of elephant grass.

"They are not going to carry it," Jan Cheroot told him, squeezing the rain from his woolly eyebrows with his thumb. "I told you they would refuse."

"They'll carry it." Zouga's eyes were cold and green as cut emeralds, and his expression was fierce. "They carry it—or they'll stay here with it, dead!"

He had carefully selected the best specimen of the carved stone birds, the only one that was completely undamaged and the one on which the carving was the most artistically executed, and he had packed and prepared it for porterage himself.

For Zouga the carving was physical proof of the existence of the ancient abandoned city, proof that could not be denied when even the most cynical critic read his account in faraway London. Zouga guessed that the intrinsic value of this relic probably surpassed the equivalent weight in pure gold. The value of the artifact was not the most important consideration in Zouga's determination to carry the carving out to civilization. The stone birds had come to have a special significance to him. They symbolized for him the success of his endeavors, and by possessing one of them he had in some strange manner taken possession of this entire savage and beautiful land. He would return for the others, but he must have this single perfect specimen. It was his talisman.

"You and you." He picked two of his strongest and his usually most willing porters, and when they still hesitated, he unslung the heavy elephant gun from his shoulder. They saw his expression and knew that his intention was serious, deadly serious. Sulkily they began breaking down their own loads and distributing them among their comrades.

"At least let us leave this other thundering piece of rubbish." The rain and the cold had affected Jan Cheroot as much as the others, and he indicated the tin box that contained Zouga's dress uniform with a hatred and contempt usually reserved for animate objects. Zouga did not bother to reply, but gestured to Matthew to take it up.

It was noon before the bedraggled little column struggled through the long sodden grass that choked the valley floor and began to climb the far side, slipping and cursing in the mud.

It rained for five days and five nights. Sometimes thick drumming bursts seemed to fall in solid sheets of water from the sky; at other times it was a cold drizzling mist, that swirled gently about them as they trudged on in the soft treacherous footing, a fine silver mist that blanketed and muted all sound except the eternal dripping of the forest and the soft sighing passage of the wind in the upper branches.

The fever vapors seemed to rise from the very ground, entering their lungs with each breath, and in the icy cold mornings they writhed and twisted like the wraiths of tormented souls down in the hollows of the valleys. The porters were the first to show the symptoms of the disease, for the fever was in their bones and the cold rain brought it out so they shivered in uncontrollable spasms and their teeth chattered in their jaws until it seemed they might crack like porcelain. However, they were seasoned to the rigors of the disease and they were still able to march.

The bulky statue in its ungainly packing of grass and bark was borne painfully up the rocky ridges and down the other side by half-naked men staggering like drunks from the fever boiling in their veins, and when they reached the bank of another water course they dropped it gratefully and fell in the mud to rest without the will to cover themselves from the relentless rain.

Where there had been dried riverbeds, with drifts of white sand shining like alpine snowfields in the sun, with quiet pools of still green water, there were now maddened torrents of racing brown water, which brimmed over the high banks and carved out the roots of tall trees, toppling them into the flood and whisking them away as though they were mere twigs.

There was no possible means by which a man could cross these racing, foaming deluges; the corpse of a drowned buffalo with bloated pink belly and its limbs sticking stiffly into the air was borne downstream at the speed of a galloping horse, while Zouga stood morosely on the bank, and knew that he had left it too late. They were trapped by the spate.

"We will have to follow the river," he grunted, and wiped his streaming face on the sleeve of his sodden hunting jacket.

"It goes towards the west," Jan Cheroot pointed out with morbid relish, and it was not necessary for him to expand on the thought.

To the west lay the kingdom of Mzilikazi, King of the Matabele, and already they must be close to that vaguely defined area that old Tom Harkness had marked on his map.

"The Burnt Land—here Mzilikazi's impis kill all travelers."

"What do you suggest, my ray of golden Hottentot sunshine?" Zouga demanded bitterly. "Have you got wings to fly this?" He indicated the broad expanse of wild water, where the curled waves stood as stationary as carved sculptures as they marked the position of submerged rocks and hidden snags. "Or what about gills and fins?" Zouga went on. "Let me see you swim, or if you have neither wings nor fins, then surely you have good advice for me?"

"Yes," Jan Cheroot answered as bitterly. "My advice is that you listen to good advice when first it is given, and second that you drop those in the river." He indicated the bundled statue and the sealed uniform box. Zouga did not wait for the rest of it, but turned his back and shouted.

"Safari! On your feet, all of you! We march!"

They worked slowly west and a little south, but too much westward for even Zouga's peace of mind, though his route was dictated by the network of rivers and flooded valleys.

On the sixth day the rain relented, and the clouds broke open, revealing a sky of deep aquamarine blue and a fierce swollen sun that made their clothing steam, and stilled the fever shakes of the porters.

Even with the accuracy of his chronometer in doubt, Zouga was able to observe the meridian passage that local noon and establish his latitude. He was not as far south as he had calculated by dead reckoning, so he was probably even further west than his suspect calculations of longitude suggested.

"The land of the Mzilikazi is drier," Zouga consoled himself, as he wrapped his navigational instruments in their oilskin covers, "and I am an Englishman, and the grandson of Tshedi. Not even a Matabele would dare deny me passage, despite what old Tom writes." And he had his talisman, the stone bird, to add its protection.

Resolutely he faced west again, and drove his caravan onward. There was one other misery to add to their sufferings. There was no meat, and there had been none since the day they left the abandoned city.

With the first onslaught of the rains, the great herds of game that had been concentrated upon the last few pools and waterholes had been freed to scatter widely across the vast land where every ditch and irregularity was now at last brimming with fresh sweet water and where the baked and sun-seared plains were already blooming green with the tender first shoots of new growth.

In five days' march in the rain, Zouga had seen only one small herd of waterbuck, the least palatable of all African game with its rank turpentine-scented musk which permeates the flesh. The heavily built bull, in his shaggy plum-brown coat, led his small troop of hornless females at a frantic gallop across Zouga's front with his wide lyre-shaped horns cocked high and the perfect white circle over his buttocks flashing with each bound. He tore through the drizzling rain and dense wild ebony bush not twenty paces from Zouga. Zouga threw up the heavy gun and led on his driving shoulder.

Behind him his hungry, exhausted porters yipped like a pack of hunting dogs with anticipation, and Zouga held his aim for an instant to make certain and then squeezed off the trigger.

With a sharp crack, the cap exploded under the falling hammer, but there was not the long spurt of flame from the muzzle and the clangor of the shot, followed by the heavy thumping impact of the lead ball into flesh. The gun had misfired. The handsome antelope led his harem away at full gallop, disappearing almost immediately into the bush and rain while the dwindling clatter of their hooves mocked Zouga. He swore with frustration. He laboriously drew the ball and charge with the corkscrew tool fitted to his ramrod, and found that the insidious rain had somehow entered the barrel, probably through the nipple. The powder was as wet as though he had dipped it in the raging brown floodwaters.

Those few hours of fierce sunlight on the sixth day gave Zouga and Jan Cheroot an opportunity to spread the coarse gray contents of their powder bags on a flat rock and dry the

377

powder out so there would be less chance of another disastrous misfire, and while they did so the porters let drop their packs and limped off to find a dry spot to stretch their aching limbs.

Then too swiftly the sunlight was blotted out once more, and hurriedly they scooped the powder back into the pouches and as the fat raindrops began to hiss and splat about them they wrapped them in the worn oilskins, tucked them under their voluminous leather capes and resumed the westward trudge, heads bowed, silent and hungry and cold and miserable, Zouga's ears singing with the quinine buzz, the first apparent side effect of massive doses of the drug taken over long periods. The quinine buzz that can lead to eventual, irreversible deafness.

Despite the heavy daily doses of the bitter powder, the morning arrived at last when Zouga woke with the deep ache in the marrow of his bones, the dull weight like a heavy stone lying behind his eyes and by midday he was shaking and shivering with the alternate flood of fierce heat and deathly sepulchre cold through his veins.

"The seasoning fever," Jan Cheroot told him philosophically, "it kills you, or hardens you."

"Some individuals would appear to have a natural resistance to the ravages of this disease," his father had written in his treatise *The Malarial Fevers of Tropical Africa: Their Causes, Symptoms and Treatment*, "and there is evidence to suggest that this resistance is hereditary."

"We'll see now if the old devil knew what he was talking about," Zouga mumbled through chattering teeth, hugging the stinking wet leather coat around his shoulders. It never occurred to him even briefly to halt for his affliction; he had not accorded that courtesy to any of his men, and he did not expect it himself.

He trudged on grimly, with his knees giving a rubbery little bounce at each pace, his vision blurring and starring into little pinwheels of light, then emerging again though phantom worms and gnats still wriggled across his sight. Every now and then a touch upon his shoulder from the little Hottentot who marched behind him directed Zouga's stumbling feet back onto the path from which they had strayed.

The nights were hideous with the nightmares of his fever-inflamed brain, they were filled with the buffeting thunder of dark wings and the sickly stench of snakes so that he would wake panting and screaming, often to find Jan Cheroot holding him with a comforting arm around his shaking shoulders.

The lifting of that first bout of his seasoning fever coincided with the next brief break in the rains. It seemed that the sunlight, magnified by the lingering moisture in the air, burned away the mists from his mind and the poisonous miasma from his blood, leaving him clear-headed, with a fragile sense of well-being but a weakness in his legs and arms and a dull ache up under the right-hand side of his rib cage where his liver was still swollen and hard as a rock, the typical aftereffect of the fever.

"You will be all right," Jan Cheroot prophesied. "You threw it off as quickly as I've seen any man with his first hit of the fever. *Ja!* You are a man of Africa; she will let you live here, my friend."

It was while he still walked on wavering legs, lightheaded, so that it felt as though his feet did not touch the muddy earth but danced inches above it, that they cut the spoor.

The weight of the bull had driven the spoor a foot deep into the sticky red mud, so that it was a series of deep potholes, strung across the earth like beads on a necklace. The exact impression of the huge pads had been cast in the holes as though in plaster of Paris, each crack and fissure in the skin of the sole, each irregularity, even the outline of the blunt toenails, was there in precise detail, and at one place where the soft earth had been unable to bear his weight and the elephant had sunk almost belly-deep, he had left the impression of his long thick ivories in the earth when he had used them to push himself free.

"It is him!" breathed Jan Cheroot, without looking up from the enormous spoor. "I would know that spoor anywhere." He did not need to say more to identify the great old bull that they had last seen so many months before on the high pass of the elephant road on the escarpment of the Zambezi River.

"Not an hour ahead of us," Jan Cheroot went on in a reverential whisper, like a man at prayer.

"And the wind stands fair." Zouga found he was whispering also. He remembered his premonition that he would encounter this animal again. Almost fearfully he looked up at the sky. In the east the storm clouds were rolling ponderously toward them once more, the brief respite was almost over. The next on-slaught of the storm promised to be as fierce, and even those deep and perfect prints would soon dissolve into liquid and be washed into oblivion.

"They are feeding into the wind," he went on, trying to put the threat of rain out of his mind and concentrating his still fever-dulled wits to the problem of the hunt.

The old bull and his remaining consort were feeding and

moving forward with the wind into their faces. That way they would not walk into trouble. Yet these two old veterans, with their decades of accumulated experience, would not hold steadily into the wind for long, they would turn at intervals to get below the wind of a possible tracker.

Every minute now was of vital consideration, if the hunt was to succeed—for despite the weakness in his legs and the silliness in his head, Zouga had not for a single moment considered letting the spoor go. They might be a hundred miles within the borders of Mzilikazi's country with a Matabele impi of border guards closing swiftly, and the hours lost in following the two old bulls might make all the difference between escaping from these fever-haunted forests or leaving their bones here for the hyena to crunch, but neither Zouga nor Jan Cheroot hesitated. They began to shed their unneeded equipment, they would not need water bottles for the land was overflowing, the food bags were empty anyway, and the blankets sodden. They would shelter tonight against the old bull's massive carcass.

"Follow at your best pace," Zouga shouted to his heavily burdened porters, dropping his unwanted equipment into the mud for them to pick up. "You can fill your bellies with meat and fat tonight, if you put your feet to it now."

They had to gamble all Zouga's remaining strength on the opening play, using speed to beat the rain and to reach the bulls before they made a turn into the wind and took the scent. They ran at the spoor, going hard from the first, knowing that even a healthy man could not hold that pace beyond an hour or two at the most before his heart broke.

In the first mile Zouga's vision was starring and fragmenting again, sweat drenched his lean body and he reeled like a drunkard as his legs threatened to give under him.

"Run through it," Jan Cheroot counseled him grimly.

He did it, by a sheer effort of will. He drove himself through to that place beyond the pain. Quite suddenly his vision cleared and though there was no feeling at all in his legs they drove on steadily under him so he seemed to float over the ground without effort.

Running at his side Jan Cheroot recognized the moment when Zouga broke the shackles and went clear of his own weakness. He said nothing but glanced sideways at him, eyes bright with admiration and he nodded once. Zouga did not see that nod, for his head was up and his dreaming gaze was fixed far ahead.

They ran the sun to its zenith, Jan Cheroot not daring to

break the rhythm for he knew that Zouga would drop like a man shot through the heart if they stopped to rest. They ran on as the sun began to drop, pursued by the ponderous cohorts of the oncoming storm that threatened it with extinction, and their own shadows danced ahead of them along the deeply driven elephant spoor. In a tight bunch behind Zouga, his four gunbearers matched him pace for pace, ready to hand him a weapon at the instant he required it.

The hunter's instinct warned Jan Cheroot. He twisted his head every few minutes to look back along the trail they had already run. That was how he picked them up.

They were two gray shadows, merging softly into the darker acacia shadows below the dripping trees, but they were moving with steadfast purpose, circling to strike their own spoor again, throwing a loop about their pursuers and taking the wind from them.

The bulls were half a mile away, moving with that swinging deceptively leisurely gait that would bring them, within minutes, full onto the hot trail with which the small band of hunters had overlaid their own huge pugmarks; the trail would be reeking with the rank odor of man, the air thick with it.

Jan Cheroot touched Zouga's arm, turning him back upon their own run without checking him nor breaking the driving rhythm of his numbed legs.

"We have to catch them before they cut our spoor," he called softly. He saw Zouga's eyes come back into focus and the color flare in his waxen pale cheeks as Zouga turned and saw for the first time the two huge shapes cruising serenely through the open forest, under the tall umbrella-shaped acacias, moving with a stately deliberation down toward the string of reeking man prints in the red mud.

The big bull was leading, his gaunt frame too tall and bony for the wasted flesh over which the skin hung in deep folds and bags. The huge yellow tusks were long and heavy for the ancient head, and his ears were ripped and torn into scarred tatters that dangled onto his creased cheeks. He had been wallowing in a mudhole and his body was slick and shining with wet red mud.

He stepped out on his long, heavily boned legs around which the thick loose skin bagged and drooped like a badly tailored pair of breeches, and close behind him strode his askari, a big heavily toothed elephant, but dwarfed by his leader.

Zouga and Jan Cheroot ran together, stride for stride, their breath hissing and gasping in their throats, as they spent their last reserves to get in gunshot range before the bulls took the scent.

They traded all stealth, any attempt at concealment, for speed, trusting that the weak eyesight of the old bulls would betray them. This time, the vagaries of the weather favored them, for as they ran, the storm burst about them again.

It had held off just long enough and now the thick streamers of pale-gray rain were drawn across the forest like lace curtains and the bad light beneath the cloud banks gave them cover to cross the last few hundred yards unseen, while the tapping rain and the rush of the wind in the branches of the acacias muffled their racing footfalls.

A hundred and fifty yards head of Zouga the old bull hit the man spoor, and it stopped him as though he had run into the side of an invisible cliff of glass. He flared back on his hindquarters, his back humping and his wrinkled, ivoried head flying up high, the ragged banners of his ears filling like the mainsail of a tall ship, and clapping thunderously as he flapped them against his shoulders.

He froze like that for a long moment, groping at the tainted earth with the tip of his trunk, then he lifted it to his mouth and sprayed the scent into the open pink buds of his olfactory organs. The dread and hated odor struck him like a physical force and he went back another pace, his trunk lifted straight into the air above him, and he wheeled and like a well-trained pair of coach horses his tall askari wheeled with him; shoulder to shoulder, and flank to flank, they began to run—and Zouga was still a hundred yards behind them.

Jan Cheroot dropped onto one knee into the mud, and flung up his musket. At the same instant, the askari checked slightly and swung left, crossing his leader's rear. Perhaps it was unintentional, but neither Zouga nor Jan Cheroot believed that. They knew that the younger bull was drawing fire, protecting the other with his own body.

"You want it? Take it then, you thunder!" Jan Cheroot shouted angrily; he knew he had lost too much ground by pausing to fire.

Aiming for the younger bull, Jan Cheroot took the hip shot, and the bull staggered, flecks of red mud flying from his skin where the ball struck, and he broke his stride, favoring the damaged joint, swinging out of the line of his run, broadside to the hunters, while the great bull ran on alone.

Zouga could have killed the crippled bull with a heart shot, for the animal was down to a dragging, humpbacked trot and

382

the range was less than thirty paces, but Zouga ran straight past him, never checking, hardly glancing at him, knowing he could leave Jan Cheroot to finish that business. He was after the big bull, but despite his utmost endeavor losing ground to him steadily.

Ahead, the ground dipped into a shallow open saucer, and beyond that rose to another ridge on which the wild teak trees stood like sentinels in the rain. The bull went down into the saucer, still in his initial burst of speed, stretching out so that his padfalls sounded like the steady beat of a bass drum, opening the gap between himself and his hunter—until he reached the bottom of the dip. There, he was almost halted.

His weight broke the surface of the swampy ground, and he sank through almost to his shoulders, and had to lunge for each step, with the glutinous mud sucking and squelching obscenely at each of his frantic movements.

Swiftly Zouga closed the range, and his spirits took wing, exultation driving back his weakness and fatigue. He felt intoxicated with battle lust. He reached the swampy ground, and leaped from tussock to tussock of coarse swamp grass, while the bull struggled on ahead.

Closer and closer still Zouga came up, almost to point-blank range, less than twenty yards, and at last he stopped and balanced on one of the little islands of grass roots.

Just ahead of him the bull had reached the far side of the swamp, and was heaving himself out onto the firm ground at the foot of the slope. The bull's front legs were higher than his still-bogged hindquarters, the whole slope of his back was exposed to Zouga, the knuckles of his massive spine stood out clearly through the mud-painted skin and the arched staves of his rib cage were like the frames of a Viking longboat, Zouga fancied he could actually see the pounding rhythm of the great heart beating against them.

There could be no mistake this time. In the months since their first encounter, Zouga had become a skilled huntsman, he knew the soft and vital places in the mountainous bulk of an elephant's body. At this range and from this angle, the heavy ball would shatter the spine between the shoulder blades without losing any of its velocity, and it would go on deep, to the heart, to those thick serpentine arteries that fed the lungs.

He touched the hair trigger, and with a pop like a child's toy the gun misfired. The great gray beast heaved himself clear of the mud, and went away up the slope, now at last settling

383

into the swinging ground-eating gait which would carry him fifty miles before nightfall.

Behind him Zouga reached the firm ground and flung down the useless weapon, dancing with impatience as he screamed at his bearers to bring up the second gun.

Matthew was fifty paces behind him, slipping and staggering in the swampy ground. Mark, Luke and John were strung out behind him.

"Come on! Come on!" screamed Zouga, and snatched the second gun from Matthew, and dashed away up the slope. He had to catch the bull before he reached the crest of the slope, for down the other side he would go like an eagle on the wind.

Zouga ran now with all his heart, with all his will and the very last dregs of his strength, while behind him Matthew stopped, snatched up the misfired weapon from where Zouga had thrown it down, and, acting instinctively in the heat and excitement of the chase, reloaded it. He did not think of what he had done.

He had poured another handful of black powder on top of the charge and ball already in the barrel and tamped down a second quarter-pound ball of lead on top of it all. In so doing he changed the gun from a formidable weapon to a lethal bomb that could maim or even kill the man who attempted to fire it.

Then Matthew slipped another percussion cap over the nipple and ran on up the slope after Zouga.

The bull was nearing the crest of the ridge, and Zouga was coming up on him, but slowly, the difference in their speed just barely discernible. At last Zouga's strength was failing, he could keep this pace for minutes more and he knew when he finally stopped he would be on the verge of total physical collapse.

His vision was swimming and wavering, and his feet stumbled and slipped on the wet lichen-covered rocks of the slope, and the rain beat into his face, almost blinding him. Sixty yards ahead the bull reached the crest, and there he did something that Zouga had never seen a hunted elephant do before: he turned broadside, flaring his ears, to look at his pursuers.

Perhaps he had been pushed too hard; perhaps he had been hunted too often and the hatred had accumulated like weed below the waterline of an old ship, perhaps this was his last defiance.

For a moment he stood tall, and glistening black with mud and rain, silhouetted against the sky, and Zouga hit him in the shoulder, the gun ringing like a bronze cathedral bell, and the long lick of red flame blooming briefly in the gloom.

Both man and beast reeled to the shot, Zouga driven off balance by the recoil and the bull taking the hardened lead ball through the ribs and going back on his haunches, the rheumy old eyes clenching tightly to the shock of it.

The bull took to his feet, though he was hard hit, and he opened his eyes and saw the man, that hated, evil-smelling and persistent animal that had persecuted him so relentlessly down the years.

He launched himself back down the slope, like an avalanche of dark-gray granite, and his repeated blood squeals rang against the low sky, and Zouga turned and ran from the charging bull, while the earth trembled beneath his feet at the weight and nearness of the stricken beast.

Matthew stood his ground, even in the terrible press of the moment. Zouga loved him for that. He stood to do his duty, to deliver the second gun to his master.

Zouga reached him, just ahead of the charging bull, dropped his smoking weapon, snatched the second gun from Matthew, and as he turned he thumbed the hammer back and swung up the long thick barrel.

The bull was on top of him, blotting out the rain-sodden sky, the long yellow ivories raised like roof beams over his head, and the trunk already uncoiling to reach down and snatch Zouga up.

Zouga pressed the hair trigger, and this time the gun fired. With a roar the barrel burst, the metal opening like the petals of a flower, and burning powder flew back into Zouga's face, singeing his beard and blistering the skin. The hammer was blown clean off the barrel and hit Zouga in the cheek, just under the right eye, cutting a jagged wound clean down to the bone while the shattered weapon flew out of his grasp, and slammed back into his shoulder with such force that he felt the ligaments and tendons tearing. Zouga was hurled into a backward somersault that carried him just beyond the grasp of the bull's questing trunk.

He fell heavily behind a pile of loose stone chips, and the elephant checked, going back on its hind legs to avoid the flashing flame and smoke of the explosion, blinded and un-sighted for a moment—and then it saw the gunbearer still standing.

Matthew started to run, poor, loyal, brave Matthew, but the bull had him before he had gone a dozen paces. It took him

385

about the waist with a single coil of its long trunk, and threw him into the air as though he were light as a child's rubber ball. Matthew went up forty feet, with his arms and legs windmilling, his scream of terror unheard in the deafening squeals of the elephant. It sounded like the whistle of a steam engine blown by a crazed engineer, and Matthew seemed to rise very slowly into the air, hang for a long moment and then drop just as slowly downward.

The bull caught him in midair and threw him again, this time even higher.

Zouga dragged himself into a sitting position. His right arm hung limply on its torn muscles and tendons, blood streamed from his ripped cheek into his beard and his eardrums were so tortured by the explosion that the elephant's squeals seemed muted and far off. He looked up groggily and saw Matthew high in the air, beginning to fall, saw him hit the ground, and the elephant begin to kill him.

Zouga dragged himself to his knees, and started to creep over the mound of loose stone toward the empty gun, the gun from which he had fired the first shot and which he had dropped when he snatched the double-shotted gun from Matthew. The gun lay five paces from him, five paces which seemed an infinite distance to drag his maimed body.

The elephant placed one foot on Matthew's chest and his ribs crackled like dry sticks in a fierce fire. It took his head in its trunk and plucked it from Matthew's shoulders, as easily as a farmer kills a chicken.

The elephant tossed Matthew's head aside and as it trundled down the slope close to where Zouga sat, he saw that Matthew's eyelids were blinking rapidly over his bulging eyeballs and that the nerves flickered under the skin of his cheeks.

Tearing his eyes from the gruesome object, Zouga lifted the empty gun into his lap and began to reload it. He had no use or feeling in his right arm, which still hung limply at his side.

Twenty paces away the elephant knelt over Matthew's decapitated body and drove one of the long yellow ivories through his belly.

Painfully Zouga poured a handful of powder into the gun muzzle, trying not to be distracted from his task.

Matthew's body hung impaled through the middle from the bloody tusk like a wet shirt on a laundry line. The elephant's trunk came up and coiled pythonlike about his battered body.

Zouga dropped a ball from his pouch into the barrel of the gun, and one-handed tamped it home with the ramrod.

The elephant tore an arm from the body, and it slid from the point of the tusk and dropped once more to earth.

Moaning softly with the pain of each movement, Zouga primed the gun and hauled back the hammer against the powerful tension of the spring.

The elephant was kneeling with both front legs on what remained of Matthew, grinding a red mush against the rocky earth.

Dragging the gun with him, Zouga crawled back to the mound of rock chips behind which he had fallen. Using only his left hand, he balanced the stock of the big elephant gun over the top of the mound.

The elephant was still squealing in unabated fury as it crushed Matthew's corpse.

Groveling flat on his belly, Zouga sighted over the thick barrel, but with only one hand it was almost impossible to hold the clumsy weapon true, and his vision swam and wavered in pain and exhaustion.

For an instant the shaking foresight aligned with the crude V of the backsight, and he let the shot fly, in flame and a billowing cloud of burned powder smoke.

The elephant's squeals stopped abruptly. As the smoke was blown aside on the cold breeze, Zouga saw that the bull had hoisted himself wearily upright and was swaying slowly from foot to foot. The massive head dropped under the weight of its blood-smeared tusks and its trunk hung as limply as Zouga's own damaged right arm.

The elephant was making a strange mournful humming sound deep in his chest, and from the second bullet wound just behind his bony shoulder joint, his heart blood spurted in short regular jets, to the beat of the huge heart, and poured down his body in a honey-thick stream.

The bull turned toward where Zouga lay, and shuffling like an old and very weary man came toward him, the tip of his trunk twitching with his last fading warlike instincts.

Zouga tried to drag himself away, but the bull came on faster than he could crawl, and the trunk reached out, touched Zouga's ankle, the vast bulk of the elephant filled the sky above Zouga, and he kicked out frantically but the trunk tightened its grip on his ankle with agonizing unbearable strength, and Zouga knew that it would tear his leg out of its socket at the hip.

Then the elephant groaned, a shuddering exhalation of air from the torn lungs, the grip on Zouga's ankle relaxed as the old bull died on his feet, his legs collapsing under him and he went down.

He fell with a weight and force that made the earth bounce and tremble under Zouga's prostrate body and with a thud that Jan Cheroot, who was crossing the swamp, heard clearly from a mile away.

Zouga dropped his head against the earth and closed his eyes, and the darkness overwhelmed him.

Jan Cheroot made no attempt to move Zouga from where he lay beside the old bull's carcass. He built a rough shelter of saplings and wet grass over him and then coaxed smoky flames from a fire at his head, and from another at his feet. This was all he could do to warm him until the porters came up with the blankets at sunset.

Then he helped Zouga into a sitting position, and between them they strapped the damaged arm.

"God Almighty," croaked Zouga, as he prepared the needle and thread from his sewing kit, "I'd give both the tusks for a dram of good malt whiskey."

Jan Cheroot held the hand mirror, and using one hand only Zouga stitched the flap of his torn cheek back into place. As he pulled the knot tight and snipped the thread, he collapsed back into his damp and stinking fur kaross.

"I will die rather than march again," he whispered.

"That is your choice exactly," Jan Cheroot agreed, without looking up from the chunks of elephant liver and heart that he had begun wrapping in yellow fat before stringing them on a green twig. "You can march or die here in the mud."

Outside the hut the porters were wailing and chanting the mourning dirge for Matthew. They had gathered the fragments of his horribly mutilated body and made a package of them, wrapping them in Matthew's own blanket and binding it up with bark rope.

They would bury him the following morning, but until then they would keep up the haunting cries of mourning.

Jan Cheroot scraped coals from the fire and began to grill the kebab of liver and fat and heart over them. "They will be useless until they have buried him, and we must still cut the tusks."

"I owe Matthew a night of mourning at least," Zouga whispered. "He stood the bull down. If he had run with the second gun . . ." Zouga broke off, and groaned as a fresh stab of pain transfixed his shoulder. Using his good left hand, he scratched under the skin blanket on which he lay, moving the lumps of stone which had caused the discomfort.

"He was good—stupid, but good," Jan Cheroot agreed. "A wiser man would have run." He turned the kebab slowly over the coals. "It will take all day tomorrow to bury him and then cut the tusks from both elephants. But we must march the day after that."

Jan Cheroot had killed his bull down on the plain, under the outspread branches of a giant acacia. Looking through the low opening of the hut Zouga could see the carcass of his own bull lying on its side not twenty feet away. Already it was swelling with trapped gas and the upper legs thrust out stiffly above the gray balloon of the belly. The tusks were unbelievable. Even as he stared at them Zouga thought they must be a fantasy of his exhaustion and agony. They were as thick as a girl's waist, and the spread of them must have been twelve feet from tip to tip.

"How much will they weigh?" he asked Jan Cheroot, and the Hottentot looked up and shrugged.

"I have never seen a bigger elephant," he admitted. "We will need three men to carry each of them."

"Two hundred pounds?" Zouga asked. The conversation distracting him from the agony in his shoulder.

"More," Jan Cheroot decided. "You will never see another like him."

"No," Zouga agreed. "That is true. There will never be another like him." Deep regret blended with his pain, making it more intense. Regret for the magnificent beast and sorrow for the brave man who had died with him.

The pain and the sorrow would not let him sleep that night, and in the dawn when they gathered in the rain to bury Matthew, Zouga strapped his damaged arm into a bark sling and had two men help him to his feet, then he walked unaided but slowly and stiffly up the slope to the grave, using a staff to balance himself.

They had wrapped Matthew's body in his fur blanket and placed his possessions with him, his ax and spear, his food bowl and beer calabash, to serve him on the long journey ahead.

Singing the slow mournful song of the dead, they packed the rock over and around him to so that the hyena would not dig him out. When they had finished, Zouga felt drained of strength and emotion. He staggered back to his hut and crawled under the dank blanket. He had only that day to gather his strength for the march that must be resumed in the dawn. He closed his eyes, but could not sleep for the thud of the axes into bone as Jan Cheroot supervised the chopping of the tusks from the casket of the old bull's skull.

Zouga rolled onto his back, and once again a loose rock chip dug into his aching body. He reached back and pulled it from under the blanket, was about to throw it aside when something caught his attention and he arrested the movement.

The rock was as white and as crystalline as the candied sugar that Zouga had loved so as a boy, a pretty little fragment. But that was not what had stopped his hand.

Even in the subdued light of the hut, the thin irregular seam of metal that wavered uncertainly between quartz crystals flicked a pinprick of brightness into his eyes. Zouga stared at it numbly, twisting the lump of quartz to catch the light and make it twinkle. There was a sense of unreality about the moment, as there always is when something sought for and longed for is at last held in the hand.

He found his voice at last, a hoarse croak through his swollen, blistered, powder-scorched lips, and Jan Cheroot came almost immediately.

"The grave," he whispered urgently, "Matthew's grave, it was dug so swiftly in such rocky soil."

"No," Jan Cheroot shook his head. "It was there. There are other holes like it along the ridge."

Zouga stared at him for a long moment, his face lopsided with the scabbed and stitched wound, his one eye a mere slit in the puffed and bruised flesh. He had let himself sink low from the wound. It had been under his nose and he had almost missed it. He started to drag himself out of his blanket.

"Help me!" he ordered. "I must see them. Show me these holes."

Leaning on Jan Cheroot's shoulder, stooped to favor his shoulder, he dragged himself along the ridge in the rain, and when at last he was satisfied, he limped back to the hut and used the last feeble light of that day to scrawl in his journal, holding it in his lap and bowing over it to protect the pages from the drip of rain through the rough thatching, using his left hand so the writing was barely decipherable.

"I have named it the Harkness Mine, for this must be very similar to the ancient workings that old Tom described. The reef is white sugar quartz and runs along the back of the ridge. It would appear to be very narrow but rich, for there is visible gold in many of the samples. My injury prevents me crushing and panning these, but I would estimate values well in excess of two ounces of fine gold to the ton of quartz.

"The ancient miners have driven four shafts into the hillside. There may be more that I overlooked, for they are heavily overgrown and an attempt has been made to refill the shafts, possibly to conceal them.

"The shafts are large enough to admit a small man crawling on hands and knees. Probably they used child-slaves in the diggings and the conditions of labour in these rabbit warrens must have been infernal. In any event they were only able to go down as far as the water table, and without sophisticated machinery to pump the flooded working, they would have been abandoned. This is probably what happened here at the Harkness Mine and there is almost certainly a great amount of gold-bearing ore to be recovered by modern methods.

"The rock dump on which stands my rude hut is composed almost entirely of the gold matrix, awaiting crushing and re-fining, and the miners were probably driven away by an enemy before they could complete their labours.

"I am couched upon a mattress of gold, and like King Midas all around me is the precious metal. Like that unfortunate King, there seems to be little profit in it for me that I can perceive at this moment—"

Zouga paused, and laid his pen aside, warming his icy hands at the smoky fire. He should have felt wildly elated. He picked up his pen once again. He sighed and then wrote tortuously, "I have a huge store of ivory, but it is spread across this land, buried in small caches. I have fifty pounds and more of native gold in ingot and nugget, and I have discovered the mother lode of untold fortune, but it cannot buy me a pound flask of gunpowder nor an unguent for my grievous injuries.

"I will not know until tomorrow if I have the strength remaining to me to continue the march to the south, or if I am destined to remain here with Matthew and the great elephant as my only companions."

Jan Cheroot shook him awake. It took a long time. Zouga seemed to be swimming up from depths through cold and murky water, and when at last he surfaced, he knew immediately that his gloomy prophecy written in the journal the previous evening had become reality. There was no feeling or strength in his legs. His shoulder and arm were bound rock-hard with spasmed muscle.

"Leave me here," he said to Jan Cheroot, and the Hottentot

heaved him to a sitting position, snarling at him when Zouga cried out at the agony of each movement, and forced him to drink the steaming hot soup made from elephant marrowbones.

"Leave one gun with me," Zouga whispered.

"Here." Jan Cheroot ignored the order and instead made him take the bitter white powder. Zouga gagged on the quinine.

It took two porters to get him on his feet.

"I am leaving that stone." Jan Cheroot pointed to the packaged statue. "We cannot carry both of you."

"No!" Zouga whispered fiercely. "If I go, the bird must go with me."

"How?"

Zouga shrugged off their hands.

"I will walk," he said. "Carry the bird."

They made less than five miles that day, but the following day the sun emerged again to cheer them on. Once it warmed Zouga's abused muscles, he could increase the pace.

That night he logged ten miles in his journal when they camped in open grassland. In the dawn Zouga was able to crawl from his blankets and gain his feet unaided. His injuries still stiff, he used the staff to leave the thorn scherm by its single gate and limp to the periphery of the camp. When he urinated his water was a dark amber color from the fever and the quinine, but he knew now that he was going to be able to continue the march.

He looked up at the sky. It would rain again soon. They should start at once. He was about to turn back to the camp and rouse the porters when movement in the tall grass caught his attention.

For a moment he thought it might be a troop of wild ostrich passing the camp, then suddenly he realized that the whole plain was alive with swift but stealthy movement, the fluffy grass tops rustling and nodding with the passage of many bodies. Now and again there was a brief glimpse of ruffled plumes above the grass. The movement spread swiftly around both sides of the small camp, where Zouga's men still slept.

Zouga stared uncomprehendingly, leaning on his staff, still muzzy with sleep and fever and anchored by his injuries; he did not move until the swift encircling movement had been completed, and the stillness and silence descended again so for a moment he believed he had been imagining phantoms.

Then there was a soft fluting whistle, like a blast on Pan's pipe, sweet and hauntingly melodious in the dawn, and immediately there was movement again, an encroaching movement, like a strangler's hand upon the throat. Zouga saw the ostrich plumes clearly now, snowy white and dead black they swayed and danced above the grass tops, and immediately afterward he saw the war shields, long oval shields of dappled black-and-white cowhide. The long shields—the Matabele.

Dread was a cold, heavy lump under his ribs, yet instinct warned him that to show it would mean death, just when he had once again believed in life.

There were a hundred, he calculated swiftly as he glanced around the closing ring of warriors. No, there were more than that, at least two hundred Matabele *amadoda* in full war plumage, only the plumes and their eyes showing above the tops of the long dappled shields. The gray dawn light glinted on the broad-bladed stabbing spears, held underhand so the points protruded beyond the ring of shields. The ring was unbroken, shield overlapped shield, the encircling horns of the bull, the classic tactics of the Matabele, the finest and most ruthless warriors that the continent of Africa had ever spawned.

"Here Mzilikazi's border impis kill all travellers," Tom Harkness had written.

Zouga drew himself up and stepped forward, holding up his one good arm with the palm extended toward the ring of shields.

"I am an Englishman. A commander of the great white Queen, Victoria. My name is Bakela, son of Manali, son of Tshedi—and I come in peace."

From the ranks stepped a man. He was taller than Zouga and his tossing ostrich plumes turned him into a giant. He swept aside his shield, and he was lean and muscled like a gladiator. On his upper arms he wore the tassels of ox tails, each one awarded him by his King for an act of valor. The ox tails were thick bunches, layer upon layer. His short kilt was of spotted civet-cat tails, and there were more ox tails bound around his calves just below the knees. He had the handsome smooth moon face of the true Nguni, with a broad nose and full sculptured lips. His bearing was noble, the carriage of his head proud.

He looked at Zouga slowly and with grave attention. He looked at his tattered rags, at the untidy bindings that held his damaged arm, the staff on which he leaned like an old man.

He studied Zouga's singed beard, and powder-burned cheeks, the blisters on his lips and the black scabs that clung obscenely on his swollen discolored cheek.

393

Then the Matabele laughed. It was a deep musical laugh, and he spoke.

"And I," he said, "am Matabele. An induna of two thousand. My name is Gandang, son of Mzilikazi, son of the high heavens, son of Zulu, and I come with a bright spear and a red heart."

Robyn Ballantyne realized within the first day's march that she had seriously miscalculated her father's strength and resilience when she made the decision to try for the coast. Perhaps Zouga had divined instinctively what she, a trained physician, should have known. That thought made her angry with herself. She found that since parting with Zouga her hostility and sense of rivalry toward him had, if anything, increased. It made her angry that he should have given the correct advice.

By noon of that first day Robyn had been forced to call a halt and to go into camp. Fuller Ballantyne was very weak, weaker than he had been when first she found him. His skin was burning hot and dry to the touch. The movement of the litter, the jolting and bumping over uneven ground, had aggravated Fuller's leg. It was grotesquely swollen, and so tender that he screamed and fought at the lightest touch upon the discolored skin.

Robyn had one of the bearers begin work on a cradle of green twigs and bark to place over the leg and keep the fur blanket off it, and then she sat by the litter applying a damp, cool cloth to her father's forehead and speaking to little Juba and the Mashona woman, not expecting nor receiving advice from them, but taking comfort from the human contact.

"Perhaps we should have stayed at the cave," she fretted. "At least he would have been more comfortable there, but then for how long could we have stayed?" She spoke her thoughts aloud. "The rains will be on us soon. We could not have stayed, and even if we march as slowly as this, we will still be trapped here by them. We simply must increase the pace—and yet I do not know if he can survive it."

However, on the following day Fuller seemed stronger again, the fever had cooled, and they made a full day's march, but in the evening when they went into camp he had once more sunk very low.

When Robyn removed the dressing from the leg, it seemed to be less sensitive, and she was relieved—until she saw the color of the skin around the ulceration. When she lifted the soiled dressing to her nose and sniffed it, she caught the taint that her professor of medicine at St. Matthew's had taught her to watch for. It was not the usual taint of benign pus, but a more pervasive odor, the smell of a decomposing corpse. Her alarm flared, and she threw the dressing on the fire and with foreboding returned to her examination of the leg.

From the inside of the groin, down the wasted thigh muscles, there were the unmistakable scarlet lines beneath the thin pale skin, and the extreme sensitivity of the area seemed to have passed. It was almost as though Fuller had no further feeling in the leg.

Robyn tried to console herself that the change and mortification in the leg was unconnected with having carried him two days in a litter over rough ground. But what other reasons were there? She could find no answer. Before the move, the ulceration had been stabilized, for it was almost eighteen months since the slaver's ball had shattered the bone.

The movement in the litter must have precipitated some serious change in the limb, and this was the result.

Robyn felt herself culpable. She should have listened to Zouga. She had brought this on her own father. Gas gangrene. She could only hope that she was wrong, but she knew she was not. The symptoms were unmistakable. She could only continue the march and hope they would reach the coast and civilization before the disease swept to its inevitable climax — but she knew that hope was futile.

She wished that she had been able to develop the same philosophical acceptance that most of her fellow physicians cultivated in the face of disease or injury which were beyond their training and ability to alleviate. But she knew she never could, always she would be victim of this helpless sense of frustration, and this time the patient was her own father.

She bound up the leg in a hot compress and knew that it was a pathetic gesture, like trying to hold back the tide with a child's sandcastle. In the morning the leg felt cooler to the touch, and the flesh seemed to have lost resilience so that her fingers left depressions as though she had touched unleavened bread. The smell was stronger.

They made a full day's march, and Fuller was silent and comatose in the litter as Robyn walked beside it. He no longer chanted psalms and wild exhortations to the Almighty, and she thanked God that at least there was no pain.

In the late afternoon they met a broad pathway, well traveled and running east and west as far as Robyn could see it. It fitted exactly the description and the location that her father had written of in his journal. Little Juba burst into tears and was rendered almost helpless with terror when she saw the road.

They found an encampment of deserted and dilapidated huts that might have been those used by the slave traders, and Robyn ordered camp there. She left the Mashona woman and the still sniveling and shivering Juba to tend Fuller Ballantyne, and she took only old Karanga with her. He armed himself with his long spear, and strutted like an ancient peacock to be so honored. Within two miles, the pathway climbed steeply to pass through a saddle in a line of low hills.

Robyn was seeking evidence that this was indeed the slave road, the Hyena Road, as Juba called it tearfully.

She found her evidence on the saddle, lying in the grass a few paces from the edge of the track. It was a double yoke, hewn from a forked tree trunk and roughly dressed with an ax.

Robyn had studied the sketches in her father's journal, and she recognized it immediately. When the slavemasters did not have chains and cuffs, they used these yokes to bind their captives around their necks; two slaves linked together and forced to do everything in concert, march, eat, sleep and defecate—everything except escape.

Now all that remained of the slaves who had once worn the yoke were a few fragments of bone that the vultures and hyena had overlooked. There was something terribly sad and chilling about that roughly carved fork of wood, and Robyn could not bring herself to touch it. She said a short prayer for the unfortunate slaves who had died on that spot and then, with her knowledge that she was on the slave road confirmed, she turned back toward the camp.

That night she held counsel with the Hottentot corporal, old Karanga and Juba.

"This camp and road have not been used for this many days"—Karanga showed Robyn both hands twice with fingers spread—"twenty days."

"Which way did they go?" Robyn asked. She had come to have confidence in the old man's tracking ability.

"They were moving along the road toward the sunrise, and they have not yet returned," quavered Karanga.

"It is even as he says," Juba agreed, and it must have been an effort to agree with somebody for whom she had such disdain and jealousy. "The slavers will make this the last caravan before the rains. There will be no trading after the rivers are full, and the Hyena Road will grow grass until the dry season comes again."

"So there is a caravan of slavers ahead of us," Robyn mused. "If we follow the road we may overtake them."

The Hottentot corporal interrupted. "That will not be possible, madam. They are weeks ahead of us."

"Then we will meet them returning, after having sold their slaves."

The corporal nodded and Robyn asked him, "Will you be able to defend us, if the slavers decide to attack our column?"

"Me and my men," the corporal drew himself to his full height, "are a match for a hundred dirty slavers"—he paused and then went on—"and you shoot like a man, madam!"

Robyn smiled. "All right," she nodded. "We will follow the road down to the sea."

And the corporal grinned at her. "I am sick of this country and its savages, I long to see the cloud on Table Mountain and wash the taste of dust from my throat with good Cape Smoke once again."

The hyena was an old male. There were patches of fur missing from his thick shaggy coat, and his flat, almost snake-like head was covered with scars, his ears ripped away by thorns and a hundred snapping, snarling encounters over the decomposing carcasses of men and animals. His lip had been torn up into the soft of the nostril in one of these fights and had healed askew, so that the yellow teeth in one side of his upper jaw were exposed in a hideous grin.

His teeth were worn with age, he could no longer crush the heavy bones that made up the bulk of hyena diet, and unable to compete, he had been driven from the hunting pack.

There had been no human corpses along the trail since the slave column had passed weeks before, and game was scarce in this dry country. Since then the hyena had subsisted on scrapings, the fresh dung of jackal and baboon, a nest of field mice, the long-abandoned and addled egg of an ostrich which had burst in a sulfurous geyser of gas and putrefied liquid when he pawed at it. However, even though the hyena was starving, he still stood almost three feet high at the shoulder and weighed one hundred and forty pounds.

His belly under the matted and scruffy coat was concave as that of a greyhound. From high ungainly shoulders, his spine slanted back in a bony ridge to his scraggy hindquarters.

He carried his head low, snuffling at the earth for offal and scourings, but when the scent came down on the wind to him, he lifted his head on high and flared his deformed nostrils.

There was the smell of woodsmoke, of human presence, which he had grown to associate with a source of food, but sharper, clearer than all the others, was a smell that made the saliva run from his twisted, scarred jaws in drooling silver ropes. He went lolloping into a swaying, uneven trot up into the wind following the tantalizing drift of that odor. The scent that had attracted the old dog hyena was the cloyingly sweet taint of a gangrenous leg.

The hyena lay on the outskirts of the camp. It lay like a dog, with its chin on its front paws and its hindlegs and its bushy tail drawn up under its belly, flat behind a clump of coarse elephant grass. It watched the activity about the smoking watch fires.

Only its eyes rolled in their sockets, and the ragged stumps of its ears twitched and cocked to the cadence of human voices, and the unexpected sounds of a bucket or an ax on a stump of firewood.

Once in a while a puff of wind would bring a whiff of the scent that had first attracted the hyena, and it would snuffle it, suppressing with difficulty the little anxious cries that rose in its throat.

As the evening shadows thickened, a human figure, half-naked, left the camp, and came toward its hiding place. The hyena gathered itself to fly but before she reached the place where it lay, Juba paused and looked about her carefully without seeing the animal, then she lifted the flap of her beaded apron, lowered herself and squatted. The hyena cringed and watched her. When she stood and returned to the camp, the creature, emboldened by the oncoming night, crept forward and wolfed down that which Juba had left.

Its appetite was piqued and as the night fell, it inflated its chest, curled its bushy tail up over its back and uttered its drawn-out haunting cry, ascending sharply in key, "Oooo-auw! Oooo-auw!"—a cry so familiar to every man and woman in the camp that hardly one of them bothered to look up.

Gradually the activity about the campfires subsided, the sound of human voices became drowsy and intermittent, the fires faded, the flames sinking and the night crept in upon the camp, and the hyena crept in with it.

Twice a sudden loud voice put it to flight and it galloped away into the bush, only to gather its courage at the renewed silence and creep back. It was long after midnight when the beast found a weak place in the protective scherm of thorn branches about the camp and quietly, furtively pushed its way through the opening.

The smell led it directly to an open-sided, thatched shelter in the center of the enclosure, and with its belly low to the earth the huge doglike animal slunk closer and fearfully closer.

Robyn had fallen asleep beside her father's litter, still fully dressed and in a sitting position; she merely let her head fall forward onto her crossed arms until overwhelmed by fatigue and worry and guilt she at last succumbed.

She awoke to the old man's shrill shrieks. There was complete blackness blanketing the camp, and Robyn thought for a moment that she was blinded by a nightmare. She scrambled wildly to her feet, not certain where she was, and she stumbled over the litter. Her outflung arms brushed against something big and hairy, something that stank of death and excrement, a smell that blended sickeningly with the stench of her father's leg.

She screamed also, and the animal growled, a muffled sound through clenched jaws like a wolfhound with a bone. Fuller's shrieks and her screams had roused the camp, and somebody plunged a torch of dried grass into the ashes of the watch fire. It burst into flames, and the orange light seemed bright as noonday.

The huge humpbacked animal had dragged Fuller from his litter in a welter of blankets and clothing. It had a grip on his lower body, and Robyn heard the sharp crack of bone splintering in those terrible jaws. The sound maddened her and she snatched up an ax that lay beside the pile of firewood and struck out at the misshapen body, feeling the ax strike solidly, and the hyena let out a choking howl.

The darkness and its own starvation had emboldened it. It had the taste in its mouth now, seeping through the blankets into its locked jaws, and it would not relinquish its prey.

It turned and snapped at Robyn, its huge round eyes glowing yellow in the light of the flames and those terrible yellow fangs clashing like the snap of a steel man-trap, closing on the ax handle inches from her fingers, jerking it out of her hand. Then it turned back to its prey, and once more locked its jaws onto the frail body. Fuller was so wasted that he was light as a child and the hyena dragged him swiftly toward the opening in the thorn scherm.

Still screaming for help, Robyn stumbled after them and seized her father's shoulders, while the hyena had him by the

399

belly. The woman and the animal fought over him, the blunted yellow teeth ripping and tearing through the lining of Fuller's belly as the hyena strained back on its hindquarters, the neck stretched out at the pull.

The Hottentot corporal dressed only in unlaced breeches, but brandishing his musket, ran toward them in the firelight.

"Help me," screamed Robyn. The hyena had reached the thorn fence, her feet were slipping in the loose dust, she was not able to hold Fuller.

"Don't shoot!" Robyn screamed. "Don't shoot!" The danger from the musket was as great as from the animal.

The corporal ran forward, reversing the musket, and swung the butt at the hyena's head. It struck with a sharp crack of wood on bone, and the hyena released its grip. Finally, its natural cowardice overcame its greed. It turned and shambled through the opening in the thorn hedge and disappeared into the night.

"Oh, sweet merciful God," Robyn whispered as they carried Fuller back to the litter, "has he not suffered enough?"

Fuller Ballantyne lived out that night, but an hour after dawn that tenacious and tough old man at last relinquished his grip on life without having regained consciousness. It was as though a legend had passed, and an age had died with him.

It left Robyn feeling numbed and disbelieving and she washed and dressed the frail and rotting husk for burial.

She buried him at the foot of a tall makusi tree and carved into the bark with her own hand:

FULLER MORRIS BALLANTYNE
3rd Nov. 1788   17th Oct. 1860
"In those days there were giants upon the earth."

She wished that she had been able to cut the words in marble. She wished that she had been able to embalm his body and carry it back to rest where it belonged in the great Abbey of Westminster. She wished that he had recognized and known who she was just once before he died, she wished she had been able to allay his suffering, and she was consumed with grief and guilt.

For three days she maintained the camp astride the Hyena Road, and she spent those days sitting listlessly beside the mound of newly turned earth under the makusi tree. She drove old Karanga and even little Juba away, for she needed to be alone.

On the third day she knelt beside the grave and she spoke aloud. "I make an oath to your memory, my dear father. I swear that I will devote my entire life to this land and its people, just as you did before me."

Then she rose to her feet and her jawline hardened. The time for mourning was past. Now her duty lay plain before her: to follow this Hyena Road to the sea, and then to bear witness before all the world against the monsters who used it.

When the lions are hunting, the prey animals seem able to sense it. They are seized by a restlessness and will graze for only seconds at a time before throwing up their horned heads and freezing into that peculiar antelope stillness, only the wide trumpet-shaped ears moving incessantly; then, skittering like thrown dice, they rearrange themselves upon the grassy plains, snorting and nervous, aware of danger but uncertain of its exact source.

Old Karanga had the same instinct bred into him for he was Mashona, an eater of dirt, and as such he was natural prey. He was the first to become aware that there were Matabele somewhere close at hand. He became silent, nervous and watchful, and it infected the other bearers.

Robyn saw him pick a broken ostrich plume from the grass beside the path and study it gravely, puckering his lips and hissing quietly to himself. It had not fallen from the wing of a bird.

That night he voiced his fears to Robyn.

"They are here, the stabbers of women, the abductors of children—" He spat into the fire with a bravado that was hollow as a dead tree trunk.

"You are under my protection," Robyn told him. "You and all the people in this caravan."

But when they met the Matabele war party, it was without further warning, in the dawn when the Matabele always attack.

Suddenly they were there, surrounding the camp, a solid phalanx of dappled shields and nodding plumes, the blades of the broad stabbing assegai catching the early light. Old Karanga had gone in the night, and with him had gone all the other porters and bearers. Except for the Hottentots the camp was deserted.

Karanga's warning had not been in vain, however, and behind the thorn scherm all the Hottentot guards were standing to their muskets, with their bayonets fixed.

The encircling Matabele stood silent, and still as statues

401

carved from black marble. There seemed to be thousands upon thousands of them—though common sense told Robyn that it was merely a trick of her heated imagination and the poor light. A hundred, at the most two hundred, she decided.

Beside her Juba whispered, "We are safe, Nomusa. We are beyond the Burnt Land, beyond the border of my people. They will not kill us."

Robyn wished she were as confident, and she shivered briefly, not merely from the dawn chill.

"See, Nomusa," Juba insisted. "The baggage boys are with them, and many of the *amadoda* carry their *isibamu* [firearms]. If they intended to fight, they would not so burden themselves."

Robyn saw that the girl was right, some of the warriors had rusty trade muskets slung upon their shoulders, and she remembered from her grandfather's writings that whenever the Matabele intended serious fighting they handed their muskets, which they neither trusted nor used with any accuracy, to the baggage boys and relied entirely upon the weapon that their ancestors had forged and perfected, the assegai of Chaka Zulu.

"The baggage boys carry trade goods, they are a trading party," Juba whispered. The baggage boys were the young apprentice warriors, and beyond the ranks of fighting men they were still in column. As soon as Robyn recognized the boxes and bundles that the baggage boys carried balanced on their heads, her last qualms faded to be replaced by anger.

They were traders, that she was sure of now, and returning along the road from the east there was little doubt in Robyn's mind as to what they had traded for these paltry wares.

"Slavers!" she snapped. "In God's name and mercy, these are the slavers we seek, returning from their filthy business. Juba, go and hide immediately," she ordered.

Then, with her Sharps rifle tucked under her arm, she stepped out through the opening in the wall of thornbush, and the nearest warriors in the circle lowered their shields a little and stared at her curiously. This small change in attitude confirmed Juba's guess, their intentions were not warlike.

"Where is your induna?" Robyn called, her voice sharp with her anger, and now their curiosity gave way to astonishment. Their ranks swayed and rustled, until a man came from among them, one of the most impressive men she had ever laid eyes upon.

There was no mistaking his nobility of bearing, the arrogance and pride of a warrior tried in battle and covered in .

402

honors. He stopped before her and when he spoke his voice was low and calm. He did not have to raise it to be heard.

"Where is your husband, white woman?" he asked. "Or your father?"

"I speak for myself, and all my people."

"But you are a woman," the tall induna contradicted her.

"And you are a slaver," Robyn flared at him, "a dealer in women and children."

The warrior stared at her for a moment, then lifted his chin and laughed; a low clear musical sound.

"Not only a woman," he laughed, "but an insolent one also."

He shifted his shield onto his shoulder and strode past her. He was so tall that Robyn had to lift her chin to look up at him. He moved with a sinuous balance and assurance of carriage. The muscles in his back shone as though they were covered in black velvet, the tall plumes of his headdress nodded and the war rattles on his ankles whispered with each pace.

Swiftly he moved through the gap in the thorn hedge and at Robyn's gesture the Hottentot corporal lifted the point of his bayonet into the present position and stepped back to let the induna pass.

With a sweeping gaze the induna took in the condition of the camp and laughed again.

"Your bearers have run," he said. "Those Mashona jackals can smell a real man a day's march away."

Robyn had followed him into the camp and now she demanded with anger that was not feigned, "By what right do you enter my kraal and terrify my people?"

The induna turned back to her.

"I am the King's man," he said. "On the King's business." As though that was all the explanation that was necessary.

Gandang, the induna, was a son of Mzilikazi, the King and Paramount Chief of the Matabele and all the subservient tribes.

His mother was of pure Zanzi blood, the old pure blood of the south, but she was a junior wife and as such, Gandang would never aspire to his father's estate.

However, he was one of his father's favorites. Mzilikazi, who mistrusted nearly all of his sons, and most of his hundreds of wives, trusted this son, not only because he was beautiful and clever and a warrior without fear, but because he lived in strict accordance with the law and custom of his people, and because of his unquestioned and oft-proven loyalty to his father and his King.

For this and for his deeds, he was covered in honors to

403

which the ox-tail tassels on his arms and his legs bore witness. At four and twenty summers, he was the youngest *indoda* ever to be granted the head ring of the induna and a place on the high council of the nation, where his voice was listened to with serious attention even by the old gray pates.

The aging King, crippled with gout, turned more and more toward this tall and straight young man when there was a difficult task, or a bitter battle in the offing.

So when Mzilikazi learned of the treachery of one of his indunas, a man who commanded the border guards of the south and eastern strip of the Burnt Land, he had not hesitated before summoning Gandang, the trusted son.

"Bopa, son of Bakweg, is a traitor."

It was a mark of Gandang's favor that his father condescended to explain his orders as he issued them.

"At first, as he was ordered, he slew those who trespassed in the Burnt Land. Then he grew greedy. Instead of killing, he took them as cattle and sold them in the east to the *Putukezi* [Portugese] and the *Sulumani* [Arabs] and sent word to me that they were dead." The old King shifted his swollen and painful joints and took snuff, before going on, "Then, because Bopa was a greedy man, and the men with whom he deals are greedy also, he began to seek other cattle to trade. On his own account, and secretly, he began to raid the tribes beyond the Burnt Land."

Gandang, kneeling before his father, had hissed with astonishment. It was contrary to law and custom, for the tribes of the Mashona beyond the Burnt Land were the King's "cattle," to be raided only at the King's direction. For another to usurp the powers and gather the booty that belonged to the King was the worst form of treason.

"Yes, my son," the King agreed with Gandang's horror. "But his greed was without frontiers. He hungered for the baubles and the trash which the *Sulumani* brought him, and when this supply of Mashona 'cattle' was not enough, then he turned upon his own people."

The King was silent and his expression one of deep regret, for though he was a despot with powers that were subject to neither check nor limitation, although his justice and his laws were savage, yet within those laws he was a just man.

"Bopa sent to me messengers accusing our own people, some of them nobles of Zanzi blood, one of treachery, another of witchcraft, another of stealing from the royal herds—and I sent the messengers back to Bopa ordering him to slay the offenders. But they were not slain. They and all their people were taken along the road that Bopa had opened to the east. Now their bodies will not be buried in this land and their spirits will wander homelessly for all time."

That was a terrible fate, and the King lowered his chin upon his chest, and brooded on it. Then he sighed and lifted his head. It was a small neat head and his voice was high-pitched, almost womanish, not that of a mighty conquerer and a warrior without fear.

"Take your spear to the traitor, my son, and when you have killed him, return to me."

When Gandang would have crawled from his presence, the King halted him with one finger raised.

"When you have killed Bopa, you and those of your *amadoda* who are with you when the deed is done may go in to the women."

It was the permission for which Gandang had waited for so many years, the highest privilege, the right to go in to the women and take wives.

Gandang shouted his father's praises as he crawled backward from the royal presence.

Then Gandang, the loyal son, had done what his father commanded. He had carried his spear of retribution swiftly across all of Matabeleland, across the Burnt Land, and along the Hyena Road until he had met Bopa returning from the east laden with the spoils he so dearly coveted.

They had met at a pass through a line of granite hills, not a day's march from where Gandang now confronted Robyn Ballantyne.

Gandang's *Inyati* impi (buffalo in their ostrich plumes and civet-tail skirts, carrying the dappled black-and-white oxhide shields), had surrounded the slave guards formed from selected warriors of Bopa's *Inhlambene* impi (the Swimmers). The slavers wore white egret plumes and kilts of monkey tails, while their war shields were of chocolate-red oxhide—but right was on the side of the Inyati, and after the swift *jikela* (encirclement) they raced in to crush the guilty and confused slave guards in a few terrible unholy minutes of battle.

Gandang himself had engaged the grizzle-headed but powerfully built Bopa—a wily, scarred fighter and veteran of a thousand such conflicts. Their shields, the one dappled black and the other red, collided with a thud like charging bulls, and they wrestled for the advantage until Gandang, the younger and stronger, with a shift of weight and feet, had hooked the point of his shield under the red shield of Bopa and prised it aside to open his enemy's flank.

"Ngidla—I have eaten!" Gandang sang out as he sent the broad blade cleaving between Bopa's ribs, and when it was withdrawn against the reluctant cling of flesh with a sucking noise like that of a man walking in thick ankle-deep mud, Bopa's heart blood burst out behind it and splattered against Gandang's shield, drenching the ox-tail tassels on his arms and legs.

Thus it was for good reason that Gandang had laughed when Robyn called him "Slaver."

"I am on the King's business," he repeated. "But what do you do here, white woman?" He knew very little of these strange people, for he had been a child when the impis of Mzilikazi had fought them in the land to the south, and had been driven by them northward into what was now Matabeleland.

Gandang had met only one or two of them. They had been visitors to his father's kraal at Thabas Indunas, travelers and traders and missionaries who had been "given the road" by the King and allowed to cross the strictly guarded frontiers.

Gandang was suspicious of them and their gaudy trade goods. He distrusted their habit of breaking pieces off the rocks along their path, he disliked their talk of a white man who lived in the sky and seemed to be in serious competition with the "Nkulukulu," the great God of the Matabele.

Had he met this woman and her followers in the Burnt Land, he would have followed his orders without hesitation, and killed them all.

However, they were still ten days' march from the frontier and his interest in them was casual; he was impatient to return to his father and report to him the success of his expedition. He would not waste much further time.

"What is your business, woman?"

"I come to tell you that the Great Queen will no longer allow human beings to be sold like cattle for a few beads. I come to put an end to this evil business."

"That is man's work," Gandang smiled. "And besides, it has already been seen to."

The woman amused him; at another time he might have enjoyed bantering with her.

He would have turned and strode from the camp when suddenly a small movement seen through a gap in the thin thatch of one of the temporary shelters caught his attention. With uncanny speed for such a big man, he ducked into the hut and pulled the girl out by her wrist; holding her at arm's length he studied Juba gravely.

"You are of the people, you are Matabele," he said flatly.

Juba hung her head and her face had a grayish sheen of terror. For a moment Robyn thought that Juba's legs would no longer bear her weight.

"Speak," Gandang commanded in that low but imperious voice. "You are Matabele!"

Juba looked up at him and her whisper was so soft that Robyn hardly caught it.

"Matabele," she agreed, "of Zanzi blood."

The warrior and the maid considered each other carefully. Juba lifted her chin, and the grayness vanished from her face.

"Your father?" Gandang asked at last.

"I am Juba, daughter of Tembu Tebe."

"He is dead, and all his children, at the King's orders."

Juba shook her head. "My father is dead—but his wives and his children are in the land of the *Sulumani* beyond the sea. I alone escaped."

"Bopa!" Gandang said the name as though it were a curse. He considered a moment. "It is possible that your father was wrongly sentenced, for Bopa sent false accusation to the King."

Juba made no reply, but in the silence that followed, Robyn saw a subtle change coming over the girl, something altered in the carriage of her head, she shifted her weight, thrusting out one hip, a small but provocative movement.

Her eyes, when she looked up at the tall induna, grew wider and softer, and her lips were held slightly apart so that the pink tip of her tongue just showed between them.

"What is this white woman to you?" Gandang asked, and there was just a trace of huskiness in his own voice. He held her wrist still, and she made no effort to pull away.

"She is as my mother was," Juba replied, and as the induna looked down from her face to her sweet young body the ostrich plumes fanned softly about his head, and Juba changed the angle of her shoulders slightly, offering up her breasts to his gaze.

"You are with her by your own will?" Gandang insisted, and Juba nodded.

"So be it." It seemed to require an effort for the warrior to break his gaze, but he dropped Juba's wrist and turned back to Robyn. His smile was mocking once more.

"The slavers you seek are not far from here, white woman. You will find them at the next pass in the road."

He went as swiftly and as silently as he had come, and his warriors followed him in a dense black column. Within minutes the last of them had disappeared along the winding narrow trail into the west.

Old Karanga was the first of servants to return to the camp. He came in through the thorn scherm like a bashful stork on his thin legs.

"Where were you when I needed you?" Robyn demanded.

"Nomusa, I could not trust your temper with those Matabele dogs," old Karanga quavered, but he could not meet her eyes.

Within the hour the other porters and bearers had crept down from the hills and out of the forest, all of them now endowed with amazing enthusiasm to continue the march in the opposite direction to that of the *Inyati* impi.

Robyn found the slavers where Gandang had promised her she would. They were scattered over the neck of the pass, they lay in knots and windrows, like leaves after the first storm of autumn. Nearly all of them had their death wounds in the chest or throat, proof that at the end they had fought like Matabele.

The victors had slit open the dead men's bellies to allow their spirits to escape, a last courtesy to men who had fought gallantly, but the vultures had used the openings to enter the belly pouches.

The birds hopped and flapped and squabbled raucously over the cadavers, tugging and dragging at them so that their dead limbs kicked and twitched as though they were still alive, and dust and loose feathers flew around them. The croaking and squawking of the birds was deafening.

In the trees and on the cliffs above the pass, the birds that had already gorged crouched somnolently, puffing out their feathers and hunching their naked scaly heads and necks upon their shoulders, digesting the contents of their bulging crops before returning to the feast.

The little caravan passed slowly, in fascinated horror at the carnage, speechless in the raucous chorus of the scavengers, stepping carefully over the ragged, dust-covered remains of brave men, reminded by them of their own mortality.

Once they had crossed the pass they hurried down the far slope with fearful backward glances. There was a stream at the bottom of the slope, a tiny trickle of clear water springing from the slope and threading its way from pool to small shaded pool.

Robyn went into camp upon the bank, and immediately called Juba to follow her.

She had to bathe herself, she felt as though death had touched her with its putrid fingertips and she needed to wash away the taint of it. She sat under the trickle of clear water, waist-deep in the pool below the waterfall, and let the stream flow over her head, her eyes closed trying to blank out the horrors of the battlefield. Juba was not so affected, she was no stranger to death in its most malevolent forms, and she splashed and played in the green water, completely absorbed in the moment.

At last Robyn waded to the bank, and pulled her shirt and breeches over her still-wet body. In that heat, her clothes would dry upon her within minutes, and while she twisted her wet hair into a rope on top of her head she called to Juba to come out of the pool.

In a mischievous and rebellious mood the girl ignored her, and remained rapt in her own game, singing softly as she picked wildflowers from a creeper that hung over the pool and plaited them into a necklace over her shoulders. Robyn turned away and left her, climbing back along the bank toward the camp, and the first turn hid her from view.

Now Juba looked up and hesitated. She was not certain why she had refused to obey, and she felt a little chill of disquiet at being alone. She was not yet accustomed to this new mood of hers, this strange and formless excitement, this breathless expectancy for she knew not what. With a toss of her head she returned to her song and her play.

Standing above the bank, half screened by the trailing creeper and mottled like a leopard by the slanting dappled sunlight through the leaves of the forest, a tall figure leaned against the bole of a wild fig tree and watched the girl.

He had stood there, unseen and unmoving since he had been led to the pool by the sound of splashing and singing. He had watched the two women, comparing their nakedness—the bloodless white against the luscious dark skin, the skinny angular frame against sweet and abundant flesh, the small pointed breasts tipped in the obscene pink of raw meat against the full and perfect rounds with their raised bosses, dark and shiny as new-washed coal, the narrow hips of a boy against the proud wide basin which would cradle fine sons, the mean little buttocks against the fullness and glossiness that was unmistakably woman.

Gandang was aware that by returning along the trail he was for the first time in his life neglecting his duty. He should have

409

been many hours' march away from this place, trotting at the head of his impi into the west, yet there was the madness in his blood that he had not been able to deny. So he had halted his impi and returned alone along the Hyena Road.

"I am stealing the King's time, just as surely as Bopa stole his cattle," he told himself. "But it is only a small part of a single day, and after all the years I have given to my father, he would not grudge me that." But Gandang knew that he would; favorite son or not, Mzilikazi had only one punishment for disobedience.

Gandang was risking his life to see the girl again, he was risking a traitor's death to speak a few words to a stranger, daughter of one who had himself died a traitor's death.

"How many men have dug their graves with their own *um-thondo*," he mused, as he waited for the white woman to leave the pool, and when she had covered her skinny boy's body with those stiff and ugly garments and called to the lovely child in the pool to follow her, Gandang tried to reach out with his own will to hold Juba there.

The white woman, clearly piqued, turned and disappeared among the trees and Gandang relaxed slightly, giving himself once more to the pleasure of watching the girl in the water. The wildflowers were a pale yellow against her skin, and the waterdrops clung to her breasts and shoulders like stars against the midnight sky. Juba was singing one of the children's songs that Gandang knew so well, and he found himself humming the chorus under his breath.

Below him the girl waded to the bank and standing in the sugar-white sand began to wipe the water from her body; still singing she bent forward to wipe her legs, encircling them with long slim pink-lined fingers and running her hands slowly down from thigh to ankle. Her back was to Gandang, and as she stooped he gasped aloud at what was revealed to him, and instantly the girl flew erect and spun to face him. She was trembling like a roused fawn, her eyes huge and dark with fright.

"I see you, Juba, daughter of Tembu Tebe," he said. There was a husky catch to his voice as he came down the bank to her.

The expression in her eyes changed; they glowed with golden lights like sunshine in a bowl of honey.

"I am a messenger of the King, and I demand the right of the road," he said, and touched her shoulder. She shivered

410

under his fingers. He saw the little goose bumps rise upon her skin.

The "right of the road" was a custom from the south, from the old country beside the sea. It was the same right which Senzangakhona had demanded of Nandi, "the sweet one," but Senzangakhona had not respected the law, and he had penetrated the forbidden veil. From this transgression one had been born, the bastard "Chaka," "the worm in the belly," who had grown to become both the King and the scourge of Zululand, the same Chaka from whose tyrany Mzilikazi had flown with his tribe to the north.

"I am a loyal maiden of the King," Juba answered him shyly, "and I cannot refuse to comfort one who follows the road on the King's business." The she smiled up at him. It was neither bold nor provocative, but a smile so sweet, so trusting and filled with admiration, that Gandang felt his heart squeezed afresh.

He was gentle with her, very gentle and calm and patient, so that she found herself impatient to render the service he desired, found herself desiring it as strongly as he so evidently did. When he showed her how to make a nest for him between her crossed thighs, she responded instantly to his word and touch, and there was something wrong with her throat and her breathing, for she was unable to answer him aloud.

While she held him in this nest she felt herself gradually overwhelmed by a strange wildness of heart and body. She tried to alter the angle of her pelvis, she tried to unlock her tightly crossed thighs and spread them for him, she strove to engulf him for she could no longer bear that dry and tantalizing friction against the inside of her upper legs. She wanted to feel him breast the warm and welcoming flood that she sent down for him and she wanted to feel him gliding upon it deeply up inside her. But his resolve, his respect for custom and law, was as powerful as that muscular body that drove above her, and he held her captive until the moment when she felt his grip break and his seed spring strongly from him to waste itself in the white sand beneath them. At that moment she felt such a sense of loss that she could have wept aloud.

Gandang held her still, his chest heaving and the sweat forming little shiny runnels across that smooth dark back and down the corded neck. Juba clung to him with both arms wrapped tightly about him, her face pressed into the hollow between his shoulder and his neck, and for a long time neither of them spoke.

411

"You are as soft and as beautiful as the first night of the new moon," Gandang whispered at last.

"And you are as black and as strong as the bull of the *Chawala* festival." She instinctively chose the simile that would mean most to a Matabele, the bull as the symbol of wealth and virility and the *Chawala* bull the most perfect specimen of all the King's herds.

"You will be only one of many wives," Robyn was horrified at the thought.

"Yes," agreed Juba. "First of all of them, and the others will honor me."

"I would have taken you with me to teach you many things and show you great wonders."

"I have already seen the greatest wonder."

"You will do nothing but bear children."

Juba nodded happily. "If I am truly lucky, I will bear him a hundred sons."

"I will miss you."

"I would never leave you, Nomusa, my mother, not for any person nor reason in the world, except this one."

"He wants to give me cattle."

"Since the death of my family, you are my mother," explained Juba, "and it is the marriage price."

"I cannot accept payment—as though you were a slave."

"Then you demean me. I am of Zanzi blood and he tells me that I am the most beautiful woman in Matabeleland. You should set the *lobola* as one hundred head of cattle."

So Robyn called the induna to her.

"The marriage price is one hundred head of cattle," Robyn told him sternly.

"You make a poor bargain," Gandang answered loftily. "She is worth many times that amount."

"You will keep the cattle at your kraal, against my coming. You will tend them carefully and see that they multiply."

"It will be as you say, *amekazi,* my mother." And this time Robyn had to return his smile, for it was no longer mocking and his teeth were so white and he was, as Juba had said, truly beautiful.

"Look after her well, Gandang."

Robyn embraced the young woman and their tears mingled and smeared both their cheeks. Yet when she left Juba did not look back once, but trotted behind Gandang's tall erect figure carrying her rolled sleeping mat balanced upon her head, and her buttocks jiggled merrily under the short beaded apron.

Man and woman reached the saddle of the pass and disappeared abruptly from view.

The Hyena Road led Robyn and her little party into the mountains, into the mist and the strangely desolate valleys of heather and fantastically shaped gray stone. It led her to the slave stockades which Juba had described to her, the meeting place where the white man and black man made their trade for human life, where the slaves exchanged their carved yokes for cuff and chains. But now the stockades were deserted, the thatch already sagging and falling in untidy clumps, only the sour smell of captivity lingered, and the swarming vermin that infected the empty buildings. In a futile gesture, Robyn put fire to the buildings.

From the misty mountains the road led on, down through gorges and at last to the low littoral where once more the heat clamped down upon them from a sullen overcast sky and the grotesque baobab trees lifted their twisted arthritic branches to it like crippled worshipers at a healing shrine.

The rains caught them here upon the coastal plain. The flood swept three men away at a ford, four more, including one of the Hottentots, died of fever and Robyn herself was smitten with the first onslaught of the disease. Shivering, half demented by the phantoms of malaria, she toiled on along the rapidly overgrown trail, slipping and stumbling in the mud, and cursing the fever miasma that rose from the brimming swamps and hung like a silver wraith in the sickly-green glades of fever trees through which they hurried.

Fever and the rigors of the last stage of the journey had weakened them all. They knew that they were, at the most, only a few days' march from the coast, deep into Portuguese territory and therefore under the protection of a Christian king and a government of civilized men. It was for these reasons that the Hottentot sentries slept beside the smoldering watch fire of damp wood, and it was there that they died, their throats slit with a blade sharp enough to cut off the least cry.

So Robyn woke to rough hands upon her, twisting her arms up between her shoulder blades and a bony knee in the small of her back, while steel cuffs clicked coldly upon her wrists. Then the hands released her and she was wrenched cruelly to her feet, and dragged from the leaky hut beside the Hyena Road.

The previous evening she had been too tired and feverish to undress, so now she was still clad in a stained and rumpled flannel shirt and patched moleskin breeches. She had even kept the cloth cap on her head, covering her hair; thus in the darkness her captors did not realize that she was a woman.

With her own porters and Hottentots she was bound, forced to wear the light marching chains which were proof, if proof was needed, as to who her captors were. The dawn revealed them to be half-breeds and blacks, all of them dressed in the castoff finery of European style, but carrying modern weapons.

These were the men she had crossed half a continent to meet, but now she cowered in the rags that were her only disguise. She shuddered to think on her fate if they should discover her sex, and she berated herself for having so blithely believed that she and her entourage would be safe from these predators merely because she was white and English. Their prey was human flesh, of whatever color and condition, and that was all she was now, human flesh on the hoof. A chained creature, of little real value, a few dollars on the auction block, and she knew that her captors would think nothing of taking their pleasure upon her, or of leaving her beside the road with a ball through the temple if she provoked them in any way. She kept silent and obeyed instantly the least word or gesture from her captors. Slipping and dragging in the mud they were marched on eastward, forced to carry their remaining stores and equipment which had now become slavers' booty.

They were closer to the coast than Robyn had calculated, they smelt the iodine and salt of the sea from afar, and later as night began to fall, they caught the smell of woodsmoke and the unmistakable odor of captive humanity. Then at last they saw the firelight flickering ahead, and the awful loom of the barracoons.

Their captors marched between the dark stockades of pole and daubed mud, from which the chilling dirge rose of men without hope singing of a land they would never see again.

At last they came into the central square around which the barracoons were built. It was an open area of trampled mud where a raised platform of rough-sawn planks had been built. Its purpose was immediately clear, for the first of Robyn's servants was dragged up the steps and stood upon the platform, while the fires around the clearing were heaped with dry wood to light the scene. The platform was the auction block, and it seemed that the sale was to take place immediately.

The auctioneer was clearly of pure Portuguese stock, a little man with the wrinkled, sun-browned face of a vicious gnome. He had the bland smile and the unblinking eyes of a serpent. He was dressed in elegantly cut jacket and breeches, and his boots and belt were of the finest Iberian leather, ornately tooled and with solid silver buckles. He carried a pair of expensive pistols in his belt, and wore the wide-brimmed flat-crowned hat of a Portuguese gentleman upon his small wrinkled head.

Before climbing up on the block, he sent one of his personal slaves with a casual kick to the carved wooden drum at the edge of the clearing. On it the slave began pounding out a summons to the buyers. The slave went to it lustily, his bare torso gleaming with sweat and raindrops in the firelight.

And in answer to the urgent staccato rhythm of the drum, men came from out of the shadows of the grove and from the living huts between the barracoons. Some of them had been drinking, they came arm in arm brandishing their rum bottles and bellowing in drunken chorus, others came singly and silently—but they came from every direction and gathered in a circle about the auction block.

The men who formed the circle seemed to be of every hue that the human skin is capable of assuming, from purple black through all the shades of brown and yellow to dead-shark's-belly white, and their features were African and Arabic, Asian and European. Even their dress differed widely, from the flowing robes of Arabia to the faded finery of embroidered jackets and high boots. They had only one thing in common, the hawk-fierce eyes and merciless mien of those who deal in human misery.

One at a time Robyn's servants were prodded up on to the block, and their ragged clothing ripped away to expose their physique to the buyers. One of these might come forward to feel the muscle tone, or force open a slave's mouth to examine the teeth, like a gypsy horse dealer at the fair.

Then, when the buyers had satisfied themselves as to the quality of the wares on offer, the small Portuguese would step lightly to the front of the block and begin the bidding.

The men in the circle below him called him Alphonse and though they exchanged coarse banter with him, yet they all treated him with wary respect. There could be no clearer proof of the man's reputation than fear and respect from these men.

Under his control the sale went swiftly. The Hottentots, small wiry men, butter-yellow and with flat puglike features, attracted little interest from the circle of buyers, knocked down for a few silver rupees apiece, while the porters, taller men and well muscled from many months of hard marching and porterage, fetched better prices—until they came to old Karanga, ancient and toothless, hobbling on to the block on storklike legs, seeming barely able to support the weight of his chains.

The laughter was derisive. The little Portuguese pleaded in vain for a single bid before dismissing the old man with disgust. It was only when he was hauled down off the block and dragged away into the darkness beyond the fires that Robyn realized what was about to happen to him and, forgetting her resolve not to draw attention to herself, called out "No—let him go!"

Hardly one of them glanced in her direction, and the man who held her chain hit her a careless open-handed blow across the side of her face that blinded her for a moment. She dropped to her knees in the mud, and through the buzzing in her ears heard the thud of a pistol shot.

She began quietly to weep, and still weeping she was hoisted to her feet and in her turn dragged forward into the circle of firelight and hoisted by her chain on to the block.

"A young skinny one," said the Portuguese. "But white enough to make a choice bum boy for the harems of Omani, once he has had his knackers clipped. Who will give me ten rupees?"

"Let's have a look at him," a voice shouted from the circle, and the Portuguese turned to Robyn, hooked a finger into the top button of her flannel shirt and ripped it down to the level of her belt buckle.

She doubled over, trying to conceal her upper body, but the man behind her twisted the chain and forced her upright. Her breasts pushed out pertly through the torn shirt, and the ring of watchers growled and moved restlessly; the mood changing instantly.

Alphonse touched the butt of one of the pistols in his belt significantly, and the growl of comment died, the ring of men drew back a little.

"Ten rupees?" Alphonse Pereira asked.

From across the circle a powerfully built man swaggered into the firelight. Robyn recognized him instantly. He wore a tall beaver hat tilted back on his head, and from under the brim curled thick shiny black hair. His teeth, when he opened his mouth, sparkled in the light of the flames. His face was flushed with excitement, his voice was thick with it.

"Gold," he shouted. "I'll bid gold, and gold mohur of the

East India Company, and a plague on any of you that goes above that."

"A gold mohur," called Alphonse, the slavemaster. "A gold mohur bid by my brother Camacho Pereira, and good luck to him," he chuckled. "Come now, who wants to deny my brother Camacho a fair tup at the wench?"

One of his men slapped Camacho's back.

"Sweet Christ, you always were a hot one, at that price you can have my turn on top of her."

And Camacho laughed, and came to the front of the block to stare up at Robyn; tipping the beaver hat forward he whispered, "I've had to wait a long time—"

Robyn felt the little insects of loathing crawling over her skin, and she backed away to the limit of her chain.

"Come now," Alphonse called. "Who will go beyond a gold mohur for a fine piece—"

"She's mine," Camacho told his brother. "Strike the bargain."

His brother lifted his hand to knock down the sale, when another voice stopped him.

"A double eagle, sir. Twenty golden dollars American bid." The voice was not raised, yet it carried clearly to every man there, as it could carry from quarterdeck to maintop in a force eight gale.

Robyn started, and swung her chains disbelievingly in that direction; she would have known that lazy drawling inflection if she had not heard it for a lifetime. He stood at the very edge of the firelight, but as every head in the circle turned to him, he stepped forward.

The smile had frozen on Alphonse's face, and he hesitated.

"Call the bid!" The advancing figure in plain white shirt and black breeches made the men about him seem small and grubby, and after a moment's hesitation, Alphonse obeyed.

"A double eagle bid," he said harshly. "Captain Mungo St. John of the clipper *Huron* bids a double golden eagle."

Robyn felt her legs start to sag under her with relief, but the men behind her jerked her upright by her chain. Camacho Pereira had whirled to face the American, and to stare at him furiously. Mungo St. John answered him with a smile, indulgent and patronizing. Robyn had never seen him look more handsome and dangerous, his jet, wavy hair catching the firelight, and the gaze of his yellow-flecked eyes level and unflinching in the face of Camacho's fury.

417

"A thousand rupees, Camacho," he said softly. "Can you match it?"

Camacho hesitated, and then turned back quickly to his own brother, his voice low and urgent.

"Stake me?" he asked, and Alphonse laughed.

"I never lend money."

"To a brother?" Camacho insisted.

"Especially not to a brother," Alphonse answered. "Let the wench go, you can buy a dozen better for fifty rupees each."

"I must have her." He whirled back to face Mungo St. John. "I must have her. It is a matter of honor. Do you understand?" He took the beaver from his head, and spun it away. One of his men caught it, and Camacho ran both hands through his thick black locks, and then stretched his arms down at his sides, flexing the fingers like a conjurer about to perform a sleight of hand.

"I will make one more bid," he said ominously. "I bid one mohur of gold—and ten inches of Toledo steel." The knife seemed to appear in his hand from out of the air. He lifted the point to the level of Mungo St. John's belt buckle.

"Walk away, Yankee, or I will take the woman *and* your gold double eagle."

The watchers growled, a low bloodthirsty sound, and swiftly rearranged themselves into a ring about the two men, jostling for a better view.

"One hundred rupees says Machito slits the Yankee's guts."

"Done!" And there was a rising hubbub as wagers were called and accepted.

Mungo St. John had not stopped smiling, but now he held out his right hand without once taking his eyes off the Portuguese's face.

Out of the ranks of the watchers emerged a large, toadlike figure with a head as round and bald as a cannonball. Tippoo moved with reptilian speed to Mungo St. John's right side. He placed a knife in the outstretched hand, then unknotted the embroidered sash from his waist and handed that to his captain. Mungo wrapped the sash around his left forearm, still smiling softly to himself.

He had not once looked up at Robyn, though she had not been able to tear her own eyes from his face.

He seemed godlike to her at that moment; everything about him, the darkly classical features, the wide shoulders under the white cloth of his shirt, the narrow waist clinched with a broad belt of polished leather, the strong straight legs in tightly fitted breeches and soft leather boots, seemed to have come down directly from Olympus. She would have gladly thrown herself at his feet and worshiped him.

Just below Robyn, Camacho was stripping off his own jacket and wrapping his guard arm with it. Then with the long knife in his right hand he made a low swift cut, forehand and then backhand, so the steel whispered as it dissolved into a silver blur like the wing of a dragonfly in flight. At each stroke he ducked his head slightly and flexed his knees, loosening and warming his muscles like an athlete before the contest.

Then he moved forward, stepping lightly in the treacherous mud and weaving the point of the knife to distract and intimidate his adversary.

The smile went from Mungo St. John's lips, to be replaced by a grave and attentive expression, a mathematician considering a complex problem. He kept his own knife low, advancing his wrapped forearm, and balancing easily, stood his full height and turned gently to face the Portuguese as he circled. It reminded Robyn of the night she had watched him on the dance floor at Admiralty House, so tall and graceful, so balanced and controlled in each movement.

Now at last the watchers were silent, straining eagerly for the first glimpse of blood. But as Camacho charged they roared the way the crowd roars when the bull first bursts into the ring. Mungo St. John barely seemed to move, swaying his body at the hips so the knife slid past him, and then he was facing Camacho again.

Twice more the Portuguese attacked, and both times Mungo St. John moved effortlessly aside, but each time he gave a little ground, until he was backed up to the first rank of watchers. They began to fall back to give the American room to fight, but Camacho saw his opportunity as Mungo was crowded like a prizefighter against the ropes and he swung back to attack. At the same moment, almost as though it had been rehearsed, a booted foot shot out from the crowd. Nobody was sure whose foot it was, for the throng was closely packed and the light uncertain, but the kick to the back of Mungo St. John's heel almost brought him down sprawling in the mud, he lunged to catch his balance, but before he could do so, Camacho hit him with the long bright blade. Robyn screamed and Mungo St. John spun away from the sting of the steel with scarlet spreading wetly down his shirtfront like rich Burgundy wine spilled on a damask tablecloth, and his own knife flicked out of his hand and was lost in the red mud.

The crowd bellowed, and Camacho swarmed in eagerly, following the wounded man the way a good dog hunts a pheasant with a broken wing.

Mungo was forced to give him ground, falling back, clutching the wound, dodging and weaving, catching a forehand slash on his wrapped guard arm so the embroidered cloth split almost to the flesh beneath it.

Skillfully Camacho herded him toward the auction block, and when Mungo felt the poles catch in the small of his back, he froze for a moment as he realized that he was trapped. Camacho drove in at him, going for the belly, his lips drawn back baring his perfect white teeth.

Mungo St. John caught the knife on his guard and then snatched a grip on the wrist with his right hand. The two men stood chest to chest, their arms entwined like vines on a trellis, swaying slightly as they strained together, and the effort brought a fresh flood of blood from Mungo's wound, but slowly he forced Camacho's knife hand upward, bending it at the elbow, until the point was no longer aimed at Mungo's belly but at the night sky above them.

Mungo shifted his feet, gathering himself, and then his face darkened, his jaw clenched and his breath sobbed with effort. Slowly Camacho's wrist gave to the pressure, and his eyes widened as the point of his own knife reversed toward him.

Now he also was wedged against the side of the auction block and could not break away, and infinitely slowly but inexorably, the long blade moved toward his own chest. Both men stared down at it, their hands and arms interlocked, pitting their strength to hold each other, but the point touched Camcho's chest, a drop of blood welled up at the tiny prick.

On the block beside Robyn, Alphonse Pereira drew the pistol from his belt with a furtive movement—but before she could shout a warning there was a blur of movement and Tippoo the mate towered beside him, his own huge smooth-bore pistol pressed to the side of Alphonse's skull. The little Portuguese rolled his eyes sideways at Tippoo, then hurriedly returned the weapon to his belt, and Robyn could watch again with fascinated horror the contest at her feet.

Mungo St. John's face was congested with blood, every muscle in his shoulders and arms raised in knots under the thin shirt, his whole existence concentrated on the knife, and he slid his left foot back until it was anchored against the auction block, and then using it as a pivot hurled all his weight forward

420

onto the knife, the final effort like the matador going over between the horns for the kill.

For a moment longer Camacho resisted him, and then the blade resumed its forward movement, entering Camacho's chest as slowly as a python swallows a gazelle.

Camacho's mouth opened in a cawing burst of despair, until, suddenly, his fingers opened and all resistance and strength went out of them. His own blade with Mungo St. John's full weight behind it shot its length into his chest with such force that the crosspiece of the hilt struck against his ribs with a sharp thump.

Mungo St. John released his grip and let him fall, face forward into the mud, while he himself caught at the edge of the auction block for support. Only then did he lift his chin to look up at Robyn.

"Your servant, ma'am," he murmured, and Tippo rushed forward to catch him before he fell.

Huron's seamen, all of them armed, formed a guard about them, and Tippo led them holding aloft a bull's-eye lantern which he shone into the shadows as they hurried down the path.

Mungo St. John was on his feet, but supported by Nathaniel, his bosun, and Robyn had bound up the wound roughly with a strip of linen torn from a seaman's shirt and had used the rest of the shirt to make a sling for Mungo's right arm.

Through a grove of mangroves they reached the bank of the creek on which the barracoons had been built and in the center of the stream, her bare masts and yards silhouetted against the starry sky, lay the lovely clipper.

She had lanterns in her rigging and an alert anchor watch, for at Tippoo's first hail the whaler swung away from her side and was rowed swiftly to the bank where they stood.

Mungo climbed the ship's side unaided, but sank down with a grateful sigh on to his bunk in the stern cabin, the bunk that Robyn remembered so vividly.

She tried to force the memory from her mind and keep her manner brisk and businesslike.

"They have taken my medical chest," she said as she rinsed her hands in the porcelain basin at the head of the bunk.

"Tippoo." Mungo looked up at his mate, and the bald, scarred head bobbed once. Tippoo ducked out of the cabin. Mungo and Robyn were alone, and she tried to remain remote as she made her first examination of the wound in good lantern light.

421

It was narrow, but deep. She did not like the angle of the thrust, just below the collar bone but angled in toward the point of the shoulders.

"Can you move your fingers?" she asked. He lifted his hand toward her face and touched her cheek lightly.

"Yes," he said, as he stroked her. "Very easily."

"Don't," she said weakly.

"You are sick," he said. "So thin and pale."

"It is nothing—lower your arm, please."

She was terribly conscious of her matted hair and filthy mud-stained clothing, of the yellow tinges of fever on her skin and the smudges of fatigue and terror under her eyes.

"Fever?" he asked quietly, and she nodded as she went on working on the wound.

"Strange," he murmured. "It makes you seem so young, so fragile," he paused, "so lovely."

"I forbid you to talk like that." She felt flustered, uncertain of herself.

"I said I would not forget you," he ignored the instruction, "and I did not."

"If you don't stop, I will leave immediately."

"When I saw your face tonight in the light of the fires, I could not believe it was you, and at the same time it was as though all our lives we had a rendezvous to keep here tonight. As though it had been destined from the moment of our births."

"Please," she whispered, "please stop."

"That's better—please is better. Now I will stop."

But he watched her face attentively as she worked. In the ship's medical chest which he kept in the locker below his bunk Robyn found most of what she needed.

He neither flinched nor grimaced as she laid the stitches in the wound, but went on watching her.

"You must rest now," she said as she finished, and he lay back on the bunk. At last he looked tired and drained, and she felt a rush of gratitude, of pity, and of that other emotion which she had believed that she had long ago subdued.

"You saved me." She dropped her eyes, no longer able to look at him and busied herself with repacking the ship's chest. "I will always be grateful for that, just as I will always hate you for what you are doing here."

"What am I doing here?" he challenged her lightly.

"Buying slaves," she accused. "Buying human lives, just as you bought me on the slaving block."

"But for a much lower price," he agreed as he closed his

eyes. "At twenty dollars gold a head there is not much profit in it, I assure you."

She awoke in the small cabin, the same cabin in which she had sailed the length of the Atlantic Ocean and in the same narrow uncomfortable bunk.

It was like homecoming. The first thing she saw after her eyes had adjusted to the harsh beam of sunlight through the skylight was the chests of her medical instruments, her remaining medicines and her few personal possessions.

She remembered the unspoken command that Mungo had given to the mate the previous evening. Tippoo must have gone back ashore during the night, and she wondered what price he had paid or what threat he had made to get them back for her.

She rose swiftly from her bunk, ashamed of her sloth; whoever had left the chests had also filled the enamel jug with fresh water. With relief she washed away the mud and filth and combed the tangles of her hair before finding worn but clean clothing in her chest. Then she hurried from her cabin down to the master's quarters. If Tippoo had been able to find her chests, then he might be able to find and free her people, the Hottentots and porters who had gone upon the auction block in the firelight.

Mungo's bunk was empty, the vest and bloodstained shirt bundled and thrown into a corner of the cabin, and the bedclothes in disarray. She turned swiftly for the deck, and as she came out into the sunlight she saw that it would be only a temporary respite from the monsoon, for already the thunderclouds were boiling up over the horizon.

She looked about her quickly. *Huron* lay in the center of a broad estuary, with mangroves on each bank, and the bar and the open sea was not in sight, though the tide was ebbing, rustling down the ship's hull and leaving the mud flats half exposed.

There were other vessels in the roadstead, mostly big dhow-rigged buggaloos typical of the Arab coastal traders, but there was another fully rigged ship at anchor half a mile further downstream, flying the flag of Brazil at her peak. Even as Robyn paused to watch her, there came the clank of her capstan, and men ran up the ratlines and spread out along her yards. She was getting under way. Then Robyn realized that there was unusual activity all about her. Small boats were plying from the shore to the anchored dhows, and even on *Huron* there was a huddle of men on the quarterdeck.

Robyn turned toward them, and realized that the tallest of them was Mungo St. John. His arm was in a sling and he looked drawn and pale, but his expression was forbidding, the curved brows drawn together in a frown, and the mouth a thin cruel line as he listened attentively to one of his seamen. So absorbed was he that he did not notice Robyn until she was only a few paces away. Then he swung toward her, and all the questions and demands stayed behind her lips for his voice was harsh.

"Your coming was an act of God, Dr. Ballantyne," he said.

"Why do you say that?"

"There is a plague in the barracoons," he said. "Most of the other buyers are cutting their losses, and leaving." He glanced downstream to where the Brazilian schooner had set reefed main and jib and was running down toward the bar and the open sea, and there was activity aboard most of the other vessels.

"But I have over a thousand prime blacks afattening ashore— and I'll be damned if I'll run now. At least, not until I know what it is."

Robyn stared at him. Her mind was a whirl of doubts and fears. "Plague" was a layman's word, it covered everything from the black death to syphilis, the grand pox, as it was called.

"I will go ashore immediately," she said, and Mungo St. John nodded.

"I thought you would say that," he said, "I will go with you."

"No." Her tone brooked no argument. "You will aggravate that wound, and in your weakened condition you will be easy prey to this plague, whatever it is." She glanced at Tippoo, and his face split laterally into that broad toadlike grin and he stepped up beside her.

"By God, ma'am, I've had them all," said Nathaniel, the little pockmarked bosun. "And none of them killed me yet." And he stepped up to her other hand.

Robyn sat in the stern while Tippoo and Nathaniel handled the oars, and as they pulled across the ebb the bosun explained what they would find ashore.

"Each of the traders has his own barracoon built and guarded by his own men," he told Robyn. "He buys from the Portos as the blackbirds are brought in."

As Robyn listened to Nathaniel, she realized the answers to questions that had worried her and Zouga. This was the reason why Pereira had tried so desperately to persuade them not to bring the expedition south of the Zambezi River, and why, when all else had failed, he had attacked it with his armed brigands and tried to destroy it. He had been protecting his brother's trade routes and selling area. It was not mere avarice and lust, but a logical attempt to preserve this lucrative enterprise from discovery.

She went on listening to Nathaniel.

"Each trader fattens his wares ashore, like pigs for the market. That way they are stronger for the crossing, and he makes sure that they are healthy and not going to bring sickness aboard with them.

"There are twenty-three barracoons here, some small ones with twenty blacks or so, belonging to the small traders, right on up to the big ones like *Huron*'s, with a thousand and more prime blackbirds in the cage.

"We have the slave decks set up in *Huron*'s hold, and we would have begun taking them aboard any day, but now—"

Nathaniel shrugged, and spat on the horny calloused palms of each hand in turn, and then plied himself to oars once more.

"Are you a Christian, Nathaniel?" Robyn asked softly.

"That I am, ma'am," he said proudly. "As good a Christian as ever sailed out of Martha's Vineyard."

"Do you think God approves of what you are doing here to these poor people?"

"Hewers of wood, ma'am, and drawers of water, like the Bible says," the weatherbeaten sailor told her, so glibly that she knew that the reply had been put in his mouth, and she guessed by whom.

Once they were ashore, Tippoo led the small party with Robyn in the center and Nathaniel in the rear.

Captain Mungo St. John had chosen the best site available for his barracoon, on a rise of ground at a distance from the river. The sheds were well built, with floors of sawn timber raised above the mud and good roofs thatched with palmetto leaves.

Huron's guards had not deserted, proof of the discipline which Mungo St. John maintained, and the slaves in the barracks had evidently been carefully chosen. They were all well-set-up men and women, and the copper cookers were filled with boiling farina so that their bellies bulged and their skins were glossy.

At Robyn's direction they were lined up and she passed swiftly down the ranks. There were some mild ailments, which she singled out for later treatment, but she found none of the symptoms which she so dreaded.

"There is no plague here," she decided. "Not yet."

"Come!" said Tippoo.

He led her through the palm groves, and the next barracoon had been deserted by the traders who had built it and stocked it. Already the slaves were hungry and confused by their sudden liberation.

"You are free to go," Robyn told them. "Go back to your own land."

She was not certain that they understood her. They squatted in the mud and stared at her blankly. It was as though they had lost all power of independent thought or action, and she knew that they would never be able to make their way back along the Hyena Road, even if they survived the coming epidemic.

With a flash of horror Robyn realized that without their slave-masters those poor creatures were doomed to a lingering death by starvation and disease. Their masters had cleared out the storerooms before they left; there was not a cupful of farina or cornmeal left in any of the barracoons they visited that morning.

"We will have to feed them," Robyn said.

"We have food for our own, that is all," Tippoo told her impassively.

"He is right, ma'am," Nathaniel confirmed. "We feed them, then we'll starve our own blackbirds; besides, most of them are poor goods, not worth the price of a cup of farina."

In the second barracoon Robyn thought that she had at last discovered the first plague victims, for the low thatched sheds were crammed with rows of prostrate naked figures, and their low moaning and whimpering was a heartbreaking sound, while the smell of corruption was thick and oily on the palate.

It was Tippoo who corrected her. "China birds," he grunted, and for a moment Robyn did not understand, and she stooped over the nearest body, then straightened immediately. Despite her training, cold blisters of sweat formed on her forehead.

By imperial decree from Peking, no black African slave could be landed on the shores of China unless he had been rendered incapable of reproducing his own kind. The Emperor was concerned that future generations would not be plagued by the growth of an alien population in their midst. The traders found it expedient to castrate their purchases in the barracoons,

426

so that losses caused by the operation could be absorbed before the expense of the long voyage was incurred.

It was crudely done, a tourniquet applied to the root of the scrotum and then the entire scrotal sack removed at a single knife stroke and the wound cauterized immediately with a heated iron or a daub of hot pitch. About sixty percent would survive the shock and subsequent mortification, but their price per capita was so enhanced that the trader could face forty percent losses with equanimity.

There was nothing that Robyn could do for so many; she felt overwhelmed by the suffering and misery all around her, and she stumbled out onto the muddy pathway, blinded by her own tears. In the next barracoon, the one nearest to the central auction block, she found the first plague victims.

Once again the sheds had been deserted by the slave-masters, and the dimly lit thatched sheds were filled with naked figures, some squatting motionlessly, others lying on the damp earthen floor, knees drawn up, shaking with the cold of fever, and powerless to lift themselves out of their own bodily wastes. The sound of delirium and suffering was murmurous as of insects in an English orchard on a hot summer's day.

The first sufferer that Robyn touched was a young girl, just beyond puberty, and her skin was burning hot. She rolled her head from side to side, endlessly and senselessly, mouthing snatches of gibberish. Swiftly Robyn ran her fingertips down the girl's naked bulging stomach and immediately she felt the tiny lumps under the hot skin, like pellets of buckshot. There could be no doubt.

"Smallpox," she said simply, and Tippoo drew back fearfully.

"Wait outside," she told him, and he went swiftly and with obvious relief. She turned to Nathaniel. She had noticed the little pitted scars in his folded sun-toughened skin, and now there was no fear in his expression.

"When?" she asked.

"When I was a boy," he said. "It killed my old ma and my brothers."

"We have work to do," she told him.

In the gloomy stinking shed the dead were piled with the living, and on some of the racked and furnace-heated black bodies the plague had already burst into full flower. They found it in all its stages. Papules beneath the skin had erupted into vesicles, bubbles of clear thin fluid that thickened into pustules,

427

which in turn burst and released a custard-thick trickle of matter.

"These will live," Robyn told Nathaniel. "The plague is purging from their blood." She found a man whose open pocks had already crusted over.

While Nathaniel held the man from moving, Robyn scraped away the crusty scabs with a spatula and gathered them in a wide-mouthed glass bottle that had once held quinine powder.

"This strain of the disease has been attenuated," Robyn explained impatiently, and for the first time she saw fear in the flecked eyes of Mungo St. John. "The Turks first used this method two hundred years ago."

"I would prefer to sail away from it," Mungo St. John said quietly, staring at the stoppered bottle which was half filled with damp yellow matter in which were small flecks of blood.

"It would be no use. The infection is already aboard." Robyn shook her head firmly. "In a week or less *Huron* would be turned into a stinking plague ship filled with dying men."

Mungo turned away from her and went to the ship's rail. He stood there with one hand clasped into a fist behind his back, the other still in its sling, staring at the shore where the thatched roofs of the barracoons just showed above the mangroves.

"You cannot leave those poor wretches," Robyn said. "They will starve. I alone could never find food to feed that multitude. You are responsible for them."

He did not answer her for a moment, then he turned back to study her curiously.

"If *Huron* sailed, with her holds empty, would you stay here on this fever and smallpox-ridden coast to tend this multitude of doomed savages?" he asked.

"Of course." She was still impatient, and he inclined his head. His eyes no longer mocked, but were sober, perhaps even filled with respect.

"If you will not stay for common humanity, then stay for self-interest." She scorned him with her tone. "A million dollars' worth of human cattle, and I will save them for you."

"You would save them to be sold into captivity?" he insisted.

"Even slavery is better than death," she replied.

Again, he turned away from her, taking a slow turn of the quarterdeck, frowning thoughtfully, puffing on the long black cheroot so that wreaths of tobacco smoke drifted behind him, and Robyn and half *Huron*'s crew watched him, some fearfully, others with resignation.

"You say that you have yourself undergone this—this thing." His eyes were drawn back, with loathing fascination, to the little bottle that stood in the center of his chart table.

For answer Robyn lifted the sleeve of her shirt and showed him the distinctive deeply pocked scar on her forearm.

A minute longer he hesitated, and she went on persuasively, "I will give you a strain of the disease that is "passant," that has been weakened and attenuated by passage through another man's body, rather than the virulent form of the plague which you will breathe on the very air and which will kill most of you."

"There is no risk?"

She hesitated and then replied firmly, "There is always risk, but one hundred, nay a thousand times less risk, than if you take the disease from the air."

With an abrupt gesture Mungo St. John ripped open the sleeve on his left arm with his teeth and offered it to her.

"Do it," he said. "But in God's name do it quickly, before my courage fails."

She drew the point of her scalpel across the smooth deeply tanned skin of his forearm and the tiny crimson droplets rose behind it. He did not flinch, but when she dipped the scalpel into the bottle and scraped up a speck of the noisome yellow stuff, he blanched and made as if to jerk his arm away, then with an obvious effort controlled himself. She smeared the pus over the tiny wound, and he stepped back and turned from her.

"All of you." His voice was rough with his horror and disgust. "Every last one of you," he told the gaping terrified seamen.

With Nathaniel, the bosun, there were three others who had survived the disease, and were speckled by the small dimpled scars which were its stigma.

Four men were not enough to help Robyn care for a thousand slaves, and her losses were much higher than she had expected. Perhaps this strain of the disease was more virulent, or perhaps the black men from the interior did not have the same resistance as the Europeans whose forebears had for generations been exposed to smallpox.

She introduced the crusted pus into the scratches on their limbs, working in the noon sunlight on into the gloom of dusk and then by the lantern's gleam, and they submitted with dumb resignation of the slave which she found pitiful and repugnant, but which none the less made her work much easier.

The reaction began within hours, the swelling and fever and the vomiting, and she went out into the other deserted barracoons to gather more of the loathsome pus from the bodies of those who had survived the smallpox and were now dying of starvation and neglect—resigning herself to the fact that she had only the strength and time to care for those in *Huron's* barracoons, resigning herself to the fact that there was farina to feed them only, and closing her mind to the cries and entreaty, to the silent dying stare from wizened faces that streamed pus from open pocks.

Even in her own barracoon the four of them working hour after hour, night and day, could give only perfunctory attention to each of the slaves, a handful of the cold pasty farina and a mugful of water once a day during the period of the most violent reaction to the inoculation. Those who survived this were left to care for themselves, to crawl to the water bucket when they could or to wolf a lump of farina from the spadeful that Nathaniel left on a wooden platter at intervals between the rows of supine figures.

Then when they were strong enough to stand they were put to work at piling the rotting bodies of their less fortunate peers upon a gun carriage and dragging them out of the barracoon. There was not the remotest chance of either burying or burning the bodies, and there were too many for the bloated vultures. They piled the corpses in heaps in the coconut grove, well downwind of the barracoon, and went back for more.

Twice a day Robyn went down to the edge of the creek and hailed the anchor watch on *Huron's* deck and had the whaler row her out to the ship, and she spent an hour in the stern cabin.

Mungo St. John's reaction had been frighteningly severe; perhaps he had been weakened by the knife wound. His arm had swollen to almost twice normal size, and the scratch Robyn had inflicted turned into a hideous canker with a thick black crusty scab. His fever was intense, his skin almost painfully hot to the touch, and the flesh seemed to melt off his big-boned frame like candle wax under the flame.

Tippoo, himself suffering from a raging fever, his own arm swollen grotesquely, could not be made to leave the side of Mungo's bunk.

Robyn felt easier knowing that Tippoo was there, strangely

gentle, almost like a mother with a child, to care for Mungo while she must go back ashore to the suffering multitude that choked the barracoons.

On the twelfth day when she went aboard *Huron*, Tippoo met her at the companionway with that wide toadlike grin which she had not seen for so long, and when she hurried into the cabin she saw why.

Mungo was propped up on the bolsters, thin and pale, his lips dry and purple bruises under his eyes, as though he had been beaten with a heavy club. But he was lucid and his skin cool.

"God's breath," he croaked. "You look awful!" And she felt like weeping with relief and chagrin.

When she had bathed and bandaged the shrinking canker on his forearm and was ready to leave, he took her wrist.

"You are killing yourself," he whispered. "When did you last sleep, and for how long?"

Only when he spoke did she realize the depth of her exhaustion: it had been two days previously and then only for a few hours that she had slept, and she felt *Huron*'s deck swing and lurch under her feet as though she rode a high sea and was not lying quietly at anchor in a placid creek.

Mungo drew her down gently beside him onto the bunk, and she did not have either the strength or the will to resist. He made a cradle for her head on his shoulder, and almost immediately she was asleep; her last memory was the feel of his fingers smoothing back the dank ringlets from her temples.

She awoke with a guilty start, not sure how long she had slept, and still fuzzy with sleep struggled out of Mungo St. John's arms brushing the hair out of her eyes with her fingers, trying ineffectually to straighten her rumpled and sweat-dampened clothing.

"I must go!" she blurted groggily, still exhausted and half asleep. How many had died while she slept? she wondered. Before he could prevent it, she was stumbling up the companionway to the deck calling for Nathaniel to row her ashore.

The few hours of rest had refreshed her so that she looked about the estuary with a new and lively interest again. It was the first time that she became aware that one other vessel, besides *Huron*, was still lying at anchor in the river. It was one of the small dhowrigged buggaloos, the coastal slavers similar to the one from which she had rescued Juba. On impulse, she had Nathaniel row her alongside, and when nobody answered her hail, she went aboard. The vessel had clearly

431

been overwhelmed by the plague before she could flee; perhaps she was the vessel from which the original infection had been carried ashore.

Robyn found the same conditions prevailing aboard as there were ashore: the dead, the dying, and those who would recover. Although they were slavers she was still a physician, and she had taken the Hippocratic oath. What she could do was very little, but she did it and the Arab captain, stricken and weakened, thanked her from his sleeping mat on the open deck.

"May Allah walk beside you," he whispered, "and may he give me the opportunity to return this kindness one day."

"And may Allah show you the error of your ways," Robyn told him tartly. "I will send some fresh water, before nightfall, but now there are others more deserving."

In the days that followed, the plague ran its inexorable course, the weaklings died; some of them, consumed by the terrible thirsts of fever, crawled from the abandoned barracoons on to the mud flats of the estuary to fill their bellies with the salt water. Their bodies were twisted into grotesque contortions by the cramps of the salt in their blood, and their insane rantings were like the cries of seabirds across the water, extinguished at last by the incoming tide. The surface of the river was troubled by the swirl and splash of the crocodile and the big sharks that had come upstream to gather this grisly harvest.

Others had crawled away into the forest and groves; they lay under every bush and even before they died they were covered with a red mantle of the fierce safari ants that overnight picked the skeleton to gleaming whiteness.

Some of those that survived, encouraged by Robyn, crept weakly away toward the west. Perhaps a few would complete the long hazardous journey back to their razed villages and devastated countryside, she hoped.

However, most of the survivors of the plague were too weak and confused and demoralized to move. They stayed on in the squalid stinking barracoons, pathetically dependent upon Robyn and her tiny band of helpers for every mouthful of water and farina, watching her with the eyes of dumb and suffering animals.

All this time the piles of corpses in the palm groves grew taller, and the stench more penetrating. Robyn knew too well what would happen next.

"The battlefield plagues," she explained to Mungo St. John. "They always follow when the dead are left unburied, when

432

the rivers and wells are choked with bodies. If they strike now, then none will survive. All of us are weakened, we would be unable to resist the typhoid and enteric plagues. Now is the time to leave, for we have saved all those who are for saving. We must fly before the new onslaught, for unlike the smallpox, there is no defense against them."

"Most of my crew are still sick and weak."

"They will recover swiftly out on the open ocean."

Mungo St. John turned to Nathaniel to ask, "How many slaves have survived?"

"More than eight hundred, thanks to the missus here."

"We will begin to take them aboard at dawn tomorrow," he decided.

That night Robyn came back to his cabin. She could not stay away, and he was waiting for her, she could tell by his expression and the quickness of his smile.

"I was beginning to fear that you preferred the company of eight hundred plague-ridden slaves."

"Captain St. John, I wish to make one more appeal to you. As a Christian gentleman, will you not release these poor creatures and have them escorted and fed on the journey back to where they came—"

He interrupted her, his tone light and that smile hovering on his lips.

"And will you not call me Mungo, rather than Captain St. John?"

She ignored the interruption, and went on. "After all they have suffered, that terrible march down from the highlands, the error and humiliation of slavery and now this plague. If you would consent to release them, I would lead them back to their homes."

He rose from the canvas chair and came to stand over her. His leanness and pallor made him seem even taller.

"Mungo!" he insisted.

"God would forgive you, I am sure of that, he would forgive you the sins that you have already committed against humanity—"

"Mungo!" he whispered, and placed his hands upon her shoulders. She felt herself begin to tremble uncontrollably.

He drew her to his chest. She could feel his ribs, he was so thin, and her voice choked up in her throat when she tried to continue her appeal. Slowly he stooped over her, and she

433

closed her eyes tightly, her arms stiff at her sides, her fists clenched.

"Say Mungo," he commanded quietly, and his lips were cool and soft on hers. Her trembling became uncontrolled shaking.

Her lips opened under his, and her arms went up around his neck.

"Mungo," she sobbed. "Oh, Mungo, Mungo."

She had been taught that her naked body was shameful, but it was the one lesson that she had learned imperfectly, and much of her shame had been mitigated, firstly in the lecture rooms and dissection rooms of St. Matthew's, and secondly in the company of Juba, the little Matabele dove, whose unaffected delight in her nudity she had transmitted to Robyn. Those childlike romps together in the cool green pools of an African river had served to blow away most of the cobwebs of shame.

Now Mungo St. John's delight in and admiration for her body gave her joy and, far from shame, brought her pride that she had never known before. Their lovemaking was no longer accompanied by pain, there were no longer barriers between them—so locked together they could ride the dips and swings of emotion from Himalayan heights where the great winds blew, down to the sweet languorous depths where they seemed to be drowning in honey, each movement slowed, every breath drawn out as though it would last forever, their bodies damp and hot, pressed together and without form, like clay in the hands of a child.

The night was too short, while the wick of the lantern guttered and smoked, neglected and untrimmed. In the dawn, their loving seemed to have filled them with new strength, to have driven away the weakness of fever and the exhaustion of the past weeks.

It was only the sound of the first slaves coming aboard that roused Robyn and brought her back from that far frontier to the hot and cramped little cabin on a slave ship in a fever creek on a wild and brutal continent.

She heard the whisper of bare feet and the clank and drag of slave chains, the sound of men's voices raised, hectoring and impatient, on the deck above.

"Hurry them, or we load for a week." Tippoo's voice.

Robyn raised herself on her elbow and looked down at Mungo. His eyes were closed but he was not asleep, she knew.

"Now," she whispered. "Now you cannot but release them. After last night, I know that something has changed in you."

She felt a strange joy, the zeal of the prophet looking down upon a convert for whose soul she had wrestled with the devil and won.

"Call Tippoo," she insisted, "and give him the order to free the slaves."

Mungo opened his eyes; even after the long night in which neither of them had slept, his eyes were clear. There was the shadow of new beard, dense and dark, carpeting his bony jawline. He was magnificent and she knew then that she loved him.

"Call Tippoo," she repeated, and he shook his head—a little gesture of perplexity.

"You still do not understand," he answered her. "This is my life. I cannot alter that, not for you nor for anybody."

"Eight hundred souls," she pleaded, "and you have their salvation in your hands."

"No." He shook his head again. "You are wrong, not eight hundred souls but eight hundred thousand dollars—that is what I have in my hands."

"Mungo." His name still felt awkward on her lips. "Jesus has said that it is easier for a camel to pass through the eye of a needle than that a rich man should enter the kingdom of heaven. Let them go, you cannot judge human lives in gold."

He laughed and sat up.

"With eight hundred thousand bucks, I can bribe my way into heaven, if I want to, but between us, my dear, it sounds an awfully dull place. I think the devil and I might have more to talk about."

The mocking gleam was back in his eyes again, and he swung his legs out over the edge of the bunk, and naked crossed to where his breeches hung on a wooden peg from the bulkhead.

"We have lain too long abed," he said briskly. "I must see to the loading, and you had best begin your own preparations for the voyage." He belted his breeches and stuffed his shirt into them. "It will take us three days to load, I would be obliged if you would test the water barrels." He came to sit on the edge of the bunk and began dragging on his boots, talking the while in crisp businesslike fashion, detailing the preparations that she should make for the welfare of the slaves during the voyage. "We will have less than a full cargo, which will make it easier to exercise them on deck and keep the holds clean." He stood up and looked down at her.

With a rush like a roused fawn she threw off the blanket that covered her and knelt on the edge of the bunk, seizing him about the waist with both arms.

"Mungo," she whispered urgently, "you cannot torture us so." She pressed the side of her face to his chest, feeling the harsh springing curls of his body hair even through the linen of his shirt. "I cannot offend further against my God and my conscience; unless you free these poor damned souls, then I can never marry you."

His expression changed swiftly, becoming tender and concerned. He lifted his hand to stroke the dense russet locks of her hair, still damp and tangled from the loving of the night.

"My poor darling," his lips formed the words, soundlessly, but her face was still pressed to his chest and she could not see his lips. He drew a deep breath, and though his eyes were still marked with regret and his expression sober, his tone was light and casual.

"Then it is just as well that I have no intention of freeing a single one of them—for what would my wife say otherwise?"

The words took many seconds to make sense to Robyn, and then her whole body spasmed, her grip around his waist tightened and then slowly relaxed. She released him. Slowly she sat back on her heels, naked in the midst of his disordered bunk, and she stared at him with an expression of desolation and disbelief.

"You are married?" Robyn's voice echoed strangely in her own ears, as though from the end of a long bare corridor, and Mungo nodded.

"These ten years past," he answered quietly. "A French lady of aristocratic birth, a cousin of Louis Napoleon. A lady of great beauty who with the three fine sons she has borne me awaits my return to Bannerfield." He paused and then went on with infinite regret. "I am sorry, my dear, I never dreamed that you did not know." And he reached out to touch her cheek, but she cringed away as though he held a poisonous serpent in his hand.

"Will you go away, please," she whispered.

"Robyn—" he began, but she shook her head violently.

"No," she said. "Please don't say any more. Just go. Go away! Please go away."

Robyn locked the door of her cabin and sat down at the sea chest which she used for a desk. There were no tears. Her eyes felt dry and burning as though blasted by a wind off the desert.

She had very little paper left and had to tear the end sheets from her journal. They were speckled with mildew and distorted from the heat and dryness of the highlands and the humidity of the monsoon-ridden littoral.

She smoothed out the first sheet carefully on the lid of her writing case, dipped her pen in the remaining half-inch of India ink and headed the sheet with a hand that was calm and unshaken.

> 16th November, 1860.
> Aboard the Slaver *Huron*.

My Dear Captain Codrington,

My trust in an all-merciful Providence and my belief in the true and one God, and in his gentle son and our Saviour Jesus convinces me that this will come into your hands while there is still time for you to act.

Through a series of incredible adventures and misfortunes I now find myself devoid of friends or protectors, in the power of the notorious American Slave Master and trader Mungo St. John. Against both my will and my conscience I am being forced to act as the physician for this infamous vessel which is at this moment preparing for the voyage around the Cape of Good Hope, across the Atlantic Ocean for a port in the Southern States of America.

As I write, I can hear the doleful sounds from the deck above me, and from the hold below where the poor creatures, eight hundred forsaken souls in all, wearing only their chains are being brought aboard and incarcerated for the voyage which many of them will not survive.

We are lying at anchor in a hidden creek, concealed from the open sea by a sweep of the channel and the mangrove swamps, a perfect hide-away for the nefarious business in hand.

However, I have been able to study the ship's chart and from the navigator's markings learn the name of the estuary and its exact position. The river is the Rio Save, and it lies 20° 58′ south latitude and 35° 03′ east longitude.

I will do all in my power to delay the sailing of this vessel, though at this moment I cannot think what that will be. If this letter reaches you in time, there will be no difficulty for an officer of your courage and experience to blockade the river mouth and seize this slave ship when she attempts to leave the river.

If we have sailed before your arrival, then I implore you to follow in the same course as the Captain of the *Huron* must set to round Good Hope, and I will pray for adverse winds and weather that will enable you to come up with us.

Robyn went on pouring out the tale of her capture, of the plague that had swept through the barracoons, of her fear and hatred of the slavers, the detailed accounts of their barbaric practices and cruelties, and suddenly she realized that she had filled many pages with her account, and she began her last paragraph.

You were gracious enough to express your belief that our destinies were linked in some mysterious way. I know that you share with me the same hatred of this abominable trade, and for these reasons I have made bold enough to appeal to you, confident that you will hearken to my anguished cry.

Robyn paused again, and then searched swiftly in her pen case and found the mate of the earring which she had given to Clinton Codrington so many months ago.

I enclose with this letter a token of my friendship and trust which I hope you will recognize, and I will search every day to see the topsails of your fine ship hurrying to give succor to myself and to the other unfortunates who are my ship-mates on this cursed and iniquitous voyage.

She signed it with her bold, rounded signature and stitched the folded pages and the single item of cheap jewelry into a square of duck canvas.

There was only one address that she had for it. Clinton had told her that he was under orders to call at Zanzibar Island, and she knew that Her Majesty's consul on the island was a man of substance and integrity, a staunch adversary of the slave trade, one of the few men that her father, Fuller Ballantyne, had ever written about with respect and affection.

When she had finished, she tucked the small canvas package up under her skirts, and went up on deck. Mungo St. John was on his quarterdeck, gaunt and lean and pale, and he took a step toward her, but she turned from him immediately.

"Nathaniel," she called to the bosun. "I wish to visit the buggaloo." She indicated the Arab dhow which was still anchored downstream from *Huron*.

"She's making ready to sail, ma'am." Nathaniel knuckled his forehead. "She'll be gone before we can get across—"

"She will if you continue talking," Robyn told him briskly. "I must see if there is aught they need, the poor devils, before they sail."

Nathaniel glanced at his captain, and after a moment's hesitation, Mungo nodded his assent and turned back to watch the stream of slaves coming aboard through the entry port.

The Arab captain of the dhow, just strong enough to take his place at the tiller, greeted her respectfully and listened attentively while she spoke.

Nathaniel was waiting in the gig, out of sight below the level of the dhow's deck, and Robyn made sure that they were shielded from a casual watcher on *Huron*'s deck before she passed the canvas package to the Arab, and followed it with a gold English sovereign.

"There will be another sovereign for you, from the man you deliver it to," she told him, and the Arab bit the coin, and smiled wanly as he tucked it into a fold of his turban.

"And I am Matabele. An induna of two thousand. My name is Gandang, son of Mzilikazi, son of Zulu, and I come with a bright spear and a red heart."

Zouga understood the words with difficulty, for they were spoken rapidly, in accents that were strange to his ears, but there was no misunderstanding the induna's intention. His tone was clear, the murderous determination in his voice evident, and around him the circle of long black shields was unbroken and steadfast.

Unconsciously Zouga had straightened, forcing his aching muscles erect, and he held the induna's gaze without flinching. They stared at each other, and Zouga found himself exerting all his will, all the force of his personality, trying to stay the induna's spear arm. He knew it needed only for the bright broad blade to drop and two hundred *amadoda* would sweep into the rudimentary camp. It would be over so swiftly, the resistance that Zouga and his tiny band could offer would be so puny that they would not even earn the compliment of disembowelment from the victors.

He knew that only his steady gaze and the completely fearless mien that he offered to the Matabele had so far stayed the spear arm, but the silence was drawing out. At any second the spell would snap. He must choose his next action and words as though his life depended upon them, as indeed they did.

Gandang watched the strange pale man before him with his features impassive, yet for possibly the first time in his life while on his father's service, he was uncertain.

The man who called himself Bakela had spoken familiar names. Tshedi and Manali, they were names that his own father revered, yet that in itself would not have been enough to stay his hand, for the King's orders were clear: all who entered the Burnt Land must die. It was more than that. He knew who this man was. The maiden whom he would soon take as wife had spoken of him. This was the brother of the white woman who had delivered Juba to his care, and who he had called *amekazi*, mother.

Juba had spoken of the man Bakela as she lay beside him on her sleeping mat. She had spoken of him with admiration and awe, as a mighty hunter of elephant, as a warrior honored by an all-powerful Queen who lived far beyond great waters. Juba had spoken of this man Bakela as a friend and a protector.

So Gandang paused before giving the order *"Bulala!* Kill them!"

A Matabele induna is never influenced by the words or whims of a woman; if he has fifty wives, their voices are still as the chattering of the waters over the rocks in the shallow rapids of the Nyati river, and a man does not heed them, or rather it must never be apparent that he heeds them. Yet . . .

Juba had traveled to strange places and spoken of wonders and witchery, and Gandang, while seeming not to listen, had indeed listened and been impressed. The girl was not only comely and high bred, but sensible far beyond that mere simpering giggling sexuality to which he was accustomed in other girls of her age.

Gandang was learning that a Matabele induna is never influenced by the whims and words of a woman, unless those words are spoken and the whims expressed on the privacy of the sleeping mat, by a senior wife whose good sense has been proven. Then it is folly not to hearken, for a senior wife can make a man's life unbearable, even if that man is an induna of two thousand, and the favored son of the most powerful monarch in Africa.

Behind the impassive mask of his handsome face, Gandang
440

was thinking furiously. Instinct and Juba's words had warned him that it would be folly to slay this man, yet the warriors at his back knew his orders, and if he failed to carry them out, that failure would immediately be construed as weakness, and his treason reported to the King.

Before him the tattered figure took a pace forward, his whole being ludicrously arrogant. Gandang could see no trace of fear in the steady gaze of his strangely colored eyes.

"I come as an emissary to the great King Mzilikazi, ruler of the Matabele people—and I bring greeting from the White Queen from across the waters."

At the words Gandang felt a small warm flame of relief. The fact that the white man spoke the language of the people, albeit with a strange accent, made it more plausible that he was indeed an emissary. It was plausible, also, that this Queen of his would want to seek the protection and favor of a king as powerful as his father, and that she should be so ignorant as to send her emissary through the Burnt Land instead of along the open road from the south. Zouga saw the shift of mood in the induna's eyes, that tiny crack in his determination.

"Wait," he said. "There is something that I have for you." In Zouga's writing case still reposed the impressive handwritten letters, with seals of wax and scarlet ribbon, that had been provided him by the undersecretary at the Foreign Office, in the usual form.

In the name of Her Britannic Majesty, Ruler of Great Britain and Ireland, Defender of the Faith—To the representatives of all foreign governments or to whomsoever it may concern.

We do, by these presents, request and require that our beloved Morris Zouga Ballantyne be allowed to pass freely without let or hindrance and that he be afforded that assistance of which he may stand in need.

Zouga turned his back on the silent menacing ranks of spearsmen, and walked back slowly through the gap in the scherm of cut thorn branches.

Jan Cheroot was waiting for him, his face the color of the watchfire ash. He and the gunbearers were crouched below the thorn barrier, staring through the chinks with expressions of such utter terror that Zouga felt emboldened in comparison.

"Lay down those guns," he snapped, for all the weapons were cocked and primed and a nervous finger on a hair trigger could let fly the shot that brought a solid black wave of Matabele sweeping through the camp.

Gandang suddenly found himself in a position of uncertainty. From being the merciless bearer of the King's justice, he found himself waiting like a timid suitor outside the gate in the thorn barrier, and every second detracted from his dignity.

Behind him he heard the stir of one of his men, the soft tap of assegai spear on hide shield. His men were growing restless already, sensing the passing of advantage to the little group of ragged starvelings they had surrounded. Gandang turned slowly, and his stony gaze passed over the ranks. They froze once more.

"Gandang, son of Mzilikazi, induna of two thousand. Come forward."

The hail from beyond the thorn barrier was unexpected and startlingly loud, but it came the moment before Gandang reached the limit of his patience and loosed his eager warriors. Gandang moved forward to the gateway, his plumes nodding about his head, his tread dignified, his carriage proud, so that no men might guess at his uncertainty. At the gateway he paused, and though his expression did not alter nor his gaze waver, he experienced a profound relief that his own wisdom and the words of his little dove had stayed his blade.

Before him stood a figure of almost incredible beauty. It took him many seconds to recognize the ragged individual of a few minutes previously. The figure wore cloth of that same peculiarly rich shade of red of the bush shrike's chest, brighter than the color of freshly spilled blood. Though this was enough to stop a man's breath, it was not all. Bright metal ornaments on breast and shoulders sparkled in the morning sunlight, the belt buckle was of the same metal. The belt and cross straps were of the same blinding whiteness as an egret's wing. The tall shako swept down to an elegant point between the eyes, and the helmet badge blazed like a sunrise upon the man's forehead.

There was no doubt now in Gandang's mind that here was indeed an important man, and a soldier of repute, as Juba had warned him, and he made a silent resolution to listen to her words in future with even greater attention. He felt a little shiver of dismay at the thought that he might have followed his first instincts and had this man cut down as though he were a worthless Mashona, a mere eater of dirt.

The magnificent figure took one pace toward him and lifted a hand to the peak of that beautiful helmet in a formal gesture

442

that Gandang answered instinctively with a sweeping salute of his stabbing spear.

"I, Bakela, request that my token be conveyed to your father, the honored and victorious Mzilikazi, and that he be informed that I request from him the right of the road," said the man in his atrocious Sindebele, and Gandang accepted the token from his hand, the small package with strange signs and marks upon it, bound up with strips of colored cloth so beautiful that they would have delighted the heart of even the most vain and spoiled woman.

"It shall be done," he agreed.

In the moments of his confrontation with Gandang, Zouga had been thinking as furiously as the Matabele and making his own calculations of survival. Now that he had fallen in with a border impi he knew he must put aside any thought of escaping southward. Apart from the fact that they were completely surrounded and heavily outnumbered, he knew that no unmounted man could run ahead of these warriors. They were like machines built for the pursuit and the annihilation of an enemy.

The meeting had not taken him completely unprepared. There had been many a night in the preceding weeks when he had woken in the darkest hours, and he had lain on the hard earth and dreaded a moment such as this.

He had mentally rehearsed his actions—from the concealment of any fear while he won time to don his dress uniform to the demand to be taken to the King's kraal. When it had gone as he planned it, when the tall induna had agreed, "It shall be done," it had taken another enormous extension of Zouga's will not to show relief. He had stood aloof, disinterested, while Gandang had picked and called out five of his swiftest runners and he had recited a long message that they must memorize, and take to Mzilikazi.

It began with a long recitation of the King's praises which began, "Great Black Elephant who shakes the earth with his tread," went on to list the deeds that Gandang had performed since leaving the kraal at Thabas Indunas, the march eastward, the battle at the pass and the slaying of Bopa, the slavemaster, right up to this day's encounter with the white man. After a flowery description of the man's magnificent finery (which Gandang knew would intrigue his father), it ended with a repetition of Bakela's request to be "given the road" to Thabas Indunas.

The chosen messengers each in turn repeated the long message, and though he showed no change of expression Zouga was amazed that each of them had it word-perfect. It was an impressive demonstration of the developed memory of people who do not have the art of writing and reading.

Gandang handed them the sealed parchment envelope that contained Zouga's letter of credentials, and the messengers sprang to their feet from where they had squatted, saluted their induna, formed file and trotted away toward the west.

Gandang turned back to Zouga. "You will stay encamped here until the King sends word."

"When will that be?" Zouga asked, and Gandang answered him sternly.

"Whenever the King is pleased to do so."

Zouga's little party was left unmolested. Although there were a dozen Matabele *amadoda* positioned about the camp, guarding it day and night, not one of them attempted to enter the gateway in the thorn scherm. Until the moment when they might slaughter them, the persons and property of their prisoners were inviolate.

The main body of the impi camped a quarter of a mile downstream. Each evening the tall induna visited Zouga and they sat for an hour or so across the fire from each other, speaking gravely and seriously.

As the days of waiting became weeks so the two men developed each for the other a deep respect, if not actual friendship. They were both warriors, and they had common ground when they spoke of old campaigns and of skirmishes and battles fought. They recognized in each other the strengths, the essential decencies of men who live by and respect the laws of their society, though those laws might diverge widely.

"I account him a gentleman," Zouga wrote in his journal. "One of nature's own."

While Gandang, speaking to Juba on the sleeping mat, said merely, "Bakela is a man."

Gandang allowed Zouga's bearers to leave the enclosure, to cut and bring in thatch and timber to strengthen and improve the buildings, so that at last Zouga could sleep dry and warm. This, together with the rest and respite from endless marching, brought an immediate improvement in Zouga's health. The deep wound in his cheek healed cleanly, leaving a pink shiny scar. The shoulder mended, the bruising abated, and he no longer needed a staff or a sling for his arm. Within a week he knew he was well enough to shoot the heavy four-to-the-pound.

One evening he proposed to Gandang that they hunt together, and the induna, who by this time was finding the waiting as tedious as Zouga was, agreed with alacrity. Gandang's *amadoda* surrounded a herd of Cape buffalo, and drove them down in a bellowing, stampeding black wave to where they waited. Zouga saw the tall induna rise from cover and race in, barefoot, shieldless, and kill a mature bull buffalo with a single thrust of the broad-bladed assegai through the ribs behind the heaving shoulder. Zouga knew that he lacked both the skill and the courage to emulate that feat.

Gandang watched when Zouga stood to meet the squealing, thunderous charge of an enraged bull elephant, and when the beast went down to the crash of the shot, dropping onto its knees in a storm of dust, Gandang stepped past Zouga and touched the little black hole that punctured the elephant's thick gray hide an inch above the first crease at the top of the trunk.

Gandang inspected the smear of blood on the tip of his forefinger, and said "Hau!" quietly but with force, which is an expression of amazement. For Gandang himself owned a musket, a Tower Musket manufactured in London in 1837. When he first acquired the weapon, Gandang had fired it at buffalo, elephant and Mashona, all of whom had fled headlong but unscathed.

Gandang understood that when firing it was necessary to close the eyes and the mouth firmly, to hold the breath and at the moment of discharge to shout a rebuke to the devil who lived in the gunpowder smoke, otherwise the devil could enter through the eyes or mouth and take possession of the marksman. In order to throw the musket ball to any distance, it was also necessary to pull the trigger with sudden and brutal force, as in hurling a spear. Furthermore, to minimize the recoil of the weapon, the butt should not touch the shoulder, but be held a hand's span from it. Despite all these precautions, Gandang had never succeeded in hitting the target at which he aimed, and had long abandoned the weapon to rust away, while he kept his assegai polished brightly.

Thus Gandang appreciated to the full the magnitude of the feat that Zouga performed with such apparent ease. So their mutual respect deepened with each day spent in each other's company, and became almost friendship. Almost, but not quite; there were chasms of culture and training between them that could never be bridged, and always the knowledge that on any day a swift runner might come from the west with a message for Gandang from his father.

445

"Bulala umbuna! Kill the white man!" And both of them knew that Gandang would hesitate not an instant longer.

Zouga had much time alone in camp, and he spent it planning his audience with the King. The longer he dwelt upon that the more ambitious became his plans. The memory of the ancient disused mine shafts returned to plague these idle hours, and at first merely to amuse himself, and then with truly serious intent, Zouga began to draw up a document which he headed:

"Exclusive concession to mine gold and hunt ivory in the sovereign territory of Matabeleland."

He worked on it each evening polishing and reshaping it in the gibberish that the layman takes for legal jargon and which he fondly believes will dignify his creation. "Whereas I, Mzilikazi, ruler of Matabeleland, hereinafter referred to as the party of the first part—"

Zouga had completed this document to his entire satisfaction when a fatal flaw in his plans became evident. Mzilikazi could not sign his name. Zouga pondered this for a day and then the solution occurred to him. Mzilikazi should by this time have in hand the sealed package. The crimson wax seals must surely impress him, and in his writing case Zouga had two full sticks of sealing wax.

Zouga began to design a great seal for King Mzilikazi. He sketched the design on the back cover of his journal, and the inspiration came from the first of the King's praise names.

"Great Black Elephant who shakes the earth."

In Zouga's design the center of the field depicted a bull elephant, with long tusks raised and ears spread wide. The upper border bore the legend, "Mzilikazi, King of the Matabele."

He started experimenting with various materials, clay and wood, but the results did not please him—and the following day he asked Gandang for permission to send a party of his porters under Jan Cheroot back to the ancient workings at the Harkness Mine to retrieve the ivory buried there.

It took two days of careful consideration for Gandang to agree, and when he did, he sent fifty of his men to accompany the caravan, with orders to kill them all at the first hint of flight or treachery. Jan Cheroot returned with the four huge tusks from the two bull elephants, and Zouga had not only the material from which to carve the King's great seal, but a gift fitting the King's importance.

Ivory was a treasure of which the Matabele had long ago realized the value in trade. It was, however, a scarce commodity, for even the bravest of men cannot kill a bull elephant with a stabbing spear. They had to rely on pickups from animals that had died of natural causes, or the very occasional victim of the pitfall.

Gandang's amazement when he saw the span and weight of the four tusks decided Zouga. The largest and most pleasingly shaped tusk would be Zouga's gift to Mzilikazi, if he were ever allowed to reach the great kraal at Thabas Indunas alive.

Not only was the threat of the King's wrath still hanging over him, but his supply of quinine powder was reduced to a few ounces. All around the camp steamed the swampy ground, fed each day by the interminable rains, and in the night he could even smell the evil fever-bearing vapors rising from the stagnant waters to waft over the camp. Yet he was forced to reduce his daily preventative dose of the bitter powder to perilously small quantities in an attempt to eke it out.

The inactivity and the dual threat of spear and disease wore on Zouga's nerves, until he found himself toying with suicidal plans to make an attempt to avoid the guarding impi and to escape on foot southward. He thought of seizing Gandang and holding him as hostage, or using the remaining fifty pounds of black powder to manufacture a combustible with sufficient power to destroy the entire impi host at a blast. Reluctantly, one after another, he recognized these as plans of folly and abandoned them.

Gandang's impi came again in the dawn. Zouga was awakened by a stentorian voice calling him out of the thorn scherm. Zouga threw a fur kaross over his shoulders and went out into the gray icy drizzle of rain, sloshing through the red mud to the gate, and he knew at a single glance that the King had at last sent his reply. The ranks of silent Matabele surrounded the camp, still as statues carved from the black wild ebony.

Zouga judged how swiftly he could reach the loaded gun beside his cot in the little thatched hut behind him, and guessed that he would probably be cut down before he could fire a single shot. Yet he knew he would still make the attempt.

"I see you, Bakela," Gandang stepped from the dark and silent ranks.

"I see you, Gandang."

"The King's messenger has arrived—" Gandang paused for a moment, solemn and stern, and then his perfectly square white teeth gleamed in the gray light of dawn as he smiled.

"The King has given you the road, and bids you attend him at Thabas Indunas."

The two men grinned at each other with relief: for both of them it meant life. The King had determined that Gandang had done his duty and correctly interpreted his commands, while Zouga had been accepted as an emissary, not as an enemy.

"We will march at once." Gandang smiled still. "Before the sun!" The King's summons brooked of no hesitations or delays.

"Safari!" Zouga roused his camp. "We march at once!"

A natural delicacy and tact had made Gandang keep little Juba out of sight and hearing of Zouga's camp, nor had he mentioned the girl's name to Zouga while sentence of death still hung over the white man. However, that first night of the journey to Thabas Indunas after they had camped, he brought Juba to Zouga's hut, and she knelt and greeted him as "Baba-father" and then with Gandang seated between them and listening attentively, he allowed them to talk for a short while.

Zouga was avid for news of his sister, and he listened in silence to the account of Fuller Ballantyne's death and his burial. It was better this way, and Zouga was already preparing his own fulsome tributes to the memory of his father.

While relieved also to hear that Robyn was safe, Zouga was less happy with the swift progress she seemed to be making. It must have been nearly three months since Juba last saw her, almost within sight of the eastern mountain range, and by this time Robyn must have surely reached the coast, and could be on board a Portuguese trade ship, well on her way to Good Hope and the Atlantic.

He did not know how long he would be delayed by the Matabele King, and then how long the overland journey down half the length of Africa might take him. Robyn's manuscript could be in London a year or more before his own.

Zouga had exchanged one worry for another, and on the following day's march he chivvied his porters, heavily laden though they were, to keep up with their captors. It was of little avail, and they struggled along behind the trotting impi until Zouga demanded of Gandang that his own bearers be ordered to help with the load of ivory and the even weightier package of bark and plaited grass which contained the granite bird which Zouga had plundered from the tomb of the Kings.

With each day's travel toward the west, the land became drier, and the forests thinned out and gave way to level pasturage with sparsely dotted acacias, graceful, mushroom-shaped trees from whose branches hung the big protein-rich, bean-shaped pods so dearly loved by game and domestic animals alike.

The relief from the driving and endless rainstorms lifted their spirits, and the impi sang on the march, winding like a thick black serpent through the lovely parklike lands below the bald and rounded kopjes of granite.

Soon they came across the first of the King's herds, the small humpbacked cattle whose origins lay far back beyond the veils of history; perhaps it had taken them and their drovers four thousand years to travel down from the valley of the Nile or from the fertile plains enclosed by the twin rivers of the Euphrates and the Tigris.

The cattle were sleek, for the grass was dense and sweet; even here in the drier lands the rains had been good. The animals were of every color and pattern, chocolate-red and black and white and yellow, piebald and skewbald, solid black or pure snowy white. They watched with a blank bovine stare as the column of men trotted past, and the small herd boys, naked except for the tiny apron of the *beshu,* came scampering to stare in silent wide-eyed awe at the fighting men in plume and tassel, for they were already pining for the day that they would be called into their own regiments and in turn follow the warriors' road.

They reached the first of the Matabele towns. It was situated on the banks of the Inyati River. Gandang explained that it was the headquarters of his own impi, the Inyati impi, and that it was not the largest of the regimental towns. The settlement was laid out around the central cattle pen, a vast enclosure large enough to hold ten thousand head of the King's herds. The dwellings were of identical thatched beehive construction in the tradition that the wandering tribe had preserved since leaving their native Zululand. The outer stockade was of cut mopani poles, set deep in the earth and forming a stout defensive wall. The villagers streamed out to welcome the returning impi, lining both sides of the route, a singing, clapping and laughing throng, mostly of women and children.

"Most of the men and the marriageable maidens have left already for Thabas Indunas. In the full of this moon, the *Chawala* dance begins, and all the nation will assemble at the King's kraal. We will rest here only one night and then take the road again to reach Thabas Indunas before the moon."

The road from the Inyati westward was now a populous

highway, as the nation went in toward the King's capital city to celebrate the festival of the first fruits. The men marched in their regiments, their distinctive dress and ornaments, the color of their war shields indentifying each from afar, from the scarred and silver-headed veterans who had fought the Basuto, the Griquas and the Boer in the south to the young bloods eager for their first kill, eager to learn in which direction the King would hurl his war spear at the conclusion of the *Chawala*—for that was the direction in which they would find their reputation, their manhood, their glory and possibly their deaths.

The regiments of young unmarried women interspersed those of the warriors, and as they passed each other on the road, the girls preened and giggled, casting languorous sloe eyes at the unmarried men, and the men pranced and leaped in the pantomime of battle, the *giya*, showing how they would wash their spears in blood and earn the privilege to "go in to the women" and take wives.

With each day's march toward Thabas Indunas the roads became more congested, and their pace was reduced by the throng. They might wait half a morning to take their turn across a ford of the river, for the regiments drove the cattle which were their food supply ahead of them and dragged their baggage train behind. Each warrior's finery, his tassels and plumes and feathers, was carefully packed and carried by the young apprentice who was his personal bearer.

At last in the sweltering noon of high summer, Zouga's little party, still borne along on the river of humanity, came over a crest of ground and saw laid out ahead of them the great kraal and capital city of the Matabele.

It was spread out over many square miles of open plain below the bald-headed granite hills that gave it its name "the Hills of the Chieftains." The furthest hill was "the Place of Killing," Bulawayo, and from its sheer cliffs those condemned to die were cast down.

The stockades formed concentric circles, dividing the city into its separate parts. Always the huge open cattle pens were the center of Matabele life, their cattle the source and store of their wealth, and now that the outlying herds had been brought in for the festival, every pen was filled with the multicolored herds of fat beasts.

Standing at Zouga's shoulder, Gandang used his stabbing spear to point out with pride the city's features. There were sections for the unmarried girls, and the unblooded regiments, and another huge area for the married quarters; the huts were

450

uniform in size and laid out in orderly patterns, the thatched roofs shining golden yellow in the sunlight. The earth between them was swept clean and beaten hard by the passage of bare feet.

"There is the King's hut." Gandang pointed out a single huge conical structure in its own separate enclosure. "And that is the compound of the King's wives," a hundred other huts, within a high guarding stockade, "and it is death to any man who enters that gate."

Gandang led Zouga down to a small grove of acacia trees outside the main stockade. There was a stream within a few yards of it, and for the first time in days they were free of the close press of humanity. Although the plain without the city walls was thick with the temporary dwellings of the visiting impis, the area around the grove was empty, as if it had been placed out of bounds to the common people.

"When will I see the King?" Zouga asked.

"Not until after the festival," Gandang answered. "There is ritual and cleansing that the King must undergo, but he has sent you gifts, you are much honored." And he pointed with his blade at the line of young maidens that left a gate in the stockade. Each girl carried a large earthenware pot balanced easily upon her head, and she did not use a hand to maintain that balance.

The girls moved with that peculiar straight-backed grace, hips swinging in lazy rhythm, the hard unripe fruits of their breasts jostling at each pace. They came into Zouga's little camp in the grove and knelt to offer the gifts they bore.

Some pots contained thick millet beer, tart and effervescent, others the clotted and soured cow's milk, *imaas,* that was so much a staple of the Nguni diet, and others again big chunks of fatty beef, roasted on the open coals.

"You are much honored by these gifts," Gandang repeated, apparently himself surprised by the King's generosity. "Yet Tshedi, your grandfather, was always his good and trusted friend."

Once the camp was set up, Zouga found himself again the victim of idleness, with long days of waiting to fill. Here, however, he was free to roam about the city and its surrounds, save only the forbidden areas of the royal enclosure and women's quarters. He sketched the fascinating bustle of preparation for the festival. During the heat of the day the banks of the rivers were lined with men and women, their velvety black skins shimmering with water as they bathed and cleansed themselves for the dances. Every tree for miles about was hung with the kilts and furs, the feathers and plaited ornaments that were airing, the creases and rumples of travel and packing were being allowed to drop out of them as they billowed and flapped in the light breeze.

He passed groups of young girls plaiting each other's hair, smearing and rubbing each other's bodies with oil and colored clays, and they giggled and waved at Zouga as he passed.

At first the problem of hygiene that this huge assembly presented puzzled Zouga, until he realized that there was an area of thick undergrowth beyond the city walls where both men and women went at dawn and in the short twilight. This area had its own population of crows and kites, of jackal and hyena, that served as the city's cleansing service.

Interested further in the running of the city, he found that all bathing and washing of clothing was allowed only below a certain spot on the riverbanks marked by a distinctively large tree or other feature, and that the women filled the waterpots for drinking and cooking above this point.

Even the huge cattle pen in its very heart helped to keep the city clean. It acted as a vast flytrap. The insects laid their eggs on the fresh cattle dung, but before they could hatch most of them were deeply trampled by the hooves of the milling herds. The brilliant sunlight and the untainted wind completed the process of keeping the area relatively clean and the smells interesting but not unbearable.

Zouga should have been content to have reached this haven, instead of leaving his assegai-riven corpse for a hyena's feast in the wilderness, but he was not.

He set himself tasks to fill the waiting days. He drew sketches and maps of the city, noting weaknesses in the fortifications, and where an attack would have the best chance of penetrating these and reaching the King's private quarters. He sketched the uniforms of the various impis. He noted the colors of their shields and other means of identifying them in the field. Asking innocent-seeming questions of Gandang, he was able to estimate the number of warriors each regiment contained, the ages and battle experience of the warriors, the names and personal idiosyncrasies of their indunas, and the location of their regimental towns.

He found that much had changed in Matabeleland since old Tom Harkness had drawn his map, and Zouga noted these changes and drew his conclusions from them.

* * *

As a further exercise to pass the waiting days he began drawing up a battle plan for a campaign against the old King Mzilikazi, the requirements in men and weapons, the logistics of supply and resupply, the lines of march, and the most expedient methods of bringing the impis to battle—for Zouga was a soldier, a soldier with a dream which might one day become reality only through military action.

Unsuspecting, Gandang was flattered by Zouga's interest and he answered every question with pride in his nation's might and its achievements. Despite this work Zouga had given himself, the days dragged past.

"The King will not give you audience until after the festival," Gandang repeated, but he was wrong.

The evening before the festival began, two elderly indunas, blue heron feathers nodding above the silvery woollen caps of closecropped hair, entered the camp in the acacia grove and Gandang greeted them with deep respect, listened to them attentively, and then came to Zouga.

"They have come to take you to the King," he said simply.

There were three small fires burning before the King's hut, and over the middle one crouched a wizened apelike figure who crooned a low incantation through toothless gums, rocking on his haunches and occasionally adding a pinch of powder or a sprig of herb into one of the large earthenware pots that bubbled over the flames.

The witch doctor was festooned with the grisly accoutrements of his profession, the dried skins of reptiles, the claws of eagle and leopard, the inflated bladder of a lion, the skull of ape and the teeth of crocodile, small stoppered gourds of potions and powders, the horn of duiker to be used as a blooding cup, and other unidentifiable charms and elixirs.

He was the orchestrator of the entire festival, the most important event in the Matabele calendar, the gathering of the first fruits of the harvest, the blessing of the nation's herds, and the setting of the warlike campaigns which would occupy the *amadoda* during the coming dry season. Thus the assembled indunas watched his preparations with attention and awe.

There were thirty or so men in the squatting circle of elders, the senior indunas of the nation, the King's privy council. The small courtyard was crowded. The tall thatched sloping side of the King's hut towered thirty feet or so above them all, the top of it lost in darkness.

The thatching was skillfully done, with intricate patterns worked into the grass, and before the low doorway stood an armchair of European design and construction. With a small prick of recognition Zouga realized that this must be the same chair given to the King by his own grandfather Moffat, Tshedi, nearly twenty years before.

"Bayete! Mzilikazi, the bull elephant of the Matabele."

Gandang had coached Zouga in the correct etiquette, the formal greetings and the behavior which the King would expect.

As Zouga crossed the narrow yard of bare earth, he intoned the King's praise names, not shouting them aloud, not crawling on his knees as a subject would have done, for he was an Englishman and an officer of the Queen.

Nevertheless, at a distance of ten feet from the King's chair Zouga squatted down, his own head below the level of the King's, and waited.

The figure in the chair was much smaller than he had expected for a warrior of such fearsome reputation, and as his eyes adjusted to the gloom, Zouga saw that the King's feet and hands were small and delicately shaped, almost feminine, but that his knees were grotesquely swollen and distorted by the gout and arthritis that was attacking them.

The King was an old man now, nobody knew how old, but he had been a fighting warrior at the turn of the century. His once fine muscles had sagged so that his belly bulged out onto his lap, the skin stretched and riven with striae like that of a pregnant woman.

His head seemed too big for the narrow shoulders, and the neck hardly strong enough to support it, but the eyes which watched Zouga intently from the seams of wrinkles and loose, bagged skin were black and bright and lively.

"How is my old friend Tshedi?" the King asked in a piping high-pitched voice.

Zouga had last seen his maternal grandfather twenty years previously; the only memory that persisted was of a long flowing white beard.

"He is well and happy," Zouga replied. "He sends you his greeting and respect."

The old man in the armchair nodded the big ungainly head contentedly.

"You may present your gifts," he said, and there was a buzz of comment from the indunas, and even the witch doctor at the fire looked up as the ivory tusk was carried in by three of Gandang's warriors, staggering under its weight, and laid before the King's chair.

The witch doctor clearly resented this interruption of the

454

ritual cleansing and the diversion of interest and attention from himself, and now with two of his assistants to help him he made an officious show of carrying one of the steaming pots from the fire and placing it between the King's feet.

Then he and his assistants raised a large kaross of stitched leopard skins and spread it like a tent over the King and his chair so the steam from the pot was trapped beneath it. Within a minute, there was a paroxysm of gasps and coughing from under the fur blanket, and when at last the witch doctor removed it, the King was streaming sweat and choking for breath, his eyes inflamed and pouring tears, but any demons had been expelled by the coughing, and impurities washed away by the sweat and tears.

The gathering waited in respectful silence while the King recovered his breath, and the witch doctor withdrew to prepare the next potion. With his breath still wheezing and whistling in his throat, Mzilikazi reached into the small chest beside his chair and brought out the sealed package which Zouga had sent him.

"Speak the words." The King handed it to Zouga, demanding that he read the letter.

Although he was illiterate, the King understood clearly the uses of the written word. For twenty years he had corresponded with Zouga's grandfather, who always sent one of his mission students to deliver his letters, to read them to the King and to record the King's reply.

Zouga stood erect and opened the package. He read aloud, translating from the English as he went along, and adding a few small embellishments to the original text.

When he had finished, there was a respectful silence from the tribal elders, and even the King studied the tall and magnificently attired figure before him with new attention. The firelight danced on the burnished brass buttons and badges of Zouga's dress uniform, the scarlet cloth of his coat seemed to glow like the very flames of the fire.

The witch doctor would have intervened again, coming forward with a brew of steaming medicine for the King to swallow, but Mzilikazi waved him away irritably.

Knowing that this was the moment when the King's interest was at its zenith, Zouga asked smoothly, "Does the King see these signs of my Queen? They are her special marks, and every ruler should have such a mark to prove his power and the rocklike nature of his words."

Zouga turned and beckoned the bearer who knelt in the

gateway behind him and the frightened man crawled to Zouga's feet, not daring to look up at the King, and handed to Zouga the small tea caddy that contained the carved ivory seal and the sticks of wax.

"I have prepared one of these for the King, that his dignity and power may be known to all men."

Mzilikazi was unable to contain his interest; he craned forward in his chair and called Zouga closer. Kneeling before him, Zouga prepared the wax, melting it onto the lid of the tea caddy with a taper lit from the fire. Then he made the impression of the seal upon it, and when it had hardened, handed it up to the King.

"It is an elephant." The King recognized the beast with unconcealed amazement.

"The great black bull elephant of the Matabele," Zouga agreed.

"Speak the words." The King touched the lettering on the border, and commanded Zouga to translate it.

"Mzilikazi Nkosi Nkulu!"

The King clapped his hands with delight, and passed the seal to his senior induna. Soon they were all clucking and exclaiming over the imprint, the wax impression passing from hand to hand.

"Bakela," the King told Zouga, "you must come to me again on the day following the *Chawala* ceremony. You and I have much to discuss."

Then with a wave of his hand he dismissed the splendid young man from his presence, and patiently, resignedly, gave himself up to the ministrations of the hovering doctor.

The full moon rose well past midnight, and the fires were stacked with new logs to welcome it, and the singing and drumming began. No man nor woman had dared to pick a single grain of corn from the harvest before this moment, for the rise of the moon heralded the *Chawala*, the dance of the first fruits, and the entire nation gave itself up to rejoicing.

The ceremony began in the middle of the first morning. The massed regiments assembled before their King, filing in column into the vast arena of the cattle stockade, and the earth shook to the crash of bare feet lifted in unison, twenty-five thousand at a time, lifted to the level of the shoulder and then brought down with the full force of the muscular, hardened bodies of highly trained warriors.

"Bayete!" they greeted the King with the royal salute.

"Bayete!" the crash of feet once more.

"Bayete!" a third time, and then the dancing began.

One regiment at a time coming forward in swaying, singing ranks to perform before Mzilikazi's armchair throne. The perfect timing and execution of the intricate steps made it seem as though they were a single living organism, the shields interlocking and revolving and twisting together like the scales of some gigantic reptile, the dust rising and swirling through their ranks like smoke so that they appeared as wraiths, and their cloaks of furs and their kilts of civets' tails and monkey skins, of the pelts of foxes and cats, swirled about their legs so they appeared to be divorced from earth, suspended above it on the moving cloud of dust and the soft waves of fur.

From the ranks sprang the champions and the heroes of each regiment, to *giya* in their pride, leaping as high as their own heads, and stabbing furiously at the air, screaming challenge and triumph; the sweat greased their muscles and flew in explosive droplets in the sunlight.

Mzilikazi was caught up in the building sea of excitement, and he quaffed from the beer pots that the maidens brought him until his eyes rolled in his head and he could not contain himself further. He struggled from his chair and hobbled out on his swollen and deformed legs, and the champions fell back to give him place.

"My father is the finest dancer in all of Matabeleland," said Gandang, squatting beside Zouga.

The old King tried to leap, but his feet did not leave the ground. He shuffled back and forth, making little pawing gestures, hacking at the air with his toy war spear.

"Thus I struck down Barend the Griqua, and thus his sons died."

The nation roared.

"The bull elephant dances, and the earth shakes." And the slamming of ten thousand feet goaded the King to circle in a painful and pathetic parody of the young champions' wild gyrations.

"Thus I spurned the tyrant Chaka, and thus I cut the plumes from the headdress of his messengers and sent them back to him," squealed Mzilikazi.

"Bayete!" thundered the nation. "He the father of the world."

Exhausted within minutes, the ancient King sank into the dust, and Gandang and two other of the King's sons leaped to their feet from the half circle of indunas and raced to his side. Gently they bore him up and carried him back to his chair,

457

and Lobengula, the King's senior son, held a beer pot for him to drink from. The beer dribbled from his chin and ran down the King's heaving chest.

"Let the nation dance," gasped the King, and Gandang returned to Zouga's side and squatted beside him.

"After war, my father loves best the dance," he explained.

The maidens came, rank upon lovely rank, their naked skin shimmering in the glaring sunlight of noon. The tiny beaded apron that barely covered their little triangular sex was all they wore, and their singing was sweet and clear.

Mzilikazi hoisted himself from his chair once more and hobbled out to dance with them, passing along the foremost rank, directing the singing with his ritual war spear pointed to the skies. The King danced until he dropped once more, and was again carried back to his chair by his sons.

By nightfall, Zouga was exhausted. His sweaty neck was chafed by the high stock of his dress coat, and sweat had soaked through the thick scarlet serge in patches. His eyes were bloodshot and inflamed from the dust and the glare, his head ached from the cacophony of drums and the roar of Matabele voices, his tongue felt thick and furry from the drafts of sorghum beer that had been pressed upon him and his back and legs ached from the unfamiliar squatting attitude he had been forced into all that day—but the King was still dancing, hobbling and prancing and squeaking on those twisted and deformed legs of his.

The following morning Mzilikazi was on his throne again, so undaunted by the previous day's exertions, that when the *Chawala* bull was loosed into the arena his sons had to restrain him bodily from rushing out to slay it with his bare hands.

A champion from each regiment had been chosen and stripped down to a loincloth. They waited in squatting ranks on each side of Mzilikazi's chair.

The bull came into the ring at the charge, horned head held high, red dust spurting from under his hooves and his wild eyes glaring. He was pure, untainted black, with a huge humped back and glossy burnished hide.

Carefully picked from all the King's herds, he was the finest animal in the whole of Matabeleland and he made an arrogant circuit of the arena, stepping high, snorting and dropping his head to hook with curved horns at anything in his path.

The King, held by his sons but struggling against their grip, was almost incoherent with excitement, and now he lifted his spear and his arms shook violently as he screamed, *"Bulala inkunzi!* Kill the bull!"

The waiting men leaped to their feet, saluted the King, and then raced out, spreading into a half-moon-shaped line, instinctively adopting the *jikela*, the movement of encirclement.

The black bull swung to meet them, came up short on locked front legs, his head swinging as he measured his charge; then the rounded quarters bunched under him and he surged forward, picking a man in the center of the line and thundering down on him.

The man he had chosen stood his ground, spreading his arms in a welcoming gesture, and the bull dropped his head and hit him. Clearly Zouga heard the brittle snap of bone as the warrior absorbed the shock of impact against his chest, and then locked his arms around the animal's neck and held on.

The bull tried to toss him, hooking and throwing his head high, but the man held on, and was cruelly thrown about, but his body blocked the bull's sight and brought him to a halt. The racing line closed about him instantly, and abruptly the bull's humped body was smothered by the rush of naked black men.

For long seconds the bull struggled to remain upright, but they bore him down and tore his legs out from under him so he hit the dusty earth with a heavy thump and a groan and bellow. A dozen men seized the long horns, and, using their leverage, began to twist them against the massive inert weight of his pinned body. Slowly, sweating and straining, they forced his head around, and the bull kicked his hooves in the air, his bellows becoming more desperate and strangled.

The King leaped up and down in his chair, screaming with excitement, and the roar of voices was like the sound of surf on a gale-driven coast of rock.

Inch by inch, the huge horned head revolved, and then suddenly there was no longer resistance. Zouga heard the crack of the vertebrae, sharp as a musket shot even above the thunder of the assembled nation. The horned head flicked through another half turn, the legs stiffened skyward for a moment, and the bull's bowels voided in a liquid green stream.

The sweat-drenched warriors lifted the carcass shoulder-high and bore it bodily across the arena to lay it at Mzilikazi's feet.

On the third and last day of the ceremony, Mzilikazi stalked out into the center of the cattle pen. He made a frail and bent figure in the vast open space, and the noon sun burned down from above so that there was almost no shadow under him. The nation was quiet, forty thousand human beings watching one old man, and there was not a whisper, nor a sound of breathing.

In the center of the arena Mzilikazi paused and raised his war spear above his head. The watching ranks stiffened as he revolved slowly, and then stopped facing toward the south. He drew back his spear arm, poised for a moment while the tension in the watchers was a palpable emanation from forty thousand charged bodies.

Then the King gave a little hop, and began slowly to revolve; the crowd sighed and swayed and then grew silent as again the King poised with his blade pointed toward the east. Then another little hop as he teased them deliberately, drawing out the moment with the timing of a natural showman.

Then suddenly his spear arm shot forward and the tiny toylike weapon flew from his hand in a high sparkling parabola, and dropped to bury its point in the baked earth.

"To the north!" thundered the nation. "Bayete! The great bull has chosen the north!"

"We go northward to raid the Makololo," Gandang told Zouga. "I will leave with my impi in the dawn." He paused, and then smiled briefly. "We will meet again, Bakela."

"If the gods are kind," Zouga agreed, and Gandang laid one hand on his shoulder, squeezed briefly, and then turned away.

Slowly, without looking back, Gandang walked away into the clamor of the singing and the sound of drums.

"Your guns would be terrible weapons if they did not have to be reloaded," Mzilikazi piped in his querulous old man's voice. "But to fight with them a man must have a fast horse, so that he may fire and then gallop away to reload."

Zouga squatted by the King's chair in the royal enclosure as he had for almost thirty successive days. The King sent for him each day, and he must listen to Mzilikazi's wisdom and eat huge quantities of half-raw beef washed down by pot after pot of beer.

"Without a horse my warriors will overrun them before they can reload, even as we did to the Griquas, and afterward we picked up over three hundred of their precious guns from the battlefield."

Zouga nodded his agreement, smiling inwardly as he imagined the *amadoda* trying those tactics on a square of British infantry.

Mzilikazi broke off to lift the beer pot, and then as he lowered it the sparkle of one of Zouga's tunic buttons caught his eye, and he leaned across to pluck at it. Resignedly Zouga took the clasp knife from his pocket and carefully cut the threads that held the button. He handed it to the King, and Mzilikazi grinned with pleasure and held it to the sunlight.

"Only five to go," Zouga thought ironically. He felt like the Christmas turkey being plucked a feather at a time. His lapel badges and field officer's pips had long since been taken by the King, as had his belt buckles and helmet badge.

"The paper," Zouga began and the King waved airily, dismissing the reference to the concession.

He might be on the verge of senility and certainly he was an alcoholic, drinking seven gallons of beer each day, by Zouga's count, but still Mzilikazi possessed a cunning and devious intellect with a natural grasp of his own bargaining weaknesses and strengths. He had teased Zouga for thirty days, just as he had teased the watching nation on the third day of the *Chawala*, while they had waited for him to hurl the war spear.

Now the King turned away from Zouga at the mention of the concession, and transferred his attention to the young couple who knelt before him. They had been accused, and had come before the King for judgment.

That day, in between chatting with Zouga, Mzilikazi had received emissaries bearing tribute from two of his vassal chieftains, he had rewarded a young herdboy for saving his herd from a marauding lion, he had sentenced to death another who had been seen drinking milk directly from the udder of one of his charges, he had listened to the reports of a messenger from the impis campaigning in the north against the Makololo, and now his attention was on the accused couple before him.

The girl was a lovely creature, with long delicately formed limbs and a sweetly rounded face with full flaring lips over small very white teeth. She kept her eyes tightly closed, so as not to look upon the King's wrath, and her body was shaken with tremors of terror as she knelt before him. The man was a finely muscled young warrior, from one of the unmarried regiments, who had still to win the honor of being allowed to "go in to the women."

"Rise up, woman, that the King may see your shame," the voice of the accuser rang out, and hesitantly, timidly, still with

461

her eyes tightly closed, the girl lifted her forehead from the dusty earth, and sat back on her heels.

Her naked stomach, drum tight and round as a ripening fruit, bulged out above the tiny beaded apron.

The King sat hunched in his chair, brooding silently for many minutes. Then he asked the warrior, "Do you deny this thing?"

"I do not deny it, Nkosi Nkulu."

"Do you love this wench?"

"As I love life itself, my King." The man's voice was low and husky, but firm and without a quaver to it.

The King brooded again.

Zouga had sat by and watched the King give judgment on a hundred such occasions. Sometimes the decision had been worthy of a black Solomon, at others Zouga had been appalled by the barbaric savagery of the sentence.

Now the King stared at the man before him, and he fiddled with the toy spear in his right hand, frowning and shaking his head softly. He reached a decision, and leaning forward he proffered the weapon to the man who knelt before him.

"With this blade, open the womb of the woman you love, take out from it that which offends against law and against custom—and place it in my hands."

Zouga did not sleep that night, and once he threw off his blankets and hurried to the fringe of the acacia grove to retch and heave, vomiting up his horror at what he had witnessed.

In the morning the memory of the girl's screams had not faded but the King was jocular and garrulous, pressing pot after pot of sour beer on Zouga's rebellious stomach, recounting episodes from his long and eventful life, describing vividly the scenes from his childhood and youth in far-off Zululand with an overly certain old man's wistful nostalgia.

Then suddenly, without any prior hint that he would do so, he commanded Zouga, "Speak the words of your paper."

He listened silently as Zouga translated the terms of the concession he was seeking, and at the end he mused a moment.

"To hunt elephant and to dig a hole," he mumbled at last. "It is not so very much you wish for. Write that you will do these things only in the land below the Zambezi, east of the Inyati River and above the Limpopo."

Not quite convinced that the King was this time serious, Zouga quickly added the proviso to the foot of his homegrown legal document.

462

Then he directed the King's trembling hand to form the big uncertain cross below it.

"Mzilikazi: his mark."

The King's pleasure in affixing the wax seal beside his mark was childlike and unaffected. After it was done he passed it to his indunas to admire, and leaned forward toward Zouga.

"Now that you have what you want from me, you will wish to leave." There was regret in the rheumy eyes, and Zouga felt a pang of guilt, but he replied directly.

"I cannot hunt in the rains, and there is much work for me to accomplish in my own land across the sea. I must go, but I shall return, Nkosi Nkulu."

"I give you the road to the south, Bakela the Fist. Go in peace and return to me soon, for your presence pleased me, and your words are wise for one still so young."

"Stay in peace, Great Elephant." Zouga rose and left the King's courtyard, and his step was as light as his spirits were gay. He had the concession buttoned into the breast pocket of his tunic, fifty-six pounds of native gold in his chest, the stone bird of Zimbabwe, and three fine tusks of ivory to buy his way. The road to the south, to Good Hope and to England lay open before him.

The wind was offshore, a faint backlash of the monsoon, but the sky was low and the twisting squalls of rain fell from it like pearl dust.

Ensign Ferris, *Black Joke*'s most junior officer, was taking his sights off the traverse board as the gunboat closed the land, calling them quietly to the signals yeoman who swiftly worked out the distance offshore, and wrote this down on the navigation slate, so that any moment the captain could glance down at it to confirm his own observations.

There was a man in the bows with a lead line, chanting the depth as he read it from the markings on the line, then twirling the weight and hurling it out ahead of *Black Joke*'s creeping bows, letting it sink and then reading the mark again as the ship passed over it.

"By the deep six."

Clinton Codrington was conning his ship in by the leadsman's chant, by the angles that Ferris was shooting off the land features which they had identified, by the color shadings of the water, by the break and swirl of the tide on shoal and bank, and by a seaman's instinct. The chart surveyed thirty years previously by Captain Owen, R.N., he trusted not at all.

463

"Bring her around a point," he told the helmsman quietly, and as the ship swung toward the land, they smelled it on the wind.

"Slave stink!" exclaimed Denham fiercely, and as he said it the masthead lookout sang out sharply,

"Smoke! Smoke from the right bank of the river."

"How far upstream?"

"Two miles or more, sir!"

For the first time since sailing from Zanzibar Harbor, Clinton allowed himself to believe that he was in time, that he had reached the Rio Save in time to answer the heartrending appeal of the woman he loved.

"We will clear for action, if you please, Mr. Denham, but don't run out the guns." He kept his voice level and formal, but his lieutenant grinned at him.

"A fair cop, by Jove. Congratulations, sir," and the crew laughed and skylarked as they lined up at the arms chest to receive their pistols and cutlasses.

As *Black Joke* breasted the breaking white water of the bar, touched sand bottom for a moment and then broke the grip of it, and surged forward into the green and still waters of the estuary, Clinton nodded at Denham.

"You may run out the guns now."

He had delayed until this moment to avoid altering the ship's trim during the critical passage of the bar. With the carriages rumbling ominously, *Black Joke* bared her fangs and under fighting sail, her bronze propeller thrashing exultingly, her crew armed and eager, she went into the labyrinth of the Rio Save like a ferret into the warren.

Clinton took her around the first bend, following the deep-green sweep of the channel between the paler sandbanks. It was two hours past low tide and the flood was pushing strongly, the leadsman calling good bottom, and Clinton was trying to conceal his impatience and eagerness by the calm controlled tone in which he called his orders to the helm.

"Would you just look at that!" exclaimed Ferris, and pointed over the side. Beside them floated what looked like an ebony log. It was only as they passed and it bobbed and rolled in their wake that Clinton realized that it was a human corpse, stomach distended, round and shiny with gas and limbs twisted like the branches of a tree blasted by lightning. Clinton transferred his attention back to the ship, with a small grimace of distaste.

"Meet her," he told the helmsman and then as they tore

around the broad curve of water between the mangrove forests and the full stretch of the estuary opened ahead of them, he said, "Midships!"

His voice was flat, unemotional, neither triumphant nor dejected. Smoke rose from the bank of the river, and through his glass he could see the smoldering remains of a series of long low buildings, roofs burned through and collapsed inward. They seemed to have been deliberately fired.

In the smoke soaring and circling on spread wings rose a host of birds, buzzards and kites and vultures and the carrion-eating marabou storks. They seemed to reach up with the smoke to the belly of the lowering monsoon clouds, dimming the light of day with their wings. The oppressive towering silence was broken only by the faint high cries of the birds, and the river was empty.

Clinton and his officers stared silently at the wide deserted sweep of the Rio Save, green and smooth from bank to mangroveclad bank. No one spoke as *Black Joke* bore on, close in to the ruined and blackened barracoons. They stared at the piles of corpses, their faces stiff and expressionless, concealing their horror at the foul plague that lurked there in the palm groves, concealing also their disappointment and chagrin at finding the anchorage deserted and *Huron* gone.

"Stop engine," Clinton broke the silence. "Let go port anchor."

Denham and Ferris turned to look at their captain, their carefully controlled expressions cracking with disbelieving dread; he was going to send a party ashore. They would come back aboard carrying the plague with them, they would all be doomed.

The bow anchor hit the mud of the estuary bottom, and *Black Joke* turned sharply, the flow of the tide swinging her across the narrow channel in her own length, the anchor holding her head until she was pointed directly back down the river toward the sea. Immediately Clinton gave the order, "Slow ahead," and, as the ship breasted the tide, "Up anchor," and the steam winch clattered merrily. The officers relaxed visibly, and Denham allowed himself to smile with relief. The captain had used the anchor merely to turn the ship as swiftly as possible without going through the dangerous business of backing and filling in the narrow channel against the push of the tide.

As the anchor came back aboard with the gluey black mud clinging to its flukes, Clinton gave another series of orders.

"Half ahead." That was as fast as he dared push for the open sea.

"Secure from action stations."

There was no enemy to fight and as the heavy long-barreled thirty-two-pounder guns were run in, *Black Joke* handled more easily.

"Mr. Ferris, we will fumigate the ship."

The smoke from the pails of burning sulfur would redden all their eyes and for days would taint the food and water, but Clinton's dread of smallpox outweighed such small considerations as comfort, and, besides, he smiled wryly to himself, any change to the taste of *Black Joke*'s bullied beef and hard bread could only be an improvement.

The smile was fleeting. He was sickened by his brief glimpses of the barracoons, and his anger was a cold sharp thing like the blade of the cutlass on his belt.

"Mr. Denham," he said quietly, "please plot a course for Good Hope. We'll come onto it the moment we clear the land."

He moved to the rail, half his mind on the job of conning *Black Joke* out of this stinking green river into the open sea, the other half of his mind running swiftly over the problem of bringing his ship into action against *Huron*.

How long a start did the tall clipper have? Robyn Ballantyne's letter had been dated November 16, today was November 27. Eleven days. That was too much. He could only hope that Robyn had been able to delay the sailing, as she had promised.

Clinton glanced back over his shoulder at the blue smoke column that blurred the horizon. Those fires had been burning not more than three or four days, he guessed, with more hope than conviction. Yet even that was still too long a start. He had seen *Huron* on a wind and she was swift as a swallow. Even with eight hundred slaves in her holds, and her water casks filled, she would toy with *Black Joke* in any wind better than a light breeze. His only advantage would be in the offing that *Huron* must make to get on the trades and weather the bulge of the continent, while *Black Joke* could cut across the other arm of the triangle, hugging the land. It was small advantage, a few hundred leagues, and in the end it would all depend on the wind.

Clinton found he was pounding his clenched fist on the ship's rail, that he was glaring ahead with such ferocity that the idle hands of the lee rail were watching him curiously.

With an effort he forced his features to relax, and linked his hands at the small of his back, beneath the tails of his uniform coat, but his eyes still glittered sapphire-blue and his lips were chalky with stress. It seemed too long for his patience before he could at last bring *Black Joke* onto her true course, and bend to the engine-room voice tube.

"I want all the speed you can squeeze out of her," he told his engineer. "There is twenty thousand pounds of prize money just below the horizon, but it's running like a fox and I'll need every pound of steam you can give me."

He straightened up and the wind whipped his pale hair against his sun-gilded cheeks and forehead. He glanced up at the sky and saw the ponderous role of the monsoon clouds on the wind.

Huron would have it full and boisterous on her port beam, and with that hull and rigging it was probably her best point of sailing.

He knew that there was not the remotest chance of finding the clipper on the open sea, there were millions of square miles of ocean to cover; not even a battle fleet with a full squadron of frigates ideally placed ahead of the fugitive would have much chance of finding a single ship in that infinity of water.

Clinton knew that his only chance was to reach the southern tip of the continent ahead of *Huron* and to take up station athwart the narrow shipping lane that was threaded around Cape Point. However, once *Huron* rounded the southern Cape, the whole of the wide Atlantic would lie ahead of her and she would be gone again. Clinton's jawline clenched spasmodically at the thought of the American escaping into that limitless expanse of sea. If she had indeed eleven days' lead on him with this wind holding fair, she could even at this moment be raising the rocky cliffs of Cape Point. He put the thought from his mind and concentrated on coaxing speed from his ship over the long days and nights ahead.

Robyn had searched in vain for a subterfuge to delay *Huron*'s departure from the Rio Save, even though she knew that if she succeeded she would be endangering the lives of all aboard her. However, Mungo St. John had swiftly regained his energy and determination. Affected by Robyn's warning about the danger of battlefield plagues, he forced the pace of his crew in loading. They worked through the night by the light of tar-dipped rope torches, the crew every bit as eager as their captain to be away from this cursed river. Four days after the loading began, *Huron*'s slave decks were in place and her cargo of slaves aboard, and that evening at the full of the tide, using the last of the light and the first gusts of the offshore night breeze, *Huron* slipped over the bar, shook out her reefs and settled down to make her offing during the night.

At dawn they caught the steady push of the trades and Mungo brought her around on to a more southerly heading, close hauled to make good their eastings before running for the bulge of Agulhas with the wind on the beam.

The sweet clean air of the open sea that had traveled thousands upon thousands of miles since last having touched land, swept through the ship, cleansing it of the dreadful stench, and Mungo's strict hygienic discipline helped to keep the holds free of the slave stink and impressed even Robyn, though reluctantly, with his forethought and his precautions.

By sacrificing a single slave deck, raising the space between each from the traditional twenty inches to thirty-two inches, he allowed not only greater comfort but easier access. In these mild conditions of wind and sea, the slaves were exercised during all of the daylight hours; the higher headroom and wider ladderways enabled even those in the lowest decks to be brought up on deck in batches of fifty at a time. On the main deck they were forced to dance to the rhythm of a tribal drum beaten by a tattooed naked tribesman, the rattle and clink of their chains making a mournful background music to the drum and the sweet sound of the singing slaves.

"Funny business, that tattooing." Nathaniel stopped to chat with Robyn as she stood watching the dismal show. "They started tattooing their children to make them repulsive to us slavers; some of them file or knock out their teeth—like that one there." He pointed at a muscular black man in the circle of dancing slaves whose teeth had been filed to sharp points like those of a shark. "Some of them put bones through the noses of their daughters, and others stretch their tits—begging your pardon at the plain speaking, ma'am—or they put rings of copper around their necks until they look like giraffes, all so the slavers will leave them alone. They do say now that these have become marks of beauty amongst the heathen. No accounting for taste, is there, ma'am?"

Robyn saw how the extra space and regular exercise would affect the well-being of the slaves, and while they were up on the main deck, in the open air, their empty slave decks were flushed out with sea water from the ship's pumps and then scrubbed down with a strong lye mixture, though even this was not enough to prevent the slave stink from slowly impregnating the ship.

Each slave spent two hours on deck each second day, and

while they were there, Robyn held clinic and examined each of them for any signs of disease or injury. Before going below once more, they were each forced to drink a decoction of molasses and lime juice to supplement the plain diet of boiled farina and water, and to ward off the dreaded scourge of the scurvy.

The slaves responded well to this treatment, and, incredibly, began to put on the weight that they had burned off during the fevers that were the result of the inoculation against the small-pox. The mood of the slaves was resigned and compliant, although there were isolated incidents. One morning, while a batch of slaves were being brought up, one of them, a fine-looking naked woman, managed to work free the shackle of her chain and the moment she reached the deck she rushed to *Huron*'s side and leaped over it, into the creaming blue wake of the racing clipper.

Despite the fact that she still wore the iron cuffs on her wrists, she managed to keep afloat for many long minutes; her struggles were pitiful to watch as she was slowly drawn down lower and lower in the water.

Robyn had run to the rail to watch the woman's efforts, expecting Mungo to heave to and lower a boat to rescue her, but he remained detached and silent on his quarterdeck, barely glancing over the stern before occupying himself once more with the management of his ship, while *Huron* tore away and the woman's head dwindled to a speck on the blue water, then was drawn inevitably below the surface by the weight of her iron cuffs.

Although Robyn realized that it would have been impossible to stop the clipper and reach the woman before she drowned, yet she glared at Mungo across the length of the deck, wishing that there were words to express her fury and indignation.

That night she lay awake in her tiny cabin, hour after hour, racking her imagination for some ruse that could be used to delay the tall clipper's full flight toward the southern Cape.

She thought of stealing one of the ship's boats and casting herself adrift during the night, forcing Mungo to turn back and to search for her. It took only a few minutes' reflection to realize that it would take a dozen strong men to free the whaler from its lashings and lower it on its davits over the ship's side— and even if she managed to accomplish that, it was far from certain that Mungo would delay even a minute. He was more likely to sail away and leave her, as he had left the slave woman.

She thought of setting fire to the ship, overturning a lantern in the mainsail locker, and creating so much damage that *Huron* would be obliged to call at the nearest port, Lourenço Marques or Port Natal, to effect repairs, and to give *Black Joke* an opportunity to come up with her. Then she imagined eight hundred chained slaves burning to death in the hold when the fire got out of control, and she shuddered, thrust that idea from her and hopelessly composed herself to a sleep which would not come.

In the end her opportunity came from a most unexpected source: Tippoo. The huge mate had a weakness, a single weakness that Robyn could observe. He was a trencherman and, in his own taste, a gourmet. Half the lazaretto was filled with delicacies that Tippoo had hoarded and which he shared with no others. There were dried and smoked meats and sausages, cheeses the smell of which brought tears to the eyes, and wooden crates of cans and bottles of preserved foods, though as a strict Moslem he took no alcohol. He made up what he lacked in the glass with his spoon.

His appetite was one of the ship's jokes, and Robyn had heard Mungo chaffing him across the wardroom table.

"Were it not for the tucker you brought aboard, Mr. Mate, we'd have room for another hundred blackbirds in our hold."

"I'll wager that belly of yours costs you more to sustain than a harem of extravagant wives."

"Sweet merciful heavens, Mr. Tippoo, but whatever you are eating should have been given a Christian burial a month ago."

One of Tippoo's favorite appetizers was a particularly virulent bloater paste, packed in half-pound tins. The instruction printed on the tin read "Spread thinly on biscuit or toast," and Tippoo would spoon it directly from the tin, consuming the entire half pound without once breaking the rhythmic dip and lift of his soup spoon, his eyes half closed and a cherubic smile buckling the wide line of his toad's mouth.

The fourth night out of the Rio Save he began his dinner with a can of bloater paste, but as he pierced the lid with his clasp knife, there was a sharp hiss of escaping gas, and Mungo St. John glanced up from his own plate of pea soup.

"It is blown, Mr. Tippoo. I would not eat it if I were you."

"No," Tippoo agreed. "But you not me."

They called Robyn a little before midnight. Tippoo was in convulsions, doubled up with agony, his belly swollen and hard as a yellow agate boulder. He had vomited until now he was retching only a little blood-flecked bile.

"It's ptomaine poisoning," Robyn told Mungo St. John. It was the first time she had spoken directly to him since that morning in the Rio Save, and her voice was cool and formal. "I do not have the medicines to treat it. You will have to put into a port where he can receive treatment. There is a military hospital at Port Natal."

"Dr. Ballantyne," Mungo answered her as formally, but his infuriating smile lurked behind the gold-flecked eyes. "Mr. Tippoo's mother was an ostrich, he can digest stones, nails and lumps of broken glass. Your concern, touching as it may be, is entirely misplaced. He will be ready to fight, flog or devour an ox by noon tomorrow."

"And I tell you that without proper treatment he will be dead in a week."

However, Mungo's prognosis proved to be correct, for by morning the vomiting and retching had abated and Tippoo seemed to have purged his bowels of the poisoned fish. Robyn was forced to a decision which she made on her knees in her cabin.

"Forgive me, O Lord, but there are eight hundred of your children chained below decks in this foul prison, and I will not kill him—at least, with your help, I will not kill him."

Then, off her knees she went briskly to work. She used a solution of peppermint tincture to disguise the taste, and let fall fifteen drops of essence of ipecacuanha into the medicine glass, which was three times the recommended dosage for the most powerful emetic known to the medical science.

"Drink it down," she told Tippoo. "It will soothe your stomach, and cure the diarrhea."

Late that afternoon she repeated the dose, but the wardroom steward had to help her lift Tippoo's head from the bolster and pour the draft down his throat. The effect was enough to alarm even Robyn.

An hour later she sent for Mungo, and the steward came back with the message, "Captain says as how the ship's safety demands all his attention at the moment, begging your pardon, Doctor."

When Robyn herself went on deck, Mungo was at the weather rail, sextant in hand, waiting for the sun to appear in a gap in the clouds.

"Tippoo is dying," she told him.

"And this will be my first sight of the day," Mungo replied without taking his eye from the eyepiece of the instrument.

"I at last believe that you are a monster with no human

feelings," she whispered fiercely, and at that moment blazing sunlight struck the deck as the sun showed briefly through the ragged hole in the cloud.

"Stand by the chronometer," Mungo called to the signals yeoman, and then "Mark!" as he brought the sun's image down to bounce lightly as a green rubber ball on the dark line of the horizon.

"Excellent," he murmured with satisfaction, as he lowered the sextant and read off the height of the sun, and called it to the yeoman to mark on his slate. Only then did he turn back to Robyn.

"I am sure you have misjudged the severity of Tippoo's ailment."

"See for yourself," she invited.

"That is my intention, Doctor."

Mungo stooped into Tippoo's cabin, and paused. His expression changed, suddenly the light mocking smile was gone. It was evident that Tippoo was indeed dangerously ill.

"How are you, old friend?" Mungo asked quietly. It was the first time Robyn had ever heard him use that form of address. He lifted his hand and laid it on the mate's sweat-beaded forehead.

Tippoo rolled the bald yellow cannonball of his head toward Mungo, and he tried to smile. It was a brave effort. Robyn felt a terrible guilty pang at the suffering she was inflicting and at being the witness to this private, and strangely intimate, moment between these two hard and dangerous men.

Tippoo tried to lift himself, but the effort brought a long dragging groan rattling up his throat, and he clutched at his stomach with both hands, drawing his knees up with agony, and then desperately twisting his head as a fresh bout of heaving and retching racked his body.

Mungo snatched the bucket off the deck and with one arm around Tippoo's shoulders held it for him—but all that Tippoo could bring up was a little splash of blood and brown bile, and when he fell back on the bunk he was gasping unevenly, bathed in fresh sweat, and his eyes rolled back in his skull until only a little half moon of the iris still showed.

Mungo stood beside his bunk for a full five minutes, bowed and attentive, swaying slightly to the ship's movement, but otherwise still and silent. His brow was creased with thought and his gaze remote, and watching him, Robyn knew he was making the dire decision—the throw of the dice of life, friendship against the loss of his ship and perhaps even his own

472

liberty, for to go into a British port with slaves in his holds was an awful risk.

Strange, now that he was showing this gentler side of his nature, that her affection came flooding back at full strength, she felt mean and cheap for playing on his deepest emotions, and for torturing the huge yellow Moslem on the narrow bunk.

Mungo swore quietly but decisively, and, still stooped under the low deck, strode from the cabin.

Robyn's affection turned to disgust and disappointment. Disgust that even the life of an old and loyal friend meant nothing to this cruel and merciless man whom she was doomed to love, and intense disappointment that her ruse had failed, that she had inflicted this dangerous suffering on Tippoo to no avail.

She sank down wearily and bitterly beside his bunk, took a cloth soaked in seawater and bathed the sweat-basted yellow head.

During their long voyage down the Atlantic, Robyn had grown sensitive to all *Huron*'s moods, to the feel of the deck underfoot at every point of sailing, and to the sounds that her hull made in different sea and wind conditions, and now abruptly she felt the deck cant sharply beneath her. She heard the stamp of bare feet on the deck above as her yards were trained around and *Huron*'s action became easier, the sounds of her hull and rigging muted as she took the wind in over her stern quarter and rode more easily.

"He's altered course toward the west," she breathed as she lifted her head to listen. "It worked. He is going in to Port Natal. Oh thank you, Lord, it worked."

Huron anchored well offshore, out on the thirty-fathom line of the shelving coast, so that she could not benefit from the shelter of the huge whale-backed bluff that protected Port Natal's natural harbor. Even with a powerful telescope, a watcher on the shore would be unable to make out any significant details of *Huron*'s cargo, nor of her true occupation. However, the ship paid for her offshore berth by taking the unfettered scend of the sea and the wind. She pitched and she rolled and she jerked at her anchor chain.

At her peak she flew the stars and stripes of her country— and below that the yellow "Quebec," the plague flag which warned, "Stay away from me! I have plague on board!"

Mungo St. John placed an armed watch on both sides of the ship and others at her bow and stern, and, despite Robyn's strident protest, she was confined to her cabin for the duration fo the ship's call, with another armed guard outside her door.

"You are very well aware of the reason, Dr. Ballantyne." Mungo answered her protests calmly. "I do not wish you to have any communication whatsoever with your countrymen ashore."

The whaler, when it took Tippoo ashore, was rowed by men that Mungo selected personally, and they were instructed to inform the harbormaster that there was smallpox aboard, and to request that no other vessel be allowed near *Huron*.

"I can only wait three days for you." Mungo stooped over the litter on which Tippoo was carried on deck. "That is all I can risk. If you are not sufficiently recovered by then, you will have to stay here until my return. That cannot be more than five months." He tucked a leather drawstring purse under Tippoo's blanket. "And that will pay your expenses in the meanwhile. Get well, Mr. Tippoo, I need you."

Robyn had administered another dose of the peppermint and ipecacuanha a few minutes previously, and Tippoo could reply only in an agonized whisper.

"I will wait for you, Captain Mungo, as long as she takes."

Mungo's voice was husky as he straightened and spoke to the seamen carrying the litter.

"Handle him easy, you hear me."

For three days Robyn sweated and fretted in the stuffy little cabin, trying to occupy her time with writing up her journals but distracted by any loud noise from the deck above, her heart pounding as she both hoped for and dreaded the hail from a British gunboat, or the rush of a boarding party coming in over *Huron*'s side.

On the third morning Tippoo was rowed back to the ship, and he climbed up the side and in through the entry port unaided. Without further doses of ipecacuanha, his recovery had amazed the military surgeons ashore, but he was so thin that the skin hung in folds from his jowls like a bulldog, his belly had shrunk so that he had tied his breeches with a length of rope to keep them from sinking down past his flattened belly, but still they flapped around his shrunken buttocks.

His skin was the pale yellow of ancient ivory, and he was so weak he had to pause to rest when he reached the deck.

"Welcome aboard, Mr. Tippoo," Mungo called from the quarterdeck. "And if you have finished your holiday ashore, I'll thank you to get this ship under way immediately."

Twelve days later, having struggled with fluky and variable

474

winds, Mungo St. John played the field of his glass down the open gaping maw of False Bay. On his right hand rose the distinctive curved black peak of Hangklip, shaped from this angle like a shark's dorsal fin, and directly opposite it across the mouth of the bay the southernmost tip of the African continent, Cape Point, with its lighthouse perched high above the steep wet cliffs.

It was a magnificent Cape summer's day, a light and fickle breeze scratching dark patches on the surface of the rolling deep-blue sea, leaving the rest of it with a satiny gloss. There were seabirds working, their wings twinkling like flurrying snowflakes in the sunlight, huge flocks of them that stretched low across the horizon.

Creeping along on the breeze, lying for minutes at a time completely becalmed, *Huron* took half a day to round the point and came on to west-northwest and a point north, the course that would carry her up the Atlantic, across the equator and finally into Charleston Roads.

Once they were on their new course, Mungo St. John had leisure to inspect the other sails that were in sight. There were nine, no, ten other vessels in view now, for there was another far out to sea, just her topsails showing. They were small fishing craft out from Hout Bay and Table Bay, and the seabirds clouded the air about them, most of them were between *Huron* and the land, and all of them were bare-masted or under working sail as they plied their lines or their nets. Only the vessel furthest out was carrying topsails, and though she was hull down she gave to Mungo's seaman's eye the impression of being a bigger ship than the rest of the fishing fleet.

"There's a ship for you!" Tippoo exclaimed, touching Mungo's arm to draw his attention and when he swung his glass back toward the land Mungo murmured with pleasure as a square-rigged East Indiaman came into view around the headland that guarded the entrance to Table Bay itself.

She was as splendid a sight as *Huron* was herself, canvas piled to the sky and her paintwork gleaming in snowy white and Burgundy red, the two lovely ships on reciprocal courses passed each other by two cables' length, the officers eying each other through their telescopes with professional interest and appraisal as they paid passing honors.

Robyn was also at *Huron*'s rail, pining toward the land. The proximity of the beautiful ship interested her hardly at all, it was that flat-topped mountain from which she could barely tear her gaze. It was so very close, marking as it did her one
475

hope of succor, her friends there, the British governor and the Cape Squadron, if they only knew that she was a prisoner aboard this slave ship.

The thought was interrupted by an abrupt movement that she caught from the corner of her eye—strange how receptive she was to Mungo St. John's smallest movement, to his slightest change of expression—and now she saw that he had turned his back on the East Indiaman as she dwindled away astern, and instead he was peering intently over *Huron*'s port side, his expression rapt, his whole body charged with latent energy, and the hands that gripped the barrel of the telescope ivory-knuckled with tension.

Quickly she followed his gaze, and for the first time noticed a tiny shred of white on the horizon that did not fade like the whitecaps of the waves, but stood constant and bright in the sunlight, though even as she watched it seemed to alter its shape slightly and—was it her imagination, or was it a thin dark wavering line that seemed to appear behind it and spread slowly away in the direction of the wind?

"Mr. Tippoo, what do you make of that sail?" She heard the timbre of concern and alarm in Mungo St. John's tone, and her heart leaped wildly, with hope and a Judas dread.

For Clinton Codrington it had been a desperate run down the eastern coastline of southern Africa, long days and sleepless nights of unceasing strain, when hope and despair pendulumed against each other. Each shift or change in the wind either alarmed or encouraged him, for it would either aid or hinder the tall clipper ship he was racing to head. The calms elated him, and the revival of the southeasterly prevailing winds sent his spirits plunging.

On the last days there was another worry to plague him. He had burned his coal like a spendthrift on the long thousand-mile run southward, and his engineer came up on deck, a small red-headed Scot with the grease and coal dust etched into his skin so that he seemed to be suffering from some debilitating and incurable disease.

"The stockers' shovels be hitting the bottom of the bunkers already," he told Clinton with mournful relish. "I warned ye, sir, that we'd not make it if you—"

"Burn the ship's furniture if you must," Clinton snapped at him. "You can start with my bunk, I'll not be needing it."

And when the engineer would have argued further Clinton added, "I don't care how you do it, Mr. MacDonald, but I want a full head of steam on your boiler until I reach Cape Point, and another full head of steam when I bring this ship into action."

They raised the Cape Point lighthouse a few minutes after midnight the following night, and Clinton's voice was hoarse with fatigue and relief as he stooped over the voice pipe.

"Mr. MacDonald, you can let your fires damp down, but keep your furnaces warmed and ready to stoke. When I ask for steam again, I'll need it in a hurry."

"You'll be calling at Table Bay to take on fresh bunkers, of course, sir?"

"I'll let you know when," Clinton promised him, and snapped the lid of the speaking tube closed and straightened up.

The Cape naval base, with all its amenities, lay only a few hours' steaming away. By dawn he could be filling *Black Joke* with coal and water and fresh vegetables.

However, Clinton knew that within minutes of dropping anchor in Table Bay, Admiral Kemp or one of his representatives would be on his way out to the ship, and Clinton's term of independent command would be over. He would revert to being a very junior commander, whose recent actions needed a great deal of explanation.

The closer that Clinton drew to Admiralty House, the louder the warnings of Sir John Bannerman rang in his ears, and the more soberly he was forced to review his own position. The excitement of storming Arab barracoons and of seizing slave-laden dhows on the high seas had long ago cooled, and Clinton realized that once he entered it he would not be able to escape again from Table Bay for weeks, or possibly months. It would not even suit his immediate plans to be seen and recognized from the land, for a boat would immediately be sent out by Admiral Kemp to order him in to face judgment and retribution.

Clinton felt not the least trepidation about the Navy's ultimate judgment; he was so indifferent to the threat hanging over his career that he surprised even himself. There was only one desire, one object in his mind, that overshadowed all else. He must have his ship in position to intercept *Huron* as she rounded the Cape, if she had not already done so. Nobody and nothing must prevent him from doing so. After that he would face his accusers with complete equanimity. *Huron* and Robyn Ballantyne first, beside them all else was pale and insignificant.

"Mr. Denham," he called his Lieutenant across the dark deck. "We will take up night patrol station ten miles off Cape

477

Point, and I am to be called immediately the lights of any ship are sighted."

As Clinton threw himself down, fully dressed and booted, upon his bunk, he experienced the first peace of mind since leaving Zanzibar Harbor. He had done all that was in his power to reach Cape Point ahead of *Huron*, and now the rest was in the hands of God—and his trust in God was implicit.

He fell asleep almost instantly, and his steward woke him again an hour before dawn. He left the mug of coffee to grow cold beside his bunk and hurried on deck, reaching it a few seconds ahead of Lieutenant Denham.

"No ships during the night, sir," Ferris, who had the watch, saluted him.

"Very well, Mr. Ferris," Clinton acknowledged. "We will take up our daylight patrol station immediately."

By the time the light was strong enough for a watcher on the shore to make out any details, *Black Joke* had retreated tactfully below the horizon and it would have taken a sharp eye to pick out the occasional flash of her topsails, let alone to identify the gunboat and to speed a report to Admiral Kemp that his prodigal had returned.

From *Black Joke*'s masthead the land was a low irregular distortion of the horizon, but a ship rounding the Cape would be many miles closer than the land. *Huron*'s mainmast was almost one hundred and fifty feet tall, her sails would shine like a flaming beacon and as long as the fog did not come down, which was unlikely at this season of the year, Clinton was confident that she could not slip by him.

The only disquiet that scratched him like a burr as he paced his deck, and the gunboat settled down into the regular four-sided box-patterned legs of her patrol, was that *Huron* had long ago flown northward on this fine wind that at last bore steadily out of the southeast at almost gale force, and that she was already lost in the endless watery green wastes of the southern Atlantic Ocean, leaving *Black Joke* to guard the gate of an empty cage.

He was not left long to brood. The first sighting was called down to the deck from the lookouts in the crow's nest at the main peak, and Clinton's nerves jumped tight and his expectations flared.

"What do you make of her?" he called up through the voice trumpet.

"Small lugger—" and his expectations plunged. A fishing boat out of Table Bay, there would be many of them. But each

478

time he could not control the wild surge of excitement when another sail was sighted, so that by nightfall his nerves were ragged, and his body ached with exhaustion as he gave the order for *Black Joke* to take up her inshore patrol station for the night.

Even then he could not rest, for three times during the night he was called from his bunk, and he stumbled owl-eyed on deck as *Black Joke* went down to investigate running lights that winked ruby-red and emerald-green out of the darkness.

Each time the same leap of expectation, the steeling of nerves for instant orders and swift action, and then the same letdown as the lights proved to belong to small trading vessels, and the gunboat sheered away quickly, lest she be recognized and her presence off the Cape be reported in Table Bay.

In the dawn, Clinton was on deck again, as the gunboat moved further offshore to take up her daylight patrol station. He was distracted by the sighting reports as his masthead lookout picked up the first sails of the fishing fleet coming out for the day's business, and by the lugubrious report of his coal-stained Scottish engineer.

"Ye'll not last out the day, sir," MacDonald told him. "Even though I am burning just enough coal to keep the furnace warm, we've not more than a bucket or two left."

"Mr. MacDonald," Clinton interrupted him, trying to keep his temper under control and to disguise his exhaustion. "This ship will stay on station until I give the order, I don't care what you burn, but you are to give me steam when I ask for it—or kiss good-bye to the fattest bundle of prize money that will ever come your way."

Despite this brave promise and threat, Clinton's hopes were sinking swiftly. They had been on station for more than a day and night already—he could not bring himself to believe that he had beaten the swift clipper to the Cape by that margin, not unless she had been somehow miraculously delayed—and every hour increased the certainty that she had run clear away from him, taking her cargo and the woman he loved out of his life forever.

He knew he should go below to rest, but his cabin was stifling in the rising summer heat, and in it he felt like a trapped animal. He stayed on deck, unable to keep still for more than a few moments at a time, poring over the chart table and fiddling with the navigational instruments before throwing them down and resuming his nervous pacing, shooting quick glances up at the masthead, and then roaming the ship so obviously intent

479

on finding fault or criticizing the ship's running that his officers followed his lanky figure with troubled expressions, while the watch on deck was silent and subdued, not one of them daring to glance in his direction until Clinton's voice rose in a coldly furious cry that froze them all.

"Mr. Denham"—the lieutenant almost ran to the summons—"this deck is a pigsty. What animal is responsible for this filth?"

On the white holystoned deck planking was a brown splash of tobacco juice, and Denham stared at it for an instant before wheeling away to bellow a series of orders that had a dozen men scampering. The activity was so intense, the atmosphere electric, as captain and lieutenant stood over four men on their knees scrubbing furiously at the offending stain while others carried buckets of seawater and still others rigged the deck pump, that the hail from the masthead was almost ignored.

It was left to Ferris to acknowledge it, and to inquire through the voice trumpet, "What do you make of her?"

"She's hull down, but she's a four-masted ship, square rigged—"

The activity on the deck ceased instantly, every head lifting as the lookout went on elaborating on his sighting.

"She's on a course to weather the Cape, now she's coming round on to a heading of north-northwest or thereabouts."

Clinton Codrington was the first to move. He snatched the telescope out of Lieutenant Denham's hand and ran to the ratlines. With the telescope tucked in his belt he began to climb, hand over hand.

He went up steadily, never pausing nor faltering, not even when he reached the futtock shrouds and for a few moments hung over backward one hundred feet above the swaying deck. However, when he reached the crow's nest at the main peak and tumbled into it thankfully, his breath was sawing dryly in his throat and the blood sang in his ears. He had not climbed like that since he had been a midshipman.

The lookout tried to make himself as small as possible, for they were crowded together in the canvas bucket, and he pointed out the ship to his captain.

"There she be, sir."

Black Joke's roll was emphasized up here on the tall pendulum of the mast, and the horizon swung giddily through the field of Clinton's telescope as he tried to keep it focused. It was an art that he had never completely mastered, but that was of little consequence, for the first time the little regular white pyramids popped up in the field of his glass the last doubts were dispelled, and Clinton felt his heart leap fiercely against his ribs.

His voice was strangled with triumphant emotion as he shouted down at the tiny foreshortened figures on the gleaming white quarterdeck far below.

"Bring her round to due east, Mr. Denham. Order a full head of steam on the boiler—"

Though he had not yet fully recovered his breath, he threw himself out of the crow's nest and scrambled down faster than he had climbed. In his haste he slid the last fifty feet down the backstay and barely noticed the rough hempen rope scorching the palms of his hands.

By the time his feet hit the deck, *Black Joke* was coming around onto her new heading, and in anticipation of Clinton's next order, Denham had already called the watch below, and they came boiling out onto the deck.

"And we will clear for action, Mr. Denham, if you please," gasped Clinton, his face flushed with blood under his deepwater tan and the sapphire eyes alight with battle lust.

All *Black Joke*'s officers carried swords on their belts, only Clinton had selected a cutlass, for he preferred the stouter and heavier weapon, and he fiddled with the hilt even now as he spoke to them quietly and seriously.

"Gentlemen, I have documented proof that the ship ahead of us has a cargo of slaves aboard her."

Denham coughed nervously and Clinton forestalled him. "I am also aware that she is an American vessel, and in ordinary circumstances we would be helpless to oppose her passage." Denham nodded with relief, but Clinton went on remorselessly, "However, I have received an appeal from one of Her Majesty's subjects, Dr. Robyn Ballantyne, whom you all know well, who is being abducted aboard the *Huron* against her will. I am certain what my duty is in these circumstances. I intend to board her, and if she resists me, I intend to fight her." He paused and their faces were shocked, strained. "Those of you who have objections to this course of action should immediately note them in the ship's log, and I will sign them."

Their relief and gratitude was immediate; few other captains would be so lenient.

He signed his name neatly beneath the entry in the ship's log, and then returned the pen to its holder.

"Now that the formalities have been seen to, gentlemen,
481

shall we get on with earning our hire?" And Clinton was smiling for the first time since they sailed from Zanzibar Harbor as he indicated the pile of snowy white sails that was now clearly visible from the deck ahead of *Black Joke*'s bows, and as he spoke there was an eruption of tarry-smelling smoke from the tall single stack above them, and the engine telegraph clanged sharply as the pointer moved to "engine standing by" position on the repeater. *Black Joke* had steam in her boiler.

Clinton stepped to the telegraph, thrust the handle fully around the dial to the "full ahead" position, and the deck vibrated under his feet as the propeller shaft began to spin and *Black Joke* lunged forward eagerly, breaking the swells off her shoulders in explosions of white spray.

"By God, he's got us pinned against the land." Mungo drawled the words out nonchalantly, even smiling slightly at Tippoo as he lowered the glass from his eye for a moment and polished the lens on his shirtsleeve. "We'll have to run like the very devil to get round him, and make the open sea. Mr. Tippoo, will you be good enough to shake out every last reef and crack on all the sail we can carry, right up to the skysails?" He lifted the glass to his eye again as Tippoo began bellowing the orders. "It's a little bit too much luck for any one man," Mungo murmured aloud. "It's too much coincidence that the one man I would not wish to meet be lying in the one place on all the oceans where I would not wish to meet him."

Again he lowered the glass and strode to the poop rail to look down onto the main deck.

Robyn Ballantyne was at the ship's side, staring out across the indigo-blue waters at the sail and the smear of smoke, still far out to sea, but every moment converging on them, headed to a point far ahead of *Huron*'s elegant bows where the courses of the two ships would meet. She sensed Mungo's eyes upon her, and she lifted the shawl off her head so that her russet hair tumbled out and snapped and danced around her cheeks. Her skirts were flattened against her legs by the wind, and she had to lean slightly forward to balance herself.

She lifted her chin to stare up at Mungo, her expression defiant and she watched him as he carefully bit the end off one of his long thin black cheroots and cupped his hands around the sulfurous flare of the vesta match and lit the cheroot without once breaking the steady gaze that held her own.

Then he sauntered easily down the poop ladder to her side.

"A friend of yours, Dr. Ballantyne?" The smile was on his lips alone. His eyes were frosty.

"I have prayed every night for him to come. Ever since I sent the letter that summoned him."

"You do not deny the betrayal?"

"I am proud I was able to perform my Christian duty."

"Who carried your letter?"

"No member of your crew, sir. I sent it by the master of the Omani buggaloo."

"I see." His voice was low, but stinging as dry ice. "And what of Tippoo's illness; would a physician, per chance, stoop to poisoning a patient?"

She dropped her eyes, unable to meet that accusation.

"Will you be so kind, Dr. Ballantyne, as to return to your cabin immediately and stay there until I give you permission to leave it. There will be an armed guard at the door."

"I am to be punished?"

"No man would blame me for dropping you over the side, and leaving you to be picked up by your countrymen. However, it is your safety I am thinking of. This deck could become an unhealthy spot in the very near future, and we will all be too much occupied to care for you."

His attention left her, and he was staring ahead, and then glancing back at *Black Joke*'s smoke, judging speeds and angles with a seaman's eye. Then he smiled.

"Before you go, I would like you to know that all your efforts have really been a fine waste of time—look there!" He pointed ahead along the sheer and mountainous coastline, and following his arm she saw for the first time that ahead of them the sea was as black and broken as new coal cut from the face, glittering with wild jumping wavelets, each flecked with pretty white crests.

"There is the wind," Mungo said. "That's where it comes through the mountains, and we will be into it before you are safely tucked up in your cabin." He chuckled now comfortably, confidently. "Once we get on that wind, there are few ships on all the oceans, either steam or sail, that would match *Huron* for a moment, and God knows, there are none who could run her down." He gave her a small mocking bow, parody of gracious southern manners. "Take a good look at that ugly little steam packet before you go, ma'am, you'll not be seeing her again. And now, if you'll be good enough to excuse me—"

He turned from her and ran lightly back up the poop ladder.

Tears of anger dimming her eyes, Robyn clutched the rail

and stared across the narrowing strip of sea at the bustling, puffing little gunboat. Already she could catch glimpses of the hull, and its painted checkerboard gunports. She began to hope that Mungo St. John's boast had been mere bravado, for *Black Joke* seemed to be keeping pace with the tall clipper, the wind was still a long, long way ahead.

There was a respectful touch on Robyn's shoulder, and old Nathaniel stood beside her.

"Captain's orders, ma'am, and I am to see you safe in your cabin."

Clinton leaned forward, all his weight on the balls of his feet, almost as though he were trying to urge his ship on by the balance of his body, the way a rider leans forward into the jump. He also had seen the wind pattern on the surface of the sea, and knew what it heralded.

The tall clipper ship looked lazy now, indolent in her flounces and ruffles as a lady of high fashion, and *Black Joke* was snorting and snuffling busily down the short leg of the triangle. If they both maintained this speed and course they would meet about eleven nautical miles ahead. Clinton could visualize the exact spot clearly, just beyond the spit of land marked on his chart as "Bakoven Point."

Huron was committed to her present course. She could not bear up for the land lay close under her weather rail, and the chart showed breaking shoals well offshore; there was one of them now, close on her starboard beam, showing its round black granite back and blowing like a whale. *Huron* was in a trap, and her only escape would be to find the extra turn of speed which would carry her away out of gunshot range—and there it was, the wind, less than three miles ahead of her.

There was a loud banging from the deck below Clinton's feet, and he glanced irritably at Ferris.

"See what that is," he snapped, and turned his full attention back to the clipper. Three short miles she had to go, but even as Clinton stared at her through his glass he saw her huge square mainsail quiver and then shake gently as she luffed in the fluky airs below the mountains.

"Please God!" Clinton whispered, and *Huron*'s speed bled off perceptibly, all her sails were losing their taut clean shape and she checked away, balking like a weary animal.

"She's found a hole in the wind," Lieutenant Denham called exultantly. "We've got her now, by God!"

"I'll thank you not to blaspheme on this quarterdeck, Mr.

Denham," Clinton told him sharply, and Denham's expression was instantly crestfallen.

"I beg your pardon, sir." At that moment Ferris arrived breathlessly back on deck.

"The stokers, sir," he panted. "They are knocking out all the furniture from the officers' quarters. Your bunk's gone, sir, and your desk also."

Clinton barely glanced at him, he was studying the clipper, evaluating each yard of difference in their speeds, judging as finely as he dared the angle of his interception.

Yes, he decided, with *Huron*'s loss of speed, he could edge in a touch more.

"Bring her up a point to starboard," he told the helmsman, and then he glanced up at his own sails that were helping the big bronze screws under the stern to hurl *Black Joke* forward. The alteration of course had affected them.

"Mr. Ferris, see to the trim of your jib, if you please."

Ferris bellowed an order to the foredeck watch, and watched critically as they hardened up the long triangular sail.

All *Huron*'s sails shivered, and then refilled, once more taking on their true shape, and she spurted away, a curl of white sparkling under her bows. The dark windswept water was much closer ahead of her.

It had been Denham's unnecessary blasphemy, Clinton was sure of it, and he glowered at his lieutenant, and then reluctantly gave the order.

"Let her fall off a point." *Huron* was headreaching again. If *Black Joke* held on she would be aiming to cut behind the clipper's stern. The alteration was an acknowledgment of the advantage changing hands once again.

The engine voice pipe squealed, and it was a relief to have even the small distraction.

"Engine room, Captain," he snapped into the mouthpiece. "Coal long ago gone, sir. Pressure down to a hundred pounds, sir—and falling."

"Burn everything you can find."

"Wood goes up like paper, sir. No body to it—and it chokes the flue." MacDonald seemed to relish the gloomy news, and Clinton felt his irritation turn to anger.

"Do your best, man, nobody can ask more than that," and he snapped the voice pipe closed.

Was he close enough yet to try a shot with his bow chaser, he wondered? The long sixteen-pounder had almost twice the range of the big thirty-two-pounders that made up *Black Joke*'s main armament. A lucky shot might carry away one of the clipper's spars, might even bring down a yard—and at that moment he distinctly felt the change in the engine vibrations coming up through the deck, *Black Joke* was faltering, the steam in her boilers losing pressure.

"Mr. Ferris, break out the colors, if you please."

As the ensign unfurled at the peak, spread gloriously against the pale-blue sky, crimson and silky white, shouting a challenge on the wind, Clinton felt that tightness in his chest, that swell of pride which never failed him.

"*Huron*'s replying," Denham muttered, and Clinton lifted his glass and watched the American's colors bloom like a flower high above her shimmering piles of white canvas.

"And be damned," Denham interpreted the show of colors. *Huron* was scorning their challenge.

"Mr. Ferris, we'll give her a gun now," Clinton decided grimly. "Put one over her bows." And Ferris scrambled away to the bows to supervise the loading and laying of the bow chaser.

The shot when it came was a puny little pop of sound, muted by the wind, and the long spurt of gray powder smoke was whipped away almost before it could form. Though they were all watching avidly through the telescopes, not one of them could spot the fall of shot, and Denham spoke aloud for all of them.

"She's not altering. She's ignoring us."

"Very well." Clinton kept his voice low. "We'll try one into her rigging."

The sixteen-pounder banged again, like an unlatched door in a high wind, and this time they both exclaimed in unison. A pinprick of light appeared in one of the *Huron*'s studding sails, pierced by shot; it held its shape for an instant and then burst like a paper packet and was blown to tatters.

Clinton saw the bustle of *Huron*'s seamen on the decks and yards, and before the bow chaser could be reloaded, the ruined sail was hauled down and another clean new sail spread open in its place. The speed with which the sail change was made impressed even Clinton.

"The devil is a good sailor, I'll grant him that—" And then he broke off, for *Huron* was turning boldly, seeming to aim to cut the gunboat's bows, and Clinton realized what her captain was doing. He was anticipating the rush of the wind, and as Clinton watched it struck her.

It came roaring aboard the clipper, howling through her

rigging like a pack of hunting wolves, and the tall ship heeled and seemed almost to crouch, gathering herself like a blood stallion feeling the cut of the lash, and then she hurled herself forward and was away.

The dark wind-scoured sea burst open before the long lithe knifing hull, and joyously *Huron* tossed the dashing white spray over her bows.

"She's making twenty knots," Denham cried with disbelief, as *Black Joke* seemed to come up dead in the water, a wallowing log when compared to the swift and lovely ship that cut daringly across her bows, just out of cannon shot, and dashed away into the open Atlantic Ocean.

Through his glass Clinton saw that the seamen who lined *Huron*'s yards were gamboling and waving their caps, mouths wide open, and they cheered and jeered, and then he focused the glass on *Huron*'s deck.

There was a tall figure at *Huron*'s near rail, clad in a plain blue jacket. Clinton could not make out the man's features at this distance, but he recognized the set of wide shoulders, the arrogant carriage of head, that he had last seen over the sights of a dueling pistol.

The acid bile of hatred rose to scald his throat as the figure lifted a hand in a laconic salute, a taunting gesture of farewell, and then turned away from the rail unhurriedly.

Clinton snapped his telescope closed.

"Stern chase!" he ordered. "We'll keep after her!"

He did not dare look at his officers' faces, lest one of them wore an expression of pity.

Lying on her bunk, her arms held stiffly at her sides and hands clenched painfully, Robyn heard the creak and squeal from the deck below her that meant *Huron* was altering course, and that the eight-inch-thick rudder lines were running through their blocks as the helmsman spun the wheel. It was a sound she had long become accustomed to, and she braced herself instinctively while the rudder lines attached to the pintles trained around the enormous wooden rudder under *Huron*'s stern and the ship altered her action through the water.

Seconds later there was a thunderous commotion from the deck above her, the blustering roar of the gale socking into the rigging, the crash of tackle coming up taut, the slam of the great sails when their awesome power was transferred into the hull, and Robyn was almost hurled from her bunk as *Huron* heeled wildly.

487

Then the cabin was filled with the exultant thrumming of the hull through water, as though she were the body of a violin as the bow was drawn across the bass strings, and *Huron* trembled with life, lifting and dropping to the new urgency of her run.

Very faintly Robyn could hear above it all the sound of men cheering. She jumped from the bunk and clutching for handholds crossed the cabin and pounded her fist upon the door.

"Nathaniel," she called. "Answer me this instant."

"Captain says as how I'm not to talk to you." His voice was muffled.

"You cannot torment me so," Robyn yelled back. "What is happening?"

A long pause while Nathaniel considered his duty and then weighed it against his affection for this spirited young woman.

"We are on the wind, ma'am," he told her at last. "And going like all the devils of hell with a crackerjack tied to their tails."

"What of *Black Joke?*" she pleaded. "What of the British gunboat?"

"Ain't nothing will catch us now. Reckon the puffing Billy will be out of sight before nightfall. From here she looks like she's dropped her anchor."

Slowly Robyn leaned forward until her forehead pressed against the planking of the door. She closed her eyes very tightly, and tried to fight down the black waves of despair that threatened to overwhelm her.

She stayed like that for a long time until Nathaniel's voice roused her. It was rough with concern.

"Are you all right then, missus?"

"Yes, thank you, Nathaniel. I'm just fine," she replied tightly, without opening her eyes. "I'm going to take a little nap now. Don't let anybody disturb me."

"I'll be right here, missus. Ain't nobody going to get past me," he assured her.

She opened her eyes and went back to the bunk, and knelt before it and began to pray—but for once she could not concentrate. Jumbled images kept intervening, and, when she closed her eyes, the face of Clinton Codrington was there, with those pale beautiful eyes in the tanned mahogany of his face that accentuated the sunbleached platinum of his hair. She longed for him as she had never done before; he had become a symbol for her that was good and clean and right.

Then her mind darted away and it was that distant mocking

smile, the taunting gold-flecked eyes of Mungo St. John. She trembled with humiliation, the man who had violated her and turned her own emotions traitor, who had dallied with her and allowed her to hope, nay, to pray that she could bear his children and become his wife. Her despair turned to hatred once again, and hatred armed her.

"Forgive me, Lord—I'll pray later—but now I *have* to do something!"

She started to her feet, and the cramped little cabin was a cage, suffocating and unbearable. She hammered her fists on the door and Nathaniel replied immediately.

"Nathaniel, I cannot bear it in here a moment longer," she cried. "You must let me out."

His voice was regretful but firm. "Can't do that, missus. Tippoo would have a look at my backbone!"

She flung away from the door, angry, confused, her mind in a turmoil.

"I cannot let him carry me away to—" She did not go on, for she could not imagine what awaited her at the end of this voyage unless—and she had a vivid mental image of *Huron* coming into dock, while standing on the quay was a beautiful tall and aristocratic French woman in crinolines and velvets and pearls with three small sons standing at her side waving up at the tall arrogant figure on *Huron*'s quarterdeck.

She tried to close her mind to it, and she concentrated instead on the sound that *Huron* made as she bore away joyously on the wind, the drumming of her hull, and the pop and creak of her planking, the clatter of tackle and the stamp of bare feet on her deck as a party of seamen walked away with a fall, training one of the yards more finely to the wind. From beneath her feet came another muted squeal, like a rat in the cat's jaws, one helmsman making a small adjustment to *Huron*'s heading, and the rudder tackle running protestingly through the blocks.

The sound triggered a memory, and Robyn froze, trembling again, but this time with anticipation. She remembered Clinton Codrington describing to her how as a young lieutenant he had been in command of a cutting-out party sent into a river estuary that was crammed with small slaving craft, buggaloos and dhows.

"I didn't have enough men to take them all as prize at once, so we jumped from one to the other, cut their rudder lines and left them drifting helplessly, until we could pick 'em up later— those that hadn't gone aground, that is."

Robyn roused herself from the memory and rushed to the corner of her cabin. She had to wedge her back against the bulkhead and push with both her feet to move her wooden chest into the center of the cabin. Then she dropped to her hands and knees.

There was a small trapdoor in the deck, so neatly fitted that its joints were knife edges, but there was a small iron ring let flush into the woodwork. Once on the long voyage down the Atlantic, she had been disturbed by a very apologetic carpenter's mate and she had watched with interest while he had dragged her chest aside and opened the hatch, to descend through it with a grease pot.

She tried now to open it, but the hatch was so tight fitting that it resisted her efforts. She snatched a woolen shawl from her chest and threaded it through the iron ring. Now she could get a fairer purchase. Once more she strained back, and the hatch moved inchingly and then abruptly flew open with a crash that she was sure must have alerted Nathaniel. She froze again, listening for a half minute, but there was no sound from beyond the cabin door.

On her hands and knees again she peered into the open hatchway. There was a faint breeze coming up out of the square hole, and she could smell the thick grease, the reek of the bilges and the awful slave stink that not all the lye and scrubbing had been able to cleanse—her gorge rose at the taint. As her eyes adjusted, she made out the low and narrow tunnel that housed *Huron*'s steering gear. It was just high enough for a man to crawl along, running fore and aft along the hull.

The rudder lines came down from the deck above, ran through heavy iron blocks bolted into one of *Huron*'s main frames, and then changed direction and ran directly astern down the narrow wooden tunnel. The pulley wheels of the blocks were caked with black grease, and the rudder lines were of new yellow hemp. They seemed as thick as a man's leg, and she could sense the enormous strain on them, for they were as rigid as steel bars.

She looked around for a means of damaging them, a knife, one of her scalpels, perhaps, and almost immediately realized the futility of anything so puny. Even a strong man with a double-headed ax would be hard pressed to hack his way through those cables, and there was no room in which to swing an ax in that narrow tunnel. Even if a man had succeeded in severing one of them, he would have been cut to bloody tatters as the cable whiplashed.

There was only one means, one sure means, and she quailed at the thought of what would happen if it got out of control, and if *Black Joke* was not very swiftly alongside to render assistance with her steam-driven pumps and hoses. She had once already rejected the idea of using fire, but now with help so close astern, with the last chance rapidly fading, she was ready to accept any risk.

She reached across and pulled off the wooden bunk one of her gray woolen blankets and waddled it into a bundle, then she stood up and lifted the oil lamp from its gimbals in the deck above her. Her fingers were clumsy with haste. She unscrewed the cap of the oil reservoir in the base of the lamp.

She soaked the blanket, and then looked around for anything else that was inflammable—her journals? No, not them, but she pulled her medical manuals out of the chest and ripped the pages out of them, crumpling them so they would burn more readily, and she made a sack of the oil-soaked blanket and wadded the paper into it.

She stuffed it down the hatch and it fell across the straining rudder lines, and entangled itself in the iron pulleys.

The mattress on the bunk was filled with coir; the dry coconut fiber would burn fiercely; she dragged it off the bunk and pushed it into the hatch. Then the wooden slats off the bunk followed it, then the navigational books from the narrow bookshelf behind the door. She looked about her swiftly, but there was nothing else in the cabin that would burn.

The first Swan vesta that she dropped burning down the hatchway flickered once and then went out. She tore the end sheet out of her journal and twisted it into a spill; when it was blazing strongly she let it fall into the opening, and as it floated down it illuminated the gloomy recesses of *Huron*'s bilges, and the rough planking of her underbelly.

The burning spill landed on the oil-soaked blanket, and blue flames fluttered over it as the evaporating gases flashed off, then a crumpled ball of paper caught and little orange flames peaked up and danced merrily over the blanket and the linen covering of the mattress. A rush of heat came up through the hatchway, scorching Robyn's cheeks, and the sound of the flames was higher than that of the rushing seas along the outside of the hull.

Using all her strength, Robyn swung the hatch cover over

491

and let it drop back onto its seating with a thump that alarmed her anew, but immediately the sound of the flames was cut off.

Panting with the effort and a savage excitement, Robyn backed away and leaned against the bulkhead to rest. Her heart was pounding so fiercely that the blood in her ears nearly deafened her, and suddenly she was afraid.

What if *Black Joke* had abandoned the unequal contest, and there was nobody to rescue the eight hundred miserable souls chained below *Huron*'s decks before the flames reached them?

That first wild assault of the wind, as it came boiling down off the mountains, had settled to a steady blast, not so furious, but constant and reliable.

"There will be no flukes or holes in this gale of wind," Mungo thought with satisfaction, pausing in his pacing to look up at the small scudding wind-torn shreds of cloud that seemed to scrape the tops of his masts, and then turning to survey an indigo Atlantic that stretched to every corner of the horizon, purpled with the wind rush and dappled with the prancing white horses that curled from every wave crest.

His leisurely survey ended over *Huron*'s stern rail. The land was already out of sight, so swiftly had *Huron* run the great flat-topped mountain below the horizon, and *Black Joke* was hull down. Only her topsails showed, not a trace of furnace smoke.

The absence of smoke puzzled Mungo a little and he frowned, considering it, and finding no plausible answer, he shrugged and resumed his pacing. *Black Joke* would be out of sight, even from *Huron*'s towering masthead, before sunset, and Mungo was planning the evolutions he would make during the night to confuse thoroughly any pursuit, before settling onto his final course to run through the doldrums and cross the equator.

"Deck, masthead." A faint hail reached him, breaking his line of thought, and he stopped again, threw back his head and with both hands on his hips stared up at the masthead as it dipped and swung across the sky.

Tippoo answered the hail with a bull bellow, and the lookout's voice was strained, his anxiety evident even against the wind and at that remove.

"Smoke!"

"Where away?" Tippoo's voice was angry; the reply should have given both distance and bearing from *Huron*—already

492

every man on *Huron*'s deck was twisting his head to sweep the horizon.

"Dead astern."

"That will be the gunboat," Mungo thought comfortably. "She's got her boiler going again—and much good may it do her." He dropped his fists from his hips and took one more pace before the look-out's voice rang out again.

"Smoke dead astern, we are trailing smoke!"

Mungo stopped dead in his tracks, his foot still an inch from the deck. He felt the icy spray of fear chill his guts.

"Fire!" bellowed Tippoo.

It was the one most dreaded word to men who lived their lives in the tinder hulls of wooden ships, whose seams were caulked with tar and pitch, and whose sails and rigging would burn like straw. Mungo completed that suspended pace, spinning on the ball of his foot as it struck the deck, and the next pace carried him to *Huron*'s rail. He leaned far out, peering back over the stern, and the smoke was a pale wisp, thin as sea fret, lying low against the sea, drifting away behind them, and dissipating even as he watched it.

Dry oak planks burn with a fine clean flame and little smoke, Mungo knew that, he knew also that the first thing he must do was starve the flames of air, heave the ship to, to reduce the wind of her passage while the extent of the flames could be explored and the ship's pumps—

He turned again, his mouth opening to begin shouting his commands. The quartermaster and his mate stood directly ahead of him, both of them balancing easily before the massive mahogany-and-brass wheel. Larger than the driving wheel on a steam locomotive, it required the strength of two men to hold *Huron*'s head in this wind and on this point of sailing, for the huge spread of her canvas was opposed by the massive oak-and-copper rudder under her stern.

Down in the steering tunnel, the flames were being fed by the strong breeze that the canvas scoops on *Huron*'s foredeck were directing down into her own slave decks in an attempt to keep them sweet.

The draft forced its way through the companionways and ladderways, through the ports and cracks in *Huron*'s bulkheads, and this steady breeze at last found its way into the long narrow tunnel that housed her steering gear.

The bright rustling flames were almost smokeless, but intensely hot. They frizzled the loose fibers of hemp off the thick hairy rudder lines, and then swiftly blackened the golden-brown

493

cords, began to eat through them so that here a strand parted with a snap that was lost in the rising crackle of burning timbers and the strand unraveled, spinning upon itself and bursting in another tiny new explosion of light.

The two quartermasters were ten feet from where Mungo stood, poised to give his commands, composing the orders in his head, when suddenly the massive wheel no longer resisted the thrust of the brawny men who held it over.

Deep down in *Huron*'s hull, in the long wooden tunnel that had been turned into a raging blast furnace, the rudder lines had burned through, and as they snapped, they snaked and whipped viciously, smashing through the burning deck timbers, scattering flaming brands into the hold below, and letting in a fresh whistling gush of air that forced the flames higher.

Under the helmsman's hands the wheel dissolved in a spinning blur of glittering brass and the quartermaster was hurled the length of the deck, striking the bulwark with a jar that dropped him to the planking, wriggling feebly as a crushed insect. His mate was less fortunate. His right arm was caught in the polished-mahogany spokes of the wheel and it twisted like a strip of rubber, the bone of his forearm breaking up into long sharp splinters whose points thrust out whitely through the tanned skin, and the head of the long humerus bone was plucked from its socket in the scapula and the whole upper arm screwed up in a twist of rubbery flesh.

With the press of the rudder under the stern no longer controlling the rush of *Huron*'s hull through the water, the tremendous pressure of the wind in her sails took over unopposed, and *Huron* became a giant's weathercock. She spun in almost her own length, her bows flying up into the wind, and every man on her deck was hurled to the planking with stunning force.

The yards came crashing about, tackle snapping like cotton, one of the upper yards tearing itself loose, falling in a twisted web of its own canvas and rigging, and *Huron* was taken full aback, the neat geometrical pyramids of her sails disintegrating into flapping, fluttering chaos, wrapping around the stays and halyards, flogging against their own yards and masts.

With the gale of wind flying fully into the front of the sails, from the diametrically opposite direction to that for which they had been designed, the tall masts flexed and arched dangerously backward, the backstays drooping slackly, adding to the confusion of sail and rigging, while all the forestays were humming with unbearable tension—and one of them parted with an ear-jarring crack and the foremast shifted a few degrees and then hung askew.

Mungo St. John dragged himself to his feet and clung to the rail. The screams of the maimed helmsman dinning in his ears, he looked about him, and disbelief turned to bitter despair as he found his beautiful ship transformed to an ungainly shambles. Wallowing drunkenly, *Huron* was beginning to make sternway, as the wind pushed her backward and the waves came tumbling aboard her.

For long seconds Mungo stared about him numbly. There was so much damage, so much confusion and so much mortal danger, that he did not know where to begin, what his first order must be. Then over *Huron*'s heaving bows, in the opposite direction to which he had last seen it, the distant but suddenly dreadfully threatening speck that was *Black Joke*'s topsails showed in a pale flash above the horizon, and it galvanized Mungo.

"Mr. Tippoo," Mungo called. "We'll reef the mains and send down all her top hamper."

The logical sequence of orders began to arrange themselves in his mind, and his voice was calm and clear, without the strained and panicky timbre they had expected.

"Mr. O'Brien, go below and give me a fire report, quick as you like."

"Bosun, rig port and starboard pumps, and stand by to hose down the fire."

"Mr. Tippoo, send a party to batten all her hatches and strike the air scoops." They must try to prevent air from reaching the flames; he was sealing the hull.

"Coxswain, have the whaler off her davits and launch her." He would attempt to tow the heavy boat astern, to act as a drogue, a sea anchor. He was not sure that it would provide a solution, but he intended to work *Huron*'s bows around with the delicate use of her forward sails—and with the drogue holding her tail in place of the rudder, he might be able to run directly before the wind. It was not his optimum course, and it would be fine and dangerous work with the deadly risk of gibing and broaching, but at the least it would give him respite while he rigged the emergency steering tackle to her useless rudder, and get *Huron* under control once more.

He paused for breath, but glanced forward. *Huron* was moving rapidly astern, dipping and staggering into the swells so that they came flurrying aboard her in spray and solid green gouts of water, while over her bows the British gunboat was closer—so close that Mungo glimpsed a little sliver of her painted hull, and it seemed that her action through the water was more boisterous and cocky, like a game rooster erecting its coxcomb and ruffling its feathers as it bounces across the sandy floor of the cockpit.

Unable to endure the company of his junior officers a moment longer, stifled and filled with a sense of helplessness by his inability to prevent the tall American clipper from romping away from him, desperate for some activity to help his nerves from fraying further, Clinton Codrington had taken his telescope and gone forward into *Black Joke*'s bows.

Oblivious to the spray that splattered over him, soaking the thin linen shirt and chilling him so that his teeth chattered even in the sunlight, Clinton clutched for a hand hold in the ratlines, balancing on the narrow bulwark and staring ahead through eyes that swam not only with the stinging spray and wind, but with humiliation and frustration.

Just perceptibly, *Huron*'s tower of canvas was sinking below the irregular watery horizon; by sunset she would be gone. She and Robyn Ballantyne. His chance had come and he had missed it. His spirits could sink no lower.

To add to his suffering, his steaming eyes were playing him false, and what he could still make out of the clipper became distorted, changing shape as he still stared after her. Then the hail from the lookout high above him broke the grip of his despair.

"Chase is altering!" Clinton could not yet believe the high-pitched shriek from the masthead. "She's coming about!" The hail was almost incoherent with excitement and surprise.

Clinton whipped the telescope to his eye, and once again doubted his eyesight. *Huron*'s masts had been almost dead in line, but now they showed individually. She was coming about, already *Huron* was almost broadside and Clinton stared. For a few moments more the orderly mass of sails retained their perfect snowy shape, and then the pattern began to break up. The ponderous belly of the mainsail wobbled and trembled, then began to flutter and shake like a pennant in the gale, it spilled its wind and collapsed like a bursting paper bag and lashed itself in a petulant fury around its own mainmast.

Huron was shortly a shambles. Through the glass Clinton could see her beginning to tear herself to pieces, sails ripping,

496

yards tumbling—her foremast sagging out of true, and he still could not believe it was happening.

"She's taken full aback." He heard Denham's triumphant yell, and other voices took up the cry.

"She fast in irons!"

"We've got her, by God, we've got her now!"

Though his vision blurred and the wetness running down his cheeks was not all splattered spray, Clinton went on staring incredulously through the telescope.

"There is smoke, she's on fire!" Denham again, and Clinton picked up the pale mist of smoke spreading away from her; and at that moment a fresh burst of spray over the bows drenched the lens of his telescope, and he lowered it.

He took a silk bandanna from his hip pocket, and wiped his face and eyes of spray and the other wetness, then he blew his nose noisily, stuffed the handkerchief back into his pocket, jumped onto his deck and strode back to his quarterdeck.

"Mr. Ferris," he said crisply, "please send up a flag hoist under *Huron*'s name and make the following: 'I am sending a boarding party to you.'" The eyes shone with a zealot's intensity. "'If you resist I shall fight you.'"

It was a long message, and while Ferris called for the pennants from the flag locker, Clinton turned to Denham. His voice shook with passion.

"Please clear the ship for action, Mr. Denham—and we'll run out our guns now."

Above the gale Clinton heard the clatter of the opening gunports, the rumble of the gun carriages, but all his attention was concentrated ahead upon the crippled slave ship.

He saw and understood the desperate attempts that her captain was making to get her before the wind. He knew what a feat it had been to take down that tangled mass of canvas and rope in such a short time, yet he felt no admiration, only cold fighting fury.

Huron was showing only a storm jib.

St. John was clearly trying to break the grip of the gale upon her, for she was fast "in irons," her bows to the wind, and he was attempting to bring her around, but the tall ship that was usually so compliant and obedient was balking, resisting him, and every minute *Black Joke* was swarming down upon her, closer and still closer.

"She's got serious structural damage," Denham gloated. "I'd hazard a guess that she's lost her rudder."

Clinton did not answer him, he strained ahead, half exultant, half fearful that St. John's efforts would succeed and he would watch helplessly as *Huron* turned her stern to him once more, and went plunging away at the speed which *Black Joke* could never hope to match.

Then, as he watched, it happened. *Huron* swung her long, low length nearly broadside to him, beam onto the wind once again, and hung there for infinite seconds, then she shuddered and shook herself free of the gale's grip and went through the eye of the wind. Instantly the scraps of sail on her foremast snapped open; she came around presenting her stern to *Black Joke* and was sailing again.

Even in his bitter chagrin, Clinton could at least feel admiration for that barely credible feat of seamanship, but beside him his officers were struck dumb, paralyzed with disappointment to see their prey slipping away once more.

More sails bloomed upon her tall bare masts, and the gap between the two ships was no longer narrowing; instead, it began to widen once more; slowly, infinitely slowly, *Huron* was forging away, and the night was coming.

"She's steaming a warp behind her," Denham lamented quietly.

"It's a small ship's boat," Ferris corrected him. They were already close enough to make out such details, *Huron* was only three or four nautical miles ahead of them, all her hull was in plain sight and they could even make out the tiny human figures on her decks with the naked eye. "Damned clever, what!" Ferris went on with professional interest. "Who would have believed it would work. Like as not the damned Yankee has the legs of us still."

Clinton's chagrin turned to anger at his junior's unnecessary commentary.

"Mr. Ferris, instead of chattering like a washerwoman, will you not read the signal *Huron* is flying?"

Huron's signal flags were blowing almost directly away from the watchers on *Black Joke*'s deck, making them difficult to spot and interpret, and Ferris, who had been fixing all his attention on the towing whaler, started guiltily, and then dived for his signal book and began busily scribbling on his slate.

"*Huron* sends under our name, 'Stay clear of me, or I will fire upon you.'"

"Good." Clinton nodded and drew an inch of bare steel from the scabbard of his cutlass to make sure the weapon was free before thrusting it back to the hilt. "Now we all know where we stand!"

But, slowly, inexorably, *Huron* even partially crippled, and steering only by the sails on her foremast, was drawing away from them, and she was still far out of random cannon shot.

"The fire has taken hold in the steering gear under the doctor's cabin." The third mate came hurrying back on deck to make his damage report. "I got her out of there." He jerked a thumb as Robyn came up on deck clutching her black leather valise into which she had hastily crammed her journals and other small valuables.

"It's got through into the cable tier and the lazaretto, it will be into the sternquarters in a minute." The mate's arms and face streamed with oily sweat, and the soot had blackened them like a chimneysweep.

"Put the hoses in through the poop companionway," Mungo told him calmly. "And flood the stern section abaft the main hold."

The mate hurried away and within seconds there was the tolling clangor of the pumps as a dozen men threw their combined weight on the handles and the canvas hoses filled and stiffened, ejaculating solid jets of seawater down the stifling ladderways where already the air was trembling with heat like a desert mirage. Almost immediately hissing clouds of white steam began to boil from the ports and stern lights.

Satisfied, Mungo turned away, shot one glance over the stern to make sure that the gunboat was still falling away behind the limping clipper, then let his gaze linger a moment longer on the thick hawser that was secured to the port stern stanchions and ran through the fairlead to the bobbing whaler that *Huron* was dragging half a cable's length astern. The whole complex arrangement of the wind and sails and drogue was critical and unstable, the slightest change might upset it. He decided he could not risk hoisting another square inch of canvas, nor could he send a party below to rig a jury tackle on the useless rudder until the fire was brought under control.

He lit a cheroot, frowning with concentration over the simple and familiar task, and then he raised his eyes to look directly at Robyn for the first time since she had come up on deck.

For a second they stared at each other, and then Robyn looked astern at the ugly little gunboat that was still plugging along after them.

"I keep making the mistake of trusting you," Mungo said beside her.

"I only made that mistake once—with you," she replied, and he inclined his head slightly, accepting the riposte.

"How did you get into the steering gear?" he began to inquire, then snapped his fingers irritably at his own oversight. "Of course, the inspection hatch. Yet your ingenuity, Doctor, has been of no avail. Your friends still cannot hold us and as soon as it is dark, I will have the rudder cables repaired."

For the last minute Mungo had been studying her face, oblivious to the sea and the ship and the gale. He did not see the fresh squall racing down upon *Huron*. When it struck, there was no helmsman to hold her. She saw the flash of alarm in his eyes, the realization of danger. His voice, as he yelled an order down the length of the deck, had for the first time the crack of fear in it.

"Get the sails off her, Mr. Tippoo. Quick as you can!"

For the squall had upset the nice balance of *Huron*'s drogue and sail. The ship lunged forward sharply, the long bellied length of cable trailing astern lifted itself above the broken surface of the sea, straightening and coming under such strain that the seawater spurted from the hemp cords in tiny feathery jets.

The empty whaler, with her tarpaulin cover still lashed down over her in an attempt to keep her dry, was at that instant canted steeply over the crest of a breaking swell. The shattering impact transmitted by the taut cable to her bows pitched her forward and heaved her clear of the crest, so that for a moment she was airborne, like a leaping porpoise, and then she struck bows first and was snatched below the surface.

For an instant *Huron* staggered to the enormous increase in drag upon the trailing cable, and then the whaler disintegrated in a boiling flurry of white disturbed water. Her broken planking popped to the surface and the cable, freed of its wearying weight, flicked high in the air like the tail of an angry lioness. Without restraint, *Huron* gibed fiercely, spinning once more across the wind, and this time being blown flat, her tall bare masts swinging over almost parallel to the sea's surface.

The lee rail dug deeply into the sea, and the water came aboard her in a sweeping torrent, like a bursting dam wall.

It caught Robyn and hurled her against Mungo St. John's chest; if it had not done so, she would have been carried overboard, but he caught her to him and held her as they were

500

tumbled down the steeply canted deck—and then *Huron* was righting herself again, the water cascading off her in silver spouts.

She wallowed helplessly, taking the gale-driven seas on her beam, her desperate rolling accentuated by the pendulum of her high bare masts, but at least that drenching wall of seawater had poured into her hull through every opening and had extinguished her fires on the instant.

Mungo St. John dragged Robyn by the wrist across the flooded deck, sloshing and slipping knee deep with loose tackle slithering and floating around them.

At the break of the poop he stopped, both of them panting for breath, their clothing and hair streaming seawater, the deck heaving and dropping crazily under them so he had to cling to the weather rail for support. He stared across at *Black Joke*.

The race was run. The gunboat was crowding down upon them exultantly, so close that he could see the cannon protruding from her open ports and the heads of the gunners above the bulwarks. Her challenging flag hoist still flew in her rigging, gaudy and gay as Christmas decorations. She would be up to the wallowing clipper in minutes, long before Mungo could ever hope to get his ship sailing again.

Mungo shook the water from his sodden locks like a spaniel coming ashore, and he filled his lungs.

"Mr. O'Brien, a pair of slave cuffs here," he bellowed, and Robyn, who had never heard him raise his voice, was stunned by the volume of sound that came up out of that muscular chest. She was still dazed and confused as she felt the cold kiss of iron on her wrists.

Mungo snapped the cuff on her left wrist, took two swift turns of chain around *Huron*'s rail and then snapped the second cuff on her right wrist.

"I have no doubt your friends will be delighted to see you— in the cannon's mouth," he told her, his face still set with anger, the rims of his nostrils white as bone china. He turned from her, running his fingers through his dark curls, throwing the hair back from his forehead and eyes.

"Mr. O'Brien, muskets and pistols to every hand. Run out the guns and load with ball, we'll change to grape as the range closes." The mate shouted his orders as he ran, and the crew scattered from the futile task of attempting to bring the clipper under control. They stumbled across the wave-swept deck, dodging fallen and broken tackle, hurrying to arm themselves and to man *Huron*'s guns.

501

"Mr. Tippoo!" Mungo's voice cut through the cacophony of gale and shouted orders.

"Captain Mungo!"

"Bring up the first deck of slaves."

"We deep-sixing them?" Tippoo asked, for he had served before under slave captains who, when capture by a naval vessel was imminent, would deep-six their cargo, drop them overboard, chains and all, and rid themselves of the most damning evidence against them.

"We'll chain 'em to the weather rail, Mr. Tippoo, with the woman." Mungo used neither Robyn's title nor her name. "Make the lime juicer think a spell before he opens fire." And Tippoo let an explosive chuckle of laughter come bouncing up his throat as he bounded away on those thick bowed legs, to get the gratings off the main hatch.

"Sir!" Denham's voice was incredulous, shocked. "Sir!"

"Yes, Mr. Denham," Clinton answered him quietly, without lowering his telescope. "I have seen it—"

"But, sir, that's Dr. Ballantyne—"

"And black slaves." Ferris could hold his tongue no longer. "They're chaining them to the rail."

"What manner of man is that Yankee!" Denham burst out again.

"A damned clever one," Clinton answered him quietly. He was watching the woman he had come to rescue through the glass. He could already recognize her features. Her eyes seemed too large for her deathly-white face, her sodden and rumpled clothing stuck to her body. Through a rent in her blouse he could see the skin of her shoulder and upper arm gleaming with a pearllike luster in the sunlight.

"Mr. Denham," Clinton went on speaking. "Warn the crew that we will be receiving fire in about five minutes, and we will be unable to return it."

He watched the ranks of naked black slaves still coming up onto the clipper's main deck and taking their place along the rail, their jailers fussing about them, chivvying them into place and securing their chains.

"We are fortunate in having a gale of wind, so we will be exposed to fire for a short period, but warn the men to lie flat upon the deck below the bulwark."

Black Joke's fragile eggshell plating would give some protection at extreme range, but as they closed with the slave ship, he could expect even grapeshot to penetrate their sides. One blessing, they would be spared the lethal flying splinters that were so much dreaded in wooden ships.

"I am going to lay her alongside the Yankee's stern," Clinton went on. That way she would be exposed to the clipper's broadsides while the two ships were bound to each other. "But she stands taller than we do. I want your best men with the grappling irons, Mr. Denham." *Huron*'s maindeck was ten feet higher than the gunboat's. There would be nice work ahead when they leaped the gap and scrambled up *Huron*'s stern with its pronounced tumble home.

"By God! She's running out her guns. She means to fight us after all," Denham cut in, and then, penitently, "I beg your pardon, sir." He excused himself for the interruption and the blasphemy.

Clinton lowered the telescope. They were so close now that he no longer needed it.

The clipper had six light cannons on each side of her, mounted on the main deck. The barrels were almost twice as long as *Black Joke*'s own heavy carronades. However, the bore of the muzzles was much smaller in diameter, and as Clinton watched, they began to train around toward him, one at a time beginning at the stern.

Even without the glass, Clinton could make out the tall lean figure in the plain blue jacket moving at a deceptively leisurely pace from one gun to the next, laying each of them personally, gesturing at the gun crews to strain on the tackles and traverse the long cannon onto their target.

Clinton saw St. John reach the bow gun and make a careful adjustment, working over it a few seconds longer than he had the others, and then he leaped to the clipper's bulwark and balanced there with the assurance of an acrobat against the rudderless hull's unpredictable movements.

The scene engraved itself upon Clinton's mind, it seemed so theatrical, like the cast of a stage production lined up at the end of the performance to receive the applause of the spectators. The file of naked black bodies, standing almost shoulder to shoulder with their arms extended in unison, like the trained chorus, their wrists locked to the teak rail by the slave cuffs. Then the principal, the figure of the woman, slim and somehow delicate and tiny in their midst. The bodice of her dress, a buttercup yellow, was a gay spot of color that drew Clinton's eye irresistibly. It was a distraction that he could not afford at this moment.

The American seemed to be watching Clinton, seemed to

have singled him out from the group of officers, and even across the wide stretch of water that still separated them, Clinton was aware of the mesmeric pull of those eyes, the eyes of a predator, a leopard perhaps, poised with a lithe and patient grace upon the bough above the waterhole, awaiting the moment when the prey moved beneath him.

At the level of Mungo St. John's knees were the heads of his gun crews, little knots of pale tense faces, contrasting starkly with the quiescent rank of black slaves. They crouched over their weapons, and the long slim barrels were reduced to small black circles as Clinton stared directly down the bores.

There were men also in *Huron*'s rigging, roosting in the crosstrees of the yards and masts, and the long barrels of their muskets were clear to see against the backdrop of the wind-driven sky. They would be picked marksmen, *Huron*'s best, and their preferred and special target would be the small group of officers on the gunboat's quarterdeck. Clinton hoped that the clipper's wild action in the gale would throw out their aim.

"Gentlemen, I advise you to take cover until we can bring the ship into action," he told Denham and Ferris quietly, and felt a little prick of pride when neither of them moved. It was the tradition of Drake and Nelson not to flinch from the coming storm of fire, and Clinton himself went on standing at his ease, hands clasped at the small of his back, calling a small adjustment to the helm as *Black Joke* drove in eagerly, the terrier going for the hold on the bull's nose.

He saw the American move his head, a final judgment of range, considered against the clipper's rolling, and beside him Ferris murmured the age-old blasphemy which Clinton this time could not find it in him to resent, for it was also a part of the great tradition.

"For what we are about to receive—" said Ferris, and as if he had heard the words, the American drew the sword from the scabbard on his belt, and raised it above his head. Involuntarily all three naval officers drew breath together and held it. *Huron* was at the bottom of her roll, her cannon pointing down into the sea close alongside, then she was coming up, the barrels rising—leveled, and the sword arm fell.

The six cannon leaped together, in perfect concert, and the startling white gusts of smoke shot fifty feet from her sides, completely silent, for the sound had not reached them, and for a fleeting part of a second they could believe that *Huron* had not loosed her broadside.

504

Then the very air beat in upon them, shocking the eardrums, seeming for a moment to suck their eyeballs from the sockets with the vast disruption of air caused by passing shot, and close above Clinton's head a stay parted with a whiplash crack.

That was one ball high, but under Clinton's feet, the deck jumped with the multiple impact of ball into her, and the hull rang like the strokes of a gigantic brass gong.

A single ball came through at deck level. It struck a burst of sparks from the steel hull, like Brocks fireworks at Crystal Palace, brilliant orange even in the strong sunlight, and the hole it tore through *Black Joke*'s plating was fringed with bare jagged tongues of metal like the petals of a silver sunflower.

A seaman in striped vest and baggy canvas breeches, who was kneeling behind the bulwark, took the ball full in his chest.

His severed limbs were strewn untidily across the gunboat's spotless deck and the ball went on to strike the foot of *Black Joke*'s mast, shivering it like a tall tree struck by lightning, and tearing a long white splinter from the seasoned Norwegian pine. Then, with its force mainly spent, the ball rolled the length of the deck, smoking and stinking of scorched metal until it thumped into the scuppers and rolled idly back and forth. Only then, seconds after the broadside struck, did the crash of the discharge reach their ears across the turbulent waters that separated the two vessels.

"Not bad shooting for a Yankee," Ferris grudged them, raising his voice above the gun thunder, and Denham had his watch out and was timing how long it took for the clipper's gun crews to reload.

"Forty-five seconds," Denham intoned, "and not a single gun run out again. A bunch of fairground tinkers could do better."

Clinton found himself wondering if it was merely bravado or complete indifference to danger and violent death which allowed the two younger officers to chat so casually while the seaman's severed arms still twitched on the deck, not twenty feet away.

Clinton was afraid, afraid of death and afraid of failing in his duty and afraid of being seen to be afraid, but then he was older than they, for despite their manly airs Ferris was a boy and Denham barely twenty—so perhaps it was not courage but ignorance and lack of imagination.

"Fifty-five seconds!" Denham grunted scornfully, as the

next ragged broadside crashed into *Black Joke*'s iron hull, and somebody started to scream belowdecks, a high mindless keening like steam from a kettle.

"Send somebody to stop that fellow," Ferris murmured to the seaman who crouched nearby, and doubled over still the man hurried away. Seconds later the screaming stopped abruptly.

"Good work," Ferris told the seaman as he took his place at the bulwark again.

"Dead, sir, he is, poor devil."

Ferris nodded without change of expression, and moved closer to listen to his captain.

"Mr. Denham, I am going to lead the boarding party. You are to be ready to sheer off and leave us to it, should there by any danger to the ship——" There was a sharp fluting sound, like the flight of a giant insect past their heads, and Clinton glanced up irritably. The marksmen in *Huron*'s rigging had opened fire, the pop of their muskets seemed muted and without menace. Studiedly Clinton ignored them and went on issuing his final orders, raising his voice to compete with the crash and roar of shot and the strike of it into the gunboat's hull.

As Clinton finished speaking, Denham blurted abruptly, "It's hell not being able to reply." He was staring across at the clipper whose silhouette was blurred with a bank of gunsmoke that even the gale could not disperse rapidly enough. "It's bad for the men," he corrected himself swiftly, and Clinton had his answer. Denham was afraid as he was, and the knowledge gave him no comfort at all. If only they could do something, anything, instead of having to stand here in the open and make studied conversation, while *Black Joke* tore across the last few hundred yards of white-crested sea that still separated them.

The crash of cannon shot tearing into *Black Joke*'s vitals was almost continuous now as the fastest gunners aboard *Huron* out-stripped the others. The bow cannon that the American captain was supervising and laying was firing three times to the other's twice—Clinton had been counting the plumes of muzzle smoke; this would be the sixth ball they sent into the little gunboat since the American had given the order to fire six minutes ago.

He watched the gunsmoke bloom again from the cannon's maw, and this time the gunboat's deck was swept as if by hailstones, but leaden hailstones as big as ripe grapes that pierced the thin steel bulwarks with pricks of sunlight and clawed chunks of wood from the main deck, a deck that was now threaded with meandering scarlet snakes of blood and slick little puddles of it that spread from beneath the inert and crumpled figures that seemed to be scattered in purposeless profusion wherever Clinton looked.

Black Joke was taking merciless punishment, perhaps already more than she could afford, but they were close now, very close, seconds only left to go.

He could hear the cheering of the clipper's gun crews, the terrified wailing of the slaves who were huddled down in pathetic little heaps upon *Huron*'s decks, he could clearly hear the rumble of the sixteen-pounders run out against the straining tackles, and hear the shouted commands of the gun captains.

The girl at the rail still stood rigidly erect, staring white-faced across at him, and she had seen and recognized him now. She tried to raise a hand to wave a greeting, but the iron slave cuff on her wrist hampered the movement. As Clinton stepped forward the better to see her, something tugged sharply at the sleeve of his jacket and behind him Ferris gasped.

Clinton looked down at his arm, the sleeve was torn and the white lining showed in the tear; it was only then he realized that it was a musket ball fired from *Huron*'s crosstrees which might have struck him squarely had he not moved, and he turned quickly to Ferris.

The boy was pressing a wadded handkerchief to his chest, standing very upright.

"You are wounded, Mr. Ferris," said Clinton. "You may go below."

"Thank you, sir," wheezed Ferris. "But I'd just as soon not miss the kill." As he spoke, a droplet of blood formed in the corner of his mouth, and with a chilling little jolt, Clinton realized that the boy was probably mortally struck: blood in the mouth would almost certainly mean a lung hit.

"Carry on then, Mr. Ferris," he said formally, and turned away. He must not let the doubts assail him now, he must not question whether his decision to board *Huron* had been correct, or if his execution of the attack had been properly carried out— or if he was responsible for those dismembered corpses that littered *Black Joke*'s deck, or for the dying lad who still determinedly kept erect. He must not let his resolve weaken.

Instead he slitted his eyes against the lowering sun that outlined *Huron*'s bare masts with golden halos, and stared across at her with true hatred. It was then he realized that at last her bow cannons could no longer bear the terrible battering

507

of the close-range grape shot that was abating as they sailed into *Huron*'s stern quadrant.

"Bring her up two points," he snapped, and the *Black Joke* cut in sharply under *Huron*'s stern. She loomed suddenly high above them and there was no more cannon fire from her while the clipper's tall hull shielded them from the gale. The sudden silence was ghostly, unnerving, as though the cannon fire had damaged his ears and he was rendered deaf.

Clinton shook off the sense of dreamlike unreality, and strode down the length of his deck.

"Up the Jokers!" he shouted, and his crew rose from where they had been crouching under the fragile bulwark.

"You've shown you can take it, boys, now let's show those damned Yankees we can hand it out."

"A tiger for Tongs!" yelled a voice, and suddenly they were all cheering, crowding the gunboat's side, so he had to cup his hands to his mouth to give the order.

"Helm a lee, let fly all!" and *Black Joke* spun up sharply under *Huron*'s counter, spilling her wind, while the seamen in her rigging stripped the canvas off her.

The two ships came together with a rending crackling crash, the gnashing of steel plate against timber and the shattering of glass in *Huron*'s sternlights.

A dozen of *Black Joke*'s sailors hurled the three-pronged grappling hooks high over the clipper's gunwale with the lines snaking up after them, and then heaved them up tight and made them fast to the portside cleats, and a swarm of seamen cheering wildly went up *Huron*'s stern, like a troop of vervet monkeys pursued into the trees by a hunting leopard.

"Take command, Mr. Denham," Clinton shouted above the hubbub.

"Aye, aye, sir," Denham's lips moved and he saluted as Clinton thrust his cutlass back into his scabbard and headed the next rush of his men, those who had been freed by the heaving to of her sails.

The two hulls were working against each other as viciously as millstones, grinding and bumping, the gap opening and closing as the wind and the seas tore at them.

At *Huron*'s rail a dozen of her crew were hacking at the grappling lines with axes, the clunking of the blades into her timber blended with the popping of pistols and muskets as their mates blazed down on the swarm of seamen climbing up from the gunboat's deck.

One of *Black Joke*'s sailors climbed swiftly hand over hand, pushing off with his feet from the clipper's raked stern like a mountaineer, and he had almost reached the rail when an American sailor appeared above him, an ax held high and then sent thudding down into the woodwork, severing the line at a single blow.

The sailor dropped like a windblown fruit from the bough into the gap between the hulls. He floundered for an instant in the surging water and then the two ships came together again, with the shriek of rending timbers, chewing the man like a pair of monstrous jaws.

"More lines," Clinton howled, and another grappling hook flew over his head, thrown by a stout British arm, and the line whipped around Clinton's shoulders.

He seized it, heaved once upon it to set the hook and then swung across the gap and his boots thudded on *Huron*'s stern. He had seen his seaman drop on the severed line, so he climbed with the strength and agility of terror and desperation, and only as he swung one leg over *Huron*'s rail did the battle rage seize him, the world changed color before him, seen through a reddish haze of hatred and fury, hatred for the slave stink that rose to offend his soul and fury for the death and punishment that his ship and his seamen had suffered.

His cutlass sprang from its scabbard with metallic rasp, and there was a man rushing down upon him, and the man naked to the waist with a bulging hairy belly and thick heavily muscled arms. He was brandishing a double-bladed ax above his head, and Clinton uncoiled his lanky frame, straightening as he prepared to strike. He drove the point of the cutlass through the ax man's furry silvered beard and the ax flew from his raised hands and went sliding away across the deck.

Clinton stood over the man he had killed, placed his foot on his chest and yanked the cutlass blade out of his throat. A bright-scarlet carotid fountain followed the blade out, splattering Clinton's boot.

Half a dozen of his seamen had reached *Huron*'s deck ahead of Clinton, and without a word of command spoken, they bunched to guard the grappling lines over the stern, holding off *Huron*'s ax men with cutlass and point-blank pistol fire. Behind them, *Black Joke*'s men came swarming aboard, unopposed, surging forward, their cheers rising into a triumphant chorus.

"At 'em the Jokers!"

"All together, boys," howled Clinton; the madness had taken complete hold of him now. There was no fear, no doubts, not even conscious thought. The madness was infectious, and his men howled with him; hunting as a pack like the wolf or the wild dog they swept across *Huron*'s deck to meet the wave of her own seamen rushing back from *Huron*'s bows.

The two waves of running, screaming men met just below the break of the poop, were transformed into a struggling mass of closely locked humanity, and their cries and curses mingled with the animal howl of terrified slaves. The pistols and muskets had all been discharged and there was no chance to reload. It was steel against steel now.

Black Joke's crew were battle-hardened, they had fought together fifty times in the past year, they had stormed glacis and barracoon and withstood fire and steel. They were blooded fighting men and proud of it.

Huron's men were commercial seamen, not warriors, most of them had never swung a cutlass nor fired a pistol at another man before, and the difference was evident almost immediately.

For a minute or less the closely engaged mass of men swayed and churned like the meeting of two strong currents at the tidal line of the ocean, and then *Black Joke*'s sailors began to forge forward.

"Up the Jokers!" They sensed their advantage.

"Hammer and Tongs, boys. Give 'em hell!"

At only one point was the tide of British sailors checked: at the foot of *Huron*'s mainmast where two men stood almost shoulder to shoulder.

Tippoo seemed immovable on the solid foundation of those massive bared legs. Like a Buddha carved from solid rock, he spurned the press of men around him, and their ranks parted and drew back.

His loincloth was drawn up between his legs, and his smooth belly bulged over it, again as hard as mountain rock, with the deep cyclops eye of his navel in its center.

The golden thread of his embroidered gilet sparkled in the sunlight, and he held his great round head low on his shoulders as he swung a double-bladed ax as easily as though it were a lady's parasol, and the ax hissed fiercely at every stroke and *Black Joke*'s seamen gave him ground.

A pistol ball had nicked the scarred flesh of his bald head, and blood poured copiously from the shallow wound, turning his face to a glaring gory mask.

His wide toad's slit of a mouth opened as he laughed and

shouted his contempt of the men who swarmed about him like pygmies about an ogre.

Beside him fought Mungo St. John. He had stripped off his blue jacket to free his sword arm, and his white linen shirt was open to the belt, the buttons torn from their threads by a clutching enemy hand. He had knotted a silk bandanna around his forehead to keep the sweat from running into his eyes, but sweat poured down his naked chest, and had soaked through his shirt in patches. He had a sword in his right hand, a weapon with a plain silver steel guard and pommel, and he cut and parried and thrust without a break in the rhythm of his movements.

He was unmarked; the droplets of thrown blood that stained the full sleeve of his white shirt and which had been diluted by his sweat to a dirty brown were not his blood.

"St. John!" Clinton called to him. They were both tall enough to look over the heads of the men between them, and they stared at each other for a moment.

Clinton's eyes were fanatical, and his lips white with fury. Mungo's expression was grave, thoughtful almost, and his gaze troubled, almost grieving, as though he knew he had lost his ship and that his life and the lives of most of his crew were forfeit.

"Fight me!" Clinton challenged him, his voice strident, ringing with triumph.

"Again?" Mungo asked, and the smile touched his lips fleetingly, then was gone.

Clinton shouldered his way roughly through the press of his own men. The last time it had been pistols, Mungo St. John's choice of weapon, but now Clinton had the familiar weight and balance of a naval cutlass in his right hand—his weapon, that he had first swung as a midshipman of fourteen years old, and the whipcord muscles in his long right arm were seasoned to the use of the blade, and every evolution in its use, every trick and subterfuge, had been drilled until it was instinctive.

As they came together, Clinton feinted and cut backhanded and low, going for the hip to cripple and bring the man down. As the stroke was parried he felt the strength of Mungo's sword arm for an instant before he disengaged, and switched his attack fluidly, going on the thrust leading with his right foot, a full stroke, and again the parry was strong and neat, but only just strong enough to hold the heavier, broader steel of the cutlass.

511

Those two brief contacts were enough for Clinton to judge his adversary and find his weakness. He had felt it through the steel the way a skilled angler feels the weakness of the fish through line and rod—it was the wrist. St. John did not have the steely resilience that comes only from long and dedicated exercise and practice.

He saw the flare of alarm in St. John's strangely flecked eyes. The American, too, had felt his own inadequacy, and he knew he did not dare to draw out the encounter. He must try to end it swiftly, before the Englishman's superiority could wear him down.

With the swordsman's instinct, Clinton translated the little flicker of the golden yellow eyes. He knew that Mungo St. John was going on the attack, so that as the stroke came an instant later, he caught it on the broad curved blade of the cutlass; then he shifted his weight forward and, with a twist of his own iron wrist, prevented the disengagement, forcing St. John to roll his own wrist, the two blades milling across each other, the steel screeching sharply on a harsh abrasive note that set their teeth on edge. Clinton forced two and then three turns, the classic prolonged engagement from which Mungo St. John could not break without risking the thunderbolt of the riposte, and Clinton felt the other's wrist give under the strain. He lunged his weight against it, slid the guard of the cutlass high up the blade and used the rolling momentum of two blades and the leverage of his wrist and the curved guard of the cutlass to tear the hilt out of Mungo St. John's fingers.

The American's sword clattered to the deck between them, and Mungo St. John threw up both hands, sucked in his belly and flung himself back against the mainmast in an attempt to avoid the thrust of the heavy cutlass blade which he knew would follow. In the fury of hatred that possessed Clinton, there was no thought of giving quarter to the man whom he had disarmed.

The thrust was full-blooded, driven by all the strength of wrist and arm, of shoulder and of Clinton's entire body weight, the killing stroke.

Clinton's whole being had been concentrated on the man before him, but now there was movement in the periphery of his vision. Tippoo had seen his captain disarmed in the same instant that he had just completed a swing with the ax. He was off balance, it would take only a shaded instant to recover that balance, to raise the ax again, but that instant of time would be too long, for he saw the cutlass stroke already launched, and Mungo St. John trapped helplessly against the mainmast, his belly unprotected and his empty hands held high.

Tippoo opened his huge paws and let the ax go spinning away, like a cartwheel, and then he reached out and seized the gleaming cutlass blade in one bare hand.

He felt the blade run between his fingers and the terrible sting of the razor-sharp edge cutting down to the bone, still he heaved with all his weight, pulling the point away from the helpless man against the mainmast, deflecting it but unable to hold it for the tensed tendons in his lacerated fingers parted, and the blade ran on driven by the full weight of the tall platinum-headed naval officer.

Tippoo heard the point of the cutlass scrape over one of his ribs, and then a numbness filled his chest, and he felt the steel guard of the hilt strike his rib cage, a thud like that of a butcher's cleaver striking the chopping board, as the cutlass blade reached the limit of its travel.

Even the savage force of that blow was not enough to knock Tippoo off his feet, though it drove him back a pace. He stood solidly. His eyes screwed up into slits of skin, staring down at the blade that transfixed his chest, his bleeding hands still clutching the guard of the cutlass.

Only when Clinton leaned back and pulled the blade from his flesh did Tippoo begin to sag slowly forward, his knees buckling, and he fell, his body slack and unresisting.

Clinton freed his cutlass blade, and it was thinly smeared along its full length, so that it blurred redly as he went on to the forehand cut, going once more for the man who was still pinned against the mainmast.

Clinton did not complete the stroke. He arrested it in midair, for Mungo St. John had been borne to the deck beneath a wave of struggling British seamen.

Clinton stepped back and rested on his cutlass. The fight was over, all around him the crew of *Huron* were throwing down their weapons.

"Quarter, for the love of God, quarter!"

They were dragging Mungo St. John to his feet, two seamen on each of his arms. He was unwounded, and Clinton's hatred was unabated. It took an enormous effort to prevent himself from driving the point of the cutlass into Mungo's belly. Mungo was struggling to throw off the hands of the men who held him, straining to reach the massive body of the half-naked Moslem mate that lay at his feet.

"Let me free," Mungo cried. "I must see to my mate." But they held him remorselessly, and Mungo looked up at Clinton.

"In the name of mercy," he was pleading, and Clinton had never expected that. He took a deep ragged breath, the madness began to fade.

"I give you my word, sir." Mungo was stricken, there was no mistaking his consuming grief, and Clinton hesitated. "I am your prisoner," Mungo told him. "But this man is a friend—"

Clinton let out his breath slowly, and then he nodded to the seamen who held Mungo St. John.

"He has given his word." And then to Mungo, "You may have five minutes." And the seamen released him. Mungo sank swiftly to his knees beside the inert figure.

"Old friend," he whispered, as he tore the bandanna from off his own head and pressed it to the obscene little slit between Tippoo's ribs, "old friend."

Clinton turned away, slipping the cutlass back into its scabbard and he ran across the deck to the weather rail.

Robyn Ballantyne saw him coming and she strained toward him, unable to lift her arms for the slave cuffs that still bound her, but as he embraced her she put her face against his chest and her whole body trembled and shook as she sobbed.

"Oh, I give thanks to God—"

"Find the keys," Clinton ordered brusquely, and as the cuffs fell from Robyn's wrists he snatched them up and handed them to one of his men. "Use these on the slaver's captain," he ordered.

With that gesture, the last of his madness was gone.

"Forgive me, Dr. Ballantyne. We will speak later, but now there remains much to be done." He bowed slightly and hurried away calling his orders.

"Carpenter's mate, go below immediately, I want the damage to this ship repaired at once. Bosun, disarm her crew, and have them sent below under lock and key with a guard on the companionway. Two men on her wheel, and a prize crew to work her. We'll sail her into Table Bay with the dawn, my boys, and there'll be prize money for your fancy." His men were still drunk on excitement and battle lust, and they cheered him hoarsely as they rushed to obey the string of orders.

Rubbing her chafed wrists, Robyn picked her way across the littered deck and through the throngs of bustling British seamen as they hustled their captives and the still-chained files of slaves below.

Almost timorously she approached the ill-assorted pair at

514

the foot of the ship's mainmast. Tippoo lay on his back, the mound of his naked belly pressing upward like a woman in labor, the soiled bandanna hiding the wound. His eyes were wide, staring up at the mast that towered above him, and his lower jaw sagged.

Mungo St. John held the huge bald cannonball head on his lap. He sat with his legs thrust out straight ahead of him, his back against the mast, and as Robyn approached, he closed the lids over Tippoo's staring eyes, one at a time, with his thumb. His head was bowed, his hands gentle as those of a mother with her infant as he lifted the bandanna and used it to bind up the sagging jaw.

Robyn went down on one knee and reached out to Tippoo's chest, to feel for the heart beat, but Mungo St. John raised his head and looked at her.

"Don't touch him," he said softly.

"I am a doctor—"

"He no longer needs a doctor"—Mungo's voice was low and clear—"especially if that doctor is you."

"I am sorry."

"Dr. Ballantyne," he told her, "you and I have no reason to apologize to each other, nor for that matter to speak to each other, ever again."

She stared at him, and his face was cold and set, the eyes that stared back at her were devoid of all emotion, and it was in that moment she knew she had lost him, irrevocably and forever. She had thought that was what she wanted, but now the total knowledge left her devastated, without the strength to break her gaze, without the power of speech, and he stared back at her remotely, hard and unforgiving.

"Mungo," she whispered, finding at last the strength and will to speak. "I did not mean this to happen, as the Almighty is my witness, I did not mean it."

Rough hands dragged Mungo St. John to his feet, so that Tippoo's head slipped from his lap and the skull thumped against the wooden deck.

"Captain's orders, me old cock, and you are to 'ave a taste of your own chains."

Mungo St. John did not resist as the slave cuffs were fastened on his wrists and ankles. He stood quietly, balancing to *Huron*'s wild gale-driven lunges, looking about the fire-blackened ship with its decks covered with fallen and tangled rigging, stained with the blood of his crew, and though his

515

expression did not change, there was a limitless grieving in his eyes.

"I am sorry," whispered Robyn, still kneeling beside him. "I am truly sorry."

Mungo St. John glanced down at her, his wrists fastened at the small of his back by the cold black links of chain.

"Yes," he nodded. "So am I." And a seaman thrust the palm of a horny hand between his shoulder blades, shoving him away toward the *Huron*'s forecastle, and the slave chains clanked about his ankles as he staggered.

Within a dozen paces he had recovered his balance, and shrugged off the hands of his jailers. He walked away with his back straight and his shoulders thrown back, and he did not look back at Robyn kneeling on the bloodstained deck.

Mungo St. John blinked at the sunlight as he followed the scarlet uniform coat and white cross straps of his escort out into the courtyard of the Cape Town castle.

He had not seen the sun for five days; the cell in which he had been confined since he had been escorted ashore had no external windows. Even in midsummer, the chill of the past winter still lingered in the thick stone walls, and the air that entered through the single barred opening in the oaken door was stale and sullied by the jail odors, the emanations from the dozen or so prisoners in the other cells.

Mungo filled his lungs now and paused to look up at the ramparts of the castle. The British flag spread jauntily above the Katzenellenbogen redoubt, and beyond it the seagulls planed and volleyed on the fresh southeasterly wind. Force five and standing fair for a ship to clear the bay and make the open Atlantic, Mungo noted instinctively.

"This way, please." The young subaltern who commanded the prison escort urged him on, but Mungo hesitated a moment longer. He could hear the murmurous song of the surf-break upon the beaches just beyond the castle walls, and from the ramparts he would have a clear view across Table Bay to Bloubergstrand on the far curve of the land.

Huron would be lying at anchor close inshore, still under her prize crew, and he longed for just a single glimpse of her, longed to know if the sternquarters were still smoke-blackened and gutted, or if O'Brien had been allowed to make the repairs to her hull and her steering gear.

If only Tippoo . . . he began the thought, and then stopped himself, shivered briefly in the sunlight not only from the prison chill in his bones. He squared his shoulders and nodded to the subaltern.

"Please lead the way," he agreed, and the hobnailed boots of the escort gnashed the cobbles as they crossed the courtyard and then climbed the broad flight of steps to the governor's suite of offices.

"Prisoner and escort, halt."

Upon the portico a naval lieutenant waited to receive them in his navy-blue-and-gold jacket, white breeches and cocked hat.

"Mr. St. John?" asked the lieutenant. He was old for his rank, gray and worn-looking, with a weary disinterested eye, and Mungo nodded disdainfully.

The lieutenant turned to the officer of the escort.

"Thank you, sir, I will take over from here," and then to Mungo, "Kindly follow me, Mr. St. John."

He went in through the magnificent teak doors, carved by the master craftsman Anreith, into the governor's antechamber with its polished floors of butter-colored Cape deal, the high hewn rafters of the same timber, and with the thick walls hung with the treasures of the Orient gathered so assiduously by that great plunderer, the Dutch East India Company, which had in turn succumbed to an even more powerful predator.

The lieutenant turned right, avoiding the brass and mahogany double doors of the governor's private office to which Mungo had expected to be led; instead they went to a less pretentious single door set in a corner of the antechamber. At the lieutenant's knock, a voice bade them enter, and they went in to a small office, clearly belonging to the governor's aide-de-camp whom Mungo had met before.

The aide-de-camp sat at the plain oak desk facing the door, and he did not rise nor did he smile as Mungo entered. There were two other men in the room, both seated in armchairs.

"You know Admiral Kemp," said the aide-de-camp.

"Good morning, Admiral."

Slogger Kemp inclined his head, but made no other gesture of recognition.

"And this is Sir Alfred Murray, Chief Justice of the Supreme Court of the Cape Colony."

"Your servant, sir." Mungo neither bowed nor smiled, and the judge leaned forward slightly in his armchair, both hands on the gold-and-amber handle of his walking stick, and stared at Mungo from under beetling white brows.

Mungo was pleased that an hour previously his jailer had

517

provided him with hot water and razor and that he had been allowed to contract with the ex-slave Malay washerwoman who laundered for the castle's officers. His breeches were clean, his boots polished and his shirt crisply ironed and snowy white.

The aide-de-camp picked up an official document from the desk before him.

"You are the captain and owner of the clipper *Huron?*"

"I am."

"The ship has been seized as prize by the Royal Navy under Articles Five to Eleven of the Treaty of Brussels, and presently lies under prize crew in British territorial waters."

That did not need reply, and Mungo stood silently.

"The case has been considered by the Courts of Mixed Commission for the colony, under the presidency of the Chief Justice, and after hearing evidence from the Officer Commanding the Cape Squadron and others, the Court has determined that as the *Huron* was taken on the high seas, the Cape Colony has no jurisdiction in this matter. The Chief Justice has recommended to His Excellency, the Governor of Cape Colony, that the—ahem"—the aide-de-camp paused significantly—"the cargo of the clipper ship *Huron* be impounded by Her Majesty's Government, but that the clipper be released under the command and connaissance of its owner and that the owner be ordered to proceed with all dispatch to place himself and his vessel under the jurisdiction of a properly constituted American court and there to answer such charges as the President of the United States deems fit to bring against him."

Mungo let out a long slow breath of relief. By God's breath, the limeys were going to duck the issue! They were not about to chance the wrath of the new American President-elect. They had taken his slaves, eight hundred thousand dollars' worth, but they were giving him back his ship and they were letting him go.

The aide-de-camp went on reading without looking up.

"The governor of Cape Colony has accepted the court's recommendation and has so decreed. You are required to make your ship ready and safe for the voyage with all speed. In this respect, the officer commanding the Cape Squadron has agreed to place at your disposal the repair facilities of the Naval Station."

"Thank you, Admiral." Mungo turned to him, and Slogger Kemp's brows came together, his face mottled with passion, but his voice was quiet and clear.

"Sixteen of my men dead, and as many maimed by your actions—sir—each day the smell of your filthy ship blows into the windows of my office." Admiral Kemp lifted himself with an effort from his armchair, and glared at Mungo St. John. "I say rot you and your thanks, Mr. St. John, and if I had my way we wouldn't be playing coy and cute with Mr. Lincoln, and I would have you swinging at the mainyard of a British man-of-war rather than sailing out of Table Bay in your stinking slaver."

Slogger Kemp turned away and went to stare out of the single window, into the courtyard of the castle where his carriage waited. The aide-de-camp seemed not to have noticed the outburst. He went on smoothly, "A representative of the Royal Navy will accompany you aboard your ship and remain there until he determines that your vessel is seaworthy."

The aide-de-camp reached back and tugged the bell pull behind his shoulder, and almost immediately the door opened and the naval lieutenant reappeared.

"Just one thing, Mr. St. John. The governor has declared you to be an undesirable alien and you will immediately be arrested if you are ever again so rash as to set foot in Cape Colony."

The tall figure came striding up the yellow gravel pathway, under the avenue of tall date palms, and Aletta Cartwright called gaily across the rose garden, "Here comes your beau, Robyn. He is early today."

Robyn straightened, the basket full of rose blossoms hanging on her arm, the wide straw hat shading her face from the flat glare of the Cape noonday. She watched Clinton coming toward her with the warmth of affection. He looked so gangling and boyish and impetuous, much too young ever to have led that rush of fighting seamen over *Huron*'s stern.

She had grown accustomed to him over the past weeks while she had been a guest once more of the Cartwright family, and each afternoon Clinton had walked up the hill from his modest lodgings in Waterkant Street. She looked forward to his visits, to their serious conversations after the frivolity and inconsequences of the Cartwright daughters. She found his admiration and his adoration flattering and deeply comforting. She felt it was something that would never change, something constant, a polestar in the confusion and uncertainty that had been her life to this time.

She had learned to value his good sense, and his judgment.

She had even allowed him to read the manuscript which was occupying most of her days now, and his comments and criticisms were always well based.

Then she had found that he filled a part of her life that had been empty for much too long. She needed something or someone to cherish and protect and comfort, somebody who needed her, someone on whom to lavish the bounty of her compassion.

"I do not believe I could ever live without you, my dear Dr. Ballantyne," he told her. "I do not believe I could have endured this terrible period of my life without your help."

She knew it was probably true, not just the hyperbole of the lovesick swain, and Robyn was entirely unable to resist the appeal of anybody in pain or in suffering.

It was many weeks since that heady day when *Black Joke* had sailed into Table Bay with her bulwarks and upperworks riddled with shot, her rigging in heroic and picturesque ruins, and her huge captive, blackened with smoke and limping under jury rigging and makeshift steering gear, headed submissively under the menace of her carronades to an anchorage close inshore at Rogger Bay.

How the townsfolk had swarmed to the beachfront to gawk and exclaim, and how the other naval vessels in the bay had lined their rails and yards with seamen to cheer them in.

She had been standing at Clinton Codrington's side when the two contingents of naval officers from the Cape Squadron's headquarters had been rowed out to *Black Joke*'s anchorage. The first had been headed by a naval commander, some years junior to Clinton.

"Captain Codrington," he saluted. "I am under orders to take over command of this ship from you forthwith, sir."

Clinton accepted this without change of expression.

"Very well, sir, I will have my gear removed, and in the meantime we should complete the formalities, and I will introduce you to the remaining officers."

When Clinton had shaken hands with his officers and his sea chest was at the entry port, the second longboat which had been lying on its oars a few yards off, now came alongside and a senior captain came aboard. Everyone on *Black Joke*'s deck knew what was about to happen, and Denham stepped close to Clinton and said softly, "Good luck, sir, you know you can count on me when the time comes."

They both knew what he was referring to: the day they would meet again in the court-martial chamber.

"Thank you, Mr. Denham," Clinton replied, then he went forward to where the senior captain waited.

"Captain Codrington, it is my duty to inform you that you have been called upon by the Officer Commanding the Squadron to answer certain charges concerning the conduct of your duties. Therefore, you are to consider yourself under open arrest and to hold yourself in readiness to answer those charges as soon as a courtmartial can be convened."

"I understand, sir."

Clinton saluted him, and then preceded him through the entry port and down the ladder into the waiting boat.

A single voice called out, "Give 'em hell, Tongs."

And suddenly they were all cheering, *Black Joke*'s crew lined her side and hung in her rigging and they cheered as though their throats would crack.

"Hammer and Tongs!" They tossed their caps on high.

"At 'em the Jokers!"

As the boat pulled away and rowed for the beach, Clinton Codrington stood in the stern and stared back at them without expression, and his bare head shone like a beacon fire in the sunlight.

That had been so many weeks ago. Still the opportunity of assembling enough senior officers in a small station like the Cape Colony to act as his judges might not occur for weeks still or even months.

Clinton had spent his nights in the cheap lodgings on Waterknat Street. Ostracized by his brother officers, he had spent most of his days alone upon the waterfront staring out at the little gunboat that was making her repairs at the anchorage, and at the bare-masted clipper.

He had watched while the slaves were brought ashore from *Huron*'s holds, and their chains were struck off by a blacksmith from the castle. He had seen the bewildered blacks put their marks upon the indenture contracts, and then be led away by the Dutch and Huguenot farmers to learn their new duties, and he had wondered at this other fate to which he had delivered them.

Then in the afternoons he had climbed the hill to the Cartwright mansion set in its green and pleasant garden to pay his court to Robyn Ballantyne.

This day he was early, the noonday gun banged from the top of Signal Hill as Clinton came striding up the pathway, almost breaking into a run when he saw Robyn in the rose garden. He left the pathway and cut across the velvety green carpet of the lawn.

"Robyn! Dr. Ballantyne!" His voice was strange, and his pale eyes wild.

"What is it?" Robyn handed the basket to Aletta and hurried across the lawn to meet him.

"What is it?" she repeated with concern, and he seized both her hands in his.

"The slaver!" he was stuttering with the force of his emotion. "The American—*Huron!*"

"Yes?" she demanded. "Yes?"

"She is sailing—they are letting her go!"

It was a cry of outrage and despair, and Robyn froze, her face suddenly pale.

"I do not believe it."

"Come!" said Clinton. "I have a carriage at the gate."

The coachman whipped the horses at the slope, with Clinton shouting to him to hurry still, and they came out on the crest of Signal Hill in a lather, with froth splattered on their chests and forelegs.

The moment the coach braked, Clinton jumped down and led Robyn to the side of the roadway facing down the steep hillside out over the bay. The tall American clipper slid silently and gracefully over a green sea that was speckled by the dancing whitecaps of the southeasterly wind.

As she cleared the low dark shape of Robben Island, she altered her heading a fraction and more sail bloomed upon her yards, white as the first flowers of spring. Silently, the man and the woman stared after the beautiful ship, and neither of them spoke as she merged with the milky sea fret, became a ghostly silhouette and then quite suddenly was gone.

Still in silence the couple turned back and climbed into the waiting carriage, and neither of them spoke until it drew up before the gates of the Cartwright estate. Clinton looked at her face. It was bloodless, even her lips were ivory-white and quivering with suppressed emotion.

"I know how you feel. After all we endured, to see that monster sail away. I share your distress," he said quietly, but she shook her head once vehemently and then was still again.

"I have other news," he told her when at last he judged she had recovered, and a little color had returned to her cheeks.

"There is a rear admiral on the passenger list of the East Indiaman that anchored in the bay yesterday. Slogger Kemp

522

has asked him to make up the numbers at the court-martial. It begins tomorrow."

Immediately she turned to face him, her expression softening with concern and alarm.

"Oh, I will pray for you every moment." She reached out her hand impulsively, and he seized it with both of his, and clung to it.

It was as though the contact had loosened something in her that she had locked away tightly and at last the tears welled up in her hot dry eyes.

"Oh my dear Dr. Ballantyne," Clinton whispered. "Please do not fret for me." But through the tears Robyn was still seeing the ghostly image of a tall and beautiful ship fading away into the pearly curtain of sea fret, and the first sob shook her body.

The floor of the ballroom of Admiralty House was laid out in chessboard squares of black and white marble, and the human characters like chess pieces were ranged upon it haphazard, as though by the vagaries of a hard-fought endgame.

Robyn Ballantyne in skirt and blouse of sober green stood by the head of the board, a solitary queen, while arranged opposite her were the rooks of the legal council: two naval officers in full uniform and sword who were playing the roles of prosecutor and defender. They had been chosen arbitrarily, and neither of them relished the unfamiliar task.

They had isolated themselves from the rest of the company, and each of them busied himself with the sheaf of documents he carried, not looking at the man whom they were destined to save or condemn, depending on the deliberations of the senior officers who were even now closeted behind the tall double doors at the far end of the ballroom.

The other witnesses—Denham of *Black Joke* bearing the ship's log under his arm, MacDonald the engineer hiding his gray coalstained hands behind his back, the colony's agent and honorary consul for the Sultan of Omani, a prosperous Asian trader—were like the scattered pawns of the game around the edge of the board.

Only the officer accused and on trial for his life was not at rest. Captain Clinton Codrington paced at random about the ballroom floor, his heeels clicking on the marble slabs, his cocked hat clasped under one arm, his eyes staring dead ahead. He paced without pattern, like the roving knight of the chessboard.

The tension seemed to charge even this huge room, increasing rather than lessening with every minute. Only the two red-coated marines on each side of the double doors seemed unaffected. They stood stolidly, their musket butts grounded beside the polished toe caps of their right boots, their expressions blank and their eyes fixed.

Once Clinton stopped in front of Robyn and drew his watch.

"Fifty minutes," he said.

"It could be hours yet," she answered quietly.

"I can never thank you for the evidence you gave."

"It was nothing but the truth."

"Yes," he agreed. "But without it—" He broke off, and resumed his restless pacing.

The prosecuting officer who had attempted for the two previous days to damn him and send him to the gallows glanced up at Clinton, and then hurriedly, almost guiltily, returned his eyes to the documents he held in his right hand. Robyn was the only one who watched him openly, and her eyes were dark with worry and concern, yet when he caught her eye again a few minutes later, she smiled at him bravely, trying to hide her doubts.

The four senior officers, before whom she had given her evidence, had listened attentively, but she had seen no warmth nor compassion in their faces.

"Madam," Admiral Kemp had asked her at the end, "is it true that you obtained a medical degree by impersonating a man, and if your answer is 'Yes,' would you not then believe us justified in doubting your allegiance to the truth?"

Robyn had seen the faces of the senior officers flanking Kemp harden, their eyes become remote. The Sultan's agent had been blatantly hostile, as the prosecuting officer had led him dutifully through a long list of aggressions and warlike acts against his master's sovereign territory and against his subjects.

Denham and MacDonald could only recite the facts, and their own repudiation of their captain's orders was recorded in the ship's logbook.

The only thing that surprised Robyn was that the court had deliberated so long, and then she started involuntarily as, with a crash that echoed around the walls of the empty ballroom, the double doors were thrown open, and the two marine guards stamped to attention.

Through the doors she could see the naval officers seated down the length of the long dining room table facing the ballroom. Their frogging and epaulettes gleamed with gold lace and Robyn was too far to be certain of their expressions. Though she took a step forward and craned to see the polished top of the table in front of the grim line of judges, she could not be certain of the hilt and point of the single weapon that lay upon it, and then her view was blocked by the backs of the three men who lined up facing the doors.

Clinton was in the center with the prosecution and the defending officers flanking him. At a muttered command, they marched briskly through the open doors. The doors closed behind the trio, and still Robyn could not know which way the naval dirk on the table was pointing, whether it was in its sheath or if the blade was naked.

Clinton had explained to her the significance of that weapon. It was only placed upon the table when the judges had reached their decision. If the blade was sheathed, and if the hilt was pointed toward the prisoner when he entered, then the judgment was "not guilty." When the bare blade was pointed toward him, then he knew that the wrath of the service was about to descend upon him—and he might be called to pay his penalty upon the flogging grating, or upon the gallows itself.

Clinton kept his gaze fixed upon a point above Admiral Kemp's head, while the doors were banged closed behind him, and he and the officers flanking him came to attention five paces from the long polished table behind which sat his judges.

Only then did he allow himself to glance down at the dagger upon the tabletop. The bare blade glinted a bluish-silver in the late sunlight that slanted in from the tall french windows, and the bright point was aimed at Clinton's stomach.

He felt the cold drive of despair in his guts, as though the dagger had been plunged through them. The shock of the injustice of the verdict, the disbelief that his whole life had been brought down at a single stroke, the shame and disgrace of a career shattered and a reputation indelibly besmirched, left him numbed and blind to all but the wicked blade before him, and deaf to all but the voice of Admiral Kemp.

"Guilty of flagrant disregard of the orders of his superior officer."

"Guilty of acts of piracy upon the high seas."

"Guilty of destroying the property of the subjects of a friendly power."

"Guilty of flouting the terms of a treaty between Her Britannic Majesty's Government and the Sultan of the Omani Arabs."

It must be death, Clinton realized, the verdict was too detailed, the list of his transgressions too long and his guilt too serious. It must be death by the noose.

He lifted his eyes from the accusing weapon, and he stared out of the french windows beyond his judges. The high stock of his uniform collar felt as tight as the hangman's noose as he tried to swallow.

I have never feared death, Lord, he prayed silently. There is only one thing I will regret—that I must leave the woman that I love.

To be deprived of honor and of life was sufficient punishment, but to lose his love as well was the final injustice.

"The court has deliberated at length on the sentence"— Admiral Kemp paused and shot a sideways glance at a lean, tanned and silver-haired rear admiral beside him, the passenger from the visiting East Indiaman—"and has heard and been swayed by the eloquent arguments of Admiral Reginald Curry."

He paused again and puffed out his lips, indicating clearly that he did not agree with those eloquent arguments, before going on.

"The sentence of this court is that the prisoner be stripped of all rank, privileges, and pay and that the Queen's commission which he holds shall be withdrawn, and that he be *dishonorably* discharged from the naval service."

Clinton steeled himself; the stripping of rank and discharge would precede the main body of the sentence.

"Furthermore," Kemp paused and cleared his throat. "Furthermore it is the sentence of the court that the prisoner be taken from here to the castle and that he be there—"

The castle was the place of execution, the gallows would be erected on the parade ground before the main gates.

"That he be imprisoned for a period of one year."

The judges were standing up, were filing out of the room. As the lean silver-haired admiral came level with Clinton, a small conspiratorial smile touched his lips, and for the first time Clinton realized that it was not death.

"A year," said the lieutenant who had prosecuted, as the door closed, "not a flogging, nor a hanging—damned generous, I'd say."

"Congratulations." Clinton's defending officer was grinning incredulously. "It was Curry, of course, he commanded the west coast antislavery squadron himself. What a stroke of luck to have him on the board."

Pale, voiceless, swaying slightly on his feet, Clinton was still staring blindly through the open windows.

"Come on, my dear fellow, a year will soon be past"—the defending officer touched his arm—"and after that, no more bully beef and hard bread—do pull yourself together."

Twenty miles a day since leaving Grandfather Moffat's mission station at Kuruman, Zouga had pushed the mules and his servants hard all the way, and now at the crest of the pass he reined in the tall swaybacked mule and stared out across the sweeping panorama of the Cape peninsula.

Directly below him was that strange hill of smooth rock, Die Paarl as the Dutch burghers had named it, "the Pearl," and it shone with an almost translucent luster in the Cape high summer sun.

Beyond that the wheatlands and vineyards dotted the flat land that stretched away to the Paarde Berg, the Horse Mountains, where once the wild mountain zebra had roamed, and the Tyger Berg. The leopard to the Dutch burghers was a tiger and the zebra was a horse.

"Nearly home now, Sergeant," Zouga called to Jan Cheroot.

"Just look at that—" The little Hottentot pointed to the smoky-blue flat-topped mountain that stood up tall and massive against the southern horizon.

"We will be there before dark tomorrow night."

Jan Cheroot puckered his lips and blew a kiss toward it. "Pull the cork and tell the Cape Town ladies that my mama didn't call me big cheroot for nothing."

His mule flicked its long hairy ears to the sound of his voice and gave a little halfhearted buck. "You feeling it too, you old thunder!" Jan Cheroot chuckled. "Let's go then!" and he whipped the animal up and went clattering away down the steep and rocky roadway.

Zouga stayed to watch the battered little two-wheeled Cape cart follow him at a more sedate pace, carrying its precious burden of ivory and sculptured green soapstone, as it had for a thousand miles and more.

It was a month before Robyn was allowed to pay her first visit to the castle. After the guard at the gates inspected her pass, she was led to a small whitewashed guardroom, devoid of all furniture except three high-backed uncushioned chairs.

She remained standing for ten minutes before the low door opposite her was opened and Clinton stooped through it. He stopped, facing her, and she was struck instantly by the prison pallor. His deepwater tan had faded to a tobacco stain of yellow, and the roots of his hair, no longer bleached by salt and strong sunlight, had darkened.

He looked older, tired and dejected.

"You at least have not deserted me in my disgrace," he said simply.

The subaltern of the guard took the third chair and tried to look as though he were not listening to their conversation. Robyn and Clinton sat facing each other stiffly, on the uncomfortable chairs, and their conversation was at first as stilted, a polite series of inquiries after each other's health.

Then Robyn asked, "Have you received the newspapers?"

"Yes. The warder has been good to me."

"Then you have read what the new American President has promised at his inauguration."

"Lincoln was always a staunch enemy of the trade," Clinton nodded.

"He has granted the ships of the Royal Navy the right of search at last."

"And six of the Southern states have seceded already," Clinton told her grimly. "There will be fighting, if he tries to force it."

"It's so unfair," Robyn cried. "Just a few short weeks and you would have been a hero instead of a—" she broke off with her hand to her mouth, "I am sorry, Captain Codrington."

"Captain no longer," he said.

"I feel so much to blame—had I not sent that letter—"

"You are so kind, so good," then he blurted abruptly, "and so beautiful that I can scarcely bear to look at you."

Robyn found herself blushing hotly, and she glanced at the listening guard officer. He was studying the rough plaster ceiling.

"Do you know what I thought when I entered the chamber and saw the dirk pointed at me?" Clinton went on, and she shook her head. "I thought I was going to lose you. That they would hang me and I would never see you again." His voice was shaking with such emotion that the listening officer rose to his feet.

"Dr. Ballantyne, I will leave the room for five minutes," he said. "Do I have your word that you will not attempt to pass a weapon or a tool to the prisoner in my absence?"

Robyn nodded jerkily and whispered, "Thank you."

The moment the door closed, Clinton launched himself across the gap between them and dropped to his knees before Robyn. He encircled her waist with both arms and pressed his cheek to her bosom.

"But now I have nothing to offer you, I have nothing to share with you but my disgrace."

Robyn found herself stroking his hair as though he were a child.

"Soon I will go back to that beautiful land below the Zambezi River. I know now that is where my destiny lies," she said quietly. "To minister to the souls and the bodies of those who live there."

She paused a moment and looked down fondly on his hair.

"You say you have nothing to offer, nothing to share, but I have something to offer you, and to share with you."

He raised his head and looked up at her questioningly, hope starting to dawn in his eyes.

"Will you not offer yourself to be ordained in God's service as a missionary, and come with me into the wilderness, to the land of Zambezia?"

"To share my life with you, and with God." His voice was husky and choked. "I never dreamed I was worthy of such an honor."

"The fellow is a prig," said Zouga firmly. "And, damn me, but now he is a jailbird to boot. Neither of you will be able to hold up your heads in society."

"He has a true and noble spirit, and now he has found his true calling in God's service," Robyn replied hotly. "Neither of us intends spending much of our time in society, you may be certain of that."

Zouga shrugged and smiled. "Of course, that is your affair. At least he has made a pretty packet of prize money which they can't take away from him."

"I assure you that money had nothing to do with my decision."

"I will believe that." Zouga's smile infuriated her, but before she could find a scathing enough retort, he turned away and sauntered the length of the long veranda under the trellised vines and stood with his hands thrust into his pockets, staring out across the Cartwrights' gardens to the far glimpses of blue bay seen through the oaks and the rustling palms.

Robyn's anger subsided and gave way to regret. It seemed

now that the two of them must always be squabbling, their desires and their motives always directly opposed.

At first her relief at his safety had been almost as strong as her sisterly delight at seeing him again. She had barely recognized him as he rode the bony swaybacked mule up the path to the Cartwright mansion. It was only when he dismounted and lifted the stained old hat from his head that she screamed with joy, leaped up from the luncheon table and ran down off the terrace to hug him.

He was so lean and hard and bronzed, and somehow endowed with new authority, charged with purpose and presence, that she glowed with pride as he recounted his experiences and all the company hung avidly on each word.

"He is like a Greek god!" Aletta Cartwright had whispered to Robyn, which was not an original description—but then Aletta did not run much to original thought, and Robyn had to agree that in this case it was accurate.

She had followed his description of the land of the Matabele, and of the long trek southward with all her attention, asking such acute questions that Zouga had asked sharply, "I hope that you will not be using any of this in your own account, sissy?"

"Of course not," she assured him, but still that had been the first sour note, and he had not spoken further of his adventures, except to give her the greetings and news of their grandfather, Robert Moffat at Kuruman.

"You would never believe that he was seventy-five years old this past December. He is so bright and alive that he has just finished translating the Bible into the Sechuan language. He gave me every courtesy and help, and it was he who arranged for mules and for the cart which made the last portion of the journey so much easier. He remembered you as a little girl of three years old, and he has received your letters and gave me this in reply." It was a thick packet. "He tells me that you have asked him about leading a missionary expedition to Zambezia or Matabeleland."

"That is correct."

"Sissy, I do not think that a woman on her own," he had begun, but she had forestalled him.

"I shall not be alone. Captain Clinton Codrington has decided to seek ordination as a missionary, and I have consented to become his wife."

That had led to the explosion which had once more marred

their relationship. As her anger faded, she made another determined effort to avert the new clash of temperament.

"Zouga." She went down the length of the terrace and took his arm. "I would be grateful if you would consent to give me away at the wedding."

Some of the hardness went out of his arm as his muscles relaxed.

"When will that be, sissy?"

"Not for seven months. Clinton has that much longer of his sentence."

Zouga shook his head. "I will not be here. I have booked passage on the P. & O. steamer that sails for home at the beginning of next month." They were both silent, and then Zouga went on, "But I wish you joy and happiness—and I apologize for the remark I made about your future husband."

"I understand." She squeezed his arm. "He is a different kind of man from you."

Zouga almost exclaimed, Thank God for that, but caught the blasphemy before it reached his lips, and again they were silent.

Zouga was considering the problem that had concerned him so intimately since his return to Cape Town: how to find out from Robyn what she had written in her manuscript, and if possible to influence her into amending those portions of it which might offend the family reputation.

Now that he had learned that she would not be returning to England, the natural opportunity had presented itself.

"Sissy, if your manuscript is prepared, I will be happy to take it with me and to make certain that it is delivered safely to Oliver Wicks."

The voyage to England would give Zouga ample opportunity to study Robyn's work, and if the delivery was delayed for a month or so after his arrival, then Zouga's own published account of the expedition would skim the cream off the pool of interest and critical literary attention.

"Oh, did I not mention it to you?" Robyn lifted her chin, and her smile was spiced with a little spiteful relish. "I sent my manuscript on the mail steamer a month before your arrival here. It will be in London already, and I should not be surprised if Mr. Wicks has published it already. I expect he will have sent the reviews, and we will have them on the next mailship."

Zouga jerked his arm out of her grip, and his eyes were steely as he glared down at her.

"I really should have mentioned it," she added sweetly. His

reaction confirmed her suspicions, and she knew that what last small chance they had was finished. From now on they would be enemies, and somehow she knew that the center of their enmity would always be the land and peoples of that faraway country between two great rivers which Zouga had named Zambezia.

At the end of the Woodstock Road, on the bank of the Liesbeeck River, not far from the domed roof of the Royal Astronomical Observatory, stands the Cartwright warehouse. It is a rambling whitewashed building of unburnt Kimberley brick with a corrugated iron roof.

Against the rear wall of the main storeroom stood three articles left there in storage and for later collection by Major Morris Zouga Ballantyne, presently on passage aboard the Peninsular and Orient Steamship S.S. *Bombay* from India to the Pool of London. The three bulky articles were almost completely screened by the bays and hillocks of bales and crates, and of barrels and bags, which reached almost to the high ceiling.

The two huge elephant tusks formed a perfect frame with their curved yellow ivories for the third package. The carved soapstone figure was still contained in its protective covering of plaited elephant grass and twisted bark rope. It stood upright on its wide heavy base, and it was merely chance that it faced toward the north.

The grass covering had been torn away from the head by careless handling and long months of travel on the shoulders of porters and on the buckboards of an unsprung Cape cart.

The cruel proud head of the bird of prey protruded from its wrappings. The stony sightless eyes stared across forest and mountain and desert, one thousand five hundred miles, to a walled and ruined city, and the words of the Umlimo's prophecy seemed to hover in the air above the graven head of the bird like living things.

"The white eagle has stooped on the stone falcons, and cast them to earth. Now the eagle shall lift them up again and they will fly afar. There shall be no peace in the kingdoms of the Mambos or the Monomatapas until they return. For the white eagle will war with the black bull until the stone falcons return to roost."

About the Author

Wilbur Smith was born in Zambia and educated in Michaelhouse and Rhodes University. He has lived all his life in Africa and his commitment to that continent is deep.

A full-time writer since 1964, he is the author of 15 novels. He also finds time to travel out of Africa and enjoy his other interests—such as numismatics, wildlife photography and big game fishing. He and his wife make an annual safari into the dwindling wilderness of Central Africa, and at other seasons he fishes by boat in the Indian Ocean for tuna and other game fish.

Mr. Smith lives with his wife in Constantia, South Africa.